WASHINGTON

*Small Town Romance
in Four Distinct Novels*

WANDA E. BRUNSTETTER
LAURAINE SNELLING

BARBOUR
PUBLISHING

The Neighborly Thing © 2003 by Wanda E. Brunstetter
Talking for Two © 2002 by Wanda E. Brunstetter
Race for the Roses © 2001 by Lauraine Snelling
Song of Laughter © 1992 by Lauraine Snelling

ISBN 1-59310-903-2

Cover art by Corbis and Index Stock

Published by Barbour Publishing, Inc., P.O. Box 719, Uhrichsville, Ohio 44683, www.barbourbooks.com

Our mission is to publish and distribute inspirational products offering exceptional value and biblical encouragement to the masses.

 Member of the
Evangelical Christian
Publishers Association

Printed in the United States of America.
5 4 3 2 1

The Neighborly Thing

by Wanda E. Brunstetter

In loving memory of my father,
William E. Cumby,
who helped me with the legalities of
opening my first doll hospital.

Chapter 1

"The perfect home," Sinda Shull murmured as she stood on the sagging front porch of her new house. "Perfect for my needs, but oh, what a dump!"

Her friend, Carol Riggins, drew Sinda close for a hug. "Seattle's loss is Elmwood's gain, and now the town won't be the same." She snickered, then her expression sobered. "I'm really glad you decided to leave the past behind and move here for a fresh start."

Sinda's thoughts fluttered toward the past, then quickly shut down. That was part of her life better left uninvited. She pulled away from her friend, choosing not to comment on her reasons for moving from Seattle. "Sure hope I can figure out some way to turn this monstrosity into a real home."

"I thought you bought the place to use for your business."

"I did, but I have to live here, too."

Carol nodded. "True, and fixing it up should help get your mind off the past."

Pushing back a strand of hair that had escaped her ponytail, Sinda frowned. Carol might think she knew all about Sinda's past, but the truth was, her friend knew very little about what had transpired in the Shull home over the years. When the Rigginses moved into their north Seattle neighborhood, Sinda and Carol were both twelve. By then Sinda and her father had already been living alone for two years. Dad didn't like her to have friends over, so Sinda usually played at Carol's house. It was probably better that way. . .less chance of Carol finding out her secrets.

Sinda heard footsteps and glanced to the left. A tall man wearing a mail carrier's uniform was walking up the sidewalk leading to the house next door. The sight of him pulled Sinda's mind back to the present, and she slapped at the dirt on her blue jeans. "Let's not spoil our day by talking about the past, okay?"

Carol pulled her fingers through her short blond curls and nodded. "We've managed to get you pretty well moved in with no problems, so I'd better get going before I ruin everything by dredging up old memories." She patted Sinda's arm. "I can't imagine what it must feel like to lose a parent, let alone both of them."

The image of her father and his recent death from a heart attack burned deep into Sinda's soul. In order to force the painful memories into submission, Sinda had to swallow hard and refocus her thoughts. "I—I appreciate all you've done today, Carol."

5

"What are friends for?" Carol gave Sinda another hug, then she turned to go. "Give a holler if you need my help with anything else," she called over her shoulder.

Sinda grimaced. "With the way this place looks, you can probably count on it."

❧

Glen Olsen poured himself a tall glass of milk, then another one for his ten-year-old daughter, Tara. It had been a long day, and he was bone tired. He'd encountered two new dogs on his route, been chewed out by an irate woman whose disability check hadn't arrived on time, and he had a blister the size of a silver dollar on his left foot. All Glen wanted to do was sit down, kick off his boots, and try to unwind before he had to fix supper.

He handed Tara her glass of milk and placed a jar of ginger cookies they'd baked the day before in the center of the kitchen table. "Have a seat and let's have a snack."

"Dad, have you met our new next-door neighbors yet?" Tara reached into the container and grabbed two cookies, which she promptly stuffed into her mouth.

Glen followed suit and washed his cookies down with a gulp of milk. "Nope, but when I got home this afternoon, I saw two women standing on the front porch."

Tara's brown eyes brightened. "Really? What were they doing?"

Glen dropped into the chair across from her and bent over to unlace his boots. "They were talking, Nosey Rosey."

"Dad!" Tara wrinkled her freckled nose and looked at him as though he'd lost his mind. "Did you see any kids my age?"

He gingerly slipped his left foot free and wiggled his toes. "Like I said. . .just the two women. I saw one of them drive off in a red sports car, and the other lady probably went inside."

Tara tapped her fingernails along the checkered tablecloth. "That doesn't tell me much. When it comes to detective work, you're definitely not one of the top ten."

Glen chuckled. "What do you mean? I told you all I know. Just because I'm not as good at neighborhood snooping as some people I know. . ."

"I'm not a snoop! The correct word for my career is 'detective'!"

"Detective—snoop—what's the difference?" Glen wagged his finger. "You need to mind your own business, young lady. People don't like it when you spy on them."

"What makes you think I've been spying on the neighbors?"

"Elementary, my dear daughter. Elementary." Glen gulped down the rest of his milk and grabbed a napkin out of the wicker basket on the table. "May I remind you that you've done it before? I'm surprised you don't have the full history on our new neighbors by now."

Tara's mahogany eyes, so like her mother's, seemed to be challenging him, but surprisingly, she took their conversation in another direction. "These cookies are great, Dad. You're probably the best cook in the entire world!"

Glen raised his eyebrows. "I might be the best cook in our neighborhood, or maybe even the whole town of Elmwood, but certainly not the entire world. Besides, you usually help me with the cooking." He reached across the table and gave Tara's hand a gentle squeeze.

She smiled in response, revealing a pair of perfectly matched dimples. "Say, I've got a terrific idea!"

"Oh, no!" Glen slapped one hand against the side of his head. "Should I call out the Coast Guard, or does that come later?"

"Quit teasing, Dad."

"Okay, okay. What's your terrific idea, Kiddo?"

Tara's eyes lit up like a sunbeam as a slow smile swept across her face. "I think we should take some of these yummy cookies over there." Tara marched over to the cupboard and brought a heavy paper plate to the table, then piled it high with cookies.

Glen reached down to rub his sore foot and asked absently, "Over where?"

She smacked her hand against the table, and a couple cookies flew off the plate. "Over to our new neighbor's house. You're always lecturing me about being kind to our neighbors, so I thought it would be the neighborly thing to do."

"Let me get this straight," Glen said, reaching for one of the cookies that had fallen to the table. "You want to take some of our delicious, best-in-the-whole-neighborhood cookies, and go over to meet our new neighbors. Is that right?"

Tara jumped to her feet. "Exactly! That way we can find out if they have any kids my age." She tipped her head to one side. "Of course, if you're too scared—"

"Me? Scared? Now what would I have to be scared of?"

"That big old house is pretty creepy looking."

"For you, maybe," Glen said with a hearty laugh. "As for me—I'm not only a great cook, but I'm also a fearless warrior."

"Can we go now, Dad?"

Glen studied his daughter intently. It was obvious from the determined tilt of her chin that she was completely serious about this. Whenever Tara came up with one of her bright ideas, he knew she wasn't about to let it drop until he either agreed or laid down the law. In this case he thought her plan had merit. "I suppose your idea does beat spying over the garden fence," he said, sucking in his bottom lip in order to hold back the laughter that threatened to bubble over.

"I don't spy," she retorted as her hands went to her hips.

"I've heard through the grapevine that you're always spying on someone with those binoculars I made the mistake of buying you last Christmas. If you had your way, you'd probably be going over every square inch of our new neighbor's house with a fine-tooth comb." Glen waved his hand for emphasis.

"I would not!" Tara went back to the cupboard, took out some plastic wrap, and covered the plate of cookies. "Ready?"

Glen stood up. "I'm game if you are." He grabbed a light jacket from the coat tree near the back door, stepped into his slippers, and threw Tara her sweater. "Come on. I'll show you how brave I can be."

Glen glanced over his shoulder and saw that Tara was following his lead out the back door. As they stepped off the porch, he felt her jab him in the ribs. "Just in case you do get scared, remember that I'll be with you, Dad."

A catchy comeback flitted through Glen's mind, but he decided against saying anything more.

They moved across the grass, and Glen opened the high gate that separated their backyard from the neighbor's. The dilapidated, three-story home was in sharp contrast to the rest of the houses in their neighborhood. Dark, ragged-looking curtains hung at the windows, peeling green paint made the siding resemble alligator skin, and a sagging back porch indicated the whole house was desperately in need of an overhaul. The yard was equally run-down; the flower-beds were filled with choking weeds, and the grass was so tall it looked like it hadn't been mowed for at least a year.

"This place gives me the creeps," Tara whispered as she knocked on the wooden edge of the rickety screen door. "I don't know why anyone would buy such a dump."

Glen shrugged. "It's not so bad, really. Nothing a few coats of paint and a little elbow grease wouldn't cure."

"Yeah, right," Tara muttered.

When the back door opened, a woman who appeared to be in her thirties stood before them holding a small vinyl doll in one hand. She was dressed in a pair of faded blue jeans and a bright orange sweatshirt smudged with dirt. Her long auburn hair was in a ponytail, and iridescent green eyes, peeking out of long eyelashes, revealed her obvious surprise. "May I help you?" she asked, quickly placing the doll on one end of the kitchen counter.

With a casualness he didn't feel, Glen leaned against the porch railing and offered the woman what he hoped was a pleasant smile. He cleared his throat a few times, wondering why it suddenly felt so dry. "My name's Glen Olsen, and this is my daughter, Tara. We're your next-door neighbors. We dropped by to welcome you to the neighborhood."

Tara held out the paper plate. "And to give you these."

The woman smiled slightly and took the offered cookies. "I'd invite you in, but the place is a mess right now." She fidgeted, and her gaze kept darting back and forth between Glen and Tara, making him wonder if she felt as nervous about meeting them as he did her.

"That's all right, Mrs.—"

"My name's Sinda Shull, and I'm not married," she said with a definite edge to her voice.

"I guess that means you don't have any kids," Tara interjected.

Glen gave his daughter a warning nudge, but before she could say anything more, the woman answered, "I have no children."

"But what about the—"

"We'd better get going," Glen said, cutting Tara off in mid-sentence. "Miss Shull is probably trying to get unpacked and settled in." His fingers twitched as he struggled with an unexplained urge to reach out and brush a wayward strand of tawny hair away from Sinda's face. Shifting his weight from one foot to the other, he quickly rubbed his sweaty palm against his jacket pocket and extended his hand. "It was nice meeting you."

As they shook, Glen noticed how small her hand was compared to his. And it was ice cold. *She really must be nervous.* He moistened his lips, then smiled. "If you need anything, please let me know."

She let go and took a step backward. "Thanks, but I'm sure I won't need anything."

Glen felt a tug on his jacket sleeve. "Come on, Dad. Let's go home."

"Sure. Okay." He nodded at Sinda Shull. "Good night, then."

❧

Sinda didn't usually allow self-pity to take control of her thoughts, but tonight she couldn't seem to help herself. She'd only been living in Elmwood one day, and already she missed home—and yes, even Dad. In spite of her father's possessive, controlling, and sometimes harsh ways, until his death he'd been her whole world. He'd taken her to church, supplied food for the table, and put clothes on their backs. He had taught Sinda respect, obedience, and. . .

Sinda moved away from the kitchen table, placing her supper dishes in the sink. She was doing it again. . .thinking about the past. Dad was dead now, and for the first time in her life she was on her own. For the last year she'd learned to become independent, so what difference did her past make now? She blinked back tears and clenched her teeth. "I won't dwell on the things I can't change."

As she turned toward the cupboard, Sinda spotted the plate of cookies lying next to the doll she'd put there earlier. "Why was I so rude to the neighbors?" she moaned. "I don't think I even thanked them for the goodies."

She squeezed her eyes shut as a mental picture of her father flashed onto the screen of her mind. *How would Dad have reacted if he'd witnessed me being rude?* She took a deep breath, holding her sides for several seconds and willing the pain to go away. There was no point wasting time on these reflections, and there was no time for neighborly things. She had a house that would take a lot of work to make it livable, much less serve as a place of business. So what if she'd been rude to Glen Olsen and his little girl? They'd be living their lives, and she'd be living hers. If they never spoke again, what would it matter?

Sinda ran warm water into the sink and added some liquid detergent, staring at the tiny bubbles as they floated toward the plaster ceiling. "I came here to get away from the past, and I've got a job to do. So that's that!"

❧

"Our new neighbor seems kind of weird, doesn't she, Dad?" Tara asked as the two of them were finishing their supper of macaroni and cheese.

Glen had other thoughts on his mind, and even though he'd heard her question, he chose not to answer.

"Dad!"

He looked up from his half-eaten plate of food. "Yes, Tara?"

"Don't you think Sinda Shull is weird? Did you see the way she was dressed?"

Glen lifted his fork but didn't take a bite. "What's wrong with the way she was dressed? She just moved in, and those were obviously her working clothes."

Tara gazed at the ceiling. "She looked like a pumpkin in that goofy orange sweatshirt, and—"

"Do I need to remind you what the Bible says about loving our neighbors and judging others?" he interrupted. "The woman seemed nice enough to me, and it's not our place to pass judgment, even if she should turn out to be not so nice."

Tara groaned. "You would say that. You always try to look for the good in others."

"That's exactly what God wants us to do." Glen shoveled some macaroni into his mouth, then washed it down with a gulp of water.

She frowned at him. "What if the person you think is good turns out to be rotten to the core?"

"I hardly think Sinda Shull is rotten to the core." Glen shook his head. "Besides, only God knows what's in someone's heart."

Tara wrinkled her nose. "You can believe whatever you like, but I've got a bad feeling about that woman. I'm trusting my instincts on this one."

"I say your instincts are way off!" He scowled. "And don't go getting any ridiculous notions about spying on Miss Shull. It's not the—"

"I know, I know," she interrupted. "It's not the neighborly thing to do."

He nodded.

Tara tapped a fingernail against her chin. "Can I ask you a question?"

"I suppose."

"Why would a woman who isn't married and has no kids be holding a doll when she answered the door?"

Glen shrugged. "Maybe she has relatives or friends with children."

Tara remained silent for several seconds, as though she were in deep thought. "She acted kind of nervous, didn't you think? And did you see those green eyes of hers?"

Glen smiled. Oh, he'd seen them all right. Even for the few minutes they'd been standing on Sinda's back porch, it had been hard to keep from staring into those pools of liquid emerald. *Get a grip,* he scolded himself. *You can't let some new neighbor woman make you start acting like a high school kid—especially not in front of your impressionable young daughter.*

"Sinda's eyes remind me of Jake," Tara said, jolting Glen out of his musings.

"Jake? What are you talking about, Tara?"

"She's got cat's eyes. She could probably hypnotize someone with those weird eyes."

Glen leaned on the table, casting a frown at his daughter. "I think you, Little Miss Detective, have an overactive imagination. You watch way too much TV, and I plan to speak to Mrs. Mayer about it. While I'm at work, she needs to watch you a bit more closely."

Tara's lower lip protruded. "I don't watch too much TV. I just have a sixth sense about people. Right now my senses are telling me that Sinda Shull is one weird lady, and she needs to be watched!"

Chapter 2

S inda pulled her white minivan into the driveway and stopped in front of the basement door. She had more than enough work to do today. There were boxes to unload, stacks of paperwork to go through, and numerous phone calls to make. The list seemed endless, and there was no telling how long it might take to get everything accomplished.

With mustered enthusiasm, Sinda climbed out of the van and went around to open the tailgate. There were five large boxes in back. Knowing they wouldn't unload themselves, she pulled the first one toward her and began to carefully lift it.

"Hi, there!"

Sinda jumped at the sound of a child's voice. The same little girl who had brought her cookies the other night was crouched in the picture-perfect flower bed next door. She had a shovel in one of her gloved hands and appeared to be weeding.

"Were you speaking to me?" Sinda asked from across the small white picket fence.

"I said 'hi.'" The child stood up and brushed a clump of dirt from the knees of her dark blue overalls.

"Hello. It's Tara, right?"

The young girl wore her cinnamon brown hair in a ponytail, and it bounced with each step she took toward Sinda. "Yeah, my name's Tara." She pressed her body against the fence, and her dark eyes looked at Sinda with such intensity it made her feel like she was on trial.

Sinda glanced down at her blue cutoffs and yellow T-shirt, gave her ponytail a self-conscious flip with one hand, then lifted the box. "I guess we're both doing chores today, Tara."

Tara pushed a loose strand of hair away from her face. "Would you like me to see if Dad can come over and carry some of those boxes into the house? The one you're holding looks kind of heavy."

Sinda clutched the box tightly to her chest. She hated to admit it, but it was a bit weighty. Accepting help from a neighbor she hardly knew was not her style, though. It hadn't been Dad's style either. In fact, if he'd had his way, she wouldn't have associated with any of their Seattle neighbors during her adolescence. It was lucky for Sinda that she and Carol had gone to school together. That's when they'd become good friends, and Sinda had decided to play at Carol's house as often as she could. Of course, it was usually after school, when Dad was still at work, or on a Saturday, when he was busy running errands.

"You look really tired. Should I call Dad or what?"

Tara's persistence jolted Sinda out of her musings. "No, I'm fine. Don't trouble your father."

"I'm sure it wouldn't be any trouble. Dad likes to help people in need."

Sinda grunted. "What makes you think I'm in need?"

Tara moved quickly away from the fence, looking as though she'd been stung by a wasp. "Okay, whatever."

"I'm sorry I snapped," Sinda called as she started up the driveway toward her basement entrance. "Thanks for the offer of help."

Tara went back to her weeding, but Sinda had an inkling she hadn't seen or heard the last of the extroverted child.

A short time later, when she'd finished unloading the back of the van, Sinda went around front and opened the passenger door. She blew the dust off her watch and checked the time, then withdrew a large wicker basket and carried it into the house. "How I wish this was the last load," she muttered, "but I'll probably be hauling boxes from my storage unit for weeks."

❧

"Just what do you think you're doing, young lady?" Glen barked when he entered Tara's bedroom and found her gazing out the window with binoculars pointing at the front yard of their new neighbor's house.

Tara jumped, nearly dropping the binoculars. "Dad! Don't scare me like that!"

"Sorry, but I did knock first. You obviously didn't hear me, because you were too busy spying."

"I was watching Sinda Shull." Tara turned away from the window. "I don't trust her. I think she's up to something."

Glen planted both hands on his hips. "Up to something? What do you think the woman's up to?"

Tara dropped the binoculars onto the bed and moved closer to Glen. She spoke in a hushed tone, as though they might be overheard. "I don't think I have quite enough evidence yet, but with a little more time, maybe I can get something incriminating on her."

He raised his eyebrows. *Where does this kid learn such big words?* "Honestly, Tara. What kind of incriminating evidence could you possibly have on someone as nice as Sinda Shull?"

Tara flopped onto the bed with a groan. "Nice? How do you know she's nice? You don't even know her."

13

Glen reached up to rub the back of his neck. He was beginning to feel a headache coming on, and he sure didn't need an argument with his mischievous daughter right now. "Sinda seemed nice enough to me."

"You've only met her once," Tara argued. "If you knew her better, you'd soon see that my intuition is right."

Glen's lips curved into a smile. "You know, Kiddo, you might be right about that."

"You think she's up to something?"

He shook his head. "No, but I think we should get to know her better."

"Oh. I guess that would help."

"In fact, I believe I'll invite her over here for dinner. Tomorrow afternoon sounds good to me."

Tara's expression turned to sheer panic. "You're kidding, right?"

"I'm totally serious. What better way to get acquainted than over a nice candlelit dinner?"

"Candlelit?" Tara came straight off the bed. "Don't you think that might be carrying neighborliness a bit too far?" She sniffed deeply. "Besides, Sunday is our day to be together. We don't want to spoil it by having some stranger around, do we?"

Glen bent down, so his eyes were level with Tara's. "You said you thought it would help if we got better acquainted with the neighbor."

"I know, but—"

"Then don't throw cold water on my plans. I think I should go over there right now and ask her. If Sinda agrees to join us for dinner, I'll fix fried chicken, and maybe some of those flaky buttermilk biscuits you like so well." He clasped his hands together and flexed his fingers until several of them popped. "Let's see. . . what shall we have for dessert?"

Tara grabbed his arm and gave it a firm shake. "Dad, get a grip! It's just one little dinner, so we can find out more about the weirdo neighbor. You don't have to make such a big deal out of it."

"No more 'weird neighbor' comments. In the book of Luke we are told to love our neighbors as ourselves, and Romans 10:13 reminds us that love does no harm to its neighbor. That includes not making unkind comments about our neighbors." He started for the door, but hesitated. "I'm going over to Sinda's, and when I get back, you should be doing something constructive. And put those binoculars away."

"Can I borrow the camcorder for a while?"

"No."

"But, Dad, I—"

"You've done enough spying for one day."

The back door of Sinda's house hung wide open, with only the rickety old screen door to offer protection from the cool spring breeze whistling under the porch eaves. Glen's feet brought him to the door as his thoughts wandered. *Is this really a good idea? Will Sinda be receptive to my dinner invitation?* With a resolve to go through with the plan, he looked around for a doorbell but found none. He rapped lightly on the side of the screen door, and when there was no response, he called out, "Hello! Anybody home?" Still nothing. He leaned forward and peered through a hole in the screen, listening for any sounds that might be coming from within. "Hello!"

There were no lights on in the kitchen, and he couldn't see much past the table and chairs sitting near the door. The thought crossed his mind to see if the screen was unlocked, and if it wasn't, maybe he'd poke his head inside. *That would be categorized as snooping,* he reminded himself. *I'm getting as bad as that would-be detective daughter of mine.*

Glen had about decided to give up when another thought popped into his mind. Maybe Sinda's out front. That's where Tara was spying on her.

He stepped off the back porch, nearly tripping on one of the loose boards, then started around the side of the house. He had just rounded the corner when he ran straight into Sinda. She held a bulky cardboard box in her arms and appeared to be heading for the front door.

"Excuse me!" the two said in unison, each taking a step backward.

"That box looks kind of heavy. Would you like me to carry it for you?" Glen offered.

She shook her head. "It's not that heavy. Besides, I've already made several trips to my storage unit today, and I can manage fine on my own."

Glen eyed her speculatively. Tara was right about one thing. Sinda's green eyes did look sort of catlike. It was difficult not to stare at them. He drew from his inner reserve and lowered his gaze. *Get yourself under control. You didn't come over here to ask for a date or anything. It's just a simple home-cooked meal, done purely as a neighborly gesture.*

Glen cleared his throat a few times, and Sinda gave him a questioning look. "Is there something I can do for you, Mr. Olsen?"

"Glen. Please call me Glen." Now that he'd found his voice again, he decided to plunge ahead. "I was wondering—that is, my daughter and I would like to invite you over for dinner tomorrow afternoon." He rushed on. "I make some pretty tasty fried chicken, and there's always plenty. Please say you'll come."

Sinda shifted the box in her arms. He could tell it was much too heavy for her, but if she didn't want his help, what could he do about it?

"I wouldn't want to put you or your wife out any," Sinda stated as she moved toward the house.

Glen followed. "My wife?"

She nodded but kept on walking.

"Oh, I'm not married. I mean, I was married, but my wife died of leukemia when Tara was a year old."

Sinda stopped in her tracks and turned to face him. Her green eyes had darkened, and if he wasn't mistaken, a few tears were gathering in the corners of those gorgeous orbs.

"I'm so sorry, Mr. Olsen. . .I mean, Glen. I'm sure it must be difficult for you to be raising a daughter all alone."

"It can be challenging at times," he admitted.

"I'm surprised you haven't remarried," Sinda remarked. "A child really does need a mother, you know."

An odd statement coming from a single lady, and her tone sounded almost reprimanding. Glen shrugged. "Guess I've never found a woman who could put up with me." *Or my daughter,* he added mentally. The truth was, he had dated a few women over the years, but Tara always managed to scare them off. She was more than a little possessive of him and had made his dates feel uncomfortable with her unfriendly attitude and constant interrogations. Most of them backed away before he could deal with Tara's jealousy.

"How 'bout it?" Glen asked, returning to the question at hand. "Will you come for dinner? It'll give us a chance to get better acquainted."

"Fried chicken does sound rather tasty." Sinda paused and flicked her tongue across her lower lip. "Okay, I'll come."

Glen could hardly believe she had accepted his invitation. The other night Sinda seemed rather standoffish. Maybe she'd just been tired. "How does one o'clock sound?" he asked.

"That'll be fine. Can I bring anything?"

"Just a hearty appetite." He turned toward his own yard. "See you tomorrow, Sinda."

Chapter 3

I still don't see why we've gotta have that woman over for dinner," Tara whined as Glen drove them home from church Sunday afternoon.

"You're the one who gave me the idea of getting to know her better." He smiled. "Who knows, you might even find you'll actually enjoy yourself."

"I doubt it," Tara mumbled.

"Just try," he said through clenched teeth. "Oh, and Tara?"

"Yeah, Dad?"

"Be on your best behavior today. No prying into Sinda's private life. If she volunteers any information about herself, that's one thing, but I don't want you bombarding her with a bunch of silly questions. Is that clear?" He glanced at her out of the corner of his eye.

She shrugged. "How are we gonna find out what she's up to in that creepy old house if we don't ask a few questions?"

Glen's patience was waning, and he scowled at Tara. "Sinda is not up to anything."

"I saw her carrying a wicker basket into her house the other day," she persisted. "And you know what I heard?"

"There's nothing unusual about a wicker basket."

"But I know I heard a—"

"Tara Mae Olsen!" Glen usually had more patience with his daughter, but today she was pushing too far. "I don't want to hear another word. Sinda Shull is our neighbor, and we're going to enjoy dinner while we try to get to know her better."

Tara sniffed deeply. "I'm just glad you didn't ask her to go to church with us."

A pair of amazing green eyes flashed into Glen's mind, and he smiled. "I should have thought of that. Maybe next time I will ask her. If she hasn't already found a church home, that is."

❧

Sinda glanced at her reflection in the bay window as she stood on the front porch of the neighbor's split-level rambler. She'd decided to wear a pair of khaki slacks and an off-white knit top for dinner at the Olsens'. She'd chosen a pair of amber-colored tortoise shell combs to hold her hair away from her face, and even though she might look presentable, she felt like a fish out of water. *Probably as out of place as my archaic house looks next to this modern one,* she mused. *What on earth possessed me to accept Glen's dinner invitation?* It wasn't like her to be sociable with people she barely knew. Dad had taught her to be wary of strangers and not to let anyone know much about their personal business.

With that thought in mind, Sinda was on the verge of turning for home, but the front door unexpectedly swung open. "You're ten minutes late," Tara grumbled as she motioned Sinda inside.

Sinda studied the child a few seconds. A thick mane of brown hair fell freely down Tara's back, and she was dressed in a red jumper with a white blouse. The freckles dotting the girl's nose made her look like a cute little pixie, even if she did seem to have a chip on both shoulders. *Such a rude young lady. Why, if I'd talked to someone like that when I was a child. . .*

With determination, Sinda refocused her thoughts. "I'm sorry about being late. I hope I haven't ruined dinner."

"It would take more than ten minutes to wreck one of Dad's great meals. He's the best cook in the whole state of Washington."

"Then I guess I'm in for a treat," Sinda responded with a forced smile.

"Dad's out in the kitchen getting everything served up. He said for us to go into the dining room."

Sinda followed Tara down the hall and into a cozy but formal eating area. It was tastefully decorated, with a large oak table and six matching chairs occupying the center of the room. The walls were painted off-white, with a border of pale pink roses running along the top. A small pot of purple pansies sat in the middle of the table with two pink taper candles on either side. The atmosphere was soft and subtle. Hardly something most men would have a hand in, Sinda noted. She offered Tara another guarded smile. "The flowers are lovely."

"They're from my mother's garden. She planted lots of flowers the year before I was born. Dad takes good care of them, so they keep coming back every year. He says as long as the flowers are alive, we'll have a part of Mom with us." Tara lifted her chin and stared at Sinda with a look of defiance. "Dad loved her a lot."

"I'm sure he did." Sinda swallowed against the constriction she felt tightening her throat. She had to blink several times to keep unwanted tears from spilling over. *What's wrong with me today? I should be able to get through a simple thing like dinner at the neighbor's without turning into a basket case.*

"Have a seat," Tara said. "I'll go tell Dad you're here."

The young girl sashayed out of the room, and Sinda pulled out a chair and sat down. Tara returned a few minutes later, carrying a glass pitcher full of ice water. She filled the three glasses, placed the pitcher on the table, then flopped into the seat directly across from Sinda.

"Something smells good," Sinda murmured, for lack of anything better to say. Why was Tara staring at her like that? It made her feel like a bug under a microscope.

"That would be Dad's fried chicken. He wanted me to tell you that he'll be right in." Tara plunked her elbows on the table, rested her chin in her palms, and continued to stare.

"Is there something I can do to help?" Sinda asked hopefully.

"Nope. Dad's got everything under control."

"What grade are you in?" Sinda was hoping a change in subject might ease some of the tension.

Tara began playing with the napkin beside her plate. She folded it in several different directions, opened it, and then refolded it. "I'm in the fourth grade," she finally answered without looking up from her strange-looking work of art.

"Do you like school?"

"It's okay, but I can't wait for summer break in June. Dad and I always do lots of fun stuff in the summer time. We usually spend all our Sundays together, too." Tara looked pointedly at Sinda.

Refusing to let the child intimidate her, Sinda asked, "Who looks out for you when your father's at work?"

"Mrs. Mayer. She's been my baby-sitter ever since I can remember."

"Is your dad a mailman?" Sinda asked, taking the conversation in another direction. "I've seen him dressed in a uniform, and it looked like the kind mail carriers usually wear."

Tara nodded. "Yep, he's a mailman all right. Dad has a walking route on the other side of town."

No wonder he looks so physically fit. Sinda had noticed a whole lot more about Glen Olsen than the uniform he wore, but she'd never have admitted it—especially not to his daughter.

"Now that you know everything about us, tell me something about you," Tara blurted out.

Sinda felt her face flush. She wasn't about to disclose anything from her past. Her life was not a book, left open for anyone to read. "There—isn't much to tell."

"Why did you buy that creepy old house?"

Sinda gave Tara a blank stare. Where were the child's manners, anyway?

"I heard that all the property on this block belonged to the first owner of your house. They built new homes all around it." Tara wrinkled her nose, as though a putrid smell had suddenly invaded the room. "Your house looks really weird sitting on the same block with a bunch of nice homes."

How could Sinda argue with that? Especially when she'd thought the same thing herself. "You're probably right," she agreed. "However, I got the house for a reasonable price, and it's perfect for my needs."

Tara's eyes brightened as she leaned forward on her elbows. "What exactly are those needs?"

Sinda blinked rapidly. *Why is she asking so many questions?*

"What do you do in that big old house?"

"Do?"

"Yeah. What I really want to know is why you—"

Tara's words were cut off when her father stepped through the swinging door separating the kitchen from the dining room. "Sorry to keep you lovely ladies waiting. It took some time to get everything dished up." Glen looked over at Sinda and offered her a friendly grin. "I hope you'll soon see—or rather taste that the wait was worth it." He placed a huge platter of fried chicken on the table. "I'm glad you could join us today, Sinda."

"It was nice of you to invite me, Glen."

Glen took a seat at the head of the table. "Tara, would you please run out to the kitchen and bring in the salad and potatoes?"

"Can't you do it?"

Sinda sucked in her breath, waiting to see how Glen would respond to his daughter's sassy remark.

"I'll be lighting the candles," he said patiently.

Sinda could hardly believe how soft-spoken he was. She'd expected him to shout at Tara and tell her she was being insolent.

"Dad, you're really not going to turn this into a fancy dinner, are you?" Tara asked, casting her father a pleading glance.

Glen turned toward Sinda and gave her a quick wink. "It isn't every day that the Olsens get to entertain someone so charming."

Sinda felt the heat of embarrassment creep up the back of her neck. There was no denying it—Glen was quite a handsome man. His wavy, dark hair and sparkling blue eyes were enough to turn any woman's head. She averted her gaze and pretended to study the floral pattern on the dinner plate in front of her.

"Tara, I asked you to bring in the salad and potatoes."

"Okay, okay. . .I'm going."

Tara left the room, and Glen pulled a book of matches from the front pocket of his pale blue dress shirt. He proceeded to light the candles and had just finished when Tara returned, carrying a bowl of mashed potatoes.

"Don't forget the salad," he reminded.

The child gave him a disgruntled look, then she stomped off toward the kitchen. A few minutes later she was back with a tossed green salad.

"Thank you, Tara. Great, we're all set now," Glen said, offering Sinda another warm smile. She was beginning to wonder if he ever quit smiling. Even when his daughter was acting like a brat, he kept a pleasant look on his face. It was a little disconcerting.

Tara reached for a piece of chicken, but Glen stopped her. "We haven't prayed yet."

"Sorry. I forgot."

When Glen and Tara bowed their heads, Sinda did the same. It had been awhile since she'd prayed—even for a meal. She knew why she'd given up praying; she just wasn't sure exactly when it had happened. Somehow it felt right to pray today, though. Glen seemed so earnest in his praises to God. Of course. . .

"Amen."

When she realized the blessing was over, Sinda opened her eyes and helped herself to a drumstick. "Everything looks and smells wonderful." She bit into the succulent meat and wasn't disappointed.

Tara sniffed the air. "Speaking of smells—I think something's burning."

Glen jumped up, nearly knocking over his glass of water. "My buttermilk biscuits!" He raced from the room, leaving Sinda alone with his daughter one more time.

Sinda spooned some mashed potatoes onto her plate and added a pat of butter from the butter dish sitting near her. She was about to take a bite, when the next question came.

"Do you know who Mrs. Higgins was?"

"My Realtor said she was the previous owner of my house."

"Yep, and she was really weird, too."

Sinda wasn't sure if Tara had emphasized the word *she* on purpose or not, but with a slight shrug, she decided to ignore the remark.

"Mrs. Higgins hardly ever left that creepy old house, and sometimes you could hear strange noises coming from over there." Tara's forehead wrinkled. "Some of the neighborhood kids think your house is haunted."

"What do you believe, Tara?"

"Dad says the noises were probably her old blind dog, howlin' at the moon. He thinks I shouldn't believe what other kids say—especially stuff like that." The child tore a piece of dark meat from the chicken leg she'd speared with her fork. "You couldn't pay me enough money to live in that creepy old place." She tapped the tines of her fork against the edge of her plate.

Glen stepped back into the dining room, interrupting Tara a second time. "That was close! My biscuits were just seconds from being ruined." He set the basket of rolls and a jar of strawberry jam on the table, then took his seat. "I believe I can finally join you in eating this meal."

"The fried chicken is wonderful," Sinda said, licking her lips. "I think Tara's right. You are the best cook in Washington."

Glen transmitted a smile that could have melted the ice cubes in Sinda's glass of water. "You'll have to try some of my famous barbecued chicken this summer."

"Oh, great," Tara muttered.

Glen shot his daughter a look that Sinda construed as a warning, and she swallowed so hard she nearly choked. Maybe Tara's dad wasn't quite as pleasant or patient as he first let on. "What did you say, Tara?" Glen's voice had raised at least an octave.

"I said, 'That sounds great.' "

Glen nodded at Tara, then Sinda. "I think so, too."

Sinda dipped her head, unsure of what to think or how to respond.

"So, how about it, Sinda? Would you be interested in trying some of my barbecued chicken sometime this summer?"

Without even thinking, she replied, "I always enjoy a good barbecue." *Now, what made me say that?*

"Great!" Glen declared with another winning smile. "The first time I do barbecued chicken, I'll be sure to let you know."

Chapter 4

Glen couldn't believe his eyes! Tara was peering through the cracks in the tall fence that separated their backyard from Sinda's. He'd just paid Mrs. Mayer her monthly check for watching Tara and seen her to her car. Now he had to deal with this? Slowly, he snuck up behind Tara and dropped one hand to her shoulder. "At it again, Miss Olsen?"

She spun around. "Dad! You've gotta quit sneakin' up on me like that. I'm too young to die of a heart attack."

"Maybe so, but you're not too young to be turned over my knee," he said, biting back a smile. While Glen did believe in discipline, he'd never had to resort to spanking Tara. Ever since she was old enough to sit in front of the TV, and he'd discovered how much she enjoyed it, he had used restrictions from television whenever she got out of line. It had always been fairly effective, too.

With hands planted firmly on her small hips, Tara stared up at him. "Dad, I was only—"

"Don't say anything more," he interrupted. "I'm not interested in your excuses." He glanced down at the ground. "Look where you're standing! You're going to ruin your mother's flowers if you're not careful."

Tara hopped out of the flower bed, just missing the toe of his boot. "Sorry," she mumbled. "I'll try to be more careful when I'm doing my investigating."

"I think you should leave the detective work to the Elmwood Police Department and try acting your age, Tara—keeping in mind that you're only ten years old and should be playing, not spying." Glen pointed toward the house. "Why don't you go play with your dolls for a while?"

Tara's forehead wrinkled. "I can't waste my time playing, Dad. I'm on a case right now. Besides, dolls are dumb. I put mine away in the hall closet ages ago."

He drew in a deep breath, reached for Tara's hand, and led her to the picnic table on the other side of the yard. "Why don't we have some cookies and lemonade? After we've filled our stomachs with something sweet, maybe we can talk about this some more." He guided her to one of the wooden benches.

Tara's eyes brightened. "That's a great idea, Dad. Mrs. Mayer made fresh lemonade when I got home from school. I think there's still a few ginger cookies left, too." She smiled up at him. "Of course, you're gonna have to make more pretty soon. Can't have an empty cookie jar, now can we?"

"No, that would never do," Glen said with a chuckle. "Maybe one evening this week I'll do some more baking, but that's only if you can stay out of trouble."

She offered him a sheepish grin. "I think I can manage."

"Good girl." Glen gave one of her braids a light tug. "Don't move from this spot. I'll be right back with cookies and lemonade."

When he returned a few minutes later, Glen was relieved to see that Tara was still sitting at the picnic table, and Jake was lying in her lap, purring like a motorboat.

"That cat sure has it easy," Glen said as he placed a tray loaded with cookies, napkins, a pitcher of lemonade, and two glasses in the center of the table. "All he ever does is laze around."

Tara stroked the gray and white cat behind its ears. "Yeah, he's got life made most of the time. Of course, he does work pretty hard when he chases down mice or poor, defenseless birds."

Glen took a seat on the bench across from her and studied the cat. "His green eyes sure are pretty."

Tara reached for a cookie. "Speaking of green eyes—I need to tell you something about our green-eyed neighbor lady."

Glen snapped to attention. "Sinda?" Against his will, and probably better judgment, he'd been thinking about Sinda ever since she'd come to dinner.

"Uh-huh."

"What about her?"

Tara leaned as far across the table as she could and whispered, "I saw her carrying more boxes into the house today."

"Sinda only moved in a few weeks ago, Tara. She told me the other day that she still has some things in storage and is bringing them home a little at a time."

"You don't understand," Tara asserted. "There was something really strange about one of those boxes."

Glen raised his eyebrows. "Strange? In what way?"

"Well, there was a—"

Tara's words were halted when Jake screeched, leaped off her lap, sailed across the yard, then scampered up the maple tree. Tara jumped up. "Ow! Stupid cat! He dug his claws into my legs!"

"I wonder what's gotten into him?" Glen shook his head. "It's not like Jake to carry on like that for no reason."

"That's why," Tara said, pointing to the gate that separated their backyard from Sinda's. It was open slightly, and a puny black dog poked its head through the opening. "Oh, great! You know how much Jake hates dogs."

A smile lifted the corners of Glen's mouth. "Yeah, and that little dog looks so ferocious."

Before Tara could respond, the dog took off like a streak of lightning, heading into the Olsens' yard, straight for the maple tree. Sinda was right behind him, calling, "Bad dog! Sparky, come back here right now!"

Glen's smile grew wider as he watched Sinda chase the small dog around his yard. He left the picnic table and moved toward her. "Is that your dog?"

"Yes," Sinda answered breathlessly. "He's a bundle of fury, too! He won't come when I call him, and I've already discovered that he likes to sneak out of the yard. No wonder he was advertised as 'free to good home.'"

Sparky was now poised under the maple tree, barking furiously and looking as though he could devour a mountain lion.

"He's after Jake!" Tara screamed, running toward the dog. "Dad, do something, quick!"

Sinda gave Glen a questioning look. "Jake?"

"Jake is Tara's cat. He ran up the tree when your pooch poked his head into our yard."

"I'm sorry," Sinda apologized. She moved in on Sparky, bent down, and scooped the yapping terrier into her arms.

"I didn't even know you owned a dog," Glen remarked. "We haven't seen or heard anything of him until a few minutes ago."

"Actually, I don't. I mean, I didn't have a dog before today." Sinda had to yell in order to be heard above the dog's frantic barking.

"He's kind of cute. Probably good company for you," Glen said in an equally loud voice.

"I did get him for companionship, but I also wanted a watchdog." Sinda held on tightly to the squirming, yapping terrier.

"He sure does bark loud. That should be enough to scare anyone off," Tara put in.

"Maybe he'll calm down if we move away from the tree." Glen took Sinda's arm and guided her toward the picnic table. "Would you like to join us for some cookies and lemonade? I'll go inside and get another glass."

Sinda looked down at the bundle of fur in her arms. "Thanks, but I'd better get this little rascal back home." She started moving toward the gate.

"Why do you need a watchdog?" Tara asked, stepping in front of Sinda. "Is there something weird going on in that creepy old house of yours?"

"Tara!"

"No, no. I mean, everything's fine," Sinda stammered.

Glen couldn't help but notice how flustered she was. Her face was red as a tomato, her hair was in complete disarray, and she looked like she was on the verge of tears. "Tara, move out of Sinda's way so she can take the dog back to her yard."

Tara stepped aside, but Glen could see by the stubborn set of her jaw that she was none too happy about it.

Sinda offered Glen the briefest of smiles, then she disappeared into her yard.

"What's that scowl you're wearing about?" Glen asked as Tara slumped onto the picnic table bench.

"Don't you see it, Dad?"

"See what?"

Tara squinted her eyes at him. "Can't you see how weird Sinda is?"

"I don't think she's weird." Glen snorted. "You, on the other hand, are apparently getting some weird ideas from watching too much TV. I'm going to speak to Mrs. Mayer about putting a limit on how much television you can watch after school."

"But, Dad, I—"

"A girl your age should be playing with her friends, not sitting in front of the TV all afternoon." Glen made an arch with his hand. "Instead, you're trying to dig up something on the neighbors!" He glanced across the yard searching for inspiration. "The flower beds could use some investigating. As soon as you finish your snack, you can get busy tending the garden."

Tara stuck out her lower lip and folded her arms across her chest. "I didn't do anything wrong."

Glen held up one finger. "You were spying." A second finger joined the first. "You were rude to Sinda." A third finger came up. "Then you said she's weird." He frowned deeply. "We keep discussing these same manners problems over and over, Tara. I'm going inside to start supper. You need to have that weeding finished before it's ready."

❧

By the time Sinda clipped a leash to Sparky's collar and secured him to a long chain hooked to the end of her clothesline, she was all done in. "Maybe getting a dog was a bad idea," she mumbled as she gave the furry creature a gentle pat. "So far, you've been nothing but trouble."

The little dog tipped his head and looked up at her as though he was truly sorry. Sinda couldn't help but smile. "I'll bring you inside after awhile." She turned and headed for the house. Sparky let out a pathetic whine, and she almost changed her mind about bringing him in before she fixed supper. When she was growing up, Sinda had always wanted a dog, but her father would never allow it. He used to say that pets were nothing but trouble, and after today Sinda thought he might have been right. Still, dogs were supposed to be companions and loyal friends. At least the mutts she'd seen on TV had been devoted to their masters.

When Sinda reached the back porch, she stopped beside the outside faucet and turned on the spigot. They hadn't had much rain yet this spring, and she figured the yard, though overgrown, could use a good drink. As the sprinkler came on, a spray of water shot into the air, and a miniature rainbow glistened through the mist.

She swallowed against the nodule that had formed in her throat. Rainbows always made Sinda think of her mother and, like it was only yesterday, she could hear Mother saying, "Rainbows are a reminder of God's promises. Whenever you see one, remember how much He loves you."

"Do You love me, God?" Sinda whispered as she looked up at the cloudless sky. "Has anyone ever truly loved me?"

The telephone was ringing when Sinda entered the kitchen a few minutes later. She grabbed the receiver with one hand while she reached for a towel with the other. In the process of turning on the hose, she'd managed to get her hand and both sneakers wet. Of course, when a faucet leaked like a sieve, what else could she expect?

"Hello," she said breathlessly into the cordless phone.

"Hi, Sinda, it's me."

Sinda dropped into a chair at the kitchen table. "Hey, Carol, how are you?"

"I was going to ask you the same question. I haven't heard from you in a while, and I was worried you might have worked yourself to death."

"Not quite, but from the looks of things, I'll be forever trying to get the rest of my things unpacked, not to mention getting this old place fixed up so it's livable."

"Know what I think you need?"

"What?"

"A break from all that work."

Sinda couldn't argue with that. She'd been working around the clock ever since she moved into the monstrosity she was dumb enough to call home.

"How about meeting me for lunch at Elmwood City Park tomorrow afternoon? If you don't take a little break, you'll end up cranky as a bear who's lost all his hair."

"I guess I could spare an hour or so."

"Great! See you at one, and be ready for fun!"

Sinda grinned. Carol had always thought she was a poet. Over the years, her friend's goofy rhymes and lighthearted banter had gotten Sinda through more than one pity party. *At least Carol taught me how to laugh.* Sinda wondered what her life would have been like if she'd been raised in a normal home with two loving parents. Instead, her childhood had been filled with loneliness, disappointment, countless rules, and sometimes hostility. But it was all Mother's fault. Dad went through so much because of her.

"Sinda, are you still there?"

Carol's question drove Sinda's thoughts back to the present, and she felt grateful. She was tired of living in the past. Tired of dwelling on the negative. She'd come to Elmwood to begin a new life, and she was determined to at least make her business venture successful.

"I'm here, Carol," she murmured. "I'll see you tomorrow at one."

Chapter 5

I'm glad you suggested this little outing," Sinda told Carol as they settled onto a park bench. She leaned back with a contented sigh. "It's such a beautiful spring day, and everything is so lush and green."

"It's that time of year, my dear." Carol poked Sinda in the ribs. "We usually get lots of liquid sunshine in the spring, but this year we're falling short of our average rainfall, so it won't stay green long if we don't get some rain soon."

Sinda made no comment, and Carol took their conversation in another direction. "You know, I was beginning to worry about you."

"How come?"

"Ever since you moved here, all you've done is work. It's been nearly a month, so I thought it was time you got out of that stuffy old house and did something fun."

Sinda opened her lunch sack and withdrew the ham sandwich she'd thrown together for their Saturday afternoon picnic. "For your information, I have gotten out of the house a few times."

"Really? Where did you go, Miss Social Butterfly?" Carol laughed and gave Sinda's arm a little squeeze.

"I've been shopping a few times, made several trips to my storage unit, stopped at the department of licensing, and I had dinner at the neighbor's one Sunday afternoon."

Carol raised her eyebrows. "Which neighbor was that?"

"The one next door. I'm sure I told you about Glen and his daughter bringing me some cookies the day I moved in."

"Yes, you did, but you didn't say anything about having dinner with them." Carol puckered her lips. "I'm surprised to hear you're seeing a man. You've never been much for dating."

"I'm not seeing anyone," Sinda said, choosing to ignore her friend's reminder about her lack of a social life. "It was just a friendly, get-to-know-your-neighbor dinner. Don't read any more into it than that."

Carol shook her head slowly. "I'm glad to have you living closer, but I'd be even happier if I knew you were truly at peace. You've had moods of melancholy as long as I've known you, and any time I've asked what's wrong, you've always avoided the subject."

"I appreciate your concern—always have, in fact. I've just never wanted to talk about my problems." Sinda stared off into space. "Besides, talking doesn't change anything."

"Maybe not, but it's good for the soul, which in turn brings happier thoughts," Carol responded.

Sinda glanced back at her friend. "My work keeps me plenty busy. And I have a good friend who meets me at the park for lunch whenever she thinks I'm working too much." She paused and winked at Carol. "That's all the happiness I need. Besides, you should concern yourself with your own love life and quit worrying about me."

Carol smiled and crossed her fingers. "I think I may have found my man."

"Is it the guy you told me about who works at the bank?"

"Gary Tarrol is our new loan officer." Carol elbowed Sinda in the ribs. "I don't know what I'll do if we should start dating and things get serious."

For a minute Sinda wondered if her friend was as leery of marriage as she was, but then she remembered how boy crazy Carol had been when they were teenagers. In fact, Sinda was amazed that Carol wasn't already married and raising a family.

"My motto is: Find the right guy and let your heart fly!" Carol continued. She batted her eyelashes dramatically. "Can you imagine me living the rest of my life with a name like Carol Tarrol?"

Sinda giggled. "It might be kind of cute. Especially since you like rhyming so well."

Her friend grimaced and opened her can of soda. "Not that well. Maybe I should look for someone with a better last name." She took a drink, then wiped her mouth on a napkin. "Now tell me—how's business?"

Sinda frowned. "I haven't done much advertising yet, so things are still kind of slow. There are lots of kids in this world, though, and just as many eager adults. I'm sure I'll do okay once the word gets out. In fact, I'll probably do as well here in Oregon as I did in Seattle."

"I have a friend who might need your services," Carol said. "She has a four-year-old daughter."

"Tell her to give me a call. I'm sure we can work something out." Sinda tossed her empty sandwich wrapper in the garbage and stood up. "Let's take a quick hike around the lake, then I need to get back home." As they started to walk away, she glanced over her shoulder. There were two young girls crouched in the bushes, not far from the bench where she and Carol had been sitting. One of the children wore her brown hair in pigtails. *That's Tara Olsen. Now, why would she be hiding in the bushes?*

❧

Sinda stood in front of her open kitchen window, talking on the phone. "Yes, they're quite safe in my basement. I'd be happy to take her off your hands," she said into the receiver. "We can discuss the price further once I've taken a good look at her." Sinda jotted a few notes on a tablet she kept near the phone, said good-bye, and hung up. Mrs. Kramer would be by soon with her delivery, then Sinda could grab a quick bite of dinner and try to get a few bills paid.

"Oh, to be wealthy and carefree," she murmured. "Even carefree would be nice."

Sinda could feel a cord of tension grip her body, like a confining belt after a heavy meal. Her mouth compressed into a tight line as her mind dragged her unwillingly back to the past. Dad had always stressed the importance of good stewardship. In his words that meant "Pay every bill on time, give God His ten percent, and never spend money foolishly." Sinda tried to be prompt about bill paying, but now that Dad was gone, she no longer worried about giving God any money. Why should she? God hadn't done much for her. First she'd lost Mother, and now Dad was dead. Didn't God see her pain? Didn't He care at all? Must the misery in her life keep on growing like yeast rising in bread?

She glanced around the kitchen, noting the faded yellow paint on the walls. The cream-colored linoleum was coming up in several places, and all the appliances were outdated. *Was I wrong to buy this place? If Dad were still alive, would he lecture me for spending my inheritance foolishly?*

The sound of a car door slamming shut drew Sinda's contemplations to a halt. It was probably Mrs. Kramer, since she only lived a mile away. *I'll worry about my ill-chosen spending some other time. Right now I've got business to tend to.*

❧

Glen stepped inside the back door, his arms full of groceries. He'd no more than set the bags on the table when Tara burst into the room. "Am I ever glad to see you!"

"Why, thank you, Miss Olsen. I'm happy to see you, too." Glen rubbed his hands briskly together. "It's been a long Saturday, and after work I had to run some errands and grocery shop. Scoot on into the living room and tell Mrs. Mayer I'm home now. I'll put away the groceries, then we'll see what we can pull together for supper. What appeals to you, honey? Tacos? Pizza?"

Tara tugged on his shirtsleeve. "I need to talk to you."

"In a minute," he said as he opened the first sack and withdrew a bag of apples. "Now do as I said."

Tara turned on her heels and was about to exit the room when Mrs. Mayer poked her head through the doorway. A radiant smile filled her broad face, and her pale blue eyes twinkled. Glen often thanked God for providing this pleasant, Christian woman to watch Tara every afternoon and on the Saturdays he was scheduled to work. "Do you need me to do anything else before I head for home?" the older woman asked.

Glen shook his head and placed the apples into the fruit bowl. "Can't think of a thing, Mrs. Mayer, thanks. Tara and I will see you at church tomorrow morning."

"Sure enough. Enjoy the rest of your evening." Mrs. Mayer waved her hand and exited through the back door.

Tara inched closer to her father. "Now can we talk?"

Glen put the perishable items in the refrigerator, then withdrew a carton of milk. "Are there any donuts left from the picnic you'd planned this afternoon with Penny, or did the two of you eat them all?" he asked, ignoring his daughter's perturbed look.

Tara shook her head. "We left a few, but Dad, we need to talk!"

Glen knew that Tara tended to be overly dramatic about most things. For some time now he had been trying to teach her to be patient and give him a chance to settle in so they could chat over a snack. Whatever she had to say could wait at least that long. "You get the donuts, and I'll pour us each a glass of milk. We'll sit at the table, and you can tell me what's on your mind. Then I've got to finish putting away the groceries and get busy making supper."

He started toward the table, but Tara halted his steps by positioning herself directly in front of him. "I think you should call the police."

Glen's eyebrows furrowed. "The police? What are you talking about?"

"Our neighbor. I'm talking about our new neighbor."

"Sinda?"

Tara's nose twitched as she pursed her lips. "She's the only new neighbor we have, isn't she?"

Glen frowned. "What's Sinda got to do with the police? Did she ask you to have me call them? Is she having some kind of problem?" Even though he didn't know Sinda very well, his heart squeezed at the thought of her being in some kind of trouble. "I'd better go over there and check on her." He placed the carton of milk on the table and started for the back door.

"No, don't!" Tara's tone was pleading, and she grabbed his hand. "Let the police handle this, Dad."

"Handle what?"

Tara pointed at the table. "Sit down, and I'll tell you all about it."

As soon as they were both seated, Tara leaned forward with her elbows on the table, and in her most serious voice she announced, "There's a little kid in Sinda's house."

Glen drew in a deep breath and mentally counted to ten. "So there's a kid visiting Sinda. I see. And we should call the police because. . . ?"

"Sinda is buying and selling children!" Tara exclaimed. "That's against the law, and she's gotta be stopped."

Glen massaged the bridge of his nose. "Could we talk about this after dinner?"

"I'm telling you the truth!" Tara shouted. "Now, are you going to call the police or not?"

"What should I tell them?"

"Sinda is committing a crime. When people commit crimes, you're supposed to call the police."

He looked at her pointedly. "What crime has Sinda supposedly committed?"

"I just told you. She's buying and selling kids! I know of at least one who's locked in her basement right now."

Glen was tempted to laugh at the absurd accusation. "What were you watching on TV today?"

Tara gave him an icy stare. "I know what you're thinking, but I'm not making this up. That woman is a criminal."

"What sort of proof do you have?"

"I saw a lady bring a kid over to Sinda's house a little while ago. When the woman left, the kid wasn't with her."

Glen slowly shook his head. This story was getting better and better. "So tell me again, what is it that's illegal about baby-sitting someone's child?"

"Sinda drove off in her minivan a few minutes after the lady left, but the kid wasn't with her. She left it all alone in that creepy old house."

"Maybe you just didn't see the child leave with her."

"There's more, Dad."

"More?"

"I've been watching Sinda for several weeks now, and—"

"You mean spying, don't you?" Before Tara could respond, Glen rushed on. "I've warned you repeatedly about that—"

"But I've gathered some incriminating evidence," Tara interrupted.

Glen clicked his tongue. "Incriminating—such a big word for a little girl."

"Would you quit teasing and listen to me?"

"Okay, okay," he conceded. "What incriminating evidence do you have on our new neighbor?"

"I've seen her bring other kids into that house." Tara frowned deeply. "Once she even brought in a baby who was in a wicker basket. I heard it crying." She paused a moment and swallowed hard. "Remember when Sinda first moved in and we went over to meet her and took her a plate of cookies?"

Glen nodded. "I remember."

"She was holding a doll when she opened the door, and she put it down really quick after she saw us. I thought maybe she had kids of her own, but then she told us she wasn't even married."

"So you naturally concluded that Sinda is up to no good." Glen shook his head. "What else haven't you told me?"

"I think that doll belonged to one of the kids she bought and sold. Today Penny and I saw Sinda and some lady with curly blond hair at the park. Sinda was telling the woman about her business, and she said she thought she was going to do okay because there are lots of kids in the world."

"Come on, kiddo. You don't seriously think—"

"That's not all," Tara asserted. "Sinda keeps the children in her basement. I was checking her place out earlier, and I heard her talking on the phone. She was telling one of her customers that's where she puts them." Tara sucked in her breath. "Who knows how many innocent children are being held in that house, only to be sold on the black market?"

Glen leaned his head back and laughed. "Black market? You don't really expect me to believe that a nice woman like Sinda Shull is involved in something like that!"

"Yes, I do." Tara's eyes filled with tears.

Glen sat there for several seconds, trying to decide how best to handle the situation. His daughter had always been prone to exaggerate, but this story was a bit too much. Perhaps Tara's increasingly wild stories were just her way of getting his attention.

"Well, young lady," he finally said, "there seems to be only one way to settle the matter."

Her eyes brightened. "You're gonna call the cops?"

He shook his head. "No, I'm not. We are heading over to Sinda's. We're going to get to the bottom of this once and for all!"

Chapter 6

A knock at the front door, followed by the sound of Sparky's frantic barking, drew Sinda out of the kitchen. She bent down and scooped the little dog into her arms and opened the door. She was surprised to discover Glen and Tara standing on her front porch. "What can I do for you?" she asked hesitantly.

Glen cleared his throat a couple of times and shuffled his feet. "There's a little matter I'd like to get cleared up. I'm sure it's just a silly misunderstanding, though."

"A misunderstanding?" Sinda repeated.

He nodded. "Tara, uh, thinks she's seen something going on over here."

Sinda shifted her weight from one foot to the other as she studied the fading rays of the evening sun dancing across Glen's jet-black hair. Her gaze roamed over his face next. He looked so nervous she almost felt sorry for him. "What do you think is going on?" she asked, shifting her gaze from Glen to his daughter.

"I want to know why you're buying and selling kids!" the child blurted out.

Sinda's mouth dropped open, and she blinked several times. "What?"

Tara narrowed her eyes in an icy stare. It was obvious by the tilt of her head and her crossed arms that the girl was not going to leave without some answers. "Don't try to deny it," Tara huffed. "I've been watching you. I know exactly what you're up to, and we're gonna call the police."

Glen backed away slightly, jamming his hands into the pockets of his blue jeans and staring down at the porch. "My detective daughter thinks you're involved with the black market."

Sinda could see that Glen was embarrassed, yet if there was even a chance that he thought. . . She forced her attention back to Tara. "I imagine you've seen a few people come and go from my house with small children."

Tara's eyes widened and she nodded. "That's right, and you can't get away with a thing like that! See, Dad? She admits it!"

"You're an excellent detective," Sinda admitted.

Tara looked up at her father with a satisfied smile. "I told you. Now can we call the police?"

Glen groaned and slapped his palm against his forehead.

Sinda gently touched Tara's arm, but the child pulled away as though she'd been slapped. "I think you both should come inside and follow me."

"Follow you where?" Glen asked, lifting his dark eyebrows.

The intensity of his gaze sent shivers of apprehension up Sinda's spine. Was he angry? Should she be inviting them inside? Her mouth compressed into a tight line as she considered her options. Did she really want the police coming to her house? Police officers had made her feel uncomfortable ever since. . .

"Where do you want us to follow you to?"

Glen's deep voice invaded Sinda's thoughts, and she jerked her attention back to the situation at hand. "To my basement." She stepped onto the porch and set Sparky down. "Did you close the gate between our yards when you came over?"

Glen nodded, and Sinda motioned them inside. She led the way downstairs, and when they reached the bottom step she snapped on the overhead light.

Tara gasped and grabbed her dad's hand as the beam of light brought into view several small babies and two toddlers lying on a table in the center of the room.

"What in the world?" Glen's open mouth told Sinda how surprised he was by the unusual sight.

"I know this might appear a bit strange, but it's really quite simple." Sinda gestured toward the array of bodies. "You see, I'm a doll doctor, and these are my patients."

Tara's face turned ashen. "But, I–I thought—"

"The children you thought were coming and going from my house were dolls, Tara," Sinda explained. "I don't have my business sign nailed up on the house yet, but I do have a business license and a permit from the city to operate a doll hospital here."

Tara hung her head. "I–I guess I sort of got things mixed up."

"I would say so." Glen gave his daughter a nudge. "Don't you think you owe Sinda an apology?"

"It's all right. There was no harm done," Sinda said quickly. Despite Tara's accusation, she couldn't help but feel sorry for the child. Sinda had made her share of blunders when she was growing up, and Dad had never treated it lightly.

"Tara," Glen stated with a scowl on his face, "you owe Sinda an apology. We'll discuss the consequences of your behavior at home."

Tara continued to stare at the concrete floor. "I'm sorry, Sinda."

Sinda took a few steps toward the child. She wanted to give Tara a hug but didn't think it would be appreciated. Instead, she merely patted the child on top of her head. "It was an honest mistake. Any intelligent little girl could have gotten the wrong impression by what you saw."

Tara's head shot up. "I am not a little girl!"

"Good, then you won't mind doing some honest work to make up for your error," Glen asserted.

Tara's gaze darted to her dad. "What kind of work?"

Glen motioned toward Sinda. "I'm sure the doll doctor can find something for you to do right here in her workshop."

Sinda sucked in her lower lip. "I might be able to use some help." Although she wasn't sure she wanted the help to come in the form of a child's punishment.

"Dad, you know I don't play with dolls anymore," Tara said with a moan.

"You wouldn't be playing, Tara," Sinda insisted. "You'd be helping me with some necessary repairs."

Tara's eyes filled with sudden tears. "It's not fair. This old house is creepy, and I hate dolls!"

Glen bent down so he was making direct eye contact with his daughter. "This case is closed, Tara."

⊱

Glen stood in front of the dresser in his bedroom, studying Tara's most recent school picture. *She's such a cute kid, even though she can be a little stinker at times.* He drew in a deep breath as he reflected on the happenings of the evening. He should never have listened to Tara's crazy idea about Sinda selling kids on the black market, much less gone over there and made a complete fool of himself. He and Tara had been on their own for nine years, and it was hard not to indulge her. He knew he'd let her get too carried away, and tonight's fiasco made him realize how necessary it was to gain control. After they'd come home from Sinda's, he'd fixed dinner, seen to it that Tara did her weekend homework, then sent her to bed without any dessert. All her pouting, pleading, and crying over the idea of going to Sinda's to help repair dolls had nearly been his undoing, but Glen remained strong.

As he moved toward the window and stared at the house next door, Glen's thoughts shifted to Sinda. He hadn't dated much since his wife's death, but of the few women he had gone out with, none had captured his interest the way Sinda had in the short time since they'd met. Some unseen pull made him want to seek out ways to spend more time with her. He wasn't sure if it was the need he sensed in her or merely physical attraction. The vulnerable side of Sinda drew him, but he would need to be cautious. She was like a jigsaw puzzle. So many pieces looked the same, but each time he tried to make them match, the pieces didn't fit. Sinda could be friendly one minute and downright rude the next. He had a hunch she was hiding something, only it was far beyond anything Tara had conjured up in her imagination. Glen's sixth sense told him that Sinda Shull had been hurt and might even be running from someone or something.

The fact that Sinda was a doll doctor had been a real surprise, but even more astonishing was that she'd given no evidence of her unusual occupation until Tara made her ridiculous accusations. Except for having dinner with them that one Sunday afternoon, Sinda had kept pretty much to herself.

"Sure wish I could get to know her better," Glen mumbled as he leaned against the windowpane. *Is Sinda a Christian?* He hoped so, because it would be wrong to begin a relationship with her if she wasn't. He raked a hand through his hair as confusion clouded his thinking. "I'd better pray about this before I approach Sinda with any questions about her faith."

❧

Sinda sat at the long metal table in her basement workshop, watching Tara sand an old doll leg. She couldn't help but notice the forlorn expression on the child's face, and without warning, vague memories from the past bobbed to the surface of her mind. She'd been sad most of her childhood. . .at least after her mother had gone. She'd tried hard to be the best daughter she could, but she'd apparently fallen short since she was never able to please her father.

I won't think about that now, she scolded herself. *I have work to do.* Quickly reaching for the doll head that went with the leg Tara was sanding, Sinda asked, "Do you recognize this doll?"

The girl's only response was a shake of her head.

"It's one of the original Shirley Temple dolls. It's a true collectable and quite valuable."

Tara squinted her dark eyes at Sinda. "You mean it's like an antique or something?"

Sinda nodded. "Right. See the cracks in her composition body?"

A glimmer of interest flashed across the young girl's face. "What's composition?"

"It's compressed sawdust and wood filler that's been poured into a mold. It has the look and feel of wood, but each part is actually hollow," Sinda explained. She ran her fingers gently along the antique doll's face, relishing the notion that she had the power to transform an old relic into a work of art. "When composition ages, it often cracks or peels. Then it needs to be sanded, patched, and repainted."

"Who's Shirley Temple?" Tara asked as she continued to sand the doll leg.

"She was a child star who used to act in a lot of movies. When she became famous, the Ideal Toy Company created a line of dolls to look like her. Today Shirley Temple dolls are worth a lot of money."

Tara shrugged, as though she'd become bored with the topic. "Say, where are you from, anyway?" she asked suddenly.

"I grew up in Seattle."

"Did you run a doll hospital there?"

Sinda nodded, then picked up a new wig for the doll and applied a thin layer of white glue to the bald head. "I took a home study course and started working on dolls when I was a teenager."

"Did you make lots of money? Enough to buy this creepy old house?"

Sinda clenched her teeth so hard her jaw ached. Tara's inquisition was beginning to get on her nerves. "I've never made enough money repairing dolls to entirely support myself, but after my dad died, I started buying and selling old dolls and a few other antiques."

"So, that's how you could afford this place?"

"My father left me his entire estate, and I used the money from the sale of our house in Seattle to purchase my new home and a minivan."

Tara's freckled nose crinkled, and Sinda was pretty sure more questions were forthcoming. "How come your dad didn't leave everything to your mother? Isn't that how it's supposed to be when a husband dies?"

Sinda's mouth fell open. She hadn't expected such a direct question, not even from her nosey little neighbor. "Uh—well—my mother's gone, too." She secured the doll wig in place, fastened a rubber band around the head to keep it from slipping while it dried, then grabbed the other composition leg and gave it a few swipes with a piece of sandpaper.

"When did your mother die?" Tara prompted.

"She's been gone since I was ten."

"I was only a year old when my mother died, so I don't even remember her." Tara shrugged her slim shoulders. "If you have to lose someone, I guess that's the best way—when you're too young to remember."

Sinda's eyes filled with unexpected tears, and unable to stop the thoughts, her mind drifted back in time. Painful memories. So many painful memories. . .

Sinda had been small at the time. . .maybe five or six years old, but she remembered hearing a resonating cry waft through the house, followed by muffled sobs. She closed her eyes and saw herself halt on the stairs. There it was again. Her skin tingled, and her heart began to beat rapidly. A man and a woman were arguing. She held her breath. The woman's pleading escalated, then it abruptly stopped.

Silence.

Sinda's muscles tensed.

The woman screamed.

"What's wrong with Mama?" young Sinda had murmured. "Did she fall?" She hurried up the stairs. . . .

Sinda felt a tug on the sleeve of her sweatshirt. She blinked several times, and the vision drifted slowly away. "What's wrong? I asked you a question, and you spaced off on me," Tara said, giving Sinda a curious stare.

"I—I must have been in deep thought."

"Yeah, I'll say."

"What was your question?"

"I was asking if your doll hospital did so well in Seattle, how come you moved?"

Sinda frowned deeply. How many more questions was Tara going to fire at her? "I thought Elmwood would be a good place to start over," she answered through tight lips.

Tara leaned forward with her elbows on the table. "Why would you need to start over?"

Before Sinda could think of a reply, the telephone rang upstairs. She jumped to her feet, a sense of relief washing over her. "Keep working on that doll. I'll be right back," Sinda said, then she scurried up the steps.

Chapter 7

Several minutes later, Sinda hung up the phone. She smiled to herself. There was no telling when she might get another offer as good as the one she'd just had. The owner of a local antique shop wanted her to restore five old dolls. Two of them were bisque, and the other three were made of composition. The work was extensive and would bring in a fairly large sum of money. It looked as though Sinda's Doll Hospital was finally on its way.

Too bad Tara hates being here, she thought ruefully. *With all this extra work, I could probably use her help even after she's worked off her debt for spying on me. I wonder if she might be willing to extend the time if I offer some payment.*

Sinda crossed to the other side of the kitchen and opened a cupboard door. Tara might enjoy a treat, and it would certainly keep her too busy to ask any more personal questions.

She piled a few peanut butter cookies onto a plate, then filled a glass with cold milk. She placed the snack on a tray, picked up the cordless phone she'd left in the kitchen, and headed downstairs. She'd only descended two steps when she ran into Tara, nearly knocking the tray out of her hand.

"I—I heard a noise," the child squeaked.

Sinda's eyebrows furrowed. "What kind of noise?"

"A rustling sound. It was coming from one of the boxes over there." Tara pointed toward the wall lined with long shelves, but she never moved from her spot on the stairs.

"It's probably a mouse," Sinda said with a small laugh. "Should we go investigate?"

Tara's eyes grew wide. "No way!"

Sinda tipped her head to one side and listened. "Sparky's barking. Someone may be at the front door." She handed the tray to Tara. "Why don't you go back to the worktable and eat this snack? I'll be right down, then we'll check on that noise." She disappeared before Tara could argue the point.

When Sinda opened the front door, she discovered Glen standing on the porch. He held a loaf of gingerbread covered in plastic wrap. "This is for you," he said as Sparky darted between his legs and ran into the yard.

Little crinkles formed at the corners of his eyes when he smiled, and Sinda swallowed hard while she brushed a layer of sandpaper dust from the front of her overalls. *I wish he wouldn't look at me like that.* "Thanks, I love gingerbread," she murmured, taking the offered gift.

"Has anyone ever told you what gorgeous eyes you have?"

"What?" Sinda's heartbeat quickened.

"You have beautiful eyes."

She felt herself blush and knew it wasn't a delicate flush, but a searing red, covering her entire face. She quickly averted his gaze. "Shall I call Tara?"

Glen shook his head. "I didn't come over to get Tara."

"You—you didn't?" She glanced back up at him, feeling small and shy, like when she was a child. She wished he would quit staring at her. It filled her with a strange mixture of longing and fear.

"I came to bring you the bread, but I also wanted to ask you something."

"What did you want to ask?"

"Do you like Chinese?"

She stood there looking at him for several seconds, then realized he was waiting for her answer. "As in Chinese food?"

He nodded.

"I love Oriental cuisine."

He shuffled his feet a few times, bringing him a few inches closer. "I was wondering if you'd like to go out to dinner with me this Friday night."

Sinda could see the longing in Glen's eyes, and it frightened her. The scent of his aftershave stirred something deep inside her as well. "Just the two of us?" she rasped.

"Yep. I have other plans for my detective daughter."

Warning bells went off in Sinda's head. *Say no. Don't go out with Glen. Do not encourage him in any way!* When she opened her mouth to respond, the words that came out were quite different from those in her head, however. "I'd love to go."

Glen smacked his hands together, and she jumped. "Great! I'll pick you up around six-thirty." He bounded off the porch, calling, "Send Tara home when she's done for the day."

Sinda stood in the doorway, basking in the tingly sensation that danced through her veins. A question popped into her mind. *Would Dad approve of me going out with Glen Olsen?* She shook her head. *I shouldn't be thinking about Dad again.* Sinda was so innocent when it came to dealing with men, but she wanted to find out what Glen was really like. He appeared to be nice enough, but appearances could be deceiving. To the world her father had been a wonderful man, faithful in attending church, and attentive to Sinda's needs. But if Dad had truly loved God, wouldn't his actions at home have revealed it? Wasn't Christianity meant to be practiced in one's personal life, not just at church? As a child Sinda had practically worshiped her dad, but about the time she started into puberty she'd begun to question his motives. Driving the disturbing thoughts to the back of her mind, Sinda focused on the gingerbread Glen had given her. It needed to be put away.

When she returned to the basement, Sinda found Tara sitting on the third step from the bottom. She'd eaten all the cookies and was just finishing her milk. "What are you doing on the steps? I thought you would take the tray over to the table."

"I wasn't going near that box with the weird noise," Tara said, lifting her chin in defiance.

Sinda stepped around the child. "Let's go check it out."

Tara remained seated, arms folded across her chest as though daring Sinda to make her move. "You check it out. I'll wait here."

Sinda shrugged and started across the room. "And I thought you were a detective."

"I am!"

"Then come help."

Sinda glanced over her shoulder and was pleased to see Tara following her. However, it was obvious by the child's hunched shoulders and the scowl on her face that she was anything but thrilled about the prospect of trying to determine the nature of the strange noise.

When they came to the box in question, Tara stepped back as Sinda searched through the contents. "If it is a mouse, aren't you afraid it'll jump out and bite you?"

Sinda glanced over at Tara, who was cowering near the table. "I don't like mice, but I'm not afraid of them. I can't have a bunch of rodents chewing up my valuable doll parts."

"Why not set some traps?" Tara suggested. "That's what we used to do before we got Jake."

"Jake's your cat, right?"

"Yep, and he can get really feisty when there's a mouse around. I'd offer to lend him to you, but he wouldn't get along with your dog."

"You're probably right," Sinda agreed. She rummaged quickly through the rest of the doll parts, then set the box back on the shelf. "There's no sign of any mice. If there was one, it's gone now." She turned to face Tara. "That phone call I had earlier was an antique dealer. She has several old dolls for me to restore."

"Business is picking up, huh?"

Sinda nodded. "It would seem so, and I was wondering if you'd be interested in helping me here two or three afternoons a week."

"I thought I was helping."

"You are. I had a more permanent arrangement in mind," Sinda said. "Of course, I would pay you."

Tara frowned. "I don't like working with dolls. I'd much rather be watching TV or doin' some detective work."

"I really could use your help."

The child shook her head. "Not interested."

It was obvious that little Miss Olsen was not going to budge.

❧

"You're taking Sinda Shull where?" Tara shouted from across the room.

Glen was standing at the stove, stirring a pot of savory stew, but he turned to face his daughter. "I'm taking Sinda out to dinner, and I've arranged for you to stay overnight at Penny's."

Tara scowled at him. "This was Sinda's idea, wasn't it?"

"No, it was not her idea. I asked Sinda out when I took a loaf of gingerbread over there earlier today."

"What time was that?"

"Around four-thirty."

Tara tapped her toe against the linoleum. "I was over there then, and she never told me you stopped by. She didn't say she was going on a date with you, either."

Glen turned back to the stove and started humming his favorite hymn, "Amazing Grace."

"Dad, why are you doing this?"

He kept on humming and stirring the stew.

Tara marched across the room and stopped next to the stove. "Why are you doing this?"

He winked at her. "Doing what?"

She grabbed his hand and gave it a shake. "Dad!"

He pushed her hand away. "Watch out, Tara. You're gonna fool around and get burned."

Tara took a step back, and she stared up at him accusingly. "Why did you invite Sinda to dinner?"

He smiled. "Because, it was the neighborly—"

"Thing to do," she said, finishing his sentence. "It's those green eyes of hers, isn't it?"

"What are you talking about?"

"I'll bet she's got you hypnotized. I saw it happen on a TV show once." Waving her hand in a crisscross motion, Tara said, "She zapped you senseless and put you under some kind of a spell."

Glen looked upward. "Oh, Lord, please give me the wisdom of Solomon." He wondered if he should lecture Tara about watching too much TV again, or would it be better to give her a Bible verse to memorize? After a few seconds' deliberation, he chose a different approach. "You're absolutely right, kiddo. Sinda hypnotized me this afternoon. In fact, she put me so far under that I actually thought I was a dog."

"Dad, be serious! Sinda may not be buying and selling kids, but I don't trust her. I still think she's up to something."

"I would advise you to avoid detective work, Miss Olsen," he threatened. "Your last mistake got you thirty days of no TV and apprentice work in Sinda's Doll Hospital, remember?"

Tara's forehead wrinkled. "I'm too old to play with dolls, and Sinda's house is creepy and full of weird noises." She stomped her foot. "There's no way I'd keep working for her after my thirty days are up."

"She asked you to? What'd you tell her?" Glen asked with interest. If Tara kept working for their new neighbor, he might get to see Sinda more often. Besides, it would be a good way for Tara to learn about responsibility.

"I said no." Tara shrugged. "She offered to pay me, but I'm not going to spend my free time sanding and painting a bunch of old dolls!" She scrunched up her nose. "I'm going to discover Sinda's secrets, then we'll see who has the last laugh."

Glen chuckled. "We sure will, and it will probably be me."

Chapter 8

"Tara, it's time to go!" Glen called from the hallway outside his daughter's open bedroom door.

Tara slammed her suitcase lid shut when Glen stepped into the room. "Would you like me to walk you over to Penny's?"

Tara shook her head. "I'm not a baby, Dad. You can just watch me walk across the street to Penny's if it makes you feel better."

Glen ran his fingers through his freshly combed hair. He thought the offer to walk with her might ease some of the tension between them. Ever since he'd told Tara about his date with Sinda, she'd been irritable. He straightened his tie and smoothed the lapel on his gray sport coat. "Do I look okay? I'm not overdressed, am I?"

"I guess it all depends on where you're goin'," Tara answered curtly. She sauntered out of the room, leaving her suitcase sitting on the floor.

Glen frowned but picked up the suitcase and followed. "I made reservations at the Silver Moon," he called after her.

Tara made no comment until she reached the bottom step. Then she turned and glared up at him. "I don't think you should go to the Silver Moon."

"Why not?"

"That place is too expensive!"

He smiled in response. "I'm sure I can scrape together enough money to pay for two dinners."

"How do you even know Sinda likes Chinese food?"

"She said so. What's this sudden concern about restaurant prices?" Glen exhaled a puff of frustration. He was not in the mood for this conversation.

She shrugged.

Glen bent down and planted a kiss on her forehead. "I'll watch you cross the street." He paused a moment. "Oh, and Tara?"

"Yeah, Dad?"

"You'd better behave yourself tonight."

She pursed her lips. "Don't I always?"

Glen knew it was time to get tough. He couldn't let Tara continue behaving like a spoiled, sassy brat. No matter how much he loved her or how sorry he was that she'd grown up without her mother, he had to remain firm. "I'm serious.

You're already on restrictions, and if you pull anything funny at Penny's, I'll add another thirty days to your punishment."

Tara picked up her suitcase and marched out the front door. "Be careful tonight," she called. "Whatever you do, don't look directly into Sinda's weird green eyes!"

❧

Sinda paced between the fireplace and the grandfather clock. Glen wasn't late yet, but she almost hoped he would be. It would give her a few more minutes to compose herself. It had been almost three years since her last date, and that one had ended badly. She could still see the look on Todd Abernathy's face when her father gave him the third degree before they left for the theater. Even worse was when Todd brought her home and was about to kiss her good night. They'd been standing on the front porch, but the light wasn't on, so Sinda figured her father had gone to bed. She found out otherwise when he snapped on the porch light, jerked open the front door, and hollered, "You're late! I can't trust you on anything, can I?" His face was a mask of anger. "You're just like your mother, you know that?" It was the last time Todd ever came around.

Swallowing the pain, Sinda drove the unpleasant memories to the back of her mind and peered into the hallway mirror. Dad wouldn't be waiting for her tonight. If she embarrassed herself in front of Glen Olsen, it would be her own doing.

"I hope I look all right," she murmured as she studied her reflection. She'd chosen a rust-colored, full-length dress to wear and left her hair hanging long, pulled away from her face with a large beaded barrette at the nape of her neck. She didn't know what had possessed her to agree to this date, but she had, so there was no backing out now. When a knock at the front door sounded, her heart fluttered like a frightened baby bird. She drew in a deep breath as she moved to the hallway and reached for the doorknob.

Glen stood on the porch, dressed in a pair of black slacks, a white shirt with black pinstripes, and a gray jacket. He was smiling from ear to ear and holding a bouquet of pink and white carnations.

Sinda tried to smile but failed. Except for the corsage Dad had given her when she graduated from high school, no one had ever given her flowers before.

A crease formed between his brows. "You're not allergic to flowers, I hope."

"No, no, they're lovely. Let me put them in some water, then I'll be ready to go." Her voice was strained as his gaze probed hers. How could this man's presence affect her so?

Sinda left Glen waiting in the living room while she went to the kitchen to get a vase. When she returned a few minutes later, she found him with his hands stuffed inside his jacket pockets, strolling around the room. He seemed to be studying every nook and cranny. Sinda knew the wallpaper was peeling badly, the dark painted woodwork was chipped in several places, and the plastered ceiling needed to be patched and repainted. And this was just one room! The rest of the house was equally in need of repairs.

"The place is a mess," she said, placing the bouquet on a small antique table near her colonial-style couch.

Glen nodded and blew out his breath. "I'll bet nothing has been done to this old house in years."

Sinda shrugged. She didn't want to spoil the evening by talking about her albatross. "I'm ready to go if you are."

⁂

The Silver Moon restaurant was bustling with activity, but since Glen had made reservations, they were immediately ushered to a table. Like a true gentleman, Glen pulled out a chair for Sinda, then took the seat directly across from her.

She shifted uneasily, unsure of what to say, but was relieved when their waiter came and handed them each a menu. At least it gave her something to do with her hands.

"I think we'll have a plate of barbecued pork as an appetizer," Glen told the young man. He gestured toward Sinda. "Does that appeal to you?"

She licked her lips and struggled with words that wouldn't be a lie. At the moment, nothing appealed. *I probably shouldn't have accepted Glen's dinner invitation,* she silently berated herself. She was attracted to the man, and that worried her a lot. "Barbecued pork will be fine," she said with a nod.

When the waiter left, Glen leaned forward and smiled. "You look beautiful tonight."

Heat crept up Sinda's neck and flooded her face. "Thanks. You look nice, too."

"Tell me, Doctor Shull, how's that daughter of mine doing in your doll hospital? Is Tara any help at all, or does she get in the way?"

Sinda smiled, and the tension in her neck muscles eased as she began to relax. "I don't think she likes the work, but she has been a big help. I even offered to pay her if she'd keep working for me a few afternoons a week."

Glen's blue eyes sparkled in the candlelight. "Tara told me."

Sinda laughed dryly. "She hated the idea and turned me down flat."

The waiter returned with a plate of barbecued pork surrounded by sesame seeds and a small dish of hot mustard.

Glen placed their dinner order, and as soon as the waiter left, he prayed his thanks for the food. Reaching for his glass of water, he said, "I have a proposition for you, Sinda."

"Oh?" She placed one hand against her stomach, hoping to calm the butterflies that seemed determined to tap dance the night away, and forced her ragged breathing to return to normal.

"It's a business proposition," he said in a serious tone.

A business proposition. Now that might be something to consider. "What kind of business proposition?"

"It's about doll repairing."

"You want to become a doll doctor?"

Glen had just popped a piece of pork into his mouth. He swallowed, coughed, and grabbed for his water again. "Too much mustard," he sputtered.

Sinda bit back a smile. "That's why I prefer ketchup."

"I'm afraid I wouldn't make much of a doll doctor," Glen said after his fit of coughing subsided.

"Why not? I've read about some men who repair dolls in one of my doll magazines."

He nodded. "I'm sure that's true, but it isn't what I had in mind."

"What then?"

"Tara's mother had an old doll that belonged to her grandmother. The doll's been in a box under my bed for years. Tara doesn't even know about it."

"It could be quite valuable."

"I don't know about that, but it does need fixing. When Tara was born, Connie was so excited about having a little girl. She was sure she'd be able to pass the old doll down to our daughter someday." Glen's face was pinched with obvious pain. "Of course that never happened. Connie died a year later."

"It's not too late. You can still give Tara the doll her mother wanted her to have," Sinda said softly.

"I never gave it to her before because I didn't know where to take it for repairs."

"And now you do," she said with a smile. "So, what's the proposition you had in mind?"

Glen took a sip of his hot tea before answering. "The doll's a mess, and I'm sure it'll be expensive to fix." He massaged the bridge of his nose and grimaced. "I'm not even sure it's worth fixing—especially since my daughter isn't too thrilled about dolls these days."

"I'm certain that once Tara finds out it was her mother's, she'll be glad to have it."

"I was thinking maybe we could trade services in payment."

Her eyebrows shot up. "What service might you have to offer me?"

He grinned. "Your place could use a few repairs and some fresh paint. I'm pretty handy with a paintbrush. My carpentry skills aren't half bad either."

It only took Sinda a few seconds to think about his offer. Except for some new kitchen curtains Carol had helped her make, she hadn't done much in the way of fixing up the old place. "I do need some work done." She drew in a deep breath and expelled it quickly. "Without seeing the doll and assessing an estimate to restore it, I can't be sure our trade would be a fair one."

"I'm sure you can find enough work for me to do, should the cost be too high."

Sinda suppressed a giggle. "I didn't mean the price of the doll repairs would be too high. I meant the amount of work I need to have done far exceeds anything I could ever do for one antique doll."

Glen eyed her curiously. "I'm not concerned about balancing it out. If I come up short on the deal, maybe you can even things out a bit by agreeing to cook me dinner sometime."

Sinda reached for a piece of pork. What was there about Glen that made her feel so comfortable? Did she dare allow herself to begin a relationship with him—even a working one? She popped the meat into her mouth, wiped her fingers on her napkin, and extended her hand across the table. "You've got yourself a deal."

He looked pleased. At least she thought it was a look of pleasure she saw on his face. Maybe he had indigestion and was merely trying to be polite.

Chapter 9

Thanks for the nice evening, Glen. I ate so much I probably won't need to eat again all weekend." Sinda leaned her head against the vinyl headrest in the front seat of Glen's station wagon and sighed deeply.

"It doesn't have to end yet," he said, a promising gleam in his eyes. "We could take a drive out to Elmwood Lake. It's beautiful there in the spring."

With only a slight hesitation, she gave her consent. *What am I doing?* an inner voice warned. *I should really go home.*

Glen turned on the radio and slipped a cassette into place. The rich, melodious strains of a Christian gospel singer poured from the speakers. "This song, about our soul finding rest, is one of my favorites," he commented.

Sinda closed her eyes and let the music wash over her like a gentle waterfall. It had been so long since she'd listened to any kind of Christian music, and the tape had such a calming effect. "Umm. . .I do enjoy this type of music."

By the time the song ended, Glen had pulled into the parking lot. "We still have a hint of daylight. Want to take a walk around the lake?"

"That sounds nice. I need to work off some of my dinner," Sinda said with a nervous laugh. *I really should be home in bed. . .or working on a doll. . .any place but here.*

"It's getting kind of chilly," Glen remarked. "Want to wear my jacket?"

She shook her head. "No thanks, I'm fine."

They walked along quietly for a while, then Glen broke the silence. "I was wondering if you'd like to go to church on Sunday with me and Tara."

Sinda's shoulders sagged, and she shook her head. "Thanks for asking, but I'd better not."

"Have you already found a church home?"

She stopped walking and turned to face him. "What makes you think I'm a churchgoer?"

He studied her intently for a few seconds. "I—uh—saw an old Bible on your coffee table, so I just assumed—"

"Looks can be deceiving."

He drew back, as though she'd offended him, and she started walking again, a little faster this time.

"You're upset about something, aren't you?" Glen asked when he caught up to her.

A curt nod was all she could manage.

"What is it? What's wrong?"

Unexpected tears spilled over, and she blinked several times trying to dispel them.

Suddenly Sinda's steps were halted as Glen drew her into his arms. "Are you angry with me?"

"No," she muttered against his jacket. She couldn't tell him what was really bothering her.

He pulled slightly away and lifted her chin with his thumb. "It might help to talk about it."

She sniffed deeply and took a step back. "I'd rather not."

"Maybe some other time."

She shrugged. "Maybe."

Then, as if the topic of church had never been mentioned, Glen changed the subject. "So, when would you like to begin?"

She blinked. "Begin?"

"On your house repairs?"

"Oh. I guess you can start whenever it's convenient. When can I take a look at the doll?"

"Whenever it's convenient," he said with a deep chuckle. "How about tonight? Tara's staying over at her friend Penny's, so it would be the perfect time to show you."

Sinda shivered and rubbed her hands briskly over her bare arms. "I suppose that would be all right."

"You are cold." Glen draped one arm across her shoulders, and she shivered again, only this time she knew it wasn't from the cold.

"Tara mentioned that you moved here from Seattle," Glen remarked. "She said you used to run a doll hospital there, too."

Sinda nodded. *I wonder what else Tara told her dad.*

"I understand your father passed away, and your mother died when you were Tara's age?"

Sinda skidded to a stop. The camaraderie they'd begun to share had been blown away like a puff of smoke. "We've certainly done our homework, haven't we? I guess your daughter isn't the only detective in the family."

"She is the only one. At least, she thinks she is." Glen chuckled, apparently unaware of her annoyance.

"If you wanted a rundown on my past, why not ask me yourself?" she snapped. "Wouldn't it have been better than getting secondhand information from a child?"

"I did not ask my daughter to get the lowdown on you. She volunteered it—plain and simple."

Glen's tone had cooled some, and Sinda suddenly felt like an idiot. Maybe she was making a big deal out of his questions. Perhaps Dad had taught her too well about keeping to herself. "I guess I jumped to conclusions," Sinda said apologetically. "I think that's enough about me for one night, anyway. Why don't you tell me something about yourself?"

"Let's see now. . . .I'm thirty-four years old. I've been a Christian since I was twelve. My parents are missionaries in New Guinea. I have one brother, who is two years younger than me. I'm a mailman who loves his job but hates the blisters he gets when he wears new boots. I love to look for bargains at yard sales and thrift stores. I've been a widower for nine years. My daughter is the official neighborhood snoop, and I'm the best cook in Elmwood." He wiggled his eyebrows. "Anything else you'd like to know?"

Sinda couldn't help but smile. She and Glen Olsen had more in common than she would have guessed. At least she liked yard sales and thrift shops, and they did enjoy the same kind of music and eating Chinese food. Glen was like a breath of fresh air—able to make her smile and even temporarily forget the pain from her past. "How come a good-looking, great cook like you has never remarried?" she asked.

"I have dated a few women since my wife's death," he acknowledged. "I was in too much pain the first few years to even think about another woman, but when I did finally start dating, Tara didn't like it." He reached for Sinda's hand and gave it a gentle squeeze. "To be perfectly honest, until recently I've never met a woman besides my wife, Connie, who could hold my interest."

Until recently? Did he mean her? Dare she ask? She was about to, but he threw a question at her instead.

"How about you? Have there been many men in your life?"

She shook her head, hoping, almost praying, he wouldn't pursue the subject. "It's getting dark. Maybe we should go. You did say you wanted me to take a look at that doll, right?"

Glen nodded, and they turned back toward his car.

❦

Sinda waited in the living room while Glen went upstairs to get the doll. When he returned a short time later, she was standing in front of the fireplace, looking at a photograph on the mantel.

"That was the last picture ever taken of Connie," he said, stepping up beside Sinda. "It was about a year before she died."

She placed the photograph back on the mantel. "She was lovely."

A few tears shimmered in Glen's sapphire blue eyes as he replied, "Her sweet attitude and Christian faith never wavered—not even when the end came near."

Sinda swallowed hard, trying not to feel his pain, yet in spite of her resolve, her heart went out to Glen. What would it be like to raise a child alone? Her father knew, but she'd never asked him. She hadn't dared to ask any personal questions, especially about her mother.

Yanking her attention away from the captivating, dark-eyed brunette in the picture, Sinda leaned over the coffee table to examine the old doll Glen had placed there.

The bisque-head, ball-jointed doll lay in pieces, and the blond mohair wig was nearly threadbare. Several fingers and toes were missing as well. Sinda held the head gently, turning it over to see if it had any special markings that might indicate who had made it. "Ah. . .a German doll," she murmured. "She's quite old and a real treasure."

"You mean the doll could be worth something?" he asked, lifting his eyebrows in obvious surprise.

"Several hundred dollars, I'd say."

Glen frowned. "It needs a lot of work, though."

She shrugged her shoulders. "Nothing I haven't done before."

"How long do you think it would take?"

"Probably a month or two."

He nodded and gave her another one of his heart-melting smiles. "Then for the next month you'll have my handyman services." They shook on it to make it official, and Sinda said she should be getting home.

As Glen walked her next door, Sinda could hear Sparky barking from inside the house.

"Be quiet, you dumb dog. You'll alert the whole neighborhood," a child's shrill voice hissed.

"Alert them to what?" Glen bellowed.

Tara, who was crouched in one corner of Sinda's front porch, jumped in obvious surprise, and so did Sinda. "Dad! What are you doing here?"

"I think the question should be 'What are you doing here, Miss Olsen?' Aren't you supposed to be at Penny's?"

Tara rocked back and forth on her heels, clasping her hands tightly together. "I–I—that is—"

Sinda's gaze swung from Tara, to Glen, to a strange-looking object on her front porch. She leaned over for a closer look. "Where did this old trunk come from?" she asked, glancing back at Tara.

The child rubbed the palms of her hands over her blue jeans and licked her lips before she replied. "I—uh—was upstairs in Penny's room, and I happened to glance out the window, when—"

"I'll bet you just happened to," Glen interrupted.

"Go on, Tara," Sinda prompted.

At her father's nod, Tara touched the trunk with the toe of her sneaker and continued. "I saw a dark-colored van pull into your driveway. A man got out, and he took this big thing out of the back. He carried it up the walk and set it on your front porch. Then he knocked on the door, but when nobody answered, he left it and drove away."

"Did you get a good look at the man? Did you see any markings on the van or anything that might give us some clue?" Glen questioned.

Tara shook her head. "No, but I decided to come over here and see if he left a note or anything."

Sinda dropped to her knees beside the trunk. She thought she recognized it, but under the dim porch light she couldn't be sure. "There's a shipping tag attached to the side. It has my name and address on it." She glanced up at Tara. "The man you saw was probably from the freight company who sent the trunk."

"Who's it from, and what's inside?" Tara asked excitedly.

"That is none of our business, young lady." Glen offered Sinda his hand, and she stood up again. "That thing looks kind of heavy. Want me to carry it into the house for you?"

"I'd appreciate it," she replied.

Glen pointed at Tara. "Get on back to Penny's. We're going to have a little talk about this in the morning."

Tara bounded off the porch, but she turned back when she reached the sidewalk. "Say, Dad, what's in that cardboard box you're holding?"

Glen nodded in the direction of Penny's house. "Go!"

Sinda waited until Tara was safely across the street and had entered her friend's house before she opened the front door. Glen handed Sinda the box with the antique doll in it, then he hoisted the trunk to his broad shoulders and followed her inside.

At her suggestion, Glen set the trunk in the hallway, then moved toward the door, hesitating slightly. To her surprise, he lifted his hand and gently touched the side of her face, sending shivers of delight up her spine. She breathed in the musky scent of his aftershave and held her breath as he bent his head toward her. Their lips touched briefly in a warm kiss as delicate as butterfly wings.

"I guess I should apologize for that," Glen whispered when he pulled away. "I'm not usually so forward."

Sinda's cheeks flamed as she realized how much she'd enjoyed the brief kiss. "Good night, Glen," was all she managed to say.

With hands in his pockets and shoulders slightly slumped, Glen ambled out the front door. Did he think she was angry? Should she have said something more?

Sinda shut the door, shuffled to the living room, and slumped to the couch with a groan. She sat there, staring vacantly at the unlit fireplace, then reached up to touch her mouth, still feeling the warmth of Glen's lips. As extraordinary as the kiss felt, she could never let it happen again!

She closed her eyes momentarily, and when she opened them, her gaze rested on the massive trunk sitting in the hallway. Who sent it and why? Should she open it now or wait until morning?

Sinda forced herself to get up from the couch, and she moved slowly across the room. *"Why put off until tomorrow what you can do today?"* She could hear her father's words as if he were standing right beside her. How many times had he reprimanded her for procrastinating? How many times had he screamed at her for forgetting things? Why was it so important to do things right away? Worse yet, why was she still doing things his way? He was dead. Shouldn't she be able to make her own decisions and do things her way?

"I guess old habits die hard," Sinda said as she knelt beside the trunk. With trembling fingers she grasped the handle and pulled. It didn't budge. That's when she noticed the hasp was held securely in place by a padlock. The key! Where was the key?

It had been many years since Sinda had seen the trunk, though she'd never viewed any of its contents. She was certain it was her mother's trunk, which she'd seen in her closet on several occasions. She'd always figured Dad had thrown it out after Mother left. Seeing it now was a painful reminder that her mother was gone forever. It made her feel as if she were ten years old again. . .sad, betrayed, and confused by everything that had happened.

Driving the troubling thoughts to the back of her mind, Sinda directed her focus to the old trunk. On closer examination, she discovered a business card attached to the handle. A light finally dawned. Alex Masters, their family lawyer, must have had access to the trunk, for it was his name and address inscribed on the card.

Without a key Sinda had no way of getting into the trunk tonight. She may as well go up to bed. In the morning she'd give Alex a call and see if he had the key. She was in no hurry to open up old wounds, anyway. There were too many hurts from her past, and after such a lovely evening with Glen, she would rather not think about them.

Chapter 10

It was Saturday morning, and Tara, recently home from Penny's, had been sent outside to do more weeding in the flowerbeds. Glen watched her wipe the dampness from her forehead and heard her mutter, "If my mother was still alive, she'd be out here in the garden with me. Dad wouldn't be acting so goofy around our weird neighbor either."

"Who are you talking to?" Glen tapped his daughter on the shoulder, and she whirled around to face him.

"Myself." She glanced at the toolbox in his hand. "What's that for?"

"Starting today I'll be helping Sinda do some repairs on her house during my free time, so if you need me just give a holler."

Tara's mouth dropped open like a broken hinge. "I thought you and I were goin' shopping today. Summer will be here soon, and I need new clothes."

Glen shrugged. "I had planned to take you to Fuller's Mall, but since you snuck out of Penny's house last night, you'll be spending the entire day doing chores. I've also decided that when your time is up at Sinda's, you can do another thirty days of doll repairs." Tara's eyes widened, and he drew in a deep breath, wondering if he was being too hard on her. He knew he was lenient at times, but there were other times, like right now, when he snapped like a turtle. *I have good reason to be stern with her,* he reasoned. *Tara disobeyed me, in spite of my warnings.*

Tara looked up at him as though she might burst into tears, and he chastised himself for feeling guilty. He leveled her with a look he hoped was admonishing. "If Sinda and I ever go out again, you'll be staying with Mrs. Mayer or at Uncle Phil's."

Tara thrust out her chin. "Aw, Dad, Uncle Phil lives in a dinky little apartment. He has no kids, and there's never anything fun to do there."

Glen couldn't argue with that. His younger, unmarried brother had his own successful business and was hardly ever home, so Phil didn't need a large place to live.

Tara's lower lip protruded. "And I don't see why I have to do more work for that weir—"

"Don't even say it," Glen interrupted. He motioned toward the flower beds. "When you're done weeding here, you can start out front."

"But, I did those a few weeks ago," she argued.

"Then do them again!" Glen disappeared, forcing all thoughts of his disobedient daughter to the back of his mind. Right now all he wanted to do was get over to Sinda's and start working.

He opened the gate and trudged through her overgrown yard. *I should offer to mow this mess.* Glen set the toolbox on Sinda's porch and knocked on her back door. She opened it right away, but he was disappointed when she didn't return his smile. She was wearing a pair of dark green overalls and a pale green T-shirt that deepened the color of her eyes, and her hair was pulled up into a ponytail. A strange sensation spread through Glen's chest. Despite her casual attire and sullen expression, he thought she looked beautiful.

"Good morning, Glen," Sinda said with downcast eyes. What was wrong? Why wouldn't she look at him?

"Morning," he responded cheerfully. He hoped his positive mood might rub off on her. "You have my services for most of the day, so where would you like me to begin?"

"You sound rather anxious to work up a sweat on such a warm spring day."

"Just keeping true to my word." He gave her a quick wink, but there was no response. Not even a smile. *It might be that she's upset because Tara was snooping around on her front porch last night. Or maybe it was that unplanned kiss. Should I ask?*

"I haven't started on your wife's old doll yet," Sinda said, breaking into Glen's contemplations.

He shrugged. "I just gave it to you last night."

"Before you tackle any of my house repairs, would you mind moving that old trunk upstairs?" she asked, changing the subject.

"No problem." He stepped inside, hoisted the trunk to his shoulders, and followed Sinda up the stairs.

When they came to the first room, she moved aside. "This room is full of boxes and things I haven't had time to find a place for yet, so let's put it here." She frowned deeply. "I don't even have a key that will open the trunk."

Glen raised his eyebrows. "No key came with it?"

She shook her head. "I have several old keys with some of my antiques, but nothing fits. I found my lawyer's business card on the handle last night, so I'll contact him to see if he has the key."

"Would you like me to break it open? I don't think it would be too difficult."

At first Sinda looked as though she might be considering the offer, but to his surprise she replied, "I'll wait and see what my lawyer has to say. There's no sense ruining a perfectly good padlock if it's not necessary."

Glen turned toward the door. "Where would you like me to begin? Should I start by mowing the lawn?"

"I think I can handle that myself," she said. "Why don't you try to do something about the front porch? It's even more dilapidated than the back porch, and since my customers come to the front door, I'd rather not have someone trip on a loose board and sue me for everything I don't own."

The expression on her face softened, and it made Glen's heart race. He grinned and started back down the stairs with Sinda following on his heels. He was glad the tension he'd felt when he first arrived seemed to be abating. "By the time you finish your breakfast, I should have a fairly good start on the project."

Her forehead wrinkled. "How'd you know I was about to eat breakfast?"

They were at the bottom of the stairs now, and Glen turned to face her. "My daughter's always telling me that I'm the best cook in the world. What kind of cook would I be if I couldn't smell scrambled eggs and sausage?"

Sinda grimaced and covered her face with her hands. "Guess I'm caught. If you haven't eaten yet, you're welcome to join me."

Glen held his stomach and gave her what he hoped was his best grin. He'd eaten a bowl of cereal and a piece of toast around seven, and it was a little after nine now. He could probably eat again.

❧

"Please, Dad, not another Sunday dinner with Sinda!"

Glen was putting away the leftovers from their Saturday evening supper of pizza and salad, while Tara cleared the table.

"Tara Mae Olsen, what is wrong with you? It seems like all you do anymore is whine and complain. What is your problem?"

"It's actually your problem, Dad, not mine," she answered sullenly.

"What is that supposed to mean?"

"Sinda's the problem, not me." Now Tara looked like she was going to cry, and she flopped into a chair and lowered her head to the table.

Glen took the seat across from her and reached out to take her hand, suddenly feeling like a big heel. He hadn't meant to make her cry. "What kind of problem do you see attached to Sinda Shull?"

Tara's head shot up, and tears rolled down her cheeks. "Can't you see it, Dad? She's out to get you."

His mouth dropped open. "You actually think Sinda is out to get me?"

The pathetic look on Tara's face told him that was exactly what she thought. "I saw her kiss you last night."

Glen's ears were burning. He didn't see how Tara could have known they were kissing. He'd seen her go into Penny's house. Furthermore, he and Sinda had kissed when they were standing in the hallway, in front of the door. Maybe she was only guessing. She was pretty good at that.

Tara stared at the table, her lower lip quivering like a leaf in the wind. "Just how did you manage to see us kissing?"

She sniffed deeply. "I was looking out Penny's bedroom window."

"It was dark when you went back to the Spauldings'," Glen reminded. "And Sinda and I were. . ." He paused and reached up to scratch the back of his head. "You were using those binoculars again, weren't you?"

Tara's face turned pink.

"How many times have I told you to stop spying on people?"

"I wasn't exactly spying," she defended. "I was looking outside. The binoculars just picked you up through that little window in Sinda's front door."

"First, you need to give those binoculars to me until you show yourself trustworthy and ready to respect others' privacy. Second, for the record, Sinda did not kiss me. It was the other way around."

Tara jumped out of her seat, nearly knocking the chair over. "Dad, how could you do such a thing? You hardly even know her!"

"I know her well enough to realize I enjoy her company." He shrugged. "Besides, it's no big deal. It was just an innocent good night kiss." *One that shouldn't have happened*, his conscience reminded. *Sinda refused your invitation to church, and you still don't know if she's ever had a personal relationship with Christ.*

"She's got you hypnotized!"

"Don't start that again, Tara. I'm in perfect control of my faculties." But even as he spoke the words Glen wondered if they were true. Not that he believed he'd actually been hypnotized by Sinda's green eyes. But there was something about the woman that held him captive. Whenever he was with Sinda he had a strange sense of some kind of mystery awaiting him. It was exciting and troubling at the same time.

"The Bible tells us to love our neighbors as ourselves, and I've invited Sinda to come for Sunday dinner again," he said with authority. "She's graciously accepted, and you will be courteous to our dinner guest. Is that clear?"

Tara hung her head. "Yeah, I understand. I wish you did."

❧

Sinda sat at her kitchen table, toying with the piece of salmon on her plate. She loved fish, especially salmon. Tonight she had no appetite, though. She hadn't been able to reach Alex Masters by phone today, and she had mixed feelings about it. Since this was Saturday, her lawyer obviously wasn't in his office, but she'd also gotten his answering machine at home. Even though she wasn't thrilled about the prospect of opening the trunk, there was a part of her that wanted to see what was inside. If it was her mother's trunk, maybe there was something within the contents that could help heal some of her pain.

Resigned to the fact that she'd have to wait until next week to call Alex again, Sinda let her thoughts carry her in another direction. Against her better judgment she had accepted another dinner invitation from Glen. She felt apprehensive about going—especially since she knew better than to allow herself to get close to a man.

Sinda thought about how Glen had spent most of the day working on her house. He'd replaced rotten boards on the front porch steps, repaired a broken railing, and helped her strip the torn wallpaper in the dining room. Then, shortly before he left, he had extended the dinner invitation. Sinda had been so appreciative of all this work that she'd accepted without even thinking.

What kind of power does that man hold over me? she fumed. *I should know better than to let my guard down because Glen seems kind and is easy to talk to. By his actions he appears to be nice, but is he all he claims to be?*

Sirens in the distance drove Sinda's thoughts unwillingly back to the past. Whenever she heard that shrill whine she remembered the frightening night when the police showed up at their door, demanding to know if someone had been injured. Sinda had heard one of the police officers say they'd had a report from a neighbor about hearing loud voices coming from the Shulls' home. Dad was able to convince the officer that everything was fine, and the shouting the neighbor heard was probably just the TV turned up too loud. Sinda remembered hearing her parents hollering at each other that night. Of course, that had been a regular occurrence, even though her mother always assured her there was nothing to worry about.

As the sound of the sirens diminished, so did Sinda's thoughts from the past. She jabbed at the fish on her plate and exclaimed, "I'll go to dinner tomorrow because I promised, but after that I won't accept any more social invitations from Glen!"

Chapter 11

As Sinda rang the Olsens' doorbell the following day, she noticed that she felt a bit more relaxed than she had the previous time she'd come to dinner. Not only did she know Glen and Tara better, but she had a sense of peace about her decision last night. She would try to be a good neighbor, but nothing more.

When Tara opened the front door, the distinctive aroma of oregano assaulted Sinda's senses, and she sniffed the air. "Something smells good."

"Dad's fixing spaghetti."

"I love most any kind of pasta dish." Sinda stepped inside, even though she hadn't been invited.

Tara gave her an icy stare, but she led the way to the kitchen without another word. When Glen turned from the stove and offered her a warm smile, Sinda squeezed her lips together to keep her mouth from falling open. How could any man look so good or so masculine when he was wearing an oversized apron and holding a wooden spoon in one hand?

"You're right on time. Dinner's almost ready, and I thought we'd eat in here." Glen nodded toward the kitchen table, which had already been set.

"Is there anything I can do to help?" Sinda asked hopefully. Anything would be better than standing here like a ninny, gawking at Glen and wishing. . . What was she wishing for anyway?

Using his spoon, Glen motioned toward the table. "Have a seat, and we can talk while I finish dishing things up." He glanced at Tara, who was leaning against the cupboard with her arms folded across her chest. "Honey, would you please fill the glasses with water?"

The child did as he requested, but Sinda could tell by Tara's deep sigh and slow movements that she was not happy about it.

"Your kitchen looks so clean and orderly." Sinda laughed self-consciously. "I love to cook, but you should see my kitchen clutter after I'm done with a meal. It looks like a tornado blew in from the east."

Glen chuckled. "I wasn't always this efficient. I've had lots of practice, and lots of help from Tara, which is probably why I appear so capable."

Sinda toyed with the fork lying beside her plate. "I've been cooking since I was a young girl, and I still make messes. I guess some people tend to be neater than others."

Tara came to Sinda's water glass, and Sinda quickly moved to one side, barely in time to avoid being caught in the dribbles that weren't quite making it into her glass. "Sorry about that," the child mumbled.

"Tara, why don't you go out to the living room until dinner is served?"

"There's nothing to do out there," the child moaned. "I can't watch TV, and—"

"Read a book or play with Jake. Sinda and I want to visit."

Tara stomped out of the room, and Glen turned to face Sinda. "Returning to our discussion about your cooking abilities—I thought the breakfast you fixed yesterday tasted great, and I never even looked at your kitchen clutter."

Sinda grimaced. "That meal wasn't much to write home about."

"Maybe you'd like the chance to cook a real meal for me. Then I can judge for myself how well you cook." Glen winked at her. "And I promise not to critique your cleaning skills."

Sinda felt her face flame as she sat there silently watching his nimble fingers drop angel-hair pasta into the pot of boiling water on the stove. When he finished, he looked her way again. "Guess a guy shouldn't go around inviting himself to dinner, huh?"

"It's not that," Sinda was quick to say. "It's just—I've been thinking maybe we might be seeing too much of each other."

"I enjoy your company, and I kind of hoped you liked being with me. After all, we both like to cook, love to go to yard sales and thrift stores, and even enjoy the same kind of relaxing music." A deep, crescent-shaped dimple sprang out on the right side of Glen's mouth as he smiled. Funny, she'd never noticed it before.

Sinda's face grew even warmer. "I do enjoy being with you, Glen, but—"

"Then let's get better acquainted."

Sinda could feel her resolve fly right out the window, and she swallowed hard. Glen was right; they did have a few things in common. "Maybe we can try dinner at my house next Sunday. Tara's invited, too, of course," she added quickly.

"Sounds great, and the invitation to attend church with us is still open if you're interested."

Sinda's heart began to race, and she wasn't sure if it was Glen's smile or the mention of church. "I think it would be best to stick with dinner," she said, feeling as though she couldn't quite get her breath.

"I was hoping you might have changed your mind about going to church."

Sinda reached for her glass and took a sip of water before she answered. "I went to church every Sunday with my dad."

"Did you ever commit your life to Christ?"

She nodded slowly. "When I was ten years old and went to Bible school, I accepted Jesus as my Savior." Was that a look of relief she saw on Glen's face?

"That's great, and it gives us one more thing in common." He frowned slightly. "So, if you're a Christian, how come you're not interested in finding a church home?"

Sinda licked her lips, searching for the right words. How could she tell Glen, a man she was just getting to know, what had happened to her faith in God? "I—uh—could we please change the subject?"

Glen nodded and began to drain the spaghetti into the strainer he'd placed in the sink. "Is there anything you'd like me to bring to dinner next Sunday. . . maybe some dessert?"

You are dessert, Glen Olsen. It's just too bad I'm on a diet, Sinda thought as she shrugged her shoulders. "Some dessert would be nice."

❧

The following week, Sinda became even more fretful than usual. It wasn't until Thursday when she finally heard from her lawyer. Then it was only to say that he'd been on vacation when she'd called. When Sinda questioned him about the trunk, he informed her that it had been in storage for several years. Though not mentioned in the will, it was her father's verbal request that she should have it after he died. Alex had forgotten all about the trunk until a bill arrived from the storage company a few weeks ago. When she asked him about the key, he said he hadn't been given one.

Wondering if she should break the lock or keep looking for a key that might fit, Sinda decided to do nothing for the time being. She wasn't even sure she wanted to see the contents of the trunk, so maybe more time was what she needed.

Another reason for Sinda's stress was Tara Olsen. The child's most recent act of disobedience had extended her time working in Sinda's doll hospital to another four weeks. While Sinda did appreciate the extra help, having Tara around seemed to add to her problems. She had to be extra careful not to let the girl see the antique doll Glen had asked her to repair. She'd have to do those restorations whenever Tara wasn't around. The sullen child was also sneaking around, nosing into places that were none of her business. Sinda had no idea what the would-be detective was looking for, but it irritated her, nonetheless.

Today was Saturday, and Tara was in the basement, cleaning the body of an ink-stained vinyl doll. Glen was up on the second floor, working in the bathroom, and Sinda was in the kitchen, making a pitcher of iced tea. She could hear him moving around overhead—a thump here—the piercing whine of a drill there. She could only imagine how he must look right now, bent over the sink, tools in hand, trying to make it usable.

Sinda placed the tea in the refrigerator and opened the basement door. She had to check on Tara and quit thinking about Glen Olsen!

When she entered the doll hospital a few minutes later, Sinda found Tara scrubbing the stomach of the vinyl doll with diluted bleach and a toothbrush, an effective treatment for ink stains.

"How's it going?" Sinda asked, peering over the child's shoulder.

Tara shrugged. "Okay, I guess."

"Have you heard any more strange noises down here?"

"Not today, but I still think this old house is creepy. Aren't you afraid to live here alone?"

Sinda shook her head. Even if she were a bit apprehensive at times, she'd never admit it to Tara. She sat down in the chair on the other side of the table. "I have Sparky for protection, so there's no reason to be afraid."

Tara lifted her gaze to the ceiling. "You'd never catch me living in a place like this."

"Maybe when your dad's finished with the critical repairs it will look less creepy."

Tara's head lurched forward as she let out a reverberating sneeze.

Sinda felt immediate concern. "Is that bleach smell getting to you?"

Tara sneezed again. "I think it is."

"Why don't you set it aside and work on something else?" Sinda placed the doll on a shelf and handed Tara another one. "This little lady needs her hair washed and combed." She gave the child a bottle of dry shampoo, used expressly for wigs. "You can work on it while I run upstairs and tend to a few things. I'll call you in about fifteen minutes, then we can have a snack. How's that sound?"

"Whatever," Tara mumbled.

Glen leaned over the antiquated bathroom sink, wondering if he'd be able to fix the continual drip, drop, drip. From the looks of the nasty green stain, it had been leaking quite awhile. In a house this old, where little or no repairs had been done, Glen figured he'd be helping out for a good many weeks. He smiled to himself. It would mean more time spent with Sinda. Maybe he'd be able to find out what was bothering her, and why, if she was a Christian, she had no interest in church.

"Dad! Dad!" Tara rounded the corner of the bathroom and skidded to a stop next to him.

Glen knew right away that something was wrong—Tara's eyes were huge, and he felt her tremble as she clung to him. "What's wrong, honey? You scared me half to death, screaming like that."

"You're scared?" she sobbed. "Go to that spooky basement by yourself, then you'll be scared!"

Glen pulled away slightly so he could get a better look at her face. "What are you talking about?"

"Strange noises! Moving doll parts! I'm telling you, Dad, this house has to be haunted!"

Glen gave Tara's shoulders a gentle shake. "Take a deep breath and calm down."

"I heard a noise! A doll leg jumped out of a box! This place is creepy, and I want to go home." Tara's voice was pleading, and she squeezed Glen around the waist with a strength that surprised him. He wasn't sure how to deal with her hysteria and wondered if she might even be making the story up just to get him away from Sinda. He gritted his teeth. *If this is a ploy, she's not going to get away with it.*

Sinda entered the bathroom, but stopped short when she saw Tara clinging to her father. "I thought you were in the basement, Tara."

"She heard a noise." Glen shrugged his shoulders and looked at Sinda with a helpless expression. "She thinks your house is haunted."

Tara seemed close to tears, and Sinda felt sorry for her. She was about to ask for an explanation, when Tara blurted, "A doll leg jumped right out of a box! I saw it with my own eyes."

Glen held up his hands. "What can I say?"

"I think I can take care of this little problem." Sinda started for the door.

"You're not going down there, are you?" Tara cried.

"Yes, I am. Me and Panther."

"Panther?" Glen and Tara said in unison.

"Panther's my new cat," Sinda explained as she started down the stairs.

Glen and Tara were right behind her. "I never knew you had a cat," Tara said. "You've got a dog, and cats and dogs don't usually get along."

Sinda nodded but kept descending the stairs. "You're right. Sparky's not the least bit fond of Panther, and I'm quite sure the cat returns his feelings. I try to keep them separated as much as possible." By now they were in the hallway, and Sinda began calling, "Here, kitty, kitty!"

"When did you get a cat?" Glen asked, moving toward Sinda.

"A few days ago. One of my customers is moving. She can't take Panther along, so I adopted him." She drew in a deep breath. "Since I'm having some trouble, I thought having a cat might be a good idea."

Glen slipped his arm around Sinda's waist, and she found the gesture comforting yet a bit disarming. "Trouble? What kind of trouble are you having?"

"I'll explain it all later," she said, moving away from Glen. "Right now I need to find that cat." Sinda stepped into the living room and called, "Panther! Come, kitty, kitty!"

Glen turned to Tara. "You're good with cats. Why don't you see if you can help?"

Tara shook her head and gave him an imploring look. "We need to get out of this house!"

"Tara Mae Olsen, would you quit being so melodramatic? Sinda needs our help, and it's the neighborly thing—"

Tara shook her head. "I just want to go home."

"We'll go as soon as we've helped Sinda solve her problem."

Sinda offered Glen a grateful smile. How could the man be so helpful and kind? Was it all an act, or did Glen Olsen really want to help?

Chapter 12

A green-eyed ebony cat streaked through the living room with the speed of lightning. "That was Panther," Sinda announced.

"I sure hope he won't fight with Jake," Tara mumbled.

"You're fast on your feet, Tara. Go after him!" Glen pointed to the staircase where Panther had bounded.

Tara scrambled after the cat, and Glen followed Sinda to the kitchen. Five minutes later Tara came running in, holding tightly to the cat, its ears lying flat against its head in irritation.

Sinda had been sitting beside Glen at the table, drinking a cup of coffee, and just as he reached for her hand, Tara marched across the room and dropped Panther into her lap.

"You found him!" Sinda exclaimed. "Where was he?"

"Hiding inside a box in that room full of junk." Tara gave her ponytail a flip and scrunched up her nose.

Glen's forehead wrinkled as he looked at his daughter. "I hope you didn't disturb anything."

Tara flopped into a chair. "Nothing except the dumb old cat."

"Now that he's been found, let's put him to work." Sinda stood up and hurried to the basement door. Glen and Tara followed. She placed Panther on the first step and gave him a little nudge. "Go get 'em, boy!" Sinda slammed the door. "That should take care of our little basement ghosts."

"You're sending a cat to chase ghosts?" Tara's eyes were wide, and her mouth hung slightly open.

"Panther's on a mouse hunt," Sinda explained, moving back toward the kitchen.

Tara was right on her heels. "Mice? You think there are mice in the basement?"

Sinda nodded. "I told you that before. I think the jumping doll leg was a lively mouse who has taken up residence in the box of doll parts. You probably frightened him, and when he jumped, it caused the doll leg to go flying."

Glen nodded. "In an old house like this, it's not uncommon to find a few mice scurrying around. We don't want them overrunning the place, though, so I think we should set some traps."

Sinda leaned against the cupboard. "That might help, but I'd rather let the cat take care of things naturally. I don't want to take the chance of either Sparky or Panther getting their noses caught in a trap."

"Or their tails," Tara added. Her gaze shifted to her father. "Remember when Jake got his tail caught in a mouse trap? That was awful!"

Glen held up his hands. "Okay, ladies. . .I get the point. We'll forget about setting any traps." He pulled Tara to his side and gave her a squeeze. "Guess what?"

She shrugged. "What?"

"Last Sunday, when Sinda came to our house for dinner, she invited us to eat at her place this Sunday." Glen smiled and winked at Sinda. "Now we get to try out some of her cooking."

Sinda was surprised Glen hadn't told his daughter about her dinner invitation until now, and the troubled look on Tara's face told Sinda all she needed to know. The child was not happy about this bit of news. *What have I done now?* she silently moaned.

❧

It had been raining all morning, and Sinda could see out the kitchen window where the water was running off the roof like it was being released from a dam. "We do need the rain, but now new gutters will have to be put up. Another job for poor, overworked Glen. Is there no end to the work needing to be done around this old place?" She groaned. "I can't believe I invited the Olsens over for dinner today." Tara didn't want to come, and when he'd phoned last night, Glen had once more tried to convince Sinda to go to church with them. As much as she enjoyed Glen's company, she couldn't go. The last time she'd gone to church. . .

Sinda turned away from the window and grabbed her recipe for scalloped potatoes from the cupboard. *I will not allow myself to think about the past today. Thinking about it won't change a thing, and it will only cause me more pain.* She wiped a stray hair away from her face and moaned. "Why don't children get to choose their parents? Life is so unfair."

Sinda heard a knock on the front door and hurried to the hall mirror to check her appearance. She was wearing her hair up in a French roll and had chosen to wear a beige, short-sleeved cotton dress that just touched her ankles. The prim and proper look was a far cry from her normal ponytail and cutoffs.

Sinda's hands trembled as she opened the door. Glen smiled and gave her an approving nod. "You look nice today." He was dressed in a pair of navy blue slacks and a light blue cotton shirt, which made his indigo eyes seem even more intense than usual. He handed Sinda a plate of chocolate chip cookies and a bouquet of miniature red roses.

"Thank you, they're lovely." She opened the door wider, bidding him entrance. "Where's Tara?"

"She'll be here soon. She couldn't decide whether to stay in her church clothes or change into something more comfortable."

"Why don't you put the cookies on the kitchen counter? I'll find a vase for these beauties and use them as our centerpiece. I bought some lemon sherbet the other day, so the cookies should go well with that." Sinda knew she was babbling, but she seemed unable to stop herself. *If Glen would only quit staring at me, I might not feel as nervous as a baby robin being chased by a cat.*

"What's for dinner?" Glen asked, lifting his dark eyebrows and sniffing the air. "Something smells pretty good."

"Nothing fancy. Just scalloped potatoes."

"I'm sure they'll be great." He cleared his throat a few times, as though he might be trying to work up the courage to say something more. "I—uh—have a question for you."

"What is it?" she asked as she filled the vase with water.

Glen moved slowly toward Sinda. Her mouth went dry, and she swallowed so hard she almost choked. *What's he doing? I hope he's not...*

He took the vase from her hands and placed it on the counter. Then he pulled her into his arms. "My question is, how come you're so beautiful?"

Before Sinda could open her mouth to reply, his lips captured hers. The unexpected kiss left her weak in the knees and fighting for breath. When it ended, she pulled back slightly, gazing up at his handsome face. She pressed her head against his shoulder, breathing in the masculine scent of his subtle aftershave. She could feel the steady beat of Glen's heart against her ear, and she closed her eyes, feeling relaxed and safe in his embrace. Safer than she'd felt in a long time. What had happened to her resolve to keep her neighbor at arm's length? It was fading faster than a photograph left out in the sun, and she seemed powerless to stop it.

"I haven't felt this way about any woman since Connie died," Glen whispered. "I realize we haven't known each other very long, but I find myself thinking about you all the time." He lifted her chin with one hand, bent his head, and captured her mouth again.

How long the kiss might have lasted, Sinda would never know, for a shrill voice sliced through the air like a razor blade. "Dad, what are you doing?"

Glen pulled away first. He seemed almost in a daze as he stared at his daughter with a blank look on his face. Several awkward seconds ticked by, then he shook his head, as though coming out of a trance. "Tara, how'd you get here?"

"I walked. We live next door, remember?"

Glen's eyelids closed partway, and he shook his finger at Tara. "Don't get smart with me, young lady! I meant, why didn't you knock? You don't just walk into someone's house. I've taught you better manners than that."

Tara blinked several times, and Sinda wondered if the child was going to cry. "I did knock. Nobody answered, but since you were already here, I tried the door. It was open, so I thought it was okay to come in. Then I found you. . . ." Tara touched her lips with the tips of her fingers and grimaced. "That was really gross, Dad."

Sinda reached up with shaky fingers and brushed her own trembling lips. *What can I say or do to help ease this tension?*

Glen moved away from her and knelt in front of his daughter. "Sinda and I are both adults, and if we want to share a kiss, it shouldn't concern you."

Tara's eyes were wide, and she waved her hands in the air. "Why not? Dad, can't you see that Sinda's got you—"

Glen held up one hand. "That will be enough, Tara. I want you to apologize to Sinda for being so rude."

"It's okay." Sinda spoke softly, hoping to calm Glen down. From the angry scowl on his face, she was afraid he might be about to slap his daughter. She couldn't stand to witness such a scene, and she'd do almost anything to stop it from happening. Sinda touched Glen on the shoulder. "We didn't hear her knock, so she did the only thing she could think to do."

He stood up and put his arm around Sinda, but his gaze was fixed on Tara. "I'm glad Sinda is kind enough to forgive you, but you do need to apologize for your behavior," he said in a more subdued tone of voice.

Tara hung her head. "I–I'm sorry for coming into your house without being invited." She glanced up at Sinda, and tears shimmered in her dark eyes.

Sinda had the sudden urge to wrap the child in her arms and offer comfort, but she was sure it would not be appreciated. Tara obviously didn't like her, and she didn't think there was anything she could do to change that fact.

"I don't know about the rest of you, but I'm hungry," Glen said, changing the subject and breaking into Sinda's thoughts. "Is dinner ready yet?"

Sinda nodded. "I think so." She moved away from Glen and busied herself at the stove. *Inviting my neighbors to dinner was a terrible mistake, and it must never happen again.*

Chapter 13

"There's only one way to get Glen Olsen out of my mind," Sinda fumed, "and that's to keep busy."

She was alone in the doll hospital, working on an antique bisque doll. Panther, who was sleeping under the table, meowed softly, as though in response to her grumbling.

In spite of her determination not to think about Glen, Sinda's thoughts swirled around in her head like a blender running at full speed. It had been four weeks since she'd had Glen and Tara over for dinner, and during those four weeks she'd been miserable.

Sinda swallowed hard and fought the urge to give in to her tears. Glen had called her after he'd gone home that night, apologizing for Tara's behavior and suggesting that they try dinner the following Sunday at his place. When Sinda told him she didn't want to see him anymore, he seemed confused. She'd even said she didn't want him doing any more work on her house, and he had argued about that as well. Sinda knew having Glen around would be too much temptation, and she might weaken and agree to go out with him again. Or worse yet, let him kiss her again. Of course her decision meant she would either have to do all her own home repairs or pay someone else to do them. Until business picked up and she had a steady cash flow, she would forget about all repairs that weren't absolutely necessary.

Sinda could still hear Glen's final words before she'd hung up the phone that night. "I care about you, Sinda, and I really want to help."

She'd almost weakened, but an image of her mother had jumped into her mind. There was no future for her and Glen, so why lead him on? And even if her past wasn't working against her, Tara certainly was!

The telephone rang, and Sinda's mind snapped back to the present. She reached for it, thankful that she'd remembered to bring the cordless phone downstairs this time. "Sinda's Doll Hospital." Her eyebrows shot up. "You want to run a story about me in your newspaper? I—I guess it would be all right. Yes, I'd like it to be a human interest story, too." *That would no doubt be good for my business.*

Several minutes later she hung up the phone, having agreed to let a reporter from the *Daily Herald* interview her the following morning. She hoped it was the right decision.

The interview with the newspaper columnist went better than Sinda had expected, but she was relieved when he and his photographer said they had all they needed and left her house shortly before noon. Even though she knew the article they planned to print about her doll hospital would be good for business, Sinda had some reservations about having so much attention drawn to her. She'd always tried to stay out of the limelight, and during her childhood none of her friends except Carol had been invited to her home. Carol had only come over a few times, and that was always whenever Sinda's father was gone.

Thinking about her friend reminded Sinda that Carol had promised to come over after work today and help her paint the kitchen cabinets. After lunch she would go to the nearest hardware store and buy some paint.

Sinda knew Glen probably could paint the cabinets much faster and probably a whole lot neater than she or Carol, but she couldn't ask for his help. . .not after his daughter had seen them kissing and thrown such a fit. No matter how much it pained her, she had to keep her distance.

Glen paced back and forth in front of the counter at the hardware store, waiting for his brother to finish with a customer. He'd been promising himself for the last several weeks to repaint the barbecue and had decided to stop by Phil's Hardware on the way home from work and pick up what he needed for the project. He hoped to have several barbecues this summer and was getting a late start. *Too bad they won't include Sinda Shull,* he fumed inwardly. *I know the woman likes me, and she's just being stubborn, refusing to see me or even let me continue with the repairs on her home. If only there were some way I could convince her that my jealous daughter will eventually come around. I know Sinda has some issues she needs to resolve, but that's even more reason I should keep seeing her. I might be able to help.*

"Hey, big brother, it's good to see you!"

Glen turned toward Phil, who was finally finished with his customer. He grabbed his brother in a bear hug. "It's good to see you, too. It's been awhile, huh?"

Phil swiped a hand across his bearded chin and frowned. "I'll say. Where have you been keeping yourself, anyway?"

Glen was tempted to tell Phil about his new neighbor, and that up until a few weeks ago, he'd been helping Sinda with some repairs on her rambling old house, but he thought better of it. Phil was a confirmed bachelor, and whenever he discovered that Glen had dated any woman, Phil bombarded him with a bunch of wisecracks and unwanted advice.

"I've been busy." Glen nodded at Phil. "What's new in your life?"

Phil shrugged, and his blue eyes twinkled. "Until a few minutes ago, nothing was new."

Glen's interest was piqued. "What's that supposed to mean?"

"I've met the woman of my dreams," Phil said, running his fingers through his curly black hair. "She came in a while ago, looking for some paint, and it was love at first sight."

Glen chuckled. How many times had he heard his goofy brother say he'd found the perfect woman, only to drop her flat when he became bored? Glen was sure this latest attraction would be no different than the others had been.

"You're not going to say anything?" Phil asked expectantly.

Glen shrugged his shoulders. "What would you like me to say?"

Phil wiggled his dark, bushy eyebrows, and Glen had a vision of his kid brother as an enormous teddy bear. "How about, 'Wow, brother, that's great. When do I get to meet this woman of your dreams?' "

"Okay, okay," Glen said, laughing. "When do I get to meet her?"

Phil turned his hands palm up. "Maybe you already have. She's your next-door neighbor."

Glen felt his jaw drop. "Sinda Shull?"

Phil nodded. "Like I said, she came in looking for some paint for her kitchen, and we got to talking. She told me she wants a new screen for her back door, and since the size she needs is out of stock, I promised to order one today and deliver it to her house as soon as it comes in." He smiled triumphantly. "That's how I got her address and discovered she lives next door to you. Small world, isn't it?"

"Too small if you ask me," Glen mumbled as he moved toward the front door.

"Hey, where are you going?"

"Home. Tara's probably starving, and I need to get dinner started."

"But you never said what you came in for."

Glen hunched his shoulders and offered his brother a halfhearted wave. "I came by for some heat-resistant paint, but it can wait. See you later, Phil." He left the hardware store feeling like someone had punched him in the stomach. Not only had Sinda decided to do some painting without his help, but she'd gone to his brother's store to buy the paint. As if that wasn't bad enough, Phil suddenly had a big crush on a woman he didn't even know, and he was obviously looking forward to delivering Sinda's new screen door. Glen loved his little brother, but he cared too much for Sinda to let her be taken in by Phil the Pill. He would do whatever it took to prevent her from being hurt. Trouble was, with her refusing to see him, he didn't have a clue what he could do other than pray. "That's it," he muttered under his breath. "I'll pray for answers until they come."

❧

Tara let out a low whistle. "Wow! Take a look at this, Dad!"

"What is it?" Glen asked as he continued to chop mushrooms for the omelet he was making.

"Our weirdo neighbor lady made the newspaper. Listen to what it says: 'Doll Doctor Has Heavy Caseload.' " Tara stifled a giggle behind the paper. "Pretty impressive, huh?"

Glen wiped his hands on a paper towel and sauntered over to the kitchen table. "Let me see that." He snatched the newspaper out of Tara's hands. "I want you to stop referring to Sinda as 'our weirdo neighbor lady.' She's not weird!" He was still upset over the conversation he'd had with Phil the day before, and he didn't need anything else to get riled about.

Tara shook her head. "She plays with dolls, Dad. Don't you think that's kinda weird?"

"No, I don't, and how many times must I remind you what the Bible says about loving our neighbor?"

Tara shrugged. "I know, but—"

"Sinda is kind, sensitive, and reserved." Glen frowned. "And she doesn't play with dolls; she repairs them." His eyes quickly scanned the article about Sinda Shull who'd recently opened a doll hospital in the basement of her home. The story went on to say that almost any doll, no matter how old or badly damaged, could be repaired by an expert such as Doll Doctor Shull. There was a picture of Sinda sitting at her workbench, sanding a wooden doll head.

"She looks great," Glen murmured.

Tara groaned. "Where's Sinda been lately? I haven't seen her since I finished my punishment in her creepy basement. She hasn't been around making eyes at you, and it makes me wonder what's up."

Methodically, Glen pulled on his left earlobe. He knew exactly how long it had been since he'd last talked to Sinda. He'd seen her a few times out in the yard, but whenever he tried to make conversation, she always concocted some lame excuse to go back inside. Just when he and Sinda seemed to be getting closer, she'd pulled away. He didn't like this hot and cold stuff. *Well, maybe it's for the best. Even though Sinda says she's a Christian, she doesn't want anything to do with church. It might be better for all concerned if I bow out graciously.*

He shook his head, hoping to clear away the troubling thoughts. Who was he kidding? He didn't want to let Sinda walk out of his life. She was afraid of something, and it was probably more than concern over Tara's reaction to their relationship. Besides, he had to protect Sinda from his little brother. Phil might look like a teddy bear, but he acted more like a grizzly bear.

"Dad, are you listening to me?"

Glen lifted both elbows and flexed his shoulders as he stretched, then dropped the newspaper to the table. "What were you saying?"

"I asked about Sinda. Why do you think she hasn't been around lately?"

"I'm sure she's been busy." He pointed to the newspaper. "That article even says so."

"I guess a lot of people have broken dolls, huh?"

Glen gave a noncommittal grunt, thinking of the doll he'd given Sinda to repair. He wondered if she would still make good on it, even though she'd changed her mind and wouldn't allow him to do any more repairs on her house. If she did finish repairing it, he would gladly pay her whatever it cost.

"I'm sure happy I don't have to help in that doll hospital anymore." Tara looked at him pointedly. "It was awful!"

"I thought you liked fixing broken dolls."

"It was okay at first, but that house is creepy and full of strange noises. Besides, I don't like Sinda. She's w— I mean, different."

"God created each of us differently," Glen said patiently. "The world would be a boring place if we were all alike."

Tara scrunched up her nose. "Sinda is way different."

"Are you sure you aren't jealous?" Glen asked, taking a seat at the table.

"Why would I be?"

He raised his eyebrows. "Maybe you're envious of the attention I've shown Sinda."

"You can't help yourself because she's got you hypnotized with those green cat's eyes."

"Don't start with that again."

Tara held up both hands. "Okay, okay. I'm just glad Sinda hasn't been hanging around. I'm happy you're not going over there anymore, either."

"It's your fault I'm not," Glen blurted without thinking.

Tara flinched, making him feel like a rotten father. "What do you mean, it's my fault?"

"One of the reasons—probably the main one—Sinda won't see me anymore, is because she thinks you don't like her."

"She's right about that," Tara muttered. "I'm glad she's not around anymore."

"Tara Mae Olsen, that's an awful thing to say!" He leveled her with a look he hoped would make her realize the seriousness of the situation. "In the book of Proverbs we are told that he who despises his neighbor, sins."

"I don't despise Sinda, Dad. It's just that I know she's after you." Tara grabbed hold of his shirtsleeve. "She's trying to win you over with compliments and flirty looks."

"Flirty looks? What would a little girl know about flirty looks?"

She grinned at him. "I'm not a baby, you know."

Glen smiled, in spite of his irritation. "That's right, you're not." He patted the top of her head. "So try not to act like one."

Chapter 14

As Glen knelt on the patio to begin scraping the rusted paint off his barbecue, he heard a noisy vehicle pull into Sinda's driveway. He straightened, rubbed the kinks out of his back, and moved casually around the side of the house. He didn't want to be seen or have anyone get the idea he was spying, so he crouched down by his front porch and peeked into Sinda's yard. It was just as he feared. . .a truck bearing the name "Phil's Hardware" was parked in her driveway, and Phil the Pill was climbing down from the driver's seat. Glen watched as his brother went around to the back of the pickup and withdrew a screen door. He whistled as he walked toward Sinda's front door, and it was all Glen could do to keep from jumping up, dashing through the gate, and grabbing Phil by the shirttail.

That would be ridiculous, Glen reprimanded himself. *It's a free country, and my brother's only doing his job. If Sinda ordered the screen door, Phil has every right to deliver it.*

"Why don't you use my binoculars, Dad?"

Glen whirled around at the sound of his daughter's voice. "Tara, you scared me! Why are you sneaking up on me like that?"

Tara snickered. "It looks like you were spying on someone." She shook her head and clicked her tongue. "Is it Sinda?"

Glen stood up straight and faced his daughter. "I wasn't spying on Sinda."

"Who then?"

"Uncle Phil."

Tara's forehead wrinkled. "Huh?"

Glen took Tara by the arm and led her around back, so they wouldn't be overheard. "I heard a vehicle pull into Sinda's driveway, and I thought I recognized the sound of Uncle Phil's truck. So, I went around front to check it out, and sure enough, he's delivering a new screen door to Sinda."

"That's good. Her old one was about to fall."

Glen opened his mouth to comment, but Tara cut him off. "Why don't we go over and tell Uncle Phil hello? We haven't seen him in ages."

He smiled. For once Tara had a good idea, and since this was her idea, Glen had a legitimate excuse to see Sinda.

❧

Sinda came upstairs at the sound of a truck in her driveway, then peeked out the living room window. "Ah, my screen door has arrived." She hurried to open the front door, and Phil from Phil's Hardware met her on the porch. He leaned the screen door against the side of the house and grinned. "Where do you want this beauty?"

"Around back, please."

Phil hoisted it again like it weighed no more than a feather and stepped off the porch. Sinda followed.

"You got anyone lined up to install this?" Phil asked when they reached the backyard.

Install it? Sinda hadn't even thought about how she would replace her old screen with the new one. She gnawed on her lower lip as she contemplated the problem. "I guess I could try to put it up myself." Even as the words slipped off her tongue, Sinda realized it was a bad idea. She knew as much about putting up a screen door as a child understood the mechanics of driving a car.

"I'd be happy to install it for you," Phil offered as he set it down, leaning it against the porch railing. "In fact, I've got my helper working at the store all afternoon, so I could do it now if you like."

"How much would you charge?"

Phil shrugged his broad shoulders and gave her a lopsided grin. "Tell you what, I'll put up the door while I work up the nerve to ask you out to dinner."

Sinda swallowed hard. "Dinner?"

"Yeah, maybe some beer and pizza. I know this great place—"

She held up her hand. "I don't drink alcoholic beverages. I also don't go out with men I hardly know." *Except Glen Olsen,* her conscience reminded. *You went out with Glen a few weeks after you met.*

Phil took a step toward Sinda. "We introduced ourselves when you came into my store the other day, and sharing dinner would give us a chance to get better acquainted." He winked at her, and she was about to reply when Glen and Tara came bounding into the yard.

"Hey, Brother, I heard the unmistakable rumble of your truck and thought I'd come over and say hi." Glen gave Phil a hearty slap on the back, then he turned to face Sinda.

She eyed him curiously. "You and Phil are brothers?" Except for the dark hair and blue eyes, the two men didn't look anything alike. Glen was slender and clean-shaven while Phil was stocky and sported a full beard. He also had a cocky attitude, which was the total opposite of Glen.

Before Glen could answer Sinda's question, Tara spoke up. "Uncle Phil's Dad's little brother." She looked up at her uncle and gave his loose shirttail a good yank. "How come you haven't been over to see us in such a long time?"

"Guess I've been too busy to socialize," Phil said, tugging on Tara's ponytail in response. His gaze swung back to Sinda, and he gave her another flirtatious wink. "I'm hoping to remedy that now that I've met your beautiful new neighbor." He glanced at his brother, and Sinda noticed that Glen wasn't smiling. In fact, he looked downright irritated.

"I plan to install Sinda's new screen door, then she's going out to dinner with me," Phil remarked with a smirk.

Sinda opened her mouth, but she never got a word out. "Is that so?" Glen interrupted. "Don't you have a store to run?"

Phil tucked his thumbs inside his jeans pockets and rocked back and forth on his heels. "Gabe's workin' for me all day, so I can spare a few minutes to put up Sinda's door." He reached out and grabbed hold of the screen, still leaning against the porch railing.

Before he could take a step, Glen seized the door and jerked it right out of Phil's hands. "Sinda hired me to do some repairs on her house in exchange for—" Glen paused and glanced down at his daughter. "Uh, I mean—I agreed to help her out, so putting up the screen door is my job."

Phil looked at Sinda, then back at Glen. "She said she had nobody to install the screen, and I volunteered."

"Is that a fact?"

Phil nodded and reached for the screen door.

Sinda wasn't sure what she should do or say. Glen and Phil were arguing over who would complete the task, but she had a feeling the tug-of-war had more to do with her than it did the door. She'd never had two men fight for her attention before, and it was a bit unnerving.

"I've got an idea," Tara interjected. "Dad, why don't you and Uncle Phil both put Sinda's screen door up? That way the job will get done twice as fast."

Glen shrugged. "I guess we could do that."

Phil nodded. "You know what they say—four hands are better than two."

"I think that's 'two heads are better than one,' Uncle Phil." Tara giggled and jabbed her uncle in the ribs.

He chortled. "Yeah, whatever."

A thought popped into Sinda's head, and she wondered why the idea hadn't come to her sooner. "I'll appreciate the help no matter who sets the screen door in place, but I won't be going out with anyone. I've got some work to do. So if you men will excuse me, I'm going downstairs to my workshop." With that, she stepped into the house and closed the door.

❧

It was another warm Saturday, and Glen was outside mowing his lawn. He waved at Tara, who was across the street visiting her friend Penny, then he stopped to fill the mower with gas. A bloodcurdling scream, which sounded like it had come from Sinda's house, halted his actions.

Sinda's terrier, Sparky, was yapping through the fence, and Glen turned his head in that direction. Maybe Sinda had come face-to-face with an intruder. She might be hurt and in need of his help. *Maybe that goofy brother of mine is back, and he's bugging Sinda to go out with him again.*

With no further thought, Glen tore open the gate and raced into Sinda's backyard, nearly tripping over the black dog. There was another shrill scream, and Glen was sure it was coming from Sinda's basement. He made a dash for the door and gave the handle a firm yank. It didn't budge. "Must be locked," he muttered. He pounded on the door, calling out Sinda's name.

The door flew open, and Sinda threw herself into his arms. Glen felt like his heart had jumped right into his throat. Something was terribly wrong. "What is it? What happened down there?"

"I think Tara may be right about this spooky old house being haunted," she said with a deep moan.

Glen held her at arm's length as he studied her tear-streaked face. Sinda's deadpan expression and quivering lower lip told him how serious she was. *At least my bear of a brother wasn't the reason for her panic.* "Tell me what happened," he said as he took hold of her trembling hand.

She hiccuped. "A doll head. I saw a doll head."

"You screamed loud enough to wake a sleeping hound dog, and you're telling me it was just a doll head that scared you?" Glen knew women were prone to hysterics, but this was ridiculous.

"It was in my freezer," Sinda whimpered. "I found a vinyl doll head in the freezer."

Glen stood there several seconds, trying to digest this strange piece of information. He could understand what a shock it would be to open the freezer, fully intending to retrieve a package of meat, and discover a doll head staring back at him instead. "Someone's probably playing a trick on you." Glen's thoughts went immediately to his daughter, even though Tara hadn't been working in Sinda's doll hospital for several weeks. *Unless she planted it there on her last day.* "How long has it been since you opened the freezer?"

She shrugged. "A week—maybe two."

"Are you sure? It hasn't been any longer?"

"I think I took some ice cream out last Saturday." She nodded and swiped her hand across her chin. "Yes, that's the last time I opened it."

"And there was no doll head then?"

"I'm sure there wasn't."

A feeling of relief washed over Glen. He didn't see how it could have been Tara. He led Sinda into the basement. "Is the doll head still in the freezer?"

"Yes. When I first saw it, I screamed and slammed the door. Then I thought I must have been seeing things, so I opened the freezer again, but it was still there." She leaned heavily against him and drew in a shuddering breath. "I heard someone pounding on the basement door, and when I opened it and saw you, I kind of fell apart."

And right into my arms, Glen thought with a wry smile. At least something good came out of this whole weird experience. "Why don't you show me the doll?" he suggested.

Sinda gripped Glen's hand tightly as she led the way to the utility room. "Would you mind opening the freezer? I don't think I have the strength."

Glen grasped the handle and jerked the freezer door open. A round head with brown painted hair and bright blue eyes stared back at him. It was so creepy he almost let out a yelp himself. He reached inside to remove the icy-cold doll head. "Looks a little chilly, doesn't it?"

"I've been looking everywhere for that!" Sinda exclaimed. "It and several other doll parts have been missing for a few weeks."

Glen scratched the back of his head. "Hmm. . .sounds like a bit of a mystery to me. Maybe we should put Detective Tara Mae Olsen on the case. She'd love something as weird as this to sink her teeth into."

Sinda was obviously not amused by his comment. She was scared to death, and it showed clearly on her ashen face. Glen placed the doll head on top of the dryer and drew her into his arms. It felt so right to hold her like this. Too bad she didn't realize how good they could be for each other.

"Glen—"

"Sinda—"

Glen chuckled. "Go ahead."

"No, you first."

"I know there has to be a simple answer to this whole thing."

She looked up at him expectantly. "What could it be?"

He shrugged. "I don't know. Do you think you could have accidentally put the head into the freezer? I've done some pretty strange things when I'm preoccupied." He grinned. "Like putting dishwasher soap in the refrigerator instead of the cupboard."

She gave him a weak smile. "I know everyone is absentminded at times, but I don't even remember picking the doll head up, much less putting it in the freezer. Besides, what about the other missing doll parts?"

Glen frowned. "Maybe you misplaced them. I do that with my car keys a lot."

"You think I'm getting forgetful in my old age?"

"Hardly," he said with a wink. "Seriously, though, even if I'm not sure what's going on with the doll parts, I don't want anything to happen to our friendship."

He brushed her cheek with the back of his hand. "I know you said you didn't want to see me anymore, but I'm hoping you'll reconsider. Please don't let Tara's resistance be a deciding factor."

Sinda licked her lips. "I want to see you, Glen, but it's not a good idea."

"Why not?"

"There are things in my past that prevent me from making a commitment to you—or any other man."

His eyebrows arched. "Are you trying to tell me that you lied about not being married?"

"No, of course not! I'm as single as any woman could be."

"And you're a Christian?"

Sinda nodded. "I am, but—"

"Then what's the problem?" Glen's finger curved under her trembling chin, and she met his gaze with a look that went straight to his heart. He felt as if her pain was his, and he wondered what he could do to help ease her discomfort. Instinctively, he bent his head to kiss her. When they broke away, he whispered, "I don't care about your past, Sinda. If you're a Christian, and you care for me, that's all that counts. We can work through any problems you have from your past." He kissed the tip of her nose. "No matter what you say, I'm not giving up on you. So there!"

Chapter 15

"Where do we go from here?" Sinda asked Glen as she took a chair directly across from him.

Glen rapped his knuckles on the kitchen table and looked thoughtful. "I want to get to the bottom of the missing doll parts, but first I think we need to figure out some way to get our relationship back on track."

"I let you put up my screen door," she reminded.

"I'm talking about our personal relationship."

A film of tears obscured her vision. "But, Glen—"

He held up one hand. "I know. You have secrets from your past and can't make any kind of commitment."

She nodded in response and clasped her hands around her knees to keep them from shaking.

"We all have things from our past that we'd like to forget," he said softly. "But God doesn't want us to dwell on the past. So why don't we pray about this, then we'll deal with one problem at a time." He paused and flicked a crumb off the table. "I think it might help to talk about what's troubling you before we pray."

She counted on her fingers. "Lost doll parts. . .a vinyl head in the freezer. . . how's that for starters?"

He nodded. "We'll take care of that in good time, but right now we need to deal with the reason you won't allow me into your life."

Sinda wiped away the unwanted tears she felt on her cheeks and avoided his gaze. Silence wove around her, filling up the space between them. "I—I haven't dated much, and I've never been in love. Even the thought of it scares me." She swallowed hard. "I'm not sure I could ever love a man, so there's no point in leading you on."

"What are you afraid of, Sinda?"

"I'm afraid of love. I'm afraid of being hurt."

Glen's thumb stroked the top of her hand, and her skin tingled with each feathery touch. "Who are you angry with?" he coaxed.

Sinda jerked her hand away. Glen was treading on dangerous territory now. "What makes you think I'm angry?"

He leaned forward and studied her intently. "It's written all over your face. I hear it in the tone of your voice."

"Your daughter thinks she's a detective, and now you're moonlighting as a psychologist," she said sarcastically.

"I'm only trying to help, but I can't if you won't let me."

Sinda's nerves were tight like a rubber band. Angry, troubled thoughts tumbled around in her head, and she stared off into space. She wanted to run, to hide, and never have to deal with her pain. "My mother! I'm angry with my mother!" Sinda's hand went instinctively to her mouth. She hadn't meant to say that. It wasn't for Glen to know.

Glen seemed unaffected by her outrage. "What did your mother do?" he prompted.

Sinda sniffed deeply. She'd already let the cat out of the bag, so she may as well get the rest off her chest. "She left my father when I was ten years old."

"Left him? You mean she died?"

Sinda shook her head, swallowing back the pain and humiliation. "She walked out."

"Was there another man involved?"

A shuddering sigh escaped Sinda's trembling lips, and she was powerless to stop it. "No!" She gulped in a deep breath. "At least, I don't think so. She left us a note, but it didn't explain her reason for abandoning us. Her message said only that she was going and would never come back. There was no other explanation—not even an apology." Sinda picked at an imaginary piece of fuzz on her peach-colored T-shirt. "Mother was there when I went to bed one night, and she was gone the next morning when I awoke."

Glen reached for her hand again, and this time she didn't pull away. "I'm so sorry, Sinda."

"My father was devastated by her betrayal, and he. . ." Her voice trailed off. How could she explain about Dad? She'd never fully understood him herself.

"I'm sure it must have been hard on both you and your father," Glen acknowledged. "If you're ready, I'd like to pray now, then we can talk some more."

She shrugged. "I–I guess so."

With her hand held firmly in his, Sinda bowed her head. "Dear Lord," Glen prayed, "Sinda has some pain from her past that needs to be healed. We know You are the Great Physician and it's within Your power to heal physically and emotionally. Please touch Sinda's heart and let her feel Your presence. Help us get to the bottom of the missing doll parts, and we thank You in advance for Your answers. Amen."

When Sinda opened her eyes, she was able to offer Glen a brief smile. She felt a bit better after his beseeching prayer. It was a relief to have him know some of her past, and it was comforting to sit with him here in her kitchen. "Whenever anyone asks about Mother, I sort of leave the impression that she died," she said with a shrug of her shoulders. "To me she is dead. I hate what she did to Dad."

"To your dad?" Glen exclaimed. "What about what she did to you? Have you ever dealt with that?"

Sinda shook her head. "I try not to think about it. Dad was all I had, and until he died, I devoted my whole life to him." She gulped and tried to regain her composure. "I hadn't thought about Mother in years. Not until that stupid trunk arrived. It was hers, but I thought Dad threw it out after she left."

"Have you looked through it yet? It might help heal some of your pain."

Sinda jumped up and began pacing the floor. "I still can't find a key that fits the lock. My lawyer said Dad wanted me to have the trunk, but he didn't give him a key."

"I'm sure the lock can be broken. I'd be happy to do it for you," Glen offered.

Sinda stopped pacing and turned to face him. "I'm not sure I want to look at her things. I've spent most of my life trying to forget my mother. She wanted out of our lives and never made any effort to contact us, so why should I care about anything that belonged to her?"

"I'll stay with you. We can deal with this together."

"What about the missing doll parts?" Sinda grasped the back of a chair and grimaced. "I thought we were going to get to the bottom of that problem."

He nodded. "We are, but right now I think you should look through the trunk."

She held up her hands in defeat. "Okay, let's get this over with."

❧

Sinda clicked on the overhead light in the storage room upstairs, and the bulky trunk came into view. She couldn't believe she'd actually told Glen the story of how Mother had abandoned her and Dad. It was a secret she'd promised never to share with anyone. Even her best friend Carol didn't know the truth. *Glen Olsen must have a powerful effect on me.*

Glen knelt beside the trunk and studied the lock. "I'd better go home and get a hacksaw." He glanced up at Sinda. "Unless you have one."

She shook her head. "I don't think so. After Dad died, I sold most of his tools. All I kept were the basics—a hammer, screwdriver, and a few other small items."

"Okay. I'll be back in a flash." Glen stood up. Her face lifted to meet his gaze, and she wanted to melt in the warmth of his sapphire blue eyes. "If you're nervous about being here alone, you're welcome to come along," he said, giving her shoulder a gentle squeeze.

"I'll be okay—as long as I stay away from the basement."

Glen dropped a kiss to her forehead, then he was gone. She stared down at the trunk and, giving her thoughts free reign, an image of her mother came to mind. Sinda closed her eyes, trying to shut out the vision, but her mother's face, so much like her own, was as clear as the antique crystal vase sitting on her fireplace mantel.

"You did this to me, Mother," Sinda sobbed. "Why couldn't you let the past stay in the past?" She trembled. Was there something wrong with her? Hadn't Dad accused her of being just like Mother? Hadn't he told her that if she didn't exercise control over her emotions, she'd end up hurting some poor unsuspecting man, the way Mother had hurt him?

In spite of the pain he'd often inflicted upon her, Sinda's heart ached for her dad. He'd been the victim of his wife's abandonment. Marla Shull had given no thought to anyone but herself, leaving him to care for their only child. *What a heartless thing to do,* Sinda thought bitterly. *Mother couldn't have felt any love for me, or you, either, Dad. You don't walk out on someone you love.*

Sinda leaned over and fingered the lock on the trunk. "You made Dad the way he was, Mother, and I'm the one who suffered for it." *If only I hadn't been so much like you. If only. . .*

The prayer Glen prayed earlier replayed itself in her mind. It seemed like a genuine prayer—a plea to God for help. Dad's prayers always seemed genuine, too—at least those he prayed at church meetings.

Sinda thought about the last time she'd gone to church. It was the night before Dad's heart attack, and they'd gone to a revival service. She would never forget the sight of her father kneeling at the altar during the close of the meeting. Had it been for show, like all the other times, or was Dad truly repentant for his sins?

Her mind took her back to the evening before the revival, when she and Dad had argued about the steak she'd fixed for dinner. He said it was overly done, and she'd tried to explain that the oven was too hot and needed repairing. She could still see the hostility on Dad's face when his hand connected to the side of her head. She could feel the pain and humiliation as she rushed to her room in tears.

That night at church, with Dad lying prostrate before the wooden altar, Sinda had been convinced that his display of emotions was only for attention, and at that moment, she vowed never to step inside another church. There were hypocrites there, and even those who weren't didn't seem able to discern when someone was physically and emotionally abusing their daughter. Whenever Dad walked into the sanctuary, he put on his "Mr. Christian" mask, but it fell off the moment they returned home.

Sinda hated her father's cruel treatment and hypocrisy at church, but she hated herself even more. After all, it was because she reminded him so much of her mother that Dad treated her the way he did.

Glen entered the room again, carrying a small hacksaw, and Sinda was thankful for the interruption. She'd spent enough time reliving the past and its painful memories.

"It's time to go to work," Glen announced. He knelt beside the trunk and quickly put the saw to good use. A few minutes later the lock snapped in two and fell to the floor with a thud.

Sinda took a deep breath to steady her nerves, and Glen moved aside. "You can open it now."

She knelt in front of the trunk, grasped the handle, and slowly opened the lid. There were a few items of clothing on top—a faded bridal veil, several lace handkerchiefs, and a delicate satin christening gown with a matching bonnet. Sinda fingered the soft material, remembering pictures that proved it had been her own. She moved the clothes aside and continued to explore.

"Would you rather be alone?" Glen asked, offering her a sympathetic smile.

She gazed at him through her pain and confusion. "No, please stay. I need the moral support."

He reached out and touched her arm. "I'll be here as long as you need me."

There was a small, green velvet box underneath the clothes. Sinda opened it, revealing several pieces of jewelry she recognized as her mother's. She placed the jewelry box and the clothes on a chair, then carried on with her search through the trunk. A few seconds later, she pulled out an old photo album. "There's probably a lot of pictures in here, and I'd like to look at them. Maybe we should go downstairs where it's more comfortable."

Glen shrugged. "Tara's spending the day with her friend across the street, so you've got me all to yourself."

"Let's go to the living room." She stood, then moved quickly toward the door.

They sat on the couch for over an hour, going through the album and talking about Sinda's childhood before her mother walked out.

"Your mother was a beautiful woman," Glen remarked. "You look a lot like her."

"I do have her green eyes and auburn hair," Sinda agreed. She drew in a deep breath and let it out in a rush. "Dad used to say I had her personality, too."

"I'm sure he meant it as a compliment."

Sinda snapped the album shut, nearly catching his fingers inside. "He didn't mean it that way at all! He meant it as a warning. He used to tell me that if I wasn't careful, I'd end up wrecking some poor man's life the way Mother ruined his."

"You didn't believe him, I hope."

She bit down hard on her bottom lip, until she tasted blood. "I had no reason not to."

Glen took her hand and gave it a gentle squeeze. "Who can discern his errors? Forgive my hidden faults," he said softly.

She tipped her head to one side. "What?"

"It's a quote from the book of Psalms," he explained, "and it means—"

"Never mind," she said, cutting him off. She placed the album on the coffee table and stood up. "I've had enough reminiscing for one day. I'd really like to look for those missing doll parts."

"Let's start in the basement," Glen suggested.

She was glad he hadn't kept prying into her past. There was too much pain there to deal with right now.

Glen led the way, and when they reached their destination, Sinda turned on a light in the room where she worked. "As you can see," she said, motioning with her hand, "I keep the dolls that come in for repairs on the shelf marked Emergency Room."

Glen whistled. "Pretty impressive!"

"I use the wooden table in the center of the room to do the work, then when a doll is done, I place it over there." She pointed to a shelf labeled Recovery Room.

"What about the parts and supplies you use for repairing? Where do you keep those?"

"Right there." She indicated another row of shelves on the opposite wall.

Glen nodded. "Are the missing pieces from a particular doll patient or from your supply of parts?"

"From my supply. Why do you ask?"

"Isn't it possible that you've already used the missing parts to repair some doll? Maybe you forgot which ones you used and thought they were still in a box. It could be that they're not really missing at all."

"There's just one flaw in your theory, Glen."

"What's that?"

"I keep good track of my inventory. To have three or four different parts missing at the same time doesn't add up."

Glen shrugged his shoulders. "It was only an idea."

"And let's not forget about that doll head in the freezer," Sinda reminded.

"How could I? It even gave me the creeps." He clapped his hands together. "Let's get to work. Those parts have to be down here someplace."

Chapter 16

The search for the missing doll parts turned up nothing. Glen was a bit frustrated, but Sinda seemed to be filled with despair. They'd given up for the day and left the basement for the comfort of her living room, and now Glen sat on the couch with his arm draped across her shoulders. "I'm sorry we didn't find anything. I can't figure it out."

Sinda lifted her head slightly and looked at him. "It's not your fault."

"We still have no doll parts, and from the way you're looking at me, I'd say I haven't done much to help alleviate your fears."

"Just having you here has helped."

They sat in silence for a while, then Glen came up with a plan. "Since being down in the basement makes you so uptight, why not let me come over and give you a hand?"

Her forehead wrinkled. "Doing what?"

"Repairing dolls. I'm sure there's something I can do to help."

"Are you teasing me?"

He saw the skepticism in her squinted eyes and shook his head. "Who knows, it might even prove to be kind of fun."

"Oh, Glen," Sinda said shakily, "that's such a sweet offer, but—"

"I can come over every evening for a few hours, and on the Saturdays I'm not on my mail route."

"I couldn't let you do that."

"Why not? Are you afraid I'll make your doll patients even sicker?" he asked with a grin.

"It's not that. I'm sure you'd do fine, but you've got your own life. You have responsibilities to your daughter."

"Maybe Tara could tag along," he suggested.

"You two have better things to do than repair dolls and hold my shaking hand. Just because I'm acting like a big chicken doesn't mean you have to baby-sit me." Sinda paused as she slid her tongue across her lower lip. "Besides, you can't always be down there with me."

"Why not? I'd gladly spend my free time helping if it would make you feel better."

"I go to the basement for lots of things that don't involve doll repairing," she reminded him. "My washer and dryer are down there, and so is my freezer."

Glen lifted Sinda's chin with his thumb. "I think I'm falling in love with you, and I believe God brought you to Elmwood for a purpose," he said, changing the subject.

She opened her mouth to say something, but he touched her lips with the tips of his fingers and whispered, "If we give this relationship a chance, we might even have a future together."

Sinda sat up straight, her back rigid, and her lips set in a thin line. "We can't have a future together, Glen. I can't love you."

"Can't, or won't?"

She averted his steady gaze. "I want to love you, but I can't. My life is all mixed up, and my past would always be in our way. Please don't pressure me."

The depth of sadness he saw reflected in her green eyes made his stomach clench, and he nodded in mock defeat. "I'll drop the subject." *For now, anyway.*

&

It had been three days since Sinda found the doll head in the freezer, and three days since Glen had declared his feelings for her. He'd phoned several times, and he'd come over twice to see how she was doing. She'd assured him that everything was fine, but it was a lie. How could anything be fine when she had doll parts unaccounted for and love burning in her heart for a man with whom she could never have a future?

Sinda had only been to the basement twice in the last three days. Once to retrieve clothes from the dryer, and another time to bring up a doll that needed some work. She planned to put the finishing touches on the painted face while working at her kitchen table. She knew she couldn't keep it up forever, but for now, until her nerves settled down, she'd do more of the doll repairs upstairs, only going to the basement to get necessary items or do laundry.

A Girl Scout leader had called yesterday, wanting to bring her troop to the doll hospital as a field trip. Sinda turned her down, saying she was too busy right now. The truth was, the idea of having a bunch of inquisitive girls roaming around her basement would have been too much to handle.

In spite of Sinda's emotional state, she had managed to go to a local swap meet this morning where she'd sold a few antiques and picked up some old doll parts. She'd even met with two new customers who wanted dolls restored before Christmas.

Her chores were done for the day now, and she stood in the spare bedroom, prepared to check out the rest of the contents of her mother's trunk. She glanced around the room. Everything was exactly as she'd left it on Saturday. The jewelry box and items of clothing were still on the chair. The trunk lid was closed, though no longer locked.

She ground her teeth together and opened the lid. Did she really want to do this? An inner voice seemed to be urging her on. With trembling hands she withdrew a white Bible, which had her mother's name engraved in gold letters on the front cover. A burgundy bookmark hung partway out, and Sinda opened it to the marked page. "Psalm 19:12. 'Who can discern his errors? Forgive my hidden faults,' " she read aloud. She could hardly believe it was the same verse Glen had quoted to her the other day. "Mother must have felt guilty about something," she muttered. *Was Glen trying to tell me that I shouldn't feel guilty about anything, or was he referring to Dad? God knows, he had plenty to feel guilty about, but he always made me feel remorseful because I reminded him of Mother.*

Sinda closed the Bible and placed it on the chair next to the jewelry box and clothes. She reached inside the trunk and withdrew a small, black diary. It was fastened with a miniature padlock, but Sinda knew she could easily pry it open.

She went downstairs to the kitchen and took a pair of needle-nosed pliers from a drawer, then dropped to a seat at the table. In short order she had the lock open. *Would this be considered an invasion of privacy?* she wondered. *How could it be? Mother's gone, and after what she did to Dad and me, I have every right to read it.*

She opened the diary to the first entry, dated October 30, just a few days after Sinda's third birthday. With one hand cupped under her chin, she began to read.

Dear Diary:

Today I received some wonderful news. A visit to the doctor confirmed my suspicions—I'm pregnant again. The baby is due the middle of April. It will be nice for Sinda to have a sibling. Another child might be good for our marriage, too. William was thrilled with the news. He wants a boy this time.

Sinda felt a headache coming on, and she began to rub her forehead in slow, circular motions. "Mother was pregnant when I was three years old? I'm an only child. What happened to the baby?"

She read on, finding the next entry dated several months later.

Dear Diary:

Christmas is behind us for another year. This was probably one of the happiest holidays we've ever had. We had friends over for dinner, and all William could talk about was the child we're expecting in the spring. Sometimes my husband can be a bit harsh, but I'm hoping our baby will soften his heart.

The pain in Sinda's head escalated, and she wondered if she should quit reading and go to bed. A part of her wanted to escape from the past, but another part needed to know what happened to the child her mother had carried—the one her father hoped was a boy; so she read on.

Dear Diary:
My heart feels as though it is breaking in two. A terrible thing happened, and I wonder if I'll ever recover from the pain. I gave birth to William Shull Jr. one week ago, but he lived only three days, never leaving the confines of his tiny incubator. The child was born two months prematurely, and William is inconsolable. He blames me for the baby's death and says I did too much during my pregnancy. He's convinced that if I'd rested more the child would not have come early.

Sinda covered her mouth with her hand as she choked on a sob. She'd had a baby brother! A child she'd never met and had no memory of. That in itself was painful, but the stark reality of her father wanting a son and blaming her mother for denying him the right was a terrible blow. She wrapped her arms around her stomach and bent into the pain. "Could this have been the reason Mother left?" she moaned. As the thought began to take hold, she reminded herself that she'd been ten years old when her mother abandoned them. That was seven years after William Jr. died. There had to be some other reason Mother had gone. Sinda was sure her only hope of discovering the truth lay in her mother's diary. She would get to the bottom of it, even if it took all night!

❧

Sinda read the diary until the early morning hours, but the impact of her mother's final entry had been too much to bear. She'd fallen asleep on the couch, with the diary draped across her chest.

A resonant pounding roused her from a deep sleep. The diary fell to the floor as she clambered off the couch and staggered to the front door in a stupor. She wasn't aware that she'd spent the night in her blue jeans and sweatshirt, or that her eyes were bloodshot and her hair a disheveled mess until she glanced at her reflection in the hall mirror.

She opened the door and was surprised to see Glen standing on the front porch with a desperate look on his face. "Glen, what is it?"

His forehead wrinkled. "I need a favor, but I can see by looking at you that you're probably not the best one to ask."

"I didn't sleep well last night," she stated flatly.

"I'm sorry. Why didn't you call?"

She shrugged. "I'm fine now. What do you need?"

"A baby-sitter."

"What?" She stared at him blankly, trying to force the cobwebs out of her muddled brain.

"I need someone to watch Tara," Glen explained. "Mrs. Mayer phoned early this morning. She's sick with the flu."

"Won't Tara be in school all day?"

Glen shook his head. "She's off for the summer."

"Oh, I forgot." Sinda ran her fingers through her tangled hair, wishing she hadn't answered the door. "There's no point in you losing a whole day's pay. Send Tara over."

"I would have asked Penny's mother, Gwen, but they're on vacation at the beach this week. So if you're sure it wouldn't be too much of an inconvenience, I'd really appreciate your help today."

Of course it was inconvenient, but she would do it. Glen had done her plenty of favors, so turnabout was fair play. "It's fine. I had a bad night, but it won't keep me from watching Tara."

Glen's worried expression seemed to relax. "Thanks so much, Sinda." He touched her shoulder lightly. "How about coming over for supper tonight? I'll make my famous pasta, and I could fix a Caesar salad to go with it."

She reached up to rub the side of her unwashed face. "You're not obligated to cook for me, Glen. After walking your mail route all day you shouldn't have to come home and cook for me, anyway. Why don't you come over here tonight? I'll do the cooking."

"Are you sure you don't mind?"

She pushed an irritating lock of hair away from her face. "Positive."

He grinned. "You're wonderful. I'll send Tara over right away."

Glen leaned toward Sinda, and she thought he might be about to kiss her. She pulled quickly away when she remembered she hadn't yet brushed her teeth. "No problem. See you later."

He hesitated a moment, then with a wave of his hand, Glen turned and left. Sinda closed the door with a sigh, wishing she had time to shower and change before Tara arrived. A quick trip to the bathroom to wash her face and run a brush through her unruly curls was all she was able to manage before she heard another loud knock.

When Sinda opened the door Tara thrust a piece of paper into her hand. "Dad told me to come over here for the day and said I was supposed to give you this." The child was wearing a white blouse under a pair of green overalls, and she held a silver skateboard under the other arm.

Sinda motioned her inside and glanced at the document. It was a form giving Sinda permission to authorize emergency medical care for Tara. Great. "Uh, I'd rather you not do any skateboarding today."

Tara frowned. "Why not? I skateboard all the time."

"I know. I've watched you out front, and you've taken a few spills. You're in my care today, so I won't be responsible for you getting hurt."

Tara ambled into the living room and flopped onto the couch, wrapping her arms tightly around the skateboard, as though it were some kind of lifeline. "You're not my mother, you know. I don't have to do what you say."

Sinda felt her irritation begin to mount. She'd discovered some terrible things yesterday, spent a restless night on the couch, had been awakened by a desperate man, and now this? She was near the end of her rope, and one more good tug would probably cause it to snap right in two. She clenched her teeth and leveled Tara with what she hoped was a look of authority. "Your dad asked me to watch you today. This is my house, and I'll make the decisions. Is that clear?"

Tara nodded and dropped the skateboard to the floor. "What am I supposed to do all day?"

"Maybe we can work on some dolls." Sinda feigned a smile. "You did such a good job helping before."

Tara shrugged. "I never did anything that great. Besides, dolls are for kids."

"No, they're not," Sinda countered. "Lots of grown women, and even some men, collect dolls. Some are worth a lot of money. As you well know, many of the ones I repair are for collectors and antique dealers."

"I saw your picture in the paper a few weeks ago," Tara said, changing the subject. "That must have been really great for business."

Sinda nodded. "It was good advertisement. Several people have brought in dolls they want restored for Christmas."

"Christmas is a long ways off."

"Some dolls need lots of work. It takes time to repair them."

Tara wrinkled her nose. "People give away old dolls as presents?"

"Often a parent or grandparent will have a doll from their childhood that they want to pass on to a younger family member." Sinda took a seat in the over-stuffed chair directly across from Tara. *I wonder if the girl knows anything about the doll her father asked me to fix.* "Did your mother have any dolls?" she casually questioned.

The child shrugged her shoulders. "I wouldn't know. I was only a year old when she died. I thought you knew that."

Sinda felt her face flush. Of course she knew it, but she wasn't about to tell Tara why she was fishing for information. Learning whether she knew about the doll wasn't all she planned to fish for, either. Since she had Tara alone for the day, maybe she could ask her some questions that would give an accurate picture of the way Glen was at home, when no one could see if his mask of Christianity had slipped or not.

"All I have are some pictures to prove that my mother even existed," Tara went on to say. "To tell you the truth, I don't feel like I ever had a mother."

"I know what you mean," Sinda said softly. "As I told you before, I lost my mother when I was young."

Tara didn't seem to be listening anymore. She was looking at something lying on the floor next to her skateboard. She reached down to pick it up. "What's this—some kind of diary?"

Sinda jumped up. "Give me that!" She snatched the book away so quickly that Tara's hand flew up, and she nearly slapped herself in the face.

"Hey, what'd you do that for? I wasn't gonna hurt the dumb thing!"

Sinda snapped the cover shut and held it close to her throbbing chest.

"What's in there?" Tara squinted dramatically. "Some deep, dark secrets from your past?"

"It's none of your business! Diaries are someone's private thoughts, and this one is not for snoopy little girls!" Sinda bolted for the door. "I'm going upstairs to take a shower. You can watch TV if you like." She stormed up the steps, painfully aware that it was going to be a very long day.

Chapter 17

It was almost six o'clock when Glen arrived at Sinda's for supper. Her hair was piled up on her head in loose curls, and she was wearing a long, rust-colored skirt with a soft beige blouse.

Glen gave a low whistle when she opened the door. "You look great!"

She smiled and felt the heat of a blush creep up the back of her neck. "A far cry from the mess that greeted you at the door this morning, huh?" Sinda was feeling a bit friendlier toward Glen this evening. After questioning Tara today about her dad, she'd learned that he had never been physically abusive. If anything, Glen was sometimes too permissive, which explained why Tara got away with being so sassy.

Glen reached for her hand. "I know you don't always sleep in your clothes. Can you tell me about it now?"

"Not this minute." Sinda motioned toward the living room where Tara sat, two feet from the TV set.

Glen nodded. "You're right. Little pitchers have big ears, and mine probably holds a world record." He followed Sinda into the kitchen. "What's on the menu?"

"Lasagna." She opened the oven door to take a peek at its progress.

He sniffed the air appreciatively. "It smells terrific."

"I hope it's fit to eat," she said. "I found the recipe in a magazine, and it said not to precook the noodles, so I can only hope it'll be all right."

"Even if the noodles turn out chewy as rubber bands, I won't care." Glen's voice dropped to a whisper, and he moved closer. "Have you been praying about us?"

Sinda edged away from him, until her hip smacked the edge of the cupboard. "Ouch!"

He pulled her quickly into his arms. "Are you okay?"

She tried to push away, but her backside was pressed against the cupboard, and she had no place else to go. Her heartbeat picked up speed, and her mind became a clouded haze as he bent to kiss her. *Glen is a great dad; Tara said so today. Glen is a good neighbor; his actions have proven it to be so. Glen is a wonderful kisser. . .*

"No! No kissing!"

Glen and Sinda both whirled to face Tara.

"Young lady, that's enough!" Glen's face was red as a cherry, and a vein on the side of his neck bulged slightly.

Tara lifted her chin defiantly. "Can we go home now?"

"No, we certainly cannot go home! I just got here, and Sinda's worked hard to fix us a nice supper. We're going to sit down and enjoy the meal, just like any normal family."

What does a normal family look like? Sinda wondered. Appearances had always been so important to her father. She and Dad used to look like the picture of happiness, and she was sure everyone at their church had thought they were content. *If they'd only known what went on in our home.*

Tara's reply broke into Sinda's troubling thoughts. "We're not a family. I mean, we are, but Sinda's not part of it."

"I'm hoping she will be someday," Glen announced.

Sinda's mouth dropped open, and Tara began to cry. "Don't you love me anymore, Dad?"

Glen left Sinda's side and bent down to wrap his arms around Tara. "Of course I love you, but I also love Sinda."

"Why?" Tara wailed. "Why do you love her?"

Glen glanced over at Sinda, and she gripped the edge of the cupboard for support. "Sinda is a beautiful, sweet lady," he said, nodding toward her.

Sinda's ears were burning. Glen was telling Tara things she had no right to hear. Especially when they weren't true. She wasn't sweet. She had bitterness in her heart and wasn't able to trust. Besides, even if Glen was all he appeared to be, and even if she were able to set her fear of hurting him aside, Tara was still an issue. The child didn't like sharing her father, and Sinda was sure Tara would never accept the fact that Glen was in love with her. There was no future for her and Glen. Not now, not ever.

❧

Sinda pulled back the covers and crawled into bed as a low groan escaped her lips. The last twenty-four hours had felt like the longest in history—her history, at least. It had begun with the reading of her mother's Bible and diary. Next, her day had been interrupted and rearranged when Glen showed up on her doorstep needing a baby-sitter for his inquisitive child. Then Tara had taken up most of her day with nosey questions and a bad attitude. The final straw came in the kitchen, where Glen professed his love for her in front of Tara. The child's predictable reaction nearly ruined dinner, even if the lasagna had turned out well. Glen and Tara went home shortly after the meal, and Sinda had been grateful. At least she wasn't forced to tell Glen what was troubling her so much that she'd slept on the couch in her clothes last night.

Sinda tucked the sheet under her chin and shifted her body to the right, then the left, trying to find a comfortable position. "I can't have a serious relationship with Glen, no matter how much my heart cries for it."

Sinda had never known the heady feeling of being in love before, and even though she found it exhilarating, she couldn't succumb to it. She was scared of marriage. She'd spent her whole life afraid of her father, blocking out his verbal and physical abuses by telling herself that even if he was doing wrong, she deserved it because she was like her mother. She'd convinced herself that Dad was the way he was because of the pain Mother had inflicted on him. Sinda had vacillated between blaming her mother, her father, and even herself. She knew the truth now, though—her mother's diary had finally brought everything into focus.

Sinda turned her head to the right, and her gaze came to rest on the diary, lying on the bedside table. She was thankful Tara hadn't read any of it. She reached out and grabbed it, thumbing through several pages, forcing herself to read her mother's final words one more time.

Dear Diary:

William and I had another argument. He continues to blame me for the death of our son, even though it's been two years. He wishes we'd never married and says even the sight of me makes him sick.

"Were you sickened by the sight of me, Dad?" Sinda whispered into the night. She sniffed deeply and forced herself to read on.

What did I do to cause William to feel such animosity? He even said he and Sinda would be better off without me. I love my daughter, and I can't bear to think of leaving her. Besides, where would I go? How would I support myself? I have no relatives to turn to, and no money of my own. William handles all the finances. I'm only allowed enough cash for household expenses. If I need personal things or clothes for Sinda, I have to make an itemized list, then he decides how much I'll be allowed to spend. William makes good money at his accounting firm, yet he acts as though we are paupers.

Sinda felt a knot form in her stomach as she tried to visualize her mother begging for money. The poor woman must have had no self-esteem. *Of course, I had no self-esteem when Dad was alive, either. If I had, I'd have left home and made a life of my own. Instead, I felt obligated to take care of Dad and try to make up for what Mother did to him.* Tears slipped from her eyes and landed on the next entry.

Dear Diary:

    William's abuse has escalated. Last night, during another heated argument, he hit me. I didn't see it coming in time, so the blow landed on my jaw. It left an ugly bruise, and this morning I can barely open my mouth.

    Thankfully, Sinda was asleep when it happened. I hope she never discovers the awful truth about her father. She seems devoted to him, and he to her.

A sob ripped from Sinda's throat, and tears coursed down her cheeks. "It's true, Mother. My loyalty was always with Dad. I did everything he told me to do. I remember hearing the two of you arguing, but I refused to accept what was really happening." She drew in a deep breath and turned to the last entry in her mother's diary.

Dear Diary:

    I know what I must do, and it's breaking my heart. It's been seven years since William Jr.'s death, yet I've been reminded of it nearly every day. My husband won't let me forget, nor will he quit laying the blame at my feet. He's become more and more physically abusive, and I fear for my life. William gave me an ultimatum last night. He said I must move out of our house and leave Sinda with him.

    I've become William's enemy, and it seems as if he wants it that way. I've tried to reestablish what we once had, but he's built a wall of indifference and hatred around himself. I've seen a counselor and even suggested that we try to have another baby, but he won't hear of it. He says I had my chance and failed. He insists that I take on a new identity and begin another life. One that won't include my precious little girl. He says that I have no other choice, and if I refuse, he'll tell Sinda I killed her baby brother. She's too young to understand. I'm afraid she would side with her father.

    He said that if I don't leave, he will force me to watch while he doles out my punishments to Sinda. After suffering years of his abuse, I know well what William is capable of doing. I would do anything to protect our daughter.

Sinda's throat felt constricted, and it became difficult to swallow. "Oh, Mother, why didn't you tell me the truth? Or why didn't you at least take me with you? You left me with a bitter, angry man." She shook her head slowly. She'd practically idolized her father when she was a child, and even if her mother had told the truth, she wouldn't have believed it. Dad had said everything was Mother's fault, and Sinda had accepted it as fact.

"I didn't see the truth because I didn't want to," she moaned. "Dad was more of a hypocrite than I'd ever begun to imagine!" She blinked away her tears, as she continued to read.

I've decided I must go in the morning, before Sinda wakes up. I'll leave a note on the kitchen table, stating only that I'm leaving and will never return. God forgive me for not having the courage to stand up to William. I have no family living nearby, and I don't even know if I can support myself. Taking Sinda with me would be a selfish thing to do. As much as I'll miss her, I know she will be better off with her father.

Sinda drew in a shuddering breath and tried to free her mind of the agonizing pain that held her in its grasp. "Dad used to tell me I would end up like you, Mother. I only dated a few times, and never more than once with the same man. Dad convinced me that, should I ever marry, I'd end up hurting my husband the way you hurt him." She covered her face with her hands and sobbed. Like mother, like daughter. Her father's accusing words rang in her head as she rocked back and forth, clutching a pillow to her chest. She'd lost so much. If only she'd been able to see through her father's charade. If she could just go back and change the past. Was it possible that Dad really had repented that night at the revival service? Why had he told Alex Masters to see that Sinda was given her mother's trunk? Could Dad have been trying to make restitution?

Sinda knew that only God could have seen what was in her father's heart. What mattered now was what she planned to do with her future. She hadn't known Glen very long, but in the short time they'd been together, she knew one thing for certain. She loved him as much as she was capable of loving anyone.

Chapter 18

Sinda awoke the following morning feeling groggy and disoriented. A barrage of troublesome dreams had left her mind in a jumble. She forced herself to shower and change into a pair of blue jeans and a white T-shirt. There were several dolls that needed to be finished, and she knew staying busy would be the best remedy for her negative thoughts and self-pity.

She and Tara had done some work in the basement yesterday. Since nothing unusual had happened, she'd talked herself into going back down there again today. She had to conquer her fears, and facing them head-on was the only way.

After breakfast Sinda cleaned up the kitchen, made a few phone calls to customers, balanced her checkbook, took out the garbage, fed the dog and cat, and watered all her houseplants. By the time she finished her chores, it was noon and she was ready for lunch. This gave her an excuse to put off going to the basement awhile longer.

Panther rubbed against Sinda's leg as she stood at the kitchen sink, peeling a carrot to add to her shrimp salad. The cat purred softly when she lifted her foot to rub the top of his sleek head with the toe of her sneaker. "Would you like to go downstairs with me?" she murmured.

The feline meowed and turned so she could rub the other side of his body. Sinda was glad Panther had come to live with her. He'd already proven to be quite the mouser. No more strange noises in the basement, and no more jumping doll parts! Sinda had been hoping her two pets would become friends, but so far it didn't appear as if that would happen. She tried to keep them separated as much as possible, alternating Sparky and Panther from the house to the yard. She probably should find another home for one of them, but right now she had more pressing matters to worry about. The first one—to get some dolls ready to go home.

A short time later, Sinda flicked the basement light on and proceeded into the doll hospital. She had little enthusiasm, but at least she was going to get something accomplished.

Sinda knew she'd become good at her craft, but on days like today she had little energy, limited confidence in her abilities, and no feeling of self-worth. In fact, she wondered if her life had any meaning at all. Where would she be living and what would she be doing twenty years from now? Would she still be here in this old house, stringing dolls, gluing on synthetic wigs, and pining for a love she could never have? Except for Carol, she had no real friends, although Glen wanted to be her friend. In fact, he wanted more than friendship.

Before she abandoned me and Dad, I thought Mother and I were friends, Sinda thought wistfully. She massaged her forehead with the tips of her fingers, hoping to halt the troubling thoughts. *I wonder if Mother's still alive. It's been almost twenty-three years since she left. Would it be a mistake to try to look for her after all this time?*

"Maybe I'm not her only daughter. If Mother took on another identity, she might have gotten married again and could even have a whole new family by now. She's probably forgotten she ever had a daughter named Sinda." She moaned and shook her head. "And what would I say if I found her?"

As intriguing as the idea was, because of Dad, Sinda felt sure her mother would want nothing to do with her. Mother no doubt thought Sinda was on his side. After all, during the time her mother had been living with them, Sinda and her father had been close. *Does Mother even know that Dad is dead?*

Sinda pushed all thoughts of her mother aside and forced her mind to focus on the Raggedy Ann doll, whose face was missing its black button eyes. In short order she completed the job of sewing on new eyes, then she went to work on an old composition baby doll. One leg was missing, so Sinda rummaged for the part in a box marked Composition Doll Legs. She searched thoroughly, knowing there had been a match the last time she looked.

"I can't figure it out," she fumed. "I showed Mrs. Allen the leg I'd be using as a replacement the day she brought the doll in. Where could it be?"

Thinking she might have taken it out earlier and placed it somewhere, Sinda looked on all the shelves and through every box of composition parts. When she still couldn't locate the leg, she set the doll aside to work on something else.

Another doll needed a new wig. Her old one was made of mohair and had been badly moth-eaten. Sinda opened the top drawer of an old dresser used exclusively for doll wigs. She knew the right size and color would be there because she'd recently received an order from one of her suppliers. She searched through every package of wigs, but couldn't find the one she needed. "I don't understand this!" She slammed the drawer shut with such force it caused the drawer below to fly open.

Sinda gasped. Wedged between two boxes of open-and-close eyes was a vinyl doll arm. It was the one she'd been looking for the other day, when Glen helped her search for missing doll parts. "What in the world is going on?"

Icy fingers of fear crept up her spine as she closed the drawer then opened the one below. She kept stringing-cord in several sizes here, along with wooden neck buttons used on the older bisque dolls. Lying in the middle of a coil of elastic cord was a composition doll arm. It was also one she had been looking for.

"I've got to get out of here!" Sinda banged the drawer shut and bolted for the stairs. A few minutes later, she stood in the kitchen, willing her heartbeat to return to a normal, steady rhythm. She wiped her clammy hands on the front of her jeans and sank wearily into a chair. Leaning both elbows on the table, Sinda let her head fall forward into her hands.

Several minutes later, she lifted her head and glanced at the clock above the refrigerator. It was only three o'clock. Glen wouldn't be home for at least two hours. Sinda shook her head. *Why am I thinking of him?*

"Maybe a nap will help," Sinda mumbled. She left the kitchen and curled up on the couch in the living room, with Panther lying at her feet.

For the first half hour, sleep eluded her. Fears and troubled thoughts hissed at her like corn popping over hot coals. *Help me, Lord. Please help me.* The words exploded in her head, and she realized that she was praying. Maybe she hadn't strayed as far from the Lord as she'd thought. Maybe He did still care about her.

When Sinda finally fell asleep, her thoughts mingled with her dreams and she could no longer distinguish between what was real and what wasn't.

Glen. . .

Tara. . .

Missing dolls. . .

Mother. . .

Sinda was awakened to the resonating chime of the grandfather clock, letting her know it was half past five. She sat up, yawned, and stretched like a cat. "Some little nap we took, huh, Panther?" The cat didn't budge, so she left him alone on the couch.

Her stomach rumbled as she plodded toward the kitchen. "I think I'd better have something to eat."

Her nerves were a bit steadier now, though she still felt physically fatigued and mentally drained. Some nourishment would hopefully recharge her batteries and get her thinking clearly.

Sinda opened the refrigerator to get some milk for the makings of clam chowder. She picked up the carton and halted. Her world was spinning out of control. With a piercing wail, she dropped the milk to the floor, turned, and rushed out the back door.

❧

Glen was standing at the stove frying lamb chops for supper when he heard a sharp rapping on the door. Knowing Tara was engrossed in her favorite TV show in the living room, he turned the burner down and went to see who it was.

When he opened the door, startling green eyes flashed with obvious fear, and Sinda practically fell into his arms. He held her for several seconds, letting her wet the front of his T-shirt with her tears. When he could stand it no longer, Glen pulled back slightly. "What is it? Why are you crying?"

"I think I'm going crazy!" Sinda shifted her weight from one foot to the other, and he noticed how badly she was trembling.

"Come, have a seat at the table." Glen led Sinda to the kitchen, offered her a chair, then handed her a napkin. "Dry your eyes, take a deep breath, and tell me what has you so upset."

"Remember the missing doll parts we hunted for the other day?" she asked, her voice quivering.

He nodded and sat down beside her.

"I found some of them today."

"That's great! See, I told you not to worry."

She grasped his arm. "It's not great! I found the parts accidentally—in some really weird places!"

She went on to give him the details, and he listened quietly until he thought she was finished. "I still don't see why you think you're going crazy. We all misplace things. The other day I lost my car keys again, and Tara found them lying on the living room floor."

"It's not the same thing. I haven't even told you the worst part."

"There's more?"

She lowered her gaze to the table. "I was about to fix some chowder for supper, and when I opened the refrigerator to take out the milk, I found a doll body—one that's also been missing." She sucked in her lower lip. "It wasn't there earlier when I fixed lunch. Do you see now why I think I'm losing my mind?"

"I'm sure there has to be some logical explanation," he said with an assurance he didn't really feel.

She looked at him hopefully. "What do you think it is?"

He reached for her hand and gave it a gentle squeeze. "I don't know."

She hung her head dejectedly, and it pulled at his heartstrings. What was there about this woman that made him want to protect her? Was it the tilt of her head, that cute little nose, those gorgeous green eyes, her soft auburn hair? Or was it Sinda's vulnerability that touched the core of Glen's being? Had God sent her to him, or was it the other way around? Perhaps they needed each other more than either of them realized.

Glen shook his thoughts aside and focused on Sinda's immediate need. "Why don't you stay here for supper? Afterward, we'll go back to your house, and I'll help you look for more doll parts, or at least some clues that might tell us something about what's been going on."

Sinda raised her head. "Thanks, but I have to tell you, I don't have much hope of finding anything."

He studied her face a few seconds. Her smile was the saddest one he'd ever seen. It nearly broke his heart to see her suffering like this.

Prayer. That's what they both needed now. Lots and lots of prayer.

Chapter 19

W hy can't I come, too?" Tara whined after Glen informed her that he was going over to Sinda's house.

"Because you have dishes to do."

"There aren't that many," she argued. "I could do them when we get back."

Since when is Tara so anxious to go to Sinda's? Glen wondered. *She's got to be up to something.* He pointed to the sink. "I want you to do the dishes now, Tara."

Tara's lower lip protruded. "Please, Dad."

"Pouting will not help."

"Maybe we could use some help on this case," Sinda suggested. "After all, Tara has been practicing to be a detective."

The child jumped up and down excitedly. "A case? What kind of case are we on?"

"We are not on any case," Glen answered firmly. "I am going to help Sinda look for a few things she's misplaced." He turned so only Sinda could see his face, and he held one finger to his lips. When she nodded, he faced Tara again. "If we run into problems we can't handle, I'll call you."

"Promise?"

"I said so, didn't I?"

Before the child could reply, Glen grabbed Sinda by the hand and led her out the back door.

"Are you sure you have time for this?" Sinda asked when they reached her back porch.

"I'll always make time for you." Glen's answer was followed by a quick kiss.

"I wish you wouldn't do that."

He wrapped his arms around her. "You mean this?" When he bestowed her with another kiss, he noticed she was blushing.

"I think we'd better go inside. Our neighbors might get the wrong idea." Sinda opened the back door and motioned toward her kitchen floor. "Excuse the mess. When I saw the doll body in the refrigerator, I dropped a carton of milk. I was so scared, I just ran out the door." She grabbed some paper towels, then dropped to her knees.

Glen skirted around her, heading for the refrigerator. Sure enough, there was a pink doll body lying on the top shelf. He reached inside and pulled it out, hardly

104

batting an eyelash over this latest phenomenon.

"Be careful with that," Sinda cautioned. "It's quite valuable."

He carried it gingerly across the room and placed it on the table.

She stood up and moved to his side. "So what do you think?"

Glen drew in a deep breath. "I'd say someone is playing a pretty mean trick on you, and I've got a good idea who that someone might be."

"You do?" She clutched his arm as though her life depended on it. "Who is it, Glen? Who could be hiding my doll parts?"

"My daughter."

Sinda's eyes widened. "You think Tara did it?"

"She's the only one with opportunity or motive."

"You make it sound as though she's some kind of a criminal."

He shrugged. "I wouldn't put it quite like that, but Tara does resent you. I think finding out I'm in love with you might have pushed her over the edge." He cleared his throat a few times. "Now you know why I didn't want her coming over here yet. I needed to discuss this with you in private." He wiped his forehead with the back of his hand. "Of course, she is the only one who can help us find the rest of the missing doll parts."

Sinda stood there, slowly shaking her head. "But how? When could she have done all this?"

"When she was helping you repair dolls," he answered. "She was here for several hours at a time, then again when you kept her while Mrs. Mayer was sick."

Sinda pulled out a chair at the table and almost fell into it. "I did catch her nosing around the place a few times, while she was helping out with the dolls." She clicked her tongue. "I can't believe Tara would do something so cruel."

"Was she ever alone? Were you out of her sight long enough for her to hide the parts?"

"Several times, but—"

Glen snapped his fingers. "Case solved!" He pulled out the chair next to Sinda and took a seat.

"It's not as simple as you might think," Sinda said, toying with a strand of her hair.

"It seems like an open-and-shut case to me. The only thing left to do is have a little heart-to-heart talk with that daughter of mine."

She touched his arm. "Tara was not in my house today, Glen."

"So?"

"She couldn't have put the bisque doll in my refrigerator."

Glen squeezed his eyes shut, praying for guidance as he tried to put the pieces of the puzzle together. "Maybe she did it yesterday."

Sinda shook her head. "The doll wasn't there before my nap. Tara hasn't been here today, and neither has anyone else."

Glen's forehead wrinkled. "I'll tell you what I think."

"What's that?"

"I think the doll body was in the refrigerator earlier, and you just didn't see it."

"I don't think so," she argued. "If it had been there, I'm sure I would have noticed."

He pursed his lips. "I'm convinced that Tara has something to do with this. She could have come over here while you were taking your nap. Was the back door unlocked?"

Sinda shrugged her shoulders. "I don't know. I usually lock it, but it's possible that I forgot after I took out the garbage."

"If the door was unlocked, Tara could have come inside, crept down to the basement, picked up the doll body, and put it in your refrigerator." Glen turned his hands palms up. "It makes perfect sense to me. Tara's jealous and she's taking it out on you."

Sinda's body sagged with obvious relief, and she gave him a wide smile. "Glen Olsen, you're beginning to sound more like a detective than your nosey daughter." She emitted a small sigh. "If you're right about this, and Tara is responsible, what do we do now?"

He stood up. "I'm going to call my detective daughter on the phone and tell her to get over here right now."

"Could you wait awhile on that?"

"What for?"

"I'd like to discuss a few other things. That is, if you have the time to listen."

Glen chuckled in response to her question. "For you, I have all the time in the world."

❧

Sinda handed Glen a glass of iced tea as they took a seat on the couch in her living room. She was about to bare her soul, because she couldn't carry the pain any longer. Her nerves were shot, her confidence gone, and she was afraid she might be close to a complete mental breakdown. "You know that old trunk of my mother's?" she asked as she pushed a stack of magazines aside and set her glass down on the coffee table.

Glen nodded.

"I looked through the rest of it the other day, and I found her Bible, as well as an old diary."

"Have you read any of it?"

Her eyes filled with unwanted tears. "All of it."

"I assume the content was upsetting?"

Sinda reached for her glass and took a sip of tea before answering. "Terribly upsetting."

"Is that what you wanted to talk about?"

She swallowed hard and nodded. "Remember when I told you that Mother left when I was ten years old?"

"I remember."

"Her diary revealed some things I didn't know before. Some alarming things." Sinda paused and licked her lips. "Mother didn't leave because she wanted to. She was forced to go."

Glen's eyebrows shot up. "Forced? How so?"

"When I was three years old, Mother had a baby boy, but he was born prematurely and died a few days later. If not for that diary, I would never have known I'd even had a brother." Tears coursed down Sinda's cheeks, and she wiped them away with the back of her hand. "Dad blamed Mother for the death of the baby."

Glen frowned as he set his glass of tea down on the table. "I don't understand. How could your mother be held accountable for a premature baby dying?"

"As far as I can tell, she wasn't responsible. Her diary says Dad accused her of doing too much while she was pregnant. He hounded her about it for years—even to the point of verbal and physical abuse."

"Your dad must have wanted a son badly to be so bitter and hostile. I think he needed professional help."

Sinda closed her eyes and drew in a deep breath. "He took me to church every Sunday and claimed to be a Christian."

"Just because someone goes to church doesn't make him a Christian. Christianity is a relationship with God." Glen flexed his fingers. "Far too many people go to church only for show."

She nodded in agreement. "I was shocked to learn it was Dad's blackmailing scheme that drove Mother away." Sinda choked back the sob rising in her throat.

Glen's eyes clouded with obvious confusion. "Blackmailing?"

Sinda set her glass down on the coffee table and stood up. She began to pace the length of the room. "Apparently Dad demanded that Mother move away and take on a new identity. He threatened to tell me that she'd killed my baby brother if she didn't." She hung her head. "He also threatened to hurt me."

When Glen stood up and guided her to stand in front of the fireplace, she leaned her head against his arm. "I can't believe I was so taken in by his lies. If I had only known the truth."

"You were just a child. Children usually believe what their parents tell them, whether it's right or wrong."

Sinda's eyes pooled with a fresh set of tears. "I grew up thinking I was just like my mother, and Dad reminded me of it nearly every day."

Glen quickly embraced her. "You can't let the words of a bitter, hateful man control your life. God created you, and He gave you the ability to love and be loved."

"I can't," she sobbed. "After what Dad did, I can never trust another man."

Glen kissed her forehead. "You can trust me."

"I wish it were that simple."

"It can be. Let me help you, Sinda. Let me show you how much I care."

She moved away from him. "I need more time. I need to work through all the things I've just learned. Dad pretended to be such a good Christian, all the while blaming Mother for everything. He was abusive to her, and as much as I hate to admit it, there were times when he abused me." She shuddered. "It was not normal discipline, Glen, but hair pulling, smacks across the face, a belt that could connect most anywhere on my body, and once, he even choked me."

Glen's eyes darkened. "I'm beginning to understand your reluctance to let me get close," he said, resting his forehead against hers. "I'm so sorry for all you've been through."

She sniffed deeply. "I've never discussed this with anyone. Our family secrets were well hidden. No one knew how controlling Dad could be." The strength drained from Sinda's legs, and she dropped into a nearby chair. "I covered for him because I thought everything was Mother's fault. If she hadn't gone, he might have been kinder. If I hadn't reminded him of her, maybe. . ." Her voice trailed off, and she closed her eyes against the pain.

Glen snorted. "Each of us is responsible for our own actions, and not all men are like your father." He moved to stand behind her, then began to knead the kinks from her shoulders and neck. "You've been through so much and discovered a lot in the last few days."

She shivered involuntarily. "There's still the matter of the missing doll parts. The mystery hasn't been solved yet, and until it is. . ."

"It will be solved soon," Glen said with assurance. "By the end of this evening, we'll have some answers."

Chapter 20

When Tara arrived at Sinda's, she was wearing a satisfied smile, but Glen glared at her, and it quickly faded.

"What's wrong, Dad? I thought you called me over to help solve a case."

He ushered Tara into the living room and motioned her to take a seat, then he joined Sinda on the couch.

"What's up?" Tara asked, dropping into the antique rocker.

Seconds of uneasy silence ticked by, then Glen glanced at Sinda. "Do you want to tell her or shall I?"

She shrugged. "She's your daughter."

Glen leaned forward, raked his fingers through his hair, then stared at Tara accusingly. "Sinda has some doll parts that are missing. Would you care to tell us where they are?"

Tara rapped her fingers on the arm of the chair. "Where were they last seen?"

Glen jumped up and moved swiftly across the room. "Don't play coy with me, young lady. You know perfectly well where they were last seen. Tell us where they are now!"

Tara's mouth dropped open, and her eyes widened. "You think I took some doll parts?"

"Didn't you?"

She shook her head.

"Come on, Tara! This has gone on long enough! Sinda needs those parts, and I want you to tell her where they are!"

Feeling a sudden need to protect Tara from her father's wrath, Sinda stood up and knelt in front of the child's chair. Even if Glen wasn't going to strike his daughter, he was yelling, and that upset her. "We're not mad at you, Tara," she said softly.

"Speak for yourself!" Glen shouted.

Tara looked up at her father, and her eyes filled with tears. "I haven't done anything wrong, and I don't know a thing about any missing doll parts."

"Are you saying you haven't hidden doll parts in some rather unusual places?" Sinda asked.

"Like maybe a freezer or the refrigerator?" Glen interjected.

Tara's mouth was set in a thin line. "I don't know what you're talking about."

"Tara Mae Olsen, I'm warning you. . . ."

"Maybe she's telling the truth," Sinda interjected.

Glen shook his head. "She has to be the guilty party. She's the only one with a motive."

"What kind of motive would I have?" Tara asked shakily.

"Do you really have to ask? You're jealous of Sinda, and you're trying to scare her away with ghost stories and disappearing doll parts."

Sinda looked the child full in the face. "Please believe me, I'm not trying to come between you and your father."

Tara glared back at her. "I think you've got him hypnotized into believing he loves you."

Glen held up his hands. "See, what'd I tell you? She hid those doll parts out of spite!" He gave Tara another warning look. "Are you going to show us where they are or not?"

The child squared her shoulders. "I can't, because I don't know."

"I believe her, Glen," Sinda said as she pulled herself to her feet.

"Well, I don't, and if she doesn't confess, she's going to be punished!"

Sinda flinched. She closed her eyes, trying to dispel the vision of her father coming at her with his belt. *You're a bad girl—just like your mother, and you deserve to be punished.* Dad's angry words echoed in Sinda's head, as though he were standing right beside her. She cupped her hands against her ears, hoping to drown out the past.

Sinda felt Glen's hand touch her shoulder. "I'm sorry. I'm a little upset with my daughter right now, but I shouldn't be snapping at you."

When Sinda made no reply, he added, "It's okay. No one's going to get hurt." He gave Tara an icy stare. "Even if they do deserve to be spanked."

Tara shrugged, apparently unconvinced of the possibility of being taken over her father's knee. "I can't make you believe me, but I am a good detective. So if you'd like my help solving this mystery, I'm at your service."

Sinda offered the child what she hoped was a reassuring smile. "We appreciate that."

"Where do we start?" Tara asked eagerly.

"I think we should wait until tomorrow," Glen said. "It's getting late, and we'll all function better after a good night's rest."

Sinda gulped. "You might be able to get a good night's rest, but I sure won't. I haven't slept well in weeks. Not since this whole frightening mess started."

"I've got an idea. Tara and I can spend the night over here," Glen suggested. "That way you won't be alone."

Before Sinda could respond, Tara grabbed her father's arm and begged,

"You've got to be kidding!"

Glen brushed her hand aside. "I'm completely serious. You can sleep upstairs in one of Sinda's spare rooms, and I'll sleep down here on the couch." He smiled at Sinda. "Since tomorrow's my day off, and Tara's on summer vacation, we can sleep in if we like. I'll fix us a hearty breakfast, and afterward we'll turn this house upside down until we find all those doll parts. How's that sound?"

It sounded wonderful to Sinda, but she hated to admit it. "I–I couldn't put you out like that, Glen."

"I'm more than happy to stay." He glanced down at Tara, who stood by his side with a frown on her face. "Let's think of this as an adventure. Who knows, it could even prove to be fun."

❧

Sinda sat on the edge of her bed with her mother's diary in her lap. She blinked against the tide of tears that had begun to spill over. *Mother, if you are still alive, where are you now? Do you ever think of me? Have you tried to get in touch with me?* She didn't know why she kept running this over and over in her mind, or why it seemed so important to her now. She glanced at the diary again and knew the reason. *Mother didn't leave because she wanted to. She left because she was afraid of Dad. She thought he would turn me against her, and she was right, that's exactly what happened.* Thoughts of her father's betrayal seemed to be just under the surface of her mind, like an itch needing to be scratched, and she groaned.

Throughout her youth, Sinda's resentment toward her mother had festered. It wasn't anger she was feeling now, though. It was sadness and a deep sense of loss, but she knew there was no going back. What was in the past was history. She would have to find the strength to forgive both of her parents and move on with her life.

She snapped off the light by her bed and collapsed against the pillow. What she needed now was a long talk with her heavenly Father, followed by a good night's sleep.

❧

Glen punched his pillow for the third time and tried to find a comfortable position on the narrow couch he was using as a bed. He hoped they would find some answers to the doll mystery soon. Sinda needed to feel safe in her own home. He didn't relish the idea of making her living room a permanent bedroom every night, either. He gave the pillow one more jab and decided he could tough it for one night.

Glen fought sleep for several hours, and just as he was dozing off, a strange noise jolted him awake. He glanced at the grandfather clock across the room, noting that it was one in the morning. He sat up and swung his legs over the edge of the couch. His body felt stiff and unyielding as he attempted to stretch

111

his limbs. He listened intently but heard no more noises. Since he was already awake, he decided to get a drink of water.

Glen entered the kitchen and was about to turn on the faucet at the sink when he heard the basement door open and click shut. He whirled around in time to see Sinda walk into the room. He hadn't turned on the light, so he could only make out her outline, but it was obvious that she was wearing a long nightgown. She padded across the room in her bare feet. It looked like she was holding something in her hands.

Glen squinted, trying to make out what it was. "Sinda? What are you doing?"

She made no reply as she bent to open the oven door.

"You're not planning to do any middle-of-the-night baking, I hope," he teased.

When she still didn't answer, he snapped on the overhead light. "What on earth?" Sinda was putting a vinyl doll leg into the oven! He moved in for a closer look, watching in fascination as she closed the oven door and turned to leave.

Glen followed her through the hallway. She opened the door that led to the basement and descended the stairs in the dark. Afraid she might fall, he turned on the light over the stairwell and followed.

Sinda walked slowly and deliberately into the doll hospital, apparently unaware of his presence. Glen watched in amazement as she pulled one of the boxes from a shelf and retrieved a small composition arm. She set the box on her workbench, turned, and made her way back to the stairs. When she reached the top, she headed toward the next flight of steps.

Glen stayed close behind, holding his breath as Sinda entered the guest room where Tara lay sleeping.

Sinda walked over to the dresser, bent down, and opened the bottom drawer, then placed the doll arm inside. When she banged the drawer shut, Tara bolted upright in bed. "Who's there?"

"It's me, Tara," Glen whispered. "Me and Sinda."

Tara snapped on the light by her bed. "What's going on, Dad? What are you doing in my room in the middle of the night?"

"Go back to sleep. I'll explain everything in the morning." Glen took Sinda's hand and led her toward the door.

"Wait a minute!" Tara called. "If something weird's going on, I want to know about it! After all, I was forced to spend the night in this creepy house, and I'm supposed to be helping you solve a big mystery."

Glen nodded. "You do deserve an explanation, but now's not the time. I need to get Sinda back to her own room."

"What's she doing in here again?"

Glen's forehead wrinkled. "Again? What do you mean?"

"She was in here earlier. I asked what she wanted, but she didn't answer. She walked over to the window, stood there a few minutes, then left. It was really creepy, Dad."

Sinda stood there, staring off into space and holding Glen's hand as though she didn't have a care in the world. Glen glanced over at her before he spoke to Tara again. "I think Sinda's been sleepwalking," he whispered. "I found her in the kitchen, then followed her to the basement."

"What was she doing down there?"

"Getting a doll part. She put one in the oven, and just now she placed a doll arm in that drawer." He pointed to the dresser and frowned.

"How weird!" Tara exclaimed. She nodded her head toward Sinda. "Just look at her. She's staring off into space like she doesn't know where she is."

"She doesn't," Glen said. "She has no idea what she's done, or even that she's out of her bed."

"Then wake her up."

"I don't think that's a good idea. I heard somewhere that waking a sleepwalker might cause them some kind of emotional trauma." He glanced at Sinda again, feeling a deep sense of concern. "I don't know if it's true or not, but to be on the safe side, I think I'll wait and tell her in the morning."

Suddenly Sinda began swaying back and forth, hollering, "Oh, my head! It hurts so bad!"

Glen held her steady, afraid she might topple to the floor.

She blinked several times, then looked right at him. "Glen? What are you doing in my room?"

"This isn't your room," he answered. "It's the guest room."

Sinda's face was a mask of confusion. "I'm in the guest room?"

He nodded. "I followed you here. You were sleepwalking."

❧

Sinda sat at the kitchen table, holding a cup of hot chocolate in one hand. "I still can't believe I'm the one responsible for all those missing doll parts." She looked over at Glen, who sat in the chair beside her. "Do you think I'm losing my mind?"

He reached out and took hold of her free hand. "No, but I believe you're deeply troubled about that diary you found in your mother's trunk."

Sinda feigned a smile. "I don't think I've ever walked in my sleep before. In fact, the doll parts didn't turn up missing until that stupid trunk arrived. Maybe that's when all the sleepwalking began."

She saw Glen glance at the clock across the room. It was nearly two in the morning. Tara was back in bed, but Sinda needed to talk, so Glen had suggested they come to the kitchen for hot chocolate.

"Sinda," Glen said hesitantly, "I know you're upset about your recent discoveries, and I think maybe your subconscious has chosen to deal with it in a rather unusual way."

Sinda blew on her cocoa before taking a tentative sip. "I'll bet there are doll parts hidden all over this house. How am I ever going to make it stop happening?" A sickening wave of dread flowed through her. She looked at Glen, hoping he could give her some answers. "I can't go on living like this. Doll repairing and selling antiques is my livelihood. I can't keep losing doll parts or wandering around the house at all hours of the night like a raving lunatic."

"You're not a lunatic," Glen said softly. "I think the best thing for you to do is try to put the past behind you and start looking to the future."

"The future?" she shot back. "Do I even have a future?"

A tear trickled down her cheek, and Glen dried it with his thumb. "Of course you have a future. One with me, I hope."

Sinda rested her head on his shoulder and a low moan escaped her lips. "I only wish it were that simple."

"It can be," he whispered.

She lifted her head. "You have a spirited daughter to raise, Glen. Do you really want to take on the responsibility of baby-sitting your neurotic neighbor?"

Glen graced her with a tender smile. "It would give me nothing but pleasure."

"What about Tara?"

"What about her?"

"She doesn't like me. And this discovery won't help."

Glen leaned over and gently kissed her. "She'll grow to love you as much as I do." He wiggled his eyebrows. "Well, maybe not quite that much."

Sinda smiled in spite of her nagging doubts. She glanced at the clock again. "I've kept you up half the night. I'm sorry for causing so much trouble."

"I'd do it all over if you'd promise to think about a future with me," he said.

She studied him intently, realizing he had a much softer heart than she'd ever imagined. "You're serious, aren't you?"

"Couldn't be more serious." He drew her into his arms. "I don't want to rush you into a relationship you're not ready for."

"Thanks," she murmured. "I've still got a lot of things to work out."

"I'm here if you need me, and when the time's right, I hope to make you my wife."

Her eyes filled with tears. "You'd be willing to marry a crazy sleepwalker who can't deal with her past?"

He snickered. "I'm not worried about that. I think as you begin to trust God fully and let Him help you work through the pain, there'll be no need for your nightly treks."

"I hope you're right, Glen," she murmured. "I really hope you're right."

Chapter 21

For the next several weeks, things went better. Sinda was able to locate most of the missing doll parts, her sleepwalking had lessened, and Tara, though reluctantly, did seem a bit more resigned to the fact that Glen and Sinda planned to keep seeing one another. Sinda and Glen had gone to a couple of yard sales, and they'd even taken Tara on a picnic at the lake. They had also started praying regularly and studying the Bible together several evenings a week.

Sinda's biggest hurdle came when she agreed to attend church with the Olsens on the first Sunday of August. Today would be the first time she'd been in church since her father died, and just the thought of it set her nerves on edge. Would she fit in? Would the memory of Dad and his hypocrisy keep her from worshiping God?

She stood in front of the living room window, waiting for Glen to pick her up, and when she closed her eyes briefly, she could see her father sitting in his church pew with a pious look on his face. "How could I have been so blind? I knew how harsh Dad was with me. Every sharp word. . .every physical blow. . . Why didn't I realize he'd been the same way with Mother? Why did I blame her for his actions?"

A knock on the front door drew Sinda away from the window. Glen was waiting. It was time to go to church.

⁓

Sinda glanced over at Glen, then past him to Tara, who sat on his other side. He was smiling and nodding at the pastor's words. An occasional "Amen" would escape his lips. Was Glen really all he seemed to be? How could she be sure he wasn't merely pretending to be a good Christian, the way her father had? Could she ever learn to fully trust again?

"God's Word says, 'Don't worry about anything; instead, pray about everything. Tell God what you need, and thank him for all he has done.' " Pastor Benton's quote from Philippians 4:6 (NLT) rocked Sinda to her soul. She'd spent so many years worrying about everything, praying about little, and never thanking God for the answers she'd received to those prayers she had uttered. Hadn't it been God, working through Glen, who showed her the facts regarding the missing doll parts? Hadn't she learned the truth about her mother because God allowed her the opportunity to read that diary?

The pastor's next words resounded in her head like the gong of her grandfather clock. "In Hebrews 11:1 we are told that faith is being sure of what we hope for and certain of what we do not see. The sixth verse of the same chapter reminds us that without faith it's impossible to please God." Pastor Benton looked out at the congregation. "How is your faith today? Are you sure of God's love? Have you put your hope in Him? Are you certain of the things which you cannot see?"

Sinda knew her faith had been weak for a long time. She'd allowed her father's deceit and abusive ways to poison her mind and cloud her judgment. She couldn't trust men because she hadn't been trusting the Lord.

As though he sensed her confusion, Glen reached over and gave her hand a gentle squeeze. She smiled and clasped his fingers in response. It was time to leave the past behind. Sinda was ready to look to the future and begin to trust again. She felt an overwhelming sense of gratitude to God.

❧

The pungent, spicy smell of Glen's homemade barbecue sauce simmering in the Crock-Pot permeated the air as Sinda and Glen entered his kitchen after church. Tara was out in the living room watching TV, and Sinda was glad they could be alone for a few minutes. "Need help with anything?" she asked.

He nodded toward the nearest cupboard. "I guess you can set out some paper plates and cups while I start forming the hamburger patties and get the chicken out of the refrigerator."

Glen headed for the refrigerator, and Sinda moved toward the cupboard he'd indicated. They collided somewhere in the middle of the room, and Glen quickly wrapped his arms around her. "Hey, I could get used to this kind of thing," he murmured.

She smiled up at him. "You think so?"

"Does this answer your question?" He bent his head, and his lips eagerly sought hers. The kiss only lasted a few seconds because they were interrupted by a deep voice.

"Ah-ha! So this is how you spend your Sunday afternoons!"

Sinda pulled away and turned to see Glen's brother standing inside the kitchen doorway, arms folded across his broad chest and a smirk on his bearded face.

"Phil! How'd you get in here?" Glen asked, brushing his fingers across his lips.

"I came to the front door, and Tara let me in. The kid said you were fixing hamburgers and chicken to put on the grill, but it looks to me like you were having dessert." Phil chuckled and winked at Sinda. Her face flamed, and she turned away.

"If you'd been in church this morning I might have asked you to join our barbecue," Glen said in a none-too-friendly tone.

The day Phil delivered her screen door Sinda had noticed the tension between the brothers, and she'd wondered what caused it. After hearing Glen's comment about church, she surmised that the problem could be about Phil's lack of interest in spiritual things.

"I was forced to go to Sunday school every day until I moved out of Mom and Dad's house, so I'm not about to spend all my Sundays sitting on hard pews, listening to doom and gloom from a pastor who should have retired ten years ago," Phil said with a sweeping gesture.

Glen made no comment, but when Sinda chanced a peek at him, she saw that his face was flushed.

Phil sniffed the air. "Something sure smells good. How about inviting me to join your little barbecue, even if I was a bad boy and skipped church this morning?"

Glen marched over to the cupboard and withdrew a glass pitcher and a jar of pre-mixed tea. He handed it to Phil. "Here, if you're going to join us, you may as well make yourself useful."

❧

As Glen flipped burgers on the grill, then checked the chicken on the rack above, he felt a trickle of sweat roll down his forehead and land on his nose. It was a warm day, and the barbecue was certainly hot enough to make a man perspire, but he knew the reason he felt so hot was because he was irritated about his brother joining them for lunch. Ever since Phil had shown up unannounced, he'd been hanging around Sinda, bombarding her with stupid jokes, and dropping hints about taking her out sometime. If Glen hadn't been trying to be a good Christian witness, he'd have booted his brother right out the garden gate.

Tara seemed to be enjoying her uncle's company, but Glen wondered if she was really glad to see Uncle Phil—or was she delighting in the fact that he was keeping Sinda away from her dad?

The meat was done, and Glen was about to tell his guests they could sit at the picnic table when he saw Sinda move toward the gate that separated their backyards. Was she leaving? Had she had all she could take of Phil the Pill?

He set the platter of chicken and burgers on the table and followed her. "Sinda, where are you going?"

She turned to face him. "I think I heard a car pull into my driveway. I'd better see who it is."

"I'll come with you," Glen offered.

She eyed him curiously. "Don't you want to stay and entertain your brother?"

"Phil's a big boy. He can take care of himself until we get back."

She shrugged, opened the gate, and Glen followed her around front. A sporty red car was parked in Sinda's driveway, and an attractive woman with short blond hair was heading toward the house.

"Carol!" Sinda waved. "What are you doing here?"

"I stopped by to see if you wanted to go to the mall, and maybe stop by my favorite pizza place for something to eat afterward."

"Actually, I was next door, about to sink my teeth into a juicy piece of barbecued chicken." Sinda gave Glen a quick glance, then swung her gaze back to her friend. "I guess you two haven't met."

"Not in person, but if this is the handsome mailman I've heard so much about, then I feel like I already know you," Carol announced.

Glen bit back the laughter bubbling in his throat. So Sinda had been talking about him. He smiled at Carol and extended his hand. "I'm Glen Olsen."

"Carol Riggins. It's nice to finally meet you."

"Carol and I have been friends since we were children," Sinda said. "Carol went to college while I stayed home repairing dolls and catering to my dad. Shortly after her graduation she moved from Seattle to Elmwood, and she's been after me to move here ever since."

"I'm glad you were finally persuaded," Glen said, placing his hand against the small of Sinda's back.

Carol started moving toward her car. "I should probably get going. The mall will only be open until six, and I don't want to keep you from your barbecue."

"Why don't you join us?" Sinda turned to face Glen. "You wouldn't mind one more at the table, would you?"

"I've got plenty of everything so you're more than welcome, Carol," he eagerly agreed.

Carol smiled. "I appreciate the offer, and I gladly accept."

A few minutes later Carol and Phil had been introduced, and everyone was seated at the picnic table. Glen said the blessing, then passed the plate of barbecued chicken to his guests.

❧

Sinda bit into a juicy drumstick and smacked her lips. "Umm. . .this is delicious."

"Dad can cook just about anything and make it taste great," Tara put in.

"He certainly did a good job with this," Carol agreed. "Everything from the potato salad to the baked beans tastes wonderful." She giggled and poked Sinda in the ribs with her elbow. "Don't look any deeper, 'cause this one's a keeper."

Sinda smiled and nodded. She couldn't agree more.

"Dad, where's the mustard?"

"Oops, I must have forgotten to set it out. Guess you'll have to run inside and get the bottle out of the refrigerator."

Tara frowned. "How come I always have to do everything?"

"You don't have to do everything, Tara." Glen pointed toward the house.

Sinda jumped up. "I'll get the mustard."

"That's not necessary, Sinda," Glen said quickly.

Sinda held up one hand. "It's okay. I'm happy to go."

Once inside the house, Sinda went immediately to the kitchen and retrieved a squeeze bottle of mustard from the refrigerator. *At least there aren't any doll parts in here,* she thought ruefully. She closed the door and moved over to the window that overlooked the backyard. She didn't see Glen sitting beside Tara anymore and figured he'd probably gone back to the barbecue for more meat. Much to her surprise, Carol had moved from her spot and was now seated beside Phil.

Sinda smiled. "Maybe Phil's found another interest. That should take some of the pressure off me. Guess Carol showing up was a good thing."

"You're right, it was. Now I don't have to share you with my woman-crazy brother for the rest of the day."

Sinda whirled around at the sound of Glen's voice. She clasped her hand against her mouth. "Glen, I didn't hear you come in!"

He grinned, and her heart skipped a beat. "I thought you might need help finding the ketchup."

"It's mustard," she said, holding up the bottle.

"Oh, right." Glen moved slowly toward her, and Sinda could hear the echo of her heartbeat hammering in her ears.

Glen bent his head to kiss her, and she melted into his embrace. "I want to marry you, Sinda Shull," he murmured.

She licked her lips and offered him a faint smile. "I—I don't know what to say, Glen."

He gave her a crooked smile. "How about, 'Yes, I'd be happy to marry you'?"

She studied his handsome face, but before she could open her mouth to respond, there was a high-pitched scream, followed by, "Dad, you can't marry Sinda!"

Sinda and Glen both turned to face Tara. Her face was bright red, and her eyes were mere slits. "Can you give me one good reason why I shouldn't marry her?" Glen asked.

Tara marched across the room and stopped in front of her father. "Yes, I can."

Sinda knelt next to Tara. "Listen, Tara, I—"

"Dad's gotten along fine without a wife for nine whole years, and he doesn't need one now!" Tara shouted. "Especially not some sleepwalking, doll-collecting weirdo!"

A muscle in Glen's jaw quivered. "Tara Mae Olsen, you apologize to Sinda this minute!"

"It's okay, Glen," Sinda said, standing up again. "She needs more time."

Tara stomped her foot. "I don't need more time. I do not want a mother, and Dad doesn't need a wife!" She pivoted on her heel and bolted for the hall door, slamming it with such force that the Welcome plaque fell off the wall and toppled to the floor.

Glen cleared his throat. "That sure went well."

Sinda's eyes filled with unwanted tears. "We'd better face the facts, Glen. It's not going to work for us. Tara isn't going to accept me."

He shrugged. "I think she's simply jealous. I'm sure she'll calm down and listen to reason."

Sinda dropped her gaze to the floor. "What if that never happens?"

He gave her shoulder a gentle squeeze, but she could see a look of defeat written on his face. "Guess I'll have to deal with it."

"Sorry about the barbecue being ruined, but I think I'd better go home so you can get things straightened out with Tara."

"I'll talk to her and try to help her understand."

Sinda blinked back her tears of frustration. She doubted that anything Glen had to say would penetrate Tara's wall of defense. She hated to admit it, but there was no future for her and Glen Olsen. Just when she'd made peace with God and had begun to trust, the rug was being yanked out from under her. Would she ever know real joy? Was it even possible to experience the kind of love God planned for a man and a woman?

Chapter 22

Glen found Tara in her room, lying across the bed, crying as if her heart were breaking. He approached her slowly. "Tara, I need you to listen to me."

"Go away."

"I'm in love with Sinda. Won't you try to understand?" He took a seat on the edge of her bed and reached out to gently touch her back.

She jerked away. "Do you love her more than me?"

"Of course not. I love her in a different way, that's all." Glen sighed deeply. "It's been nine years since your mother died, and—"

Tara sat up suddenly. "Did you love her?"

"Connie?"

Her only reply was a curt nod.

"Of course I loved her. When she died, I thought I'd never recover, but God was good, and He filled my life with you."

She sniffed deeply. "Then how come I'm not enough for you now?"

Several seconds passed, as Glen tried to come up with an answer that might make sense to his distraught daughter. "God's plan was for a man to have a wife," he said softly. "I've waited a long time to find someone I could love enough to want for my wife."

Tara jumped up and stalked over to the window. She stood there, looking out at Sinda's house. "If you marry her, it'll never be the same."

"Tara, I know—"

She reeled around to face him. "I could never love Sinda."

How could he choose between Sinda and his daughter? He was in love with Sinda, but Tara was his only child. Until Tara calmed down and they worked through her jealousy, he'd have to keep Sinda Shull at arm's length. He hoped she would understand, but could he ask her to wait?

❧

Sinda moped around the house for the next several weeks, unable to get much work done or even fix a decent meal. She'd heard from Carol, with news that she and Phil had gone bowling. This should have brought her joy, since it obviously meant Phil's interest had shifted from her to Carol. However, Glen had called, too, informing her that he'd tried to reason with Tara, but it was to no avail. The child wouldn't accept the prospect of their marriage. Sinda understood, but the question foremost on her mind was what to do with the rest of her life. Even though Glen had tried to convince her that Tara would come around someday, she knew in her heart that their romance was over.

As she stood there staring out the living room window, Sinda caught a glimpse of the man she loved leaving for his mail route. She'd never meant to fall in love, and every encounter with Glen was something she both dreaded and anticipated. How could she stand seeing him like this, knowing they had no future together? Each time they met and uttered a casual greeting, a part of her heart crumbled a bit more. Sinda wanted to jerk the front door open and call out to Glen, but she knew it would be a mistake. She couldn't live here any longer, hoping, praying things would change. She wasn't growing younger, and she had no desire to wait around until Tara matured.

"The best thing I can do is move out of this house and get as far away from Elmwood as possible," she muttered. As soon as she had some breakfast, Sinda planned to phone the Realtor. *No point putting off until tomorrow what you can do today.* Her father's favorite expression rang in her ears. This time, however, she would do it because it was the only way, not because it was something Dad would have expected.

It was nearly noon when Sinda called the Realtor's office, but she was informed that the Realtor who'd sold her the house was on vacation and wouldn't be back for two weeks. Sinda could either call someone else or wait.

"Guess a few more weeks won't matter," she muttered as she hung up the phone. "It will give me a chance to spruce the place up a bit so it looks more appealing to any prospective buyers."

Sinda left the kitchen and went out front to do some weeding. The flower beds were in terrible shape, and she knew a thorough going over should help. Dropping to her knees, with a shovel in her hand, Sinda filled her mind with determination. She glanced up when she heard laughter. Tara and her friend Penny were skateboarding on the sidewalk in front of her place. They had made some kind of crazy ramp out of plywood and a bucket. Penny waved, but Tara didn't even look her way.

A pang of regret stabbed Sinda's heart as she was reminded of how much she had lost. Not only had she been forced to give Glen up, but she'd been cheated out of having a stepdaughter. If only she and Tara could have become friends.

Sinda thrust the shovel into the damp soil, forcing her thoughts back to the job at hand. It would do no good to think about the what-ifs.

A verse of Scripture she'd read that morning popped into her mind, and she recited it. " 'And we know that in all things God works for the good of those who love him, who have been called according to his purpose,' Romans 8:28." Surely

God had something good planned for her. It simply wasn't going to be here, in this neighborhood, in the town where Glen Olsen lived. She'd have to move on with her life, even if it meant going back to Seattle, where she was born and raised.

Another thought came to mind. If she did go home, maybe she could discover the whereabouts of her mother. Perhaps she was still living in Seattle. Sinda knew she was grasping at straws, but in her present condition, she needed something to hang on to.

She grabbed a handful of weeds and gave them a yank. It felt good to take her frustrations out on the neglected flower bed. Half an hour later, she'd finished up one bed and was about to move to another when she heard a scream.

Her head snapped up. Sparky, who'd been lying peacefully at her side, ran toward the fence, barking frantically.

Sinda scrambled to her feet and followed the dog. She was surprised to see Tara sprawled on the sidewalk. Her skateboard was tipped on its side, a few feet away.

With no hesitation, Sinda jerked the gate open and hurried down the steps. Tara's friend Penny was standing over Tara, sobbing hysterically. "I only gave her a little push down the ramp, and I didn't mean for her to get hurt."

Sinda moved Penny gently aside and knelt next to Tara. Her eyes were shut, and she was moaning. "What is it, Tara? Where are you hurt?" She couldn't see any blood, yet it was obvious from the agonized expression on the young girl's face that she was in a great deal of pain.

When Tara spoke, her words came out in a whisper. "My head. . .my arm. . . they hurt." She opened her eyes, then squeezed them shut again.

Sinda's mouth went dry. One look at the girl's swollen, distorted-looking wrist told her it was most likely broken. She knew how to put broken dolls back together, but she didn't know the first thing about giving first aid to an injured child. Sinda looked up at Penny, who was still whimpering. "Penny, go tell Tara's baby-sitter to call 9-1-1. Tell her I think Tara has a broken arm and could have a concussion."

"Tara's staying at my house this week while her dad's at work."

"Then ask your mother to call for help."

Penny muttered something about it being all her fault, then she bolted across the street. Sinda leaned closer to Tara. "It's going to be okay. The paramedics will be here soon."

"Don't leave me," Tara wailed. "Please don't go."

An onslaught of tears rolled down the child's pale cheek, and Sinda wiped them away. "I won't leave you, honey, I promise."

❧

As Sinda began to pace the length of the hospital waiting room, the numbness she'd felt earlier began to wear off. Penny's mother offered to call the post office to see if they could track Glen down, and Sinda had been allowed to ride with Tara in the ambulance. Once Glen arrived, Sinda had taken a seat in the waiting room.

She had just picked up a magazine when a nurse stepped to her side. "Are you Tara Olsen's baby-sitter?"

"I'm their next-door neighbor. Why do you ask?"

"Tara asked me to come get you," the nurse said. "She wants both you and her dad to be there when the doctor sets the bone."

The room began to spin, and Sinda closed her eyes for a moment, hoping to right her world again.

"The X-rays confirmed she broke her wrist," the nurse explained.

"Does she have a concussion?"

The nurse shook her head. "She's one lucky girl. I've seen some skateboard accidents that left the victim in much worse shape. Kids sure don't know the meaning of the word careful." She patted Sinda's arm in a motherly fashion. "It's a good thing you were there when it happened."

"I was only doing the neighborly thing," Sinda said absently. Her brain felt like it was on overload. Tara's wrist was broken, the doctor was about to set it, and the child wanted her to be there.

Sinda squared her shoulders and followed the nurse down the hall.

Chapter 23

It was the last Saturday of October, and today was Sinda's thirty-third birthday. She found it hard to believe how much her life had changed in the last few months. Everything wasn't perfect as far as her emotional state, but thanks to God's love and Glen's friendship, she was beginning to heal. She was confident that the days ahead held great promise.

As Sinda checked her appearance in the full-length mirror on the back of her bedroom door, her thoughts began to drift. *I wish you were here to share in my joy, Mother. If only things had been different between you and Dad. I wish. . .*

There was a soft knock on the door, and she was grateful for the interruption. There was no point in dwelling on the past again. Not today. "Come in," she called.

Tara, dressed in a full-length pale yellow gown and matching slippers, entered the room. Her hair was left long, but pulled away from her face with a cluster of yellow and white ribbons holding it at the back of her head.

"You look beautiful," Sinda murmured. "Just like a flower in your mother's garden."

"Thanks. You look pretty, too," the child replied.

Sinda glanced back at the mirror. She was wearing an ivory-colored full-length satin gown, detailed with tiny pearls sewn into the bodice. Her hair, piled on top of her head, was covered with a filmy veil held in place by a ring of miniature peach-colored carnations. "I'm glad you agreed to be my maid of honor. It means a lot to me," she said, moving away from the mirror.

Tara's cheeks flamed. "I suppose since you're gonna be my stepmom, we should try to help each other out." The child sniffed deeply, and Sinda wondered if she might be about to cry. "Like you did the day I broke my wrist. After all, I am supposed to love my neighbor."

Sinda reached for Tara's hand, glad that the cast was off now and the wrist had healed so nicely. "Your dad loves you very much. That's not going to change because he's marrying me." She swallowed hard, hoping to hold back the wall of tears threatening to spill over. "I love you, Tara, and I'll never do anything to come between you and your father. I hope you'll give me the chance to prove that." Sinda blotted the tears rolling down her cheeks with her lace handkerchief. "I've always been more comfortable with dolls than I have with people, but I'm going to try hard to be a good wife to your dad, and I really want to be your friend."

Tara's lower lip quivered slightly. "Am I supposed to call you Mom now?"

Sinda shook her head. "Sinda will be fine."

"I know it was dumb, but for a while I thought you had Dad under some kind of spell." Tara gave Sinda an unexpected grin. "I'm sure glad you didn't talk Dad into living in this old house."

"My house will work out well for my business, but your house is a much nicer place to live." Sinda smiled. "And Sparky is getting along quite well at Carol's." She bent down and pulled a cardboard box from under the bed.

"What's in there?" Tara asked, taking a step closer.

"Something for you." Sinda placed the box on top of the bed and nodded toward Tara. "Go ahead, open it."

Tara lifted the lid, her dark eyes filled with wonder as she pulled out the restored antique doll. "It's beautiful. Was it yours?"

Sinda shook her head. "It was your grandmother's doll, and your mother wanted you to have it. It needed some repairs, so your dad brought it to me several months ago. We've been saving it for just the right time."

Tara's eyes pooled with tears as she stroked the doll's delicate, porcelain face. "I'll take good care of it."

Sinda slipped her arm around Tara's shoulders, and when the child didn't pull away, she whispered a prayer of thanks. There was another knock, and she called, "Come in."

The door opened, and Carol poked her head inside. "You two about ready? I think the groom is going to have a nervous breakdown if we don't get this show on the road." She chuckled. "No show—the groom might go."

Tara giggled as she moved away from Sinda. "Should we be mean and make Dad wait?"

Sinda shook her head. "I want to start this marriage off on the right foot. No lies, no secrets, and no tricks." She extended her hand toward Tara. "Ready?"

"Ready as I'll ever be," the child answered as she slipped her hand into Sinda's.

The ladies descended the stairs, and Sinda scanned her living room, decorated with bouquets of autumn flowers and candles in shades of yellow and orange. *Some might think this an odd place for a wedding,* Sinda thought with a smile, *but I wanted my marriage to begin in the house where I learned what trust and true love really mean.*

As her gaze left the decorations, Sinda spotted her groom, dressed in a stunning black tux, standing in front of the fireplace. He looked so handsome. The minister stood on one side of Glen, and Phil stood on the other side. Tara and

Carol had joined the bridal party and stood to the right of the men. Beside Sinda's friend was a petite older woman with short auburn hair, streaked with gray. Her green eyes shimmered in the candlelight, and her smile looked so familiar. Sinda swallowed against the knot that had lodged in her throat. No, it couldn't be. "Mother?" she mouthed.

The woman nodded, tears pooling in her eyes, and her chin trembled as she smiled.

But how? When? Sinda, so full of questions, took her place beside Glen. She looked at her mother, then back at Glen, hoping for some answers.

"I'll tell you about it after the ceremony," he whispered.

Sinda could hardly contain herself. Here she was standing in the living room of her rambling old house, about to marry the most wonderful man in the world, and her mother was here to witness the joyful event. It was too much to comprehend.

Feeling as if she were in a daze, Sinda tried to focus on the pastor's words about marriage and the responsibilities of a husband and wife. She'd spent her whole life wondering if all men were alike, and now, as she repeated her vows, Sinda's heart swelled with a joy she'd never known. Glen sealed their love with a kiss, and she found comfort in the warmth of his arms.

As soon as the minister announced, "I now present to you Mr. and Mrs. Glen Olsen," Glen grasped Sinda's hand, and they moved to the back of the room to greet their guests.

Sinda's mother was the last one through the receiving line, and she and Sinda clung to each other and wept. "How did you find me?" Sinda asked through her tears.

Her mother looked over at Glen. "I didn't. Your groom found me."

Sinda cast a questioning look at her husband. "How? When? Where?"

He lifted her chin so she was gazing into his eyes. "I hired a detective, and he found your mother living in Spokane, where she'd moved several years ago. She didn't know your father was dead or that you'd moved away."

Sinda turned to look at her mother again, and her vision clouded with tears. "How come you never came to see me?"

Clutching Sinda's arm, she replied, "Your father threatened to hurt you if I did. He was an angry, confused man, and I was afraid to stand up to him for fear of what he might do." She sniffed deeply. "Even though William filed for divorce, I never remarried. In order to support myself, I took a job as a maid at a local hotel. I never missed any of your school or church programs."

Sinda's eyebrows furrowed. "How did you manage to see my programs and not show yourself?"

Her mother dropped her gaze to the floor. "I wore a wig and dark glasses. Nobody recognized me, not even your father." She shook her head slowly. "I never stopped loving you or praying for you, Sinda. Please believe me, I had your best interest at heart."

Sinda was tempted to tell her mother that living with an abusive father could not have been the best thing for her, but she realized with regret that her mother had no idea Dad had mistreated her—no one else ever had. *It doesn't matter now*, Sinda mused. *I have Mother back again, and I'm thankful to God for that.* Through a sheen of tears, she smiled at Glen. "You're remarkable, and I love you so much."

He bent his head and kissed her so tenderly she thought she would drown in his love. "I wanted to give you a combined birthday and wedding present—something you would never forget." Then, taking Sinda's hand in his left hand, and her mother's hand in his right hand, he announced, "I thought it was the neighborly thing to do."

Talking for

Two

by Wanda E. Brunstetter

To my son, Richard, Jr.,
who first suggested I learn ventriloquism.
To my daughter, Lorine,
the best ventriloquist student I ever had.
To Clinton Detweiler,
a talented ventriloquist:
Much thanks for all your helpful insights.

Chapter 1

"Miss Johnson, will you make Roscoe talk to us again?" Four-year-old Ricky Evans squinted his pale blue eyes and offered up a toothy grin so appealing that Tabitha knew it would be impossible for her to say no.

She pulled the floppy-eared dog puppet from its home in the bottom drawer of her desk and quickly inserted her hand. Thankful she was wearing blue jeans and not a dress today, she dropped to her knees and hid behind the desk, bringing only the puppet into view. Roscoe let out a couple of loud barks, which brought several more children running to see the program. Then Tabitha launched into her routine.

"Did you know I used to belong to a flea circus?" the scruffy-looking puppet asked. The children now sat on the floor, completely mesmerized, waiting for what was to come next.

"Really and truly?" a young girl called out.

Roscoe's dark head bobbed up and down. "That's right, and before long, I ran away and stole that whole itchy show!"

The children giggled, and Roscoe howled in response.

Tabitha smiled to herself. She was always glad for the chance to entertain the day care kids, even if she was doing it behind a desk, with a puppet that looked like he'd seen better days.

Five minutes and several jokes later, she ended her routine and sent all the children to their tables for a snack of chocolate chip cookies and milk.

"You're really good with that goofy puppet," came a woman's soft voice behind her.

Tabitha turned to face her coworker and best friend, Donna Hartley. "I enjoy making the kids laugh," she said, pushing an irritating strand of hair away from her face. "It makes me feel like I'm doing something meaningful."

Always confident, always consoling, Donna offered her a bright smile. "Just helping me run Caring Christian Day Care is meaningful."

Tabitha blinked. "You really think so?"

Donna pulled out a chair and motioned Tabitha to do the same. "You know what you need, Tabby?"

Tabitha took a seat and offered up a faint smile, relishing the warm, familiar way her friend said her nickname. Donna began calling her that when she and

131

her parents moved next door to the Johnsons, nearly twenty-three years ago. That was when Tabitha had been a happy, outgoing child. That was when she'd been an only child.

Shortly after she turned six, her whole life suddenly changed. The birth of blond-haired, blue-eyed sister Lois had turned talkative, confident Tabby into a timid, stuttering, introverted child. Her father, who'd once doted on her, now had eyes only for the little girl who looked so much like him. Tabby's mother was a meek, subservient woman; rather than stand up to her controlling husband and his blatant acts of favoritism, she had merely chosen to keep silent while Tabby turned into a near recluse.

"Are you listening to me?" Donna asked, jerking Tabby's thoughts back to the present.

"Huh? What were you saying?"

"Do you know what you need?"

Tabby drew in a deep breath and blew it out quickly. "No, but I'm sure you can't wait to tell me."

Donna snickered. "Okay, so I'm not able to keep my big mouth shut where you're concerned. Old habits die hard, you know."

Tabby tapped her foot impatiently. "So, what do I need?"

"You need to attend that Christian workers' conference we heard about a few weeks ago."

"You know I don't do well in crowds," Tabby grumbled. "Especially with a bunch of strangers. I stutter whenever I talk to anyone but you or the day care kids, and—"

"But you won't be in a crowd," Donna reminded. "You'll be in a workshop, learning puppetry. You can hide behind a puppet box."

Tabby shrugged, letting her gaze travel to the group of happy children sitting at the table across the room. "No promises, but I'll think about it."

≈

Seth Beyers had never figured out why anyone would want to buy an ugly dummy, but the customer he was waiting on right now wanted exactly that.

"The uglier the better," the young man said with a deep chuckle. "The audiences at the clubs where I often perform seem to like ugly and crude."

Seth had been a Christian for more than half of his twenty-six years, and he'd been interested in ventriloquism nearly that long as well. It just didn't set right with him when someone used a God-given talent to fill people's heads with all kinds of garbage. While most of Seth's customers were Christians, a few secular people, like Alan Capshaw, came to his shop to either purchase a ventriloquist dummy or have one repaired.

"Okay, I'll do my best for ugly," Seth said with a slight nod. "How does

Dumbo ears, a long nose, and lots of freckles sound?"

"The big ears and extended nose is fine, but skip the freckles and stick a big ugly wart on the end of the dummy's snout." Alan grinned, revealing a set of pearly white teeth.

The dummy may turn out ugly, but this guy must really attract women, Seth mentally noted. Alan Capshaw not only had perfect teeth, but his slightly curly blond hair, brilliant blue eyes, and muscular body made Seth feel like he was the ugly dummy. He never could figure out why he'd been cursed with red hair and a slender build.

Seth waited until the self-assured customer placed a sizable down payment on his dummy order and sauntered out the door—and then he allowed himself the privilege of self-analysis. Sure, he'd had a few girlfriends over the past several years, and if he were really honest with himself, he guessed maybe he wasn't too bad looking, either. *At least not compared to the ugly dummy I'll soon be constructing.*

Whenever Seth went anywhere with his little buddy, Rudy Right, folks of all ages seemed to flock around him. Of course, he was pretty sure it was the winking dummy to whom they were actually drawn and not the hopeful ventriloquist.

Seth scratched the back of his head and moved over to the workbench. This was the place where he felt most comfortable. This was where he could become so engrossed in work that his troubles were left behind. He'd started fooling around with a homemade sock puppet and a library book on ventriloquism soon after he was old enough to read. When he turned twelve, his parents enrolled him in a home-study course on ventriloquism. In no time at all, Seth Beyers, normal, active teenager, had turned into a humorous, much sought-after ventriloquist. It wasn't long after that when he began performing at local fairs, school functions, and numerous church programs. About that time, he also decided he would like to learn how to make and repair dummies for a living. He'd always been good with his hands, and with a little help from a couple of books, it didn't take long before he completed his first ventriloquist figure.

Seth now owned and operated his own place of business, and people from all over the United States either brought or sent their ventriloquist figures to him for repairs. When he wasn't performing or teaching a class on ventriloquism, Seth filled special orders for various kinds of dummies. All but one of Seth's goals had been reached.

He wanted a wife and family. He'd been raised as an only child and had always longed for brothers and sisters. Instead of playing with a sibling, Seth's best friend was his sock puppet. Then Mom and Dad had been killed in a plane crash when he was fourteen, and he'd been forced to move from Seattle to Tacoma to live with Grandpa and Grandma Beyers. He loved them both a lot, but it wasn't the same as having his own family. Besides, his grandparents were getting on in years and wouldn't be around forever.

Seth groaned and reached for a piece of sandpaper to begin working on a wooden leg. "What I really need is to find someone who shares my love for Christ and wants to serve Him the way I do." He shook his head. "I wonder if such a woman even exists."

The telephone rang, pulling him out of his reflections. He reached for it quickly, before the answering machine had a chance to click on. "Beyers' Ventriloquist Studio." Seth frowned as he listened. "Glen Harrington's had a family emergency and you want me to fill in?" There was a long pause. "Yeah, I suppose I could work it into my schedule."

Seth wrote down a few particulars, then hung up the phone. The last thing he needed was another seminar to teach, but he didn't have the heart to say no. He'd check his notes from the workshop he'd done in Portland a few months ago, and if everything seemed up to date, maybe there wouldn't be too much preliminary work. Since the seminar was only for one day, he was sure he could make the time.

He closed his eyes briefly as his lips curled into a smile. *Who knows, maybe I'll be able to help some young, talented kid hone his skills and use ventriloquism as a tool to serve the Lord.*

❧

Tabby stared dismally out the living room window in the converted garage apartment she shared with Donna. It was raining again, but then this was late spring, and she did live in the suburbs of Tacoma, Washington. Liquid sunshine was a common occurrence here in the beautiful Evergreen State.

Normally the rain didn't bother her much, but on this particular Saturday it seemed as though every drop of water falling outside was landing on her instead of on the emerald grass and budding trees. She felt as if it were filling up her soul with agonizing depression and loneliness.

Tabby wrapped her arms tightly around her chest, as a deep moan escaped her lips. "Maybe I should have gone to Seattle with Donna and her parents after all." She shivered involuntarily. Tabby disliked crowds, and there was always a huge flock of people at the Seattle Center. No, she was better off here at home, even if she was lonely and miserable.

A sharp rap on the front door brought Tabby's musings to a halt. She moved away from the window and shuffled toward the sound. Standing on tiptoes, she peered through the small peephole, positioned much too high for her short stature.

Tabby's heart took a dive, and her stomach churned like whipping cream about to become butter. She didn't receive many surprise visits from her sister. Maybe this one would go better than the last. At least she hoped it would. Tabby drew in a deep breath, grasped the door handle, then yanked it open.

A blond-haired, blue-eyed beauty, holding a black, rain-soaked umbrella and ensconced in a silver gray raincoat, greeted her with a wide smile. "Hi, Timid Tabitha. How's everything going?"

Tabby stepped aside as Lois rushed in, giving her umbrella a good shake and scattering droplets of cold water all over Tabby's faded blue jeans. Lois snapped the umbrella closed and dropped it into the wrought-iron stand by the front door. With no invitation, she slipped off her raincoat, hung it on the nearby clothes tree, then headed for the living room. Sitting carefully on the well-worn couch, she hand-pressed a wrinkle out of her pale blue slacks.

Tabby studied her sister. It must be nice to have her good looks, great taste in clothes, and a bubbling personality besides. Compared to Lois's long, carefully curled, silky tresses, Tabby knew her own drab brown, shoulder-length hair must look a mess.

"So, where's your roommate?" Lois asked. "On a rainy day like this, I figured the two of you would probably be curled up on the couch watching one of your favorite boring videos."

"Donna w–went to S–Seattle with her f–folks, and *L–Little W–Women* is not b–boring." Tabby glanced at the video, lying on top of the TV, then she flopped into the rocking chair directly across from her sister. "The b–book is a c–c–classic, and s–s–so is the m–movie."

"Yeah, yeah, I know—little perfect women find their perfect happiness, even though they're poor as scrawny little church mice." Lois sniffed, as though some foul odor had suddenly permeated the room. "The only part of that corny movie I can even relate to is where Jo finally finds her perfect man."

"You've f–found the p–p–perfect man?" Tabby echoed.

Lois nodded. "Definitely. Only mine's not poor. Mike is loaded to the gills, and I'm about to hit pay dirt." She leaned forward, stuck out her left hand, and wiggled her ring finger in front of Tabby's face.

"Wow, w–what a r–r–rock! Does th–this m–m–mean what I th–th–think?"

"It sure as tootin' does, big sister! Mike popped the all-important question last night, right in the middle of a romantic candlelight dinner at Roberto's Restaurant." Lois leaned her head against the back of the couch and sighed deeply. "Six months from now, I'll be Mrs. Michael G. Yehley, lady of leisure. No more humdrum life as a small potatoes secretary. I plan to spend the rest of my days shopping 'til I drop."

"You're g–getting m–married that s–soon?"

"Don't look so surprised, Shabby Tabby." Lois squinted her eyes. "And for crying out loud, stop that stupid stuttering!"

"I—I c–can't h–h–help it." Tabby hung her head. "I d–don't d–do it on p–purpose, you—you know."

"Give me a break! You could control it and get over your backward bashfulness if you really wanted to. I think you just do it for attention." Lois pursed her lips. "Your little ploy has never worked on me, though. I would think you'd know that by now."

"I d–do not d–do it for a—attention." Tabby stood up and moved slowly toward the window, a wisp of her sister's expensive perfume filling her nostrils. She grimaced and clasped her trembling hands tightly together. *Now I know I should have gone to Seattle. Even a thousand people closing in around me would have been easier to take than five minutes alone with Lois the Lioness.*

"Are you going to congratulate me or not?"

Tabby forced herself to turn and face her sister again. Lois was tapping her perfectly manicured, long red fingernails along the arm of the couch. "Well?"

"C–c–congratulations," Tabby mumbled.

"C–c–congratulations? Is that all you've got to say?"

"Wh–wh–what else is th–there to s–say?"

"How about, 'I'm very happy for you, Lois'? Or, 'Wow, Sis, I sure wish it were me getting married. Especially since I'm six years older and quickly turning into a dried-up, mousy old maid.' "

Lois's cutting words sliced through Tabby's heart, and a well of emotion rose in her chest, like Mount Saint Helens about to explode. How could anyone be so cruel? So unfeeling? She wished now she had never opened the front door. This visit from her sister wasn't going any better than the last one had. Blinking back unwanted tears, Tabby tried to think of an appropriate comeback.

"Say something. Has the cat grabbed your tongue again?" Lois prompted.

Tabby shrugged. "I–I th–think you'd better just g–g–go."

Her sister stood up quickly, knocking one of the sofa pillows to the floor. "Fine then! Be that way, you little wimp! I'm sorry I even bothered to stop by and share my good news." She swooped her raincoat off the clothes tree, grabbed the umbrella with a snap of her wrist, and stormed out the front door without so much as a backward glance.

Tabby stood staring at the door. "My little sister doesn't think I'll ever amount to anything," she muttered. "Why does she treat me that way?"

Lois is not a Christian, a small voice reminded.

Tabby shuddered. Why was it that whenever she felt sorry for herself, the Lord always came along and gave her a nudge? Tabby's parents weren't churchgoers, either. In fact, they had never understood why, even as a child, Tabby had gotten herself up every Sunday morning and walked to the church two blocks from home. Without Jesus' hand to hold, and the encouragement she got from Donna, she doubted if she would even be working at the day care center.

With a determination she didn't really feel, Tabby squared her shoulders and lifted her chin. "I'll show Lois. I'll show everyone." But even as the words poured out of her mouth, she wondered if it was an impossible dream. What could she, Timid Tabitha, do that would prove to her family that she really was a woman of worth?

Chapter 2

I still can't believe I let you talk me into this," Tabby groaned as she settled herself into the passenger seat of Donna's little red car.

Donna put the key in the ignition, then reached over to give Tabby's arm a reassuring squeeze. "It's gonna be fine. Just allow yourself to relax and have a good time. That's what today is all about, you know."

A frown twisted Tabby's lips. "That's easy enough for you to say. You're always so laid back about everything."

"Not always. Remember that blind date my cousin Tom fixed me up with last month? I was a nervous wreck from the beginning to the end of that horrendous evening."

Tabby laughed. "Come on now. It couldn't have been all that bad."

"Oh, yeah?" Donna countered as she pulled out into traffic. "How would you have felt if the most gorgeous guy you'd ever met took you on a bowling date, only because your matchmaking cousin set it all up? I didn't mention it before, but the conceited creep never said more than three words to me all night."

Tabby shrugged. "That would never happen to me, because I'm not about to go on any blind dates. Besides, have you thought maybe the poor guy was just shy? It could be that he wasn't able to conjure up more than three words."

Donna gave the steering wheel a slap with the palm of her hand. "Humph! Rod Thompson was anything but shy. In fact, he spent most of the evening flirting with Carol, my cousin's date."

Tabby squinted her eyes. "You're kidding."

"I'm not. It was probably the worst night of my life." Donna wiggled her eyebrows. "It was nearly enough to throw me straight into the arms of our preacher's son."

"Alex? Has Alex asked you out?"

"Many times, and my answer is always no."

"Why? Alex Hanson is cute."

Donna released a low moan. "I know, but he's a PK, for crying out loud! Nobody in their right mind wants to date a preacher's kid."

Tabby's forehead wrinkled, and she pushed a lock of hair away from her face. "Why not? What's wrong with a preacher's kid?"

Donna laughed. "Haven't you heard? The pastor and his entire family live in a fish bowl. Everyone expects them to be perfect."

"If Alex is perfect, then what's the big problem?"

"I said, he's supposed to be perfect. Most of the PKs I've ever known are far from perfect."

Tabby chuckled. "I have a feeling you really like Alex."

"I do not!"

"Do so!"

"Do not!"

Their childish banter went on until Tabby finally called a truce by changing the subject. "Which workshop are you going to register for at the seminar?" she asked.

Donna smiled. "Chalk art drawing. I've always been interested in art, and if I can manage to use my meager talent in that form of Christian ministry, then I'm ready, able, and more than willing."

Tabby glanced down at the scruffy little puppet lying in her lap. "I sure hope I won't have to talk to anyone. Unless I'm behind a puppet box, that is." She slipped Roscoe onto her hand. "If I'm well hidden and can talk through this little guy, I might actually learn something today."

"You're just too self-conscious for your own good. You've got such potential, and I hate to see you waste it."

"Potential? You must have me mixed up with someone else."

Donna clicked her tongue. "Would you please stop? You'll never build your confidence or get over being shy if you keep putting yourself down all the time."

"What am I supposed to do? Brag about how cute, smart, and talented I am?" Tabby grimaced. "Take a good look at me, Donna. I'm the plainest Jane around town, and as I've reminded you before, I can barely say two words to anyone but you or the day care kids without stuttering and making a complete fool of myself."

"You want people to accept you, but you don't think you can ever measure up. Am I right?"

Tabby nodded.

"That will all change," Donna insisted. "Just as soon as you realize your full potential. Repeat after me—I can do it. I can do it. I can do it!"

Tabby held Roscoe up and squeaked, "I can do it, but that's just because I'm a dumb little dog."

❧

The foyer of Alliance Community Church was crammed with people. Tabby gulped down a wave of nausea and steadied herself against the sign-up table for the puppet workshop. She was sure that coming here had been a terrible mistake. If not for the fact that Donna was already in line at the chalk art registration table, she might have turned around and bolted for the door.

"Sorry, but this class is filled up," said a soft-spoken older woman behind the puppet registration table.

"It—it—is?" Tabby stammered.

"I'm afraid so. You might try the ventriloquist workshop." The woman motioned toward a table across the room. "If you like puppetry, I'm sure you'd love to try talking for two."

Tabby slipped quietly away from the table, holding Roscoe so tightly her hand ached. There was no more room in the puppet workshop. Now she had a viable excuse to get out of this crowded place. She turned toward the front door and started to run. Pushing her way past several people, she came to a halt when she ran straight into a man.

"Whoa!" his deep voice exclaimed. "What's your hurry?"

Tabby stared up at him in stunned silence. She was rewarded with a wide smile.

Her plan had been to make a hasty exit, but this young man with soft auburn hair and seeking green eyes had blocked her path.

He nodded toward the puppet she was clutching. "Are you signed up for my class?"

Her gaze was drawn to the stark white piece of paper he held in his hand. "I—uh—th–that is—"

"I hope you're not self-conscious about using a hand puppet instead of a dummy. Many ventriloquists use puppets quite effectively."

Tabby gulped and felt the strength drain from her shaky legs. The guy thought she wanted to learn ventriloquism, and apparently he was the teacher for that workshop. The idea of talking for two and learning to throw her voice did have a certain measure of appeal, but could she? Would she have the nerve to sit in a class with people she didn't even know? Could she talk for her puppet without a puppet box to hide behind? *Maybe I could just sit quietly and observe. Maybe I'd never have to say a word.*

❧

As she studied the handout sheet she'd just been given, Tabby wondered what on earth had possessed her to take a ventriloquist class, of all things! She felt about as dumb as a box of rocks, but as she pondered the matter, an idea burst into her head. Maybe she could do some short ventriloquist skits for the day care kids. If they liked Roscoe popping up from behind a desk, how much more might they enjoy seeing him out in plain view? If she could speak without moving her lips, the kids would think Roscoe really could talk.

From her seat at the back of the classroom, Tabby let her gaze travel toward the front. The young man with short-cropped auburn hair had just introduced himself as Seth Beyers, owner and operator of Beyers' Ventriloquist Studio. He was holding a full-sized, professional ventriloquist figure with one hand.

"I'd like to give you a little rundown on the background of ventriloquism before we begin," Seth said. "Some history books try to date ventriloquism back to biblical times, citing the story of Saul's visit to the witch of Endor as a basis for their claim." He frowned. "I disagree with this theory, though. As a believer in Christ, I take the scriptural account literally for what it says. In fact, I don't think the Bible makes any reference to ventriloquism at all.

"Ventriloquism is nothing more than an illusion. A ventriloquist talks and creates the impression that a voice is coming from somewhere other than its true source. People are often fooled into believing the ventriloquist is throwing his voice. Ventriloquism has been around a long time. Even the ancient Greeks did it. Romans thought ventriloquists spoke from their stomachs. In fact, the word ventriloquism comes from two Latin roots—*venter*—meaning belly, and *loqui*—the past participle of the verb *locuts*, which means to speak."

Seth smiled. "So, the word ventriloquism is actually a misnomer, for there is really no such thing as stomach talking. A ventriloquist's voice comes from only one place—his own throat. Everything the ventriloquist does and says makes the onlooker believe his voice comes from someplace else."

Positioning his foot on the seat of an empty folding chair, Seth placed the dummy on top of his knee. "Most of you will probably start by using an inexpensive plastic figure, or even a hand puppet." Gesturing toward the dummy, Seth added, "Later on, as you become more comfortable doing ventriloquism, you might want to purchase a professional figure like my woodenheaded friend, Rudy."

Suddenly it was as though the dummy had jumped to life. "Hi, folks! My name's Rudy Right, and I'm always right!"

A few snickers filtered through the room, and Seth reprimanded his little friend. "No way, Rudy. No one but God is always right."

"Is that so? Well, in the dummy world, I'm always right!" Rudy shot back.

Tabby leaned forward, watching intently. Seth's lips didn't move at all, and the sound supposedly coming from Rudy Right was nothing like the instructor's deep voice. If common sense hadn't taken over, she might have actually believed the dummy could talk. *A child would surely believe it. Kids probably relate well to what the dummy says, too.*

Yanking her wayward thoughts back to the happenings at the front of the room, Tabby giggled behind her hand when Rudy Right accused his owner of being a bigger dummy than he was.

"Yep," spouted Rudy, "you'd have to be really dumb to wanna be around dummies all the time." With the wink of one doeskin eye, the woodenhead added, "Maybe I should start pullin' your strings and see how you like it!"

When the laughter died down, Seth made Rudy say good-bye, then promptly put him back in the suitcase from which he'd first appeared. With a muffled voice from inside the case, Rudy hollered, "Hey, who turned out the lights?"

In the moment of enjoyment, Tabby laughed out loud, temporarily forgetting her uncomfortable shyness. Everyone clapped, and the expert ventriloquist took a bow.

"I see a few of you have brought along a puppet or dummy this morning," Seth said. "So, who would like to be the first to come up and try saying the easy alphabet with the use of your ventriloquist partner?"

When no one volunteered, Seth pointed right at Tabby. "How about you, there in the back row?"

Her heart fluttered like a bird's wings. She bit her bottom lip, then ducked her head, wanting to speak but afraid to do so.

Seth took a few steps toward her. "I'm referring to the young woman with the cute little dog puppet."

If there had only been a hole in the floor, Tabby would have crawled straight into it. She felt trapped, like a caged animal at the Point Defiance Zoo. She wanted to tell Seth Beyers that she wasn't ready to try the easy alphabet yet. However, she knew what would happen if she even tried to speak. Everything would come out in a jumble of incoherent, stuttering words, and she'd be completely mortified. Slinking down in her chair, face red as a vine-ripened tomato, she merely shook her head.

"I guess the little lady's not quite up to the task yet," Seth responded with a chuckle. "Is there someone else brave enough to let us critique you?"

One hand from the front row shot up. Seth nodded. "Okay, you're on!"

An attractive young woman with long red hair took her place next to Seth. She was holding a small boy dummy and wearing a smile that stretched from ear to ear. "Hi, my name's Cheryl Stone, and this is my friend Oscar."

"Have you done any ventriloquism before?" Seth questioned.

Cheryl snickered. "Just in front of my bedroom mirror. I've read a book about throwing your voice, but I haven't mastered all the techniques yet."

"Then you have a bit of an advantage." Seth flashed her a reassuring smile.

Tabby felt a surge of envy course through her veins. Here were two good-looking redheads, standing in front of an audience with their dummies, and neither one looked the least bit nervous. Why in the world did she have to be so paralyzed with fear? What kept her locked in the confines of "Timid Tabitha"?

"Okay, let's begin with that easy alphabet," Seth said, breaking into Tabby's troubling thoughts. "All the letters printed on the blackboard can be said without moving your lips. I'll point to each one, and Cheryl will have her dummy repeat after me."

Cheryl nodded. "We're ready when you are."

Seth moved toward the portable blackboard positioned at Cheryl's left. "Don't forget to keep your mouth relaxed and slightly open, biting your top teeth lightly down on the bottom teeth." Using a pointer-stick, Seth began to call out the letters of the easy alphabet.

Cheryl made Oscar repeat each one. "A C D E G H I J K L N O Q R S T U X Y Z."

She'd done it almost perfectly, and Seth smiled in response. "Sometimes the letter Y can be a problem, but it's easy enough if you just say ooh-eye."

"What about the other letters in the alphabet?" an older man in the audience asked. "What are we supposed to do when we say a word that has B, F, M, P, V, or W in it?"

"That's a good question," Seth replied. "Those all get sound substitutions, and we'll be dealing with that problem shortly."

Oh, no, Tabby groaned inwardly. *This class is going to be anything but easy.*

"Let's have Cheryl and her little friend read some sentences for us," Seth continued. Below the easy alphabet letters he wrote a few lines. "Okay, have a go at it."

"Yes, I can do it." Cheryl opened and closed her dummy's mouth in perfect lip sync. "She had a red silk hat, and that is no joke!"

Everyone laughed, and Cheryl took a bow.

Seth erased the words, then wrote a few more sentences. "Now try these."

"I ran across the yard, heading to the zoo. I need to get a key and unlock the car."

Tabby wrestled with her feelings of jealousy as Cheryl stood there looking so confident and saying everything with no lip movement at all. Tabby sucked in her bottom lip and tried to concentrate on learning the easy alphabet. After all, it wasn't Cheryl's fault she was talented and Tabby wasn't.

"That was great, Cheryl!" Seth gave her a pat on the back.

She smiled in response. "Thanks. It was fun."

The next few hours flew by, with only one fifteen-minute break for snacks and use of the restrooms. Tabby's plan had been to sneak out during this time and wait for Donna in the car. The whole concept of ventriloquism had her fascinated, though, and even if she wasn't going to actively participate, she knew she simply couldn't leave now.

By the time the class finally wound down, everyone had been given a video tape, an audiocassette, and several handouts. Everything from the easy alphabet to proper breathing and sound substitutions had been covered. Now all Tabby had to do was go home and practice. Only then would she know if she could ever learn to talk for two.

Chapter 3

"You're awfully quiet," Donna said, as they began their drive home from the seminar. "Didn't you enjoy the puppet workshop?"

"I never went," Tabby replied.

"Never went?"

"Nope. The class was filled up."

"If you didn't go to the workshop, then where have you been all morning, and why are you holding a bunch of handouts and tapes?"

"I was learning ventriloquism."

Donna's dark eyebrows shot up. "Ventriloquism? You mean you took the workshop on how to throw your voice?"

"Yeah, and I think I threw mine away for good."

"It went that badly, huh?"

Tabby's only reply was a slow sweep of her hand.

"What on earth possessed you to take something as difficult as ventriloquism?" Donna questioned. "I'm the adventuresome type, and I'd never try anything like that."

Tabby crossed her arms. "Beats me."

"Did you learn anything?"

"I learned that in order to talk for two, I'd need talent and nerves of steel." Tabby groaned. "Neither of which I happen to have."

Donna gave the steering wheel a light rap with her knuckles. "Tabitha Johnson, will you please quit putting yourself down? You've got plenty of talent. You just need to begin utilizing it."

"You didn't say anything about nerves of steel, though," Tabby reminded. "Being shy is definitely my worst shortcoming, and without self-confidence, I could never be a ventriloquist."

"I wouldn't be so sure about that."

"Right! Can't you just see it? Timid Tabitha shuffles on stage, takes one look at the audience, and closes up like a razor clam." She wrinkled her nose. "Or worse yet, I'd start to speak, then get so tongue-tied every word would come out in a jumble of uncontrollable stuttering."

Donna seemed to be mulling things over. "Hmm. . ."

"Hmm. . .what?"

"Why don't you practice your ventriloquism skills on me, then put on a little program for the day care kids?"

"I've already thought about that. It's probably the only way I could ever talk for two." Tabby shrugged. "Who knows—it might even be kind of fun."

"Now that's the spirit! I think we should stop by the Burger Barn and celebrate."

"You call that a place of celebration?"

Donna laughed. "Sure, if you love the triple-decker cheeseburger—and I do!"

Tabby slipped Roscoe onto her hand. "Okay, girls; Burger Barn, here we come!"

⁓

In spite of the fact that he'd lost a whole morning of work, Seth had actually enjoyed teaching the ventriloquism workshop. With the exception of that one extremely shy young woman, it had been exciting to see how many in the class caught on so quickly. The little gal holding a scruffy dog puppet had remained in the back row, scrunched down in her seat, looking like she was afraid of her own shadow. She never participated in any way.

Seth had encountered a few bashful people over the years, but no one seemed as self-restricted as that poor woman. Whenever he tried to make eye contact or ask her a question, she seemed to freeze. After a few tries he'd finally given up, afraid she might bolt for the door and miss the whole workshop.

A muscle twitched in his jaw. *I really wish I could have gotten through somehow. What was the point in her taking the class, if she wasn't going to join in? But then, who knows, the shy one might actually take the tapes and handouts home, practice like crazy, and become the next Shari Lewis.*

He chuckled out loud. "Naw, that might be stretching things a bit."

Gathering up his notes, Seth grabbed Rudy's suitcase. He needed to get back to the shop and resume work on Alan Capshaw's ugly dummy. There would be another full day tomorrow, since he was going to be part of a Christian workers' demonstration at a church in the north end of Tacoma.

Seth didn't get to worship at his home church much anymore. He was frequently asked to do programs for other churches' Sunday schools, junior church, or special services that might help generate more interest in Christian ministry. Between that and his full-time business, there wasn't much time left for socializing. Seth hoped that would all change some day. Not that he planned to quit serving the Lord with the talents he'd been generously given. No, as long as the opportunity arose, he would try to follow God's leading and remain faithfully in His service.

What Seth really wanted to modify was his social life. Keeping company with a bunch of dummies was not all that stimulating, and even performing for large crowds wasn't the same as a meaningful one-on-one conversation with someone who shared his interests and love for God.

"Well, Rudy Right," Seth said, glancing at the suitcase in his hand, "I guess it's just you and me for the rest of the day."

❧

The Burger Barn was crowded. Hoping to avoid the mass of people, Tabby suggested they use the drive-thru.

"Part of the fun of going in is being able to check out all the good-looking guys," Donna argued.

Tabby wrinkled her nose. "You do the checking out, and I'll just eat."

A short time later they were munching their food and discussing the workshop.

"Tell me about the chalk art class," Tabby said. "Did you learn anything helpful?"

Donna's face lit up. "It was wonderful! In fact, I think I'm gonna try my hand at black light."

"Black light?"

"You hook a thin, black light over the top of your easel. The pictures you draw with fluorescent chalk almost come to life." Donna motioned with her hand, as though she were drawing an imaginary illustration. "I wish you could have seen some of the beautiful compositions our instructor put together. She draws well anyway, but under the black light, her pictures were absolutely gorgeous!"

Tabby smiled. "I can see she really inspired you to use your artistic talent."

"I'll say. I thought maybe you and I could combine our talents and put on a little program during Sunday school opening sometime."

"You're kidding, right?"

"I'm not kidding at all. I could do a chalk art drawing, and you could put on a puppet show. You might be able to use that old puppet box down in the church storage room." Donna gulped down her lemonade and rushed on. "It's not like you'd have to try your new ventriloquist skills or anything. You could hide behind the puppet box, and—"

Tabby held up one hand. "Whoa! In the first place, I have no ventriloquist skills. Furthermore, I've never done puppets anywhere but at the day care. I'm not sure I could ever do anything for church."

"Sure you could," Donna insisted. "Tomorrow, during our morning worship service, we're going to be entertained and inspired by some of the best Christian education workers in the Puget Sound area."

Tabby's interest was piqued. "We are? I hadn't heard. Guess I've been spending too much time helping out in the church nursery lately."

Donna smiled. "There will be a puppet team from Edmonds, Washington, a chalk artist from Seattle, a ventriloquist, who I hear is a local guy, and several others."

Tabby stared out the window. *Hmm. . .seeing some professionals perform might be kind of interesting. No way does it mean I'll agree to Donna's harebrained idea of us performing at Sunday school, though. I'll just find a seat in the back row and simply enjoy the show.*

⚓︎

The church service would be starting soon, and Seth hurried through the hall toward the sanctuary. Someone had just come out of the ladies' restroom, head down and feet shuffling in his direction. Thump! She bumped straight into his arm, nearly knocking little Rudy to the floor.

From the startled expression on her face, Seth could tell she was just as surprised to see him as he was to see her. "Oh, excuse me!" he apologized.

"It's—it's o–o–okay," the young woman stammered. "It w–w–was probably m–m–my fault."

Seth smiled, trying to put her at ease. "I was the instructor at the ventriloquism workshop you took yesterday; do you remember?"

She hung her head and mumbled, "Y–y–yes, I kn–kn–know who y–y–you are. S–s–sorry for g–g–getting in the w–way."

"Naw, it was all my owner's fault," Seth made his dummy say in a high-pitched voice. "He's got two left feet, and I guess he wasn't watchin' where he was goin'." The vent figure gave her a quick wink, then added, "My name's Rudy Right, and I'm always right. What's your name, Sister?"

"My name's Tabitha Johnson, but you can call me Tabby." She reached out to grasp one of the dummy's small wooden hands.

Seth grinned. By talking to her through his partner, Tabby seemed much more relaxed. She was even able to make eye contact—at least with the dummy. *I should have tried that in the workshop yesterday. She might have been a bit more receptive.*

Seth had used his ventriloquist figure to reach frightened, sick, and even a few autistic children on more than one occasion. They had always been able to relate better to the dummy than they had to him, so maybe the concept would work as well on adults who had a problem with shyness. He also remembered recently reading an article on stuttering, which seemed to be Tabby's problem. One of the most important things a person could do when talking to someone who stuttered was to be patient and listen well. He thought he could do both, so Seth decided to try a little experiment. "It was nice having you in my workshop," he said, speaking for himself this time.

Tabby's gaze dropped immediately to the floor. "It w–w–was good."

"Did ya learn anything?" This question came from Rudy.

Tabby nodded, looking right at the dummy, whose eyes were now flitting from side to side.

"What'd ya learn?" Rudy prompted.

"I learned that ventriloquism is not as easy as it looks."

No stuttering at all this time, Seth noted. *Hmm. . .I think I may be on to something here.*

"Are you gonna be a ven-trick-o-list?" Rudy asked, giving Tabby a wink.

Tabby giggled. "I'd like to be, but I'm not sure I'd have the nerve to stand up in front of people and talk."

"Aw, it's a piece of cake," Rudy drawled. "All ya have to do is smile, grit your teeth, and let your dummy do most of the talkin'." The figure's head cranked to the left. "Of course, ya need to find a better-lookin' dummy than the one I got stuck with!"

At this, Rudy began to howl, and Tabby laughed right along with him.

Seth's experiment had worked, and he felt as if he'd just climbed to the summit of Mount Rainier.

"I'm surprised to see you here today," Tabby said, directing her comment at Rudy.

The dummy's head swiveled, and his blue eyes rolled back and forth again. "My dummy was asked to give a little demonstration during your worship time. I just came along to keep him in line."

"And to be sure I don't flirt with all the cute women," Seth added in his own voice.

Tabby's face flushed. "I—uh—it's been n–nice t–t–talking to you. I th–think I sh–should g–go find a s–seat in the s–s–sanctuary now."

"Maybe I'll see you later," Seth called to her retreating form.

❧

Tabby slid into a back-row pew, next to Donna.

"What took you so long? I thought I might have to send out the Coast Guard, just in case you'd fallen overboard or something."

Tabby groaned at Donna's tasteless comment. "I ran into the ventriloquist who taught the workshop I took yesterday."

"You did? What's he doing here?"

"He's part of the demonstration. He brought along his cute little dummy."

"I guess he would, if he's going to do ventriloquism." Donna sent a quick jab to Tabby's ribs with her elbow. "Did he talk to you?"

"Who?"

Another jab to the ribs. "The ventriloquist, of course."

"Actually, it was the dummy who did most of the talking. He was so funny, too."

Donna nodded. "I guess in order to be a ventriloquist, you'd need a good sense of humor."

Tabby twisted her hands together in her lap. How in the world did she think she could ever talk for two? Humor and wisecracking didn't come easy for someone like her. She was about to relay that to Donna, but the church service had begun. She turned her full attention to the front of the room instead.

Mr. Hartung, the middle-aged song leader, led the congregation in several praise choruses, followed by a few hymns. Announcements were given next, then the offering was taken. After that, Pastor Hanson encouraged the congregation to use their talents to serve the Lord, and he introduced the group who had come to inspire others to use their talents in the area of Christian ministry.

The first to perform was Mark Taylor, a Christian magician from Portland, Oregon. He did a few sleight-of-hand tricks, showing how sin can seriously affect one's life. Using another illusion, he showed the way to be shed of sin, through Jesus Christ.

Next up was Gail Stevens, a chalk artist from Seattle. She amazed the congregation with her beautiful chalk drawing of Christ's ascension into heaven, adding a special touch by using the black light Donna had been so enthusiastic about. This illuminated the entire picture and seemed to bring the illustration to life, as Jesus rose in a vibrant, fluorescent pink cloud.

There were oohs and ahs all around the room, and Donna nudged Tabby again. "That's what I want to be able to do someday."

Tabby nodded. "I'm sure you will, too."

A group of puppeteers put on a short musical routine, using several Muppet-style puppets, who sang to a taped version of "Bullfrogs and Butterflies." Tabby enjoyed their skit but was most anxious for the upcoming ventriloquist routine.

Joe Richey, a gospel clown from Olympia, did a short pantomime, which he followed with a demonstration on balloon sculpting. He made a simple dog with a long body, a colorful bouquet of flowers, and ended the routine by making a seal balancing a ball on the end of its nose. Everyone clapped as Slow-Joe the Clown handed out his balloon creations to several excited children in the audience.

Seth Beyers finally took his place in the center of the platform.

"There he is," Tabby whispered breathlessly. "And that's his cute little dummy, Rudy."

Seth had already begun to speak, and Tabby chose to ignore her friend when she asked, "Who do you really think is cute? The funny-looking dummy or the good-looking guy who's pulling his strings?"

"I would like you all to meet my little buddy, Rudy," Seth boomed into the microphone.

"That's right—I'm Rudy Right, and I'm always right!"

"Now, Rudy, I've told you many times that no one but God is always right."

Rudy's glass eyes moved from side to side. "Is that so? I guess we must be related then!"

"The Bible says that God made people in His own image, and you're certainly not a person."

There was a long pause, as if Rudy might be mulling over what the ventriloquist had said. Finally, the dummy's mouth dropped open. "I may be just a dummy, but I'm smart enough to pull your strings!"

Seth laughed, and so did the audience.

Donna leaned close to Tabby. "This guy's really good. His lips don't move at all."

Tabby smiled. "I know." Oh, how she wished she could perform like that, without stuttering or passing out from stage fright. What a wonderful way ventriloquism was to teach Bible stories and the important lessons of life.

A troubling thought popped into Tabby's head, pushing aside her excitement over the ventriloquism routine. *What would it feel like to have someone as good-looking, talented, and friendly as Seth Beyers be interested in someone as dull and uninteresting as me?*

Chapter 4

Wasn't that program great?" Donna asked, as she steered her car out of the church parking lot. "Could you believe how gorgeous the chalk art picture was under the black light?"

"Uh-huh," Tabby mumbled.

"And did you see how quickly Gail Stevens drew that picture? If I drew even half that fast, I'd probably end up with more chalk on me than the paper."

"Hmm. . ."

Donna glanced Tabby's way. "Is that all you've got to say? What's wrong with you, anyway? Ever since we walked out the door, you've been acting like you're a million miles away."

Tabby merely shrugged her shoulders in reply.

"Since my folks are out of town this weekend, and Mom won't be cooking us her usual Sunday dinner, should we eat out or fend for ourselves at home?"

Tabby shrugged again. "Whatever you think. I'm not all that hungry anyway."

"What? Tabitha Johnson not hungry?" Donna raised her eyebrows. "Surely you jest!"

Tucking a thumbnail between her teeth, Tabby mumbled, "I've never been much into 'jesting.' "

Donna reached across the short span of her car to give Tabby's arm a quick jab. "I've seen the little puppet skits you put on for the kids at our day care. I think they're quite humorous, and so do the children."

Tabby felt her jaw tense. "You're just saying that to make me feel better."

"Uh-uh, I really do think your puppet routines are funny."

"That's because I'm well out of sight, and only the silly-looking dog is in the limelight." Tabby grimaced. "If I had to stand up in front of an audience the way Seth Beyers did today, I think I'd curl up and die right on the spot."

"You know, Tabby, ventriloquism might be the very thing to help you overcome your shyness."

"How can you say that, Donna? I'd have to talk in front of people."

"Yes, but you'd be talking through your dummy."

"Dummy? What dummy? I don't even have a dummy?"

"I know, but you could get one."

"In case you haven't heard—those lifelike things are really expensive. Besides, I'm only going to be doing ventriloquism for the kids at day care. Roscoe's good enough for that." She inhaled deeply. "Of course I have to start practicing first, and only time will tell whether I can actually learn to talk for two.

❧

As Seth Beyers drove home from church, a keen sense of disappointment flooded his soul. The realization that he hadn't seen Tabby Johnson after the morning service didn't hit him until now.

During his little performance with Rudy, he'd spotted her sitting in the very back row. After the service he had been swarmed by people full of questions about ventriloquism and asking for all kinds of information about the dummies he created and repaired.

Tabby had obviously slipped out the door while he'd been occupied. He would probably never see her again. For reasons beyond his comprehension, that thought made him sad.

He reflected on something Grandpa had recently told him: "Everyone needs to feel as if they count for something, Seth. If you recognize that need in dealing with people, you might be able to help someone learn to like themselves a bit more."

Seth knew his grandfather's advice was good, and as much as he'd like to help Tabby, he also knew all he could really do was pray for the introverted young woman. He promised himself he would remember to do so.

❧

Tabby had been practicing ventriloquism for several weeks. She'd often sit in front of the full-length mirror in her bedroom, completely alone except for Roscoe Puppet. Not even Donna had been allowed to see her struggle through those first few difficult attempts at talking for two. If Tabby were ever going to perform for the day care kids, it wouldn't be until she had complete control of her lip movement and had perfected those horrible sound substitutions. There was *th* for v and f, *d* for b, and *n* for m. It was anything but easy, and it was enough to make her crazy!

Tabby took a seat in front of the mirror, slipped Roscoe onto her hand, and held him next to her face. "What do you think, little buddy? Can we ever learn to do ventriloquism well enough to put on a short skit for the kids?"

Manipulating the puppet's mouth, she made him say, "I think we can. . . I think we can. . . I think I have a bang-up plan. You throw your voice, and let me say all the funny stuff."

Tabby smiled triumphantly. "I did it! I said the sound substitutions without any lip movement!" She jumped to her feet, jerked open the door, and bolted into the living room. Donna was there, working on a chalk drawing taped to her easel. Tabby held Roscoe in front of her face. "I think I'm finally getting the hang of it!"

Donna kept on drawing. "The hang of what?"

Tabby dropped to the couch with a groan. "I'm trying to tell you that I can talk without moving my lips."

Donna finally set her work aside and turned to face Tabby. "That's great. How about a little demonstration?"

Tabby swallowed hard, and a few tears rolled unexpectedly down her cheeks.

Donna was at her side immediately. "What's wrong? I thought you'd be thrilled about your new talent."

"I am, but I wonder if I'll ever have the nerve to actually use it." She swiped at the tears and sniffed. "I really do want to serve God using ventriloquism, but it seems so hard."

"God never promised that serving Him in any way would be easy," Donna said. "And may I remind you of the acts you already do to serve the Lord?"

Tabby sucked in her bottom lip. "Like what?"

"You teach the day care kids about Jesus. You bake cookies for the residents of Rose Park Convalescent Center. You also read your Bible, pray, and—"

Tabby held up one hand. "Okay, okay. . .I get the picture. What I want to know is, are you saying I should be content to serve God in those ways and forget all about ventriloquism?"

Donna shook her head. "No, of course not. You just need to keep on trying and never give up. I believe God wants all Christians to use their talents and serve Him through whatever means they can."

Running a hand through her hair, Tabby nodded. "All right. I'll try."

With fear and trembling, Tabby forced herself to do a short ventriloquist routine the following day for the day care kids. Fifteen little ones sat cross-legged on the carpeted floor, looking up at her expectantly.

Tabby put Roscoe on one hand, and in the other hand she held a small bag of dog food. Drawing in a deep breath, she began. "R–R–Roscoe wants to tell you a little st–st–story today."

Tabby couldn't believe she was stuttering. She never stuttered in front of the kids. *It's only my nerves. They'll settle down in a few minutes.*

Several children clapped, and one little freckle-faced, redheaded boy called out, "Go, Roscoe! Go!"

Tabby gulped. It was now or never.

"Hey, kids—what's up?" the puppet said in a gravelly voice.

So far so good. No lip movement, and Roscoe's lip sync was right on.

"We just had lunch," a young girl shouted.

Tabby chuckled, feeling herself beginning to relax. "That's right," she said to the puppet. "The kids had macaroni and cheese today."

Pointing Roscoe's nose in the air, Tabby made him say, "I think I smell somethin' else."

"They had hot dogs, too. That's probably what you smell."

"Hot dogs? They had hot dogs?"

Tabby nodded. "That's right. Now it's time for your lunch."

"Oh, boy! I get a nice, big, juicy hot dog!"

"No, I have your favorite kind of dog food." Tabby held the bag high in the air.

Roscoe's furry head shook from side to side. "No way! I hate dog food! It's for dogs!"

The children laughed, and Donna, standing at the back of the room, gave Tabby an approving nod.

Tabby's enthusiasm began to soar as she plunged ahead. "But, Roscoe, you are a dog. Dogs are supposed to eat dog food, not people food."

"That's easy for you to say," Roscoe croaked. "Have you ever chomped down on a stale piece of dry old dog food?"

"I can't say as I have."

"Dog food makes me sick," Roscoe whined.

"I never knew that."

Roscoe's head bobbed up and down. "It's the truth. In fact, I was so sick the other day, I had to go to the vet."

"Really?"

"Yep! The vet took my temperature and everything."

"What'd he say?" Tabby prompted.

"He said, 'Hot dog!'" The puppet's head tipped back, and he let out a high-pitched howl.

By the time Tabby was done with her routine, Donna was laughing so hard she had tears rolling down her cheeks. As soon as the children went down for their afternoon naps, she took Tabby aside. "That was great. You're really good at talking for two."

"You think so?"

"Yes, I do. Not only have you mastered lip control and sound substitutions, but your routine was hilarious. Where did you come up with all those cute lines?"

Tabby shrugged. "Beats me. I just kind of ad-libbed as I went along."

Donna gave Tabby a quick hug. "Now all you need is a good ventriloquist dummy."

With an exasperated groan, Tabby dropped into one of the kiddy chairs. "Let's not get into that again. I can't afford one of those professional figures, and since I'll only be performing here at the day care, Roscoe will work just fine!"

Seth was nearly finished with the ugly dummy he was making for Alan Capshaw. While it had turned out well enough, it wasn't to his personal liking. A good ventriloquist didn't need an ugly dummy in order to captivate an audience. A professional ventriloquist needed talent, humor, and a purpose. For Seth, that purpose was sharing the gospel and helping others find a meaningful relationship with Christ.

In deep concentration at his workbench, Seth didn't even hear the overhead bell ring when a customer entered his shop. Not until he smelled the faint lilac scent of a woman's perfume and heard a polite "Ahem" did he finally look up from his work.

A young, attractive woman with short, dark curls stood on the other side of the long wooden counter.

Seth placed the ugly dummy aside and skirted quickly around his workbench. "May I help you?"

"Yes. I was wondering if you have gift certificates for the dummies you sell."

Seth smiled. "Sure. For what value did you want it?"

"Would three hundred dollars buy a fairly nice dummy?"

He nodded. "Prices for ventriloquist figures range anywhere from one hundred dollars for a small, inexpensive model to seven hundred dollars for one with all the extras."

"I'd like a gift certificate for three hundred dollars then."

Seth went to his desk, retrieved the gift certificate book, accepted the young woman's check, and in short order the business was concluded.

"Are you a ventriloquist?" he asked when she put the certificate in her purse and started to turn away.

She hesitated, then pivoted to face him. "No, but a friend of mine is, and she's got a birthday coming up soon."

"You're giving her a professional figure?"

"Sort of. She'll actually be the one forced to come in here and pick it up."

"Forced?" Seth's eyebrows arched upwards. "Why would anyone have to be forced to cash in a gift certificate for a ventriloquist dummy?"

"My friend is extremely shy," the woman explained. "It's hard for her to talk to people."

"Your friend's name wouldn't happen to be Tabby Johnson, would it?"

"How did you know that?"

"I thought I recognized you when you first came in. Now I know from where." Seth extended his right hand. "I'm Seth Beyers. I saw Tabby sitting with you during the Christian workers' program at your church a few weeks ago."

"I'm Donna Hartley, and Tabby and I have been friends since we were kids. She said she spoke with you. Well, actually, I guess it was more to your dummy."

Seth nodded. "I could hardly get her to make eye contact."

"That's not surprising."

"Whenever she talked to me, she stuttered." His forehead wrinkled. "She could talk a blue streak to my little pal, Rudy, and never miss a syllable."

Donna shrugged. "To be perfectly honest, besides me, the day care kids are the only ones she can talk to without stuttering."

"Day care kids?"

"Our church has a day care center, and Tabby and I manage it. It's about the only kind of work Tabby can do. Her self-esteem is really low, and I seriously doubt she'd ever make it around adults all day."

Seth couldn't begin to imagine how Tabby must feel. He usually didn't suffer from low self-esteem—unless you could count the fact that he hadn't found the right woman yet. Occasionally he found himself wondering if he had some kind of personality defect.

"Do you think ventriloquism might help Tabby?" Donna asked, breaking into his thoughts.

He shrugged. "Maybe."

"Tabby did a short routine at the day care the other day. It went really well, and I think it gave her a bit more confidence."

Seth scratched the back of his head. He felt like taking on a new challenge. "Hmm. . . Maybe we could work on this problem together."

Donna's eyebrows furrowed. "What do you mean?"

"You keep encouraging her to perform more, and when she comes in to pick out her new dummy, I'll try to work on her from this end."

Donna's expression revealed her obvious surprise. "You'd do that for a complete stranger?"

" 'Whatever you did for one of the least of these brothers of mine, you did for me,' " Seth quoted from the Book of Matthew.

"I like your Christian attitude," Donna said as she turned to leave. "Thanks for everything." After the door closed behind her, Seth let out a piercing whoop. He would soon be seeing Tabby again. Maybe he could actually help her. Maybe this was the answer to his prayers.

Chapter 5

I wish you weren't making such a big deal over my birthday," Tabby grumbled as she and Donna drove home from the grocery store one evening after work. This time they were in Tabby's blue hatchback, and she was in the driver's seat.

"It's just gonna be a barbecue in my parents' backyard," Donna argued. "How can that be labeled a big deal?"

Tabby grimaced. "You ordered a fancy cake, bought three flavors of ice cream, and invited half the city of Tacoma!"

"Oh, please! Your folks, Lois, her boyfriend, your grandma, me, and my folks—that's half of Tacoma?" Donna poked Tabby on the arm. "Besides, your folks live in Olympia now."

"I know, but being with my family more than twenty minutes makes me feel like it's half of Tacoma," Tabby argued.

"It isn't every day that my best friend turns twenty-five," Donna persisted. "If I want to throw her a big party, then it's my right to do so."

"I don't mean to sound ungrateful, but you know how things are between me and my family," Tabby reminded.

Donna nodded. "Yes, I do, and I know your parents often hurt you by the unkind things they say and do, but you can't pull away from them and stay in your cocoon of shyness. You don't have to like what they say and do, but you've got to love your family anyway." She sighed. "What I'm trying to say is, you've gotta love 'em, but you can't let them run your life or destroy your confidence, the way you've been doing for so long. It's high time for you to stand up and be counted."

"Yeah, right. Like that could ever happen."

"It could if you gained some self-confidence and quit letting Lois overshadow you."

"Fat chance! Just wait till you see the size of her engagement ring. It looks like Mount Rainier!"

Donna laughed. "How you do exaggerate."

"She's only marrying this guy for his money. Did I tell you that?"

"Only about a hundred times."

"I think it's disgusting." Tabby frowned. "I'd never marry anyone unless I loved him. Of course, he'd have to be a Christian," she quickly added.

"I'm beginning to think neither of us will ever find a husband," Donna said. "You're too shy, and I'm too picky."

"I can't argue with that. Unless I find a man who's either just a big kid or a real dummy, I'd never be able to talk to him."

"Maybe you can find a ventriloquist to marry, then let your dummies do all the talking."

Tabby groaned. "Now there's a brilliant idea. I can see it now—me, walking down the aisle, carrying a dummy instead of a bouquet. My groom would be waiting at the altar, holding his own dummy, of course."

Donna chuckled. "You are so funny today. Too bad the rest of the world can't see the real Tabitha Johnson."

❧

The birthday party was set to begin at six o'clock on Saturday night, in the backyard of Donna's parents, Carl and Irene.

"I still say this is a bad idea," Tabby grumbled, as she stepped into the living room, where Donna waited on the couch.

"Should we do something special with your hair?" Donna asked. "We could pull it away from your face with some pretty pearl combs."

Tabby wrinkled her nose. "I like it plain. Besides, I'm not trying to make an impression on anyone." She flopped down next to Donna. "Even if I were, it would never work. Dad and Mom won't even know I'm alive once Lois shows up with her fiancé."

"I've got a great idea!" Donna exclaimed. "Why don't you bring Roscoe to the barbecue? After we eat, you can entertain us with a cute little routine."

Tabby frowned. "You're kidding, right?"

"No. I think it would be a lot of fun. Besides, what better way to show your family that you really do have some talent?"

"Talent? What talent?"

"There you go again." Donna shook a finger in Tabby's face. "Self-doubting will never get you over being shy."

Tabby stood up. She knew Donna was probably right, but it was time to change the subject. "Do you think this outfit looks okay?" She brushed a hand across her beige-colored slacks.

"Well, now that you asked. . .I was thinking you might look better in that soft peach sundress of mine."

"No thanks. I'm going like I am, and that's final."

❧

The warm spring evening was a bit unusual for May in rainy Tacoma, but Tabby wasn't about to complain. The glorious weather was probably the only part of her birthday that would be pleasant.

The smoky aroma of hot dogs and juicy burgers sizzling on the grill greeted Tabby as she and Donna entered the Hartleys' backyard. Donna's father, wearing a long, white apron with a matching chef's hat, was busy flipping burgers, then covering them with tangy barbecue sauce. He stopped long enough to give both girls a quick peck on the cheek but quickly returned to the job at hand.

His petite wife, who looked like an older version of Donna, was setting the picnic table with floral paper plates and matching cups.

"Is th—there anything I can d—do to help?" Tabby questioned.

Irene waved her hand toward the porch swing. "Nope. I've got it all covered. Go relax, Birthday Girl."

"That's a good idea," Donna agreed. "You swing, and I'll help Mom."

Tabby didn't have to be asked twice. The Hartleys' old porch swing had been her favorite ever since she was a child. Soon she was rocking back and forth, eyes closed, and thoughts drifting to the past.

She and Donna had spent many hours in the quaint but peaceful swing, playing with their dolls, making up silly songs, and whispering shared secrets. *If only life could have stayed this simple. If only I could always feel as contented as when I'm in this old swing.*

"Hey, Big Sister. . . Wake up and come to the party!"

Lois's shrill voice jolted Tabby out of her reverie, and she jerked her eyes open with a start. "Oh, I—I d—didn't kn—know you w—w—were here."

"Just got here." Lois gave Tabby an appraising look. "I thought you'd be a little more dressed for tonight's occasion."

Tabby glanced down at her drab slacks and pale yellow blouse, then she lifted her face to study Lois's long, pastel blue skirt, accented by a soft white silk blouse. By comparison, Tabby knew she looked like Little Orphan Annie.

Lois grabbed her hand and catapulted her off the swing. "Mom and Dad aren't here yet, but I want you to meet my fiancé, the successful lawyer, whose parents have big bucks."

Tabby was practically dragged across the lawn and over to the picnic table, where a dark-haired, distinguished-looking young man sat. A pair of stylish metal-framed glasses were perched on his aristocratic nose, and he was wearing a suit, of all things!

"Mike, honey, this is the birthday girl—my big sister, Tabitha." Lois leaned over and dropped a kiss on the end of his nose.

He smiled up at her, then turned to face Tabby. "Hi. Happy birthday."

"Th—th—thanks," she murmured.

Michael gave her an odd look, but Lois grabbed his hand and pulled him off toward the porch swing before he could say anything more.

Donna, who had been pouring lemonade into the paper cups, moved toward

Tabby. "Looks like your sister brought you over here just so she could grab the old swing."

Tabby watched her beautiful, self-assured sister swagger across the lawn, laughing and clinging to Michael like she didn't have a care in the world. She shrugged. "Lois can have the silly swing. She can have that rich boyfriend of hers, too."

"Oh, oh. Do I detect a hint of jealousy?"

Tabby knew Donna was right, and she was about to say so, but her parents and grandmother had just come through the gate, and she figured it would be rude to ignore them.

"So glad you two could make it." Donna's father shook hands with Tabby's parents, then turned to her grandmother and planted a noisy kiss on her slightly wrinkled cheek. "You're sure lookin' chipper, Dottie."

"Carl Hartley, you still know how to pour on the charm, don't you?" Grandma Haskins raked a wrinkled hand through her short, silver-gray hair and grinned at him.

Up to this point, no one had even spoken to Tabby. She stood off to one side, head down, eyes focused on her beige sneakers.

Grandma Haskins was the first to notice her. "And here's our guest of honor. Happy twenty-fifth, Tabitha."

Tabby feigned a smile. "Th–thanks, Grandma."

"Yes, happy birthday," Mom added, placing a gift on one end of the table.

Tabby glanced up at her mother. She knew she looked a lot like Mom. They had the same mousy brown hair, dark brown eyes, and were both short of stature. That was where the similarities ended, though. Mom was much more socially secure than Tabby. She was soft-spoken, but unlike Tabby, her words didn't come out in a mumble-jumble of stammering and stuttering.

Tabby's gaze went to her father then. He was still visiting with Donna's dad and never even looked her way. Lois got her good looks from him, that was for sure. His blond hair, though beginning to recede, and those vivid blue eyes were enough to turn any woman's head. *No wonder Mom fell for Dad.*

Donna's mother, Irene, the ever-gracious hostess, instructed the guests to be seated at the picnic table, while she scurried about to serve them all beverages.

Even though Tabby was the only one in her family who professed Christianity, they all sat quietly through Carl's prayer. When he asked God to bless Tabby and give her many good years to serve Him, she heard Lois snicker.

Tabby had a compelling urge to dash back home to her apartment—where she'd be free of Lois's scrutiny and her dad's indifference. She knew it would be rude, and besides, the aroma of barbecued meat and the sight of several eye-catching salads made her feel as if she were starving. The promise of cake, ice cream, and gifts made her appreciate the special party Donna had planned, too. It was more than her own family would have done. With the exception of Grandma, she doubted whether any of them even cared that today was her birthday.

"Please don't sing 'Happy Birthday' and make me blow out the dumb candles," Tabby whispered when Donna set a huge cake in front of her a short time later. It was a beautiful cake—a work of art, really—German chocolate, Tabby's favorite, and it was covered with thick cream-cheese frosting. Delicate pink roses bordered the edges, and right in the middle sat a giant-sized heart with the words "Happy Birthday, Tabby."

"Don't spoil everyone's fun," Donna said softly.

Tabby bit back a caustic comeback, forcing herself to sit patiently through the strains of "Happy Birthday."

"Okay, it's time to open the presents." Donna moved the cake aside, then placed the gifts directly in front of Tabby. The first one was from Lois. Inside a gold foil-wrapped gift box was a pale green silk blouse and a makeup kit. It was filled with lipstick, blush, eyeliner, mascara, and a bottle of expensive perfume.

At Tabby's questioning look, Lois said, "I thought it might spark you up a bit. You always wear such drab colors and no makeup at all."

Tabby could have argued, since she did wear a touch of lipstick now and then. "Th–thanks, L–Lois," she mumbled instead.

Grandma Haskins reached over with her small gift bag. "Open mine next."

Tabby read the card first, then removed a small journal from the sack.

"I thought you might enjoy writing down some of your personal thoughts," Grandma explained. "I've kept a diary for many years, and I find it to be quite therapeutic."

Tabby and her maternal grandmother exchanged a look of understanding. Despite the fact that Grandma, who'd been widowed for the last ten years, wasn't a Christian, she was a good woman. Tabby felt that Grandma loved her, in spite of all her insecurities.

"Thank you, Grandma. I th–think it'll be f–fun."

"This one's from your folks," Donna said, pushing the other two gifts aside.

There was no card, just a small tag tied to the handle of the bag. It read: "To Tabitha, From Mom and Dad."

Tabby swallowed past the lump lodged in her throat. *They couldn't even write "love." That's because they don't feel any love for me. They only wanted me until Lois came along; then I became nothing but a nuisance.*

"Well, don't just sit there like a dunce. Open it!" her father bellowed.

Tabby ground her teeth together and jerked open the bag. Why did Dad always have to make her feel like such an idiot? As she withdrew a set of white bath towels, edged with black ribbon trim, her heart sank. Towels were always practical, but white? What in the world had Mom been thinking? She was sure it had been her mother's choice because Dad rarely shopped for anything.

"Th—thanks. Th—these will go g—good in our b—b—bathroom," she stuttered.

"I was hoping you'd put them in your hope chest," Mom remarked.

Tabby shook her head. "I d—don't have a h—hope chest."

"It's high time you started one then," Dad roared. "Lois is only nineteen, and she's planning to be married soon."

As if on cue, Lois smiled sweetly and held up her left hand.

"Your engagement ring is beautiful," Donna's mother exclaimed. "Congratulations to both of you."

Michael beamed and leaned over to kiss his bride-to-be.

Tabby blushed, as though she'd been kissed herself. Not that she knew what it felt like to be kissed. The only men's lips to have ever touched her face had been her dad's, when she was young, and Carl Hartley's, whenever he greeted her and Donna.

Donna cleared her throat. "Ahem! This is from Mom, Dad, and me." She handed Tabby a large white envelope.

Tabby's forehead wrinkled. Donna always went all out for her birthday. A card? Was that all she was giving her this year?

"Go ahead, open it," Donna coached. She was smiling like a cat who had just cornered a robin. Carl and Irene were looking at her expectantly, too.

Tabby shrugged and tore open the envelope. She removed the lovely religious card that was signed, "With love, Donna, Irene, and Carl." A small slip of paper fell out of the card and landed on the table, just missing the piece of cake Grandma Haskins had placed in front of Tabby. Tabby picked it up, and her mouth dropped open. "A gift certificate for a ventriloquist dummy?"

"Ventriloquist dummy?" Lois repeated. "What in the world would you need a dummy for?"

Before Tabby could respond, Donna blurted out, "Tabby's recently learned how to talk for two. She's quite good at it, I might add."

If ever there had been a time when Tabby wanted to find a hole to crawl into, it was now. She swallowed hard and said in a high-pitched squeak which sounded much like her puppet, "I—I'm just l—l—learning."

❧

By the time Tabby and Donna returned to their apartment, Tabby's shock over the surprise gift certificate had worn off. It had been replaced with irritation. She knew Donna's heart was in the right place, and Tabby didn't want to make an issue out of it, but what in the world was she going to do?

Tabby placed her birthday gifts on the kitchen table and went out to the living room. Donna was busy closing the mini-blinds, and she smiled when she turned and saw Tabby. "I hope you enjoyed your party."

Tabby forced a smile in response. "It was nice, and I really do appreciate the expensive gift you and your folks gave me."

Donna nodded. "I sense there's a 'but' in there someplace."

Tabby flopped into the rocking chair and began to pump back and forth, hoping the momentum might help her conjure up the courage to say what was on her mind. "It was an expensive birthday present," she said again.

Donna took a seat on the couch, just opposite her. "You're worth every penny of it."

Tabby shrugged. "I don't know about that, but—"

"There's that 'but.'" Donna laughed. "Okay, let me have it. What don't you like about the idea of getting a professional ventriloquist dummy?"

Tabby stopped rocking and leaned forward. "I—uh—"

"Come on, Tabby, just spit it out. Are you mad because my folks and I gave you that certificate?"

"Not mad, exactly. I guess it really would be kind of fun to own a dummy, even if I'm only going to use it at the day care."

"That's exactly what I thought," Donna said with a satisfied smile.

"The gift certificate says it's redeemable at Beyers' Ventriloquist Studio."

"That's the only place in Tacoma where ventriloquist dummies are bought, sold, and repaired."

"I know, but Seth Beyers owns the business, and he—"

"Oh, I get it! You have a thing for this guy, and the thought of being alone with him makes you nervous."

Tabby bolted out of the rocking chair, nearly knocking it over. "I do not have a thing for him! I just can't go in there and talk to him alone, that's all. You know how hard it is for me to speak to anyone but you or the kids. Wasn't that obvious tonight at the party?" She began to pace the length of the living room. "I couldn't even get through a complete sentence without stuttering and making a complete fool of myself. No wonder my family thinks I'm an idiot."

Donna moved quickly to Tabby's side and offered her a hug. "You're a big girl now, Tabby. I can't go everywhere with you or always be there to hold your shaking hand."

Donna's words stung like fire, but Tabby knew they were spoken in love. "What do you suggest I do—call Seth Beyers and see if I can place an order over the phone?"

Donna shook her head. "Of course not. You need to take a look at what he's got in stock. If there isn't anything suitable, he has a catalog you can look through."

"But I'll stutter and stammer all over the place."

Donna stepped directly in front of Tabby. "I suppose you could always take little Roscoe along for added courage," she said with a teasing grin.

Tabby's face brightened. "Say, that's a great idea! I don't know why I didn't think of it myself!"

Chapter 6

Tabby knew there was no point in procrastinating. If she didn't go to Beyers' Ventriloquist Studio right away, she'd have to endure the agony of Donna's persistent nagging. Since today was Friday, and she had an hour off for lunch, it might as well be now.

Tabby slipped Roscoe into the pocket of her raincoat, said good-bye to Donna, and rushed out the door. She stepped carefully to avoid several large puddles, then made a mad dash for her car, because, as usual, it was raining.

"Why couldn't it have done this last night?" she moaned. "Maybe then my birthday party would have been canceled." She slid into the driver's seat, closed the door with a bang, and pulled Roscoe out of her pocket. "Okay, little buddy, it's just you and me. I'm counting on you to get me through this, so please don't let me down."

❧

Seth had been up late the night before, putting the finishing touches on a grandpa dummy someone in Colorado had ordered from his catalog. He'd had trouble getting the moving glass eyes to shift to the right without sticking. Determined to see it through to completion, Seth had gone to bed shortly after midnight. Now he was feeling the effects of lost sleep and wondered if he shouldn't just close up shop for the rest of the day. He didn't have any scheduled customers that afternoon, and since it was raining so hard, it wasn't likely there would be any walk-ins, either.

Seth was heading over to put the CLOSED sign in the window, when the door flew open, nearly knocking him off his feet. Looking like a drenched puppy, Tabby Johnson stood there, holding her purse in one hand and a small, scruffy dog puppet in the other.

"Come in," he said, stepping quickly aside. "Here, let me take your coat."

"My—my c–coat is f–fine. It's w–w–waterproof."

Seth smiled, hoping to make her feel more at ease, but it didn't seem to have any effect on the trembling young woman. "I've been expecting you," he said softly.

"You—h–have?"

"Well, maybe not today, but I knew you'd be coming in sometime soon."

Tabby slipped Roscoe onto her hand and held him in front of her face. "How did you know Tabby would be coming here?" she made the puppet say.

Seth had no idea what she was up to, but he decided to play along. "Tabby's friend was in the other day," he answered, looking right at the puppet. "She bought a gift certificate for a dummy and said it was for Tabby's birthday."

Tabby's hand slipped slightly, and Roscoe's head dropped below her chin.

Now Seth could see her face clearly, and he had to force himself to keep talking to the puppet and not her. "Say, what's your name, little fellow?"

"Woof! Woof! I'm Roscoe Dog!"

She's actually doing ventriloquism, Seth noted. *Doing a pretty good job at it, too. Should I compliment her? Maybe give her a few encouraging words about her newfound talent? No, I'd better play along for a while and see if I can gain her confidence.*

Seth moved over to the counter where he usually did business with customers. He stepped behind it and retrieved one of his catalogs from the shelf underneath. "Are you planning to help Tabby pick out a dummy?" he asked, again directing his question to the puppet.

Roscoe's head bounced up and down. "Sure am. Have ya got anything on hand?"

"You don't want to look at the catalog?" This time Seth looked right at Tabby.

She squirmed under his scrutiny, but in a well-spoken ventriloquist voice she made the puppet say, "I'd rather see what you've got first."

Seth frowned. Tabby seemed unable to carry on a conversation without either stuttering or using the puppet, and she still hadn't looked him in the eye when he spoke directly to her. What was this little woman's problem, anyhow?

Tabby tapped the toe of her sneaker against the concrete floor as she waited for Seth's response to her request.

"Okay, I'll go in the back room and see what I can find," he finally mumbled. When Seth disappeared, she took a seat in one of the folding chairs near the front door. She didn't know what had possessed her to use Roscoe Puppet to speak to Seth Beyers. He probably thought she was out of her mind or acting like a little kid. If she'd tried to talk to him on her own, though, she'd have ended up stuttering like a woodpecker tapping on a tree. Tabby knew it was stupid, but using the puppet helped her relax, and she was able to speak clearly with no stammering at all. *Guess this little experience will be something to write about in my new journal,* she thought with a wry smile.

The telephone rang sharply, causing Tabby to jump. She glanced around anxiously, wondering whether Seth would hear it ringing and return to answer it. For a fleeting moment she thought of answering it herself but quickly dismissed the idea, knowing she'd only stutter and wouldn't have the foggiest idea of what to say.

She was rescued from her dilemma when Seth reappeared, carrying a large trunk, which he set on one end of the counter. "Be right with you," he said, reaching for the phone.

Tabby waited impatiently as he finished his business. She was dying to know what was inside that huge chest.

Five minutes later, Seth finally hung up. "Sorry about the interruption. That was a special order, and I had to be sure of all the details."

Tabby moved back to the counter, waiting expectantly as Seth opened the trunk lid. "I didn't know if you wanted a girl, boy, or animal figure, so I brought a few of each," he explained. Tabby's eyes widened as Seth pulled out several dummies and puppets, placing them on the counter for her inspection.

"They all have open-close mouths and eyes that move from side to side. Would you like to try one?"

Roscoe was dropped to the counter as Tabby picked up a small girl dummy dressed in blue overalls and a pink shirt. The figure's moving glass eyes were blue, and her brown hair was braided. Tabby held the figure awkwardly with one hand, unsure of what to say or do with it. The telltale sign of embarrassment crept up the back of her neck, flooding her entire face with familiar heat. "H—how do you w—work it?"

"Here, let me show you." Seth moved quickly around the counter until he was standing right beside Tabby. She could feel his warm breath against her neck, and she shivered when his hand brushed lightly against her arm. She wondered if she might be coming down with a cold.

Seth pulled the slit on the dummy's overalls apart, so Tabby could see inside the hollow, hard plastic body. "See here. . .that's where the wooden control stick is hidden. You turn the rod to the right or left for the figure's head to move." He demonstrated, while Tabby held the dummy.

"When you want to make her talk, you need to pull sharply down on this." He gave the small metal handle a few tugs. "The right lever makes the eyes move from side to side."

When Tabby nodded, Seth stepped away, allowing her access to the inside of the figure's body. "Okay, now you try it."

The control stick felt stiff and foreign beneath Tabby's trembling fingers, and it took a few tries before she got the hang of it. "Hi, my name's Rosie," she made the dummy say in a high-pitched, little-girl voice. "Will you take me home with you?"

Tabby pretended to whisper something into the figure's ear.

"She wants to know how much I cost," Rosie said to Seth.

His sudden frown made Tabby wonder if the girl dummy cost a lot more than the value of her gift certificate.

"This little game has been fun," Seth said kindly, "but if we're gonna do business, I think Tabby should speak for herself."

Seth's words hadn't been spoken harshly, but they still had an impact, causing Tabby to flinch, as though she'd been slapped.

"I'm sorry, but I get in enough dummy talk of my own," he apologized. "I'd really like to speak to you one-on-one."

Tabby lifted her gaze to finally meet his, and their eyes met and held. "I—I h–have a ph–phobia about sp–speaking in p–public or to p–people I–I'm uncomfortable w–w–with."

Seth grinned, but his eyes remained serious. "I know all about phobias."

"Y–you do?"

"Yep. I studied them in one of my college psychology classes." He pointed at Tabby. "Your phobia is called phonophobia—fear of speaking aloud. I think everyone has at least one phobia, so it's really not such a big deal."

"W–we do? I m–mean, other p–people have ph–phobias, too?"

"Oh, sure. In fact, I believe I'm plagued with one of the worst phobias of all."

Tabby shot him a quizzical look. "R–really? W–what's your ph–ph–phobia?"

"It's arachibutyrophobia—peanut butter, sticking to the roof of my mouth."

She giggled, in spite of her self-consciousness. "Y–you're m–making that up."

He shook his head. "No, that's the correct terminology for my phobia."

Tabby eyed him suspiciously.

He raised his hand. "I'm completely serious. I really do freak out every time I try to eat peanut butter. If it gets stuck to the roof of my mouth, which it usually does, I panic."

If Seth was trying to put her at ease, it was working, because Tabby felt more relaxed than she had all day. She tipped her head toward Rosie. "So, h–how much does she cost?" she asked, stuttering over only one word this time.

"Three hundred dollars. Your gift certificate should pretty well cover it."

"W–what about tax?"

He rewarded her with a quick wink. "My treat."

"Oh, no, I c–couldn't let you do th–that."

Seth shrugged. "Okay. You treat me to a cup of coffee and a piece of pie, and we'll call it even."

"I—I have to get b–back to w–w–work," she hedged, beginning to feel less relaxed and fully aware that she was stuttering heavily again.

"You can give me your address and phone number, which I'll need for my customer records anyway," Seth said with a grin. "I'll come by your house tonight and pick you up."

Tabby's heartbeat picked up considerably. "P–p–pick me u–up?" Her knees felt like they could buckle at any moment, and she leaned heavily against the counter for support.

Seth's grin widened. "How's seven o'clock sound?"

She was keenly aware of his probing gaze, and it made her feel even more uneasy. All she could do was nod mutely.

"Great! It's a date!"

❧

"How'd it go? Did you get a dummy? Where is it, and how come you don't look overjoyed?"

"You'd better go take your lunch break," Tabby said as she hung her wet raincoat over the back of a chair. "We can talk later."

Donna shook her head. "I ate with the kids, and now they're resting. We have plenty of time to talk."

With a sigh of resignation, Tabby dropped into one of the little chairs.

Donna pulled out the chair next to her and took a seat, too. "Don't keep me in suspense a moment longer. Where's the dummy?"

"Right here," Tabby said, pointing to herself. "I'm the biggest dummy of all."

Donna's forehead wrinkled. "I don't get it."

"I'm supposed to take Seth Beyers out for pie and coffee tonight." Tabby's lower lip began to tremble, and her eyes filled with unwanted tears.

"You've got a date with Seth Beyers, and you're crying about it? I sure hope those are tears of joy."

Tabby dropped her head into her hands and began to sob.

"Please don't cry," Donna said softly. "I would think you'd be thrilled to have a date with someone as good-looking and talented as Seth."

Tabby sniffed deeply. "It's not really a date."

"It's not? What is it then?"

"He covered the tax for Rosie, so I owe him pie and coffee."

Donna shook her head. "I have absolutely no idea what you're talking about. Who's Rosie?"

Tabby sat up straight, dashing away the tears with the back of her hand. "Rosie's my new dummy. She's out in the car."

"Okay, I get that much. What I don't get is why you would owe Seth pie and coffee."

"I just told you. He covered the tax. My gift certificate was the right amount for the dummy, but not enough for the tax. Seth said if I treated him to pie and coffee, he'd call it even."

Donna smiled smugly. "Sounds like a date to me."

❧

Seth had spent the better part of his day thinking about the pie and coffee date he'd made with Tabby. He wasn't sure why the thought of seeing the shy young woman again made his heart pound like a jackhammer. His mouth felt as though he'd just come from the dentist's office after a root canal. Maybe his interest in Tabby went deeper than a simple desire to help her climb out of the internal cell that obviously held her prisoner. If Seth were being completely honest, he'd have to admit that he was strangely attracted to Tabby. She might not be a beauty queen, but she was a long way from being ugly. In fact, he thought she was kind of cute. Even so, it wasn't her looks that held him captive. *What is it then?* he wondered.

Seth shrugged into a lightweight jacket and started out the door. "Guess I'll try to figure it all out tonight, over a piece of apple pie and a cup of coffee."

⁂

Tabby passed in front of her full-length bedroom mirror and stopped short. For a fleeting moment she thought she saw a smiling, beautiful woman staring back at her. No, that wasn't possible, because she was ugly. *Well, maybe not actually ugly,* she supposed. *Just ordinary. Shy and ordinary.* How could timid, stuttering Tabitha Johnson with mousy-colored brown hair and doe eyes ever look beautiful? Tabby's navy blue cotton dress slacks with matching blue flats weren't anything spectacular. Neither was the red-and-white pin-striped blouse she wore. She'd curled her hair for a change, and it fell in loose waves across her shoulders. It was nothing compared to her sister's soft, golden locks, though. What, then, had caused her to think she looked beautiful?

Tabby studied her reflection more closely. A hint of pink lipstick was all the makeup she wore. However, her cheeks glowed, and her eyes sparkled with. . . what? Excitement? Anticipation? What was she feeling as she prepared for this outing with Seth Beyers?

"Nervous, that's what I'm feeling!" Tabby exclaimed, pushing that elusive lock of hair away from her face. She reached for the doorknob. "Guess there's no turning back now. A promise is a promise," she muttered as she stepped into the living room. She began to pace, wondering if the butterflies, so insistent on attacking her insides, would ever settle down.

"Would you please stop pacing and sit down? You're making me nervous!" Donna patted the sofa cushion beside her. "Have a seat."

Tabby flopped onto the couch with a groan. "I hate waiting."

When the doorbell rang, Tabby jumped up like someone who'd been stung by a wasp. "Do you think I look okay?"

"You're fine. Now go answer that door."

As soon as Tabby opened the front door, her mouth went dry. Seth stood there, wearing a beige jacket, an off-white shirt, and a pair of brown slacks. His auburn hair looked freshly washed, and his green eyes sparkled with the kind of happiness she so often wished for. "Hope I'm not late," he said in a jovial tone.

"I–I th–think you're r–right on time."

"Are you ready to go?"

Tabby hesitated. "I—uh—let me g–get my d–dummy first."

Seth's eyebrows shot up. "I thought this was a pie and coffee thing." Without waiting for an invitation, he pushed past Tabby and sauntered into the living room. His gaze went to Donna, sitting on the couch. "You're Tabby's friend, right?"

She nodded. "Last time I checked."

"Can't you talk some sense into her?"

Donna shrugged and gave him a half-smile. "She's your date."

"Quit talking about me like I'm not even in the room!" Tabby shouted. "I need the dummy so I don't stutter."

Seth and Donna were both grinning at her. "What? What's so funny?" she hollered.

"You're not stuttering now," Seth said, taking a seat in the overstuffed chair nearest the door.

"I–I was angry," Tabby shot back. "I usually d–don't stutter when I'm mad."

Seth chuckled and gave Donna a quick wink. "Guess maybe we should keep her mad at us."

Donna wiggled her eyebrows. "You think that might be the answer?"

Tabby dropped to the couch. "Would you please stop? This is no l–laughing m–matter."

Donna looked at Seth and smiled, then she glanced back at Tabby. "Can't you see yourself sitting at the pastry shop, holding your dummy and talking for two?" She grabbed a throw pillow and held it against her chest, making a feeble attempt at holding back the waves of laughter that were shaking her entire body.

"You never know," Seth said with a chuckle. "We might draw quite a crowd, and Tabby could become famous overnight. I'd probably drum up some ventriloquist business in the process, too."

Tabby didn't know whether to laugh or cry. She sat there several seconds, watching her best friend and so-called date howling at her expense. When she'd had all she could take, Tabby jumped up and stormed out of the living room. Jerking open her bedroom door, she stalked across the carpet and flung herself on the bed. "I may never speak to Donna again," she wailed. "Forget about the dumb old tax. Seth Beyers can buy his own pie and coffee!"

Chapter 7

A stream of tears ran down Tabby's face, trickling toward her ears. She jumped off the bed, fully intending to go back into the living room and give Seth and Donna a piece of her mind, but she stopped short just after she opened the door.

"Tabby has real potential," she heard Donna say. "She's just afraid to use her talents."

"She needs lots of encouragement," Seth responded. "I can see how shy she is, but I didn't think taking the dummy along on our date would help her any. In fact, if someone were to laugh at Tabby, it might make things even worse. I really do want to help her be all she can be, but I'm not sure how to go about it."

"I think you're right," Donna said. "Taking the dummy along would be a bad idea."

Tabby peered around the corner. She could only see the back of Seth's head, but Donna was in plain view. She ducked inside her room. Now probably wasn't a good time to reappear. Not with the two of them talking about her.

Tabby crawled onto her bed again and stared at the ceiling. When she heard a knock at the door, she chose to ignore it. The door opened anyway, but she turned her face to the wall.

"Tabby, I'm sorry." The bed moved under Donna's weight, and Tabby felt a gentle hand touch her trembling shoulder. "Seth and I were wrong to laugh at you. It was all in fun, and we didn't expect you to get so upset."

Tabby released a sob and hiccupped. "Seth must think I'm a real dummy."

"I'm sure he doesn't. He only wants to help you."

Tabby rolled over, jerking into an upright position. "Help me? You mean he thinks I'm some kind of neurotic nut who needs counseling?" She swiped the back of her hand across her face. "Is he still here, or has he split by now?"

"He's still here."

Tabby bit her lip and closed her eyes with the strain of trying to get her emotions under control. "Just tell him the pie and coffee date is off."

Donna hopped off the bed and started for the door. "He's your date, not mine, so you can tell him yourself."

Tabby grabbed one of her pillows and let it sail across the room, just as the door clicked shut.

✤

Seth paced back and forth across the living room—waiting, hoping, praying Tabby would come out of her room. He needed to apologize for his rude behavior. The last thing he wanted was to hurt Tabby's feelings.

"Maybe I should have kept my big mouth shut and let her drag the dumb dummy along on our date. The worst thing that could have happened is we'd be the laughingstock of the pastry shop," he mumbled. "It sure wouldn't be the first time I've been laughed at. Probably not the last, either."

When Tabby's bedroom door opened, Seth snapped to attention. His expectancy turned to disappointment when Donna stepped from the room without Tabby. Seth began to knead the back of his neck. "She's really hoppin' mad, huh?"

Donna nodded. "Afraid so. She wouldn't even listen to me."

"Will she talk to me?"

Donna shrugged and took a seat on the couch. "I doubt it, Seth. She wanted me to tell you that the date is off, but I told her she'd have to tell you herself."

Seth chewed on his lower lip. "And?"

"She threw a pillow at me, but it hit the door instead."

Seth groaned. "She may be shy, but she's obviously got quite a temper."

Donna shook her head. "Not really. In fact, I've never seen her this angry before. She usually holds in her feelings. She must have it pretty bad."

Seth lowered himself into a chair. "Have what pretty bad?"

Donna opened her mouth to reply, but was stopped short when Tabby stepped into the room.

Seth could see she'd been crying. Her eyes were red, and her face looked kind of swollen. It made him feel like such a heel. He jumped up from his chair and moved swiftly toward her. "Tabby, I—"

She raised her hand, and he noticed she was holding a checkbook. He fell silent. It was obvious that a simple apology was not going to be enough.

✤

Tabby shifted from one leg to the other, wondering what to say. She was keenly aware of Seth's probing gaze, and it made her feel uneasy. She was sure he already thought she was an idiot, so it shouldn't really matter what she said at this point. After tonight, Seth would probably never want to see her again anyway.

Tabby continued to stand there, shoulders hunched, arms crossed over her chest. She felt totally defeated. "Y—you h—hurt me," she squeaked. "You h—hurt me b—bad."

Seth nodded. "I know, and I'm sorry for laughing at you. It's just that—"

"You d—don't have to—to explain," Tabby said with a wave of her hand. "I know it w—would embarrass you if I t—took my d—dummy, but I can't t—talk right w—without her."

Seth took a few steps toward Tabby, which brought his face mere inches from hers. "Your stuttering doesn't bother me, but if you'd be more comfortable bringing Rosie, then I'm okay with it."

Tabby gulped and drew in a deep breath. She was sure Seth was only trying to humor her. Taking the dummy into the pastry shop would be even dumber than taking her puppet to Seth's place of business earlier that day. She held out her checkbook. "Let's forget about pie and coffee, okay? I'll write you a check to cover the tax due on Rosie."

Combing his fingers through his hair, Seth frowned. "You don't want to go out with me?"

She glanced at him anxiously, then dipped her head, afraid of the rejection she might see on his face. "I d–don't w–want to embarrass y–you."

"Look, if it would make you feel more at ease, we can get our pie and coffee to go. We could take it to the park and eat it in the car."

Tabby shifted uneasily. She really did want to go, but—

Donna, who'd been sitting silently on the couch, spoke up. "Would you just go already? You two are driving me nuts!"

"I th–think she w–wants to get rid of me," Tabby said, giving Seth a sidelong glance.

He wiggled his eyebrows playfully. "Her loss is my gain."

Tabby's heartbeat quickened at his sincere tone. He did seem to be genuinely sorry. "Okay, l–let's go. Without R–Rosie, though. One d–dummy is enough for y–you to h–handle."

"I hope you're not referring to yourself," he said with a puckered brow.

"She is," Donna said, before Tabby had a chance to answer. "She's always putting herself down."

Tabby shot her friend a look of irritation before retrieving her raincoat from the hall closet. "We'll talk about this later."

Donna shrugged. "You two have fun!"

"We will," Seth called over his shoulder.

❧

"I was impressed with your ventriloquism abilities when you were in my shop today," Seth said. He and Tabby were sitting in his black Jeep, at a viewpoint along the five-mile drive in Point Defiance Park.

Tabby took a sip of her mocha latte. "I'm just a beginner, and I know I still have lots to learn."

"But you're a quick learner. I saw no lip movement at all."

She shrugged. "That's what Donna's been telling me. She thinks I should do a ventriloquist routine for our Sunday school opening sometime."

Seth's face broke into a smile. "That's a terrific idea!"

"Oh, I couldn't."

"Why not?"

"I stutter."

Seth chuckled. "Not when you're really mad. . .or doing ventriloquism." He snapped his fingers. "Do you realize that you haven't stuttered once since we pulled into this parking spot? I don't know if it's the awesome sight of the lights on Narrows Bridge that has put you at ease, or if you're just beginning to feel more comfortable around me."

Tabby contemplated that for a few seconds. Seth was right; she hadn't been stuttering. For the first time all evening Tabby didn't feel nervous. In fact, she felt more relaxed than she had all day. Donna and the day care kids were the only people she'd ever felt this comfortable around. Maybe Seth could be her friend. Maybe. . .

Tabby grimaced. Who was she kidding? Seth was confident, good-looking, and talented. He'd never want someone like her as a friend. In his line of work, he met all sorts of people. Probably had lots of close friends. She was sure none of them stuttered or turned cherry red every time someone looked at them. Why did she allow herself to hope or have foolish dreams? Would she spend the rest of her life wishing for the impossible?

"Tabby, did you hear what I said?" Seth's deep voice broke into her thoughts, and she forced herself to look at him.

"Huh?"

He rested his palm on her trembling hand. "You don't have to be nervous around me. I'm just plain old Seth Beyers, fearful of eating sticky peanut butter."

Tabby swallowed hard. Seth's gentle touch made her insides quiver, and she looked away quickly, hoping to hide the blush she knew had come to her cheeks. At this moment, she felt as though *her* mouth was full of gooey peanut butter. How could she not be nervous when he was touching her hand and looking at her with those gorgeous green eyes? She closed her own eyes and found herself wondering how Seth's lips would feel against her own.

"My fear may not affect my relationship with people," Seth continued, "but it's real, nonetheless." He trailed his thumb across her knuckles, marching a brigade of butterflies through her stomach. "I'd like to be your friend, Tabby. I want to help you overcome your shyness. You have potential, and if you'll let Him, I know the Lord can use you in a mighty way."

Tabby blinked away stinging tears. How she wished it were true. She'd give anything to face the world with confidence. It would make her life complete if she could serve God without fear or bashfulness—even if it wasn't in a mighty way, like Seth was doing with his ventriloquist skills.

"Will you allow me to help?" Seth asked.

Tabby felt drawn to his compassionate eyes, and she sensed he could see right through her. *I could drown in that sea of green.*

"Tabby?"

She nodded. "I–I'm not expecting any big m–miracles, but yes, I w–would like your help."

❧

For the next several days Seth's offer of help played itself over and over in Tabby's mind. When he dropped her off at the apartment that night, after pie and coffee, he'd said he would give her a call, but he never explained how he planned to help her. Would he offer to get her speech therapy? If so, that would never work. Her parents had sent her for all kinds of therapy when she was growing up. Nothing helped. There wasn't a thing wrong with Tabby's speech. If there had been, she would have stuttered all the time, not just in the presence of those who made her feel uncomfortable. It was her low self-esteem and shyness that caused her to stutter, and she was sure there wasn't anything that could be done about it.

"You're awfully quiet today," Donna remarked, pulling Tabby out of her musings.

Tabby glanced over at her friend in the passenger seat. They took turns driving to work, and today they'd taken Tabby's car.

Tabby gave the steering wheel a few taps. "I was just thinking."

Donna laughed. "Thinking's okay, as long as you pay attention to where you're going."

"I am."

"Oh, yeah? Then how come you drove right past the church?"

Tabby groaned as she glanced to the left and saw the corner of Elm Street. She cranked the wheel and made a U-turn.

"Oh, great, now you're trying to get yourself a big, fat ticket," Donna complained. "What's with you this morning?"

"Nothing. I'm just preoccupied." Tabby pulled into the church parking lot and turned off the ignition.

"Thinking about Seth Beyers, I'll bet."

Tabby opened her mouth, but before she could get any words out, Donna cut her off. "I think that guy really likes you."

"Seth's just friendly. He likes everyone." Tabby didn't like where this conversation was going, and she'd have to steer it in another direction soon, or they might end up in an argument.

"I know Seth is friendly," Donna persisted, "but I think he's taken a special interest in you. You should have seen how upset he was when you ran into your room the other night."

"How about this weather? Can you believe it hasn't rained in the last half hour? We'd better get inside before it changes its mind and sends us another downpour."

Donna clicked her tongue. "You're trying to avoid the subject, and it won't work. I have something to say, and you're gonna hear me out."

"We'll be late for work."

Donna glanced at her watch. "We're ten minutes early. So, if you'll quit interrupting, we still have plenty of time to talk."

Tabby drew in a deep breath and let it out in a rush. "Okay, get whatever it is off your chest. I really want to get on with my day."

Donna gave her a reproachful look. "What I have to say isn't all that bad."

"All right then, let me have it."

Donna blinked. "My, my, you're sure testy. It's Seth, isn't it?"

Tabby remained silent.

"I really do think the guy likes you."

Tabby wrinkled her nose. "You already said that. I think Seth's the type of person who's kind to everyone. It's obvious that he takes his relationship with Christ seriously."

Donna raised her dark eyebrows. "And you don't?"

Tabby shrugged. "I try to, but I'm not outgoing and self-confident the way he is. I don't think I'm a very good Christian witness."

"You could be, Tabby. You have a wonderful new talent, which you should be using to serve the Lord."

"I—I still don't feel ready to do ventriloquism in front of a crowd."

"Maybe you need to take a few more lessons. I'm sure if you asked, Seth would be more than willing to help you."

Tabby drew in another long breath, and this one came out as a shuddering rasp. "He said he'd help, and I even agreed."

"That's great. I'm glad to hear it."

"I've thought it over thoroughly," Tabby said. "I like Seth too much to expect him to waste his time on someone like me."

Donna shook her head. "Now that's the most ridiculous thing I've ever heard. If you like the guy, then why not jump at any opportunity you have to be with him?"

"Aren't you getting this picture? I don't stand a chance with someone like Seth Beyers. He's totally out of my league."

Donna held up both hands. "I give up! You don't want to see your potential or do anything constructive to better yourself, so there's nothing more I can say." She jerked open the car door and sprinted off toward the church.

Tabby moaned and leaned against the headrest. "Maybe she's right. Maybe I need to pray about this."

Chapter 8

Seth had been thinking of Tabby for the past few days. In fact, he couldn't get her out of his mind. The other night she'd told him where she worked, and he had decided to stop by the day care for a little visit. One of the fringe benefits of being self-employed was the fact he could pretty much set his own hours and come and go whenever he felt like it. Today he'd decided to take an early lunch and had put a note in his shop window saying he wouldn't be back until one.

Seth pulled his Jeep into the church parking lot, turned off the engine, and got out. He scanned the fenced-in area on one side of the building. There were several children playing on the swings, so he figured that must be part of the Caring Christian Day Care.

He ambled up the sidewalk, and was about to open the gate on the chain-link fence, when he caught sight of Tabby. She was kneeling on the grass, and a group of children sat in a semicircle around her, listening to a Bible story. The soft drone of her voice mesmerized him, as well as the kids, who were watching Tabby with rapt attention. She wasn't stuttering at all, he noticed. It was uncanny, the way she could speak so fluently with these children, yet stutter and hang her head in embarrassment whenever she was with him.

"And so, little ones," Tabby said as she closed the Bible, "Jonah truly learned his lesson that day."

"He never went on a boat again, right, Teacher?" a little red-haired, freckle-faced boy hollered out.

Tabby smiled sweetly, and Seth chuckled behind his hand. She still didn't know he was watching her, and he decided to keep it that way for a few more minutes.

"Jonah's lesson," Tabby explained, "was to obey God in all things. He could have drowned in that stormy sea, but God saved him by bringing the big fish along in time."

"I wonder if the fishy had bad breath," a little, blond-haired girl piped up.

Tabby nodded. "The inside of that fish probably smelled pretty bad, but Jonah was kept safe and warm for three whole days. When the fish finally spit him out on dry land, Jonah was happy to be alive."

"And I'll bet he never went fishing after that," said the freckle-faced boy.

Tabby laughed softly. Her voice sounded like music to Seth's ears. How could anyone so introverted around adults be so at ease with children? *She'll make a good mother some day*, Seth found himself thinking. *She has a sweet, loving spirit, and the kids seem to relate really well to her.*

Seth opened the gate and stepped inside the enclosure just as Tabby stood up. She brushed a few blades of grass from her denim skirt, and the children all stood, too.

"It's time to go inside," she instructed. "Miss Donna is probably ready for us to bake those cookies now."

A chorus of cheering voices went up, and the kids, including those who had been swinging, raced off toward the basement door.

Tabby started to follow, but Seth cleared his throat loudly, and she whirled around to face him. "Oh, you—you sc–scared me. I d–didn't know you w–were h–here. How l–long have you–you been st–standing there?"

Seth grinned at her. "Just long enough to hear the end of a great story. The biblical account of Jonah and the big fish is one of my favorites."

"It's m–my favorite, too," she murmured.

"You're really good with the kids," he said, nodding in the direction of the disappearing pack of children.

"Th–thanks. I love w–working w–with them."

"It shows."

There was a moment of silence, as Seth stood there staring at Tabby, and she shifted from one foot to the other.

"Wh–what br–brings you here?" she finally asked.

"I came to see you," he said with a wide smile.

Her only response was a soft, "Oh."

"But now that I'm here, I think maybe I should follow the kids into the day care and see what kind of cookies they'll be making." Seth offered her a wink, and she blushed, dropping her gaze to her white sneakers.

"We're m–making chocolate ch–chip," Tabby said. "We'll be t–taking them to R–Rose Park Convalescent C–Center tomorrow m–morning."

He nodded. "Ah, so you're not only a great storyteller, but you're full of good deeds."

Her blush deepened, and she dipped her head even further. "It's n–nothing, really."

"I think you're too modest," Seth replied, taking a few steps toward her. When he was only inches away, he reached out and gently touched her chin. Slowly, he raised it, until her dark eyes were staring right into his. "There, that's better. It's kind of hard to carry on a conversation with someone who's staring at her feet."

Tabby giggled, obviously self-conscious, and it reminded him of one of her day care kids. "Wh—what did you w—want to see m—me about, Se—Se—Seth?"

"I thought maybe we could have lunch and talk about something," he answered, stepping away. "I saw a little deli just down the street, and I'm on my lunch hour, so—"

"Th—that would be nice, but I've got c—cookies to b—bake," she interrupted. "D—Donna and I w—will pr—probably be baking l—long after the k—kids go down for their n—naps."

Seth blew out his breath. "Okay, I guess I can call you later on. Will that be all right?"

She nodded. "Sure, th—that will be f—fine. Do y—you have m—my ph—phone number?"

"It's on the invoice I made out for your dummy purchase the other day."

"Oh." She turned toward the church. "I—I'd better g—get inside now. T—talk to you l—later, Seth."

He waved to her retreating form. "Yeah, later."

❧

"You're wanted on the phone, Tabby!"

Tabby dried her hands on a towel and left the kitchen. When she entered the living room, Donna was holding the receiver, a Cheshire-cat grin on her pixie face.

"Who is it?"

"Seth."

Taking in a deep breath, Tabby accepted the phone, then motioned Donna out of the room.

Donna winked and sauntered into the kitchen.

"H—hello, Seth," Tabby said hesitantly. Her palms were so moist, she hoped she could hold onto the receiver.

"Hi, Tabby. How are you?"

"I'm o—okay."

"I'm sorry we couldn't have lunch today, but I said I'd call later. Is this a good time for you to talk?"

She nodded, then realizing he couldn't see her, she squeaked, "Sure, it's—it's f—fine."

"Good. You see, the reason I wanted to talk to you is, Saturday afternoon I'll be doing an advanced ventriloquism class," Seth said. "I was hoping you'd agree to come."

Tabby twirled the end of the phone cord between her fingers. "I—uh—really c—can't, Seth."

"Can't or won't?"

179

She flinched, wondering if Seth could read her mind.

"Tabby?"

"I—I wouldn't feel comfortable trying to do v—v—ventriloquism in front of a b—bunch of strangers," she answered truthfully. "You know h—how bad I stutter. They'd probably l—laugh at me."

There was a long pause, then, "How 'bout I give you some private lessons?"

"P—private lessons?"

"Sure. We could meet once a week, either at your apartment or in my shop."

"Well. . ."

"I'd really like to see your talent perfected. Besides, it would be a good excuse to be with you again."

He wants to be with me. Tabby squirmed restlessly. Did Seth really see her in some other light than a mere charity case? Could he possibly see her as a woman? An image of little Ryan O'Conner, the freckle-faced boy from day care, flashed through her mind. He had a crop of red hair, just like Seth. *I wonder if our son would look like that?*

"Tabby, are you still there?" Seth's deep voice drew Tabby back to their conversation.

"Yes, I'm—I'm h—here," she mumbled, wondering what on earth had been going on in her head. She hardly knew Seth Beyers, and fantasizing about a child who looked like him was absolutely absurd!

"Are you thinking about my proposal?" Seth asked, breaking into her thoughts a second time.

"Pro—proposal?" she rasped. Even though she knew Seth wasn't talking about a marriage proposal, her heart skipped a beat. They'd only met a short time ago. Besides, they were exact opposites. Seth would never want someone as dull as her.

"So, what's it gonna be?" he prompted.

She sent up a silent prayer. *What should I do, Lord?* A few seconds later, as if she had no power over her tongue, Tabby murmured, "O—okay."

"Your place or mine?"

Tabby caught a glimpse of Donna lurking in the hallway. "You c—could come here, but we'll p—probably have an audience."

"An audience?"

"Donna—my r—roommate."

Seth laughed. "Oh, yeah. Well, I don't mind, if it doesn't bother you."

Actually, the thought of Donna hanging around while Seth gave her lessons did make Tabby feel uncomfortable. It was probably preferable to being alone with Seth at his shop, though. "When do you w—want to b—begin?" she asked.

"Is tomorrow night too soon?"

She scanned the small calendar next to the phone. Tomorrow was Friday, and like most other Friday nights, she had no plans. "Tomorrow n—night will be f—fine. I d—don't get home till six-thirty or seven, and I'll need t—time to change and eat d—dinner."

"Let's make it seven-thirty then. See you soon, Tabby."

❧

Seth hung up the phone and shook his head. He could just imagine how Tabby must have looked during their phone conversation. Eyes downcast, shoulders drooping, hair hanging in her face.

His heart went out to her whenever she stuttered. He felt a hunger, a need really, to help the self-conscious little woman. He wanted to help her be all she could be. Maybe the advanced ventriloquism lessons would enable her to gain more confidence.

Seth turned away from the phone. *If I work hard enough, Tabby might actually become the woman of my dreams.* He slapped his palm against the side of his head. "Now where did that thought come from? I can't possibly be falling for this shy, introverted woman."

Back when he was a teen, Seth had made a commitment to serve God with his ventriloquist talents. He'd also asked the Lord for a helpmate—someone with whom he could share his life and his talent. Since he'd never found that perfect someone, maybe he could make it happen.

He sighed deeply. The way Tabby was now, he knew she'd only be a hindrance to his plans. He could just imagine what it would be like being married to someone who couldn't even talk to a stranger without stuttering or hiding behind a dummy. Unless he could draw her out of that cocoon, there was no possibility of them ever having a future together.

"What am I saying?" Seth lamented. "I hardly even know the woman, and I'm thinking about a future with her!" He shook his head. "Get a grip, Seth Beyers. She's just a friend—someone to help, that's all. You'd better watch yourself, because you're beginning to act like one of your dummies."

❧

"I don't know what you're so nervous about. You've already mastered the basic techniques of ventriloquism, so the rest should be a piece of cake," Donna said with a reassuring smile.

Tabby nodded mutely as she flopped onto the couch beside Donna. The truth was, she was a lot more nervous about seeing Seth than she was about perfecting her ventriloquism skills. She liked him—a lot. That's what frightened her the most. She'd never felt this way about a guy before. She knew her child-ish fantasies about her and Seth, and children who looked like him, were totally absurd, but she just couldn't seem to help herself.

"Tabby, the door!"

181

Donna's voice broke through Tabby's thoughts, and she jumped. She hadn't even heard the doorbell. "Oh, he's here? Let him in, okay?"

Donna grinned. "Since he's come to tutor you, don't you think *you* should answer the door?"

Tabby felt a sense of rising panic. "You're not staying, I hope."

"If you're gonna do ventriloquism, then you'll need an audience," Donna said.

The doorbell rang again, and Tabby stood up. When she opened the front door, she found Seth standing on the porch, little Rudy cradled in the crook of one arm and a three-ring binder in his hand. "Ready for a lesson?"

She nodded, then motioned toward the living room. "We h–have our audience, j–just as I expected."

"That's okay. It's good for you to have an audience," Seth answered. "It'll give you a feel for when you're on stage."

Tabby's mouth dropped open. "On st–st–stage?"

Seth laughed. "Don't look so worried. I'm not suggesting you perform for a large crowd in the next day or two. Someday you might, though, and—"

"No, I won't!" Tabby shouted. "I'm only d–doing this so I can per–perform better for the kids at the d–day care."

Seth shrugged. "Whatever." He followed her into the living room. "Where's your dummy?"

"In my room. I'll go get her." Tabby made a hasty exit, leaving Seth and Donna alone.

❧

"She's a nervous wreck," Donna remarked as Seth placed the notebook on the coffee table, then took a seat on the couch.

"Because you're here?"

She shook her head. "I think you make her nervous."

"Me? Why would I make Tabby nervous?"

"Well, I'm pretty sure. . ."

"I–I'm ready," Tabby announced as she entered the room carrying Rosie.

Seth stood up. "Great! Let's get started."

"Sh–should I sit or st–stand?"

"However you're the most comfortable." Seth nodded toward the couch. "Why not sit awhile, until you're ready to put on a little performance for us?"

"I–I may never be r–ready for that."

"Sure you will," Seth said with assurance. He wanted her to have enough confidence to be able to stand up in front of an audience, but from the way she was acting tonight, he wondered if that would ever happen.

"Tabby, show Seth how you can make Rosie's head turn backwards," Donna suggested.

Tabby dropped to the couch and held her dummy on one knee. She inserted her hand in the opening at the back of the hard plastic body and grabbed the control stick. With a quick turn of the stick, Rosie was looking backwards. "Hey, where'd everybody go!" the childlike voice squealed.

Not one stuttering word, Seth noted, as he propped one foot on the footstool by Donna's chair. *Talking for two seems to be the best way Tabby can converse without stammering.* "We're right here, Rosie. Come join the party." This came from Rudy Right, who was balanced on Seth's knee.

"Party?" Rosie shot back. "We're havin' a party?"

"Sure, and only dummies are invited." Rudy gave Tabby a quick wink.

She giggled, then made Rosie say, "Guess that means we'll have to leave, 'cause the only dummies I see are pullin' someone else's strings."

Seth chuckled. "I think we've been had, Tabby." He scooted closer to her. "Would you like to learn a little something about the near and far voice?"

"Near and far? What's that?" The question came from Donna.

"The near voice is what you use when your dummy is talking directly to you or someone else. Like Tabby and I just did with our two figures," Seth explained. "The far voice would be when you want your audience to believe they're hearing the dummy talking from someplace other than directly in front of them." He pointed to the telephone on the table by the couch. "Let's say you just received a phone call from your dummy, and you want the audience to hear the conversation." Seth reached over and grabbed the receiver off the hook.

"Hi, Seth, can I come over?" A far-sounding, high-pitched voice seemed to be coming from the phone.

"Sure, why don't you?" Seth said into the receiver. "We're having a party over at Tabby and Donna's tonight, so you're more than welcome to join us."

"That's great! I love parties!" the far voice said. "Be right there!"

Seth hung up the phone and turned to face Tabby. "Do you have any idea how I did that?"

"You used the power of suggestion," Donna said, before Tabby had a chance to open her mouth. "We saw a phone and heard a voice, so it makes sense that we thought the sound was coming from the receiver."

Seth looked at Tabby. "What do you think?"

"I–I'm not sure, but I think m–maybe you did something different in your th–throat."

Seth grinned. "You catch on fast. I tightened my vocal chords so my voice sounded a bit pinched or strained. There's an exercise you can do to help make this sound."

"Oh, great! I love to exercise," Donna said, slapping her hands together.

Seth could tell from Tabby's expression that she was more than a bit irritated with Donna's constant interrupting. He wished there was some way to politely ask her well-meaning friend to leave.

"Actually, Donna, it's not the kind of exercise you're thinking of. It's only for ventriloquists, so. . ."

Donna held up both hands. "Okay, I get the picture. You want me to keep my big mouth shut, right?"

"You are kind of a nuisance," Tabby replied.

Wow, she can get assertive when she wants to. Seth wondered what other traits lay hidden behind Tabby's mask of shyness.

"I'll keep quiet," Donna promised.

Tabby raised her eyebrows at Seth, and he grinned in response. "Now, let's see. . . . Where were we?"

"An exercise." Donna ducked her head. "Sorry."

"The first thing you do is lean over as far as you can," Seth said as he demonstrated. "Try to take in as much air as possible, while making the *uh* sound."

Tabby did what he asked, and he noticed her face was turning red. How much was from embarrassment and how much from the exercise, he couldn't be sure, but he hoped it wouldn't deter her from trying.

"Now sit up again and try the same amount of pressure in your stomach as you make the *uh* sound." He placed one hand against his own stomach. "You'll need to push hard with these muscles as you speak for your far-sounding voice. Oh, and one more thing. It's best to keep your tongue far back in your mouth, like when you gargle. Doing all that, try talking in a high, whisper-like voice."

"Wow, that's a lot to think about all at once!" The comment came from Donna again, and Seth wondered if Tabby might be about to bolt from the room.

"There is a lot to think about," he agreed, "but with practice, it gets easier." He leaned close to Tabby and whispered, "Ready to try it now?"

She sucked in her bottom lip and nodded. "Hi, I'm glad you're home. I was afraid nobody would answer the phone."

Seth grabbed her free hand and gave it a squeeze. "That was awesome, Tabby! You catch on quick. A natural born ventriloquist, that's what you are."

A stain of red crept to her cheeks, but she looked pleased. "Th–thanks."

Seth pulled his hand away and reached for the notebook he'd placed on the coffee table. "I have some handout sheets to give you. Things for you to practice during this next week and a few short distant-voice routines to work on."

Tabby only nodded, but Donna jumped up and bounded across the room. "Can I see? This has all been so interesting! I'm wondering if maybe I should put away my art supplies and come back to your shop to look at dummies." She grinned at Tabby. "What do you say? Should I take up ventriloquism so we can do some joint routines?"

Chapter 9

By the time Tabby closed the door behind Seth, she felt emotionally drained and physically exhausted. Tonight's fiasco would definitely be recorded in that journal Grandma had given her. Donna had done nothing but interrupt, offer dumb opinions, and flirt with Seth. At least that's how Tabby saw it. Her best friend was obviously interested in the good-looking ventriloquist. What other reason could she have for making such a nuisance of herself?

Well, she's not going to get away with it, Tabby fumed. She headed for the living room, resolved to make things right. *Friend or no friend, I'm telling Donna exactly what I think.*

Donna was sitting on the couch, fiddling with the collar on Rosie's shirt. "You know what, Tabby? I think your dummy might look cuter in a frilly dress. You could curl her hair and—"

"Rosie looks just fine the way she is!" Tabby jerked the ventriloquist figure out of Donna's hands and plunked it in the rocking chair. "I'd appreciate it if you'd mind your own business, too."

Donna blinked. "What's your problem? I wasn't hurting Rosie. I was only trying to help."

Tabby moved toward the window, though she didn't know why. It was dark outside, and there was nothing to look at but the inky black sky. "I've had about enough of your opinions to last all year," she fumed.

Donna joined Tabby at the window. "I thought your lesson went really well. What's got you so uptight?"

Tabby turned to face her. "I'm not uptight. I'm irritated."

"With me?"

Tabby nodded. "You like him, don't you?"

"Who?"

"Seth. I'm talking about Seth Beyers!"

Donna tipped her head. "Huh?"

"Don't play dumb. You know perfectly well who I mean, and why I think you like him."

"I think Seth's a nice guy, but—"

"Are you interested in him romantically?"

"Romantically?" Donna frowned. "You've gotta be kidding."

Tabby sniffed deeply. "No, I'm not. You hung around him all night and kept asking all sorts of dumb questions."

Donna's forehead wrinkled. "You're really serious, aren't you?"

"I sure am."

"I think we'd better have a little talk about this. Let's sit down." Donna motioned toward the couch.

Tabby didn't budge. "There's nothing to talk about."

"I think there is."

"Whatever," Tabby mumbled with a shrug.

Donna sat on the couch, but Tabby opted for the rocking chair, lifting Rosie up, then placing the dummy in her lap after she was seated.

"I'm not trying to steal your guy," Donna insisted. "He's not my type, and even if he were, you should know that I'd never sabotage my best friend."

The rocking chair creaked as Tabby shifted, then she began to pump her legs back and forth. "Seth is not my guy."

A smile played at the corner of Donna's lips. "Maybe not now, but I think he'd like to be."

Tabby folded her arms across her chest and scowled. "Fat chance."

"There might be, if you'd meet him halfway."

"Like you did tonight—with twenty questions and goofy remarks?"

"I was only trying to help."

"How?"

"Before Seth arrived, you said you were nervous."

"And?"

"I was trying to put you at ease."

"By butting in every few minutes?" Tabby gulped and tried to regain her composure. "How was that supposed to put me at ease?"

Before Donna could say anything, Tabby stood up. "All you succeeded in doing tonight was making me more nervous."

"Sorry."

Donna's soft-spoken apology was Tabby's undoing. She raced to the couch, leaned over, and wrapped her friend in a bear hug. "I'm sorry, too. I—I'm just not myself these days. I think maybe I. . ." Her voice trailed off, and she blinked away tears threatening to spill over. "Let's forget about tonight, okay?"

Donna nodded. "Just don't let it ruin anything between you and Seth."

Tabby groaned. "There's nothing to ruin. As I said before, there isn't anything going on. Seth and I are just friends—at least I think we are. Maybe our relationship is strictly business."

Donna shrugged. "Whatever you say."

"I think I'll take my next ventriloquist lesson at Seth's shop," Tabby said as

186

she started toward her room. "Tonight made me fully aware that I'm not even ready for an audience of one yet."

❧

Seth wasn't the least bit surprised when Tabby called the following week and asked to have her next lesson at his place of business. Her friend Donna had turned out to be more than a helpful audience, and he was sure that was the reason for the change of plans. The way he saw it, Donna had actually been a deterrent, and it had been obvious that her constant interruptions made Tabby uptight and less able to grasp what he was trying to teach her. Even though they might be interrupted by a phone call or two, Beyers' Ventriloquist Studio was probably the best place to have Tabby's private lessons.

A glance at the clock told Seth it was almost seven. That was when Tabby had agreed to come over. His shop was closed for the day, so they should have all the privacy they needed.

"She'll be here any minute," he mumbled. "I'd better get this place cleaned up a bit."

Not that it was all that dirty, but at least it would give him something to do while he waited. If things went really well, he planned to ask her on a date, and truthfully, he was more than a little anxious about it. What if she turned him down? Could his male ego take the rejection, especially when he'd planned everything out so carefully?

Seth grabbed a broom out of the storage closet and started sweeping up a pile of sawdust left over from a repair job he'd recently done on an all-wooden dummy brought in a few weeks ago.

As he worked, he glanced over at Rudy Right, sitting in a folding chair nearby. "Well, little buddy, your girlfriend, Rosie, ought to be here any minute. I sure hope you're not as nervous as I am."

The wooden-headed dummy sat motionless, glass eyes staring straight ahead.

"So you're not talking today, huh?" Seth said with a shake of his head. "I'll bet you won't be able to keep your slot jaw shut once Tabby and her vent pal arrive."

Talking to Rudy like this was nothing new for Seth. He found that he rather enjoyed the one-way conversation. It was good therapy to talk things out with yourself, even if you were looking at a dummy when you spoke. He was glad there was no one around to witness the scene, though. If there had been, he might be accused of being a bit eccentric.

Seth chuckled. "Maybe I am kind of an oddball, but at least I'm having fun at my profession."

The bell above his shop door jingled, disrupting his one-way conversation.

He grinned when Tabby stepped into the room, carrying Rosie in her arms. "Hi, Tabby."

"I–I hope I'm not l–late," she said. "Traffic was r–really bad."

Seth glanced at the clock again. "Nope, you're right on time."

"Are—are you r–ready for my l–lesson? You l–look kind of b–busy."

"Oh, you mean this?" Seth lifted the broom. "I was just killing time till you got here. My shop gets pretty dirty after I've been working on a dummy."

She nodded. "I g–guess it w–would."

Seth put the broom back in the closet and turned to face Tabby. "Are you ready for lesson number two?"

"I–I th–think so."

"Let's get started then." He motioned toward one of the folding chairs. "Have a seat and I'll get my notes."

&

Tabby watched as Seth went to his desk and shuffled through a stack of papers. *Why is he taking time out of his busy schedule to work with me?* she asked herself. *I'm sure he has much better things to do than give some introverted, stuttering woman private ventriloquist lessons.*

"Okay, all set." Seth dropped into a chair and graced her with a pleasant smile. "Did you get a chance to practice your near and far voices?"

"I p–practiced a little."

"How about a demonstration then?"

"N–n–now?"

"Sure, now's as good a time as any." Seth pointed at Rosie. "If it would be any easier, you can talk through her instead of a pretend object or the telephone."

"How c–can I do th–that?" Tabby asked. "If I t–talk for R–Rosie, won't that be m–my near v–voice?"

Seth scratched his head. "Good point. I'll tell you what—why don't you set Rosie on a chair across the room, then talk for her. Make it sound as though her voice is coming from over there, and not where you're sitting."

Tabby bit down on her bottom lip and squeezed her eyes tightly shut. She wasn't sure she could do what Seth was asking, and she certainly didn't want to make a fool of herself. She'd already done that a few times in Seth's presence.

"You can do this," Seth urged. "Just give it a try."

Tabby opened her eyes and blew out the breath she'd been holding. "All r–right." She stood up and carried Rosie and a chair across the room, then placed the dummy down and returned to her own seat. "Hey, how come you put me way over here?" she made Rosie say in a childlike voice.

"You're in time-out."

"That's not fair, I'm just a dummy. Dummies should never be in time-out."

"Oh, and why's that?"

"Dummies are too dumb to know how to behave."

Tabby opened her mouth, but Seth's round of applause stopped her. She turned to look at him and was surprised when he gave her "thumbs-up."

"D–did I do o–okay?"

He grinned from ear to ear. "It was more than 'okay.' It was fantastic, and you never stuttered once. I'm proud of you, Tabby."

Tabby could feel the warmth of a blush as it started at her neckline and crept upward. She wasn't used to such compliments and was unsure how to respond.

"In all the years I've been teaching ventriloquism, I don't think I have ever met anyone who caught on as quickly as you," Seth said sincerely. "You mastered the basics like they were nothing, and now this—it's totally awesome!"

"You really th–think so?"

"I know so. Why, you—"

Seth's words were cut off when the shop door opened, jingling the bell. In walked Cheryl Stone, the attractive redhead who had demonstrated her talents at Seth's beginning ventriloquism workshop, where Tabby first met him.

Cheryl gave Seth a smile so bright Tabby was sure the sun must still be shining. "Hi, Seth, I was in the neighborhood and saw your lights on. I was wondering if you've finished that new granny figure for me yet?"

Seth gave Tabby an apologetic look. "Sorry about the interruption," he whispered. "I wasn't expecting anyone else tonight, and I forgot to put the closed sign in my window."

"It's o–okay," Tabby murmured. "I'll j–just w–wait over th–there with R–Rosie w–while you take c–care of b–business." She was stuttering heavily again, and it made her uncomfortable.

Seth nodded. "This will only take a minute."

Tabby moved quickly toward Rosie, hoping Cheryl wouldn't stay long. She watched painfully as the vibrant young woman chatted nonstop and batted her eyelashes at Seth. *She likes him, I can tell. I wonder if they've been seeing each other socially.*

Tabby shook her head. It was none of her business who Seth chose to see. Besides, if she were being totally honest, she'd have to admit that Seth and Cheryl did make a striking pair. They were both redheads, had bubbling personalities, and could do ventriloquism. What more could Seth ask for in a woman?

Chapter 10

It was nearly half an hour later when Cheryl finally walked out the door. Seth gave Tabby an apologetic look. "Sorry about that. Guess she's a little anxious to get her new dummy." He offered Tabby one of the most beautiful smiles she'd ever seen. "Before we continue with your lesson, I'd like to ask you a question."

Her heart quickened. Why was he staring at her that way? She swallowed against the tightening in her throat. "What question?" she squeaked.

Seth dropped into the seat beside her. "I have to go to Seattle tomorrow—to pick up an old dummy at the Dummy Depot. I was wondering if you'd like to go along."

Tabby's mouth went dry. He was asking her to go to Seattle. Was this a date? No, it couldn't be. Seth wouldn't want to go out with someone as plain as her. Why didn't he ask someone like cute Cheryl Stone? From the way the redhead kept flirting with him, Tabby was sure she would have jumped at the chance.

"Tabby?" Seth's deep voice cut into her thoughts.

"H–huh?"

"Are you busy tomorrow? Would you like to go to Seattle?"

She blinked. "Really? You w–want m–me to go along?"

He nodded. "I thought after I finish my business at the Dummy Depot we could go down by the waterfront. Maybe eat lunch at Ivar's Fish Bar and check out some of the gift shops along the wharf. I think it would be fun, don't you?"

Tabby gazed at the floor as she mulled this idea over. Tomorrow was Saturday. She wouldn't be working, and she had no other plans. She hadn't been to the Seattle waterfront in ages. Despite the amount of people usually there, it wasn't closed in the way so many of the buildings in Seattle Center were. The waterfront was open and smelled salty like the sea. Besides, it was an opportunity to spend an entire day with Seth.

"Tabby?"

She looked up. "Y–yes. I'd l–like to go."

❧

Tabby didn't sleep well that night. Excitement over spending a whole day with Seth occupied her thoughts and kept her tossing and turning. She was sure Seth wouldn't appreciate her taking Rosie to talk through, but she was concerned about her stuttering. Seth had told her several times that her speech impediment didn't bother him. It bothered her, though—a lot. She'd have given nearly anything to be confident and capable like normal people.

If only God hadn't made me so different, she wrote in her journal before turning off the light by her bed.

Tabby let her head fall back as she leaned into the pillow. *Maybe it wasn't God who made me different. It's all Lois's fault. If she just wasn't so beautiful and confident—everything Mom and Dad want in a daughter—everything I'm not.* She squeezed her eyes tightly shut. *Guess I can't really blame Lois, either. She can't help being beautiful and confident. It would take a miracle to make Mom and Dad love me the way they do her. They think I'm a failure.*

The thrill of her upcoming date with Seth was overshadowed by pain. She needed to work on her attitude. It wasn't a good Christian example, not even to herself. She released a shuddering sigh, whispered a short prayer asking God to help her accept things as they were, then drifted off to sleep.

～✦～

When Tabby entered the kitchen the following morning, she found Donna sitting at the table, sketching a black-and-white picture of a bowl of fruit.

"All ready for your big date?"

Tabby shrugged. "It's not a real date."

"What would you call it?"

"I'd call it a day in Seattle to—" She giggled. "Maybe it is kind of a date."

Donna laughed, too. "You came home last night all excited about going, and it sure sounded like a date to me. I'm kind of surprised, though."

"About what?"

"I didn't think you liked Seattle."

Tabby dropped into a chair. "I don't like the Seattle Center, or shopping downtown, but we're going to the waterfront. I love it there, even with all the people."

Donna grinned. "I think you'd go to the moon and back if Seth Beyers was going."

"Don't even go there," Tabby warned. "I've told you before, Seth and I are just friends."

Donna shrugged. "Whatever you say."

Tabby glanced at the clock above the refrigerator. "Seth will be here in an hour, and I still need to eat breakfast, shower, and find something to wear." She reached for a banana from the fruit bowl in the center of the table.

"Hey! You're destroying my picture! Why don't you fix a fried egg or something?"

Tabby pulled the peel off the banana and took a bite. "Eggs have too much artery-clogging cholesterol. Fruit's better for you." She glanced at Donna's drawing. "Besides, you've already got some bananas sketched, so you shouldn't miss this one."

Donna puckered her lips. "You never worry about cholesterol when you're chomping down a burger or some greasy fries."

Tabby gave her a silly grin. "Guess you've got me there."

"How'd the lesson go yesterday? You never really said," Donna asked.

Tabby was tempted to tell her about Cheryl's interruption and how much it had bothered her to see the two redheads talking and laughing together. She knew it would only lead to further accusations about her being interested in Seth.

She flicked an imaginary piece of lint from the sleeve of her robe and replied, "It went fine."

"Great. I'm glad."

Tabby felt a stab of guilt pierce her heart. She was lying to her best friend. Well, not lying exactly, just not telling the whole story. "Seth got an unexpected customer, and we were interrupted before we really got much done."

"But you continued on with the lesson after they left, didn't you?"

Tabby grabbed an orange from the fruit bowl and began to strip away the peel. "The customer was a redheaded woman named Cheryl. I think Seth likes her."

"But it's you he invited to Seattle," Donna reminded.

"He probably feels sorry for me."

Donna dropped her pencil to the table. "Is there any hope for you at all?"

Tabby sighed. "I wish I knew. Sometimes I think there might be, and other times I'm so full of self-doubts."

"What makes you think Seth likes this redhead, anyway?" Donna asked.

"She's cute, talented, and outgoing. What guy wouldn't like that?" Tabby wrinkled her nose. "They looked like a pair of matching bookends."

Donna snickered. "Well, there you have it! If Seth can look at this redheaded gal and see himself, then he's bound to fall head over heels in love with her."

Tabby pushed away from the table. "Seth and Cheryl make a perfect couple, and I'm just a millstone around Seth's neck."

"If he saw you as a millstone, he sure wouldn't be asking you out. Normal people don't go around asking millstones to accompany them to Seattle for the day."

Tabby stared off into space. "Maybe you're right."

❧

Seth arrived on time. Not wishing to give Donna the chance to say anything to him, Tabby raced out the front door and climbed into his Jeep before he even had a chance to get out.

"I was planning to come in and get you," Seth said as she slid into the passenger seat.

She smiled shyly. "That's okay. I was r–ready, so I f–figured I may as w–well s–save you the b–bother."

Seth smiled. "You look nice and comfortable."

Tabby glanced down at her faded blue jeans and peach-colored sweatshirt, wondering if she was dressed too casually. Maybe she should have chosen something else. She considered Seth for a moment. He was wearing a pair of perfectly pressed khaki-colored pants and a black polo shirt. His hair was combed neatly in place, parted on the left side. He looked way too good to be seen with someone as dowdy as her.

"So, w–where exactly is th–this Dummy Depot, and w–what kind of d–dummy are you b–buying there?" she asked, hoping to drag her thoughts away from how great Seth looked today.

Seth pulled away from the curb. "The Dummy Depot sells mostly used dummies. Harry Marks, the guy who runs the place, recently got one in that needs some repairs. He asked if I'd come get it, since his car isn't running and he didn't want to catch a bus to Tacoma. I thought it might be kind of nice to mix a little pleasure with business," Seth said, giving Tabby another one of his heart-melting smiles.

Tabby nodded. "Makes sense to me." She leaned her head against the headrest and released a contented sigh. Maybe he really did want to be with her. Maybe there was a chance that. . .

"Have you known Donna long?" Seth asked, breaking into her thoughts.

"Huh?"

"How long have you and Donna been friends?"

"Ever since we w–were kids. Her folks m–moved next-door to us when we were b–both two."

"Tell me a little about your family," he pried.

"There's nothing m–much to tell."

"There has to be something." Seth tapped the steering wheel with his long fingers. "Do your folks live nearby? Do you have any brothers and sisters?"

Tabby swallowed hard. The last thing she wanted to do was talk about her family. This was supposed to be a fun day, wasn't it? "My—uh—p–parents live in Olympia, and I h–have one s–sister. She l–lives in a high-rise apartment in d–downtown Tacoma, and sh–she's a secretary. There's n–nothing m–more to tell."

"You're lucky to have a sister," Seth commented. "I grew up as an only child. My folks were killed in a car wreck when I was fourteen, and my grandparents took me in."

"I'm so s–sorry," she murmured.

"Grandma and Grandpa Beyers were good to me, though. They taught me about Christ and helped me learn to use my talents for Him." Seth smiled. "I'll never forget the day Grandpa informed me that when he and Grandma were gone, the house would be mine."

Tabby knew the house he was referring to was the one he lived in now. The basement had been converted into his ventriloquist shop. Seth had told her that much when she'd had her lesson the evening before. What he hadn't told her was that the house had been his grandparents', or that they'd passed away.

"I'm s–sorry your g–grandparents aren't l–living anymore. It must be h–hard not to h–have any family," she said with feeling. As much as she disliked many of the things her own family said or did, she couldn't imagine what it must have been like growing up as an only child or not having her parents around at all, even if they did make her feel like dirt most of the time.

Seth chuckled. "Grandma and Grandpa aren't dead yet."

"They're n–not?"

"No, they moved into a retirement home a few years ago. Said the old house was too much for them to handle." Seth cast her a sidelong glance. "Grandpa thought the place would be well suited to my business, not to mention a great place to raise a bunch of kids someday."

Tabby wasn't sure how to respond to that statement. She'd always dreamed of having a big family herself, but the possibility didn't seem very likely.

"There sure is a l–lot of traffic on the f–freeway today, isn't there?" she said, changing the subject again.

Seth nodded. "Always is a steady flow of cars on I–5, but the weekends are even worse. Things will level off a bit once we get away from the city."

Tabby turned to look out the passenger window. They had just entered the freeway and were traveling over a new overpass. As busy as the freeway was here, she knew it would be even worse once they got closer to Seattle. It made her thankful Seth was driving. She'd be a ball of nerves if she were in the driver's seat.

"Mind if I put a cassette in the tape player?" Seth asked.

"Go a–ahead."

When the soft strains of a familiar Christian song came on, Tabby smiled. Seth liked the same kind of music she did. She closed her eyes and felt her body begin to relax. She wasn't sure if it was because of Seth's rich baritone accompanying the tape, or simply the fact that she was with him today. Tabby was glad she'd accepted Seth's invitation to go to Seattle.

❧

Seth glanced over at Tabby. Her eyes were shut, and she was sitting silent and still. He wished he could read her mind. Find out what thoughts were circling around in her head. *She reminds me of a broken toy. She didn't have much to say about her family. I wonder if something from her past is the reason for her terrible shyness. If she's hurting, then maybe her heart can be mended. There's even a chance she could actually be better than new.*

The only trouble was, Seth wasn't sure how to find out what kind of pain from the past held Tabby in its grip. She was a mystery he wanted to solve. Since Tabby seemed so reserved and unable to communicate her feelings to him, maybe he should talk to Donna about it. Tabby said they'd been friends most of their lives. Surely Donna would know what made Tabitha Johnson tick. A little bit of insight might help him know what direction to take in making her over into his perfect woman.

Seth hugged the knowledge to himself and smiled. *As soon as I get the chance, I'll get together with Donna and find out what gives.*

Chapter 11

The Dummy Depot was located in downtown Seattle, in a small shop near the busy shopping area. While Seth talked business with the owner, Tabby walked around the room studying all the figures for sale. It didn't take long to realize she could have bought a used dummy for half the price she'd paid for Rosie. She consoled herself with the fact that most of the figures looked well-used and had lost their sparkle. Rosie, on the other hand, was brand new, without a scratch, dent, or paint chip on her entire little body. Besides, she'd purchased the dummy with the birthday gift certificate from Donna and her parents. They'd wanted her to have a new one or else they wouldn't have given it to her.

"Ready to go?" Seth asked suddenly.

"Sure, if y–you are."

Holding the damaged dummy under one arm, Seth opened the shop door with his free hand. "I don't know about you, but I'm getting hungry. I think I can actually smell those fish-and-chips wafting up from the waterfront."

Tabby's mouth watered at the mention of eating succulent cod, deep-fried to perfection, and golden brown fries, dipped in tangy fry sauce. "Guess I'm kinda h–hungry, too," she admitted.

Ten minutes later they were parking in one of the huge lots near the waterfront. Seth reached for Tabby's hand as they crossed the street with the light.

Her hand tingled with his touch. *This does feel like a date,* she thought, though she didn't have a whole lot to gauge it by, considering she'd only been on a couple of dates since she graduated from high school. Those had been set up by Donna, and none of the guys had held her hand or acted the least bit interested in her. Of course, she hadn't said more than a few words, and those had come out in a mishmash of stammering and stuttering.

Groups of people were milling about the waterfront. Tabby clung tightly to Seth's hand, not wishing to get separated. As they headed down the sidewalk toward one of the fish bars, she spotted a young man walking a few feet ahead of them. He had two sizable holes in the back of his faded blue jeans, and long, scraggly brown hair hung halfway down the back of his discolored orange T-shirt. That was not what drew her attention to him, however. What made this man so unique was the colorful parrot sitting on his shoulder. With each step the man took, the parrot would either let out an ear-piercing squawk or imitate something someone had just said.

"I'm hungry! I'm hungry!" the feathered creature screeched. "The ferry's coming! The ferry's coming! Awk!"

Tabby glanced to her left. Sure enough, the Vashon Island ferry was heading toward one of the piers. Enthusiastic children jumped up and down, hollering that the ferry was coming, and the noisy parrot kept right on mimicking.

"I don't know who's more interesting—that guy with the long hair or his obnoxious bird," Seth whispered to Tabby.

She giggled. "The b–bird has my vote."

"I heard this story about a guy who owned a belligerent parrot," Seth remarked.

She looked up at him expectantly. "And?"

"The parrot had a bad attitude, not to mention a very foul mouth."

"So, what h–happened?"

"The guy tried everything from playing soft music to saying only polite words in front of the bird, but nothing worked at all."

"Did he s–sell the parrot then?"

Seth shook his head. "Nope. He put him in the freezer."

Tabby's mouth dropped open. "The freezer?"

"Yep, for about five minutes. When he opened the door again, the parrot calmly stepped out onto the guy's shoulder, a changed bird."

"He didn't use b–bad words anymore?"

"Nope. In fact, the parrot said, 'I'm truly sorry for being so rude.' Then the colorful creature added, 'Say, I saw a naked chicken in that icebox. What'd that poor bird do?' "

Tabby laughed, feeling happy and carefree and wishing the fun of today could last forever.

Seth sobered, nodding toward the edge of the sidewalk. "You see all kinds down here."

Tabby watched with interest as a group of peddlers offered their wares to anyone who would listen. Everything from costume jewelry to painted T-shirts was being sold. Several men lay on the grass, holding signs announcing that they were out of work and needed money. An empty coffee can sat nearby—a place for donations. Tabby thought it sad to see people who were homeless or out of a job, reduced to begging. These few along the waterfront were just the tip of the iceberg, too.

"It's hard to distinguish between who really needs help and who's merely panhandling," Seth whispered in her ear.

She nodded, wondering if he could read her mind.

"Ivar's has a long line of people waiting to get in," Seth said. "Is it okay with you if we try Steamer's Fish Bar instead?"

Tabby glanced at the restaurant he'd mentioned. The aroma of deep-fried fish drifted out the open door and filled her senses. "One fish-and-chips place is probably as good as another," she replied.

They entered the restaurant and placed their orders at the counter, then found a seat near a window overlooking the water. Tabby watched in fascination as several boats pulled away from the dock, taking tourists on a journey through Puget Sound Bay. It was a beautiful, sunny day—perfect weather for boating.

"Would you like to go?"

Seth's sudden question drew Tabby's attention away from the window. "G—go? But we j—just got here," she said, frowning.

Seth grinned. "I didn't mean go home. I meant, would you like to go for a ride on one of those tour boats you're watching so intently? We could do that after we eat, instead of browsing through the gift shops."

"Do w—we have t—time for th—that?"

Seth glanced at his watch. "I don't see why not. My shop's closed for the day, and I don't have to be back at any set time. How about you?"

Tabby shook her head. "I have all d—day."

"Then would you like me to see about getting a couple of tour-boat tickets?"

Tabby felt the tension begin to seep from her body as she reached for her glass of lemonade. "Actually, if I h—had a choice, I think I'd r—rather take the ferry over to V—Vashon, then ferry from there b—back to Tacoma."

Seth's face brightened. "Now that's a great idea! I haven't ridden the ferry in quite a while."

❧

Tabby hung tightly to the rail as she leaned over to stare into the choppy waters of Puget Sound Bay. The wind whipped against her face, slapping the ends of her hair in every direction. It was exhilarating, and she felt very much alive. Seagulls soared in the cloudless sky, squawking and screeching, as though vying for the attention of everyone on board the ferry. It was a peaceful scene, and Tabby felt a deep sense of contentment fill her soul.

Seth was standing directly behind Tabby, and he leaned into her, wrapping his arms around her waist. "Warm enough?" he asked, his mouth pressed against her ear.

Tabby shivered, and she knew it was not from the cool breeze. "I'm fine."

Seth rested his chin on top of her head. "This was a great idea. I've had a lot of fun today."

"Me, too," she murmured.

"It doesn't have to end when we dock at Point Defiance."

"It doesn't?"

"Nope. We could have dinner at the Harbor Lights."

Tabby glanced down at her outfit and grimaced. "I'm not exactly dressed for a fancy restaurant, Seth."

He chuckled. "Me neither, but I don't think it matters much. A lot of boaters pull into the docks at the restaurants along Tacoma's waterfront. I'm sure many people will be dressed as casually as we are."

Tabby shrugged. She was having such a good time and didn't want the day to end yet. "Okay. . .if you're sure."

"I'm positive," Seth said, nuzzling her neck.

She sucked in her breath. If this was a dream, she hoped it would last forever.

⁓

Seth sat directly across from Tabby, studying her instead of the menu he held in his hands. She was gazing intently at her own menu, which gave him the perfect opportunity to look at her without being noticed. When had she taken on such a glow? When had her eyes begun to sparkle? He shook his head. Maybe it was just the reflection from the candle in the center of the table. Maybe he was imagining things.

Tabby looked up and caught him staring. "What's wrong?" she asked with furrowed brows. "Don't you see anything you like?"

Seth's lips curved into a slow smile.

"What's so funny?"

He reached across the table and grasped her hand. "Two things are making me smile."

She gave him a quizzical look.

"You haven't stuttered once since we left Seattle."

Tabby's face turned crimson, making Seth wonder if he should have said anything. "I didn't mean to embarrass you. It makes me happy to know you're finally beginning to relax in my presence."

She returned his smile. "I do feel pretty calm tonight."

He ran his thumb across the top of her hand and felt relief when she didn't pull it away.

"You said there were two things making you smile. What's the second one?"

He leaned farther across the table. "Just looking at you makes me smile."

A tiny frown marred her forehead. "Am I that goofy looking?"

Seth shook his head. "No, of course not! In fact, I was sitting here thinking how beautiful you look in the candlelight."

"No one has ever c–called me b–beautiful before," she said, a blush staining her cheeks.

Great! Now she's stuttering again. So much for making her feel relaxed. Seth dropped her hand and picked up his menu. "Guess I'd better decide what to order before our waiter comes back. Have you found anything you like yet?"

Tabby nodded. "I think I'll have a crab salad."

"You can order whatever you want," Seth said quickly. "Lobster, steak, or prime rib—just say the word."

"Crab salad is all I want," she insisted.

Seth was about to comment when the waiter returned to their table.

"Have you two decided?" the young man asked.

"I'll have prime rib, and the lady wants a crab salad." Seth handed both menus back to the waiter. "I think we'll have two glasses of iced tea as well."

As soon as the waiter left, Seth reached for Tabby's hand again. "I didn't mean to make you blush a few minutes ago. How come you always do that, anyway?"

"Do what?"

"Turn red like a cherry and hang your head whenever you're paid a compliment."

Her forehead wrinkled. "I–I don't know. I'm not used to getting compliments. You don't have to try and make me feel good, you know."

"Is that what you think—that I'm just trying to make you feel good?"

"Well, isn't it?"

His throat tightened. "I don't pass out false compliments so someone will feel good, Tabby."

Her gaze dropped to the tablecloth. "Let's forget it, okay?"

Seth offered up a silent prayer. *Should I let this drop, Lord, or should I try to convince her that I'm really interested in her as a woman, and that. . .* He swallowed hard. What did he really want from this relationship? When he'd first met Tabby, he'd felt sorry for her. He could sense her need for encouragement and maybe even a friend, but when had he started thinking of her as a woman and not just someone to help? There was a great yearning, deep within him, and he wondered if it could be filled by a woman's love. Tabby might be that woman. He had thought about her nearly every day since they first met. That had to mean something, didn't it?

Seth felt a sense of peace settle over him as he heard the words in his head say, *Go slow, Seth. Go slow.*

Chapter 12

"I can't believe you were gone all day!" Donna exclaimed when Tabby entered their apartment.

Tabby dropped to the couch beside her and released a sigh of contentment. "Today was probably the best day of my life."

Donna's eyebrows shot up. "Did Seth kiss you?"

"Of course not!"

"You're turning red like a radish. He must have kissed you." Donna poked Tabby in the ribs. "Tell me all about it, and don't leave out one single detail."

Tabby slid out of Donna's reach. "Don't get so excited. There's not that much to tell."

"Then start with when Seth picked you up this morning and end with a detailed description of his kiss."

Tabby grimaced. "I told you, there was no kiss!" Her inexperience with men was an embarrassment. If she'd been more coy, like that cute little redhead, Cheryl, maybe Seth would have kissed her.

"Then what has you glowing like a Christmas tree?" Donna asked, pulling Tabby out of her musings.

"Seth is a lot of fun, and I had a good time today," she mumbled.

Donna released a sigh. "That sure doesn't tell me much."

Tabby leaned her head against the back of the couch. "Let's see. . . We drove to Seattle, and freeway traffic was terrible." A long pause followed.

"And?"

"When we got to Seattle, we went to the Dummy Depot to pick up a ventriloquist figure Seth needs to repair." Another long pause.

"Then what?"

"We went down to the waterfront, where we had a great lunch of fish-and-chips."

"You must have done more than that. You've been gone all day."

Tabby glanced at her watch and wrinkled her nose. "It's only a little after eight. Besides, you're not my mother, and I'm not on any kind of a curfew."

Donna squinted her eyes. "You look like you're on cloud nine, so I figure you must have done something really exciting today."

Tabby grinned. "We did. We rode the ferry from Seattle to Vashon Island, then we caught another one to Point Defiance." She closed her eyes and thought about Seth's arms around her waist and his mouth pressed against her ear. She could still feel his warm breath on her neck and smell his woodsy aftershave lotion. That part of the day had been the most exciting thing of all. She wasn't about to share such a private moment with Donna—even if she was her best friend.

"What'd you do after you left Point Defiance?" Donna asked.

"We went to dinner at the Harbor Lights."

Donna let out a low whistle. "Wow! Things must be getting pretty serious between you two. The Harbor Lights costs big bucks!"

Tabby groaned. "It's not that expensive. Besides, going there doesn't mean anything special."

Donna gave her a knowing look. "Yeah, right."

"It's true," Tabby insisted. "I'm the queen of simplicity, so why would a great guy like Seth be attracted to someone like me?"

Donna clicked her tongue. "Are you ever going to see your true potential?"

Crossing her arms in front of her chest, Tabby shrugged. "I don't know. Maybe I do have some worth."

❧

After their day in Seattle, Tabby had hoped Seth might call and ask her out again. That would have let her know if he really was interested in seeing her on a personal level or not. However, the week went by without a single word from him. Today was Thursday, and she had another, previously scheduled ventriloquism lesson that evening. Thinking about it had very little appeal, though. If only Seth had called. If only. . .

As she drove across town, Tabby forced her thoughts away from Seth and onto the routine she'd been practicing with Rosie. She was determined to do her very best this time. Even if Seth never saw her as a desirable woman, at least she could dazzle the socks off him with her new talent.

When she arrived at Seth's, Tabby was relieved to see he had no customers. The thought of performing before an audience held no appeal whatsoever.

Seth greeted her with a warm smile. "I'll be with you in just a minute. I have to make a few phone calls."

Tabby nodded and took a seat, placing Rosie on her lap. Mentally, she began to rehearse the lines of her routine, hoping she had them memorized so well she wouldn't have to use her notes. Watching Seth as he stood across the room talking on the phone was a big enough distraction, but when the bell above the shop door rang, announcing a customer, Tabby froze.

In walked Cheryl Stone carrying her dummy, Oscar. She hurried past Tabby as though she hadn't even seen her and rushed up to Seth just as he was hanging up the phone. "Seth, you've got to help me!" she exclaimed.

"What do you need help with?" Seth asked.

"Oscar's mouth is stuck in the open position, and I can't get it to work." Cheryl handed him the dummy. "I'm supposed to do a vent routine at a family gathering tonight, and I was hoping you'd have time to fix Oscar for me."

Seth glanced at Tabby. "Actually, I was just about to begin teaching a lesson. Why don't you use your new dummy tonight—the one you recently bought from me?"

Cheryl shook her head. "I haven't gotten used to that one yet. Besides, Oscar's so cute, he's always a hit wherever I perform."

"Have a seat then," Seth said, motioning toward the row of chairs along the wall where Tabby sat. "I'll take Oscar in the back room and see what I can do."

Cheryl smiled sweetly. "Thank you, Seth. You're the nicest man."

The chocolate bar Tabby had eaten on her drive over to Seth's suddenly felt like a lump of clay in her stomach. Cheryl obviously had her eye on Seth. For all Tabby knew, he might have more than a passing interest in the vibrant redhead, too.

Cheryl took a seat next to Tabby, opened her purse, withdrew a nail file, and began to shape her nails. The silence closing in around them was broken only by the steady ticking of the wall clock across the room and the irritating scrape of nail file against fingernails.

Should I say something to her? Tabby wondered. Just sitting here like this felt so awkward. Given her problem with stuttering, she decided that unless Cheryl spoke first, she would remain quiet.

Several minutes went by, and then Cheryl returned the nail file to her purse and turned toward Tabby. "Cute little dummy you've got there."

"Th–thanks."

"Are you here to see about getting it repaired?"

Tabby shook her head. "I–I'm t–taking l–lessons." She glanced toward the back room, hoping Seth would return soon. There was something about Cheryl's confidence and good looks that shattered any hope Tabby might have of ever becoming a successful ventriloquist, much less the object of Seth's affections.

Cheryl tapped her fingers along the arm of the chair. "I wonder what's taking so long? Seth must be having quite a time with Oscar's stubborn little mouth." She eyed Tabby curiously. "How long have you been taking ventriloquism lessons?"

"Not l–long."

"Guess you'll be at it for a while, what with your stuttering problem and all." Cheryl offered Tabby a sympathetic smile. "It must be difficult for you."

Hot tears stung Tabby's eyes as she squirmed in her seat, then hunkered down as if succumbing to a predator. She bit her lower lip to stop the flow of tears that seemed insistent on spilling onto her flaming cheeks. She was used to her family making fun of her speech impediment, but seeing the pity on Cheryl's face was almost worse than reproach.

Dear Lord, she prayed silently, *please help me say something without stuttering.*

With newfound courage, Tabby stuck her hand into the opening at the back of Rosie's overalls, grabbed the control stick, opened her own mouth slightly, and said in a falsetto voice, "Tabby may have a problem with shyness, but I don't stutter at all." It was true, Tabby noted with satisfaction. Whenever she did ventriloquism, the voice she used for her dummy never missed a syllable.

Cheryl leaned forward, squinting her eyes and watching intently as Tabby continued to make her dummy talk.

"My name's Rosie; what's yours?"

"Cheryl Stone, and my dummy, Oscar, is in there getting his mouth worked on." Cheryl pointed toward the room where Seth had disappeared.

Tabby smiled. She could hardly believe it, but Cheryl was actually talking to her dummy like it was real. Of course, Cheryl was a ventriloquist, and people who talked for two did seem to have the childlike ability to get into the whole dummy scene.

"How long have you been doing ventriloquism?" little Rosie asked Cheryl.

Cheryl smiled in response. "I learned the basics on my own a few years ago. Since I met Seth, he's taught me several advanced techniques."

I wonder what else he's taught you. Tabby opened Rosie's mouth, actually planning to voice the question, but Seth entered the room in the nick of time.

"I think Oscar's good to go," he said, handing the dummy to Cheryl.

Cheryl jumped up. "How can I ever thank you, Seth?" She stood on tiptoes and planted a kiss right on Seth's lips!

Tabby wasn't sure who was more surprised—she or Seth. He stood there for several seconds, face red and mouth hanging open. Finally, he grinned, embarrassed-like, then mumbled, "I'll send you a bill."

Cheryl giggled and gave his arm a squeeze. "You're so cute." As she started for the door, she called over her shoulder, "See you on Saturday, Seth!" The door clicked shut, and Cheryl Stone was gone.

Tabby wished she had the courage to ask Seth why he'd be seeing Cheryl on Saturday, but it didn't seem appropriate. Besides, she had no claim on him, and if he chose to date someone else, who was she to ask questions?

"Sorry about the interruption," Seth said in a business-like tone of voice. "We can begin now, if you're ready."

Tabby swallowed hard. Cheryl was gone, but the image of her lovely face rolled around in Tabby's mind. She'd been more than ready for a lesson when she came into Seth's shop, but now, after seeing the interchange between Seth and Cheryl, the only thing she was ready for was home!

Chapter 13

Seth eased into a chair and leaned forward until his head was resting in his hands. He couldn't believe how terrible Tabby's lesson had gone. Beside the fact that there had been an air of tension between them ever since Cheryl left, Tabby seemed unable to stay focused. What had gone wrong? Was he failing as a teacher, or was she simply losing interest in ventriloquism? Did she have any personal feelings for him, or had he read more into their Seattle trip than there actually was? Tabby seemed so relaxed that day, and when he'd held her hand, she hadn't pulled away. In fact, as near as he could tell, she'd enjoyed it as much as he had.

Seth groaned and stood up again. He wasn't sure how or even when it happened, but Tabitha Johnson definitely meant more to him than just someone to help. After seeing the way she was with her day care kids the other day, and after spending time with her in Seattle, he really was beginning to hope she was the woman he'd been waiting for. If he could only make Tabby see what potential she had. If she could just get past all that shyness and stuttering, he was sure she'd be perfect for him.

He moved toward the telephone. Tabby wouldn't be home yet. Maybe it was time for that talk with her friend.

Donna answered on the second ring. Seth quickly related the reason for his call, and a few minutes later he hung up the phone, happy in the knowledge that he'd be meeting Donna for lunch tomorrow. Between the two of them, maybe Tabby could become a confident woman who would use all her abilities to serve the Lord.

~

"I am so glad this is Friday," Tabby murmured, as she prepared to eat her sack lunch at one of the small tables where the day care kids often sat.

"Me, too," Donna agreed. She grabbed her sweater and umbrella and started for the door. "See you later."

"Hey, wait a minute," Tabby called. "Where are you going?"

"Out to lunch, and I'd better hurry."

"Say, why don't I join you?"

"See you at one." Donna waved and disappeared out the door before Tabby could say another word and without even answering her question.

Tabby's forehead wrinkled. Donna hardly ever went out to lunch on a weekday. When she did, she always arranged for one of their helpers to take over the day care so Tabby could come along. What was up, anyway?

Tabby snapped her fingers. "Maybe Donna has a date and doesn't want me to know about it. I'll bet there's a mystery man in my friend's life."

"Who are you talking to, Teacher?"

Tabby jerked her head at the sound of four-year-old Mary Stevens's sweet voice.

"I—uh—was kind of talking to myself."

Mary grinned. "Like you do when you use Roscoe or little Rosie?"

Tabby nodded. "Something like that." She patted the child on top of her curly blond head. "What are you doing up, Missy? It's nap time, you know."

The child nodded soberly. "I'm not sleepy."

"Maybe not, but you need to rest your eyes." Tabby placed her ham sandwich back inside its plastic wrapper and stood up. "Come on, sweetie, I'll walk you back to your sleeping mat."

❧

Seth tapped the edge of his water glass with the tip of his spoon as he waited impatiently for Donna to show up. She'd promised to meet him at Garrison's Deli shortly after noon. It was only a few doors down from the church where she and Tabby ran their day care center. It shouldn't take her more than a few minutes to get here.

He glanced at his watch again. Twelve-twenty. Where was she anyway? Maybe she'd forgotten. Maybe she'd changed her mind. He was just about to leave the table and go to the counter to place his order, when he saw Donna come rushing into the deli.

She waved, then hurried toward his table. Her face was flushed, and her dark curls looked windblown. "Sorry I'm late," she panted. "Just as I was leaving the day care, Tabby started plying me with all sorts of questions about where I was having lunch, and she even suggested she come along. I chose to ignore her and hurried out of the room. Then I got detained a few more minutes on my way out of the church."

Seth gave her a questioning look as she took the seat directly across from him.

"One of the kids' parents came to pick him up early. She stopped me on the steps to say Bobby had a dental appointment and she'd forgotten to tell us about it," Donna explained.

Seth nodded toward the counter. "I was about to order. Do you know what you want, or do you need a few minutes to look at the menu?"

"Chicken salad in pita bread and a glass of iced tea sounds good to me," she replied.

"I'll be right back," Seth said, pushing away from the table. He placed Donna's order first, then ordered a turkey club sandwich on whole wheat with a glass of apple juice for himself. When he returned to the table, he found Donna staring out the window.

"Looks like it could rain again," he noted.

She held up the umbrella she'd placed on one end of the table. "I came prepared."

Seth decided there was no point in wasting time talking about the weather. "I was wondering if we could discuss Tabby," he blurted out. "That day you came into my shop to get the gift certificate for Tabby's dummy, we agreed that we'd work together to help her. I've really been trying, but to tell you the truth, I kind of feel like a salmon swimming upstream."

Donna giggled. "How can I help?"

"I have a few questions for you," he answered.

"What do you want to know?"

"I've never met anyone quite as shy as Tabby," he said. "Can you tell me why that is and what makes her stutter?"

Donna drew in a deep breath and exhaled it with such force that her napkin blew off the table. "Whew. . .that's kind of a long story." She bent down to retrieve the napkin, then glanced at her watch. "This will have to be a scaled down version, because I have to be back at work by one."

Seth leaned forward with his elbows on the table. "I'm all ears."

"I've known Tabby ever since we were little tykes," Donna began. "Up until she turned six, Tabby was a fun-loving, outgoing child."

"What happened when she turned six?"

"Her sister was born." Donna grimaced. "Tabby's dad favored Lois right from the start. I can't explain why, but he started giving Tabby putdowns and harsh words. She turned inward, became introverted, and began to lack confidence in most areas of her life." She drummed her fingers along the edge of the table. "That's when she began stuttering."

Seth was about to reply, but their order was being called. He excused himself to pick up their food. When he returned to the table, Seth offered a word of prayer, and they both grabbed their sandwiches. "Do you think you can eat and talk at the same time?" he asked.

"Oh, sure, I've had lots of practice," Donna mumbled around her pita bread.

"I've noticed that Tabby stutters more at certain times, and other times she hardly stutters at all."

Donna nodded. "It has to do with how well she knows you, and how comfortable she feels in your presence."

"So, if Tabby felt more confident and had more self-esteem, she probably wouldn't stutter as much—or at all."

Donna shrugged. "Could be. Tabby's worst stuttering takes place when she's around her family. They intimidate her, and she's never learned to stand up for herself."

Seth took a swallow of apple juice, and his eyebrows furrowed. "Tabby doesn't stutter at all when she does ventriloquism. It's almost like she's a different person when she's speaking through her dummy."

Donna shrugged. "In a way, I guess she is."

"Just when I think I've got her figured out, she does something to muddle my brain."

"Like what?"

"Last night was a good example," Seth answered. "Tabby arrived at my shop for another lesson, and I thought she was in a good mood, ready to learn and all excited about it."

"She was excited," Donna agreed. "She's been enthusiastic about everything since the two of you went to Seattle."

Seth brightened some. "Really? I thought she'd had a good time, but I wasn't sure."

Donna grinned. "Tabby was on cloud nine when she came home that night." Her hand went quickly to her mouth. "Oops. . . Guess I wasn't supposed to tell you that."

Seth felt his face flush. That was the trouble with being fair skinned and redheaded. He flushed way too easily. *Tabby must have some feelings for me. At least she did until. . .*

"Tell me what happened last night to make you wonder about Tabby," Donna said, interrupting his thoughts.

He took a bite of his sandwich, then washed it down with more juice before answering. "As I said before, Tabby was in a good mood when she first came in."

"And?"

"Then an unexpected customer showed up, and after she left, Tabby closed up like a razor clam."

"Hmm. . ."

"Hmm. . .what?"

Donna frowned. "Tabby was in kind of a sour mood when she came home last night. I asked her what was wrong, and she mumbled something about not being able to compete with Cheryl." She eyed Seth speculatively. "Cheryl wouldn't happen to be that unexpected customer, would she?"

"Afraid so. Cheryl Stone is a confident young woman with lots of talent as a ventriloquist."

"Is she pretty?"

He nodded. Cheryl was beautiful, vivacious, and talented. *That perfect woman you've been looking for,* a little voice taunted. *If Cheryl is perfect, then why do I think I need to remake Tabby?*

"Will you be seeing Tabby again?" Donna asked.

He swallowed hard, searching for the right words. Did he love her? Did she love him? He enjoyed being with her, that much he knew. Was it love he was feeling, though? It was probably too soon to tell.

"I–I don't know if we'll see each other again," he finally answered. "Guess that all depends on Tabby."

"On whether she wants more lessons?" Donna asked.

Seth shrugged. "That and a few other things."

Donna didn't pry, and he was glad. He wasn't in the mood to try to explain his feelings for Tabitha Johnson, or this compelling need he felt to make her into the woman he thought he needed.

"Well," Donna said a few minutes later, "I really do need to get back to work." She finished her iced tea and stood up. "Thanks for lunch, Seth. I hope some of the things we've talked about have been helpful. Tabby's my best friend, and I care a lot about her." She looked at him pointedly. "She carries a lot of pain from the past. I don't want to see her hurt anymore."

Seth stood up, too. "My car's parked right out front. I'll walk you out," he said, making no reference to the possibility that he might add further hurt to Tabby's already battered mental state. He was so confused about everything right now, and some things were better left unsaid. Especially when he hadn't fully sorted out his feelings for her and didn't have a clue how she really felt about him.

❧

With a bag of trash in her arms, Tabby left Gail, their eighteen-year-old helper, in charge of the day care kids while she carried the garbage out to the curb. The garbage truck always came around three on Friday afternoons, which meant she still had enough time to get one more bag put out.

Tabby stepped up beside the two cans by the curb and had just opened the lid of one, when she heard voices coming from down the street. She turned her head to the right and froze in place, one hand holding the garbage can lid, the other clutching the plastic garbage bag.

She could see a man and woman standing outside Garrison's Deli. She'd have recognized them anywhere—Seth for his red hair, Donna for her high-pitched laugh. What were they doing together? Tabby's mouth dropped open like a broken hinge on a screen door. Her body began to sway. She blinked rapidly, hoping her eyes had deceived her. Seth was actually hugging her best friend!

Chapter 14

Tabby dropped the garbage sack into the can, slammed the lid down, whirled around, and bolted for the church. She didn't want Donna or Seth to see her. She had to think. . .to decide the best way to handle this little matter. Would it be better to come right out and ask Donna what she was doing with Seth, or should she merely ply her with a few questions, hoping the answers would come voluntarily?

Tabby returned to the day care center with a heavy heart. Were Seth and Donna seeing each other socially? Was he Donna's lunch date? Was he the mystery man in her best friend's life? As much as the truth might hurt, she had to know.

Tabby was setting out small tubs of modeling clay when Donna sauntered into the room humming "Jesus Loves Me." She looked about as blissful as a kitten with a ball of string, and not the least bit guilty, either.

"How was lunch?" Tabby asked after Donna had put her purse and umbrella in the desk drawer.

"It was good. I had pita bread stuffed with chicken salad."

"What did your date have?"

Donna spun around, and her eyebrows shot up. "My date?"

"Yeah, the person you met for lunch."

"Did I say I was meeting someone?"

Tabby shrugged. "Not in so many words, but you acted kind of secretive. Are you seeing some guy you don't want me to know about?"

Donna lowered herself into one of the kiddy chairs, keeping her eyes averted from Tabby's penetrating gaze. "Let's just say I'm checking him out. I need to see how well we get along. I want to find out what he's really like."

Tabby opened one of the clay lids and slapped it down on the table. "Why didn't you just ask me? I know exactly what he's like!"

Donna's forehead wrinkled, and she pursed her lips. "Since when do you have the inside scoop on our pastor's son?"

"Who?"

"Alex Hanson."

"Alex? What's Alex got to do with this?"

"I had lunch with Alex the Saturday you and Seth went to Seattle," Donna explained.

Tabby's insides began to quiver. What was going on here, anyway? "That's fine. I'm happy you finally agreed to go out with Alex, but what about today? Did you or did you not have lunch with someone over at Garrison's Deli?"

Donna's face grew red, and little beads of perspiration gathered on her forehead. "Well, I—"

"You don't have to hem and haw or beat around the bush with me." Tabby grunted. "I know perfectly well who you had lunch with today."

"You do?"

Tabby nodded. "I took some garbage outside a little while ago. I heard voices, and when I looked down the street, there stood Seth—with his arms around my best friend!" She flopped into a chair and buried her face in her hands.

Donna reached over and laid a hand on Tabby's trembling shoulder, but Tabby jerked it away. "How could you go behind my back like that?"

"You're wrong. Things aren't the way they appear."

Tabby snapped her head up. "Are you going to deny having lunch with Seth?"

"No, but—"

"Was it you and Seth standing in front of the deli?"

"Yes, but—"

"You can't argue the fact that he was hugging you, either, can you?"

Donna shook her head. "No, I can't deny any of those things, but I'm not the least bit interested in Seth. We've been through all this before, Tabby, and—"

"Just how do you explain the secret lunch. . .or that tender little embrace?"

Donna's eyes filled with tears. "I didn't want you to know I was meeting Seth, because I didn't want you to think we were ganging up on you."

Tabby bit her bottom lip, sucking it inside her mouth when she tasted blood. "In what way are you ganging up on me?"

"Can't we talk about this later? The kids will be up from their naps soon," Donna said, glancing toward the adjoining room.

Tabby lifted her arm, then held it so her watch was a few inches from Donna's face. "We still have three minutes. I think you can answer my question in that amount of time, don't you?"

Donna pulled a tissue from her skirt pocket and blew her nose. "Guess you don't leave me much choice."

Tabby's only response was a curt nod.

"It's like this. . .Seth was concerned about your actions last night. He said you didn't do well at your lesson, and that you seemed kinda remote. He's trying hard to help you overcome your shyness, and perfect your—"

"So the two of you are in cahoots, trying to fix poor, pitiful, timid Tabitha!" Tabby could feel the pulse hammering in her neck, and her hands had begun to shake.

Donna's eyelids fluttered. "Calm down. You'll wake the kids."

Tabby pointed to her watch. "It's almost time for them to get up anyway."

"That may be true, but you don't want to scare the little tykes with your screeching, do you?"

Tabby sniffed deeply. "Of course not. But I'm really upset right now, and I'm not sure who I should be angrier with—you or Seth."

Donna grimaced. "Sorry. I didn't mean to get you all riled up. I just thought—"

Donna's sentence was interrupted when a group of children came trooping into the room, chattering and giggling all the way to the table.

Donna gave Tabby a look. For now, this conversation was over.

⋙⋘

Seth hung up the phone, wondering why he'd ever agreed to recruit another ventriloquist to perform with him at the Clearview Church Family Crusade. The female ventriloquist who'd originally been scheduled to perform had just canceled out. Now they were asking him to find a replacement.

Seth knew plenty of ventriloquists. The trouble was, it was so last-minute. The crusade was set for next Friday night, and finding someone at this late date would be next to impossible. If only he could come up with. . .

The bell above his shop door rang sharply as a customer entered the shop. It was almost closing time, and the last thing Seth needed was one more problem he didn't know how to fix. He glanced up, and his heart seemed as though it had quit beating. It was Tabby, and she didn't look any too happy.

"Hi," Seth said cheerfully. "I'm glad to see you. You never called about having another lesson, and—"

Tabby held up one hand. "I've decided I don't need any more lessons."

"Then why are you here? You're not having a problem with Rosie, I hope."

She shook her head. "No, I w–wanted to talk about—"

Seth snapped his fingers, cutting her off in mid-sentence. "Say, you just might be the answer to my prayers!"

She furrowed her brows and turned her hands, palm up. "I d–don't get it."

He motioned toward a folding chair. "Have a seat, and I'll tell you about it."

When Tabby sat down, Seth took the chair next to her.

"Well, h–how am I an answer t–to your prayers?" she asked.

He reached for her hand. This was not going to be easy. Only a God-given miracle would make Tabby willing to do what he asked.

⋙⋘

Tabby was tempted to pull her hand from Seth's, but she didn't. It felt good. In fact, she wished she'd never have to let go. She stared up at him, searching his face for answers.

"I—uh—will be doing a vent routine at Clearview Community Church next

Friday night," Seth began slowly.

"What's that got to do with me?"

"I'm getting to that." He smiled sheepishly. "The thing is, Sarah McDonald, the other ventriloquist who was originally scheduled, has had a family emergency and was forced to bow out." Seth ran his thumb along the inside of Tabby's palm, making it that much harder for her to concentrate on what he was saying. "I was hoping you might be willing to go with me next week—to fill in for Sarah."

Tabby's throat constricted, and she drew in a deep, unsteady breath. Did Seth actually think she could stand up in front of an audience and talk for two? He should be smart enough to realize she wasn't ready for something like that. The truth was, even though she had gained a bit more confidence, she might never be able to do ventriloquism for a large audience.

"I know it's short notice," Seth said, jerking her thoughts aside, "but we could begin practicing right now, then do more throughout the week. I'm sure—"

The rest of Seth's sentence was lost, as Tabby closed her eyes and tried to imagine what it would be like to perform before a crowd. She could visualize herself freezing up and not being able to utter a single word. Or worse yet, stuttering and stammering all over the place.

"Tabby, are you listening to me?" Seth's mellow voice pulled her out of the make-believe situation, and she popped her eyes open.

"I c–can't d–do it, Seth."

He pulled her to her feet, then placed both his hands on her shoulders. "You can do it, so don't be discouraged because you believe you have no ability. Each of us has much to offer. It's what you do with your abilities that really matters. Now, repeat after me. . .'I can do everything through him who gives me strength.' "

In a trembling voice, Tabby repeated the verse of Scripture from Philippians 4:13. When she was done, Seth tipped her chin up slightly, so they were making direct eye contact. "I know you can do this, Tabby."

She merely shrugged in response.

"You're a talented ventriloquist, and it's time to let your light shine," Seth said with feeling. He leaned his head down until his lips were mere inches from hers. "Do this for me, please."

Tabby's eyelids fluttered, then drifted shut. She felt the warmth of Seth's lips against her own. His kiss was gentle like a butterfly, but as intense as anything she'd ever felt. Of course, her inexperience in the kissing department didn't offer much for comparison. Tabby knew she was falling for Seth Beyers, and she wanted desperately to please him. She'd come over here this evening to give him a piece of her mind, but now all such thoughts had melted away, like spring's last snow. She reveled in the joy of being held in Seth's arms and delighted in the warmth of his lips caressing her own.

When they pulled apart moments later, Tabby felt as if all the breath had been squeezed out of her lungs.

"Kissing is good for you, did you know that?" Seth murmured against her ear.

Numbly she shook her head.

"Yep. It helps relieve stress and tension. Just think about it—when your mouth is kissing, you're almost smiling. Everyone knows it's impossible to smile and feel tense at the same time."

Tabby leaned her head against his shoulder. She did feel relaxed, happy, and almost confident. In a voice sounding much like her dummy's, she rasped, "Okay, I'll do it. Rosie and I will p—perform a vent routine."

He grinned and clasped his hands together. "Great! I know you'll be perfect."

Chapter 15

Tabby awoke the following morning wondering if she'd completely lost her mind. What in the world had come over her last night? Not only had she not told Seth what she thought about him trying to change her, but she'd actually agreed to do a vent routine next week—in front of a large audience, no less!

"It was that kiss," Tabby moaned as she threw back the covers and crawled out of bed. "If only he hadn't kissed me, I could have said no."

She winced as though she'd been slapped. Would she really rather he hadn't kissed her? In all honesty, if Seth would offer another of his sweet kisses, she'd probably say yes all over again.

Feeling more like a dummy than a ventriloquist, Tabby padded in her bare feet over to the window and peered through the mini-blinds. The sun was shining. The birds were singing. It was going to be a beautiful day. Too bad her heart felt no joy. She turned and headed for the kitchen, feeling as though she was part of a death march.

Discovering Donna sitting at the table, talking on the cordless phone, Tabby dropped into a chair. When Donna offered her a warm smile, she only grunted in response.

By the time Donna's conversation was over, Tabby had eaten an orange, along with a handful of grapes, and she was about to tackle a banana. "Good morning, sleepyhead. I thought you were never going to get up."

"I got in late last night," Tabby mumbled as she bit into the piece of fruit.

"Tell me about it!" Donna exclaimed. "I finally gave up waiting for you and went to bed. You said you had an errand to run after work. Where were you anyway?"

Tabby swallowed the chunk of banana and frowned. "I'm afraid my errand turned into more of an error."

Donna's eyebrows lifted in question.

"I went to Beyers' Ventriloquist Studio, planning to put Seth in his place for trying to run my life."

"And did you?"

Tabby sucked in her bottom lip and squared her shoulders. "Afraid not. I ended up promising to do a vent routine at the Clearview Church Family Crusade next Friday."

Donna slapped her hand down on the table, and Tabby's banana peel flew into the air, landing on the floor. "Awesome! That's the best news I've had all year. Maybe even in the last ten years!"

Tabby shook her head. "Don't get so excited. I haven't done it yet."

"Oh, but you will," Donna said excitedly. She pointed to the phone. "That call was from Alex Hanson. He asked me to go out with him again, and guess where we're going?"

"Please don't tell me it's the crusade," Tabby said, already knowing the answer.

"Okay, I won't tell you. I'll just let you be surprised when you look out into the audience and see your best friend and your pastor's son cheering you on."

Tabby gazed at the ceiling. "I think I need a doctor to examine my head more than I need a cheering section." She groaned. "I can't believe I let Seth talk me into such a thing!"

"You'll do just fine," Donna said with an assurance Tabby sure didn't feel. "I imagine you and Seth did some practicing last night?"

Yeah, that and a few other things. Tabby wasn't about to discuss Seth's kiss. Donna would probably go ballistic if she knew that had happened. "We had a bite of supper at the café near Seth's shop, then we worked on my routine till almost midnight." Tabby grimaced. "I'm lucky I even have any voice left after all that talking. Maybe I could get out of this if I had laryngitis or something. Seth asked me to do him a favor by filling in for someone else, and—"

"And you love the guy so much, you couldn't say no," Donna said, finishing Tabby's sentence.

Tabby's eyes filled with tears. "He wants me to be something I'm not."

"Which is?"

"Confident, talented, and ready to serve the Lord."

Donna reached across the table and patted Tabby's hand. "I've seen you do ventriloquism, so I know how talented you are. I also know you want to serve the Lord."

Tabby nodded and swiped at her face with the backs of her hands.

"The confident part will come if you give yourself half a chance," Donna assured her. "If you wallow around in self-pity the rest of your life, you'll never realize your full potential."

Tabby released a shuddering breath. "I know you're right, but I still stutter when I'm nervous or with people I don't know well. How can I become truly confident when I can't even talk right?"

"Philippians 4:13: 'I can do everything through him who gives me strength,'" Donna reminded.

Tabby sniffed. "Seth quoted that same verse last night."

"See," Donna said with a smile. "The Lord wants you to lean on Him. If you keep your focus on Jesus and not the audience, I know you can do that routine next week."

Tabby smiled weakly. "I hope so." Her eyes filled with fresh tears. "I owe you an apology for the other day. We've been friends a long time, and I should have known you'd never try to make a play for Seth behind my back."

Donna nodded. "You're right; I wouldn't. And you are forgiven."

❧

Tabby and Seth met every evening for the next week to practice their routines for the crusade. Not only was it helpful for Tabby to memorize her lines and work on her fear of talking for two in public, but it was an opportunity to spend more time with Seth. Sometimes, after they were done for the night, he'd take her out for pie and coffee, and a few times they just sat and talked. They were drawing closer, there was no doubt in Tabby's mind, but much to her disappointment, Seth hadn't tried to kiss her again. Maybe he thought it best to keep things on a strictly business basis, since they were preparing to do a program and shouldn't be playing the game of romance when they needed to be working.

As she entered the Clearview Community Church that Friday night, carrying Rosie in a small suitcase, Tabby's heart thumped so hard she was sure everyone around could hear it. The driving force that enabled her to make the trip across town was the fact that Seth was counting on her, and she didn't want to let him down.

She spotted Seth talking to a man in the foyer. When he noticed Tabby, he motioned her to come over.

"Tabby, I'd like you to meet Pastor Tom Fletcher," Seth said, placing his arm around her waist. "He's heading up the program tonight."

"It's nice to meet you," the pastor said, reaching out to shake her hand.

She nodded and forced a smile. "N–nice to m–meet you, too."

"Seth was just telling me that you've graciously agreed to fill in for Sarah McDonald. I sure do appreciate this."

Tabby cringed, wishing she could tell Pastor Fletcher the truth—she wasn't graciously filling in. She'd been coerced by Seth's honeyed words and his heart-melting kiss.

"Tabby's new at ventriloquism," Seth said to the preacher. "She's got lots of talent, though. Doesn't move her lips at all."

Right now I wish my lips were glued shut, she fretted. *I wish Seth would quit bragging about me. It'll only make the pastor expect more than I'm able to give.*

"Why don't we go backstage now?" Seth suggested, giving Tabby a little nudge.

She let herself be led along, feeling like a sheep heading straight for the slaughterhouse. If she lived through this ordeal, she'd be eternally grateful. She caught sight of Donna and her blond-haired date as they were entering the sanctuary. Donna waved, and Alex gave her a thumbs-up. She managed a weak smile, but the truth was, she felt like crying.

As though he could read her mind, Seth bent down and whispered, "Relax. You'll do fine."

"I wish everyone would quit telling me that."

Seth offered her a reassuring smile. "Do you realize that your last sentence was spoken without one bit of stuttering?"

She shook her head. Right at this moment she could barely remember what her last sentence had been about, much less focus on the fact that she hadn't stuttered.

Seth led her through a door, and a few minutes later they were in a small room with several other performers. Tabby recognized a few of them who'd been part of the demonstration for Christian workers at her own church a few months ago. There were Mark Taylor, the magician from Portland, Oregon, and Gail Stevens, the chalk artist from Seattle. Tabby knew Donna would be glad to see her. She'd probably be practicing her chalk art in earnest after tonight's performance. Slow-Joe the Clown was busy practicing his animal twisting skills, and some puppeteers were lining up to do their puppet skit. Tabby envied them. . .partly because they were going first and could get their routine over with, but mostly because they had the advantage of a puppet box to hide behind. If only she didn't have to face that crowd out there in the sanctuary!

"Now remember," Seth said, pulling Tabby aside, "I'll go out first and do my routine with Rudy; then you'll come out with Rosie, and we'll do a little bantering with our dummies. By then your confidence should be bolstered, so I'll just bow out, and you'll be on your own."

She looked up at him with pleading eyes. "That's the part that has me so worried, Seth. Couldn't you stay by my side the whole time?"

He shrugged. "I suppose I could, but I think the audience will appreciate your talent more if they see you perform solo."

Who cares if the audience appreciates my talent? I just want to get through this ordeal and live to tell about it. Tabby's heart fluttered like a frightened baby bird, and she fidgeted with the bow on Rosie's new pink dress. Donna would be glad to see she'd taken her advice and dressed the dummy up a bit.

Seth reached for her hand and squeezed it. "Your fingers feel like icicles, Tabby. Take a deep breath, and try to relax."

"That's easy enough for you to say," she muttered. "You're an old pro at this."

It seemed like no time at all that Seth was being announced by Pastor Fletcher. He grabbed Rudy and his stand, blew Tabby a kiss, and walked confidently onto the stage.

Tabby stood as close to the stage door as she could without being seen. She didn't want to miss her cue and end up embarrassing both Seth and herself. Seth was doing a bang-up job with his routine, but she was too nervous to appreciate any of it. All too soon, Seth announced her.

Holding Rosie with one hand and balancing the metal stand Seth had given her with the other, Tabby swallowed the panic rising in her throat and moved slowly across the stage. Applause sounded from the audience, and she felt her face flame.

"Rudy and I both needed dates for tonight," Seth told the crowd. "This is my friend, Tabitha Johnson, and I'll let her introduce her little pal."

Tabby opened her mouth, but nothing came out. She just stood there, feeling like some kind of frozen snow woman, unable to remember her lines and too afraid to speak them if she had.

Coming quickly to her rescue, Seth opened Rudy's mouth. "I think Tabby's waiting for me to introduce her friend. After all, she is my date, so it's probably the right thing to do." The dummy's head swiveled to the left, and one of his doe eyes winked at Rosie. "This is Rosie Wrong, but someday I hope to right that wrong and make her my bride. Then she'll be Rosie Right, who's always right, because she married me—Rudy Right!"

The audience roared and clapped their approval. Tabby felt herself begin to relax a little, and she was even able to make her dummy say a few words.

"What makes you think I'd marry a dummy?" Rosie announced. "Do I look stupid?"

"No, but you sure are cute!" Rudy shot back.

More laughter from the audience. This was fun—almost. What was Tabby going to do once Seth and Rudy left the stage? So far, she'd only spoken for Rosie. How would things go when she was forced to speak herself?

Rudy and Rosie bantered back and forth a bit longer, then finally Seth said the words Tabby had been dreading. "Well, folks, I think it's time for Rudy and me to say good-bye. I'll leave you in the capable hands of Tabby and her friend, Rosie. I'm sure they have lots of fun up their sleeves." With that, Seth grabbed Rudy and his stand and marched off the stage. The audience clapped, and Tabby nearly panicked. She forgot to pray, and in her own strength, she tried to concentrate on her routine. Everything Seth had told her seemed like ancient history. She couldn't think of anything except trying to please the audience and the paralyzing fear that held her in its grip.

"Say, R–Rosie, h–have you h–heard any good elephant j–jokes lately?" she finally squeaked.

"Oh, sure. Would you like to hear them?" Rosie responded.

Tabby only nodded. One less sentence to stammer through.

"Why do elephants have wrinkles?" Rosie asked.

"I d–don't know."

"Well, for goodness' sake, have you ever tried to iron one?"

A few snickers came from the audience, but it was nothing compared to the belly laughs Seth had gotten. This did little to bolster Tabby's confidence, and she struggled to remember the rest of her performance.

"I sure wish I had enough money to buy an elephant," Rosie said.

"Why w–would you—you w–want an el–elephant?"

"I don't. I just want the money."

Tabby paused, hoping the audience would catch on to the little joke, but they didn't. Not even Donna laughed. Tabby felt like a deflated balloon. So much for the confidence she thought she might have gained. She was failing miserably at entertaining this audience, much less bringing any glory to God through her so-called talent. Then there was Seth. What must he think of his star pupil now? He was probably as mortified as she was, and she couldn't blame him one little bit.

"M–money isn't everything, R–Rosie," Tabby said.

"It's all I need."

"Do y–you know w–what the Bible says about m–money?"

"No, do you?"

Tabby did know what it said, but for the life of her, she couldn't remember. In fact, she had no idea what to say or do next. The audience looked bored with her routine, and she'd done nothing but tell stale jokes and stutter ever since Seth took his leave. Her hands were shaking so badly she could hardly hold Rosie still, and her legs felt like two sticks made of rubber. If she didn't get off this platform soon, she would probably pass out cold.

Tabby drew in a deep breath, grabbed Rosie up in one quick swoop, and darted off the stage.

Chapter 16

Tabby was sobbing hysterically by the time she reached the room offstage. With all Seth's encouragement, she'd almost begun to believe she did have some talent, but she'd blown it big time. She had let God down, disappointed Seth, and made a complete fool of herself in front of nearly two hundred people! How could she have let this happen? Why hadn't she just told Seth no? All she wanted to do was go home, jump into bed, and bury her head under the covers.

She felt Seth's arms go around her waist. "It's okay, Tabby," he murmured against her ear. "This was your first time, and you were a little nervous, that's all. It's happened to everyone, and it will get easier with time and practice." He slid his hand up to her back and began patting it, as though that would somehow bring her comfort. "You'll do better next time, I'm sure of it."

Tabby pulled away sharply. "There won't be a next time, Seth! Except for the day care kids, I'll never have another audience."

"Yes, you will. You could be perfect if you'd give yourself half a chance. Please, let me help you. . . ."

It seemed as though Seth was asking her to be perfect at ventriloquism, but some of the things she'd heard him say to both Donna and herself made Tabby wonder if what Seth really wanted was for her to be perfect.

"You've helped me enough!" she cried. "Thanks to you, I made myself look like a total idiot out there!"

Before Seth could offer a rebuttal, Tabby jerked the door open. "Find someone else to help," she called over her shoulder. "I'll never be perfect, and I'm not the woman you need!" Slamming the door, she dashed down the hall. Despite the tears blinding her eyes, Tabby could see someone standing by the front door of the church. It was Donna.

Tabby shook her head. "Don't even say it. I don't want your pity or any kind of sappy pep talk about how things will go better next time."

Donna opened her mouth to say something, but Tabby yanked on the door handle, raced down the steps, and headed straight for her car. All she wanted was to be left alone.

❧

The next few weeks were filled with mounting tension. Tabby barely spoke to anyone, and Donna kept trying to draw her into a conversation. Seth phoned several times, but Tabby wouldn't accept any of his calls. He even dropped by the day care on two occasions, but she refused to talk to him. It pained her to think she'd fallen in love with a man who couldn't accept her for the way she was. If he wanted "perfect," then he might be better off with someone like Cheryl Stone. Why hadn't he asked her to fill in for the ventriloquist who couldn't do the routine for the crusade? At least Cheryl wouldn't have humiliated herself or Seth in front of a church full of people.

A phone call from her parents a week later threw Tabby into deeper depression. On Friday night they would be hosting an engagement party for Lois. Tabby was expected to come, of course. She had always been obligated to attend family functions, even if no one seemed to notice she was there. If she didn't go, she'd probably never hear the end of it, but it irked her that they waited until the last minute to extend an invitation. There was hardly enough time to buy a suitable gift.

The party was set for six-thirty, and it was a good forty-five-minute drive from Tacoma to Olympia. That was barring any unforeseen traffic jams on the freeway. Tabby knew she'd have to leave for Olympia by five-thirty. The day care was open until six-thirty, but Donna said she and their helper could manage alone for an hour.

⊱

Seth was fit to be tied. His phone calls to Tabby and his trips to the day care had been for nothing. No matter how much he pleaded, she still refused to talk to him. He could understand her being upset about the routine she'd botched at the crusade. That didn't excuse her for staying mad at him, though.

Sitting at his workbench, mechanically sanding the arm of a new vent figure, Seth sulked. At first he'd only thought of Tabby as someone who needed his help. Then he began to see her as a friend. Finally, he realized he could love her, but she just didn't fit his mold for the "perfect" wife.

Even though they hadn't known each other very long, Seth cared a lot about Tabby and only wanted the best for her. She'd accused him of trying to change her. Maybe it was true. If he were being totally honest, he'd have to admit he did want her to be different—to fit into his special design and become the kind of person he wanted her to be. Tabby might be right. Perhaps he should find someone more suited to him. Maybe Cheryl Stone would be a better match. She had talent, confidence, and beauty. There was just one problem. . . . He wasn't in love with Cheryl. The truth of this revelation slammed into Seth with such force, it left him with a splitting headache. Until this very moment, he'd never really admitted it. He was actually in love with Tabby Johnson, and not for what she could be, but rather for who she was—gentle and sweet-spirited with children, humble and never bragging, compassionate and helpful—all the qualities of a true Christian.

Seth left his seat and moved toward the front door of his shop. He put the CLOSED sign in the window, then turned off the lights. What he really needed was a long talk with God, followed by a good night's sleep. Maybe he could think things through more clearly in the morning.

⊷

"Are you sure you don't want me to go with you tonight?" Donna asked Tabby as she prepared to leave the day care center.

Tabby shook her head. "This shindig is for family members only—our side and the groom's. Besides, you've got another date with Alex, remember?"

Donna shrugged. "I know how much you dread being with your family. If I were there, it might buffer things a bit. I could call Alex and cancel."

"Not on your life! It's taken you forever to get past your fear of dating a PK. Don't ruin it by breaking a date when it's totally unnecessary." Tabby waved her hand. "Besides, I'm a grown woman. As you've pointed out many times, it's high time I learn to deal with my family without having someone there to hold my hand."

Donna squeezed Tabby's arm. "Okay, try to have fun tonight, and please, drive carefully."

Tabby wrinkled her nose. "Don't I always?"

"It's not your driving I'm worried about. It's all those maniacs who exceed the speed limit and act as if they own the whole road."

"I'll be careful," Tabby promised as she went out the door.

⊷

Tabby was glad she'd left in plenty of time, because the freeway was terrible this night. She was tempted to take the next exit and travel the back roads, but the traffic was so congested, she wasn't sure she could even move over a lane in order to get off. By the time she finally pulled off at the Olympia exit, Tabby was a bundle of nerves.

She knew part of her apprehension was because she was about to enter the lions' den. At least, that's the way it always felt whenever she did anything that involved her family. If only Mom and Dad could love and accept her the way they did Lois. If only she was the kind of daughter they wanted. What exactly did they want? Beauty. . .brains. . .boldness? Lois had all three, and she'd been Dad's favorite ever since she was born. But what parent in their right mind would love one child more than another?

Tabby clenched her teeth. Everyone wanted her to change. Was there anyone willing to accept her just the way she was? Donna used to, but lately she'd been pressing Tabby to step out in faith and begin using her talents to serve the Lord. *If I ever have any children of my own, I'll love them all the same, no matter how different they might be.*

Then there was Seth. Tabby thought at first he just wanted to help her, but she was quite sure now he'd been trying to make her over ever since they first met. Was she really so unappealing the way she was? Must she become a whole new person in order for her family and friends to love and accept her?

A verse of Scripture from 2 Corinthians popped into her mind: "Therefore, if anyone is in Christ, he is a new creation; the old has gone, the new has come!"

Tabby had accepted the Lord at an early age. She knew she'd been cleansed of her sins, which made her a "new creation." Her stuttering problem and lack of confidence had made her unwilling to completely surrender her life to Christ and let Him use all her talents, though. If she were really a new creation, shouldn't she be praying and asking the Lord's help to become all she could be? She hadn't prayed or kept her focus on Jesus the other night at the church program. Instead, she'd been trying to impress the audience.

"I'll think about this later," Tabby murmured as she turned into her parents' driveway. Her primary concern right now was making it through Lois's engagement party.

❧

Seth was tired of dodging his problems. With Bible in hand and a glass of cold lemonade, he took a seat at the kitchen table, determined to relinquish his own selfish desires and seek God's will for his life.

The first passage of Scripture he came to was in Matthew. Jesus was teaching the Beatitudes to a crowd of people. Seth read verse five aloud. " 'Blessed are the meek, for they will inherit the earth.' "

He propped his elbows on the table and leaned his chin against his palms. "Hmm. . .Tabby fits that category, all right."

He jumped down to verse eight. " 'Blessed are the pure in heart, for they will see God.' " How could he have been so blind? Purity seemed to emanate from Tabby. Morally, she seemed like a clear, crisp mountain stream, untouched by the world's pollution.

Seth turned to the Book of Proverbs, knowing the thirty-first chapter addressed the subject of an honorable wife. " 'A wife of noble character who can find? She is worth far more than rubies.' " He scanned the rest of the chapter, stopping to read verse thirty. " 'Charm is deceptive, and beauty is fleeting; but a woman who fears the LORD is to be praised.' "

Praised. Not ridiculed, coerced, or changed into something other than what she was. Seth placed one hand on the open Bible. He knew he'd found a good thing when he met Tabitha Johnson. Even though she was shy and couldn't always speak without stuttering, she had a generous heart and loved the Lord. Wasn't that what he really wanted in a wife?

Seth bowed his head and closed his eyes. "Dear Lord, forgive me for wanting Tabby to change. You love her just as she is, and I should, too. Please give me the chance to make amends. If she's the woman You have in mind for me, then work out the details and make her heart receptive to my love. Amen."

Unexpected tears fell from Seth's eyes, and he sniffed. He had to talk to Tabby right away, while the truth of God's Word was still fresh on his heart. Praying as he dialed the telephone, Seth petitioned God to give him the right words.

When Donna answered, Seth asked for Tabby.

"She's not home," Donna said. She sounded as though she was either in a hurry or trying to put him off. Was Tabby still too angry to speak with him? Had she asked Donna to continue monitoring her phone calls?

"I really do need to speak with her," Seth said with a catch in his voice. "It's important."

"I'm not giving you the runaround, Seth. Tabby isn't home right now."

"Where is she?"

"She left work a little early and drove to Olympia."

"Why'd she go there?"

"It's where her parents live. They're having an engagement party for her sister, Lois."

"Oh." Seth blew out his breath. If Tabby was in Olympia, she probably wouldn't get home until late. There would be no chance of talking to her until tomorrow.

"I'd like to talk more, Seth, but my date just arrived," Donna said.

He groaned. "Yeah, okay. Tell Tabby I'll call her tomorrow." Seth hung up the phone and leaned his head on the table. Why was it that whenever he made a decision to do something, there always seemed to be some kind of roadblock? If only he'd committed this situation to God a bit sooner.

"Guess all I can do is put things in Your hands, Lord. . .which is exactly where they should have been in the first place."

Chapter 17

Tabby's mother greeted her at the door with a frown. "You're late. Everyone else is here already."

Tabby glanced at her watch. It was ten minutes to seven. She was only twenty minutes late. She chose not to make an issue of it, though, merely shrugging and handing her mother the small bag she was holding. "Here's my g–gift for L–Lois."

Mom took the gift and placed it on a table just inside the living room door. "Come in. Everyone's in the backyard, waiting for your father to finish barbecuing the sirloin steaks."

Tabby grimaced. Apparently Dad was going all out for his favorite daughter. *If I were engaged, I doubt I'd even be given an engagement party, much less one with all the trimmings. And even if there were a party in my honor, Dad would probably fix plain old hamburgers, instead of a select, choice cut of meat.*

"How was the freeway tonight?" Mom asked as she and Tabby made their way down the hallway, leading to the back of their modest but comfortable split-level home.

"Bad. R–really bad. That's w–why I'm l–late," Tabby mumbled.

Mom didn't seem to be listening. She was scurrying about the kitchen, looking through every drawer and cupboard as if her life depended upon finding whatever it was she was searching for.

"C–can I help w–with anything?" Tabby asked.

"I suppose you can get the jug of iced tea from the refrigerator. I've got to find the long-handled fork for your father. He sent me in here five minutes ago to look for it."

Tabby crossed the room, opened the refrigerator, grabbed the iced tea, and started for the back door.

"Wait a minute," Mom called. "I found the fork. Would you take it out to Dad?"

"Aren't you c–coming?" Tabby took the fork from her mother and waited expectantly.

"I'll be out in a minute. I just need to check on my pan of baked beans."

Tabby shrugged and headed out the door, wishing she could be anywhere else but here.

About twenty people were milling around the Johnsons' backyard. Some she recognized as aunts, uncles, and cousins. Then there was Grandma Haskins, Dad, Lois, and her sister's wealthy fiancé, Michael Yehley. Some faces were new to her. She assumed those were people related to the groom.

"I see you finally decided to join us," Dad said gruffly, when Tabby handed him the barbecue fork. "Ever since you were a kid, you've been slow. Yep, slower than a turtle plowing through peanut butter. How come you're always late for everything?"

Peanut butter, Tabby mused. *That's what Seth has a fear of eating.* It seemed that lately everything made her think about Seth. She wouldn't even allow Dad's little put-down to rattle her as much as usual. She was too much in love. There, she'd finally admitted it—at least to herself. *For all the good it will do me. Seth doesn't have a clue how I feel, and even if he did, it wouldn't matter. He sees me only as a friend—someone to help out of her shell.* She frowned. *Besides, I'm still mad at him for coercing me into doing that dumb vent routine.*

"Are you just going to stand there like a dummy, or is there some justification for you being so late?" Dad bellowed, snapping Tabby out of her musings.

"I w–wasn't l–l–late on pur–pur–purpose," she stammered. She always stuttered worse around Dad. Maybe it was because he was the one person she wanted most to please. "Tr–traffic was r–really h–h–heavy."

"Why didn't you take off work early so you could get here on time?" Dad said, jerking the fork out of Tabby's hand.

She winced. "I—I d–did l–leave early." Tears hung on her lashes, but she refused to cry.

Dad turned back to the barbecue grill without saying anything more. Tabby pirouetted toward her grandmother, knowing she would at least have a kind word or two.

Grandma Haskins, cheerfully dressed in a long floral skirt and a pink ruffled blouse, greeted Tabby with a peck on the cheek. "It's good to see you, dear." She tipped her silver-gray head to one side. "You're looking kind of peaked. Are you eating right and getting plenty of sleep? You're not coming down with anything, I hope."

Tabby couldn't help but smile. Grandma was always worrying about something. Since she saw Tabby so seldom, it was only fitting that she'd be her target tonight. Tabby didn't really mind, though. It felt kind of nice to have someone fussing over her. Ever since she'd made a fool of herself at the crusade, she had been wallowing in self-pity. Maybe a few minutes with Grandma would make her feel better. "I'm f–fine, Grandma, r–really," she mumbled.

Tabby and Grandma were about to find a place to sit down, when Lois came rushing up. Her face was flushed, and she looked as though she might have been crying.

"What's wrong, Lois?" Grandma asked in a tone of obvious concern.

Lois sniffed deeply and motioned them toward one of the empty tables. As soon as they sat down, she began to cry.

Tabby gave her sister's arm a gentle squeeze. "C–can you t–tell us about it?"

Lois hiccupped loudly and wiped at her eyes, which only smudged her black mascara, making the tears look like little drops of mud rolling down her cheeks. "It's Mike!" she wailed.

"Is something wrong with Michael?" Grandma asked. "I saw him a little while ago, and he looked fine to me."

"Oh, he's fine all right," Lois ranted. "He's so fine that he's decided to take over the planning of our wedding."

"Isn't that the b–bride's job?" Tabby inquired.

"I thought so, until this evening." Lois blew her nose on a napkin and scowled. She didn't look nearly as beautiful tonight as she had the last time Tabby had seen her. That was the night of Tabby's birthday party. Lois didn't have little rivulets of coal-colored tears streaming down her face then.

"Tell us what happened," Grandma prompted.

Lois looked around the yard anxiously. Her gaze came to rest on her fiancé, sitting with some of his family at another table.

Tabby glanced that way as well. She was surprised when Mike looked over and scowled. At least she thought it was a scowl. Maybe he'd just eaten one of Mom's famous stuffed mushrooms. Tabby didn't know why, but those mushrooms always tasted like they'd been filled with toothpaste instead of cream cheese.

"Mike doesn't want us to get married the first Saturday in October after all," Lois whined, jerking Tabby's thoughts back to the situation at hand.

"He doesn't?" Grandma handed Lois another napkin. "Does he want to call the whole thing off?"

Lois drew in a shuddering breath. "He says not, but I have to wonder. Mike thinks we should have more time to get to know one another before we tie the knot. He wants to postpone the wedding until June, and he waited till tonight to drop the bomb."

"June?" Grandma exclaimed. "Why, that's ten months away!"

"That's not a b–bad idea," Tabby interjected. "I mean, s–sometimes you th–think you know a p–person, and then he g–goes and does something to r–really throw you a c–curve ball."

Grandma and Lois both turned their attention on Tabby. "Are you talking about anyone in particular?" Grandma asked.

Tabby shook her head. "No, n–not r–really." She had no intention of telling them about Seth. They'd never understand the way things were. Besides, they weren't supposed to be talking about her right now. This was Lois's engagement party, and apparently there wasn't going to be a wedding. . .at least not this year. "Do M–Mom and D–Dad know yet?" she asked.

Lois shook her head. "I only found out myself a few minutes ago." She reached for Tabby's hand and gripped it tightly. "What am I going to do?"

Tabby swallowed hard. She could hardly believe that her confident, all-knowing little sister was asking her advice. If only she had the right answers. Thinking back to the devotions she'd done that morning, Tabby quoted the following Scripture: " 'Do not let your heart be troubled. Trust in God, trust also in me.' "

Lois's face was pinched, and her eyes were mere slits. "What on earth are you talking about? Why would I trust in you? What can you do to help my situation?"

Tabby bit back the laughter rising in her throat. Even though she and Lois had both gone to Sunday school when they were children, Lois had never shown much interest in the things of God. In fact, she'd quit going to church when she turned thirteen. "That verse from the Book of John is saying you should trust God and not allow your troubles to overtake you. 'Trust in God; trust also in Me.' That was Jesus speaking, and He was telling His followers to trust in Him, as well as in God." Tabby smiled at her sister. "As I'm sure you already know, Jesus and God are one and the same. So, if you put your trust in God, you're trusting Jesus, too."

Lois's mouth was hanging wide open, and Grandma was looking at Tabby as though she'd never seen her before.

"What? What's wrong?" Tabby questioned.

"Do you realize you just quoted that Bible verse and gave me a little pep talk without missing a single word? No stuttering, no stammering, nothing," Lois announced. "I think that must be a first, don't you, Grandma?"

Grandma smiled. "I wouldn't say it was a first, because I can remember when Tabby was a little girl and didn't have a problem with stuttering." She reached over and gave Tabby's hand a gentle pat. "I think it's safe to say when Tabby feels convicted about something, she forgets her insecurities, so her words flow uninterrupted."

Tabby wasn't sure how to respond to Grandma's comment, but she never had a chance to, because Lois cut right in. "Well, be that as it may, it doesn't solve my problem with Mike. How am I going to convince him to marry me in two months? I'll just die if I have to wait until next summer."

Grandma's hand made an arc as it left Tabby's and landed on Lois's. "Everything will work out, dear. Just do as Tabby says, and put your trust in the Lord."

Tabby looked over at her grandmother, and her heart swelled with love. If Grandma was beginning to believe, maybe there was some hope for the rest of the family. With more prayer and reliance on God, there might even be some hope for her. Perhaps she just needed to trust the Lord a bit more.

Chapter 18

When rain started falling around eight o'clock, everyone went inside. Tabby decided to head for home, knowing the roads would probably be bad. Besides, she was anxious to be by herself. This had been some evening. First, her parents' little put-downs, then the news that Lois wasn't getting married in October, followed by that special time she, Grandma, and Lois had shared. For a few brief moments, Tabby had felt lifted out of her problems and experienced a sense of joy by offering support to her sister. If only Lois hadn't ended up throwing a temper tantrum right before the party ended. She and Mike had spent most of the evening arguing, and when they weren't quarreling, Lois was crying. Tabby couldn't help but feel sorry for her.

"No matter when the wedding is, you can keep the automatic two-cup coffeemaker I gave you tonight," Tabby told Lois just before she left. She said good-bye to the rest of the family and climbed into her car. It had been a long week, and she'd be so glad to get home and into bed. Maybe some reading in the Psalms would help, too. Despite his troubles, David had a way of searching his soul and looking to God for all the answers to his problems and frustrations. Tabby needed that daily reminder as well.

❧

The freeway was still crowded, though it was not quite as bad as it had been earlier. To make matters worse, the rain was coming down so hard Tabby could barely see out her windshield. She gripped the steering wheel with determination and prayed for all she was worth.

By the time Tabby reached the Lakewood exit, she'd had enough. She turned on her right blinker and signaled to get off. Traveling the back roads through Lakewood, Fircrest, then into Tacoma would be easier than trying to navigate the freeway traffic and torrential rains. At least she could travel at a more leisurely pace, and she'd be able to pull off the road if necessary.

Tabby clicked on her car radio as she headed down the old highway. The local Christian station was playing a song by a new female artist. The words played over and over in Tabby's head. *Jesus is your strength, give to Him your all. . . . Jesus wants your talents, please listen to His call. . . .*

The lyrical tune soothed Tabby's soul and made her think about Seth again. For weeks he'd been telling her to use her talents for the Lord. "That's because he's trying to change me," she murmured. "Seth's more concerned about finding the perfect woman than he is about me using my talents for God."

Even as she said the words, Tabby wondered if they were true. Maybe Seth really did care about her. It could be that he only wanted her to succeed as a ventriloquist so she could serve the Lord better.

"But I am serving the Lord," Tabby moaned. "I bake cookies for shut-ins, take my turn in the church nursery, teach the day care kids about Jesus, tithe regularly, and pray for the missionaries. Shouldn't that be enough?"

As Tabby mulled all this over, she noticed the car in front of her begin to swerve. Was the driver of the small white vehicle drunk, or was it merely the slick road causing the problem? *Maybe the man or woman is driving too fast for these hazardous conditions,* she reasoned. Tabby eased up on the gas pedal, keeping a safe distance from the car ahead. If the driver decided to slam on his brakes unexpectedly, she wanted plenty of room to stop.

She was on a long stretch of road now, with no houses or places of business nearby. Only giant fir trees and bushy shrubs dotted the edge of the highway. The vehicle ahead was still swerving, and just as it rounded the next corner, the unthinkable happened. The little car lurched, spun around twice, then headed straight for an embankment. Tabby let out a piercing scream as she watched it disappear over the hill.

Tapping her brakes lightly so they wouldn't lock, Tabby pulled to the side of the road. Her heart was thumping so hard she thought it might burst, and her palms were so sweaty she could barely open the car door. Stepping out into the rain, Tabby prayed, "Oh, Lord, please let the passengers in that car be okay."

Tabby stood on the edge of the muddy embankment, gazing at the gully below. She could see the white car, flipped upside down. She glanced up at the sky. Tree branches swayed overhead in a crazy green blur, mixed with pelting raindrops. She took a guarded step forward; then with no thought for her own safety, she scrambled down the hill, slipping and sliding with each step. Unmindful of the navy blue flats she wore on her feet or the fact that her long denim skirt was getting splattered with mud, she inched her way toward the overturned vehicle.

When she reached the site of the accident, Tabby noticed the wheels of the car were still spinning, and one tire had the rubber ripped away. Apparently there had been a blowout, which would account for the car's sudden swerving.

Tabby dashed to the driver's side. The window was broken, and she could see a young woman with short brown hair lying on her stomach across the upside-down steering wheel. There was only a few inches between her head and the roof of the car. She could see from the rise and fall of the woman's back that she was breathing, but her eyes were closed, and she didn't respond when Tabby called out to her.

A pathetic whine drew Tabby's attention to the backseat. A young child, also on her stomach, called, "Mommy. . . Mommy, help me!"

Tabby's brain felt fuzzy, and her legs were weak and rubbery. She had no idea how to help the woman or her child. She certainly wouldn't be able to get them out by herself, and even if she could, she knew from the recent CPR training she'd taken, it wasn't a good idea to move an accident victim who might have serious injuries. What this woman and child needed was professional help. She'd have to go back to the car and call 911 on her cell phone. If only she'd thought to grab it before she made her spontaneous descent.

"D—don't be afraid, little g—girl," Tabby called to the child. "I'm g—going to my c—car and c—call for help. I'll b—be right b—back."

The blond-haired girl, who appeared to be about five years old, began to sob. "I don't know you, and you talk funny. Go away!"

A feeling of frustration, mixed with icy fingers of fear, held Tabby in its grip. She hated to leave but knew she had to. "I'll b—be right b—back," she promised.

As she scrambled up the hill, Tabby could still hear the child's panicked screams. They tore at her heart and made her move as quickly as possible. By the time she reached her car, Tabby was panting, and her fears were mounting. What if the car was leaking gas? What if it caught on fire and she couldn't get the passengers out in time? The stark terror that had inched its way into her head was now fully in control. She felt paralyzed of both body and mind.

She offered up another quick prayer and slid into the car, then reached into the glove box for her cell phone. With trembling fingers, she dialed 911. When an operator came on, Tabby stuttered and stammered so badly the woman had to ask her to repeat the information several times. Tabby was finally assured that help was on the way and was instructed to go back to the car and try to keep the occupants calm.

How in the world am I going to do that? she wondered. *The little girl didn't even want to talk to me.*

Suddenly, Tabby remembered Rosie, who was in the backseat. She'd taken the dummy to work that day, in order to put on a short routine for the day care kids. *Maybe the child will feel less threatened talking to Rosie than she would me.*

Tabby reached over the seat and grabbed the dummy. "Well, Rosie, you're really gonna be put to the test this time."

Back down the hill she went, feeling the squish of mud as it seeped inside her soft leather shoes and worked its way down to her toes. Her clothes were drenched, and her soggy hair hung limply on her shoulders. In the process of her descent, Tabby fell twice. The second time, Rosie flipped out of her arms and landed with a thud on an uprooted tree. Tabby picked her up, only to discover that Rosie's face was dirty and scratched, her head had come loose, and the control stick was jammed. Not only would Rosie's slot-jaw mouth no longer move, but the poor dummy looked a mess!

"Now what am I going to do?" Tabby lamented. "Rosie was my only hope of reaching that child."

"I can do everything through him who gives me strength." The Scripture verse that popped into Tabby's mind offered some comfort and hope. She closed her eyes briefly and pictured the Lord gathering her into His strong arms. He loved her. He cared about her, as well as the two accident victims in that car down there. With His help, Tabby would step boldly out of her shell and serve Him in whatever way He showed her. She could do all things, because of His strength.

"Lord, I really do need Your strength right now. Please calm my heart and let me speak without stuttering, so I can help the little girl not be so afraid."

When Tabby hurried to the car, the child was still crying. She knelt next to the open window and turned Rosie upside down, hoping the sight of the small dummy might make the girl feel better. "This is my friend, Rosie. She wants to be your friend, too," Tabby said softly. "Can you tell me your name, sweetie?"

The child turned her head slightly, and her lips parted in a faint smile. "It's Katie, and I'm almost six."

Tabby released the breath she'd been holding. Progress. They were making a little bit of progress. "Rosie's been hurt, so she can't talk right now," she said. "Why don't the two of us talk, though? Rosie can just listen."

Katie squinted her blue eyes, but finally nodded. "Okay."

Tabby's confidence was being handed over to her. She could feel it. She hadn't expected such a dramatic answer to her prayer, but the doors of timidity were finally swinging open. *Thank You, Lord.* Tabby tipped her head to one side and leaned closer to the window. Now Rosie's head was poking partway in. "Are you hurting anywhere?" she asked Katie.

"My arm's bleedin', and my head kinda hurts," the child said, her blue eyes filling with fresh tears.

"I used my cell phone to call for help," Tabby explained. "The paramedics should be here soon. Then they'll help you and your mommy get out of the car."

Katie choked on a sob. "Mommy won't wake up. I keep callin' her, but she don't answer."

Tabby wasn't sure how to respond. Even though Katie's mom was breathing, she could still be seriously hurt. She might even die. Katie had good reason to be scared.

"Listen, honey," she said with assurance, "I've been praying for you and your mommy. The Lord is here with us, and help is on the way. Let's talk about other things for now, okay?"

Katie nodded, but tears kept streaming down her bruised cheeks. It tore at

Tabby's heartstrings, but she was thankful the child was willing to talk to her now. She was also grateful for answered prayer. Since she'd returned to the battered car, she hadn't stuttered even once.

"What's your last name, Katie?"

There was a long pause, then finally Katie smiled and said, "It's Duncan. My name's Katie Duncan."

"What's your mommy's name?"

"Mommy."

In spite of the stressful circumstances, Tabby had to bite back the laughter bubbling in her throat. Children were so precious. That's why she loved working with the kids at the day care. She'd probably never marry and have children of her own, and being around those little ones helped fill a void in her heart.

"I have a dolly, too, but she's not half as big as yours," Katie said, looking at Rosie.

Tabby chuckled. "Rosie's a ventriloquist dummy. Do you know what that means?"

Katie shook her head.

"She's kind of like a big puppet. I make her talk by pulling a lever inside her body."

"Can you make her talk right now?"

Tabby sucked in her bottom lip. "Rosie's control stick broke when she fell down the hill."

Katie's chin began to quiver, as a fresh set of tears started to seep from her eyes.

"I suppose I could make her talk," Tabby said quickly. "Her mouth won't move, though. Could you pretend Rosie's mouth is moving?"

"Uh-huh. I like to pretend. Mommy and I do pretend tea parties."

"That's good. I like to play make-believe, too." Tabby tipped Rosie's head, so Katie could see her better. Using her childlike ventriloquist voice, she said, "I'm Rosie Right, and I'm always right." *Now what made me say that? That's the line Seth always uses with his dummy, Rudy.*

"Nobody but God is always right. Mommy said so," Katie remarked.

Tabby nodded. "Your mommy's right. Rosie's just a puppet. She can't always be right, and neither can people. Only God has all the answers."

"Do you go to school, Rosie?" Katie asked the dummy.

"Sometimes I go to day care," Rosie answered. "Tabby works there."

The next few minutes were spent in friendly banter between Rosie, Tabby, and Katie. Tabby was glad she could keep the child's mind off the accident and her unconscious mother in the front seat, but when a low moan escaped the woman's lips, Tabby froze. Now she had two people to try to keep calm.

Chapter 19

O h! Oh! I can't breathe," Katie's mother moaned. "My seat belt. . .it's too tight."

Tabby pulled Rosie quickly away from the window and placed one hand on the woman's outstretched arm. "Please, try to remain calm."

The woman moaned again. "Who are you?"

"I'm Tabitha Johnson. I was in the car behind you, and I saw your car swerve, then run off the road. You ended up going over the embankment, and now the car's upside down."

"My name is Rachel Duncan, and I need to get this seat belt off. Do you have a knife?"

Tabby shook her head. "That's not a good idea. If we cut the belt loose, your head will hit the roof, and that might cause serious damage if there's a neck injury."

Rachel's eyelids closed, and she groaned. "Katie. . . Where's Katie?"

"Your little girl is still in the backseat," Tabby answered. "We've been visiting while we wait for the paramedics."

"Mommy, Mommy, I'm here!" Katie called.

Rachel's eyes shot open. "I'm so sorry about this, Katie. Mommy doesn't know what happened."

"From the looks of your right front tire, I'd say you had a blowout," Tabby said.

Rachel's swollen lips emitted a shuddering sob. "I told Rick we needed to buy a new set of tires."

"Rick?"

"Rick's my husband. He had to work late tonight, so Katie and I went to a movie in Lakewood. We were on our way home when it started raining really hard." She grimaced. "I hope someone gets us out of here real soon. I don't think I can stand being in this position much longer."

"Are you in pain?" Tabby asked with concern.

"My left leg feels like it might be broken, and my head's pounding something awful."

"Would you mind if I prayed for you?" Tabby didn't know where she'd gotten the courage to ask that question. It wasn't like her to be so bold.

"I'd really appreciate the prayer," Rachel answered. Tears were coursing down her cheeks, but she offered Tabby a weak smile. "I'm a Christian, I know how much prayer can help."

Tabby placed Rosie on the ground and leaned in as far as she could. "Heavenly Father," she prayed, "Rachel and Katie are in pain and need medical attention as soon as possible. I'm asking You to bring the paramedics here quickly. Please give them both a sense of peace and awareness that You are right here beside them."

Tabby had just said "amen" when she heard the piercing whine of sirens in the distance. "That must be the rescue vehicles," she told Rachel. "I think I should go back up the hill to be sure they know where we are. Will you be all right for a few minutes?"

"Jesus is with us," Katie squeaked.

"Yes, He's by our side," Rachel agreed.

"All right then, I'll be back as quick as I can." Tabby pulled away from the window and started up the hill as fast as she could, thankful the rain had finally eased up.

A police car, a fire truck, and the paramedics' rig were pulling off the road by her car when she came over the hill. Gasping for breath, she dashed over to one of the firemen. "There's a car down there," she panted, pointing to the ravine. "It's upside down, and there's a woman and a little girl trapped inside."

"Could you tell if they were seriously injured?" one of the paramedics asked as he stepped up beside her.

"Rachel—she's the mother—said her head hurt real bad, and she thinks her leg might be broken. Katie's only five, and she complained of her head hurting, too. She also said her arm was bleeding."

He nodded, then turned to his partner. "Let's grab our gear and get down there."

The rescue squad descended the hill much faster than Tabby had, but she figured they'd had a good deal more practice doing this kind of thing.

Tabby followed, keeping a safe distance once they were at the scene of the accident. She did move in to grab Rosie when a fireman stepped on one of the dummy's hands. Poor, dirty Rosie had enough injuries to keep her in Seth's shop for at least a month. Right now Tabby's concerns were for Rachel and her precious daughter, though. She kept watching and praying as the rescuers struggled to free the trapped victims.

When they finally had Rachel and Katie loaded into the ambulance, Tabby breathed a sigh of relief. The paramedics said it didn't appear as though either of them had any life-threatening injuries, although there would be tests done at the hospital. Before the ambulance pulled away, Tabby promised Rachel she would call her husband and let him know what happened.

One of the policemen, who identified himself as Officer Jensen, asked Tabby a series of questions about the accident, since she'd been the only witness.

"You are one special young lady," the officer said. "Not only did you call for help, but you stayed to comfort that woman and her daughter." He glanced down at the bedraggled dummy Tabby was holding. "From the looks of your little friend, I'd say you went the extra mile, using your talent in a time of need."

Tabby smiled, although she felt like crying. For the first time in a long while, she'd forgotten her fears and self-consciousness, allowing God to speak through her in a way she never thought possible. Throughout the entire ordeal, she'd never stuttered once. It seemed like a miracle—one she hoped would last forever. Up until now, she believed that unless her family treated her with love and respect, she could never become confident. How wrong she'd been. How grateful to God she felt now.

When Tabby got into her car, she reached for the cell phone and called Rick Duncan at the number Rachel had given her. He was shocked to hear about the accident but thankful Tabby had called. He told her he'd leave work right away and head straight for Tacoma General Hospital. Tabby could finally go home, knowing Rachel, Katie, and Rick were in God's hands.

❧

Tabby awoke the following morning feeling as though she'd run a ten-mile marathon and hadn't been in shape for it. The emotional impact of the night before hit her hard. If she could get through something so frightening, she was sure the Lord would see her through anything—even dealing with her unfeeling parents and self-centered sister. Instead of shying away from family gatherings or letting someone's harsh words cut her to the quick, Tabby's plan was to stand behind the Lord's shield of protection. She could do all things through Him, and as soon as she had some breakfast, she planned to phone Tacoma General Hospital and check on Rachel's and Katie's conditions. Then her next order of business would be to visit Beyers' Ventriloquist Studio.

❧

Seth had dialed Tabby's phone number four times in the last fifteen minutes, and it was always busy. "Who is on the phone, and who could she be talking to?" he muttered. "Maybe I should get in my car and drive on over there."

Seth figured Tabby was still mad at him, and he wondered if she'd even let him into her apartment. Well, he didn't care if she was mad. He'd made up his mind to see her today.

Seth left the red-nosed clown dummy he'd been working on and walked into the main part of his shop just as the bell on the front door jingled. In walked Cheryl Stone.

"Good morning, Seth," she purred. "How are you today?"

Seth's heart sank. The blue-eyed woman staring up at him with a hopeful smile was not the person he most wanted to see. "Hi, Cheryl. What brings you here this morning?"

"Does there have to be a reason?" Cheryl tipped her head to one side and offered him another coquettish smile.

Seth felt the force of her softly spoken words like a blow to the stomach. Cheryl was obviously interested in him. "Most people don't come to my shop without a good reason," he mumbled. "Are you having a problem with Oscar again?"

Cheryl gave the ends of her long red hair a little flick and moved slowly toward Seth. "Actually, I'm not here about either one of my dummies."

Seth swallowed hard and took a few steps back. *Now here's a perfect woman. She's talented, confident, poised, and beautiful. How come I don't go after her?* He groaned inwardly. *I'm in love with Tabby Johnson, that's why.* There was no denying it, either. Shy, stuttering Tabitha, with eyes that reminded him of a wounded deer, had stolen his heart, and he'd been powerless to stop it.

With determination, Seth pulled his thoughts away from Tabby and onto the matter at hand. "Why are you here, Cheryl?"

"I've been asked to be part of a talent contest sponsored by Valley Foods. My father works in the corporate office there," Cheryl explained.

"What's that got to do with me?"

"I was hoping you'd be willing to give me a few extra lessons." She giggled. "I know I'm already a good ventriloquist, but I think you're about the best around. Some more helpful tips from you might help me win that contest."

Seth cleared his throat, hoping to stall for time. At least long enough so he could come up with some legitimate excuse for not helping Cheryl. He had an inkling she had a bit more in mind than just ventriloquist lessons.

His suspicions were confirmed when she stepped forward and threw her arms around his neck. The smell of apricot shampoo filled his nostrils, as a wisp of her soft red hair brushed against his cheek.

"Please say you'll do this for me, Seth," Cheryl pleaded. "Pretty please. . . with sugar and spice. . .now don't make me ask twice."

Seth moaned. Cheryl was mere inches from his face now, but all he could think about was Tabby. He opened his mouth to give Cheryl his answer, when the bell on the door jingled. Over the top of Cheryl's head, he saw the door swing wide open.

It was Tabitha Johnson.

Chapter 20

Seth expected Tabby to turn around and run out the door once she saw Cheryl in his arms. She didn't, though. Instead, she marched up to the counter and plunked her dummy down. "I'm sorry to interrupt," she said in a voice filled with surprising confidence, "but I need you to take a look at Rosie. Do you think you can spare a few minutes, Seth?"

Seth reached up to pull Cheryl's arms away from his neck. He was guilty of nothing, yet he felt like a kid who'd been caught with his hand inside a candy dish. He could only imagine what Tabby must be thinking, walking in and seeing what looked like a romantic interlude between him and Cheryl.

He studied Tabby for a few seconds. She looked different today—cute and kind of spunky. Her hair was curled, too, and it didn't hang in her face the way it usually did. Her blue jeans and yellow T-shirt were neatly pressed, and she stood straighter than normal.

"Do you have time to look at Rosie or not?" Tabby asked again.

Seth nodded, feeling as if he were in a daze. Tabby wasn't even stuttering. What happened to Timid Tabitha with the doe eyes? He glanced down at Cheryl and noticed she was frowning. "Excuse me, but I have to take care of business," he said, hoping she'd get the hint and leave.

Cheryl planted both hands on her slim hips and whirled around to face Tabby. "Can't you see that Seth and I are busy?"

"I'll only keep Seth a few minutes; then he's all yours," Tabby said through tight lips.

A muscle in Seth's jaw twitched. "I'll call you later, Cheryl," he said, turning toward the counter where the dummy lay.

"Yeah, okay," Cheryl mumbled.

When he heard the door close, Seth heaved a sigh of relief. At least one problem had been resolved.

❧

Tabby was trembling inwardly, but outwardly she was holding up quite well—thanks to the Lord and the prayer she'd uttered when she first walked into Seth's shop. Seeing Cheryl Stone in Seth's arms had nearly been her undoing. Only God's grace kept her from retreating into her old shell and allowing her tongue to run wild with a bunch of stuttering and stammering. It still amazed her that ever since the car accident last night she hadn't stuttered once. God really had changed her life.

"What in the world happened to Rosie?" Seth asked, breaking into Tabby's thoughts. "She looks like she got roped into a game of mud wrestling. I'd say she came out on the losing end of things."

Tabby snickered. "It was something like that." Then, feeling the need to talk about what happened last night, she opened up and shared the entire story of the accident she'd witnessed.

Seth listened intently as he examined the dummy. When Tabby finished talking, he looked up from his work and groaned softly. "I'm sure thankful you're okay. You were smart to keep a safe distance from that car when it began to swerve. It could have been your little hatchback rolling down the hill."

Tabby swallowed hard. Was Seth really concerned about her welfare? Was that frown he wore proof of his anxiety?

"Now about Rosie. . . ," Seth said, pulling her back to the immediate need.

"How bad is the damage? Will Rosie ever talk again?"

Seth's green eyes met Tabby's with a gaze that bore straight into her soul. "She will if you want her to."

Tabby blinked. "Of course I do. Why wouldn't I?"

Seth cleared his throat a few times, as though searching for the right words. "After that program at the crusade, you didn't seem any too anxious to continue using your ventriloquistic talents."

She nodded. "You're right about that, but since last night I'm seeing things in a whole new light."

He raised his eyebrows. "You are? In what way?"

"For one thing, God showed me that I don't have to be afraid of people or circumstances which might seem a bit unusual or disturbing," she explained. "I was really scared when that car went over the embankment. When I found Rachel and her daughter trapped inside their overturned vehicle, I nearly panicked." Tabby drew in a deep breath and squeezed her lips together. "Little Katie wouldn't even respond to me at first. I was stuttering so much I scared her. Then I thought about Rosie in the backseat of my car, and I climbed back up the hill to get her."

Seth nodded. "Kids will react to a dummy much quicker than they will an adult." He smiled. "Guess we're a bit too intimidating."

"I dropped Rosie on the way down the hill, and by the time I got to the wreck, I realized her mouth control was broken." Tabby shrugged. "I had to talk on my own, and I asked God to help me do it without stuttering. I wanted Katie to be able to understand every word, so she wouldn't be afraid."

"So poor Rosie took a trip down the muddy incline for nothing?" Seth asked, giving the dummy's head a few taps with his knuckle.

Tabby shook her head. "Not really. After Katie and I talked awhile, I began to gain her confidence. Then I put Rosie up to the window and made her talk, without even moving her lips."

Seth tipped his head back and roared.

"What's so funny?"

"If Rosie's lips weren't moving, then who was the ventriloquist, and who was the dummy?"

Tabby giggled and reached out to poke Seth playfully in the ribs. "Ha! Very funny!" She wiggled her nose. "I'll have you know, Mr. Beyers, my dummy is so talented, she can talk for two without moving her lips!"

Seth grinned, and his eyes sparkled mischievously. "And you, Miss Tabitha Johnson, are speaking quite well on your own today."

Tabby felt herself blush. "I haven't stuttered once since last night." She placed her palms against her burning cheeks. "God gave me confidence I never thought I would have, and I'm so grateful."

"I think it was because you finally put yourself fully in His hands."

Tabby was tempted to ask Seth if he thought she was worthy of his love now. After all, he'd wanted her to change. Instead of voicing her thoughts, she nodded toward Rosie. "Is there any hope for her?"

Seth scratched the back of his head and smiled. "I think with a little help from some of my tools and a new coat of paint, Rosie will be up and around in no time at all."

Tabby smiled gratefully, but then she sobered. "Will the repairs be expensive?"

Seth winked, and she pressed a hand to a heart that was beating much too fast.

"Let's see now. . . The price for parts will be reimbursed with two or three dinners out, and labor. . .well, I'm sure we can work something out for that as well," Seth said, never taking his gaze off her. "Something that will be agreeable to both of us." He moved slowly toward her, with both arms extended.

Tabby had an overwhelming desire to rush into those strong arms and declare her undying love, but she held herself in check, remembering the little scene she'd encountered when she first entered Seth's shop. It was obvious that Seth had more than a business relationship with Cheryl.

Seth kept moving closer, until she could feel his warm breath on her upturned face. She trembled, and her eyelids drifted shut. Tabby knew she shouldn't let Seth kiss her—not when he was seeing someone else. Her heart said something entirely different, though, and it was with her whole heart that Tabby offered her lips willingly to Seth's inviting kiss.

Tabby relished the warmth of Seth's embrace, until the sharp ringing of the telephone pulled them apart.

"Uh, guess I'd better get that," Seth mumbled. He stepped away from Tabby and moved across the room toward the desk where the phone sat.

Tabby looked down at Rosie and muttered, "I think I was just saved by the bell."

As Seth answered the phone, his thoughts were focused on Tabby. He'd wanted to hold her longer and tell her everything that was tumbling around in his mind. He needed to express his feelings about the way he'd treated her in the past and share the Scriptures the Lord had shown him. Maybe they'd be able to pick up where they left off when he hung up the phone. Maybe. . .

"Seth Beyers," he said numbly into the receiver. "Huh? Oh, yeah, I'd be happy to take a look at your dummy. I'm about to close shop for the day, but you can bring it by on Monday."

Relieved to be off the phone, Seth returned to Tabby. She was standing over Rosie, looking as though she'd lost her best friend. "She'll be okay, I promise," he said, reaching out to pull Tabby into his arms. He leaned over and placed a kiss on her forehead. Her hair felt feathery soft against his lips, and it smelled like sunshine.

She pulled sharply away, taking him by surprise. She'd seemed willing a few minutes ago. What had happened in the space of a few minutes to make her so cold?

"How long till she's done?" Tabby asked.

"I could probably get her ready to go home in about a week. How's that sound?"

She shrugged. "That'll be fine, I guess." She turned and started for the door.

"Hey, where are you going?" he called after her.

"Home. I left the apartment before Donna got up, and since I came home so late last night, I promised to fill her in on the accident details this morning."

Seth rushed to her side. "Don't tell me I'll be taking the day off for nothing."

She blinked several times. "I don't get it. What's your taking the day off got to do with me?"

"I'd really like to spend the day with you. That is, if you're not tied up."

"I just told you. . ."

"I know. You want to tell Donna about last night." Seth grabbed Tabby's arm and pulled her to his side again. "Can't that wait awhile? We have some important things to discuss, and I thought we could do it at the park."

"Point Defiance?"

He nodded.

Tabby hung her head. He knew she was weakening, because she'd told him before how much she loved going to Point Defiance Park.

"Wouldn't that be kind of like a date?" she murmured.

He laughed. "Not kind of, Tabby. . .it is a date."

"Oh. Well, I guess my answer has to be no."

His forehead creased. "Why, for goodness' sake? Are you still mad at me for coercing you into doing that vent routine?"

She shook her head. "No, I've done what the Bible says and forgiven you. Besides, what happened at the crusade was really my own fault. I could have said no when you asked me to perform. I could have prayed more and allowed God to speak through me, instead of letting myself get all tied up in knots, and ending up making my routine and me look completely ridiculous."

Seth gently touched her arm. "Neither you nor your routine was ridiculous, Tabby." He chewed on his lower lip, praying silently for the right words to express his true feelings. "Tabby, you're not the only one God's been working on lately."

"What do you mean?"

"Through the Scriptures, He's showed me that I've been expecting too much. I wanted the perfect woman. . .one who'd fit into my preconceived mold. I thought I needed someone who would radiate with confidence and who'd have the same burning desire I do to share her talents with others by telling them about the Savior."

Tabby nodded. "I was pretty sure you felt that way, and I really couldn't blame you, but it did make me mad. I knew I could never be that perfect woman, so I was angry at you, myself, and even God."

Tears welled up in her dark eyes, and when they ran down her cheeks, Seth reached up to wipe them away with his thumb. "You don't have to be the perfect woman, Tabby. Not for me or anyone else. All God wants is for us to give Him our best." He kneaded the back of his neck, trying to work out the kinks. "I tried to call you last night. I wanted to tell you what God had revealed to me. I was planning to tell you that it didn't matter if you stuttered, had no confidence, or never did ventriloquism again. I just wanted you to know that I love you, and I accept you for the person you are. . .one full of love and compassion."

"Love?" Tabby looked up at him with questioning eyes.

He nodded. "I know we haven't known each other very long, but I really do love you, Tabby."

"But what about Cheryl Stone?"

His brows furrowed. "What about her?"

"After seeing the two of you together, I thought—"

"That we were in love?"

She only nodded in response.

Seth's lips curved into a smile, then he let out a loud whoop.

"What was that for?"

"I don't love Cheryl," Seth said sincerely. He dropped to one knee. "This might seem kind of sudden, and if you need time to think about it, I'll understand." He smiled up at her. "If you wouldn't mind being married to a dummy, I'd sure be honored to make you my wife. After we've had a bit more time to go on a few more dates and get better acquainted," he quickly added.

Tabby trembled slightly. "You—you w–want to marry me?"

Seth reached for her hand and kissed the palm of it. "You're stuttering again. I think maybe I'm a bad influence on you."

She blushed. "I'm just so surprised."

"That I could love you, or that I'd want to marry you?"

"Both." Tabby smiled through her tears. "I love you so much, Seth. I never thought I could be this happy."

"Is that a yes?" he asked hopefully.

She nodded as he stood up again. "Yes! Yes! A thousand times, yes!"

"How about a December wedding? Or is that too soon?"

"December? Why that month?"

"I can't think of a better Christmas present to give myself than you," he said.

She sighed deeply and leaned against his chest. "That only gives us four months to plan a wedding. Do you think we can choose our colors, pick out invitations, order a cake, and get everything else done by then?"

A dimple creased her cheek when he kissed it. "I'm sure we can." There was a long pause, then he whispered, "There is one little thing, though."

"What's that?"

"I don't want our wedding cake to have peanut butter filling."

Tabby pulled back and gave him a curious look.

"My peanut-butter phobia, remember?"

She giggled. "Oh, yes. Now how could I forget something so important?"

Seth bent down and kissed her full on the mouth. When the kiss ended, he grinned.

"What?"

"I must be the most blessed man alive."

"Why's that?"

"If a man is lucky, he finds a wife who can communicate her needs to him. Me. . .well, I'll always know what my wife needs, because she can talk for two." He winked at her. "Now that we've had our little talk, do you still want to go to the park?"

She smiled. "Of course I do. I can't think of a better place for us to start making plans for our future."

Epilogue

Tabby had never been more nervous, yet she'd never felt such a sense of peace before. Next to the day she opened her heart to Christ, today was the most important day in her life.

Much to her sister's disappointment, Tabby had beaten her to the marriage altar. Tabby took no pleasure in this fact, but it did feel pretty wonderful to be married to the man she loved. Lois would find the same joy when it was her turn to walk down the aisle. By then, maybe she'd even be a Christian.

Tabby glanced at her younger sister, sitting beside Mike and her parents at a table near the front of the room. Thanks to Tabby's gentle prodding, Lois had recently started going to church. Now if they could just get her fiancé to attend.

The wedding reception was in full swing, and Tabby and Seth were about to do a joint ventriloquist routine. It was the first time she'd ever done ventriloquism in front of her family. Tabby gazed into her groom's sea-green eyes and smiled. If someone had told her a year ago she'd be standing in front of more than a hundred people, married to a terrific guy like Seth, she'd never have believed them. It still amazed her that she no longer stuttered or was hampered by her shyness. God was so good, and she was glad for the opportunity to serve Him with her new talent.

She felt the warmth of Seth's hand as he placed Rosie into her arms. He probably knew she was a bit nervous about this particular performance. He bent down and pulled Rudy from the trunk. With a reassuring smile, he quickly launched into their routine.

"How do you feel about me being a married man?" Seth asked his dummy.

Rudy's head swiveled toward Tabby. "I can see why you married her, but what's she doin' with a guy like you?"

Before Seth could respond, Rosie piped up with, "Don't talk about Seth that way, Rudy. I think he's real sweet."

"I think so, too," Tabby put in.

Rudy snorted. "He's not nearly as sweet as me." The dummy's head moved closer to Tabby. "How 'bout a little kiss to celebrate your wedding day?"

Tabby wiggled her eyebrows up and down. "Well. . ."

"Now, Rudy, what makes you think my wife would want to kiss a dummy?"

Rudy's wooden head snapped back to face Seth. "She kisses you, doesn't she?"

The audience roared, and Tabby felt herself begin to relax. Even Dad was laughing, and Mom was looking at her as though she was the most special person in the whole world. Maybe she wasn't such a disappointment to them after all. Maybe her newfound confidence could even help win her parents to the Lord.

"You know, Seth," Rudy drawled, "I hear tell that once a man ties the knot, his life is never the same."

"In what way?" Seth asked.

"Yeah, in what way?" Rosie echoed.

Rudy's eyes moved from side to side. "For one thing, some women talk too much. What if Tabby starts speaking for you, now that you're married?"

Tabby leaned over and planted a kiss on Rudy's cheek, then did the same to Seth. "Yep," she quipped, "from now on, I'll definitely be talking for two!"

WANDA E. BRUNSTETTER

Wanda E. Brunstetter lives in a small town in Central Washington with her husband, Richard, who is a pastor. They have two grown children and six grandchildren. Wanda is a professional ventriloquist and puppeteer, and she and her husband enjoy doing programs for children of all ages. Wanda's greatest joy as a Christian author is to hear from a reader that something she wrote has touched that person's heart or helped them in some special way. Her published works include eleven novels with Barbour Publishing's **Heartsong Presents**, five novellas, and an Amish romance novel, *The Storekeeper's Daughter*—a bestseller! Wanda believes the Amish people's simple lifestyle and commitment to God can be a reminder of something we all need. Visit her Web page at www.wandabrunstetter.com.

Race for the Roses

by Lauraine Snelling

Prologue

I'm sorry, Son, but I have to leave now."

"But, Daddy." Seven-year-old Dane Morgan looked up at his father, tears swimming in blue eyes that matched his father's. "I don't want you to go."

"I know, Son, neither do I." Hubert Morgan ignored the creasing of his dress khakis as he knelt and gathered his son into his arms. "But I have to." He tipped his son's face up with one caring finger under the quivering chin. "You must be the man of our house until I come home again; do you understand?"

The boy shook his head and tried to bury his face in his father's shoulder.

Hubert kept a firm hold on his son's chin. "That means you must take care of your mother and sister, keep them safe until I return."

"I. . .I w–will, Daddy." The small boy straightened and touched two fingers to his forehead in the salute his father had taught him. "Yes, sir." His chin quivered again. One tear trickled over the curve of his round cheek. "I will t–take care of Mama and Sissy." He snapped his arm back to his side.

Hubert Morgan stood and returned the salute. "Bye, Son. See you in a few months. I'll be praying for you every day."

"Me, too. Bye, Daddy," the boy whispered as his father, shoulders and back straight as the Marine Corps demanded, walked toward the waiting plane. While Dane felt his mother's hand on his shoulder, he never took his eyes off the plane until he could see it no longer.

Chapter 1

thirty years later

Wispy veils of ground fog hovered over the oval track and white-fenced infield of Portland Meadows Racetrack. As Robynn O'Dell trotted the bay Thoroughbred onto the sandy course, the horses galloping in front of the grandstand appeared legless, phantom creatures floating on a drifting sea.

"Easy, fella," she crooned, her musical voice a counterpoint to the grunts of the straining horse. "You can let it out later." Robynn gentled him with her voice, rising in the short stirrups to gain greater control.

With the sensitive hands and perfect balance of a born horsewoman, she kept the seventeen-hand colt at the easy lope she knew would build the greatest endurance. As her mount settled down to serious work, Robynn glanced at the overcast sky.

"Do not rain," she ordered the scurrying clouds. *Heavenly Father, we need a good fast track, not ankle-deep mud. I'm tired of washing half of Oregon down the drain after every race.* While she knew the prayer was only a holdover from early days, still it didn't hurt to invoke the name of the Almighty, in case He might be listening—not that she was convinced He cared about such a mundane request.

As if on cue, a silver disk of pale sun appeared low in the east, floating behind thin clouds. A few strides later, the cloud bank blotted it out again.

When Robynn and her mount swept by the entry gate, she felt a tingling up her spine. The desire to turn and see who was watching her almost broke her concentration on the animal she rode so effortlessly. After several more circuits of the track, she pulled the steaming horse down to a sidestepping trot.

Robynn switched her one-piece rein to her left hand so she could push up her goggles and wipe her dripping eyes on her other sleeve. October mornings in the Pacific Northwest had a real bite to them. In all her twenty-five years of living there, she hadn't adjusted to it.

Steam billowed from the tired horse as she slowed him to a walk just before they exited for the stables.

The tingling sensation rippled up her back again. Startled, Robynn searched every face until her violet eyes locked with the electric blue gaze of a tall, broad-shouldered man in a sheepskin jacket. He leaned against the fence as if he owned it. Her breathing quickened as the moment stretched to include the sun breaking through just in time to set the fog droplets sparkling in his blue-black hair. The tingle spread to her middle, then up to her face. She could feel the heat warring with her chilled skin.

As her horse sidestepped through the gate, Robynn could still feel the man's gaze on her back. The desire to turn and look at him again ate at her mind, singing out to her fingers. She clenched her hands on the reins, willing them and herself to behave. Why, she'd never even seen the guy before, let alone met him. Who was he? He acted as if he owned not only the track but the entire world. He'd stared at her and her horse as though they were on display just for him.

❦

Who was she? Dane Morgan couldn't keep his gaze off her. The petite woman rode with the effortless skill of a natural rider, but that wasn't the only thing that drew his attention. He could barely see her face, hidden by the goggles and racing helmet, so it wasn't that.

Maybe it was the control he sensed. Control and power were entities he'd understood. He'd used both in building Morgan, Inc., to its present level of success. While he fully credited his employees with implementing the team-management principles long before the concept became a buzzword, he knew the personal power it took to make everything come together. Plus the time. And the effort.

Which was why he'd finally taken some time to indulge in his hobby, Thoroughbred horse racing. He came by the love of horses naturally: His grandfather bred them, his uncle Josh trained them, and his mother had been a steeplechase jockey—before the accident. Now she only jockeyed her wheelchair.

His gaze kept returning to the woman slow galloping her feisty mount around the track. *Wouldn't you know?* He shook his head. *She rides Thoroughbreds.* Well, he'd make sure he met her before he left, to get rid of the attraction if nothing else. Just like all the other attractive women he'd met, once she opened her mouth, he'd lose interest. Maybe his mother was right: No flesh and blood woman could ever measure up to his fantasy of perfection.

He shook his head. He was here to look for horses, and he hadn't even noticed the mount she rode. Maybe he was just tired. Or lonely. Or both.

❦

"You and Dandy looked real good out there, Princess." Josh MacDonald, the trainer Robynn rode for, took hold of the colt's bridle. "I've entered the two of you in the third race day after tomorrow. If it clears off like it looks like it might, you've got a real good chance."

"Thanks." Robynn pulled herself back to the moment. "He really feels ready." She concentrated on the white-haired man walking beside them. Tingles no longer tantalized the edges of her mind.

Robynn kicked her feet free of the stirrups and slid to the cedar shaving-covered walk in front of the long row of stalls belonging to Opal McKecknen. As Robynn unhooked the cinch to the tiny racing saddle, her mind flicked back to the stranger at the fence. *Wonder who he is? Why haven't I seen him around before?* Questions sparked like the dew glinting in his hair. That black hair. Crisp curls, cut short to control them. Control. The word fit him.

You idiot, she scolded herself. *You're acting like a dopey teenager, panting after every new boy on the block.*

No, not every one, she answered herself. *You've had the blinders on for seven years.*

"And I'll keep them on."

"What'd you say?" Josh finished cross-tying the steaming gelding.

"Nothing." Robynn shook her head. "I mean. . ."

"You all right?" The aging trainer lifted the saddle from her arms. "Ye're acting kinda strange."

"No. No. I'm fine. Or at least I will be when we get done with the workout. I'm so hungry I could eat burnt toast."

Josh handed her a scraper. "If you help me wash the horses down, I'll treat."

"You're on." Robynn stuck the scraper in the back pocket of her jeans.

By the time she had Jim Dandy sponged down, Josh had her next mount, a filly, saddled and ready. "Now take it easy with her." He cupped his hands to boost her into the saddle. "Just loosen her up. You two are scheduled for the fourth race tomorrow."

"Okay." Robynn slid her scuffed boots into the short stirrups. As Josh unclipped the tie rope, she gathered the rein in her gloved fingers and settled into the saddle. "You better have the next one ready when I get back." She grinned down at the former jockey. "Or I'll order the steak and eggs special."

"You know, the way you eat. . ."

"You'd think I'd weigh a ton. I know." Her chuckle rippled on the morning breeze. "It's my royal blood. Keeps me skinny."

"Skinny you ain't," Josh muttered as he patted the filly on the rump. "Now get goin'."

By the time the remaining horses were exercised and clipped to the hot walker, Robynn had nearly asked Josh about the stranger a hundred times. *Keep this up and I won't have any tongue left,* she thought as she rubbed the offending member against the inside of her teeth. Remembering those soul-searching blue eyes caused shivers to play tag up and down her spine.

"Who else ye ridin' for today?" Josh asked as they crossed the asphalt road to the cafeteria.

"Well, besides the three for you, I'm up on two for Dr. Benson and one for

Brandenburg. It'll be a good day."

Josh chewed on the straw he kept in his teeth in place of the cigar he'd given up several years before. "That one for Brandenburg. It ain't that cantankerous gray of his?"

Robynn didn't answer.

"Princess." Josh stopped her with a hand on her arm. "You know. . ."

"I know what you've told me. The lecture's been often enough." She straightened to her full five feet, three inches and assumed the regal bearing that had earned her the nickname. "But Josh, I *need* that ride today. My house and car payments are due, the quarterlies for Jeremy's school are coming up, and so are the taxes. My so-called savings account is flatter'n the bankbook since this is the beginning of the season. You know what it's like." She rammed her flying hands in her pockets. "Besides, that monster likes a good dry track, and I can handle him."

"Yeah, if you can get him straight outta the gate and he got up on the right side of the bed this morning and it's the thirty-second day of May."

"Now, Josh." Robynn pulled out all the stops on her charm. "You've told me over and over that I handle the hard ones with an Irishman's insight. I know what those horses are gonna do before they do."

"Sure, and you'd use an auld man's words agin'im," Josh muttered, but the beginnings of a smile teased the corners of his mouth.

"Oh, go on with ye." Robynn lapsed into the brogue the two used when they wanted to tease. "And an auld man you'd be calling yourself. Auld is only when. . ."

"But Princess. . ." The man's smile disappeared. "You'll be extra careful—takin' no chances?"

"I'll be careful," she agreed. *But if there's a hole to get through*, she promised herself, *I'll take it. I need a win.* Ten percent of a couple good purses today would sure take the pressure off.

❧

Bacon and egg perfume overlaid with cigarette smoke assailed their nostrils as Josh pulled open the cafeteria door. People relaxed around the small square tables, rehashing the morning workouts. The din crashed on their ears. Robynn glanced quickly around the huge room. Disappointment settled over her. *Well, whoever he was, he didn't feel the need for a coffee break or breakfast. But then, what do I care?*

She followed Josh to the counter and automatically slid a tray onto the ledge. In slow motion she chose a grapefruit half before Josh poked her with his elbow. "Come back to the real world, lass. The man wants your order."

"Uh, oh, sorry." Robynn shook her head to erase the penetrating blue eyes. "That'll be fine."

"That'll be fine?" Josh hooted as the white-aproned man behind the counter shrugged. "Maybe we'll be lettin' you starve if you can't pay better attention'n that." He nodded to the counterman. "Ask her again."

"Do you want the special or. . .?" The cook's grin took the sting out of the tone of his voice. He enunciated carefully as if she were slightly dim-witted.

"All right, you two." Robynn forced herself to pay attention to their clowning. "I'll have my usual, one boiled egg, four minutes, two slices wheat toast, dry."

"Thought you said you was hungry." Josh slid his tray down to the coffee urns. "Something about even burnt toast sounding good."

"That was before." She poured herself both a glass of orange juice and a steaming cup of coffee. "Let's sit over there." She pointed to any empty table in the far corner.

"Before what?" Josh removed his dishes from the tray and stacked both trays on another table. Robynn ignored him as she dug into the presectioned grapefruit. "Lady, you sure make an exciting meal partner." Josh buttered his pancakes after the waitress delivered their hot order. "A body'd think you was mad or something."

"Nope." Robynn smiled as she sipped her coffee. "Just following your instructions. Getting up for the race." *Liar*, the little voice perched on her shoulder scolded. *You can't get your mind off that stranger. Maybe you could find him again if you ran up and down the barns and around the track.*

"You gotta be kidding," she muttered under her breath.

"What'd you say?" Josh forked another bit of pancake into his mouth.

Robynn shook her head. "Nothing." She took a deep breath. "Nothing important."

"You know, if I didn't know you better. . ."

"Is this seat taken?" The stranger's voice was as deep as she knew it would be.

"Dane! You old coot!" Josh's chair slammed to the floor when he shoved it back. He ignored the crash as he leaped to his feet and, between hugs, pounded the newcomer on the back. "When'd you get here?"

"About an hour ago. Your string is looking good."

"Here." Josh pulled out the adjoining chair before righting his own. "Sit down, son, sit down."

Robynn felt like she'd come in at the middle of the second act at the theater. Everyone knew the action but her. One thing for certain: Her nervous system hit overload. There were no naps in sight for her nerve ends. To prove her exterior nonchalance, she reached for her just-refilled coffee cup. Sipping the scalding brew eased the crick in her neck earned while staring at the two ecstatic men.

Josh clapped a hand on her shoulder. "This here's my nephew, you know, the one from California. I told you about him before."

"The name's Morgan. Dane Morgan." Those startling blue eyes twinkled at Josh's chagrin. "This old buzzard forgot to tell you my name."

Robynn shook the proffered hand. And wished she hadn't.

"According to the man I asked," he continued, "they call you Princess."

Robynn nodded. She pulled her focus from the heat pulsing from her fingers to her wrist and up her arm. That same heat glued her tongue to the roof of her mouth. With precise concentration, she articulated a word in spite of her useless vocal cords. "Yes." Her inner voice was shocked into silence by her reaction. But only for a moment. *What in the world...* She could feel that voice gearing up for a full-blown assault.

Instead of listening, she searched Dane's eyes. They shimmered like high mountain lakes in the summer sun. When he smiled at her perusal, laugh lines crinkled at the corners of his eyes and white teeth emphasized his deep tan. A tan one would never find on anyone who lived in the Willamette Valley.

Abruptly he released her hand and with the easy grace of a man who knows his own body, settled into the chair next to her. "I watched you this morning. You ride well."

"She's one of the best." Josh winked at her. "I trained her just like I trained you."

"Do you have horses here?" Robynn straightened in her chair and tried for a friendly smile on her dry lips.

"Not yet." Dane leaned his elbows on the table. "I'm up here looking for a farm and another string of animals. Know any that are for sale?"

"Could be." Josh waved to the waitress to refill their cups. "In fact, there are several. You thinking of moving up here?"

"Yes. My company headquarters will remain in San Francisco, but I'm ready for something different. I need a new operation, and you've always raved about the Pacific Northwest, so here I am."

Robynn's eyes widened at the sheer arrogance of the man. She stared at Josh, willing him to look up at her.

Instead, he drew circles in the droplets of water on the Formica-topped table. "How big an operation you want?"

"Well, since it seems to me I paid for half of that Stealth fighter with my tax dollars alone, I know I need new shelters."

"Yeah, you and King Midas might be related. . . ."

"Not quite. But things have gone well."

What an egotist. Robynn stared from one man to the other. Only sheer will-power kept her from laughing out loud. But they were serious. A tiny nod from Dane made her aware that her thoughts must be showing on her face again.

"You planning on moving your ponies up here?" Josh continued the discussion.

"All depends." Dane leaned back in his chair, teetering on the back two legs. "On?"

"On what's available. It would be nice to race the entire coast season. I have an appointment with a Realtor in half an hour."

"You're planning on staying around for a time then?"

"Yes." Dane turned to Robynn, who carefully wiped the derision off her face. "I think I'm going to be around a lot."

"You about finished, Princess?" Josh seemed to stress the nickname. "We got a pile of work to do before the afternoon program."

Robynn nodded. "Nice to meet you, Dane." All her mother's schooling on company manners came to her aid. She smiled, a formal smile that tried to hide the mischief dancing in her eyes, as she pushed back her chair. Before she could finish the action, Dane was on his feet behind her. He pulled out her chair, making her feel like the royalty her name proclaimed. As she turned to leave, his hand on her arm stopped her.

"How about dinner tonight?" He turned her to face him.

Her gaze started at the mother-of-pearl snap midchest on his royal blue plaid western shirt, traveled up past the springy hair showing in the open V, paused at the cleft chin and smiling lips, and then locked into his direct gaze. The tingle from the ride earlier jangled a warning over her entire nervous system. Danger! Danger! It was as if a siren went off.

"I don't think so, but thank you anyway."

"Come on, Princess, he's safe. After all, he is my nephew."

"But Josh." He knew she didn't date. What was the matter with him?

"Please." Since Josh rarely asked anything of her, his pleading look went straight to her heart.

"All right, I'd be glad to." She ignored the internal shock. *Glad to? Give me a break! I only said I'd go because Josh forced me.* She just barely kept herself from shaking her head.

"What time?" He obviously didn't waste words.

"I'll be done with chores after seven."

"Come on, Princess." Josh now commanded from the door. "We got work to do."

"Catch you later, Josh." Dane waved to his impatient relative. "Princess. . ." The deep timbre of his voice held her more securely than the hand burning her arm. "What about lunch? I can be back by then."

"No." She shook her head. "No time. Why?"

"I'd like to see you."

"But you said dinner."

"I know. But that's hours away."

"You don't let any grass grow under your feet, do you?" Robynn took a deep breath, hoping to calm the quivers his nearness ignited. Instead, the tang of expensive aftershave tickled her nose.

"No, I don't. When I see something I want, I go after it."

"I've got to get to work." Robynn's voice softened in spite of herself, mesmerized by the force he exuded.

"Coffee?"

"If you bring it to the tack room at noon." She fled to the barns, hooting in amazement at her reactions. *He'll never show. Men with a line like that never do.*

～

Sucker! I thought you were off women for the duration. Dane would like to have throttled the little voice laughing hysterically on his shoulder. True, he had decided to relax by searching for a new racing string and possible farm in the Pacific Northwest. True, he had given up the quest for that perfect mythical mate in spite of his mother's pleading. And true, he had informed *all* friends and family to quit playing matchmaker. He slid into the seat of his silver Porsche. *Think I'll keep that appointment this morning short. There's plenty of time this afternoon. Wonder where she'd like to go for dinner?*

～

Mucking out stalls was not a job requiring any degree of concentration. It left Robynn with too much time to think, to remember. The pain was always there, just buried under the experiences of seven years of balancing a life at the track with the pain of widowhood and long-distance motherhood. Most days she wasn't sure which was worse. She could still see, hear, feel the day her husband left.

"I can't handle it," was all the slim-hipped, happy-go-lucky jockey had said. "I know I've not been that great a husband, but I'm definitely not cut out to be a daddy. You know that. See ya, kid." He grinned his heart-stopping smile, touched three fingers to his slouch hat, and roared off in his red Corvette.

The next day that same grin greeted her from the sport's section of the evening paper: *Sonny O'Dell, Top Jockey at Portland Meadows.* A day later, the same paper carried the story of his wasted death, mangled and twisted within the frame of his 'Vette. Along with the girl who rode beside him. . .a real celebration they'd had.

At eighteen she'd wanted to run, to find someplace that had no memories of Sonny. Giving up seemed an appropriate response. But the baby growing inside her deserved a chance in spite of his parents' messed-up lives, so Robynn got on with living. She bought a house with part of the insurance money so she could make a home for their son. Jeremy she called him from the first fluttering movements. While the birth wasn't easy, the moment she first held her squirming little son in her arms was a thrill like nothing else in life. He was part of her, a new person to be surrounded with all the love her heart yearned to offer. Two months later, the doctors confirmed something Robynn suspected. Jeremy was blind. She dug in for the long stretch. Handicap was a word only for the racetrack. It would not stigmatize her son.

So much for the happily-ever-after kind of life the media promised. Without her friends and family, life would have seemed like happily-never-after. But she was a survivor. Jeremy would be, too. Her mother reminded her far more often than she appreciated that letting God help her would ease the pain, but the daughter would have none of it. If God cared so much, why was Jeremy born blind? If her mother wanted to pray—fine, but Robynn had no desire to return to the God of her youth, the God who had let her down so badly.

"What is it, Princess?" Robynn jumped as Josh touched her arm. Her wheelbarrow stopped with a thump. One look at her pain-punished eyes, and the trainer hustled her into an empty stall. "What's wrong? Something happen to Jeremy?"

"No. I saw him yesterday. He's fine. I just started thinking back, and that awful pain grabbed me again. It's always back there, just waiting. . . . Oh, Josh, why won't it go away. . .permanently?" Tears shimmered at the corners of her eyes.

"Ach, lass. . ."

"And part of it *is* Jeremy. I hate leaving him down at that school."

"But you'n' the counselors figured it was for the best. . . ."

"Sure. The best school. The best training. But I only see him once a week and on vacations. Mothers are supposed to be there when their kid needs them. To tuck him in at night, to listen to his prayers. To kiss away his hurts."

"But you can't ride the circuit and drag him along. And you know he needs special training, consistently. At least for a while."

"I know all that. But still, I keep wondering. Am I doing what's best for him? Maybe I should take some office job so I can be home at regular hours." She stared at the dirt floor for an endless moment. When she raised her face, a single tear had escaped and glistened down her curved cheek.

Josh reached out with one gnarled finger and wiped the drop away. They'd been over this many times before.

"Come on, lass. You're supposed to be gettin' up for the race."

"I know." She took a deep breath, and like lifting a shade, her eyes cleared, her chin assumed its usual determined angle. Shoulders back, another chest-expanding breath, and the "Princess" took over again. "Thanks." Even the royal smile returned. "Don't be a'worryin' yerself, auld man." Her brogue thickened to distract him.

"Well, you'd be tellin' me if anything was to happen?" Bushy white brows met over his eyes. "Wouldn't ye?"

"Yes." Her shoulders sagged. "Yes. I promise."

Josh stared hard into her eyes for another millennium-like second, then turned and strode out of the stall. Robynn heard something like, "If I could just a-got my hands on that fool O'Dell. . . ," all muttered under his breath.

"Whew." Robynn breathed deeply, shrugging the cloud away. *You know better than to look back,* her inner voice scolded. *It never does any good. You swore to look forward, look only at the good things that are happening.* In a flash she saw blue eyes and hair glistening like the breast of a warbling blackbird. She sighed. *Definitely one of the good things.*

But then. . .no men, the little voice continued. *You said no man would ever cause you pain again. This one certainly could be painful if this flash of attraction is any indication. See, and you thought attraction like this only happened in the movies.*

Robynn finished dumping the loaded wheelbarrow and trundled it back to the tack room.

"Here." A steaming Styrofoam cup seemed to leap from the dimness and came to rest in her hand.

"Oh! You startled me." She leaned her back against the doorjamb, waiting for her heart to resume its normal beat. Without conscious thought, her body assumed a languid air. An errant sunbeam warmed her high cheekbones and sparked diamonds in the tendrils of hair that escaped the confining comb.

"You said noon." The shadowed stall made him loom even larger than before.

"And you're always punctual, I suppose."

"My middle name. Dane Punctual Morgan. Sounds good, don't you think? Nobody gave me a name like Princess."

Robynn eyed his blatantly masculine physique. "I should hope not. Princess would never suit you."

Dane chuckled, the warmth in his voice drawing them closer. "But it does suit you." He studied her over the rim of his coffee cup. "I think you stepped right out of a fairy-tale book."

A slight tremor shook her hand as Robynn set her half-empty cup on a shelf. The urge to stay and hear more fought with her awareness of the passing time.

"I've got to get going." She glanced a second time at the slim, silver band on her wrist. "Thanks for the coffee."

"The chores are done. Why don't you come with me instead?"

A look like he had misplaced his marbles crossed her face. She shook her head. "Sorry, but I have races to run."

"I thought, hoped you just trained for Josh. You race?"

Robynn nodded.

"Take care, then."

Robynn had no idea how heartfelt his light comment really was.

❧

Dane watched her leave. Slowly he ran his finger around the rim of his Styrofoam coffee cup. Riding was dangerous for anyone, but much more so for women. Why'd she. . .

"She's been bad hurt." Josh hung a horse sheet on the rack.

"Racing?" Dane's eyebrows shot up.

"No," Josh snorted. "By a man. She can handle the horses."

Keeping further questions to himself, Dane glanced at his watch. "See you this evening. I gotta run. And Josh, thanks for the info."

Why would anyone hurt her? The question nagged him as he strode out to the parking lot. What kind of fool had she been mixed up with?

⁓

The sun played tag with the low-floating clouds, more often than not losing the contest, as Robynn lugged her gear across the infield of the race track. Flags from the holes in the nine-hole golf course that utilized the infield snapped in the breeze. Spectators were already filing into the glass-enclosed grandstand in preparation for the day's entertainment, while the last golf cart putted out the gate.

Robynn turned and walked backwards on the sandy passage, checking to see if Mount Hood had received a fresh dusting of snow. The sharply pointed peak to the south of the broad Columbia River promised skiing in the winter. Poor, decapitated Mount St. Helens off to the north had never looked the same since the devastation from the volcano's eruption.

Seeing both mountains before a race was one of Robynn's good luck charms. She always won when both peaks were visible.

"I knew today felt good," she whispered. "A special day. A winning day." She turned, breathing deeply in the crisp clean air, not sullied with even a trace of pollution from the paper mills upriver. "Yes, a winning day." She turned for a last glimpse of the mountains, then with a light step crossed the track to the tunnel leading to the saddling area and the jockeys' locker rooms. With an effort she banished the image of broad, sheepskin-clad shoulders and a laughing grin.

Robynn blinked as the dimness of the concrete entry closed around her. After following the fenced area that kept spectators from getting too close to the horses in the saddling paddock, she opened the door to the weighing room and jockeys' locker rooms. Even the ancient green paint failed to dull her mood.

"Hey, Princess," one of the guys hailed her. "You up in the first?"

"Yeah, number six for Dr. Benson." She paused by the scale. "What about you?"

"Naw. Second race. All you old-timers get first choice."

Robynn grinned at the familiar complaint of the apprentice jockey. "I served my time," she reminded the young man not yet out of the acne stage. "You'll get yours, if you hang around long enough." She smiled at him again and turned left to the cramped dressing space for the women. Her nose wrinkled as the familiar aromas of liniment, shampoo, wet showers, and stale cigarette smoke assailed her upon opening the door. Half of the small room was taken up by the table for the resident chiropractor, who would bend and stretch the women on the table to get them in shape for the riding ahead. Benches lining the room were scattered with articles of tack and clothing.

"Hi, Princess." The girl on the chiropractor's table waved one hand, then grunted as the doctor snapped another vertebra into place.

"Still feeling the effects of that fall?" Robynn asked as she hung up her jacket.

"Ummm-hummm." The girl nodded. "I think we got clipped, or he wouldn'ta gone down like that. You watch that Romero. Talk about us women taking chances."

"Thanks for the advice. He's pretty young."

"Yeah, and money hungry. Let alone swamped by dreams of glory." She rolled onto her side. "You just be careful."

As Robynn wrapped a towel around her head and stepped into the showers, she could hear old Josh. *Keep your distance as much as you can*, he always said. *So your mount don't bang the horse's feet in front of you. That's clipping. You gotta watch who's coming up behind, too, so he don't do the same to you. Racing ain't just runnin' that nag around the track to win. You gotta develop a sixth sense about where everyone is and what they're likely to do. That's what makes a good jockey.*

Another voice and face took over her inner musings when she turned off the shower and wrapped herself in the emerald bath sheet. A face with angular planes, interesting shadows, and a well-used smile that crinkled up to his eyes. She'd already memorized that face well, even though she'd just met Dane that morning. Or had they known each other for eternity?

She could feel the rustle of her azure silk dress as it swished against her legs. First dinner, then. . .

"Hey, Princess!" A voice next to her shattered her vision. "If you're up in the first, you better quit daydreaming and get a hustle on."

Chapter 2

Dane thumped a fist on the steering wheel as he threaded the Porsche through the traffic on the way to the Realtor's office. He hadn't been impressed with the man he'd met that morning. The woman he'd spoken with later sounded suitably enthusiastic. After he'd outlined what he wanted, she promised to show him several farms.

His frustration increased as he found himself caught behind a slow-moving truck. Why'd she have to be a jockey? Training and exercising weren't so bad. Accidents were rare in the morning hours. But he'd seen some bad ones during the program, races when both riders and horses had died. Living with a mother permanently crippled during a steeplechase taught him another side of the tragedy of accidents.

And I didn't keep her safe.

He thumped the wheel again. Women should *not* be licensed as jockeys. No matter how good they were. Sheer strength counted at times. While he knew his views were considered chauvinistic in today's world, he had no intention of changing his mind.

He gunned the Porsche past the dump truck. His mother's voice came back to him. *You're acting like a chauvinist, Son.* But then, she hadn't been a spectator as he had while the pain she experienced drove the son to curse the cause. She should have been in the grandstand that fateful day, rather than in the racing saddle. He should have made sure of that, like his father had commanded him.

He switched off the dark thoughts along with the car key. Sliding from the low-slung car, he strode toward the real estate office. Now was the time to concentrate on his future. He took a deep breath and blinked hard to dispel the vision of laughing violet eyes.

❧

By the time the call came for weighing in, Robynn's resident troop of butterflies cavorted in aerial shows in her stomach. Today was a four-star performance no matter how many times she swallowed and ordered them back to their roosts.

"One hundred five pounds." The scale master handed her seven pounds of lead to insert in the slots of her saddle pad. "That brings you up to the one hundred twelve you need. Have a good one." He grinned at her. "Next."

Robynn paused a moment to scan the crowd across the entry to the paddock, hoping, in spite of what he'd said, to see a tall man in a sheepskin jacket. Instead, she grinned and waved at an appreciative wolf whistle. Even with her wavy hair tucked up under her green silk-covered racing helmet, no one could mistake her for one of the guys. The loose-fitting silks failed to conceal her slender neck and shoulders. Silky white pants curved from her narrow waist over slim but definitely feminine hips and down long legs to be tucked into knee-high riding boots. Self-assurance, obvious in the tilt of her determined chin, belied the fluttering horde of butterflies halfway up her throat.

All the horses were already in the individual stalls that spoke-wheeled from a central hub in the cavernous saddling paddock. Robynn circled to the right until she found her mount for this race. She had ridden the horse several times before, once to a second place.

Mounted on Tame Adventure, she listened to the last-minute instructions of the trainer. Finally he led the animal out to the pony riders, who led the Thoroughbreds around the track to the starting gate.

Her mount broke clean at the gate and easily swept into the lead, winning by a length. "You did it, old man." She patted the horse's steaming shoulder as she turned him back toward the winner's circle. "Good fella." The horse side-stepped his way through the spectators to stand in front of the cameras. Robynn slipped her saddle off his back as the officials draped a horseshoe wreath of red and white roses over his withers.

"Congratulations." Portly Dr. Benson pumped her hand. "You two looked really good out there."

"Thank you." Robynn smiled for the flash camera and, while searching the crowd for certain blue eyes, finished her conversation. "Tame Adventure was really ready, and so was I. You have a good horse there."

"Let's just hope this is the first of many." The doctor beamed.

Robynn smiled her agreement and stepped on the scale. A feeling of discontent niggled at her mind. Where was he? Maybe she'd been wrong. Maybe he didn't feel the same way she did. But it sure felt both ways at the time. And he *had* asked her out to dinner. But he didn't even know where she lived. The internal argument never showed on her smiling face.

By the end of the day, Robynn felt like she'd been run over by a Mack truck. Every muscle ached, and even though she'd been in the money four times, including two firsts, the hovering miasma of disappointment refused to dissipate.

"You did a good job with that gray." Josh nodded as she returned to the stalls. "Never dreamed he'd make it into the money."

"I hate to say 'I told you so' but. . ."

"Then don't. Park your hunkus on that chair for a spell." He pointed to the director's chair in the corner of the tack room. "You look like your best friend took a hike."

Robynn sat as ordered, glad of the opportunity to let down. She leaned back into the curving canvas and, with closed eyes, allowed the tiredness and the black mood to seep out through her booted toes.

"Whyn't you just head on home," Josh said, pity for the purple shadows under her closed eyes evident in his glance. "You look done in."

"What about feeding?"

"I'll manage. Been taking care of horses long before you came along."

"Thanks, Josh." The weary woman rose to her feet. "You're a real friend." She paused at the door. "If anyone should ask for me. . ."

"I'll tell him."

Robynn nodded.

The drive to her house out by Portland State passed in a blur of stops and starts. Her black Celica shifted easily and turned as if it knew the way without her assistance. Even the bronze and fiery red chrysanthemums lining her driveway failed to lift her spirits in their customary way. She unlocked the back door and, as she closed it, dropped her jacket, then sweater and shirt on her way to the bathroom. Once in the bedroom, she rammed her heel into the bootjack by her bed and, after straining to pull the boots off, flung each one in the general direction of the closet. "I'll clean them later," she promised herself as she staggered to the shower.

⤝

Minutes later Robynn slipped between cool sheets and pulled the navy down comforter up to her chin. Flashing blue eyes dominated her thoughts as she sighed her way into dreamland. *She and Dane, sitting across from each other at a restaurant. Their eyes locked. He moved his hand across the table to capture hers. There were flames from his touch; his breath, teasing her ear as he leaned forward, sent windblown sparks igniting brushfires wherever they lit. The music played countermelody to the blood pulsing through her limbs, drugging her mind.*

A buzzing—long, then short—wended its way through the rhythm. The buzz disrupted the dance, the man in her arms faded as if she watched the action through the wrong end of a telescope.

"Buzzzzzz." That nagging presence sounded again. Still in the rosy warmth of the land between waking and sleeping, Robynn knotted the belt of her royal purple robe at her waist and drifted for the front entrance. Just as an impatient finger pressed the doorbell again, she twisted the lock and swung open the door.

"Yes-s-s." Her eyes and mouth O'd as she clutched her robe more tightly around her. "D–Dane." *Oh ground, swallow me up right now!*

"Last time I looked in the mirror that's who I was."

"I. . .ah. . .I'm not ready."

"I can tell that." He leaned forward and lowered his voice. "Don't you think you should invite me in before your neighbors start to talk?"

She stepped back, the heat that fired up her neck making her wish for a fan—one powered high enough to blow this man right off the steps. She stepped back and beckoned him in. Pointing to the living room, she said in a rush, "You can wait in there." She turned and headed down the hall. "I'll just be a few minutes."

His "take your time" floated after her.

As if racing for the finish line, Robynn threw her clothes on the bed, not wasting time on the selection. With a swish, the deeply-draped neckline of her azure silk dress settled in place. She smoothed the full skirt over her hips and reveled as the fabric swirled about her legs. She loved silk, the fabric of royalty—especially princesses being taken to dinner.

A touch of dusky, gray-blue eye shadow and navy mascara set her eyes to shimmering as she outlined her perfectly bowed lips with deep rose lipstick. Peach blush emphasized her high cheekbones, and with a dusting of powder, she was finished. Swiftly she glanced over her collection of fragrances, her one feminine weakness. Which one could be termed romantic? She stared for a moment at her reflection in the mirror, grabbed a bottle of Shalimar, and sprayed it lightly on pulse points. The cut glass atomizer clinked as she set it down.

She started out of the room but stopped in front of the dresser that held her stand for pierced earrings. Only for a moment, she debated before choosing the tiny diamonds, her wedding present from. . .

Abruptly she attached them to the lobes of her ears and with a toss of the cloud of hair caressing her shoulders, flicked off the light and left the room. Pausing for a moment in the arched doorway, she unconsciously waited for a reaction from the man prowling her living room.

"Dane?"

He spun from his study of the wall decorated with framed photos of her in the winner's circle, candids of her favorite mounts, Josh and other track officials, plus a large color shot of an entire field of Thoroughbreds straining around the far turn of the track.

The now familiar tingle started at her toes and, like a Derby entry in the homestretch, raced to the top of her head.

"Princess?" Her name was a whisper on his lips as he blinked at the transition from racing to dining silks. The moment stretched until goose bumps crept up Robynn's arms from the intentness of his gaze.

"I'm ready."

"Right." Dane Morgan seemed to recall himself from some far distant land as he stepped forward to take the coat she held. She slipped her arms in the sleeves as he held her coat for her. It had been so long since anyone had held her coat. She sighed at the pleasure. His fingers sent curls of excitement coursing over her scalp when he lifted her hair from the neckline of her cream wool.

"Your chariot awaits." He squeezed her shoulders before opening the front door. "Your Highness."

Portland had donned her evening gown of lights as they cruised the wide street above the shipping center of Swan Island. The Fremont Bridge rose in all its white glory with the United States and Oregon flags snapping in the spotlights high above the crest. While the City of Roses was Portland's nickname, Robynn always felt City of Bridges would fit better, as five spans crossed the Willamette River in as many miles.

Skyscrapers from round to octagonal glittered in their formal evening dress, giving the city a distinctive skyline.

Robynn loved it all. Portland was a gutsy, growing metropolis with typical urban difficulties but room for a racetrack and breeding farms within twenty minutes of downtown.

"Where're we going?" She settled deeper into the rich leather seat of the silver Porsche.

"You'll know soon enough." Dane clicked a CD into the player. The clear tenor of John Denver's "Rocky Mountain High" filled the car.

Fifteen minutes later, after discovering mutual interests in music and food, they pulled up in front of Maggie's Olde Inn, one of Robynn's favorite restaurants.

Dane tucked her arm in his as they left the car and walked up the short flagstone path to the entry. Heavy wooden doors crossed with iron bands swung open when he pressed the latch.

Stepping inside was like walking through a time warp, back a hundred years to merry old England. Dark beams spanned the ceiling and led one's eyes to the focal point of the dining room, a man-sized fireplace set in the tabby wall. Waitresses in gathered skirts and white mobcaps rushed between the dark wooden tables surrounded by patrons.

"Two for Morgan," Dane responded to the hostess's query.

The svelte blond bypassed the main dining room and led them up a steep, narrow stair to an alcove just large enough for a table for two. Robynn could hear other diners in the individual rooms around them, but the illusion of privacy lent a mysterious air to the evening.

"Enjoy your dinner." The hostess stood two leather-bound menus in front of them. "Your waitress will be right up."

"Thanks."

Robynn took a deep breath. "Um. . ." She paused, trying to think. "How did you enjoy the races today?"

"I didn't."

"What?" Robynn shook her head.

"No, no. It's not what you think. I love horse racing."

Her held-in breath sent the candle flickering as it escaped.

"But I couldn't enjoy the races because I wasn't there." The twinkle in his eyes told her he knew what she'd thought. "I was out with that Realtor looking at farms. I told you I wanted to buy one."

"That's right. Did you see any good ones?"

"Nothing I really liked. But when I stopped by the track, Josh told me of one. He said his owner was thinking of selling out."

"Yes." Robynn sipped her iced tea again. "She's been ill."

"She?"

"Opal McKecknen. Her husband died several years ago. He was a really dedicated Thoroughbred breeder, but she loved the horses as much as he, so she kept the string going. Josh has done a good job for her. He oversees the farm and breeding stock besides running the training and racing here at the track."

"I have an appointment to talk with her tomorrow."

"It's really hard for her." Robynn frowned as she thought of the birdlike woman who rode well enough to have been a jockey herself. "Getting old is the pits."

"What do you think of Robynn O'Dell?" His question caught her by surprise.

"Um–m–m–m. . .that's. . ."

Before she could gather her wits enough to finish the sentence, Dane interrupted. "All the track was talking about him, how well he did today."

Robynn took a swallow of ice water to dispel the rock in her throat. He didn't know who she was. She stared at him, hoping to find a teasing light in his eyes. None.

"I'll need a man like that."

"Uh–h, there are other good jockeys out there, too." Robynn felt caught in a trap. "We're finding that many times women make better riders."

"No." Dane stated an absolute. "Not for me. I'll never have a woman up on one of my horses during a race."

Chapter 3

Robynn's inner warmth dropped to below zero. The tingles turned to icicles. "Did I hear you right?" Each word seemed sheathed in ice.

"What's the matter?" Dane shook his head, question marks all over his face. "I don't have anything against women exercising horses. But racing is too dangerous. Women just don't have the strength to control half a ton of hurtling horseflesh."

"And men do?"

"Well, not always." She could see he was trying to be honest. "But at least they have a better chance."

"And how many horses have *you* raced?"

"None. Princess, I don't understand—"

"Don't call me that!" Her chin had turned to steel, matching the glint in her eyes.

"What. . .?"

"Princess." Her tone was flat. "Mr. Morgan, do you know what my name is? My real name?"

He stared at her. The silence lengthened, taut as a guitar string turned once too many times. "No. I don't guess I do."

"My name is Robynn, as in Robynn O'Dell." She watched as his eyes narrowed. "You said earlier, you wanted to hire me?"

"O–h–h. . ."

"Surprised? And I'll let you in on a little secret, Mr. Fancy Horse Buyer from California. I wouldn't ride for you if you owned Citation, Seattle Slew, *and* Man O' War." She rose. Queen Elizabeth couldn't have been more regal. "And now I find I've lost my appetite. Do you want to take me home or shall I call a cab?"

"Princess!" The ice in her eyes reminded him. "All right, Robynn. I didn't know. You're a good rider."

"Just not good enough for your horses, the horses. . ." Her control cracked around the edges.

"No, that's not what I meant. Sit down so I can talk to you." He tried to stare her down. "You could have told me your real name. Not just let me run on like some babbling fool."

"If the shoe fits?" Robynn could see she'd gone about as far as was wise.

271

Straight black brows met at the scowl furrows in his forehead. His hand clenched and unclenched on the handle of the coffee mug. Anger burned from his eyes, furnace-hot rather than icy.

"Sit down!" Each consonant snapped like a rifle shot.

Robynn didn't move. "The cab?"

"No! I'll take you home." He grabbed his jacket and rammed his arms into the sleeves. This time when he held her coat, his fingers felt like they'd rather pull her hair than lift it gently. *Pull it out by the roots, most likely*, she thought. The way he hustled her down the stairs and threw some bills at the astounded waitress left Robynn in no doubt of his feelings.

"Have a good evening." The door slammed on the hostess's words.

"I am strong enough to make it to the car on my own." Robynn tried to slow him down, but the fingers clenched on her upper arm forced her to dogtrot in her high heels. "Even if I am a woman." Honey dripped from her change in tone.

Dane Morgan didn't seem to like the sweetness any better than the ice as he stuffed her into the silver Porsche.

The drive to her home passed in a silence so loud it hurt her ears. She stepped out of the car before he could open his door when the vehicle halted in her driveway. Her stiff "thank you" was lost in the roar of the engine as Dane rammed the machine into reverse and shot back into the street.

"Well, my girl," Robynn said to herself as she swung open the front door. "It sure felt good for a while. But. . ." She hung her coat in the closet. "You better stick to horses and small boys." She wandered into the bedroom and picked up the latest picture of Jeremy, framed against the backdrop of the State School for the Blind. "You seem to do better in those categories." She studied the sweet face of her son. "Oh Jeremy, I miss you so. And thanks to that *gentleman*, I didn't get to call you tonight. What a mistake." She set the picture back down and sighed.

She could feel the anger resurging. "What a stupid, chauvinistic attitude. Men!" She dropped her earrings on the dresser top. "At least this time *I* did the dumping. And before I got hurt."

As she slipped between the sheets, electric blue eyes flashed back on her inner vision. *At least I hope so.* The small voice sounded doubtful.

❦

All the tossing and turning made inroads on Robynn's alertness for the morning. She woke up feeling drained and out of sorts, and she hadn't recovered her normal good humor by the time she reached the stables. Liquid sunshine, as Portlanders call their frequent rain, misted her hair and dripped onto her neck, only adding to her depression.

"You seem down," Josh commented after watching her mope around the tack room, waiting for the horses to finish their grain.

"Yeah. To get even with a pregnant centipede, I'd have to reach up."

"That bad, huh?"

"Must be the rain."

"How is Dane this morning, or rather last night?"

She stared at the knowing twinkle in his eyes.

"Well, when he left here, he seemed mighty anxious to find your house. I just assumed. . ."

"Well, you know what assuming does. And I'm not the one to feel like a you-know-what this morning." The words poured faster as her anger returned.

"And ye're meaning he should?"

"Meaning that he wanted to hire the great Robynn O'Dell to ride his future horses until he found out Robynn O'Dell is me!"

"Hold on now, lass." Josh shook his head. "You're not making a lot of sense."

"Josh, he doesn't want a woman jockey. Afraid I can't handle these *huge* animals in a real race." She whirled from the far wall she'd been staring into. "I'd like to show him how strong. . ."

"He hasn't seen you race." Josh picked up a saddle and sat down on a bale of hay to start the never-ending cleaning.

"No. And I don't care if he ever does."

"Lass, he has an appointment with Opal McKecknen today." Josh rubbed the rag around the can of saddle soap and applied the cream to the leather.

"I know. And that's what scares me silly." She joined him on the hay bale.

"We've been a team for a long while." Josh patted her shoulder. "But you can ride for anyone now. That agent of yours'll have half the owners beating down his door after your wins this last week. You were somethin' to see."

"But. . .but. . ." She paused, trying to straighten out the thoughts careening through her brain. "It's like Opal's horses are my own. I've been with some of them since they were dropped. I broke and trained them. I want to keep on riding them, besides the others."

"Here." He handed her the rag and saddle. "Might as well be useful, 'stead of flittin' about."

Robynn continued the circular motions without a break. Her brow furrowed while she stared unseeing at the leather in her hands. The turning wheels could nearly be heard out loud as her agile brain shifted into high gear.

"Josh, Opal is serious about selling?"

"Um." He continued soaping a headstall. The squeak of leather in his hands grew loud in the silence.

Concentrating so hard on the ideas bursting in her mind, Robynn stared intently at the saddle in her lap. "Let's buy them."

"Them, who?"

"The horses. Our horses."

"Are ye daft, girl? Where'd we be gettin' that kind of money?"

"You said it yourself, we've been partners for a long time. This way we could be real partners." She dumped the half-cleaned saddle as she sprang to her feet. "Then I could keep riding them. Before Dane buys the whole shootin' match from her."

"But, Princess, we don't know for sure he's gonna buy them."

"How can he help it? He seems to have the money." With an impatient hand, she brushed back the raven wings of hair on her temples. "You know what a perfect setup it is. And besides, if not him, then someone else will."

Unbidden, thoughts of the McKecknen farm leaped into her consciousness. A split rail fence surrounded the sprawling brick ranch house. Next to the newly painted white stables, the quarter-mile track made breaking and training convenient. Acres of lush pasture dotted with grazing Thoroughbreds proclaimed the set purpose of the place. The sturdy sign with the words "McKecknen's Racing Stables" painted in green only made it official.

It was truly a horse and rider heaven. And in her mind, on the trail that circled back into the fir trees on the hills behind the farm, trotted two riders. Herself and a broad-shouldered, ebony-headed man. Laughter floated on the breeze. Knees brushed as they rode side by side, and at the spot where the alder trees kissed overhead, they stopped.

Robynn shook her head, bringing herself back to the tack room and her conversation with Josh.

"That it be. Yeah, it be that perfect." The deep crevices in his forehead revealed more than his words.

"I know I could take out a loan against my house."

"What about the payments to Jeremy's school?"

"They'd come from somewhere. I've never borrowed from my parents before. Dad might get real excited about owning part interest in the ponies." Robynn's words tumbled over themselves in her excitement.

"Whoa, lass." The old man waved a hand in front of her nonfocusing eyes. "Yer like a filly with the bit in her teeth. Slow down."

"I can't, Josh. I never thought of doing something like this before." She whirled at the corner and strode back across the room. A single lightbulb dangled on a cord from the ceiling, alternately casting shadows then highlights on her face as she paced. "You said it yourself. My agent will get plenty of mounts for me."

"Sounds like I said far too much, the way you keep turnin' my words agin me," Josh grumped at the bridle clutched in his aging fingers.

"She wouldn't want the money all at once." Robynn spun again, striding back and forth. "Would she?"

"Don't ask me." Josh hung the headstall and saddle back on the pegs in the wall. "I just work here."

Robynn stopped her pacing. "You don't think it could happen, do you?"

"Right now I think you better get out there and work them horses." He led the way to the door. "Before it's noon."

"Josh!" She grabbed his arm. "Answer me."

Absently, he patted her fingers. "I dunno, lass. Ye've surprised me, that's all." He squinted up at the still-dripping heavens as if to receive instructions from above.

Robynn waited. All the early morning sounds of a track penetrated her consciousness. Down the line a horse nickered. Another whinnied, answering a call from across the barns. In the next stall, Tame Adventure banged the door with a pawing hoof, demanding his release. The pungent aroma of ammonia, straw, and horses filled her nostrils.

"All I can promise," he patted her hand again, "is to think about it. To really think about it."

"You've always dreamed of owning a string of Thoroughbreds," she whispered. "You know you have."

"You take Finding Fun out first." He pointed to the sorrel filly with her head hanging over the stall door. "Work her easy for a couple-a miles, then breeze her for two furlongs. We'll clock her and see how she's comin' along. I'd like to enter her in that maiden race next week."

Robynn knew better than to keep pushing him. When Josh promised to think about something, she knew he would, slowly and carefully, searching every angle.

All the animals seemed bathed in a new light as she looked at them through the eyes of a possible future owner. She knew all their strengths and weaknesses, how to outsmart their quirks, how to get the best from them. Between her and Josh, they might as well have owned the string as it was—Opal had let them have such a free hand the last year. But then both Opal and her husband had depended completely on Josh to train and manage their horses and breeding farm, even before Mr. McKecknen died.

Finding Fun was one of Robynn's favorite animals. She had been at the farm the day the filly entered the world, snorting and kicking. Feisty Fun would have been a good name for her. Her inquisitive nose was always into anything new, but while she pushed and tried each restraint, she'd never been mean.

"I can't wait to race you." Robynn rubbed the white blaze on the filly's nuzzling nose. "You've got the speed and the heart. Now all you need is the experience." The filly nodded as if she agreed. Robynn chuckled while she snapped the cross ties onto the soft web halter.

After they'd groomed the filly, Josh boosted Robynn into her saddle. "You remember what I said about this workout?"

Robynn nodded down at him and lowered her goggles into place.

"Fine, then. I'll be up in the bleachers, so let her out at the pole in front."

Robynn calmed the dancing filly. "Josh." She tightened the reins even more. "You won't talk to anyone about our discussion this morning, will you?"

"Ach, lass, ye know me better'n that." He led the animal toward the track entrance.

She smiled and patted the filly's shoulder. "You're right. I think I just needed to hear myself talk." As she rode out onto the track, the drizzling mist muffled the hoofbeats of the other horses working the sandy oval. Across the field the grandstand seemed fuzzy, its outline slightly out of focus, blurred by the gloom.

Robynn tried to keep her mind on the animal she was riding, but the smooth canter the filly settled into lulled her into thinking about the evening before. The time with Dane had felt so good. Even their senses of humor were compatible. All except for the fact that he was a totally insufferable, close-minded... She slammed her mental door on the memories. As she and her mount swept easily past the gate on their first mile, she felt the now familiar tingle. "Dummy!" She scolded herself. "Even just thinking about him causes a reaction. This has got to stop."

The next time around, though, she scanned the small covered and heated bleachers where owners and trainers could get out of the rain to watch the workouts. Beside Josh, in the middle row, a sheepskin-jacketed figure leaned against the wooden bench behind them. One lazy hand lifted in greeting.

Robynn's hands loosened on the reins as her mind went into shock. Instantly aware of her rider's lack of concentration, the filly snorted and leaped forward. The jolt brought Robynn back to the present with a snap. Reflex action kept her in the saddle and had her back in control before they'd gone four more paces.

Good reaction time, she congratulated herself after her heartbeat returned to normal. *Good reaction time, my foot*, her resident critic chided. *You nearly blew that one, and all because of that man. You know, the one you said would never bother you.* Robynn mentally turned off the voices and leaned forward to pat the filly's shoulder.

"Never a dull moment with you around, is there?" Her voice gentled the excited filly. But when they reached the pole again, the horse leaned into the bit, asking for more rein. "Come on, baby! Go for it!"

The filly didn't need a second invitation. Within two paces, Finding Fun leveled out, each stride increasing her speed.

Robynn loved the speed and power so much she nearly forgot to pull up at the appointed post. "Another time, girl." Robynn leaned her weight against the reins as globs of lather from the heaving animal splattered her. As they neared the gate, Josh waved them over.

Robynn refused to meet the eyes of the man towering over Josh. Instead she beamed at her trainer. "Good, huh?" She pushed her goggles up on her helmet.

"Seventeen and a half. She sure can move." Josh stroked the filly with one hand while he held the bridle with the other. "Had a hard time getting her to stop, didn't ye?"

"Some." Robynn grinned down at him. "But she minded anyway." While the two of them discussed the ride, the tingles sprinting up and down her spine reminded her that another man stood beside the filly's head. Deliberately she kept her gaze on the trainer. At the same time, her back straightened, the tilt of her chin assumed its imperial angle.

"Well, let's get the mud off her and cool her out." Josh headed to the barn.

As Robynn nudged the filly to follow, a tanned hand grasped the reins just under the horse's jaw. "Robynn. . ."

She stared out between the sorrel ears, the exhilaration of the run evaporating. She glared down at the hand he placed on her knee. The icicles returned to spike her words. "Excuse me, I don't—"

"I'm sorry I acted the way I did last night." Dane interrupted her before she could go any farther. He removed his hand.

Robynn could hear and feel the ice shattering like an unexpected spring thaw.

"Can we please agree to disagree?" His contrite tone forced her to look at him. "Please forgive me."

"Yes." Her response caught her by surprise.

Violet eyes locked with sky blue. Robynn forgot the rain, the run, and the dampness creeping down her neck. It was as if the sun had forced its way through the clouds to shine just on them. The glow spread from the spot on her knee where his hand had been, leaped to her mouth to tug at its corners, and danced on up to twinkle in her eyes.

She spoke around the ripple of laughter in her throat. Iridescent notes of joy burst from the prison in her chest and winged their way to find the sun. "We can try to do that."

"And, Robynn." He leaned against the nudge the impatient filly gave him.

"My friends call me Princess," she interrupted him softly.

"Friends." He held out his right hand.

"Friends." She placed her own in his. She had to breathe deeply to counteract the shock of the pressure of his fingers around hers.

Finding Fun raised her head, pulling against the weight of the hand on her reins. When another nudge failed to catch their attention, she jigged sideways, staring imploringly toward the barn.

With another smile, Dane turned and led them up the road.

"I'll take her now," Josh said as they reached the row of stalls. Nodding, Robynn kicked out of the stirrups and, swinging her right leg over the filly's rump, slid to the ground. She turned and bumped into a solid wall of male chest.

"What time are you done today?"

It was the last question she expected. "Why?"

"Two things. I'd like you to look at some farms with me. You know the area, and that way you'll know what I'm looking for."

"And?"

"And I'd like to take you out to dinner again. To make up for last night. Some subjects we just won't discuss right now, okay?"

Can I really do this? Agree to disagree and not bring up the subject that means so much to me? Lord, if this is from You, aren't You asking an awful lot of me? The silence lengthened before she finally sighed.

"Right." She nodded as if to seal the bargain. "And now I'd better get back to work or Josh'll come looking for me."

"Speaking of angels. . ."

"Is that what you call him?"

Josh thrust the reins of the bay Come Runnin' in her hands. "Someone around here better get some work done or they'll be blowing Parade before we're finished." He winked at her when he saw the sunlight smile on her face. "Looks like we bypassed the centipedes."

I hope so, Robynn thought. *I'm tired of feeling down.*

Well, you've got a lot to look up to now, her sneaky little voice giggled. *Dane Morgan is pretty big and. . .* Robynn pulled her goggles into place and swung her mount out on the track. The mist blew in her face. Surprised, she licked the moisture from her lips. She'd thought sure the sun was shining.

Chapter 4

By three o'clock when Robynn finished riding for the day, she probably wouldn't remember which horse she won with and which placed third. For sure she'd put the loser out of her mind. She'd used all her powers of concentration during each race, but between them—

"Princess," the scale master had chided, "don't you think you'd better have the silks on your helmet match your shirt? Most owners appreciate that kind of uniform." Robynn dashed back to change, the red staining her cheeks not a reflection from the silks she wore.

The other women jockeys kept out of her way as Robynn broke the sound barrier showering and dressing. Impatiently she tucked the turquoise silk blouse into the waistband of black western pants, then pulled the lacy black v-neck sweater over her head. By the time she added silver loop earrings and two chains, Robynn the woman was metamorphosed from Robynn the jockey. The addition of mauve eye shadow and black mascara, plum lipstick and blush completed the transition.

"It's just not fair," grumbled one of the women.

"What's not?" Robynn halted the brush sweeping the waves back in her hair.

"You're not only a fantastic rider, but you walk out of here looking like a model."

"At five feet, three inches?" Robynn snorted. "Some model. I could maybe pose for the junior wear."

"Well, it's just not fair."

"Thanks." Robynn finished brushing her hair, shrugged into her leather hip-length jacket, and slung her duffel over her shoulder. "You make me feel good."

The wolf whistle from one of the fans that greeted her as she stepped out the door added even more to her self-confidence. But the look in Dane's eyes caused the roses to bloom on her cheeks.

"The wait was worth every minute." The tang of wood-burning stoves greeted them as they stepped onto the parking lot. The three-story structure with the lighted sign above showing perpetually running horses dominated the flatlands of Delta Park, now being taken over by retail stores, hotels, and light industry.

"This way." Dane took her elbow to guide her through the puddles left from the earlier rain.

279

Even through her jacket, Robynn could feel the warmth from his hand. But the heat that radiated from his touch had nothing to do with body temperature.

This is crazy, Robynn scolded herself. *One touch and your pulse is racing like Finding Fun in the homestretch. You've been out with good-looking guys before.*

A-a-a-h, a countervoice responded. *But the chemistry is here. You've never met someone with chemistry like this between the two of you. Not even with Sonny. This can lead to something special.*

"Are you hungry?" Dane's deep voice interrupted the small voices arguing in her brain.

"Not really. Are you?"

Dane opened the door to his Porsche and tossed her bag in the back. "Nope. But let's grab a pop as we go. Buckle your seat belt." He slammed the door and strode around the front of the car.

"Stupid thing." Robynn fussed with the black straps as Dane slid into his seat. "You need a master's degree in seat belts to ever figure them all out."

"Here, let me." Dane leaned across her, his shoulder brushing hers. Robynn froze. She sucked in her breath trying to make herself as small as possible, but the contact sent quivers to her middle.

Vaguely she realized it was taking longer than necessary to adjust the belt. At the final click, Dane turned his head. The grin that lifted the corners of his sharply etched lips slowly faded, but the twinkle in his eye invited an answer from hers.

Robynn blinked as he finally drew away, her long lashes raised to reveal violet eyes full of question marks.

"Dane—I. . ." *Was he about to kiss me? Or am I making things up?*

"You what?"

"I–I don't know you well enough to. . ."

"To?" He waited. "To what?" The twinkle returned. "To go have a pop with me?"

"No, you nut." The mood was broken, and Robynn wasn't sure if she was happy or sad—or somewhere in between. After all, she hadn't been kissed in a long, long time.

"Dane!" Robynn tried to keep a straight face but giggled instead. She settled back in her seat, contentment wrapped like a fleecy blanket around her. Being with this man felt so good.

"Here." He handed her a sheet of paper off the dash. "You be the navigator. I have no idea where we're going."

"Now I know why you brought me along. And here I thought it was because you wanted the pleasure of my company."

"Don't kid yourself, lady." Dane turned the key and the engine roared to life. "Another time and place and I'll show you just why I want you around."

"Dane."

"What?" He glanced in the rearview mirror and out both windows.

"Your seat belt." She pointed to the strap still hanging in place. "You want me to help you with it?"

Dane grinned at her innocent expression. "I think that's what got us into trouble before."

"I wouldn't call that trouble." She stared straight ahead, chewing her lip to keep from laughing at him.

"Where's the nearest watering trough?" The silver Porsche accelerated, spraying water from the puddles.

By the time they'd purchased two large Cokes at the hamburger stand and zoomed up the entrance to I-5, the northbound lanes were already slowing with the afternoon's rush-hour traffic. Dane shifted down and eased into the bumper-to-bumper flow of homeward-bound cars.

"Freeways are the same everywhere, I guess." He paused while a madman changed lanes like no one else was around. "But compared to rush hour down south, this is a Sunday afternoon drive."

"I hear they're pretty bad. Especially down around L.A."

"You ever been down in my country?"

"For vacations. You know. Rush down. See the high spots. And rush home again. My folks enjoyed taking their vacations in the Southwest and along the coast."

"Your parents live around here?"

"U-m-m. Out in Lake Oswego. I'm a born and bred Oregonian. There aren't an awful lot of us around. Seems most everyone you meet is a transplant." She turned in her seat so she could watch him. "What about you?" His profile seemed even more strongly defined when viewed against the backdrop of steel girders as they crossed the Interstate Bridge. "Oh, get in the right-hand lane. Quick. We follow the signs to Camas."

"Now you tell me." Dane checked the cars around him and roared across two lanes. "Some navigator you are."

"Sorry." Robynn opened her eyes again. She'd squeezed them shut when the bumper of a service truck tried to peer in her window.

"You take that first exit, hard to the right." Robynn pointed as she spoke. "That puts you on Highway 14." After they navigated the turn, she asked, "What kind of farm are you looking for?" As soon as she asked it, she realized he hadn't told her anything about himself. It seemed that every time they talked, he asked her questions. Was he hiding something or what?

"About fifty to one hundred acres. Large house. I'd like to find one operational if I can. Otherwise I'll buy the land and build it the way I want. That'll take longer, though. I hate to wait."

"Have you thought of east of the mountains?"

"Looked into it. But that's too far from a good track. I was thinking of the Seattle area, too, until Longacres folded. But that uncle of mine has been filling my head with stories of how wonderful Portland is for more years than I can remember."

"It is wonderful," Robynn stated emphatically.

"That's prejudice. You've never lived anywhere else."

"Nope. And don't care to."

"Opinionated, aren't you?"

"My father always said, 'Know your mind and speak it—nicely, of course.'" Robynn studied the play of Dane's broad hands on the wheel of the powerful little car. The two seemed made of one piece, man and machine. "Do you ride much?"

"Some. I love to ride along the beach. Especially in the early morning or at sunset. Of course, I never seem to have time in between."

"That's something I've always wanted to do. Instead, we went horseback packing in the mountains. Dad loves the Cascade Crest trail." Robynn closed her eyes to remember the brisk mornings, high, clear mountain lakes, and snow-capped lava peaks towering on either side of a rocky trail.

"You took your own horses?"

"No. I've never owned a horse. That's one of my major, major dreams."

"How'd you get into racing then?"

"Just showed up at the track one day, willing to do anything so I could be around the horses. Made such a pest of myself with all my questions that Josh finally hired me to shut me up. He figured a couple of days mucking out stalls and I'd conveniently forget to appear one morning."

"And?" Dane glanced over to encounter her velvet eyes watching his every move.

Robynn smiled at him, lazily, like they had all the time in the world and had known each other for centuries.

"And I never missed. The track became my second home; Josh, the grandfather I never knew."

"How do your parents feel about your racing?" Dane took a long swallow of his pop.

"At first they pitched a fit. Dad hollered and Mom cried. It didn't help. I inherited all their stubbornness combined. Now Mom figures I've worn out more than my contingent of guardian angels, but she loves to watch the ponies run. You'll see them nearly every weekend up in the stands. They're the two short, pudgy people, waving their programs and screaming, "That's our Robynn! Go get 'em, O'Dell!"

Dane laughed at the picture she created. "They sound like pretty special people."

"You turn here." Robynn pointed to the exit for northbound 205. "They are. They've always stood by me. Especially when. . ." Her smile flitted away like a dandelion puff blown by the breeze. The remembered agony doused the sparkle in her eyes. *You've got to tell him about Jeremy.* Her little voice was becoming persistent.

Dane waited for her to continue. When she didn't, he gently squeezed her hand, then released it to negotiate the curves taking them up onto the new freeway. Running straight again, he glanced back at her.

Robynn fought for control as the rough days crept back into her mind. The doctor's office had been decorated all in beiges and browns. The earth tones were supposed to be restful, but the antiseptic smell still made patients aware of their surroundings. The sleeping infant lay exhausted in her arms after all the tests. By the time the doctors were finished, he had arched his back and waved his tiny fists, a miniature prize-fighter taking on the world. His furious screams ricocheted off the walls.

His anger hadn't helped.

Nothing had helped. The verdict remained the same.

Blind.

The doctors wanted to promise hope, but there was none. For some reason, Jeremy's eyes had never finished developing. What wasn't there couldn't be repaired.

Robynn might have gone under without God's presence in her life after Sonny's departure. While her cries of "Why, God?" seemed to go spinning into the eternal black holes of space, the comfort promised in the Scriptures tiptoed in and wrapped her in the love and reassurance she needed for her baby. God's touch came to her in people: doctors, nurses, counselors, and the pastor and members of the church she had turned to.

Drifting away from that closeness had happened gradually as her busy life took over. While she tried to stifle such feelings, sometimes resentment of God's role or lack of it reared its ugly head. It was hard not to ask *Why me?* not to blame God for both the death and the blindness.

But the counsel of the medical people, her friends, and family had been correct. Jeremy grew into a delightful little boy, learning to enjoy life in spite of his disability. Now he was getting the training needed to become an independent person. Training all the mother-love in the world couldn't give him.

Dane waited patiently for Robynn to come back from the far reaches of her mind. Gently, his thumb stroked the limp hand in his.

"Who is it that hurt you?" His soft voice helped Robynn slam the door on her memories.

"It couldn't be helped." She became aware of the warmth radiating from her enclosed hand and up her arm. It would be so easy to tell him everything. No man had ever created that desire in her before. She had always kept her feelings to herself. Her air of aloofness contributed to her nickname.

Robynn took a deep breath and tilted her chin a fraction higher. After a quick smile at the man beside her, she stared straight ahead. She would manage. She always had. Robynn O'Dell did not need the care and comforting of any man, especially this one. Good feelings sometimes became weak feelings, and she was not weak. Not by a long shot. Maybe that was why she had a hard time letting God in, too: She had such a driving need to do things herself. A Bible verse from her childhood echoed softly in her ears. *"I can do all things through Christ which strengthens me."*

She chuckled to herself. *I like the first part of that verse. The last half. . .*

"Can you let me in on the joke?"

She shrugged. *So where is he in matters of faith?* She knew she wouldn't make a mistake like Sonny again. But as Josh so often reminded her, she and Sonny had both been so young. Hardships had a way of making you grow up—fast. Grow better or bitter, that was always the choice, according to her dad.

Robynn glanced at the paper in her hand. "You turn to the right up there." She changed the subject. "From the looks of this address, this farm must be out by Opal's."

"Good. Maybe we can stop there, too. I can see the others on the list another time."

"You hadn't planned on looking at all of them today, had you?" Robynn stared at the list of addresses. "It'll be dark before long."

It didn't take them two minutes to look at the first farm. Dane didn't even get out of the car. One glance at the house, rundown barn, and swampy pasture-land, and he reversed the Porsche. The powerful car threw gravel getting out of the driveway.

"So much for the Realtor's description of 'slight fixer-upper.'" Dane snorted his contempt. "You'd think after the guidelines I gave, they'd know what I want. I was very explicit." Dane detailed again the requirements he had set up.

A pang shot through Robynn as she realized what a contrast Opal's farm would be to the one they'd just seen. She was almost tempted to bypass it and take the next one on the list.

"You said the McKecknen farm is near here?" Dane shot down her idea before it crystallized into action.

"Turn right, then left at the intersection." Mechanically Robynn gave the instructions.

"What's wrong?" Dane's puzzled look made her aware again how closely she must guard her thoughts. The man was so perceptive. *Wonder what it would be like to live with someone that sensitive?*

Get a hold of yourself, girl, her inner voice scolded her. *Remember, you said no men.*

"McKecknen's Racing Stable," Dane read the sign aloud. Even in the deepening dusk, the white board fences beckoned one up the drive. The welcoming arms of the U-shaped house at the top of the rise invited all comers to enter and make themselves at home. A wide doorway and smiling window eyes radiated warmth, much as their gracious owner did.

Dane remained silent as they slowly drove up the asphalt drive. Robynn watched him as his gaze took in everything. Only his hands tensing on the wheel betrayed any feelings. She sensed his mental cash register tallying up the cost. Without a doubt, this place would be worth every penny Opal was asking.

"It's perfect," Dane finally said, with a sigh. "I feel like I've come home."

"You haven't seen the inside of the house or the barns or checked out the land or. . ." Robynn could feel herself babbling to distract him. He couldn't feel this was his home yet. She and Josh and Jeremy had to have first chance. She realized the car had been motionless for several minutes.

Turning, she found Dane regarding her with a question in his dark eyes. "You don't want me to have this farm, do you?" His tone was flat. More of a statement than a question. "Why?"

"What makes you think that?"

"Lady, you're as easy to read as a foal at feeding time."

"Would you like to see the barns?" Robynn interrupted. "Opal's car isn't here, so I don't think anyone is home. You'll have to tour the house another time." She unbuckled her seat belt and opened the door. When she hadn't heard any movement, she turned. Dane leaned against his door, staring at her. A slight frown drew his heavy black brows closer together.

Robynn discovered what a victim must feel like when mesmerized by a cobra. Dane seemed to be peeling layer after layer from her mind to get down to the core of her.

"If you'd rather not," she offered halfheartedly.

Without a word and without taking his eyes from her, Dane unsnapped his seat belt and opened the door. With a slight nod, he slid from behind the wheel and unfolded his broad frame to stand beside the vehicle.

When Robynn straightened outside the car, she found him leaning his elbows on the roof, all the while studying the lay of the land. Immaculate. A show place. Home. These were some of the words Robynn had heard used to describe this jewel of a ranch. To the east, the Cascades backdropped the rolling hills of the McKecknen place.

"On a clear day, you can see Mount St. Helens over there." She pointed at an impenetrable cloud bank toward the north. "And in the winter, even the foothills usually have snow on them. If that's important to you, that is."

"It is to you?" His soft question drew her eyes back to his. Gone was the stern face of a few moments ago. In its place was the caring look he'd worn in the car, when she'd disappeared into her memories.

"Yes." She turned and led the way up the gravel road to the stables.

The mercury yard lights were casting a bright glow by the time Dane and Robynn finished their inspection of the outbuildings and the animals. Dane watched her surrounded by her inquisitive friends in the pasture. One of the colts nuzzled her pocket, obviously used to finding treats in it.

"You do more than just ride for Opal, don't you?" Dane asked as they climbed back in the car.

"Yes. I help break the two-year-olds and work with the other stock when I can." She buckled her seat belt by herself this time. "I love the foals. Did you see that black filly run? She's going to be something one of these days." Enthusiasm brought the sparkle back to her eyes. "And that bay mare? That's Finding Fun's dam. She's bred to—"

Dane chuckled as he started the engine. "Enough, woman." He shifted into reverse. The silver car spun in a tight circle, obedient to the strong hands on the wheel. "I'm starved. How about you?"

Robynn relaxed against the seat, grateful for the return of the feeling of camaraderie. The darkness cocooned them in the rich-smelling interior as the car picked up speed on the main road. Black asphalt sparkled diamonds in the headlights when a slight sprinkle dampened the road. Even the rhythmic swish and click of the wiper blades when the drizzle turned to rain added to Robynn's sense of well-being. On hold were the fears of losing the farm and animals. She was content to enjoy the moment.

"Do you know where you're going?" she finally asked.

"We're going."

"What?"

"Not just me. Wherever I go, you go, too. You see, you're in the same car as I and—"

"Dane!" She playfully pushed his arm. "I didn't ask for a lesson in semantics. A simple answer would suffice."

"Wait and see."

"Thanks a lot."

"You're welcome." At his polite nod, a duet of laughter sang counterpoint to the wiper blades.

When they finally drew up in front of a log building, Robynn looked around with interest. A wooden bridge arched over a low waterfall that joined two ponds. Underwater lights shimmered as the raindrops splashed on the surface, dripping like tears from the weeping willow overhanging the pond's edge.

"Dane, you utterly amaze me." Robynn shook her head in astonishment. "How'd you hear about this place? I've never been here before."

"Just asked about a good place for steaks and a rustic atmosphere." He came around the car to open her door. "At your service, ma'am." Robynn placed her hand in his to rise from the low seat.

They had finished ordering before Robynn had time to inspect their surroundings. Rounded knotty-pine half-logs finished the walls and the individual booths. Steins of every size and description paraded across the heavy plank mantel above a fieldstone fireplace, complete with roaring blaze. Old-fashioned wagon wheel lights provided dim overhead illumination, while on each table small hurricane lamps flickered with any passing breath.

Dane reached across the table to cover her folded hands with his own. The sparks leaped back to life.

"You're really a special person." His words rumbled low in his throat. When he leaned forward, the lamplight cast shadows over his lean face, highlighting carved-granite cheekbones.

"Yours was the blue cheese, right, sir?" The waitress slid a chilled salad plate in front of him.

I'll come back to this later, his eyes silently promised Robynn before he smiled politely up at the cheery young woman. The fringe on her western suede vest and skirt flounced as she finished serving them.

"Can I get you anything else?" She paused.

"No. That's fine, thank you." Dane smiled in dismissal.

By the time they finished their perfectly done, charcoal-seared steaks, Robynn could feel her eyelids begin to droop. The combined effects of warm room and full stomach, plus a day that had begun at five in the morning, were wearing on her. With a sigh, she leaned back against the hard wood of the seat back.

"Tired?"

"Um. Beat. But that was a marvelous dinner."

"Dessert?"

"I'm a jockey, remember?"

"Don't remind me." Dane studied her across the table. "I think I better take you home."

Robynn only nodded.

The ride home passed quickly as the powerful machine ate up the miles. The roads were well marked, so Robynn didn't need to concentrate to give him directions. Instead, she rested her head against the soft leather seat and slipped into slumber, a soft smile curving her lips.

After he killed the engine in her driveway, Dane watched her for a moment before gently shaking her shoulder.

"Hey, sleepyhead. You're home."

Her eyelids fluttered open. The curve of her lovely lips deepened. As her eyes met his, Dane leaned forward toward her. Slowly, tantalizingly, his lips brushed hers.

"Good night, Princess," he breathed against her cheek. "Thank you for a very special evening."

He jackknifed himself from the low-slung car and came around to help her out. Her arm tucked securely in his, they strolled up the walk to the back door. The tang hanging in the air from a neighbor's fireplace sharpened the evening air like a touch of tarragon in veal cordon bleu. At the bottom of the cement steps, Dane turned her to face him, clasping both her hands in his.

Robynn waited, savoring the anticipation. Their gazes locked.

"Good night, Princess," he whispered as he finally pulled away. "I'll see you tomorrow."

Bemused, Robynn slid her key in the lock and opened her door. Reluctant to lose her rosy glow, she bypassed the light switch, making her way to the bedroom in the soft reflection from the street lamps.

A red flashing signal on her answering machine caught her attention.

She flicked the play switch while she hung her coat in the closet.

"This is Emmanuel Hospital. We admitted Josh MacDonald at nine-thirty this evening. He asked us to notify you. He'll be going into surgery shortly."

The hanger banged against the bar as Robynn ripped her coat back out of the closet and shoved her arms in the sleeves on her mad dash to the car.

Chapter 5

O God, no. Not Josh." She slammed the door behind her. "Please, let him be all right. Make him all right. Please." *Please* was the litany her mind sang as she dashed out to the garage. Within seconds her black Celica roared out into the street. Impatiently, she stopped at the lights; every one seemed to turn red as she approached. As the caution yellow appeared for the traffic coming the opposite way, she gunned the motor, the car pushing against the brake like an impatient Thoroughbred at the starting gate.

She started to release the avid machine when she heard the roar of an approaching vehicle and slammed her foot on the brake. The Celica stalled partway into the intersection. With a cheery wave, the driver of a red Corvette saluted her quick reflexes. His blinking taillights mocked her shaking hands and pounding heart.

Robynn checked both ways before she turned the key to bring the engine back to life again. Biting her lip to stop its quivering, she drove the remaining distance at a Sunday driver's pace.

"Well, my girl," she reminded herself, "you wouldn't have been much help being wheeled into the emergency room on a gurney yourself."

What right do you have asking for favors and care? the guilt side of her brain questioned. *You haven't been worshiping or reading your Bible or. . .in fact, the only time you think about God is when you need something. What kind of a relationship is that?*

But—

She turned off any excuses, telling herself she'd deal with this later.

With a sigh, Robynn acknowledged the warring factions in her mind. Swiftly she locked the door and, stuffing the key in its outside pocket, swung her shoulder bag in place. Her boots beat a double-time tattoo as she entered the hospital, the swoosh of the automatic door the only greeting.

The woman at the main desk finished a ledger entry before she looked up. "May I help you?" Her face looked as if a smile might crack it, shattering the rigid lines into slivers.

"Uh, someone here called. I'm Robynn O'Dell to see Josh MacDonald. I understand he's been in an accident."

With all the speed of a sedentary slug, the woman sorted through her notes. "Yes. Here it is." She removed her half glasses. "Go on up to five. There's a waiting room right by the elevators."

"Can I see him?"

The woman meticulously placed her glasses back on her patrician nose and consulted her notes. "You can ask at the desk up there. They'll know more than I do." The eyes peering over the flat frames of the horn-rimmed glasses might have been chipped from a glacier.

"Thank you."

The woman almost nodded as she traced back to her place in the ledger.

Robynn strode impatiently to the bank of elevators down the hall. *That woman must be a real comfort to people who come here,* she thought as she punched the UP button.

"Dr. Davis to pediatrics," the intercom echoed as she entered the metal box. "Dr. Davis to pediatrics."

Alone in the rising elevator, Robynn stared at the signs for NO SMOKING and LOAD LIMITS without consciously seeing them. She gnawed her bottom lip, willing the silent elevator to hurry, willing Josh to respond, to be all right.

The strong smell of antiseptic penetrated her concentration as she stepped into the night-dimmed hall. Somewhere down the hall, a weak voice cried, "Help me. Someone please help me?"

Robynn shuddered.

The lights created a comforting oasis at the nurses' counter. The young nurse working on reports at the lower desk looked up immediately as Robynn approached the high shelf. "Hi," she said with a smile. "What can I do for you?"

"It's about Josh MacDonald. I received word on my answering machine that he's been hurt. The receptionist said to come up here."

While Robynn talked, the nurse quickly scanned her lists. "Yes, he's in the recovery room now. They should be bringing him to his room in about half an hour."

"Er–r, can you tell me, do you know what happened?"

"I'm sorry." The voice sounded really apologetic. "I don't know any details. If you'll wait in that room over there," she pointed to a pair of swinging doors, "the doctor can tell you when he comes out."

"Thanks." Robynn turned to follow directions. "Oh." She spun on her heel. "Where can I find a phone?"

"Is it a local call?"

"Um-hmm." Robynn nodded.

"Here, you can use this one. Just don't tell anyone." The nurse winked at her.

Robynn thanked her and dialed Josh's home number. Surely Dane had made it back by this time. She glanced at her watch. It must have been half an hour since she'd heard the messages on her machine.

"Dane, this is Robynn," she announced as a groggy voice finally answered the ringing phone. "I'm at Emmanuel Hospital. Josh has been in an accident."

"How bad is it?" His voice immediately snapped with authority.

"I don't know. I haven't seen the doctor and Josh is still in recovery."

"There was surgery then?"

"Um-hmm."

"I'll be there as quick as I can. Where is it?"

"Go south on I-5. You'll see the hospital off to the left. Take the next exit." Robynn's memory flashed back to her near miss. "Drive carefully."

The empty line buzzed in her ear. When Dane went into action, he didn't waste time. Robynn smiled her thanks at the nurse as she hung up the phone. Her booted heels tapped overloud in the nighttime hush of the darkened hall. As she passed an open door, someone groaned. Robynn stepped up her pace but tried to walk more on her toes. The hovering miasma of pain and agony called for a silent passage.

In the waiting room, she tried to relax on the rigid couch but found herself looking up at every sound, hoping one would be the doctor coming out. The double swinging beige doors leading to the surgical wing had big signs: NO ADMITTANCE.

She heard rapid footsteps coming down the hall at the same moment the doors opened. A tired-looking man in green cotton surgical garb wiped a weary hand across his forehead and removed the green mask that dangled from its strings.

"Are you Robynn O'Dell?"

Robynn nodded. At the same moment, she felt her hand taken by a larger one.

"I'm Dane Morgan, Doctor. Josh's nephew. What can you tell us?"

"He has numerous superficial lacerations and contusions. But the real problem is his right leg. The force of the impact shattered the tibia. I've had to pin it, and he'll be in traction for a time."

"But he'll be all right?" Robynn asked.

"Yes, barring complications."

"What happened?" Dane questioned.

"He was brought in from an automobile accident, furious at the idiot who ran the red light. I have the feeling," the doctor smiled at them, "he's not going to be a very good patient. First thing out of the anesthetic, he demanded crutches and a walking cast. Says he has horses to race."

"When can we see him?"

"They're bringing him to Room 515 now. He'll be pretty groggy for a while, but you can talk to him if you want."

"Thank you, sir." Robynn extended her hand. "I appreciate all you've done."

"You're Robynn O'Dell, the jockey, aren't you?" the doctor asked as they turned to leave.

"Yes, I am. Why?"

"My friend, Dr. Benson, raves about what a great rider you are. He's trying to talk me into going partners with him on a horse."

"You'd enjoy it. Thanks again." Robynn felt her feet flying down the hall as Dane hurried her with a strong hand under her elbow.

As they opened the door, the nurse was just finishing adjusting the weights and pulley contraption attached to a heavy cast. Only the tense white lines around Josh's mouth spoke of the pain he suffered. One eye was swollen shut, but the other blinked open instantly when Robynn whispered his name.

"Took you long enough to get here." Josh's voice belied the weakened state of his body.

"And a thank you for coming to you, too." Robynn grinned in relief at his ill humor. "I can see you have been knocked down but not out."

"What time is it?" Josh turned his head, looking for a clock.

"Midnight." Dane checked his watch. "For whatever difference that makes."

"Fool driver hit me on my way home from the track. About nine. I've got so much to do, and now that fool doctor says I'll be laid up for weeks." Pain closed his good eye for a moment when he moved more than his head.

"It'll be okay, Josh." Robynn stroked the gnarled hand lying on the white bedspread. "I know what needs to be done. I'll manage."

"No. You can't handle it all." He struggled to move his tousled head. "Dane. You're going to have to take over for me at the track. You know the procedures. They're not any different than those down south. Robynn here'll introduce you to all the people you need to know."

"But, Josh." A note of pleading crept into her voice.

"I can handle it." Dane stepped closer to the bed.

She flashed a glance of resentment at the tall man by her side.

"And Dane." Josh raised his hand long enough for Dane to take it. "No matter what your personal beliefs, Robynn races. She's the only jockey who's ever been up on most of those animals. They go best for her."

Now it was Dane's turn to narrow his eyes and tighten his jawline. The moment stretched.

"They're not your horses—yet." The old man closed his good eye and his hand dropped back to the bed. "And now, off with both of ye. You'll be needing your sleep."

Robynn leaned over and kissed the wrinkled cheek. Josh looked twenty years older than he had that afternoon.

"Talk to you tomorrow," she whispered.

"Let me know how you do."

"Yes." She turned at the door, but Dane's tall body blocked her view. When she raised her gaze to his, ice sheathed the blue depths.

"Why are you mad at me?" she asked when they entered the elevator.

"I don't want you racing."

"It doesn't matter what you want."

"It does when I'm in charge of the horses. And giving the jockey orders." He crossed his arms over his chest.

"Well, you heard Josh."

"Yes. But I don't have to like it." Again a hand under her arm propelled her along after they reached the lobby.

Stung by his reply, Robynn seethed all the way to the cars, trying to think of some appropriately scathing reply. None came.

"Well, then." After climbing into her car, she smiled up at him so sweetly the honey dripped from each syllable. "We'll just have to agree to disagree, won't we?"

The slam of his car door was her only answer.

❧

Robynn's alarm buzzed before she'd even had time to roll over during the short night. Groggy, with sleep still locking her eyelashes together, she staggered into the bathroom and a hot shower. When even the stinging water couldn't force her eyes open, she turned on the cold. With a yelp, she was wide awake and reaching for the towel.

Dawn still snoozed when she swung her car into the rain-drenched parking lot. The drizzle let up to a light mist as she dogtrotted through the gate and to the barns.

Dane already had grain in front of all the horses as though he was used to the familiar routine.

"Didn't you go home at all?" Robynn asked when she found him in the far stall checking out the horses scheduled for racing in the afternoon.

"Of course I did." He straightened from picking the horse's hooves. "What took you so long?" The cheery note in his voice took the sting out of the words.

"Actually, I'm early. He okay?" She nodded at the huge bay calmly munching his grain.

"Sure. How about taking Finding Fun out first? She's a fast eater, just needs to be loosened up."

"Fine." Robynn stared out at the drops splashing over the eaves. "Sure wish this rain would let up. You'd think it was the middle of January or something." She followed him as he entered the next stall. "Watch this one. He bi—"

"Ouch! You stupid. . ." Dane jerked the halter of the dark gelding. "Knock it off!" The horse turned back to his manger. He'd made his point.

"Here, you hold his head." Dane turned to glare at her. Robynn could hardly hide the giggles threatening to erupt. Dane caught the laughter in her eyes. "You could have warned me sooner." He rubbed his shoulder. "At least he bites rather gently."

"Yeah, he just likes to show any new man who's boss. He's never bitten me." Robynn rubbed the tender spot up behind the horse's ears. The munch of grain and the drip of the incessant rain were the only sounds as Dane stroked down each leg, searching for hot spots and swelling.

He's thorough, that's for sure, Robynn thought as she watched him calmly go about his business. *If only he didn't have such a thing about female jockeys. For such a smart man, how can he be so stupid?*

By the time dawn had lightened the sky to dull gray, Robynn had already had three horses out. The rapport between her and Dane settled into an easy working relationship, each aware of the expertise of the other. Dane boosted her up each time, then watched the workouts from the covered bleachers.

Once, mounted on the fourth, Robynn settled herself and stroked the sleek neck of the waiting animal. Come Runnin' reached around to sniff her boot.

"Yeah, it's me." She smoothed his mane. "Did you think we were gonna pull a switch on you?" Robynn laughed at the question in Dane's eyes. "I'm the only one who's ever ridden him. I broke him last year and raced him toward the end of the season as a two-year-old." She leaned forward to pull some hair from under the headstall. "Weren't quite grown up yet, were you, old man?" She rubbed just behind his ears. Come Runnin' sighed.

"We didn't do too well." Robynn shook her head. "He was like a young teenager in the worst of the growing stages. Clumsy and just not ready." Awareness of the depth of blue in Dane's eyes penetrated her monologue. "He ah—m. . ."

My goodness, her mind filled in the gaps, *but he's a handsome hunk of man. Why'd he have to come into my life just now? I don't have time for any more complications. And I think he's going to make things really complicated.*

"He what?" Dane prompted her, stroking the horse's shoulder.

"Well, he wasn't ornery or anything, but not placid like he is now, either."

"What happened?"

Robynn shrugged her shoulders. "Well, we took a bit of a tumble one day."

"In a race?"

Robynn lifted her reins. "We better get going. I've got a lot to do."

Dane rubbed the horse's ears in the same place Robynn had. Come Runnin' leaned against him, grateful for the attention.

"Robynn, was the fall during a race?" He emphasized each word, his diction clipping the sounds. His smile had been tucked away, back where Robynn couldn't even see a glimmer.

Why'd you let yourself in for this? she scolded herself. *You knew how he felt. Get a grip, girl.*

"Dane, no one got hurt. . . ."

"That's not what I asked." A tiny muscle worked at the side of his mouth. "Was it during a race?"

"Yes! And don't say 'I told you so.' Falls sometimes go with the territory. It wasn't anyone's fault, and besides that I've learned how to fall. I'm a jockey and a good one." The tension from her voice and mind crept to her knees. Come Runnin' sidestepped and gazed longingly at the track. He pulled at the restraining hand on his bridle.

Robynn shivered as she felt the mist creeping into her bones. She pulled her goggles down and settled them in place. "Remember," she turned the horse toward the track and spoke over her shoulder, "we agreed to disagree." Come Runnin' broke into a trot at the pressure of her calves. As he cleared the gate he pulled at the bit, begging to run.

"Tomorrow you get to run, fella." Her voice fell into its easy singsong. It worked. Horses always responded to her voice and calm hands. Even the most fractious settled down. "That's one of the things that makes me a good jockey," she sang to the long pointed ears that kept turning back to listen to her, then forward to catch the sounds from in front. "And I *am* a good jockey. Someday I'll be one of the best. One of these days there'll be another O'Dell, top jock at Portland Meadows. And besides, I need the money."

Come Runnin' settled into the easy lope that ate up the miles and hardly raised a sweat. As they passed other horses, he worked the snaffle bit with his tongue, like a little kid begging for a cookie. At her insistence he relaxed but kept the same pace.

"If all my mounts were as easy as you." Robynn eased him back to a trot.

Two horses later, while Dane clipped the cross tie ropes onto a steaming horse, Robynn pulled the gloves from her freezing fingers. She tucked her hands under her armpits and jogged in place to get some feeling back in her feet.

"Cruddy weather!" she muttered to herself, low so Dane couldn't hear her.

As Robynn circled the track with her last mount, the breeze shifted to a bone-chilling wind from the east. Blowing down the Columbia Gorge, the cold weather hit the racetrack full strength. The drizzle flattened into a driving rain that plastered Robynn's down jacket to her back. One by one, the horses left the track.

When Robynn trotted her mount up to the stalls, Dane appeared out of the downpour to lift her down. "Thanks," she shivered the word out.

"Do you have dry clothes here?" He might have been speaking to a three-year-old.

Robynn was too cold to argue. "Y–y–es–s–s."

"I'll go call Josh and meet you for breakfast in half an hour. A long shower ought to warm you up."

Robynn grabbed her duffel bag from the tack room and trotted across the road to the dressing rooms.

"Hey, Princess, you look about froze clear through," Pam Highden, Robynn's best friend, called. "Didn't you have sense enough to quit?"

"Wanted to get done first."

"How's Josh?"

"He'll be laid up for a while. But he's tough."

Amazed at the speed of the track info line, Robynn dropped her soaked jacket on the bench. The bootjack made short work of her tall black boots as she pulled an old woolen sweater over her head. By the time her white turtleneck joined the pile of clothes, the warmth of the room had begun to penetrate. The goose bumps on her skin receded to mosquito bite size.

"Hey." Pam dug through her duffel. "You got any shampoo?" Robynn tossed her the plastic bottle.

"Do you ever forget anything?" Pam asked as they entered the showers.

"Yeah, I'm bad on birthdays and anniversaries. Except for Jeremy's." Robynn turned the shower to full force. Steam billowed, speeding the defrosting process, starting from the toes up.

"How's Jeremy doing?" Pam shouted above the thundering water.

"Fine. He likes the school now." Robynn turned and let the hot fingers of water massage her back. "Has a super housemother. Mrs. Cravens. Really a neat grandmother-type person."

"Sounds good."

"Yeah. Tomorrow's my day to visit."

"Speaking of visits. . ." Pam peeked around the shower stall. "Who was that hunk I saw you with this morning? Been holding out on me?"

"I just met him the other day."

"Didn't look that way to me. Or you got friendly mighty fast."

"Well, you know how fast us jockeys are."

"Oh sure. Robynn O'Dell, the untouchable princess. The only time you're fast is on the homestretch with a horse under you." Pam wrapped a towel around her bony figure. "You haven't even looked at anyone since Sonny, no matter how many great men I've introduced you to. The 'Ice Princess,' that's what some of the guys call you."

"Hey, that's not fair. I'm friendly to everyone."

"Not the kind of friendly they want. But. . .you looked pretty friendly with whatever-his-name-is."

"It's Dane Morgan." Robynn shut off the shower, wrapped the emerald green towel around her, and tucked in the ends. "He's Josh's nephew from California, looking for some horses and a farm."

"Wheee. Must be loaded. And good lookin', too." Pam rolled her hazel eyes toward the ceiling. "A winning combination." They collected their supplies and headed back to their clothes. "Is he married?"

Robynn stared at her, confusion stamped all over her expressive face.

Pam snorted. "You don't know, do you?"

Robynn shook her head. "He doesn't act married."

"Them's the worst kind, babe. Before you go losing your heart over him, you find out."

"But. . ."

"No buts, Princess." Pam snapped her skintight jeans. "Men play by different rules."

"What am I supposed to do? Walk up to him and say, 'Dane, are you married?'" Robynn slammed her feet into her ankle-high boots.

"I'm just warning you. You've been hurt enough already." Pam plugged in her blow-dryer. "Yeah, I know." Pam made a face. "I'm bossy, nosey, and. . ."

"And a good friend." Robynn applied black mascara to her lashes.

"Thanks. But you *will* be careful?"

Robynn nodded at the concerned face in the mirror. *Careful,* she thought. *That's what I've been for years, and now. . . .* She stuffed her hairbrush and toiletries back into her duffel bag.

"You ready to eat?" Robynn slung the bag over her shoulder.

"Yeah, but I'll be a few more minutes. You go ahead. Hey!" Pam called as Robynn opened the door. "You might save me a place at your table so I can meet him."

Robynn only had to step into the cafeteria when her "Dane Morgan interception system" picked up his signals. Dane lifted a beckoning hand as her eyes zeroed in on his. Robynn waved back, feeling like the sun had just peeked through the leaden skies.

By the time she had loaded her tray and approached the table, Dane and another trainer were deep in a discussion about training Thoroughbreds. Dane stood and pulled out the chair next to him, a smile brightening his face.

Robynn removed her dishes from the tray and slid it onto the table behind them. She tried to concentrate on her food, but her eyes tracked back to Dane's face, waiting for the warm smiles he seemed unable to suppress whenever he glanced at her.

"What do you think?" Dane snapped his fingers in front of her eyes. "Robynn, come back. I asked you a question."

"Um–m–m." She blinked. "I must have been daydreaming. What did you want?"

"You looked to be enjoying yourself. You were smiling, at least." Dane teased her. "I asked when you were going up to the hospital. And do you think Josh will be ready for company from some of his friends here? They've been asking."

"He'd love company, if I know him." Robynn smiled at the trainers and grooms gathered around them. Where had they all come from? Had she been that caught up in her daydreaming? "I'm going up before the afternoon program. I'm sure he's already champing at the bit."

The sound of a throat being cleared swung Robynn's attention to the slender woman standing next to her, her tray balanced on the back of a chair.

"Hey, you finally made it." Robynn indicated the chair. "Sit yourself."

When Dane stood to scoot in the chair, the other men nodded and went about their business.

"Pam Highden, this is Dane Morgan," Robynn made the introductions. "Dane is Opal's fill-in trainer."

"Trainer!" Pam sputtered. "But I thought. . ." She stared from Dane to Robynn. "Princess, you said. . ."

Dane looked at Robynn, expecting a response to the questions floating around, unasked and unanswered.

"Okay." Pam put on her no-nonsense voice. "What's going on here? In the first place, Dane, I'm glad to meet you." She stuck out her hand. "In the second place, what in the Sam Hill do they mean by trainer? Robynn said. . .ow–w–w!"

Robynn's booted toe, placed with force against Pam's shin, found its mark.

"What were you saying?" Robynn asked sweetly, her boot ready if another nudge was needed. "You don't think Dane will make a good trainer?"

"I think I better eat and keep my mouth shut." Pam dug into her grapefruit. "Don't mind me, folks."

Dane dropped his napkin on the table and scraped back his chair. "It was nice meeting you, Pam." He nodded in her direction. "But I've got to get back to the barns. Maybe you should spend the afternoon with Josh, Robynn. I can get someone else to ride for me today."

"Fat chance!" A frown settled on Robynn's brow. "I'll be back in plenty of time. And, Dane." He turned back at her tone. "*I* ride the McKecknen horses. And any others my agent puts me on."

Dane touched his fingers to the brim of his felt hat, then strode out the doors.

Was that a defeat or victory? Robynn asked herself as she stared after him.

"Wow!" Pam tapped Robynn on the arm. "He's one gorgeous creature. Gives me the chills just looking at him."

"That's not what he gives me," Robynn grumbled.

"What's that all about?" Pam asked. "Getting someone to sub for you?"

"No, not sub. He doesn't want women jockeys in the races. A slightly antiquated opinion, but one he's dead set on."

"Why does anyone who looks so good have to be so bullheaded?" Pam moaned. "And after all the work we've done to get some equality out here. What are you going to do?"

"Ride the same as usual. Josh made him promise last night. But it looks like the man won't give up without a struggle."

"How many rides you got this afternoon?" Pam spread strawberry jam on her toast. "If we don't get rained out."

"No chance, the track's not running rivers yet. But it'll be slow going and slippery. Glad I'm only up twice, once for Josh on Jim Dandy, who hates the rain. And a mudder for Dr. Benson. Got a good chance on that one."

"They scratched mine for today. Doesn't break my heart any. I hate the wet worse'n your horse does. Maybe I'll head for sunny southern California when the season starts down there. Warm breezes, waving palm trees, blue sky, sunglasses instead of slickers." She sighed a deep sigh that echoed one of Robynn's.

Robynn drew up with a start when she realized her sunny daydream included a certain tall, dark, and forceful horse owner, now trainer. "Better get going." She slung her green raincoat around her shoulders. "Josh'll be as impatient as a nag at the feed trough to hear how the morning went."

At least Dane and I are still speaking, Robynn thought as she zipped her jacket against the chill. *Even if we don't like some of the stuff we're saying. Wonder what he's going to do next?*

Chapter 6

"Hi, Josh."

Robynn pushed open the hospital room door and entered his room. Banks of flowers and a fruit basket filled every spare counter, the window ledge, and part of the floor. "What have you done? Traded racing in for the florist business?" She bent her head to inhale the fragrance of an arrangement of American Beauty roses.

"How'd you two do this morning?" Josh was not to be deflected from his main point.

"Fine. Didn't Dane call you?"

"That he did, but I wanted to hear it from you as well. Last night I was afraid you might come to blows in the parking lot. Neither one of you hide your emotions very well."

Robynn leaned over to plant a kiss on his weathered cheek. "Give us some points for civility. This morning we were all sweetness and light." As she studied him, she could see the swelling had gone down in his eye. But both eyes had the slackness pain killers give. "Do you hurt bad?"

"No. They've got me so doped up all I do is sleep."

"Well, that's good. That way you're not jawing at them to let you up."

"It was miserable out there this morning, wasn't it?"

"Yeah. But we got through. They haven't canceled the program for this afternoon. Dane invited me to stay here with you. Said he'd get a sub."

"Determined, ain't he?"

"Um—m—m." Robynn read one of the cards on the flowers. "But then, so am I."

Josh nodded. "Called Opal this morning. She'll be here to meet with us at seven, okay?"

Robynn mentally checked her calendar. "That'll be fine. Thanks, Josh. I was afraid you'd forget."

"It's my leg that's busted, not my brain. Besides, lying here gives me all kinds of time to think. . .too much time."

The two discussed the morning workout and planned strategies for the afternoon before Josh's eyes began to droop.

"I'll see you later," Robynn whispered.

300

Josh nodded. He forced his eyes open. "You be careful now, you hear?"

Robynn blew him a kiss from the door.

⁓

"Now be careful."

"I will, sir." Robynn nodded at the rounded man standing at her stirrups. His usually beaming face was creased with worry.

"Fools should have canceled the program. Maybe I'm the fool for letting you run."

"Not to worry. This is his kind of day." She stroked the mahogany shoulder of the horse under her. "You like the mud, don't you, fella?" Black ears twitched back and forth to listen to her.

"Well, you know him better'n I do, but. . ."

"See you in the winner's circle."

Dr. Benson tried to smile at her confidence, but worry clouded his gray eyes. "You just be careful." He tapped her knee with each word. "Hear me?"

As the string of horses paraded to the post, Robynn hunched her shoulders. Even so, the drizzle discovered a crack between her helmet and silks and dripped down her neck. Peevish gusts of wind blew sheets of rain across the infield like silver curtains billowing in the breeze.

The start was slow, and the slogging mud kept the pace ponderous. Robynn's mount broke free by the second furlong and ran easily ahead of the pack, head up, enjoying the scenery. As they rounded the far turn, Robynn heard someone making a bid to catch them.

She leaned forward. "Come on, old man," she called to the twitching ears. "Let's go." He leveled out some more and crossed the wire ahead by two lengths.

"Just out for a Sunday drive, weren't you," Robynn laughed as she pulled the tall bay horse down to a trot to return to the winner's circle. He snorted and tossed his head, ready to go some more.

"See? What'd I tell you?" Robynn shook the good doctor's hand. His face was now wreathed with good cheer, belying his former concern.

"He looked like he was playing out there."

"Well, we had a good time, didn't we, fella?" Robynn scratched behind the twitching ears. The colt rubbed his muddy nose on her shoulder just as the flash-bulbs clicked. Robynn grinned at all the good wishes.

"Congratulations." Dane's clipped voice and glowering expression made a lie out of his words. He took the reins and trotted off, leading the obedient animal.

Robynn shook her head as she stepped on the scale. Winning races was certainly going to be easier than winning him. Winning him? She started in surprise. Who said anything about even wanting him?

You did, the little voice inside teased her. *Think about your reactions to him. Winning with him sure is better than winning over him. Together, you two make quite a pair. Love never comes easy, you know.*

The rest of the afternoon passed in a shower of mud. Her agent had gotten her three new mounts, so Robynn was in the saddle most of the time and in the money every race she rode. The amount of her winnings kept pace with the adrenaline pumping through her system as she saw her bank account grow at each win and bring her a tiny mark closer to the reality of owning her own horses.

But exhaustion painted purple shadows under her eyes as the adrenaline dissipated after the last race. Even a shower failed to revive her. She slogged through the puddles out to her car, too weary to walk across the infield to the barns, so she drove around to the back gate.

Robynn pasted a smile on her face and forced her shoulders straight as she stepped into the stall where Dane squatted down, wrapping a horse's leg. With deft hands, he wound the bandages around the hot leg, being careful to keep them from cutting off the circulation. Even though he glanced up to see who was there, Dane began on the other foreleg without a word.

"How bad is he?" Robynn kept her voice noncommittal.

When Dane didn't answer, Robynn leaned against the wall. She closed her eyes and savored the smell of good hay, warm horseflesh, and the bite of liniment. Her green shiny jacket was the only spot of color in the dimly lit stall.

"That's all for you, boy." She heard Dane slap the blood bay horse's rump. Robynn opened her eyes to find him glaring down at her.

"You're so tired you're asleep on you feet."

"Ah. But thousands of dollars richer." Robynn knew her flippant answer was a mistake before it was out of her mouth.

Dane slammed a fist against the wall above her head.

"You're nothing but a money hungry. . ."

"Say it," Robynn flared back at him. "Money isn't important until you don't have enough."

"But you're taking your life in your hands." He reached for her waist. "I saw you nearly go down out there. Is money worth that?"

"Maybe what money can buy is." She twisted away from him. "And who made you my keeper? I've been racing for a long time without your smothering."

Dane glared down at her. The silence stretched until the curious horse nudged him in the back. "We'll discuss this later," he snapped. "I have work to do."

"What do you want me to do?"

"Nothing. Get out of here and go home to get some sleep. I'll pick you up for dinner at seven."

"No, you won't." Robynn stared at him, appalled at his ordering her around. "I already have something I have to do."

"Fine. I'll help you." He walked off as if the conversation was finished.

Robynn trotted to catch up with him. When he didn't stop, she grabbed his arm. "Dane Morgan. You don't understand. I don't want to discuss my racing with you. I don't want to go home to bed. And most of all, I don't want to have dinner with you tonight."

Dane leaned back against the barn, arms crossed over his chest. "Anything else?"

"No."

"I'll see you at seven." A twinkle peeked out of his eyes, as though testing to see if the climate were right. He un-crossed his arms and, reaching out one tanned forefinger, brushed the wavy hair back off her cheek.

Robynn forced the frown to remain in place. "Dane!" Tiny electric pulses spread from the point of contact, darting up to smooth out her brow. She sighed as if she'd been holding her breath for a long time. "I won't be there," she whispered.

"Then I'll come and find you." He grasped her by the shoulders, turned her, and gently pushed her toward the exit. "See you."

Not if I see you first, Robynn fumed to herself. She was even more disgruntled to find herself doing exactly as he said. Bed did sound good.

❧

Several hours later when she woke up, Robynn wasn't sure if she'd engaged in a shouting match with an icy-eyed Irishman or just dreamed it. The impression was so strong she found herself muttering as she pulled her clothes back on.

"I *will* keep racing. Not him, not accidents, nothing is going to stop me. After wins like today, that top jockey spot is coming closer. This year I may make it." She glared at her reflection in the mirror. "So there."

❧

The woman at the desk hadn't thawed any when Robynn entered the hospital just before seven. She'd grabbed a hamburger on the way to make sure she was out of the house when Dane arrived. She refused to analyze her motives. Orders always made her feel rebellious.

As she entered the room, she saw a diminutive, gray-haired lady perched on the edge of the visitor's chair. She and Josh were talking a mile a minute. Hesitant to interrupt, Robynn paused in the door. If possible, there were more flowers in the room than had been that morning. The pervasive aroma completely blanketed the hospital odor.

"Hi, Princess." Josh raised a hand in greeting when he finally noticed her. "You'll have to find another chair. They keep taking them out, hoping it will discourage visitors, I think."

"I take it there've been a few." Robynn gestured toward the colorful display.

"Yeah." Josh grinned. "One or two. I think some of them just needed a place out of the rain for a while."

"Josh MacDonald. You old rascal." Opal chided him. "You know better than that."

"That's right, let him have it." Robynn enjoyed the repartee between the two old friends. "How are you, Opal? Were you at the track today?"

"Of course. You rode well." Opal's precise diction harked back to her years of teaching English and speech. "I never dreamed Jim Dandy would run that well, in the mud especially."

"He's a fine colt." Robynn nodded. "You'll see him in the winner's circle more and more."

"That's what we need to talk about." Opal leaned forward. "I'm leaving next week for Phoenix. My daughter is ill. She needs me, and this is a perfect time to make the move. I've been planning it for some time. Her illness is just the catalyst."

"And. . ."

"And I want to sell the horses and the farm. You already knew that."

"Yes."

"Josh says the two of you would like a chance to purchase the animals, especially the racing stock."

"Um-m-m."

"I need a quarter million for the racing string. I haven't decided how much for the brood mares and colts. The farm is listed at 750,000 dollars. I've priced everything for a quick sale."

Robynn felt like someone had just socked her in the solar plexis. It was hard to breathe around the knot of muscles in her midriff. A quarter million! And that was just for the. . .

"I have appointments with several prospective buyers," Opal continued, "but I wanted to give you," she nodded at both of them, "the first chance."

"Would we be able to set up a contract?" Josh locked his hands behind his head. "Over a couple of years maybe?"

"The best terms I can give are seventy-five percent down and a year to pay it off. I'm sorry." She shrugged. "But I really need the money."

"When will you decide how much for the breeding stock?" Robynn asked. "Don't you have part ownership in that stud, too?"

"The other owners have already bought me out, and in answer to your first question, I'll know within the next two days."

Boy, you don't waste any time, Robynn thought. *A quarter million. Why, most people never see that amount of money all at one time in their entire life. And what about the mares? The foals? I want all of them. They're just like my kids.*

When she sells the place, there won't be any more farm for Jeremy. Where else could he ride and run and. . .why, it'll be like losing a grandma for her to go.

Robynn settled back in her chair, slipping down so she rested on her tailbone. One finger tapped the wooden arm of the chair. None of her actions calmed the swirling in her mind.

"I can tell this has taken you by surprise." Opal leaned forward in her chair. "I really hadn't planned to be so abrupt, but then I didn't know how much money we would need for my daughter's treatment."

"That's an understatement if I ever heard one." Robynn shook her head. "I feel knocked down and run over. Guess I just never totaled it up before. But I sure do understand about needing money to help your daughter."

"Can we ask a favor?" Josh lowered his gaze from contemplating the acoustical tile.

"Of course."

"Can you give us until tomorrow to think about, discuss this?"

"Tomorrow I go to see Jeremy. . . ."

"How about until Friday?" Opal interrupted. "You need to go on your visit." She nodded at Robynn. "That should give you some business hours to find backing. How does that sound?"

"You won't take any offers in the meantime?" Josh punctuated the statement with his hand.

"No. Everything will be on hold. I'll meet my appointments, but no money will change hands until I talk with you." Opal picked up her leather purse from the floor and stood. "Now, Josh, you behave yourself so you can get out of here more quickly." She patted his hand.

"See you later." Robynn smiled but remained where she was while Opal strode briskly out of the room. With a heavy sigh, Josh sank back against his pillows.

"Well, now we know." He stared glumly at the roses amassed by the sink.

"Yeah."

"You'll talk to your parents?"

"Um. Tonight, I guess. It's about time I visited them anyway. Glad Dad wasn't there today. He's a worse fussbudget than Dane."

"You given any thought to why he acts the way he does?"

"Who? Dad or Dane?"

"Either one. Both. I think the reason is the same."

"What are you talking about?"

"It's all a matter of caring."

"Josh, in case it's slipped your mind, I met Dane Morgan only the other day. It's hardly fair to compare him to my father. I've known *him* slightly longer than forty-eight, no, seventy-two hours."

Ignoring her sarcasm, Josh stared into her eyes.

The moment stretched.

"Josh!"

"I'm just calling 'em as I see 'em."

Like a frisky colt on a summer's day, Robynn's mind darted back to each of the encounters with Dane. They got along just great, in fact, better than great, she admitted as she thought of the kiss in the Porsche. That is, until the discussion got around to her racing. In reality, no man she'd ever met sent awareness racing up and out her nerves like he did.

"But I've no more chances of getting hurt than the next guy. He's just a chauvinist, thinks women'll go to pieces in a race."

"Maybe *your* being beat to pieces under some horse is the problem."

"I think it's stupid that he worries about me." Robynn slammed her palm on the chair arm and shoved the chair back. "And you can just tell him so."

"Tell who what?" A deep voice sent the aforethought of tingles back out where they made her fingers and toes feel alive again.

"Tell him yourself." Josh fumbled for the call button pinned to the edge of his bed. "I'll talk to the nurse."

Before the silence had stretched to an uncomfortable degree, the cheery nurse bustled into the room. Dane and Robynn rose and walked out the door as she whipped the sliding curtain around the bed.

"Would you like to go out to the waiting room and sit down?"

"Not particularly." His hand on her arm sent signals over her body again.

"You weren't at the house."

"Very perceptive of you."

"Are you running away from me?" He turned so she had to look at him or stare at the floor.

"I wasn't the one giving the orders."

"Is it wrong to want to take care of you?" He crossed his arms over his chest.

"What gives you the idea that I need caring for? I've managed my life pretty well up to now." Her renegade mind flashed back to the comfort, the warmth she found in his arms. "And I intend to continue the same way. I don't need you or anyone else messing me up."

"Is that what I do? Mess you up?"

Startled, Robynn stared at him. A five o'clock shadow deepened the cleft in his chin, causing his eyes to seem even bluer and his hair blacker. The force in his gaze willed her to answer.

"I think I hear my mother calling," she whispered.

Dane stared back at her, then burst into deep belly laughs. "I haven't heard

306

that one for a long time." His mirth receded into chuckles, his wide smile crinkling up the lines around his eyes. "Have dinner with me tonight?"

"Can't."

"Why not?"

"I already have a date." Mentally, Robynn crossed her fingers to cross out the lie.

"You said before you'd spend the evening with me."

"Things have changed since then."

"I think I was trying to say I'm sorry for the way I acted this afternoon." He tried to capture one of her hands in his own.

"Dane, that has nothing to do with it." Robynn drew her hand back. *You could always go out to your folks' after dinner with him,* a sneaky little voice whispered in her ear. She shook her head. "I've got business to attend to."

"I thought you said you had a date." Like a big black cat hunting in a hay field, Dane pounced on her answer.

Her gaze flicked around the room, seeking escape. "I, u–m–um." She breathed in deep. Raised her chin. Looked him straight in the eye, her head at an imperious angle. The Princess completely hid the quivering woman.

"Can't you get the point? I don't want you taking care of me. I don't need you. And I'm busy tonight."

With a snort of disgust, Dane straightened off the wall. "I'll see you tomorrow then."

"Tomorrow's my day off."

"Good. I'll pick you up at two."

"I won't be home."

"Another date?"

"Yes, with the only really important man in my life."

"Robynn. . ."

Blue eyes clashed with violet. Sparks flew—enough to start a barn burning—but Robynn refused to back down.

Muttering something uncomplimentary under his breath, Dane strode across the carpeted floor.

"Talk about messing me up," Robynn mumbled to herself as she strolled back to Josh's room. "He causes more trouble than a boa constrictor at a ladies' luncheon."

A short time after saying good night to Josh, Robynn drove up on I-5, heading for Lake Oswego. Her parents had moved there several years ago, and while she always enjoyed the visits, the house had never seemed like home to her.

Robynn had also never asked them for money before. She had always stood on her own two feet, made her own way, even though at times she'd had to do without. Before in all the hard times but not so often the good times, whenever she *really* needed something, Robynn turned heavenward. *Like Mom says,* she reminded herself, *one good thing about calling God is that His line is never busy. Never get put on hold, either.*

Resolutely she shut the door on the voice that nagged her about only praying when she was desperate, but not before it reminded her that due to her lack of faith or expressions thereof, she didn't deserve an answer.

Her eyes watched the signs and traffic while her mind went into prayer mode—in spite of her. *God, Father, help. I need money. We want the horses so bad. Please give my dad a soft heart tonight so he'll want to buy in. Help me earn all the purses I need and find us some other backers.*

She shook her head. Why on earth was she praying? Pictures of Josh lying in the hospital brought on a guilty groan. For Josh she would do anything. *Father, I blew it again, didn't I? Josh's health is so much more important than money. Please heal him quickly. And I hate being at odds with anyone, especially Dane. Why did You bring him into my life? To help now with Josh laid up? Is he the man You intend for me? If so, You'll have to work it out. All I can see is problems. Thank You for never letting me go.*

After the greetings at her parents' home, Robynn asked if she could use the phone. "I need to call Jeremy. He was still at dinner when I left home."

"Sure. Then let us talk to him." Her dad handed her the phone.

While waiting for Jeremy to come to the phone, Robynn filled her mom and dad in on Josh's condition and what had been happening at the track, carefully leaving out much about Dane. They already knew Josh's nephew had taken over for him at the barns.

"Hi, Tiger, how ya doing?"

"Good; I can type on the Braille machine better all the time. My teacher says I'm the best one in our class."

"Good for you. How's your reading doing?"

"Okay. Johnny is two books ahead of me in the contest. I got to catch up."

Robynn laughed. "I'm sure you will. You're minding Mrs. C?"

"M–o–m!"

"Hey, just had to check. You want to talk with Grammy?" At his enthusiastic response, she handed the phone to her mother. By the time they'd all talked and she'd sent him a good night kiss, the pang of being parted had settled on her shoulders like half a mountain. His squeal when she promised to be at the school to pick him up by ten in the morning helped lift the load. Mondays with Jeremy were a high point of her week.

After her mother poured the coffee, Robynn laid out the plan she and Josh had decided on. The next two hours went extremely well. Robynn's parents, after an exchange of glances, decided that owning some up-and-coming racehorses might be a lot of fun, besides being a good investment. Robynn climbed back into her car with all their good wishes and the promise of seventy-five thousand dollars in a week and another fifty thousand dollars by the end of the year should they need it. Her father would also check around for other backers.

"We've been praying for some way to help you out," her father said. "Since you're so stubborn, maybe this is it."

Robynn watched her mother. She knew that the downcast eyes meant her mother was praying, most likely for wisdom. Robynn thought about telling them she'd prayed about this, too, knowing how they desired her to return to church and her Bible study. But it seemed manipulative, just like asking God for help had. If only—

She barely kept herself from shaking her head. If onlys didn't count.

Robynn drove home in a daze. "Thanks, God," she finally whispered. "Seems like You really do care about what I care about, like Mom said. I've never seen You work so fast before." The dawning reality exploded in her mind. They would own the horses. A quarter of a million dollars didn't seem such an unreachable dream anymore.

Unable to wait, she swung her little car off at the exit to the hospital. Late-night arrivals were becoming a habit. She tiptoed down the darkened hall of the fifth floor and gently pushed open the door.

Josh turned his head at the slight sound.

"Not sleeping yet?" she whispered.

"No," came the gruff reply. "Got too much on my mind."

"I know the feeling. I went to see my parents and. . ."

"Yes. Yes."

"And they'll enjoy being part owners of our horses. Dad's been looking for something new to get into and. . ."

"How much?" Josh squeezed her hand impatiently. "How much?"

"Seventy-five thousand dollars now and more at the end of the year."

"Well, and you wouldn't be a-teasin' an old man, now would ye?" His hand gripped tighter.

"No, Josh." Robynn squeezed back, then removed her fingers to check for broken bones. "Things are looking better than a few hours ago."

"Saints be praised." He shook his head. "I never dreamed we'd get that kind of money from them."

"You get to sleep now." She smoothed the covers where she had been sitting. "I've got to get home. All of us can't sleep late in the morning like you."

"I can't believe it." He shook his head again. "Princess?" She turned back at the door. "Give Jeremy a hug for me."

Robynn blew him a kiss as she tiptoed out into the hall. She felt like an interloper in the darkened hospital. Signs on all the walls proclaimed the visiting hours were over at nine.

"Tough," she informed the down button on the elevator. "This news couldn't keep until morning."

❧

The promised sunshine broke through the clouds the next morning to find Robynn easing back in her Celica, down the I-5 freeway that was alive with braiding strands of traffic. Once past Wilsonville, the flat open country of the Willamette Valley, bound on both sides by mountains and hills, silently encouraged more speed. Robynn set the cruise control at fifty-nine. She didn't need another ticket. If she kept on like she had been going, she'd get known as a freeway jockey as well as a racetrack jockey. Major difference. Here *she* paid.

Robynn turned at the first Salem exit and followed the truck route until she saw the signs for the State School for the Blind. Whistling under her breath, she parked in the parking lot and reached in the backseat for the sack containing Jeremy's present. She knew she was trying to buy his approval when she brought a present each visiting day, but it didn't matter. He enjoyed the little surprises, and she enjoyed his enjoyment.

She glanced at her watch. Ten o'clock right on the button.

At the swinging glass door, she checked her appearance. Under her leather jacket she wore a red cashmere cowl-neck sweater because Jeremy loved the feel of it. Her gold chains were of different textures. He liked that, too. Even her perfume had been chosen with him in mind. It was Blue Grass, reminding her of open fields and warm sunny days. *People here will begin to think I don't own anything else*, she chuckled to herself as she swung the door open.

The tap of her high leather dress boots announced her arrival to the curly headed boy slumped in the leather chair even faster than her voice did.

"Mommy!" He was out of the chair like a shot and into her arms as she stooped to clutch him to her.

"Hey, Tiger." She hugged him again, aware that he wouldn't tolerate too much "mushy stuff." Today he didn't pull away. Instead he rubbed his cheek against the soft fleece of her sweater.

Robynn stroked his head, each ebony curl springing back into place after her fingers' passage. "How've you been?"

"Fine." He lifted his head. A smile curved his rosy lips and deepened the dimple in his cheek. "I've been learning on the Braille typewriter. Pretty soon I'll be able to write you a letter. I get to do it 'cause my teacher says I'm so smart." The last was said with a bit of a swagger.

"That's super-fantastic." Robynn sank down in the deep armchair in front of the windows. Today she wasn't aware of the book-lined walls. All her attention concentrated on the jeans-clad figure beside her. "What else you been doing?"

"Ah-h. I made my bed today without even being reminded. Mrs. C gave me a star." He squirmed on the seat beside her, already having sat his quota for the day. "Her dog had pups. She's gonna bring one after her day off."

"What kind?"

"Hm-m." He thought hard. "I think she called them labortory dogs."

Robynn grinned at him. "You mean Labrador?"

"That's what I said. Labortory. They're hunting dogs. Someday I'm gonna have a hunting dog." He turned so he faced her on the seat. One could never tell he was blind by looking into his sparkling blue eyes. "Did you know they give dogs to blind people to help them see? The dog takes them around. Mom, I'm gonna have one of those dogs someday. When I get lots bigger."

"Sounds like a winner to me. What gave you the idea?"

"They brought one to school. He wears a harness and everything. You shoulda been here."

Guilt made her flinch. "Maybe next time. You'll have to tell him to come on Mondays." Robynn picked up the package from where she had dropped it in the rush of greetings. "Brought you something."

Jeremy found the sack lying on her lap. He opened the top and reached inside to remove the soft, fuzzy bear.

"He's a koala bear," Robynn told him as his swift fingers explored the plush animal. "Koalas live in Australia, in eucalyptus trees. He has fur the color of dust and round black eyes."

Jeremy hugged the animal with one arm and took her hand with the other. "Where we going today? Mrs. C wants to talk with you. And my teacher says I can show you my lessons. That's this afternoon."

"Well, I thought maybe you'd like to go down to the park. The sun is shining, and it's beautiful out. Then we'll eat."

"At McDonald's?"

"At McDonald's. Aren't you getting tired of eating there?"

"Nope." He tugged on her hand. "Let's go. Now."

They spent the next couple of hours at the park on the swings and slides.

"Faster, Mom! Turn it faster," Jeremy shrieked on the merry-go-round. Robynn grabbed the bars as they came around and flung them away again with all her might.

"That's enough." She laughed. "I need to get my breath. I'll sit here, Son, and you ride it out."

Jeremy leaned back against the force of the spinning machine. His curls feathered in the breeze, and the red of his T-shirt reflected in his bright cheeks.

Like Robynn, he lifted his face to the smiling sun, seeking its warmth. When the ride finally slowed to a stop, he slid to the edge, dragging his toe in the dirt and right through a shallow puddle.

"Hey! I'm wet!" He shrieked with joy.

"You would." Robynn laughed along with him. "How come I always take you back wet or muddy? You can find a puddle faster than a duck."

"Quack, quack." Jeremy strutted toward her, confident that she would watch out for him. All his life, he'd rather bump into things than have people baby him. The playground had become very familiar to him since they came here on the nice days.

"Ready to eat?"

"Can I have a Big Mac?"

"Is there anything else?"

"Yeah. You have Chicken McNuggets so I can have one of those, too."

By late afternoon, Robynn and Jeremy had finished all he had planned for them to do. While she watched him play with the other children, the woman in charge of the school came and sat down on the playground beside her.

"Jeremy is doing very well here," she said. "You can be proud of him."

"I always am," Robynn replied softly, never taking her eyes from the slim figure in red and blue.

"All the children like him because he has such a good sense of humor. I have yet to see him hit anyone else or get really angry."

"Beware when he does," Robynn said with a laugh. "He has a temper if you push him too far."

"He's proud of you, too. Says you're a jockey. Is that true?"

Robynn turned to smile at the motherly woman beside her. "Yes, it is. One thing you'll learn, Jeremy never lies. He might get his facts mixed up sometimes, but he never lies."

"His father is a jockey, too?"

"Was."

"Oh, I'm sorry."

"Don't be. Jeremy's father died before Jeremy was born. I've told him about his dad and so have others." Robynn clasped her hands about one raised knee. "It was a long time ago."

Dinner was served family style, and Jeremy led her to his table to sit beside him. Robynn was glad she had been so meticulous about teaching Jeremy to eat properly. Some of the children were still in the mess of learning.

By the time Robynn read him his *Cat in the Hat* book, Jeremy was cuddled in her lap, sweet smelling from his bath. His eyes drooped as she tucked him and his koala bear into bed. Robynn hugged him close. She kissed his cheek, then kissed him lovingly again. Wasn't he a bit warm?

"I'll watch him close!" Mrs. C, a white-haired lady with twinkling eyes, assured her. "If there's any problem, we'll let you know right away. Maybe he just had an extra big day today."

Robynn chewed her lip as she swung out the front door. It would be so much easier on her mind if he were home where she could watch him.

"God, please watch out for him. I can't." Robynn unlocked her car and slid into the seat. "Please?" She rested her forehead on the steering wheel. Leaving Jeremy didn't get any easier. She thumped the wheel with the heel of her hand. They hadn't said his prayers, either. As she drove out of the parking lot, a thought repeated itself. *Why would you expect Jeremy to pray when you don't? He should be in Sunday school, too. Hmm.*

Chapter 7

Robynn leaped out of bed, rejuvenated after her day off, even though she'd gone to sleep stewing about Jeremy and all the muddling aspects of her situation. *If you're not careful, my girl,* she reminded herself, *you're going to feel pulled into tiny pieces.*

Each time she began to worry, she thought again of the promised money from her father. It made the load seem easier.

And Dane. Keeping him out of her thoughts would be like trying to stop the bubbles from rising in a tub full of bubble bath.

The bubbles stayed with her all the way to the track. The stars were still bright with only the faintest line of dawn in the east when she locked her car in the parking lot.

"Where were you yesterday?" Dane barked as soon as he saw her.

Stunned, Robynn tried for a moment to remember. "I told you I would be gone all day." A tentative smile tugged at the corners of her mouth.

"Yes! You said 'with the only important man in my life.' But you didn't say you'd be gone all evening, too." He threw the gear he was carrying down on the tack boxes.

"I don't understand why you're so upset. . . ."

"Upset! You call me upset! I must have dialed your number a thousand times. I finally went over there to make sure you were all right and the house was empty. Josh. . ."

"Josh knew where I was," Robynn interrupted his tirade.

That stopped Dane in his tracks. "He did?"

Maybe Josh is right flitted through her mind. *He sure acts like a man worried half out of his mind. Maybe he really does care about me. Robynn O'Dell, the person, not just keeping a woman off his horses.*

"Yes, he did." She gazed at him, the smile still hovering. "Did you have a good day?"

"Not particularly." A matching smile started in his eyes and tiptoed to his lips. "Did you?"

"Yes, a marvelous day."

"Are you going to tell me who with?" His jaw tightened again.

Robynn watched him for several moments. Doubt and indecision chased each other across her face before a smile banished them both. "Not just now." She paused. "But probably sometime. Sometime soon." *Why not now?* She consciously kept her thoughts from her eyes and face. The man was too perceptive by far. "I don't like to be hollered at."

"Then why. . .?" He paused and lowered his voice with visible effort. "Then why keep secrets from me?"

"Isn't that a bit like the pot calling the kettle black? Like you've not told me anything about yourself. And yet. . ." She sucked in a deep breath. "Forget it."

When he reached for her, she took a step back. "That isn't the answer, either."

"It is for me." He put both arms on the wall behind her, effectively trapping her between two walls, one of flesh and blood, the other solid wood.

Robynn let herself go limp. She would *not* respond to him, no matter what her jangling nerve ends screamed.

A horse whinnied. Another banged a forefoot against the door.

"I think I hear your friends calling us," she whispered.

"Is that what you call them?" Dane sighed and dropped his arms. "Then let's get going." His gaze bored into hers. "But we're not over this yet, not by a long shot."

Together they sauntered down the row of stalls bound by horses impatiently hanging their heads over the doors. Robynn greeted each one, giving special rubs and pats to her favorites.

As Dane gave her the instructions for each workout, he punctuated his words by tapping with one finger on her knee. The spot seemed eternally warm, even in the breeze from galloping through the early morning ground mist. The sun rising round and golden from behind Mount Hood inspired cheerful responses from all the people working at The Meadows. Grooms, trainers, bug boys, jockeys, everyone perked up, glad for a respite from the never-ending rain.

The good cheer extended into the afternoon's program.

The bantering between jockeys in the saddling paddock set laughter ringing against the high dusky ceiling. Robynn gave as good as she got. Dane was the recipient of secret, admiring glances from all the female contingent.

"Robynn, are you paying attention?" He spoke sharply to get her attention away from the sallies of the young jockey mounted next to her.

"Of course." Robynn sobered instantly. "I heard everything you said. Try to take him out in front from the beginning and. . ." She paused. "You realize I've ridden this horse many times. I think by now I know his little tricks better than anyone."

Dane glared up at her. "Just be careful."

"I will."

"I just bet." He led the animal out to the pony rider.

Being careful was not in Robynn's vocabulary today or any day. Her mount got off to a bad start. By the time he found his footing, the rest of the pack galloped a furlong ahead of them.

Robynn brought her stick down on his rump just once. The horse exploded and advanced on the pack like a steam engine out of control. A row of tightly packed haunches barred their way. Robynn tried to pull him up, but the horse laid back his ears and drove right down the middle.

"Coming through," Robynn yelled as she fought to get him back under control. Miraculously the horses parted without any clipping on either side. Robynn breathed a sigh of relief.

The field was clear until he caught the two front-runners neck and neck in the backstretch. Robynn guided him to the outside. He paced the leaders until she swung her bat again. With a surge, he drove for the finish line, winner by a nose.

Robynn caught the heat from Dane's snapping eyes as she slipped her saddle off the steaming animal. She smiled for the camera and nodded gracefully at all the accolades.

"That was some ride," the barrel-chested owner congratulated her. "You used real unusual strategy with him this time. Glad to see it worked." He pumped her hand again while the trainer took the animal back to the barn.

Robynn weighed in, and as she stepped from the scale, Dane let loose.

"I couldn't help it," Robynn responded when she finally got a word in edgewise. "Somehow he got the bit in his teeth. . . ."

"Sheer carelessness on your part." The white lines around his mouth announced the effort he was making at control. "If you'd been stronger. . ."

"That has nothing to do with it. I've seen it happen to men, too. Just be grateful no one got hurt. I am." She turned on her heel and stomped off to the dressing room.

"Man, oh man," Pam commiserated once they were in the dull green room. "He sure let you have it. You going to put up with that kind of harassment?"

The sigh that escaped as Robynn sat down on the bench came clear from her toes. "He's just worried about my lily-white neck. I'm trying to ignore him."

"That ain't easy." Pam joined her, leaning against the concrete wall.

"You're telling me." Robynn leaned her head from side to side, trying to loosen the kinks. "That monster animal scared me out of ten black hairs. A few more like him, and I'll have lily-white hair to match my neck."

Pam chuckled. "Well, no one could tell by looking at you. Calm, cool, and collected as always."

"For that performance today I should get an Oscar."

"I wonder if they give Dane awards."

"Pam!"

Dane remained tight-lipped and surly the rest of the day. But he didn't try to tell Robynn how to ride each mount. In fact, he hardly spoke to her at all.

That evening when Robynn visited the hospital, Josh had good news for her. He had rounded up another twenty-five thousand dollars to invest in "our string," as he already called the horses.

"See," he chortled. "Even broken I'm good for something. Have some more guys coming to see me tomorrow."

"You kinda like having them come to you, don't you?" Robynn teased. "King Josh."

"How'd it go today? Sure wish they'd broadcast it on TV. Even the radio stations don't carry the races. I feel like I'm stuck here in no-man's-land and the track is only five miles away."

"Quit your grumping. I added another fifteen hundred dollars to the kitty today. The sun shining for a change brought out the best in everybody." She studied the cuticle of her thumb. "It's at times like this that I wish you could bet on my rides—see if we could up our investment money."

"You know better than that. You haven't forgotten our pact, have you?" Josh pointed at the chair. "Sit down so I don't have to strain my neck." She sat.

"No. I know that some Christians say betting is a sin, so we don't do it, but still. . ." She raised a hand as though stopping traffic. "Don't worry, Josh, I just said I thought about it. I'm not serious."

"Good." Josh relaxed back in his pillows. "Sounded to me like you and Dane had a bit of a set-to."

"Why? Oh. You talked to Dane already. He *was* a bit put out with me." She slid down in the seat.

"I'd call it more than a bit put out."

"I'd call it furious." Dane's deep voice announced his entrance.

Robynn sank lower in her chair. She winked at Josh and licked the smile off her lips. "Why, Dane." The honey dripped. "Fancy meeting you here."

"Now, you two are supposed to be getting along." Josh punctuated each word with a slash of his hand. "Am I gonna have to come over there and referee?"

Dane pulled a chair next to Robynn's and, when he sat down, leaned his arm along the back of her chair. Each time she moved her head, she could feel the brush of her hair against his sleeve. It made concentrating on the conversation increasingly difficult.

"Well, I've got to get going," she said as she broke into the first lull. "You behave yourself, Josh. Don't go sweet-talking the nurses." She glanced at Dane. "I'll see you in the morning."

"Have you eaten yet?" He stopped her with a hand on her wrist.

"No. I have stew in the Crock-Pot at home. Would you like to come for dinner?" The words slipped out before she had time to think.

"She makes a mighty mean stew, boy." Josh leaned back against his pillows. "You better take her up on it."

"I plan to." Dane slid his hand down to her fingers. "What are we waiting for?" He rose and almost pulled her from the room. "See you later." He stuck his head back around the door and winked at the old man in the bed.

All the way home Robynn racked her brain, trying to think what else to have with the stew. Maybe a cottage cheese and pear salad, and there were home-baked rolls in the freezer. But what for dessert? She never had sweet stuff in the house. Too tempting. *Well, tough,* she finally decided. *He'll have to take what I have. Next time I'll plan a special meal.* She caught herself. Next time. Having Dane around was becoming a habit, a natural event. Was that the way love sneaked up on you? Day by day instead of fireworks and rocket explosions?

Dane's nearness caused her to fumble with her key at the door. The heat from his body permeated her jacket and clothing. Her nerve ends lit up like sparklers on the Fourth of July. Who said there were no fireworks?

The rich aroma of bubbling beef stew announced the menu even before they opened the door.

When Robynn turned to take Dane's coat after flipping on the lights, he pulled her into his arms.

"You know, I can't seem to keep my hands off you," he murmured into her fragrant hair.

"You'll have to if you want to eat." Robynn listened to his heart drumming under her ear. "Or aren't you hungry?"

"That's a tricky question." He smiled down into her upturned face. "Either way I answer it, I'll have to chew on my boot leather."

"Better chew on the stew instead." She pulled away from his embrace and opened the refrigerator door. "Here." She handed out containers. "I'll make the salad while you set the table."

At the perplexed expression furrowing his eyes, she laughed. "I'll tell you how."

"I know how to set tables." He grinned at her as she closed the door. "I thought you said I had to make the salad. I cook a mean steak and fry chicken better than the Colonel, but salads mean slicing veggies in tiny pieces. And slicing usually means blood—mine."

"Well, we certainly wouldn't want you bleeding all over the place, would we? The dishes are up there, and the silverware is in the drawer next to the dishwasher."

Robynn found herself touching Dane every time she passed him; little things like hands brushing, shoulders meeting, a hand on his arm. It was a good feeling, a right feeling. Working together like this in the evening after a day at the track made her day complete. Complete. That was the word. A part of her had been missing up until now; she just realized it. If only Jeremy could be here at home, too.

Life with Sonny had been razzle-dazzle, arguments and tears, wild reconciliations. The time with Dane, especially away from the track, grew like a river fed by small tributaries as it flowed deeper and broader.

"You're awfully quiet." He laid down his fork after finishing dinner. "Can you share the thoughts behind those beautiful violet eyes?" He waited for an answer.

"I–I. Dane, are you married?"

"Heavens, no. What made you ask that?"

"Well, Pam said I had to make sure." Confusion colored her neck to match her rose-colored shirt.

Dane's eyes narrowed, creases appeared on his forehead. "How do you figure I could be here with you like this if I were married? What kind of a man do you think I am?"

"Dane, I, um–m." Black lashes veiled her eyes, as a red stain rose to cover her cheeks. She felt hot all over. *What a stupid, stupid. . .* She swallowed. "Please," she whispered, one hand raised beseechingly. "I'm sorry."

"Robynn." Dane came around the table and took her hand. "We need to do some serious talking. I think the living room will be a better place."

When she looked up at him, she realized a smile had replaced the frown.

"Why don't you start the fire while I bring in the coffee? The matches are in the pottery bowl on the mantel." Dane nodded but seemed reluctant to release her fingers.

Robynn heard the sounds of fire building as she reached for the instant coffee. At the last moment she changed her mind and got out the jar of coffee beans instead. She dumped them in the grinder while filling the tank on her under-the-counter coffeemaker. Instantly, the aromatic scent of fresh coffee filled the air. Smiling to herself, Robynn piled the dishes in the sink, waiting for the pot to finish dripping. She entered the living room a few minutes later, carrying a pewter tray with hand-thrown pottery mugs on it.

Dane reclined in front of the now-roaring fire, orange and yellow flames casting dancing shadows over his pensive face. He had turned on the stereo so easy listening music played counterpoint to the snap and hiss of the burning logs.

"Sit here." Dane patted the spot in front of him. "I saved it just for you."

Robynn smiled as she handed him his mug. Then setting the tray on the coffee table, she surprised herself by doing just as he asked. Immediately he wrapped a strong arm about her waist and pulled her back to lean against the hard muscles of his chest. For a while they stared into the flickering firelight, sipping coffee, a feeling of peace and contentment floating on the strains of the music.

"Princess Lady."

"Um—m."

"What is there about you that's so different from anyone I've ever known before? You're feisty, fun, and funny; you make me furious, yet in the next moment I want to hold you." He paused, allowing his thoughts free rein. "You're mysterious. One of these days I hope you'll let me in on those deep thoughts and hidden hurts." All the while he talked, his fingers drew hypnotic lines up and down her arm.

"But there's more than that. Things don't seem to get you down. There's a caring that flows out of you and touches everything around. Everyone at the track is so protective of you, I can't find out much of anything. Even Josh, my own uncle."

"What did he say?" Robynn scooted down so her head could rest on his arm.

" 'Ask Robynn. When she's ready, she'll tell you.' " Dane set his cup down on the hearth. "I'm asking, love. I need to know."

"What's different about me?" Robynn stared into the fire, searching for the right words. "About that caring you said I have? It's not mine. My heavenly Father gives it to me, and I just pass it on. He's the one who keeps me steady, even when I forget to ask. My mom says He sends guardian angels, a whole platoon of them in my case, to watch over me. I like that idea. When things were really bad, when Sonny, the man I married at eighteen much against my parents' wishes, left me and then was killed the next day, I had nowhere else to turn. There's an old saying that has come to mean a great deal to me, 'When we share our sorrows they're cut in half. Share our joys and we double them.' "

"I like that." If Robynn had turned her head, she would have seen compassion and love on his face.

"To make a long story short, I am who I am because God lives up to His promises. When. . ." She paused, struggling with the idea of telling him about Jeremy. *Why don't I just tell him?*

"Robynn."

"Um—m—m."

"Look at me."

She turned her head. The moment for telling him passed. The look in his eyes made her heart speed up.

"I think I'm falling in love with you." The words hung in the air, crystal clear and perfect.

Robynn couldn't answer. She reached out with one hand, laying it gently along his jaw. Her fingertips rasped on the slight end-of-the-day stubble. With a small movement, he turned his face and, with his warm lips against warm flesh, bestowed a kiss in her palm. His eyes never left hers, holding her, cocooning her with their intensity. "That's why I can't stand to watch you race. Every time a horse falls, I see you under it. When a jockey is thrown, I'm sure it must be you."

"But. . .but I'm a good rider. Those things are just accidents. People get injured driving down the freeway just as easy—look at Josh. Besides, racing is my life."

"But accidents, as you say, can ruin a person's life." *Tell her about your mother,* his inner voice prompted. *If you want to know her secrets, you have to reveal yours.*

Tension crept into the room, snaking between them, flicking them with its ugly tongue. Dane's face assumed the tight-lipped expression he wore when pushed to the edge of his patience.

Tell her! The voice became imperative. *Tell her about Mother, about how you failed in the promise to your father.*

He rose to his feet. "Thanks for the dinner, Princess." He held out his hand to pull her up. "I'll see you at the track in the morning."

Robynn nodded, as a chill crept about her shoulder blades and settled around her heart, a chill that had nothing to do with the warmth of the room.

She handed him his jacket, then walked him to the door and stood shivering on the step until he started his car and backed out the drive. The shivers continued to attack her until long after she snuggled down under her warm comforter on the bed. "Why couldn't I say how I feel? Why couldn't I tell him about Jeremy? God, what's wrong with me?" She pounded her pillow, wishing it were her stubbornly disobedient mind.

❦

The next morning, Dane's clipped voice gave her the training instructions, but there was no warm interlude in the tack room. It was as if he had put his emotions on hold. Robynn hoped it wouldn't be for long. She'd gotten used to the brush of his hand, the pressure under her elbow when he walked her to the cafeteria.

Robynn finished exercising the horses and left for the hospital to talk to Josh. Her afternoon program was full—eight rides.

"How's it going?" she asked as she entered the room. "You behaving yourself?"

"Can't do much else long as I'm hooked up to that contraption." Josh pointed to the weights and pulleys holding his heavy cast in the air. "Doctor says another week. Then they'll X-ray it again. And it better be a-healing, is all I can say."

"Well, as you always tell me, 'Picture it the way you want it to be.' I'm sure that pertains to broken bones, too. And you know there are lots of people praying. First time for some of them."

"Thanks, lass. I know you have, and I do appreciate it." He pointed to a tablet on the table beside his bed. "There's the list of money we've been promised. Not as much as I'd hoped, but it could be worse."

"I'm on my way down to the loan officer at the bank to talk about a second mortgage on my house. If I can get fifty thousand dollars we should be in pretty good shape. I'm booked solid at the track. Winning makes everyone want me."

"You've been doing a fine job. How are you and Dane getting along? From the looks of the wins, you make a good team."

Robynn chewed her bottom lip as she studied the cuticles on her nails. Her hair waved forward, partially hiding her eyes.

"Dr. Rice to surgery. Dr. Rice to surgery" blaring from the intercom accented the silence in the flower-filled room.

"Oh, Josh." The words poured forth once she started. "He says he loves me but can't stand to watch me race. What am I going to do?"

"Do you love him?"

"I think so—oh, I don't know." She leaped from the chair and went to stand at the sink, her back to the man in the bed. "I couldn't say 'I love you' and I couldn't tell him about Jeremy." She turned, a desperate plea in her eyes, face, and voice. "What's the matter with me?"

"Give it time, lass." Josh used the same soothing tone with her as he did with high-strung horses. "Give it time. You're so impatient. If love is right, time never hurts it. Let it grow, lass, till the season is right." He paused. "Did he tell you anything about his family?"

She shook her head. "I've been meaning to ask, but something always comes up. I don't get it. Why? Is there something really important I oughta know?"

"You'll just have to ask him."

"You could tell me."

"I could, but I won't. Just like I haven't told him about Jeremy since you seem to want to keep that boy a secret here." His eyes grew piercing. "Why?"

Robynn drew circles on the bedspread. "I—I think I'm afraid of Jeremy getting hurt. What if he really likes Dane and then this, whatever this is, is over? Men leave, you know. If I get hurt, stupid me, but I can't have Jeremy hurt."

"Thought it might be somethin' like that."

She sank down on the edge of the bed beside him. Tears shimmered in her eyes and deepened her voice. "Thanks, Josh. You're about the best friend anybody could ever have."

"Now get on with ye." His brogue thickened. "Or you'll have us both a-weepin'."

"Thanks again." She leaned over and kissed him lightly on the cheek, then was gone.

❧

The loan officer was not as amicable as she had hoped. Even as he studied her credit references and her payment history at his own institution, the frown never left his forehead.

"You realize," he said, tapping the papers with a pen, "that you're in a very unstable profession. What if you were injured tomorrow and couldn't ride anymore? How would you pay this off?"

"If I were permanently disabled, my insurance would cover the mortgages on my home. Besides, we'd own some increasingly valuable horses." Robynn strove to appear businesslike and knowledgeable, but this was beginning to feel like begging. She hated begging.

He studied the papers some more. "With the market the way it is right now, I don't see that we can go with the full amount." He looked over his glasses at her. "The board approved a loan for twenty-five thousand dollars. Will that be satisfactory?"

No, it won't, Robynn wanted to shout. *I need the full amount.* She raised her chin in the unconscious gesture she used when dealing with officious people. "That will be fine. When can I sign the papers?"

"They'll be ready by Monday. Can you come in then?"

"Fine." *I'll just have to be late for Jeremy.* She could see no other way out. "I'll be here at ten."

As she rose, Robynn extended her hand. "Thank you for your time." The dishrag handshake did nothing to raise her impression of the man. "I surely hope you won't go broke over this." She turned and marched across the tiled floor, her boots tapping out her resentment.

By the time the afternoon's races were over, her mood hadn't improved much. She'd only been in the money three times, never in the winner's circle.

Back in the dressing room, she shrugged as she let the shower beat down on her back. Win some, lose some. Another day, another dollar. The platitudes didn't help.

You never seem down, whispered in her ear from the conversation the night before.

"That's all you know, Mr. Morgan." She shut off the shower. "I get down, but I never stay down. That's the difference."

By the time she dressed, brushed her hair out, and blew it dry, she found herself whistling under her breath. The tune had been playing on the stereo the night before.

Dane was in his usual place, holding up the wall, when she came out. A smile answered her jaunty grin, her shattered bits of peace drawing together like iron filings to a magnet.

"Dinner?"

"It'll have to be quick. I planned to go to church tonight." She didn't even try to repress the bubbles his nearness caused. They were together again, oh, happy day.

323

He tucked her arm in his after taking her duffel bag and slinging it over his other shoulder. "Can I come along?"

"May I?"

"Let me change that. May I take you to dinner and then to church?"

"What about the horses?"

"All done, Your Highness. Anything else?" He pushed the door open and held it for her.

"Yes. Where are we eating?"

When they entered the sanctuary of the small brick chapel at seven, Robynn allowed the strains of the organ prelude to wash over her, restoring her tranquility in preparation for the service. Why had she let so much time pass since the last service she attended? As they sat down in one of the short wooden pews, she glanced at the man beside her.

He smiled, then pulled her arm through his, drawing her closer. The service opened with the congregation singing "Just as I Am," "Amazing Grace," and other old favorites. Robynn rejoiced to hear Dane's strong baritone, singing like the words were familiar.

When he saw the question on her face, he whispered in her ear, "Mother saw to it that we all went to church as children. I just haven't been for a while." At her nod, he finished his statement. "A long while."

When the white-robed pastor rose for the sermon, Robynn turned off the thoughts rampaging through her mind and tried to concentrate on what he said. Her conscious mind caught the last words, "And the greatest of these is love." Dane turned to watch her as the pastor spoke of married love, the love between a man and a woman. Blue eyes met violet. The look they exchanged spoke the words they couldn't say.

Robynn's heart sang along as the words of the doxology closed the service. As usual, God had met her and left her feeling blessed.

"Do you come all the time?" Dane asked as they walked back to his car.

"No." She shook her head, the fresh fragrance of her perfume wafting upward. "It's so easy to get out of the habit. I just know I have a need to be here all the time again. The sermon always seems written just for me—and I need that."

The ride back to her house deepened the feeling of contentment. At the door, when Dane raised his lips from hers, he stared into her eyes for a long moment. "I meant what I said last night. I love you, Robynn O'Dell, and I'll keep at it till one of these days I'll wear you down so you'll love me back." He laid two fingers against her lips before she could respond. "Good night, Princess." And he was gone.

Robynn let herself into the dark house, the rose-hued cloud she floated in making the lights unnecessary. In the living room she switched her recorder off. She would answer calls herself.

As she undressed for bed, she felt Dane's lips against hers again. "I love you." What beautiful words.

The phone rang. She glanced at the clock by her bed. Nine. She was going to bed early for a change. On the third ring, she picked it up.

"Mrs. O'Dell?" A gentle voice spoke. "This is Mrs. Cravens, Jeremy's housemother."

"Yes. Is something wrong with Jeremy?" Fear immediately tightened her throat.

"No, no, dear. Nothing serious. Jeremy has just been feeling under the weather and wanted to talk to his mother. Here he is."

Robynn waited until a small voice said, "Mommy?"

"Yes, Tiger. I'm here. What do you need?" Robynn made her voice soothing and warm.

"My head hurts and my tummy aches." The plaintive note in his voice tore at Robynn's heart. She steeled herself to be positive.

"It's not much fun to feel crummy is it, Son? I'm sure you'll feel better tomorrow. Did I tell you Josh is in the hospital? He broke his leg and has a huge cast."

Jeremy immediately perked up. "When's he coming to see me? Can I visit him in the hospital? Did you win today?"

Robynn chuckled into the receiver. "Didn't do quite so well today. And Josh can't come to see you for a long time, but maybe we can sneak you in to visit him. I'll check, and we'll plan on doing that on Monday. How's that sound?"

"Good. Mrs. C said I could have a popsicle. Any kind I want. I like banana best."

"Good night, Tiger. You go have your popsicle and sleep tight. I love you. Let me talk to Mrs. C again, please."

"Sure. Bye, Mom." Robynn could hear him saying in the background.

"Mrs. O'Dell?"

"Please call me Robynn. Thank you for being so good to him. I wish I could be there. I can come if it would help."

"Now don't you worry. He'll be right as rain in a day or two. There's been several cases of some twenty-four-hour virus," the grandmotherly voice continued reassuringly.

"You'll let me know?"

"Of course, dear. Don't worry. Good night now."

"Bye." Robynn heard the dial tone before she hung up. What an empty sound.

Chapter 8

"Father, take care of Jeremy, please," Robynn entreated on her way to the track in the early morning hours. She gave herself a mental shake. After all, it was "only a virus."

As she locked her car, she forced her princess mask back in place. Head high, shoulders erect, she entered the gate with her customary smile for the guard.

By the third mount for the morning, she caught a puzzled look in Dane's eyes as he gave her instructions. She made sure her smile brightened and a tiny bit of sparkle found its way to her eyes. If she could just quit feeling guilty about being here when Jeremy needed her.

"Are you all right?" Dane hung onto the horse's reins.

"I'm fine, Dane." She smiled again. "Really." She could feel his gaze boring into her back as she trotted the horse out onto the track. Long years of habit helped her concentrate on the animals she rode when her desire was to be cuddling a sick little boy. That's what moms were supposed to do.

As soon as the horses were all snapped onto the hot walker, she dashed for the pay phone. When the school answered, she asked for Mrs. Cravens.

"He's much better this morning," the cheery voice reassured over the line. "He'll probably stay in bed today, at least for a while, but he ate a piece of toast for breakfast. The monkey is already asking for another popsicle."

Relief made Robynn lean against the wall. "Thank you, Mrs. C. You've just made my day. You don't think it necessary that I come down tonight then?"

"No, no, dear. Jeremy'll be fine. You have a nice day now."

After the conversation Robynn felt a nice day was a more likely possibility.

"Everything okay now?" Dane set his tray down at her table.

"Yes." Robynn bit into her toast. "Everything is just great." His warm glance sent the tingles racing to her fingertips.

By race time, Robynn realized the shutters had locked over Dane's features again. His stoic look could have been carved out of stone, the same granite that chipped off in his words. His glacier eyes refused to meet hers as he gave her the instructions for each race.

Robynn ignored what she disagreed with. She'd been riding these horses long before he arrived on the scene.

Ignoring his instructions got her in trouble that afternoon. Around the first turn, she found herself boxed in by straining Thoroughbreds and determined jockeys. The only way to keep from being knocked about was to pull her mount back. By the time he hit his stride again, the other horses ran far ahead.

"You should have gone for the outside like I said." Dane's words dripped ice water when he stopped her on the way to change.

"I know. I know." Robynn stared down at the saddle in her arms. "I thought I could get away with it. He just wasn't quick enough out of the gate."

She could hear the bricks clinking into place on the wall building between them. When she raised her eyes to smile at him, he glared at her once more and marched back to the barns.

By the end of the afternoon Robynn had added more wins to her reputation, but none of the purses were large ones. The sweepstakes of the day found her with only a third place, nothing to brag to Josh about. Tame Adventure, the favorite for the big race, had pulled a muscle and had to be scratched.

When Dane appeared in the hall waiting for her, Robynn stopped, amazed. "What are you doing here?"

"I thought we could go visit Josh. And then we'll have dinner." He lifted the duffel from her shoulder.

"Which are you today, Jekyll or Hyde?"

"What do you mean?" The warmth from his fingers seeped through, just as if they'd never itched to shake her.

"Dane." She planted her feet, refusing to go any farther. "An hour ago you wouldn't even say my name without snapping at me, and now we're friends again. This isn't making any sense to me; I don't like feeling caught at the end of a string like a yo-yo."

"I have an easy answer for that." He dropped the duffel at their feet and took both her hands in his. "Stop racing and marry me."

The silence stretched and stretched some more. Robynn stared deep into his eyes, searching out any chance at humor. Slowly she became aware of his thumbs, smoothing the backs of her hands. Marrying him would make her life so much easier. They could buy the horses and the farm. And he loved her. He kept telling her so, in fact, if persistence was any indicator. . . But did she love him? She loved the feeling of being held in his arms, she missed him if they were separated, she loved laughing with him, teasing him. But did she care enough to give up racing?

"I take it that's either/or." She finally whispered past the lump in her throat.

"I think so." He leaned back against the concrete wall, tucking her under his arm. "You could have gone down so easily out there today."

"I know that, and it was a stupid mistake. One I won't make again." She could feel the thudding of his heart through her fingertips as they played with the buttons on his shirt. Dane covered her hands with his, stilling the nervous actions, pressing them into his chest. Slowly, his eyes remaining on hers, he raised each slim hand to his mouth and breathed a feather kiss onto the palm. Then he closed her fingers over the caress and pressed them shut.

"Let's go see Josh."

Mist softened Robynn's gaze at the tenderness Dane shared with her. Now would have been as good a time as any to mention Jeremy, but the words just wouldn't come. *Either/or, what would she do? Was there really any question?*

When Dane left Josh's room for a moment, she called Jeremy's school. Mrs. C reported that Jeremy had been good all day but had been so tired he fell asleep at dinner.

"Having a bug like this takes a lot out of the little tykes," Mrs. C stated positively. "I wouldn't worry none."

It's easy to say "don't worry," Robynn thought when she recalled the report on Jeremy as she undressed for bed that night. *You're there where you can watch him, and I'm up here, wishing I were beside him. It's a good thing he's been so healthy. The only illness he's had was the chicken pox a couple of weeks ago. I couldn't handle this on a regular basis.*

❧

Robynn had come home for her break and was nearly ready to dash out the door at noon the next day when the phone rang.

"This is Mrs. Taylor. I spoke to you the other day when you visited Jeremy here at the school. I don't want to alarm you, but I have some bad news. I just took Jeremy into emergency at Capital Hospital. He started vomiting about eight last night."

"Oh, no." Robynn slumped against the wall.

"The doctor said to bring him in. I think you should come as soon as possible."

"Yes, I will." Robynn checked her watch. "I'll be there in about an hour." The phone clattered in the cradle. Wildly Robynn stared around the room, trying to decide whom to call.

Fingers shaking, she dialed Josh's number. "Josh, there's been an emergency. The school just called and Jeremy's in the hospital. They don't know what it is, but I'm leaving right away. Can you call my parents for me? I'll be at Capital Hospital."

"Of course, lass. Sure and you'll be wanting to let Dane know."

"You tell him; I can't right now. And Josh, pray hard."

"That I will. Robynn?"

"Yes." She shifted impatiently, wanting, needing, to be on the road.

"You drive carefully."

"Thanks. I'll call you when I know something."

The drive down the freeway passed in a blur of fence posts, fields, and semi-trucks. Her shiny black car wove in and out of traffic expertly, even though its driver could hardly see through her tears.

"Father God," she muttered over and over. "Please take care of him. Make him well again. Why, oh, why wasn't I there?"

What more could you have done? The calm, sensible side of her brain argued with the nagging guilt attacking her on the other.

Robynn stopped at the first gas station after turning off the freeway to ask directions to the hospital. Grateful for the lack of patrols on the streets, she sped through town, swung into the parking lot of the ancient brick hospital, and followed the signs to emergency.

The few seconds from the time she parked the car until she entered the automatic door played in slow motion.

"I'm Robynn O'Dell. They brought my son Jeremy in from the school for the blind?"

The nurse smiled up at her. "Yes, we've admitted him. You go over to the elevator," she pointed down the hall, "and up to three. Turn right."

"Thanks," Robynn called over her shoulder as she trotted along the narrow hall.

She repeated the procedure at the nurse's desk on three. The young, blond nurse in a red-checked smock didn't need to check her chart. "He's in 304," she said. "We're just getting him into his bed. Go right on in."

Strange, Robynn thought as she pushed open the door. *Two of the people I love most are in hospitals at the same time.*

Jeremy's face, except for the purple shadows under his eyes, almost matched the sheets. An IV had already been started in his arm, and the nurse was just finishing taking his blood pressure and temperature.

"How is he?" Robynn sank onto the edge of the bed beside him and smoothed the tousled hair back from his forehead. "Jeremy, Mommy's here." His blue-veined eyelids flickered.

"He's a pretty sick little boy." The nurse lifted a thin arm to check the pulse. "Little kids like this dehydrate pretty quickly, but the IV helps right away."

"Do you know what's wrong?" Robynn wanted to pick him up and hold him. He looked so small and fragile lying there.

"We're not sure. The blood work is down at the lab now. Your doctor should be in shortly. His name is Dr. Prescott, the pediatrician who takes care of the schoolchildren." She slipped her stethoscope back in the pocket of her cheery yellow top. "Can I get you anything?" she asked as she walked out. "A cup of coffee or a pop?"

"No. No, thank you." Robynn never took her eyes from the sleeping form.

When Jeremy's face contorted with the dry heaves, Robynn grabbed the basin from beside his pillow and held it for him. "Oh, Jeremy," she muttered. "Jeremy, please get well." She wiped his mouth with a washcloth dampened at the sink.

"Mommy?" A tiny whisper rewarded her efforts.

"Yes, darling, I'm here." She gathered him in her arms and hugged him close. "We're at the hospital so you can get better."

"Mrs. O'Dell?" A robust, gray-haired man with a crew cut stopped at the foot of the bed. "I'm Dr. Prescott." His warm smile inspired confidence immediately. "The blood work isn't back yet, but we started the IV to get some fluids back in him. The school gave us all the information we need. They mentioned that he had chicken pox about two weeks ago?"

"Yes." Robynn nodded. "A very light case. He had only about a dozen pox. He was only sick about a day. Do you think there's some connection?"

"We'll know more later. You didn't give him aspirin by any chance, did you?"

"No. He was at school. I came down the first two days. Then he was all right, just itched." She watched as the doctor checked Jeremy's pulse with thumb and forefinger, then eye responses with a tiny flashlight. "They said last night he just had a virus."

"And that's most likely what it is." Dr. Prescott nodded. "There's been a lot of stuff going around." He walked to the door. "Get him to take fluids if you can. Fruit juice, popsicles, anything. Just ask the nurses for whatever you need."

"Thank you, Doctor."

"I'll let you know as soon as we have some results." Robynn nodded as he left the room.

"Hey, Tiger." She patted the pale little face. "How about a piece of ice? You've always liked to munch ice chips." When he nodded the tiniest bit, she poured a couple pieces of ice into the paper cup and held it to his mouth.

"It's cold," he whispered around the crunches.

"I should hope so." His weak response made her feel giddy. "It'd be a real shame if ice were hot. How about some more?" A few more chips disappeared before the boy shook his head. Robynn felt like she'd earned her mother badge for the day. At least her being here had a good effect on him.

❦

"Where is she?" Dane stopped at the foot of the bed. The tone of his voice matched the thunder on his brow.

"She had an emergency, like I told you." Josh smacked a pillow behind his head so he could see better. "Come over here so I don't get a crick in my neck from trying to see you."

Dane complied. "I swear I'll crank up that apparatus if you don't tell me."

He pointed to the weights and pulleys holding Josh's leg up.

"Now, don't go gettin' all testy."

"You want *testy*, you just. . ."

"Sit down and behave yourself. Yer worse'n a horse with colic."

Dane took the chair he'd been pointed to and clasped his hands, elbows on his knees. He leaned closer to Josh. "Now, tell me."

"Jeremy is in the hospital in Salem, and she went to him."

"Jeremy?"

"Her seven-year-old son."

Dane leaned back like he'd been pushed. "A son? Why hasn't she told me? Why. . . ?"

Josh sighed. "Why haven't you told her about your mother?"

"Touché." It was Dane's turn to sigh. "Is he—Jeremy—going to be all right?"

"I sure pray to God so. Something happens to that boy, and I don't know how she could stand it. They're at Capital Hospital in Salem. You might spend your driving time praying for them."

"I will. Thanks, Uncle." Dane stopped on his way out the door. "Don't tell her I'm coming, okay?"

"Just get going, and give her a walloping big hug from me."

Dane found her about an hour later, stretched out on the bed, cuddling the little boy to her, both of them sound asleep. Without a sound, he sat down in the chair and waited.

Robynn awoke when the nurse came in to change the IV bag. The nurse checked Jeremy's pulse again while Robynn scrambled from the bed, an apologetic look on her face. "I just wanted to hold him, but the tubing wasn't long enough. This seemed the next best thing."

"Don't worry, Mrs. O'Dell. We don't stand on rules so much in this department; whatever helps these little ones get well."

Robynn turned to find the chair only to encounter a familiar male form rising to meet her.

"Dane," she breathed. "When did you get here?"

"Quite some time ago, but I couldn't bear to wake you. The picture the two of you made—he's beautiful, Robynn, just like you." He paused, lifting a tentative hand to brush back the ebony wings of hair framing her face. "Why didn't you tell me about him?"

Anxiety wrinkled the creases around her eyes.

"I–I." Robynn fought the conflicting emotions warring to come out. "I. . ."

"Mommy?" At the thready whisper, she spun back to the bed.

"I'm here, darling, what is it? How about more ice? A popsicle?" The little hand clung to hers.

Jeremy nodded. "Banana."

"I'll see if they have it." Dane touched her shoulder reassuringly as he left the room.

"Do you want a piece of ice in the meantime?" Robynn noticed the little animal sitting on the window ledge. "I see they brought your koala bear." A tiny smile lifted the corners of Jeremy's mouth.

"Bear's my friend." Rejoicing at any response, Robynn stood. "I'll get him for you." As she glanced out the window, her attention was caught by a stone statue of the shepherd and his sheep, banked about with scarlet chrysanthemums. "Thank You, Jesus," she whispered. "You're always here, every time I need You. And this is certainly a time of need."

She had just finished tucking the fuzzy koala under the covers, with Jeremy's arm locked around it, when Dane entered the room, triumphantly waving a yellow popsicle.

Robynn cracked it in half on the lip of the bedside table and, unwrapping it, held half to Jeremy's mouth. A tiny nibble followed another until much of it was gone. The grins that Dane and Robynn shared united them with one more silk-fine thread in the web of companionship.

The nurse brought in a dinner tray for Jeremy, but it remained untouched.

Awhile later a rounded woman with little pepper left in her hair hugged her daughter as soon as she entered the room. "Oh, Robynn, darling. We came as soon as we could." As Mary Ahern turned to her grandson, Robynn leaned against her father's chest.

"There now, girl." He patted her back. "It'll be all right. You'll see." Giving her another reassuring hug, he went around the bed to stand at Jeremy's other side.

"Grammy and Grandpa are here, Tiger. Can you wake up for them?"

Jeremy moved his head restlessly on the pillow, a frown caterpillaring his eyebrows.

Robynn stood back so that the grandparents could murmur words of love to their only grandson. Without a thought, she slipped her arm into Dane's. She leaned her head against his upper arm, the muscles contracting as he pressed her hand against his side.

"Mother, Father," Robynn said when they straightened, "I'd like you to meet Dane Morgan." Her voice had a proud ring to it. "He's my. . .uh. . .taking over for Josh. He's the nephew."

The three exchanged names and handshakes as Robynn thought, *Friend? That's not enough. Boyfriend? He would like to be, but not yet, if ever. Here I am stuttering and stammering like some fifteen-year-old with her first date.*

"Have you had anything to eat?" Dane whispered in her ear as the grandparents turned their attention back to the silent form in the bed.

"No." Robynn shook her head.

"Did you eat at all today? You weren't at the cafeteria this morning."

Robynn wrinkled her forehead trying to think. "I'm not sure. All I could think of was Jeremy. . . ."

"Why don't you come down to the cafeteria with me while your parents are here to watch him? You've got to take care of yourself, too."

"I can't leave until the doctor's been here."

Dane nodded and went out to the hall, returning a few minutes later with two more chairs. "Might as well wait comfortably."

When the doctor did arrive, he hadn't much more to say. Maybe by tomorrow the tests would be more conclusive. But perhaps then Jeremy would be much better.

Leaving her mother strict instructions to get liquids into her grandson, Robynn allowed Dane to lead her out the door.

❧

After everyone left that night, when Robynn snuggled down in the chair-bed that Dane found, she reviewed all the things he did to make this disaster easier for her. Whatever she needed, he seemed to provide before she could ask. As if she would ask. She'd have done it herself. This depending on him was getting to be a habit. She watched Jeremy breathe, the dim light from the hall their only illumination. A very nice habit.

She awoke each time during the night when a nurse came in, but only once was she able to get Jeremy to take anything. Morning found her tired and rumpled.

The look of concern on Dr. Prescott's face did nothing to make her feel better. "The tests this morning showed a rise in blood ammonia and a drop in blood sugar. That confirms my earlier fears. Jeremy has Reye's syndrome, a rare complication of some common viruses like chicken pox and flu. Some schools of thought are that aspirin may contribute to this. That's why I asked you earlier if you had given Jeremy any. But neither you nor the school gave aspirin, and the theory's controversial. That's why I tell my patients to use Tylenol just to be safe. Whatever the cause may have been, Jeremy's diagnosis is definite."

"What does that mean?" Robynn took a deep breath. "What happens next?"

"If he doesn't go comatose on us, he'll have a better chance of recovery."

"Are you saying. . ." Fear wrapped its ugly claws around her stomach and jerked. "Are you saying that Jeremy might. . .might. . .die?" The impossible word was out.

"Not if I can help it. The problem is that we can only do what we're doing. We'll start a glucose solution stat to keep his blood sugar elevated, and then we wait. Are you a praying person?"

Mutely, Robynn nodded.

"Then I suggest you bombard the lines to heaven. We never know why one makes it and another doesn't." He picked up Jeremy's hand to take the pulse as if to give himself something to do. His dark eyes warmed with compassion.

"But it doesn't make any sense." Robynn sank into the chair, the load beating her down.

"No, it doesn't. But remember, he has as good a chance as any. He's basically a healthy little boy. His school says he's done well dealing with his disability. Maybe that has given him extra staying power. He'll need it." He paused as he turned to go. "Has the chaplain been in yet?"

When Robynn shook her head, he said, "I'll send for him."

Too numb to even say "thank you," Robynn stared at the slight figure in the bed. *God, it isn't fair,* her mind raged. *You can't have Jeremy. I need him worse than You do.* Tears rolled down her cheeks unheeded.

She got herself together enough to call her parents and Josh, sharing with them the most positive side of the prognosis, holding inside the fear, the anger.

"The doctor says to pray; call anyone else you can think of. I'll let you know if there's any change."

She hung up and went to stand at the window, staring at the statue. It reminded her of a verse from childhood: "I am the good shepherd. I know my own and My own know Me." Comforted, Robynn turned to fight the battle.

By evening when Dane appeared at the door with a suitcase for her, Robynn had gotten some ice and another half a popsicle into Jeremy. Each bite he took was a victory in her mind.

"Josh told me," Dane said as he took her in his arms. Robynn clung to him, grateful for his caring.

"Thanks for bringing my things," she murmured into the comforting wall of his chest.

"Who's riding for me?" she asked after he had forced her to eat the food he brought on a tray. Some color had returned to her cheeks.

"Pam. And everyone sends their love. Why, there are people praying up there who only used God's name as an expletive before. They really care about the two of you."

Tears sprang to the corners of her eyes. She tightened her lips, willing herself not to cry. "Thank them for me, please." She stared down into her coffee cup. "And thank you for all you've done."

"Ah–h, Robynn." He pulled her onto his lap. "I've done so little when I want to do so much." Robynn curled there, comforted by the steady thud of his heart until Jeremy stirred restlessly. It was back to the fray again.

During the long night, Robynn alternated between sleeping in the chair-bed, caring for Jeremy, or pleading for his healing in the chapel.

"It's not fair, You know," she said at one point, feeling more like screaming. "You have lots of kids, and I only have one. You know You can heal him." The tears threatened to overwhelm her again. "And I—I know it, too." Her voice sank to a whisper. "But will You?"

She knotted her fingers together, as if the very action would keep her from flying into fragments. "God, he's *my* son. Please, please, don't take him from me." She stood and paced again, furious, wanting to shake her fist in His face. Her heels clicked against the tiled floor. She couldn't go back to Jeremy while she still felt like screaming. The rage erupted in chest-tearing tears, and she sank to the floor, her arms on the railing in front of the small altar. The cross hanging on the wall above drew her gaze when she could finally see again.

A voice, soft as a sigh, seemed to circle around her. *I lost My Son, too, for a time. I let Him die for you so that now you are My own. I will not let you go, nor ever forsake you. Come, rest in Me.*

"God, what else can I do?"

The picture of the shepherd statue came to her mind. *I am the good shepherd. I know My sheep and My sheep know Me. Come, My child, and rest in Me.*

"But Jeremy. . ."

Just rest.

❧

The next day Jeremy never even flinched at the ringing of the phone anymore. Dane called, then Josh not much later, and in the afternoon, her mother and father called to say they'd be down to be with her before long. She hung up to go stand at the window and look down at the shepherd. *Oh, God, you say Jesus is the shepherd of the sheep, but He doesn't seem to be here right now, when we need Him.*

Yes, I am here; I said I would never leave you nor forsake you. Just close your eyes and be with Me.

Robynn sank down in the chair, closing her eyes in both weariness and despair. The monitors bleeped along, shoes squeaked in the hall, and a voice called for someone over the loudspeaker. But Robynn felt like she was cradled in the softest down, and the heart she heard beating was not her own. She'd never felt so warm and comfortable—and comforted.

"God, please hold Jeremy like this." She wasn't sure if she whispered the words or only thought them, but she meant them with all of her heart.

"You look better, dear," her mother said when they arrived.

"I know." How could she tell them what she'd sensed? And yet she knew she wasn't going out of her mind. She'd never forget that sensation of perfect peace.

"How's our boy?" Her father touched his knuckles to Jeremy's cheek. "Come on, Tiger, we got things to do, places to see."

Robynn fought the tears that threatened to run at the sight of her father weeping without a sound. Her mother sat down on the bed and took Jeremy's left hand in her own.

"Just Grammy saying I love you and I baked your favorite cookies this morning. Brought some in case you were feeling better, but there's lots in the freezer waiting for you." She smoothed the lank hair back from Jeremy's forehead. "How about a popsicle? I checked, there's banana."

Jeremy blinked his eyes and gave the tiniest nod.

Robynn let her mother and father do the honors, knowing how much it meant to them to be able to do something. That was the hardest part, not being able to *do* anything.

"Let's go to the chapel," Dane suggested later, after he'd been there awhile. At Robynn's nod, he took her arm, and nodding to her parents, they walked down the hall.

The room waited, serene and calm as the picture on the wall. Candles flickered in squat, square glass holders that someone had left on the carpeted riser. Robynn walked into the second oaken pew from the front and took a seat sideways so she could see Dane. He sat down beside her and rested his wrists on the pew back in front of them and stared at the picture. The silence didn't beg for words but instead bestowed peace.

"He's about the same, then?"

His voice caught her by surprise. "Yes, I'd say so." Could she tell him about what had happened to her earlier?

"And you?" He reached with one finger and brushed back a lock of hair from her cheek. "You look better." The way he stared into her eyes seemed to plumb the depths of her being.

"I am. Dane, I think God held me in His arms this afternoon."

"Um—m." He nodded. "I've heard of things like that. My mother. . ." He stopped.

She waited.

"I'm glad for you."

He took her hand and rubbed the palm with his thumb. "Do you feel like talking?"

What does he want to talk about right now? Her throat clenched. Robynn blinked. "I—I guess. Is. . .is Josh all right?"

Dane snorted a little. "Can't keep him down. Pretty soon they'll pay me to take him home." He turned with one bent knee on the seat between them. "I. . ." He sighed. "I looked up Sonny O'Dell in the *Oregonian* and read about the accident and all. I hope you don't mind."

Robynn shook her head. "No, that's all history." She almost flinched at the grip he had on her hands.

He saw that and relaxed his fingers. "Could you. . .would you please tell me about you and Jeremy after that?"

And so she did, starting with when she knew she was pregnant, buying a house with the insurance money, and her shock at learning that her perfect baby boy was blind. "The doctors did all kinds of tests, hoping they could change the diagnosis with surgery." She shrugged. "But they couldn't. Mom and Dad helped care for him while I raced, and then when he got old enough, the doctor suggested I send him to a school for the blind to learn Braille and other skills he needs."

She paused, keeping her gaze on their joined hands. "I wonder if that was the right thing to do, especially now." Her eyes swam with tears as she looked up at him. "But it seemed right at the time."

"Hindsight is always twenty-twenty. That's what my mother says."

"I know." She waited again.

"I'd like you to meet my mother. She'll love Jeremy—and you."

Robynn canceled the thought that tried to take hold. *If Jeremy lives.*

"Where does she—your mother—live?"

"In Pasadena, not far from my house." Now it was his turn to pause. When he looked up, he took a deep breath and let it out. "My mother lives in a wheelchair, and it is all my fault." The words came out in a rush, as though if he didn't say them fast, he wouldn't say them at all.

"Your fault? Was there a car accident or. . .?"

He shook his head. "My father died in Vietnam, but before he left, he told me to take care of my mother. She and her mount went down in a steeplechase and she never walked again."

Robynn waited for him to go on. When he didn't, she squeezed his hands. "How old were you when your father left?"

"Seven."

"And at the accident?"

"Ten." He looked up at her, eyes dark with suffering. "I saw her fall. That's why I don't want you racing. What if the same thing happens to you?"

Robynn blew out a breath of air and shook her head. "Dane, you were a kid, she was an adult. She *chose* to steeplechase."

"Like you choose to flat race." He leaned forward. "Jockeys are injured and killed all the time. I can't bear the thought of seeing you under some horse's hooves."

"Robynn, Jeremy's asking for you." Her mother stood in the doorway.

Robynn got to her feet. "We'll continue this discussion later, my friend." She cupped his cheek in her hand for a brief moment and then led the way back to Jeremy's room.

"Bear?" Jeremy opened his eyes half-mast. "Thirsty."

Robynn snuggled the bear in the crook of his arm and slid some ice chips between his parched lips. While he munched, she smoothed some lip balm around his mouth. When Dane returned with a popsicle, they got him to take part of a half.

After they all left, Robynn stood again at the window. This time her prayers were for another boy, one who had grown to become a wounded man. "Ah, Father, the loads we all carry. Why can't we let You carry them, like You want?"

⤎

By the fifth day, Jeremy's delirium alternated with restless sleep. The purple strokes under Robynn's eyes and the lines about her mouth shouted her condition, even if one ignored her trembling hands. But now she knew where to find sanctuary, clinging to the promised rest.

Dane found her in the chapel, kneeling in front of the picture of Christ with hands raised in welcome. Her mother and father were with Jeremy.

"Dane," she whispered in a broken voice as he gathered her in his arms. "I can't even think anymore. I just keep putting one foot in front of the other. I don't even know what to pray."

"Then that's the time the rest of us pray for you." He kissed away the moisture on her eyelids. *Can I pray aloud for her—right now?* Dane cleared his throat and sniffed. "Father in heaven, thank You for the strength You have given Robynn. Thank You for the healing You are bringing to Jeremy. Thank You that You have brought this woman into my life and through her, You've brought me back to You. Forgive me for taking off on my own instead of letting You be Lord of my life. Please give us wisdom and comfort and the peace that I have sensed in here."

Robynn sniffed and added her "amen."

"I wish I could stay here with you." He held both of her hands, his thumbs rubbing the fragile skin on the backs. "But with Josh in the hospital. . ."

"There's not a whole lot you can do here, and keeping real busy makes the time go by faster." She stood on tiptoe and kissed his cheek. "Thanks for the hugs and the prayer." She watched him head down the hall to the elevator.

During the next day, Jeremy tossed restlessly and refused everything she offered. Even being held in her arms didn't pacify him. By evening the lethargy had returned, deeper than before. The doctor and nurses had a harder time being optimistic.

"How much longer can he go like this?" Robynn asked as Dr. Prescott finished his examination.

"I don't know." He pressed her hand as he left the room.

"There comes a time," the slender, soft-voiced chaplain said when he met her in the chapel that night, "when we must place our children in God's hands, resting in the assurance that He knows best."

"I thought I did that when Jeremy was baptized and then again when we discovered he was blind. I'm learning to trust Him all over again, but. . ."

"That's part of the problem," he replied. "That 'but' is always there. Remember He promised to be with us, to deliver us from evil, to bear our burdens. There are no accidents with God, and He cares about our every incident, every tiny thing. Nothing is too small for Him or too hard. And He uses it all."

"So, if I had been more faithful, you think this wouldn't have happened to Jeremy?" Admitting this fear took all the power she had.

"Oh, no, I'm not saying that. Our merciful God doesn't work that way—but He is using this illness to draw you closer, is He not?"

Robynn nodded. "For so long I've felt alone, but not now."

Robynn couldn't sleep that night. She heard nothing but each slow breath Jeremy took, each one seeming farther apart. At three she found herself at the window, looking down on the lighted statue. "But, God," she whispered against the windowpane, "I raised him for living, not for dying." A peace wrapped around her, seeping inside to quiet her soul.

The morning nurse confirmed Robynn's tentative hope. Jeremy seemed more alert. His blood test came back positive. The poison was leaving his system.

"Oh, Dane." The joy in her voice bubbled over the wire when Dane called. "Thank God, he's better. Tell everyone Jeremy's better. Now they can thank God along with us. Our boy is going to get well."

"That's wonderful. I love you, Princess." She could hardly understand him for the tears clogging his throat.

❧

Jeremy was home by the end of the week to finish recovering before he returned to school. He was so weak he could hardly lift his head after the drive. The smile on his face tore at the hearts of the adults rejoicing around him.

"You're going to bed, my girl, for twenty-four hours straight," Dane ordered as he picked up his coat that evening. "Your mother is dying to take care of Jeremy and you, too. Let her do it."

When she didn't respond, he tilted her chin up with one finger so he could look into her eyes. "Hear me?"

"Who appointed you my keeper?" The sparkle had returned to her eyes.

"Me."

Her lips parted as his mouth descended to hers. When his arms came around her, she leaned into the strength of him, savoring the fresh scent of his aftershave. Talk about bulwarks in a storm, he had been one. The words of his prayer had never left her mind. Was God using this to get to other people, too—not just her?

Chapter 9

Robynn's crystal bottle of joy shattered about her feet the next morning when she went to see Josh. One look at his face and she knew the news wasn't good.

"The farm is sold," Josh responded in answer to her query, "along with the brood mares and foals. Opal gave us an extension on the racing string but received too good an offer on the others to pass it up."

"But. . .but. . ." Robynn slumped down in the chair. "I was hoping for the breeding stock along with the racing string. I knew the farm was an impossible dream. But the colts. . ."

"It's sorry I am to be telling you such bad news. At a time like now, you should be rejoicing. Just think, lass, Jeremy's getting well again."

"I know." The sparkle returned. "I'll just be grateful for what is and not worry about tomorrow."

She rose and went to stand at the window. Seen from the south side and in the daylight, the arching white Fremont Bridge was still an awesome monument to man's ingenuity. The huge grain elevators down on the river were obscured by the crisscrossing freeways. "You had X-rays last week, didn't you?"

"Yes. And the bones are knitting together, but slowly. Said it was because of my age." Josh snorted at the thought. "He just wants to keep me in this contraption for as long as possible."

"Well, you've gotta admit it's kept you out of trouble. You know if you could hobble on crutches, you'd be down at the barns, telling everyone what to do."

Josh tried to glare at her, but his white hair going every which way made him look more endearing than angry.

"I'm sorry I wasn't more help with the boy," he said. "Can you bring him to visit me soon?"

"Will they let him in?" She pulled one of the roses out of a fresh arrangement and held it to her nose.

"Don't ask, just do it as soon as he's feeling up to it. Why don't you take some of these flowers home with you? Let 'em smell up *your* house."

"You old faker." Robynn laughed. "You know you love all the attention. And roses have always been your favorite flower."

"Yours, too."

"Aye. But mostly around the neck of a horse." She scooped up a vase of red roses and, waving, left the room.

Well, she reminded herself philosophically when visions of the farm clouded her memory. *You can't win 'em all, and this way we have time to come up with less money. I've got to get back to work. Better notify my agent to get me back on the ponies day after tomorrow. That gives me one more day with Jeremy.*

❧

"Who is that man that comes?" Jeremy asked the next morning. Dane had come for coffee the night before, after Jeremy's bedtime.

"His name is Dane Morgan, and Josh is his uncle. He's been taking Josh's place at the track, training the horses. Remember, I told you at the hospital. Why?" Robynn mashed his soft-boiled egg with a fork and seasoned it. "There, sir, your breakfast is ready." She walked to her own chair and sat down. Carefully, Jeremy held the bowl in place with one hand and spooned up the egg with the other. Robynn naturally placed all his food in the right order so he could easily locate each item.

Jeremy put his glass of milk back on the table, a white mustache decorating his upper lip. " 'Cause I think he likes you."

"What gives you that idea?" Robynn kept her voice noncommittal, but her heart cartwheeled in her chest.

"He calls me Tiger and you Princess Lady. Is he going to be my new daddy?"

"Jeremy!"

"Well, other kids get new daddies, and my old one died so. . ." It was the classic case of the seven-year-old explaining the facts of life. Robynn felt properly put in her place.

"Finish your breakfast. Grammy will be here soon."

"I don't want any more." He got down from his chair. "Do we have any popsicles?"

"Beat it, monkey." Robynn smiled at the privilege of having her pint-sized philosopher home again. He might not be able to see with his eyes, but he sure viewed the world in his own special way.

The next two days set the pattern for Robynn's days. She arrived at the track by five; exercised as many horses as she could fit in, not just the string Dane ran; home by eleven for lunch and time with Jeremy; and back to the track to ride as many mounts as she could find in the afternoon program. Her evenings she devoted to Jeremy. Each night she read him a Bible story before his prayers, just like they used to. The only way Dane got to talk with her was to come over to her house. Their miniature chaperon was always present, ready to be part of the party.

Purple smudges appeared under Robynn's eyes again. But no matter how tired she was, she continued reading the New Testament. She was up to Luke

341

and the miracles of Jesus, rejoicing in the miracle she'd seen herself.

"You're driving yourself too hard," Dane growled at her one evening when he stole her away. Grammy had agreed to spend the evening with Jeremy.

Robynn stared straight ahead, unwilling to spoil the evening with an argument. "Dane, you just don't understand."

"I understand all right. You need the money; that's what comes through loud and clear, or at least that's what you say."

"Look." She twisted in the seat so she could look him in the eye. "I'm not putting this kind of pressure on myself just for fun. I. . .Josh and I have a dream, and I'll do whatever it takes to get the cash I need." She laid a hand on his arm. "So please don't nag at me. It won't be for much longer."

Dane covered her hand with his own. "Princess Lady, we need to talk. Not just quick visits, but really talk."

She glanced at her watch. "I have to go in. Mother wants to get home, and as you so inelegantly put it, I look—"

"Beautiful," he interrupted her. "But that's not the last you'll hear from me." He climbed out of the car and came around her side to open the door. "I won't come in tonight. You need some rest." He took both her shoulders in his strong hands, then massaged his way up to her slender neck. When his thumbs brushed her parted lips, he bent his head and dusted each eye with his lips, nibbled the tip of her nose, and at last, found her mouth. His hands tangled in her hair as his breathing quickened. "Good night." He patted her on the shoulder as he turned her toward the house. Before Robynn had time to open the back door, the roar of his car's engine faded down the street.

Her mother met her at the door, coat in hand. "I'll see you in the morning, dear. Four forty-five as usual?"

"Yes." Robynn stopped her with a hand on her arm. "You could stay here, you know. We have a spare bedroom."

"I know, dear. But your father likes me home in bed with him."

"You could both stay here."

"See you later." The discussion was becoming a nightly thing.

"I'll never understand them if it takes a thousand years," Robynn muttered to herself as she shut off the lights.

With only the light from the hall, she tiptoed into Jeremy's room. He lay on his stomach, one arm wrapped around the koala bear, dark curls feathered across his forehead. The hollows were already filling in his cheeks, and the terrible pallor was disappearing. Each day his noise level seemed to rise another decibel. It was so good to have him home.

Her father came by the house at noon the next day to join them for lunch. The absence of his perennial smile triggered the worry in Robynn's mind before he even got his coat off.

"Okay, what is it?" She hung his coat in the closet.

"Hi, Grandpa." Jeremy ambled out of his room. "You gonna eat with us? Grammy fixed tuna sandwiches and chicken noodle soup. That's my favorite. Besides, hambuggers and hot dogs and. . ." He scrunched his face up, thinking hard.

Grandpa Ahern bent down to hug the little boy, then scooped him up in his arms.

Jeremy crowed with glee. Robynn laughed along, but inside, the worry gnawed at her.

With lunch over and Jeremy settled down with his talking books, she refused to be put off any longer. "All right." She refilled her father's coffee cup and sat down herself. "Let's have it."

"Well, I made a mistake with a couple of my investments and. . .well. . ." He took a deep breath. "I can't get my hands on the full amount I said I'd have for you."

Robynn stared at her hands. She heard the dreams shattering like falling glass. "How much?"

"How much can I invest?"

She nodded.

"Forty now. Twenty-five within a year, hopefully." He took a swallow of coffee. "I'm sorry, Princess. I did my best. I know that racing string is a good investment, but I'm borrowing as it is."

She stopped behind him to lay a hand on his shoulder. "Don't worry, Daddy. I'm not desperate—yet."

After the races that afternoon, Robynn called a real estate friend. "How soon could you sell my house?"

Silence weighted the line. "I'm sorry, Robynn, but right now isn't a good time to sell. Houses have been sitting on the market for months. We can hardly give them away."

Robynn groaned.

"I know. It's terrible. But what would you want to sell your house for, anyway? It's just perfect for you. Hey, this is me talking as your friend, not your favorite Realtor."

"I need the money."

"Good reason. Have you thought of a loan?"

"Yes. They gave me twenty-five thousand dollars. I need about a hundred and fifty." Robynn slumped down until she sprawled on the dusty blue carpet, her back against the wall.

"What about a personal loan at the bank?"

"For a hundred thousand? They talk in terms of ten without collateral.

Remember, my house is now mortgaged to the hilt." Jeremy came and sat down between her legs. She dropped a kiss on the top of his head. "I gotta go. Thanks anyway." She reached up to replace the phone, then gave him a squeeze. "Oh, Jeremy, I love you, love you, love you." With the final "love you," she sneaked her fingers up to his rib cage and tickled.

Jeremy's head thumped her chest as he wriggled to get free. "No, Mommy," he giggled, squirming and twisting around. He stopped suddenly, tilting his head toward the front door. "Dane's here." He leaped to his feet. "Maybe he brought me some popsicles."

"Jeremy!" Robynn followed him, laughing in exasperation. "How many times have I warned you about asking for treats."

"I didn't." Jeremy turned, hands on hips. "He asked."

Dane became the hit of the evening when he invited them out for dinner. "Well, Tiger, where would you like to go?"

"Don't ask him," Robynn said, pretend horror rounding her mouth.

"McDonald's," Jeremy stated as if there were no other place in the world, let alone Portland.

"I tried to warn you." Robynn laughed as she got their coats. "Maybe next time you'll listen to me."

When they got out of the car again, Jeremy walked in the middle, swinging both their hands like he'd grown up doing just that.

We look like any other American family out for dinner, Robynn thought as she caught their reflection in the swinging door. *Who's to know this is a first for us?* Her smile dimmed; too soon Jeremy would be going back to school. And Dane. What was it he wanted to talk to her about? Right now he probably wouldn't have any words left. He'd used them up on Jeremy.

"But why?" Jeremy asked for the umpteenth time.

"Why not?" Dane smiled down at him.

The scrunched-up look indicated Jeremy was thinking hard for a suitable reply.

"What do you want, Tiger?" Dane asked.

"A cheesebugger. . .umm. . .french fries and. . ."

"How about a chocolate shake?"

"Wow! Really? Mom never lets me have that."

Dane shrugged his shoulders apologetically, accompanied by a sheepish grin in Robynn's general direction.

"You're buying," is all she said.

"Mom wants Chicken McNuggets so I can have one," Jeremy stated. "And I like sweet and sour sauce."

"Hey, this is your mother's dinner. You already ordered yours."

"I know, but this is what we always order."

Robynn heard Dane mutter under his breath, "Lord protect us from small Caesars."

When they were seated at their table and Jeremy had said an extended grace, the conversation between Dane and Jeremy continued. Dane showed remarkable patience in answering all the questions. Robynn enjoyed it, watching both of them as she ate her dinner in peace. Usually she was the one on the answering end.

Then she began to feel left out. The two seemed to get along just great without her. *This is silly,* she scolded herself. *You want them to get to know each other, so don't interrupt. God, how come I can be so mixed up?*

By the last french fry, the question machine was wearing down, his drooping eyes testifying to his recent illness. Dane picked him up in one arm and with the other hand pulled Robynn to her feet. She was beginning to feel as drained as the child smiling over Dane's broad shoulder, one arm curled around the man's neck.

The ride home passed in silence. When Dane reached into the backseat to unbuckle Jeremy, the boy was sound asleep. Carefully he lifted the limp body out, no mean stunt in the cramped space of the low-slung car.

"We're going to need a bigger car," he grunted as he stood upright.

Robynn turned to him, startled.

"I warned you I'm a persistent man." Dane smiled back at her, his teeth flashing white in the dimness.

Robynn unlocked the back door and led the way to Jeremy's bedroom, flicking on the lights as she went.

Together they untied the knotted laces of the blue tennis shoes. Like a well-rehearsed team, they had Jeremy undressed and in bed without his ever waking. The sense of rightness persisted as they each kissed the small boy's cheek and Robynn tucked the bear in place in the crook of Jeremy's arm.

"Lord bless and keep you, my son," she whispered as she kissed his cheek again.

"Amen to that, and you, too." At the door Dane turned out the light and, leaving the door open a crack, followed Robynn into the living room.

"You're very good with him, you know." She smiled as she gestured toward the sofa. "Can you stay for a while?"

"No, I don't think I better." Dane suddenly seemed ill at ease.

Confusion creased Robynn's forehead. "What is it?"

"Robynn, loving you and leaving you, watching you ride, keeping myself under control when all I want to do is be with you and protect you—it's all driving me nuts. I can't sleep at night. A certain violet-eyed Irishwoman keeps haunting my dreams. I can't stand it much longer." He clasped her in a bear hug, then nearly ran out the door.

His words echoed in her mind as she prepared for bed. The evening had been a perfect jewel until the gem cutter slipped and destroyed the facets. Her prayers that night centered on a certain stubborn Irishman.

❧

Two days later a low-pressure bank still lay over Portland, bringing with it the ever-present drizzle. It would let up, then become showers. Robynn was never sure where one stopped and the other began. She didn't think the meteorologists on TV really knew, either.

The track was soggy, and so were everyone's tempers. Even the horses were edgy, responding to the tension. Robynn's first mount for the morning workout, Finding Fun, lived up to her name. Halfway around the track she ploughed to a stop, then crow-hopped sideways, snorting at the fallen rider in front of them. Luckily for Robynn, she was prepared or she'd have landed in the soft sand like the inexperienced jockey picking himself up and brushing off the mud.

"You okay?" She pulled the prancing filly to a standstill.

"That worthless. . ." He carried on in his native Spanish as he slogged back across the infield.

"We have a new one to train," Dane said as she slipped off Finding Fun. "He's down in the end stall. Don't go near him by yourself. He looks to be a mean one."

"Josh won't take a mean animal, says they're too much trouble." They ambled companionably down the row of stalls.

A blood-red sorrel bared his teeth and lunged at them as they approached, his forefeet thundering his anger against the door.

Robynn stopped just beyond his reach and began her sing-song, no particular words, just the crooning voice that worked wonders on animals and people alike.

This time was no different. The horse pointed his ears toward her, listening intently. The croon continued. The furious red hue left his eyes, he tossed his head one last time and stood at the door, inviting the light fingers she stroked down his nose. She rubbed his ears, his broad, flat cheekbones, and down the sweat-spotted neck. The horse blew in her hair and leaned into the stroking, his ears flicking back and forth at her singing.

Dane stood tense, ready to leap in to save her if necessary.

"I can't believe what my own eyes see," he muttered as he watched them.

When she finally gave the horse one last pat and a piece of carrot from her ever-present supply, she turned to Dane. "Shall I get the next one out before this crummy weather becomes a downpour?"

"What are you, a horse whisperer or something?"

"No. Josh calls it my gift. For some reason I've always had a way with animals."

"Well, I wouldn't have believed it if I hadn't seen it." He turned her toward him as they reached the sanctuary of the tack room. "Maybe that's how you've captured me." Removing her helmet, he drew her into his arms and laid his cheek against her hair. "You scared me out of another night's sleep just now. What am I going to do with you?"

They both knew the question was rhetorical.

Each day the sorrel colt grew calmer, tolerating Dane, even in Robynn's absence. At first, two men worked the colt on ropes as a safety precaution. After several days they discarded the practice. The horse had already been broken to the track and starting gate before Josh had agreed to finish him out.

Getting Dane's permission was the hardest part of riding the frisky colt. The first morning out on the track, Dane rode the steady quarter horse they used for training, keeping a tight hold on the lead rope. The two-year-old Sunday Driver trotted along, head high, ears flicking to listen for Robynn's voice. He watched every horse on the track, whistled and snorted when one came near. She could feel his tension—poised and ready to react at any moment.

Robynn thrilled to the horse's display of barely leashed power. She watched his ears, alert to any change of mood, and grinned at Dane when she caught his gaze.

"Wow! This is some horse." She patted the sweaty shoulder and unbuckled the girth. "Whoever named him Sunday Driver sure made a mistake. He's more like a Fireball."

Dane's jaw tensed. Ignoring her banter, he cautioned, "You just be careful. Don't let up for a minute. He might like you but. . ."

The workout passed without incident and Robynn had a hard time keeping from saying "I told you so."

"You worry too much." Robynn slipped her arm through his, leaving the now docile Thoroughbred in his stall. "We'll have him ready for the geriatric set to ride within a week."

❧

Robynn arrived at the track late the next morning. A traffic snarl had trapped her mother on the freeway. Daylight brightened the sky when she finally skidded into the lot, parked her car, and raced through the gate.

She dogtrotted down the row of stalls looking for Dane. As she ran, the high-pitched scream of an angry horse raised the hairs on the back of her neck.

The piercing whinny came again, this time with the answering challenge of another horse, lower pitched but just as furious.

Robynn dashed around the end of the barn and into the open area used to walk horses for the cooldown.

Two men clung to the rope of a dark bay. They watched as the horse rose in the air, forelegs slashing at Sunday Driver. As the bay hit the ground, the men leaped to clamp their hands on his halter. Their combined weight forced his feet to stay on the ground.

Sunday Driver charged, teeth bared. But Dane, who had one hand on the halter, raised the other hand to strike the horse's nose. "Whoa!" At the force of his hand and commanding voice, the animal stopped and shook his head.

Dane's back was turned to the other horse. Suddenly the bay reared again. A vicious forefoot dropped Dane to the ground like he'd been pole-axed.

When her stunned brain finally responded, Robynn rushed in to help. Every muscle and tendon quivered from the skirmish as Sunday Driver stood, head down, the lead rope caught beneath Dane's inert body.

Dane, Dane! her mind screamed, but she dared not take her eyes off the quivering horse until she had backed him away and handed the lead rope off to one of the waiting grooms.

By the time she moved back to Dane, two men were checking his pulse and eyes. Robynn knelt in the shavings by his head. His dark hair seemed even blacker in contrast to the pallor of his normally tan face.

"Dane, please be okay. O God, let him be all right." Her prayers to God and her entreaties to the fallen man intermingled, along with tears that flowed unheeded down her cheeks.

"I've called the ambulance," a man behind her said.

Robynn nodded, vaguely aware of who spoke. Tenderly, she explored the back of Dane's head with her fingertips. As her fingers caressed his scalp, she felt hair matted and moist. Her hand came away streaked with blood.

"He's bleeding! Someone get a bandanna quick." Robynn reached up and within seconds was handed a makeshift bandage for Dane's wound. She remembered her first aid training—apply pressure. She gently placed the dressing over the bleeding area and held it tightly against his head.

He could be dying, and you never even told him you love him, a voice from her mind jeered. *You might not get the chance now.*

But he can't die. We have too much living to do—together. Together. . .

"Dane," she whispered, "you'll be all right. Remember that. You can't leave your family."

The red and white ambulance pulled up beside them. Two men scrambled out and within moments had a stretcher on the ground, ready for the injured man.

As they lifted him onto the canvas cot, Dane's eyelids fluttered open. "Wha. . .what hit me?" he muttered, trying to raise his hand to his head. He couldn't.

"That crazy bay." Robynn had been holding both his hands in a viselike grip. Now, under his scrutiny, she slowly released her hold.

Dane sat up. "Easy now," the attendant said. "You've had a nasty crack on the head." He probed the area gently.

"Ouch!" Dane flinched. "How's that fool, Sunday Driver?"

At the disgruntled tone in his voice, laughter from sheer joy got the better of her. She tried to stifle the sound, but Dane heard her.

"What's so funny? I nearly get my head kicked off and you stand there laughing." A smile lurked in the blue of his eyes, but he grimaced when he turned his head too quickly. He stood, leaning his weight on her.

"You'll probably need X-rays," the attendant suggested. "You never know about head injuries."

"Thanks anyway, but I'll take a rain check on the ambulance. Leave the ride for those who really need it. Little Merry Sunshine here can take care of me."

"Dane Morgan! You sit down and let them take a look at that wound." Her violet eyes flashed up at him. "You may need stitches if nothing else." Surprised at the command in her voice, he obeyed.

"It's just a scalp wound, although you'll have quite a goose egg back there." The attendant cleansed the wound expertly as he gave them instructions. "If you have continuing headaches, blurred vision, or vomiting, you'd better get yourself to emergency pronto."

"He will," Robynn assured them as they replaced their equipment. By now, seeing Dane was safe, everyone else had gone back to work.

"Well, look who's giving the orders now." He stood again, letting Robynn take some of his weight as they shuffled back to the tack room.

"Somebody has to have some sense around here."

Dane chuckled carefully, trying not to move his head.

"Does it hurt terribly?" She looked up to catch the glinting amusement. "What are you laughing at?"

"You, Princess. Just listen to yourself. You order me to take it easy when you've been driving yourself to the point of exhaustion for weeks. And you're the one with sense?"

Robynn grinned sheepishly. "But, Dane, you scared me to death back there. Those horses out of control, you lying unconscious on the ground."

"To quote a very bright person I know, 'Accidents can happen just as easily on the freeway as on the track.'" He lowered himself into one of the chairs. "Ah-h-h. That's better."

Ahem, Robynn, her internal voice counseled. *Now you know how he's been feeling all this time. It tears you up inside when someone you love is hurt. You knew that for Jeremy. Now admit it for Dane. You love him. Tell him so.*

Her mind played with the words. *I love you, Dane Morgan. Dane, I love you, love you, love you. . . .*

"Dane, I. . ." She placed a hand on his shoulder and started again. "I. . ."

One of the grooms stuck his head through the doorway. "How's he doing?"

Dane nodded without opening his eyes. "Fine."

"Good. Josh said to call him as soon as you could. He phoned a few minutes ago."

"News sure travels fast around here." Dane rose from his chair. "Let's go get a cup of coffee and call him from there. Then we've got to get to work. We're running way behind."

The moment for declaring love had passed. *I'll tell him later*, Robynn promised herself. Later didn't come. Pressures of daily work increased as time flew by. The racing program had ended before they could find a moment together.

"I'll feed the horses for you tonight." She pushed him out the door after they returned to the barns. "You go home and get some sleep. You'll feel better in the morning."

"Yes, Mother Hen." A drawn smile revealed his exhaustion. "John Simms will be over in a few minutes. He asked if he could help, and I took him up on it. See you in the morning."

"Tomorrow," she promised Finding Fun as she poured grain in the filly's manger. "I'll tell him tomorrow."

Chapter 10

When she arrived back at the track after her break the next afternoon, Robynn parked the Celica and went directly to the jockeys' dressing rooms. The first race of the day was already under way, showing on the monitor screen. It looked like a mud bath. Halfway around the track, and it was almost impossible to tell who was who. When the straining horses crossed the wire, Robynn breathed a sigh of relief.

No accidents.

"Bet there's a lot of hot legs from that race." She hung her silks on the hooks above the benches. "Probably lamed half the horses out there."

By the time she stepped on the scales with all her gear in hand, Robynn felt more jittery than normal. She hated a muddy track even worse than Jim Dandy did. All the slipping and sliding. She'd had her worst fall on a day just like today. A dislocated shoulder and two cracked ribs laid her up for over a week. Sheer guts beat the pain for weeks after that.

Don't look back, she reminded herself. *Think up. Today is gonna be a great day. You've got races to win and the horses that can do it. You're a good rider with a good mind. You know you can do it.* After the pep talk, she took a deep breath and shrugged her shoulders up tight to her ears and lowered them again to relax the tense muscles.

"You okay, Princess?" John Simms waited beside her for the horses to be led into the saddling paddock.

"Sure." She put on a smile, just for his benefit, then added some life to her second. "Sure. Of course. It's a great day."

"Yeah, just marvelous if your feet are webbed and you quack instead of whinny or talk."

"Why, John, you sound downright anti-Oregon. I thought everyone developed webbed feet after awhile. I'll show you mine sometime."

"F-u-n-n-y. But if you're showing off, it isn't your webbed feet I'd like to see." *John!*

He tried to leer at her, but the sight of her scandalized face sent his crow of delight bouncing off the murky ceiling beams.

The blush that stained her cheeks stayed with her as she circled the stalls to find her mount. Dane and Jim Dandy waited on the far side.

351

"Who's been teasing you now?" He lifted the saddle from her arms and positioned it just behind the horse's withers.

"Oh, that John. . ."

"He's sure up on a mean one over there." Dane nodded over his shoulder. "That black tried to kick Dandy here as we came in."

Robynn stole a glance at the man giving her a leg up. His jaw looked clamped as a sprung bear trap, his fine lips thinned to a narrow line. When his eyes met hers, the steel of suppressed fury bolted through her like a stray lightning shaft.

Robynn shivered.

She tore her gaze from the ice blue one and concentrated on what he was saying. The shivers running up and down her back had nothing to do with the weather.

Here we go again, back to the old yo-yo. Maybe I'm the yo-yo after all. Thoughts chased each other through her brain like frisking colts on a brisk fall morning.

"You know what to do as well as anyone," Dane continued. "There're only five entered, but watch out for that black. If you can get out in front, so much the better. You know how Dandy hates mud in his face."

Robynn stroked down the satiny neck and reached forward to scratch right behind the horse's ears. "We'll be fine," she crooned as much to settle herself as the colt and the man beside her. "Not to worry."

As they walked from the dimness of the paddock into the falling mist, her horse fell into step alongside the pony rider. Jim Dandy reached out in a smooth, flat-footed walk, his ears pricked, anticipation evident in every rippling muscle.

By the time they reached the starting gates, Robynn had put Dane out of her mind. All her concentration zeroed in on Jim Dandy and the race at hand.

The horses were nearly in the gate when the black snorted in fury, slashed at the handler, and reared straight in the air. Robynn caught a glimpse of Simms clinging like a burr to the furious animal. When the black came down again, John turned him and walked him around in a tight circle.

"Easy, fella," Robynn sang her song of calm. "You don't have to pay any attention to him. He's just a troublemaker." Jim Dandy danced a moment with his front feet, then settled back on his haunches as the gate closed behind the fussing horse.

With her goggles in place, Robynn sucked in a deep lungful of air, let it out in a whoosh to relax, and tangled her fingers in a hunk of mane. The gates clanged open. Dandy leaped forward. As he found his stride, Robynn felt him slip. She tightened the reins, feeling the uncertainty in his mouth. When he felt secure again, the pack was already in front of them, pounding hooves showering everything with sloppy mud. A crack opened between the two in front, and

Robynn urged Dandy forward. Straight and true, he drove up the middle, his ears flat against his head.

As Robynn debated whether to swing around on the outside of the next two in front of her, the black slipped. In that split second, he careened against his running mate, and before anyone had time to change course, both animals and jockeys became a mass of flailing legs and thrashing bodies. No one knew whether the screams were from the horses or jockeys. Even as Robynn felt Dandy gather himself, he leaped into the air and over the fallen entries. He slipped as his feet hit the mud again, but Robynn kept the reins taut, helping him stay upright. The delayed-action panic grabbed her guts.

As they passed under the wire, Robynn heard herself crying, "Dear God, make them be all right. Please! Please!" As she slowed Jim Dandy and turned toward the winner's circle, she could see the ambulance attendants picking up both riders. One horse, head hanging down, leaned against the rail, taking the pressure off a front leg. The black was still down.

At the winner's circle, Robynn slipped from her horse's back and quickly unbuckled the saddle girth. One look at Dane's bloodless face, and she felt the fear grab her insides again. For just a moment she leaned against her mud-caked horse, waiting for the weakness to leave her knees so she could walk.

"Congratulations, O'Dell." The race master laid the horseshoe of red and white roses over Jim Dandy's withers. "That was quick thinking out there."

"Not on my part." Robynn stroked her horse's muddy neck. "It was all Jim Dandy here. I just hung on."

Robynn's smile for the cameras never made it past the twitch of her mouth. She stopped one of the owners she knew.

"How bad?"

"John's unconscious, bleeding from a head wound."

"Oh, no. . ."

"It's ribs and a leg for the other. The black broke his neck." He shook her gloved hand. "Congratulations on your quick thinking out there. It could have been worse."

Robynn forced herself not to look back at the track where the accident had happened, but her mind knew about the truck and winch that came to pick up the dead animal. There would be extra time between the two races to clean up the mess and drag the track again.

She staggered as she stepped onto the scale. The scale master's strong hand caught her and held her upright until she regained her balance.

"Thanks," she muttered past the tears clogging her throat. She wasn't sure if they were for John, the horses, or relief that she was still in one piece. Shivers attacked her again, so strong the scale refused to balance. Robynn breathed deeply, forcing herself to stand still. At the master's nod, she stepped down and slammed into a tall, rock-solid chest. Dane wrapped both arms around her, saddle and all. Robynn shivered again as his warmth penetrated her frozen bones.

"Come on, you little idiot." He took the saddle from her clenched arms. "Let's get you out of the rain." With one strong arm around her, Dane almost carried her into the shelter of the stands.

Robynn took off her helmet and, shaking out her hair, leaned against him, grateful for both his warmth and caring. She could hear his heart thundering beneath her ear. How nice it felt to be held, leaving other arms to fight off the rain and cold for her.

"Hurry and get showered and I'll take you home," Dane murmured against her hair.

"Home?" Robynn stared up at him. "But I've got three other races to run."

"After what happened out there?"

"What do you mean?" Robynn shook her head as the steel-trap jaw closed above her. "That was an accident."

"You stubborn woman." The shake he administered was not gentle. "You could have been killed out there, like that black beast."

"But I wasn't."

"No, not this time. And not any time if I have anything to say about it."

Robynn borrowed the steel from his jaw to stiffen her spine. "But you don't have anything to say about it." She stepped back, chin tilted, nostrils flaring, her princess mask back in place. "I *am* a jockey. Racing horses is my job. And accident or no, I do my job."

The force of the saddle being dumped into her arms sent Robynn reeling back against the concrete wall. The fury in his eyes impaled her in place.

When her breath returned, Robynn turned and stumbled into the dressing rooms. "Blast him," she muttered. "When is he going to quit worrying about me?" With great skill, she ignored the voice that reminded her how she had felt when Dane was struck down—and what he'd said about his mother.

"He has an overdeveloped sense of responsibility, that's all. He'll just have to get over it." She could feel her steam of anger dissipate as she muttered.

Chapter 11

The more Robynn thought about Dane's behavior, the angrier she became. Of all the high-handed—hollering at her like that with other people around—and on top of that, her head ached where she had banged it against the concrete. He'd almost thrown the saddle at her.

"Well, if that's the way he wants it, that's the way he'll have it." She glared at her reflection in the mirror. Her violet eyes sparked darts, daggers, and a promise to get even.

Each time she settled in the saddle on another horse, she pulled her mind back from the earlier disaster and tried to concentrate on the race at hand. It wasn't easy.

Reports came back from the hospital. John would be all right. The concussion was of medium severity. Having experienced a mild one herself, Robynn knew he felt like retiring from the land of feeling for a time.

The jockeys congregated by the scale in their spare moments to discuss the accident.

"He'll feel more like having visitors tomorrow," Robynn reminded them. "At least the hospital's put both jockeys in the same room. Even on the same floor as Josh. They must have had us in mind, trying to make visiting easy."

"Yeah," Pam replied. "That hospital is gonna get 'em well real fast, before they drive the nurses totally nuts."

By the last race of the day, Robynn still had not seen Dane. He'd sent the horses over with a groom. Each time, her anger boiled a little closer to the surface. Her final mount was the cantankerous gray he had warned her about. Robynn drove the animal under the wire, ahead by a length, just to spite him.

Robynn smiled amid the congratulations for a day of superior riding. The stands buzzed with the way she and Jim Dandy had avoided the fall.

However, none of the smiles, handshakes, and good wishes meant anything without Dane's special smile, his hug, his words of praise.

Anger turned to disappointment as she turned out of the locker room to face an empty wall. Somehow, she'd hoped he'd be there. The wall wasn't the only thing that needed to be held up right now.

"Pull yourself together," she ordered as she climbed into her car. "You can't go home to Jeremy looking like this. He's too sensitive to your moods."

355

"Jeremy's been a handful today!" Grammy said as she met her daughter at the door. "I finally had to send him to his room."

"I'm sorry, Mom." Robynn gave her a big hug. "Maybe the weather is affecting him, too."

"Well, something certainly is." Grammy went out the door, shaking her head.

"Bad day, huh, Tiger?" Robynn asked as she turned on the light in his bedroom. She sat down on the edge of his bed.

Jeremy buried his head in her lap. "Grammy's mad at me." His lower lip stuck out far enough to rest his koala bear on it.

"What did you do?"

"Nothing."

"What were you supposed to do?" She stroked the curling hair back from his forehead. *It's amazing,* she thought, *how much he resembles Dane. Same black, curly hair. Same blue eyes. Whoa, girl,* she commanded herself. *You're mad at that man, remember?*

"I didn't want soup for lunch. I want hot dogs."

"But we're out of hot dogs. You ate them yesterday."

The stubborn thrust of his lip revealed his state of mind. "And I asked for a popsicle."

"We're out of those, too. Tomorrow is grocery day."

"Grammy didn't want to take me to the store."

"I should guess not. You've been a pill, but. . ." Robynn wrapped both arms around him and squeezed. "I love you, anyway. And so does Grammy." She leaned over and planted a smacking kiss on his ear.

Jeremy scrubbed it off with one fist, but smiles returned to his mouth. A giggle escaped when she blew on his scrunched, closed eyelids. "When's Dane coming?" He sat up as if expecting to hear the car any moment.

"Probably not tonight." Robynn chewed her lip. "I–I think he had something else planned."

"Does he still have a bump on his head?"

"Yes."

"Maybe he has a headache. He better go to bed." Jeremy delivered his medical pronouncement with all the seriousness of a practicing physician.

"You tell him, Tiger." She took his hand, and together they walked out to the living room. "Want some pop? I'm going to have some."

Robynn read two complete books to Jeremy before he finally fell asleep. The phone hadn't rung. No silver Porsche roared up the street.

Even though she thought of calling Dane, she phoned Josh instead, hoping he might mention Dane. They talked of the day's racing, the accident, the amount of money they were short—but not about Dane.

Robynn went to bed, self-pity bickering with righteous anger. "Jesus," she prayed, "it's hard to be thankful when you're mad at someone, but I sure appreciate the way You kept everyone alive today—and yesterday." She sighed before going on. "Thank You for keeping me safe today. Can't Dane see what a miracle that was and be glad with me? What is he, a pouter? Why just yesterday everything was fine again. I hate feeling jerked around."

She thumped her pillow. "So. . .I praise You for giving my horse wings today and for sending Your Son to die for me, and for loving me when, like right now, I don't feel very lovable. God, I need a hug, a Dane hug." She smiled in the darkness. "And I bet he does, too. Yesterday. . ."

Yesterday. Her thoughts roamed. *Yesterday I almost told Dane how much I care for him.*

"Yes-ter-day. . ." The old song hummed through her mind, lulling her to sleep.

❧

Robynn woke in the morning with a different song on her mind. This was a child's song, a Bible verse set to music. "Be kind to one another, forgiving one another even as God in Christ has forgiven you." The catchy tune ran over and over as she pulled on worn jeans and a red wool sweater over her turtleneck. The song persisted as she waved good-bye to her mother. The hum of windshield wipers refused to drown out the words.

"All right!" She laughed at her reflection in the rearview mirror. "I get the message." She still whistled the tune as she skipped down the stalls, searching for the man she loved.

Ed Bannon, a longtime friend of Josh's, was feeding the horses and reading instructions from a list in his hand.

"Hey, Ed. Where's Dane?" Robynn asked, a small knot of worry tightening under her ribs.

"I don't know. All's I know is Josh called me last night and asked me to take care of the horses till he gets back. Said you'd know about the training and racing. I'm to get more instructions this morning when I see him after chores is done."

Robynn collapsed on the box in the tack room. She felt like she'd been thrown from a horse and all the wind knocked out of her. *He's gone. I know it. Dane's gone.*

"I'll be back in a bit," she called as she leaped to her feet. She ran back out the gate and flung her car door open. *He can't be gone,* she reasoned. *He must be at Josh's apartment. Somehow we've got to talk.*

The hope buoyed her until she pulled into the cul-de-sac. There were no lights and no silver Porsche. Only Josh's tired old pickup waited in the driveway. Biting her lip, she got out of the car and rang the doorbell. Finally, she leaned against the bell, willing, praying, for Dane to answer.

Nothing.

Nothing was the color of the morning as she finished her duties so she could visit Josh. She was a jockey, she reminded herself when she wanted to run away and cry. And with a jockey, the horses came first. Horses deserved more than desertion.

"I'll never be understanding it myself, Princess." The lines on Josh's face had deepened overnight. "He came in here last night like a house afire. Said on top of what was going on here, he had an emergency back in San Francisco. Ed agreed to take over." Josh slammed his fist into the mattress. "If I don't get out of here pretty soon, everything'll be shot beyond redemption.

"We'll get along, Josh." Robynn raised her chin. "You just get better. I've managed a long time without our so-called friend. I'll manage again." Shoulders back, she marched out the door.

❧

From the smiling princess mask secured on Robynn's face in the following days, no one knew what the tears were doing to her inside. "He had an emergency," she responded when questioned about Dane. Finally, Pam cornered her before she could slip out the door.

"Okay," Pam demanded as they walked out to the parking lot after the final race. "What gives with you? Did you send him packing or what?"

Robynn repeated her canned speech, "Mr. Morgan. . ."

"Stow it, Princess. This is Pam. You know, your old friend Pam. The one who can see beyond that mask of yours." She stopped abruptly at the sight of the mirrored pain in Robynn's eyes. "I'll kill him," Pam muttered. "I swear, I'll kill that man. Anyone who would hurt you like that deserves to be shot."

Robynn took a deep breath. It took all the force in her lungs to get enough air past the huge lump that had taken up permanent residence in her chest.

"Thanks for your concern, lady." She tossed the duffel bag in the backseat of the Celica. "You're a good friend."

"Go to dinner with me. Maybe talking will make you feel better."

"Thanks. But tomorrow Jeremy goes back to school, so I need to get his stuff together. Maybe another time."

Jeremy had stopped asking about Dane. But Robynn noticed that he stopped whatever he was doing to listen intently whenever a sports car roared by. Each time, the sound faded away completely before he went back to what he was doing.

"Hurry, Jeremy, or we'll be late for church."

"I don't want to go. I want Dane to come. You call him, okay?"

"Sorry, Tiger, I don't know his phone number."

"You could call information."

"You're right. I'll think about it, okay? You go wash your face, and we'll be outa here. I bet we could find a hot fudge sundae on the way home."

"Yeah." Two minutes later they were out the door.

As usual, the singing lifted her spirits and the sermon seemed written just for her. God promised again to never leave nor forsake her.

Not like some men I know, she thought before forcing her mind to concentrate on the verses being read.

Back home, after all Jeremy's clothes were packed, Robynn and her son cuddled on the sofa in front of the fireplace. If she just closed her eyes, she could see Dane lying there on the rug.

"Mommy, keep reading." Jeremy tugged at her arm.

She finished the story and closed the book. "Time for bed, Son. Go brush your teeth and I'll be right in. Oh, and make sure you get all the fudge off." Jeremy ran off, giggling.

Robynn closed her eyes again. She could feel the play of Dane's muscles as she leaned against his broad chest, smell the tang of his aftershave.

"Mom!" The tone was demanding, like this wasn't the first time Jeremy had called.

❦

The next morning, Robynn pasted her princess smile back in place and forcefully injected cheer into her voice as she and Jeremy left for school. To pass time on the drive down the Willamette Valley, she told him stories: David, the giant killer, and Samuel, a boy called by God. Jeremy's favorite was Moses.

"Let my people go," he chanted with her when they came to the part about Moses and Pharaoh. "Let my people go."

Mrs. C welcomed him back with a big hug and dishes of chocolate ice cream for the children in his cottage. Robynn kissed him good-bye and left him, the star bragging about his stay in the hospital.

She tried to brighten up for Josh the next day. His good news? He'd be graduating to crutches by the end of the week. Finally he would be able to leave the hospital.

But each of the lonely nights back at her house, she alternated between anger and hurt, worry and fear. Was Jeremy really all right at school? Where in the world was Dane? Why didn't he at least call? That always brought her back to anger, and the cycle continued.

Until she gave up and prayed it all out again.

"You must get tired of me saying the same thing every night." She swallowed the tears again and opened her Bible, searching for the promises God meant just for her. Psalm 91 helped. The thought of being safe under the pinions of His mighty wings made it possible to sleep.

She perked up a couple nights later at the hospital when Josh handed her a letter from Opal. She had accepted their new offer of half the money down and the rest within a year. The racing string was theirs. "That's great, Josh. When you get out of here, we can look for some good pastureland."

"Aye." His eyes grew dreamy. "And maybe I'll be findin' a farm I can afford. Ten acres with a wee house."

She gave him a hug. "You will."

Each evening when she returned to her house, the emptiness struck her anew. Empty. What a dismal word. One Wednesday evening she dialed the area code for Pasadena and asked for the Dane Morgan residence.

"I'm sorry, ma'am, but that is an unlisted number." She felt like slamming the phone down but set it back gently. *Tomorrow*, she promised herself, *tomorrow I ask Josh.*

At church that evening, the pastor warned about self-pity. "When you're feeling low," he said, "look up. Look to the Christ who bears our burdens. Look to His hands, nailed for our sins. Look up. Look out. There's someone who needs you."

Robynn shook his hand at the door. "Thank you," she said. "I needed that."

For the first time in days, a smile curved her lips as she fell asleep. She'd made the decision: no more yo-yo. After the races on Sunday, she would fly to San Francisco and find Dane. Josh surely must have his address. After all, they *were* related.

And if he didn't? She'd call every construction company in town if she had to. How hard would it be to find a construction company called Morgan something or other? This time *she* was going to do some talking and *he* was going to do some listening. And if he still insisted on marriage *or* racing? Well, so be it. They'd cross that bridge when they came to it. If he thought he was going to run out on her, he had another think coming. She refused to allow herself to think negative thoughts. As the pastor said, "Look up."

❧

Sunday dawned with the sun streaking gold and vermilion on scattered clouds and painting Mount Hood the rarest of pinks. When Robynn breathed deeply the crisp, stinging air, she coughed. The boulder in her throat was gone. Someone had rolled it away during the night.

As if celebrating what might be the last sunny day of the racing season, the stands filled early. The Pacific Futura, a race for maiden colts, had drawn a lot of publicity. Sunday Driver was Robynn's mount. She found it hard to believe this was the same colt who had precipitated Dane's accident.

The fiery animal broke from the gate straight and true and never looked at another horse as he leveled out, driving hard for the finish, ahead by a length.

It was a good way to start the day's program.

The day continued with Robynn in the money in every race. The tension built toward the finale, the Race for the Roses, Portland's prestigious sweepstakes. Robynn had never won this race before. Neither had Sonny.

When Ed Bannon brought Finding Fun up to the saddling paddock, Robynn felt a thrill of anticipation. The two of them were already linked as winners.

She rubbed Finding's nose and up behind her ears. With a sigh, the filly leaned into her chest, begging for more. Robynn pushed her away. "You're getting hair all over me," she laughed. Ed boosted her into the saddle. As Robynn leaned over to adjust the stirrup, she felt a tingle up her spine.

Startled, she straightened and carefully searched the sea of faces surrounding the fence. Nothing.

"Well, girl, this is it," Robynn crooned as the filly stretched out in her ground-eating walk. When they entered the starting gate, she pulled her goggles into place and wrapped one hand in a hank of mane.

"The flag is up!" the announcer blared as, at the clang of the gates, eleven horses catapulted into action. The crowds screamed for their favorites. All Robynn heard was the grunting and blowing of the straining horses. Steadily, stride by stride, Finding Fun and a bay pulled out of the pack. At the far turn, Robynn made her bid.

"Go, Finding," she yelled into her flickering ears. The bay on the rail beside them reacted at the same time.

Nose for nose, they thundered for the wire. At the last moment, Robynn tapped the sorrel's shoulder with the bat. Finding Fun leaped forward, winner by a head.

Robynn stood high in her stirrups, the thrill of victory welling like a geyser bursting from the ground. She laughed aloud. They had done it. They'd won the Race for the Roses.

Back in the winner's circle, Robynn and Finding Fun received thundering ovations. Robynn grinned and waved, feeling like the Queen of England facing her subjects.

When she slipped from the filly's back and unbuckled the girth, she again felt that familiar tingle start at her toes and race for the top of her helmet.

As the coveted horseshoe of red roses was draped over Finding's withers, Portland's mayor stepped forward. She placed a dozen long-stemmed red roses in Robynn's arms and kissed her on both cheeks.

The tingle sprinted up her spine again.

When the mayor took her arm and presented her to the roaring crowd, she saw him.

The tall, broad-shouldered man in a sheepskin jacket filled her range of vision. In his arms he carried a small, curly-headed boy with hair the color of a raven's wing, just like the man's. The two looked so alike they could be father and son.

She barely noticed the old man, leaning on crutches at their side.

It could be said she hardly noticed anything. She couldn't tear her eyes away from the shocking blue gaze of the man staring with equal intensity at her. Ideas hummed along that gaze—dreams, apologies, and forgiveness asked and received.

The crowd parted like the Red Sea, leaving her an open aisle. Robynn O'Dell, the Princess, walked it proudly, cradling the roses in her arms. Their gazes never faltered.

Dane opened his other arm and Robynn walked into the curve of it, the roses clutched in her left hand. It left the right one free to hug both the man and the little boy.

"Mommy," Jeremy's voice rang out clearly. "Dane's gonna be my new daddy and we're gonna live on Opal's farm."

Robynn's look questioned Dane, then flicked to Josh. She smiled up at Jeremy. "We'll see, Son."

"And right the laddie is." Josh beamed, a tiny bit of moisture filming his eyes. "Dane here bought out the man who bought her out." The older man studied Robynn's face for a long moment, as if searching for her response, then shook his head. "Hey, Tiger, how about grabbing on to my crutch here and we'll see about some ice cream." Dane set the boy down, never taking his eyes from Robynn's.

"You're finished here for the day?"

"Yes."

"Good, then we have some talking to do."

"Hey, Princess, you got some words for the press?"

"Be right there." She sent a questioning glance Dane's way.

"You go ahead. I'll be waiting right here."

She almost asked, "You sure you won't leave?" but smiled instead. "I'll hurry."

After answering questions for both print and television, she turned to the last man.

"So, did I hear right? There are wedding bells in the offing?"

Robynn could feel a blush work its way up her neck and over her cheeks. "I. . .we. . ." She glanced over at Dane, who lounged against the fence. He nodded and touched a finger to his forehead.

"No comment right now, Dave. Catch me later." Robynn made her way back to where Dane waited, stopping only to sign a couple programs thrust her way.

"Who's taking care of the horses?"

"Ed is, with Josh there to boss him. Your folks took Jeremy home with them.

How soon can you get changed?" He held her elbow in a firm but gentle grip, walking so fast she had to dogtrot to keep up.

"Dane. Slow down."

"Oh, sorry." He gave her a sheepish smile and at least let her feet touch the ground every few feet.

Pam hummed a few bars of "Here Comes the Bride" when Robynn darted into the dressing room. "Hear ye! Clear the way. Our princess is in a royal hurry to meet her prince."

"Pam, knock it off."

"So, when's the date?"

"I haven't said yes yet." Robynn pulled up her jeans and snapped them, grabbing a clean shirt and sweater without even a minute's pause.

"So. . .are you?"

"He's got some explaining to do." Robynn stuffed her dirty things in the duffel, then grinned at her friend. "And then I'll hog-tie him so he can't leave again." She shoved her arms in the sleeves of her leather jacket and was out the door before the women quit laughing.

Once in the car, a four-wheel-drive SUV this time, Dane started the ignition and then asked, "Are you hungry, thirsty, or. . . ?"

"Or."

"Or?"

"I've got questions, you've got answers. You've got questions, I've got answers. So start." She snapped her seat belt and settled against the leather seat.

Dane stared straight ahead, wrists draped over the steering wheel. "Me first, huh?"

"Yep." Robynn could feel her heart pounding. Surely he didn't have some deep dark secret that would prevent their life together.

"Okay." He shifted into drive and joined the line of cars leaving the parking lot. "Remember when I told you how back when I was a little kid my father left for another tour of duty in the Marine Corps and made me promise to look after my mother and my sister?"

Robynn nodded. "In the chapel at the hospital."

"I took the charge seriously, so when my mother was permanently paralyzed in a steeplechase accident, I figured it was my fault. I had let down my father, who returned from duty in a casket. I failed. I promised myself I would never let the woman I fell in love with be injured."

"Oh, Dane, I. . .I kinda figured as much."

He held up a hand. "Let me finish while I can. My mother raked me over the coals for my overbearing attitude many times, especially when I told her about you. I won't tell you what my sister said, but rest assured, they are both on your side. So I have had to do some deep thinking, and the emergency in my company was a good excuse to beat a hasty and totally ungentlemanly retreat. My mother's words."

He took the Highway 14 exit after crossing the I-5 bridge going north. "Your turn. Why didn't you tell me earlier about Jeremy?"

"I didn't want him hurt in case you decided to leave."

Dane flinched. "And I left."

She nodded.

"And he got hurt?"

Another nod.

"Will you forgive me?"

"Yes, and we both already have. I finally had to make a commitment, or recommitment if you will, to my faith in Jesus. I got sick and tired of yo-yoing back and forth. I want God at the center of my life from now on, and any relationship we have has to be based on that principle."

"I have no problem with that." He took the turnoff to Orchards.

"Where are we going?"

"You'll see. I grew up in the church like you did and, like you, let other things get in the way. Jeremy's illness was the take it or leave it point. I just mess things up without Jesus Christ as my center. And you got hurt because of it. Another thing to forgive me for."

"Done." Robynn leaned her head back against the seat and turned to watch Dane's face. "So, anything else to reveal? I am looking forward to meeting your mother and sister, by the way. I've never had a sister before."

Dane covered her hand with his. "They'll love you, but not nearly as much as I do."

The simple statement made her eyes burn. "Ah, Dane."

They turned into the drive for McKecknen Stables and parked by the pasture of young stock. Halfway out of the car, Dane leaned back to ask, "Are you coming?"

"Okay." But before she could unbuckle her seat belt, he was around to open her car door. He took her hand and waved the other in an arc to encompass the farm.

"What do you think?"

"Of what?" She gave him a puzzled look.

"Of our farm."

"You really did buy it?"

"Lock, stock, and horseflesh."

"So Jeremy wasn't just confused?" Robynn leaned against the fence. The three yearlings trotted up to nose her sleeve and beg for treats.

"Not at all, but I have one more question." He dug in his pocket and pulled out a gray ring box.

Robynn turned her back to the horses so she could watch his face.

"Robynn O'Dell, will you marry me and be the Princess of all this?"

She now understood what people meant when they said her heart stopped.

"Dane, I–I want to keep racing." There, it was out. Her heart took up an unknown rhythm.

"Okay, but how about if only on our own horses? Not racing for other stables. Would that be a fair compromise?" He paused. "You can see I've given this a lot of thought."

Robynn closed her eyes. Her *Thank You, heavenly Father* winged heavenward before she lifted her eyes to see Dane studying her. While he'd leaned one arm on the white board fence so his hand almost touched her shoulder, his face said he was anything but relaxed.

"Of course I'll marry you." She raised her face for his long overdue kiss.

"Um, one thing."

"What?" She leaned back in his arms to study his face.

"You haven't said if you love me yet."

"Oh, I do, Dane Morgan. I love you now and for always." This time she kissed him.

"Ouch." He drew back and glared at the three colts. The middle one nodded as if he'd just done something of major importance. Dane rubbed his shoulder.

"Shame on you, Rowdy. You are not to bite." Robynn looked up at her husband-to-be. "You want me to kiss it and make it better?"

Dane growled, and both hands at her waist, swung her up in a circle. "Those three better get ready to race for their own roses because we've already won ours." He kissed her again, this time leaving her breathless. "I take it you want roses in our wedding?"

"Of course, but it's a good thing there are plenty of hot-house ones year around because I'm not waiting until June."

"How about red ones for Christmas?"

Robynn nodded. "I always was partial to long-stemmed red roses or else ones braided into a blanket or horseshoe." She snuggled against his chest. "Tell me I'm not dreaming."

"You are definitely not dreaming, Mrs.-Dane-Morgan-to-be. Or else we are in the same dream together." They stepped away from the fence just as the colt stuck out his nose for another warning. "Dreams full of love and roses."

Song of Laughter

by Lauraine Snelling

To Wayne, who loved the farm as much as I did.
Thank you for encouraging me and supporting me so I can write.
With love and gratitude to Noreen Brownlie and Jerry Chan,
who gave of themselves, their home, and their time that this book could be finished
in time for the Golden Heart contest.
Friends like these are the gifts God gives us beyond measure.
Thanks also to the other members of our Portland critique group, Lynn Jordan,
Beverly Fletcher, and before she moves, Annette Broadrick.
When we're together again, it's like the years between have never been.
That's the test of true friendship.

Chapter 1

S orry, old girl—" Lareana stroked the old milk cow's velvety throat—"that's all for tonight." Then with a screech of metal on metal, the barred gate swung open and the bell cow of the Three Trees herd ambled out the door. Lareana pushed levers, closing one gate and opening another, to admit the next candidate into the milking parlor. As the idea flitted through her mind, she smiled to herself. *Other ladies dress in their finest and entertain guests in their parlors, but look at me!* Giving her faded jeans a rueful look, she pushed back a few tendrils of honey-blond hair—"If this pit can be called a parlor, that is."

She paused a moment to survey her cramped quarters. The concrete enclosure where the dairy cows were simultaneously fed and hooked up to the milking machines more nearly resembled a deep stall. The cow on her left stopped munching long enough to stare at her with baleful brown eyes, then returned to her feed bin.

Lareana stood at shoulder level with the cows' udders to slip into position the four suction cups connected to long tubes that would pipe the milk directly to the cooling tank. With a cow on either side of her, she was forced to be efficient in her movements, but she always took time for the petting and individual attention the herd had come to expect in the six long months since her husband, John, had died.

" 'Step into my parlor, said the lady to the cow.' " She parodied an old nursery rhyme. When the animal glared at her for not cranking the feed handle immediately, Lareana's laughter was music floating like dust particles in a sunbeam. "You just don't appreciate good poetry, my girl. Don't you know—"

"Know what?"

Lareana whirled. A small shriek escaped her lips and her heart raced as all the blood drained from her face. "Who. . .who—" She took a deep breath and tried again. "Who are—"

"Hey, sorry!" called the tall stranger leaning against the doorframe. "I didn't mean to frighten you."

"Well, then, you're just naturally good at it!" Seeing that the man appeared genuinely remorseful, Lareana willed her stomach back below her tonsils. "I—I just didn't hear you come in."

"How could you?" His grin crinkled the corners of sky blue eyes. "You were too busy messing up that poem."

"Didn't like my version, huh?" Her mind flew ahead of her words, cataloguing the broad shoulders that stretched a plaid shirt, worn jeans, and scuffed boots. The leather gloves, carelessly clasped in one bronzed hand, clued her in. "Why, you're the new hay hauler."

He nodded, emanating power leashed and at rest. With two fingers he tipped the brim of his sweat-darkened felt hat. "You got it."

"Where's Bud?"

"Down setting up the elevator." The man gestured toward the aging barn. "Sent me up to let someone know we're here."

"Uncle Haakan's gone for the evening. We didn't expect you until tomorrow." She turned to remove one of the machines. "I won't be done for—" she closed her eyes, calculating mentally—"for at least another hour."

"We'll manage." He smiled again and glanced down at the infant seat parked in the doorway. The device cradled a soundly sleeping four-month-old baby. "You always have an audience when you milk?"

"Yep. Johnny's my rooting section. The rhythm of the machines works better than a rocking chair."

An incoming cow bellowed, the sound ricocheting off the cement block walls. The tow-headed tot flinched, sucked once on the thumb in his mouth, and relaxed again.

"See?" Love turned her azure eyes to shimmering pools.

The man froze. Golden rays from the late sun slanted through the high windows, burnishing the slim figure before him. In the light, this rustic setting with mother and child was an artist's daydream. He blinked, then forced his mind back from the illusion.

The woman's smile again caressed the sleeping infant, then rose to warm the man's face also. She finished her sentence, "He likes it here."

"Can't say as I blame him, even with all this noise." The man grinned again as he turned to go, eyeing her appreciatively. "And by the way, I like your shirt." Whistling the opening bars of "Some Enchanted Evening," he closed the screen door softly behind him.

Lareana glanced down at the front of her navy sweatshirt. The words "Nuzzle My Muzzle" arched above two red Duroc piglets, snout to snout. She chuckled, then caught herself humming along.

"Silly," she chided herself, "you didn't even ask him his name."

Having learned through experience that she could not hurry when milking cows, Lareana continued at her habitual pace. Her mind, however, refused to stay inside the milking parlor. It flitted to the man in the barn, to the dinner she had left simmering in the Crock-Pot, and back to the recurring problems that nibbled like mice at the corners of her consciousness. How would she keep the farm operating at peak efficiency now that John was gone? Four hundred acres with 150 milking cows was. . .well, it was almost too much for *two strong men* to manage, let alone a woman and her elderly uncle. Besides, the income barely supported their two families.

To bring in some additional funds, she had considered increasing the herd, but she would have to sell that forty-acre piece of property out by the freeway first. And she needed to hire some more part-time help. She heaved a deep sigh. It seemed a catch-22 situation. Selling out might still be the best option, after all.

Shrugging aside the negative thought, she squared her shoulders. "We're going to make it," she vowed to the last cow to enter the stall. "I'm going to keep this farm. John and I worked too hard to give up now."

Little John had finished his nap and was well on his way to getting bored and fussy before Lareana gave the cow she was milking a sharp slap on the rump and sent her out the door.

"Almost done, Johnny," she crooned as she set him out of the way so she could hose down the milking parlor and holding pen, then run soapy water through the milk lines.

But soft promises were no longer sufficient, and his eyes were brimming with angry tears when she finally hoisted the infant seat onto one hip. Setting the automatic agitator for the huge stainless steel milk tank, her eye caught the date on the wall calendar—October 10. Only three more weeks before the drunk who had killed John would come to trial.

The baby in her arms kicked his feet and gurgled. Lareana unclenched her teeth and flipped the switch. "Your turn, son. You've been patient long enough." He accepted her apology with a toothless grin.

Outside, Lareana drew in a deep draught of the crisp October air. Dusk had deepened to dark, but the two mercury floodlights in the yard drove back the shadows as she walked swiftly up the graveled drive past the barn, noticing that the green semi-trailer was only half unloaded.

"Dinner will be ready when you are," she called to the man slinging hundred-pound bales of rich green alfalfa onto the electric elevator.

Bud's familiar weather-beaten face peered down from the stack of bales above her head, and he shouted over the elevator clicking and clanking the hay up to the loft. "Hi-yah, Lareana. My stomach says it's ready now, but it'll be another hour 'fore we're done here."

"That's okay. That'll give me time to feed my helper here and put him to bed." She nodded to the baby in her arms.

"Whatcha got there?" The burly man perched on a bale and squinted down. "Last time I saw you, you was big as a house. Thought you'd have triplets, for sure." He spat a brown stream of tobacco juice onto the floor.

"Thanks. You sure know how to make a woman feel good." Her chuckle was warm and throaty as she moved so he could see the baby.

"The name's Johnny, if that gives you a clue." As she turned, her eyes were drawn to the level gaze of the stranger in the loft.

"See you two later then?"

He nodded.

" 'You will see a stranger across a crowded room,' " Lareana serenaded baby Johnny as she headed for the square white house. Three ancient Douglas firs protected the two-story home from the north winds and dropped cones and needles on the pillared porch that flanked it on both sides.

Pausing in the front yard, she stopped for her evening commune with Mount Rainier, the silver sentinel standing guard at the far end of the hay fields and the undulating fir-clad hills. "Thank You, God, for another day," she murmured, "for being like that mountain, for never leaving me—ever changing yet always the same." She hugged the infant seat close. Her eyes sought the stars, poking holes in the heavens above.

Down in a pasture, a cow lowed. The wistful sound was carried on the same breeze that stirred the branches above her and gently lifted the sun-kissed strands of her bangs. Lareana waited. The sense of peace deepened, wrapping itself around her like a giant hand, holding her safely in its grasp.

Stepping quietly, so as not to shatter the moment, Lareana swung open the gate, entered her mum-fenced yard, and clicked the gate shut behind her. Samson, her sable collie, was stretched out on the porch. He thumped his tail at her approach, then rose and looked toward the door expectantly.

"Where were you when the hay truck arrived?" At the sternness in her voice, his feathery tail drooped. "You're supposed to be guarding the place." His ears followed suit. He whimpered, dejection apparent in every line of his powerful body. "Off gallivanting, I'll bet. We should just call you Romeo." The dog dropped to the porch floor.

Lareana shook her head. "You sure can put on an act." She bent down to pet the drooping ears. "That must be some hussy down the road to make you miss the hay truck." The change in her voice worked a lightning-fast transformation in the dog. He sat up, his tongue lolling to one side of his mouth, then lifted one white paw and waited.

"Oh, all right, you're forgiven," she conceded, laughing and shaking the proffered paw. "I always have been a sucker for a male with nice manners."

Samson had his nose in the door almost before she had opened it. "Sit, boy. You forgot. Women and children first."

She entered, set the infant seat down on the floor, and flicked on the light switch, bringing the delft blue and white kitchen to life. "All right, Samson.

Come." He obeyed, wagging his tail with delight.

The aroma of home-baked beans wafted around her as she stepped outside once more to pull off her boots. She could hear Johnny gurgling and chattering at the dog who always sneaked in a quick lick when her back was turned.

From force of habit, she looked back toward the milk house, expecting to see John coming for dinner any minute. As the slowly dimming pain struck forcefully again, she remembered. John was dead. A loved one can be killed in an instant, but five-year–long habits of waiting and loving take longer to die.

She shut her eyes against the pain and tried to regain her sense of peace. Failing that, she muttered through clenched teeth, "I *will* praise the Lord. I *will*." Comfort stole around her shoulders, encircled her heart, and released the tension in her jaw.

The light streaming from her open door beckoned her back to the world of cooing infants and baking beans. But her sigh drifted toward the heavens, effectively communicating her deepest needs to the Father she trusted to listen.

Pink begonias blooming on the windowsill above the sink were reflected in the darkened window as Lareana washed her hands. She smiled at her reflection—"wholesome," her uncle always said—then brushed back tendrils of hair that insisted on a life of their own. Johnny, bored with pulling patient Samson's ears, whimpered.

"I'm coming, I'm coming," she promised the restless infant as she dried her hands. "Which do you want first, dinner or dry pants?" She lifted him from the seat, and the baby's questing mouth left no doubt about his choice. "Too bad, you're soaked."

Quickly she changed him, then settled into the rocker in front of the wood stove. With one wool-stockinged toe, she twirled the handle on the door of the square black stove and opened it. The low-burning embers flamed briefly in the gust of air, and the warmth crept up her leg, bathed her face in its orange glow, and turned the collie at her feet into molten gold. It would be so easy to close her eyes and. . .a tiny fist rubbed against her chest. Baby John delivered a gargantuan belch, and his lashes fluttered softly into sleep.

Lareana gazed down at him, reluctant to let the moment go. During his four months of life, little John had grown to resemble his father more and more. The dimple in his chin matched the cleft in big John's, and the muddy gray of newborn eyes had deepened to the same cobalt blue. "Good night, darling." Then Lareana heard herself repeating the same words John had said to her every night just before they slept: "God loves you and so do I."

Carefully she eased herself and the sleeping baby from the chair. Johnny only sighed and popped a tiny thumb in his mouth as she tucked the blanket around him in the crib.

In her bedroom, Lareana dug a clean top out of the drawer and quickly donned it. On the way back to the kitchen, she stopped by the bathroom to run a brush through her hair and re-secure the leather clasp holding her ponytail in place. As an afterthought, she applied a coat of pearl pink lipstick. Shrugging, she winked at her reflection in the mirror. "What we women do for the men."

Walking into the kitchen, her eyes automatically flew to the clock above the stove. *Better hustle*, she admonished herself. *They'll be here any minute.*

She had just finished setting the table when a knock on the door announced the arrival of the two men.

"Come on in," she called as she removed the electric cord from the brown Crock-Pot and transferred it to the middle of the table. "Bud, why don't you show your friend where to wash up, and I'll have dinner on in a sec."

When they re-entered the kitchen, Lareana was pulling a pan of warm rolls from the oven. Bud sniffed appreciatively. "That smells mighty good, Miss Lareana. Trey here thinks I come to deliver hay, but really I come for some of your good homemade bread. You downright spoil me."

"Didn't notice any cut in the price of hay." She slipped the rolls into a waiting basket. "And, Bud, I haven't officially met your friend here." Shifting her basket, she put out her hand. "I'm Lareana Amundson." Tall at five feet, eight inches, she still had to tilt her head back to meet the warm blue gaze of the man towering above her. He seemed to fill the room.

"Just call me Trey." His big hand enveloped hers.

"Hey, Lareana, where's John tonight?" Bud asked as he pulled out his chair. "Down in Portland with the show string?"

"Oh, Bud, you didn't know?" Lareana bit her lip. "John died last April. . .a car accident. . . . The other driver was drunk." The pain sliced through her again, though, thank God, it came less often now. Convulsively, she clenched the hand holding hers.

Trey watched as the sparkle dimmed in Lareana's smiling face. He tightened his grip on the hand he still held, seeking to still its sudden tremor. He was surprised at the powerful urge he felt to take her in his arms. Talk about pluck, this lady had it. Even as he watched, her determined chin rose, a deep breath drained the tension from her shoulders, and she gently disengaged the hand that clutched at his.

"I'm sorry," he said and immediately felt helpless. What good would that do? What could anyone ever say to make a difference in a situation like this? She was so young, too young to suffer such a loss.

For once, Bud was speechless. Lareana glanced at him, saw the tear in the corner of his eye, and filled in the silence. "Bud, I'm the one who's sorry. . .to spring the news on you like that. I forget sometimes that everyone doesn't know.

He got to his feet and patted her shoulder awkwardly. "John was a fine man, made his daddy proud, he did."

Lareana shook her head. If only. . .but she knew by now that the "if onlys" always got her in trouble. She had to play the game the way it was dealt her. Her rose-colored glasses had been shattered with the night arrival of the state patrolman and had been buried along with her husband.

"Come on, you guys." She set the rolls on the table, but before she could pull out her chair, Trey was there, seating her, gently brushing her shoulder with a compassionate hand before seating himself.

Lareana bowed her head for grace and took another deep breath. This was just one more time when she missed John's resonant voice. "Thank You, Father, for the food we have and the friends we meet. Amen."

She glanced around the table to make sure everything was in order and encountered the intent gaze of the man sitting across from her. His look conveyed no pity, only the deep empathy of someone who has also suffered and therefore understands. She nodded. And felt comforted.

"If you'll pass your plates, I'll dish up the beans. The pot's too hot to pass." She opened the crock with a potholder.

Bud cleared his throat. "Your uncle Haakan helping you then?"

"Yes." She scooped a ladleful of the beans and rich molasses sauce onto his plate. "He does most of the chores, but he and Aunt Inga had a community Grange meeting tonight. I talked them into going out for dinner first, though. He needed a night off." She held out her hand for Trey's plate. "When it's not raining, Johnny and I don't mind milking at all."

"This looks delicious." Trey motioned when he had enough on his plate. "I can't remember when I've had real baked beans. I thought they almost always came in a can."

"Awwww, not this woman." Bud spoke around a mouthful of beans and fresh rolls. "She's the best cook in the county! Cooks from scratch, too. You oughta taste her rhubarb pie."

"That a hint, Bud?" Lareana smiled.

"No, no, 'course not," he sputtered, with a sly look and a wink at Trey, "but then again. . ." All three joined in the laughter at his innocent expression.

"Oh, I haven't offered you anything to drink," said Lareana apologetically. "What'll you have?"

"I'd like a beer," Bud replied, "if you got it, that is."

"Not anymore." A frown puckered Lareana's smooth brow. "I won't have liquor of any kind on the place. As far as I'm concerned, it can all go—"

"Okay, okay, I understand." Bud braced his elbows on the table. "Just make it coffee, tea, whatever. . ."

"Guess that's getting to be my soapbox," Lareana admitted. "But too many people are killed or have their lives really messed up by drunk drivers. Somebody's got to do something about it."

And I'll bet you're just the one, Trey thought, admiration for her growing by the moment. *I'd hate to be on the opposite side of any battle with you.* He tried to shake off the invading argument: *But people can drink and still function. You can't tell the world to lay off the booze.* He wiped his mouth with a napkin and arranged his silverware on the plate in front of him. "Thank you, ma'am. That certainly was delicious."

"You'll have coffee and dessert, won't you? Even if it isn't rhubarb pie?" She winked at Bud as she scraped the plates. But before she could get to her feet, Trey was beside her, removing the stack and setting them in the sink. She hesitated a moment, unaccustomed to such chivalry. Setting and clearing the table had always been her job.

"Where are the cups?" he asked, turning to face her as she set the bean pot on the counter.

"Up there." She pointed to the mug rack hanging on the end wall of the oak cabinet. "Do you take cream and sugar?"

He shook his head. "Just black."

She poured three cups of coffee and Trey helped carry them to the table.

"Seconds of dessert, anyone?" she asked when the men's plates were cleaned in record time. "I have nearly a whole pan of apple crisp left."

"No, thanks." Trey shook his head.

"Me, neither." Bud eyed the pan. "I sure wish I had some more room. That was mighty fine." He pushed his chair back and reached for his hat. "We gotta be hittin' the road. It's a long way to George."

"Are you going over the pass tonight?"

"Yeah. If I get too tired, this young buck here can drive. Thank you, Miss Lareana. And. . .and I'm sorry, truly sorry for what you've been goin' through." The catch was back in his throat.

Trey extended his hand and his clasp was warm and firm. "Thanks for the meal. I'll see you again." His words were more statement than question.

Lareana nodded. "Drive carefully now." The scene seemed to unfold in slow motion as he lifted his hat, secured it over his wavy, roan red hair, and finally released her hand.

That's some pair, Lareana mused as she leaned against the open door frame until she heard the gate latch click. *Mutt and Jeff.* She chuckled to herself when the floodlight picked out the two broad-shouldered men. Within moments the green semi rumbled past the fir trees, a blink of the headlights bidding her good-bye. How thoughtful. If he'd tooted that air horn, Johnny might have awakened, screaming his head off. She closed the door.

By the time she had the dishwasher loaded and the kitchen cleaned up, she heard her young son squirming in his crib, making tentative noises that would soon crescendo into loud demands for food. She gave the blue tile counters a last swipe before entering the baby's bedroom. In the light from the door, she could see him turn to watch her, his chubby fists waving in the air.

Following their familiar routine, she shrugged into her blue robe and slippers, pulled a dry sleeper on over the baby's downy head, and settled once more into the carved rocking chair by the fire.

Lulled by the flickering firelight and the nursing infant, her mind slipped back in time. Like a benediction to the day, the memories came. . .flooding her with warmth and peace. Memories of John were painfully sweet. She had met him on the fair circuit, when as young 4-H'ers they had shown their fathers' registered Ayrshires. Everyone had said they were too young for marriage.

While they waited, there had been cooking school and courses in restaurant management for Lareana.

She and John were best friends as well as lovers. After the wedding, they had combined their growing dairy herds, leased a farm with an option to buy, and begun building their future. Neither of them was afraid of hard work, and it began to pay off. Two years later they signed the purchase papers on their land.

Folks in the tiny community of Yelm, Washington, spoke of them with growing respect. John was no longer Sig Amundson's boy, he was young Amundson, an influence to be reckoned with. Lareana, too, was making a place for herself in her adopted community. She became president of the local homemakers organizations, and her 4-H club was becoming famous for its award winners.

The baby coming fulfilled all their dreams. Johnny. She nuzzled his head, breathing in the sweet baby smell.

How quickly their plans had come crashing down around them. That raining April night. . .the patrolman saying John never knew what hit—

Lareana became slowly aware of the tears slipping down her cheeks, the collie at her feet, the grandfather clock ticking away in the hall, the babe fast asleep in her arms. "Ah, John," she murmured to the picture on the mantel, "everyone says I've handled all this so well. Then why am I so lonely at night? When will the tears be over?" She closed her eyes, her head resting on the back of the rocker.

Unbidden, the more recent memory of a tall stranger intruded into her thoughts. And the refrain from "Some Enchanted Evening" echoed faintly in her ear, whistled by a man who filled the doorway.

Chapter 2

The following morning Lareana did the customary feeding at the calf barn, carrying Johnny in a navy blue pack on her back. Hanging the nipple buckets in front of each bawling calf, she spread out grain for the heifers already weaned. His own tummy full, Johnny waved and chortled at the animals. When she took the buckets back to the milk barn to wash them out, she found a white-haired, slightly stooped giant running the milking machines. "Morning, Uncle Haakan. How was your dinner last night?"

"Inga, she liked it." The rhythm of his speech, along with arctic-blue eyes, echoed the land of his origins.

"And you *didn't?*" Lareana could not resist poking a bit of fun at the scarcity of his words.

"Umm-mm."

"Was that a yes or no?" She turned to pour disinfectant in the buckets, then scrubbed them briskly. After a good rinse, she tipped them over a rail above the deep galvanized wash sinks. "The hay haulers came last night. A new man. . .Trey somebody. . .came with Bud."

Uncle Haakan mumbled something under his breath, too low for Lareana to hear.

She looked up quizzically. "You've been down to the barn?"

He nodded again.

"Want me to wash up for you?"

He shook his head. "Inga will have breakfast soon. You go on up."

Apparently she wasn't going to learn anything much about the evening from her taciturn uncle. She should have known.

The morning sun was quickly dispelling the bite in the air as Lareana and her small passenger strode across the narrow field separating the two houses, the collie bounding at her side. An early frost had set the vine maple by the drive exploding with vivid scarlet, flame, and vermilion. Spiders, artisans of the night, had decorated the hog wire fencing, now bejeweled with dewdrops that refracted sunbeams like fine prisms.

She walked backward a few paces so she could see her mountain, etched white against the deepening blue of the sky.

"Oh, baby mine," she whispered to Johnny, "God's world certainly is grand this morning." She shifted the straps biting into her shoulders as she prepared to

378

climb the sty. Johnny squealed and kicked when she jumped down lightly, pausing to catch an extra lungful of the pure air. "Hey, we're gonna have to put you in a stroller if you get any heavier, young man!"

Aunt Inga's green thumb was evident in the profusion of fall asters and mums bordering the sidewalk and surrounding the double-wide mobile home when Lareana arrived at her uncle's home. Hanging baskets and planted pots of lush greenery turned the deck into a veritable greenhouse. Lareana pulled off one boot, then the other, at the bootjack and opened the sliding glass door. She was greeted by waffle and bacon perfume and the song of a canary who was trilling his heart out in the corner.

"My, the roses are certainly blooming in your cheeks." Inga, a snow-capped dumpling of a woman, reached to help Lareana remove the backpack. "And how's my little man?" She hugged the baby to her. "Um-m-m. Such a big boy now."

"Sure smells good in here." Lareana sniffed the mouth-watering aromas. "Uncle Haakan won't be up for a while yet. He wouldn't let me hose down for him." She turned on the water in the sink to wash her hands, then leaned back against the tile counter as she dried her hands with a towel.

Aunt Inga had taken Johnny on her lap. While removing his hat and jacket, she kissed each tiny palm and patted them together. The baby answered in jumbled sounds and stuck one finger in her mouth to be chewed on and growled over. His giggles became belly laughs, deep for a baby, and as catching as a yawn.

"Sure know where I rate around here these days," Lareana teased, lifting the lid of the cast-iron skillet to check the bacon.

"Here, you take him." Inga hugged Johnny once more, then handed him back to his mother. "I'll pour the batter in the waffle iron. There's water on the stove for tea if you'd like some."

Lareana strapped the child into the high chair that always stood ready by the maple table, then accepted a plate for herself when the delicacy was done to a golden turn.

"Aren't you having any?" Lareana asked around a mouthful of waffle drowned in homemade blackberry syrup. She speared another slice of bacon and leaned back on her chair to munch in comfort.

"I ate early. Besides, I'm still full from dinner last night."

"Good food, huh?"

"We went to that new Surf and Turf in Tacoma. I think Haakan would have been just as happy at the café in Yelm, but I enjoyed myself." Inga sat down at last and sipped her coffee. "My land, they have this flaming-up grill where you watch your dinner cooking and a lobster tank—you should see the size of some of those things—claws fit to—"

"You had lobster?" Lareana's voice rose to a squeak.

"No, no. We just *looked* at them." Inga patted her hand. "They're much too ugly to eat."

Lareana shook her head. "I suppose you had ground round or—"

Inga tried to look offended, but the twinkle in her eyes belied the effort. "Halibut. About the best piece of fish I've ever eaten, too. You know, I refuse to buy steak. Our own is better. Besides, we wouldn't waste the money on—"

"I know, I know, Aunt Inga." Lareana laughed, having heard all her aunt's arguments many times before, then changed the subject. "Was the service as good as they say it is?"

"Yes, but the prices—"

"I thought the motto of that place was 'Great food, great service, at roll-back-the-years prices.' " Lareana recalled the TV commercials advertising the new place.

"Humpf. They certainly didn't roll the years back very far. But then we didn't used to go out much, either. Haakan has always preferred to eat at home."

Lareana stirred from her comfortable chair with regret. "Speaking of which, I'd better get in gear. I have all kinds of chores waiting at home, and it looks like our young friend here is ready for a nap." Johnny yawned and fought to keep his eyes open, then jerked upright when the phone rang.

"Good morning. Three Trees," Inga answered, then turned to Lareana. "It's for you, that real estate fellow," she added in a stage whisper.

Lareana took the phone, her brow arched, and spoke into the receiver. "Good morning, Mr. Horton. I sure hope you have some good news for me today." She listened for a few moments, her face lighting with a mega-candle smile. "Just a sec." She covered the receiver with her hand. "Can you watch Johnny at about eleven? Mr. Horton says he has a buyer for that freeway parcel."

"Of course."

Lareana returned to the phone. "Yes, I can make it. I'll be at your office at eleven. Umm-hum. . . 'Bye now." She whirled in place as the phone clattered back in its cradle. "I'll be there with bells on!" She hugged her aunt impulsively, then herself. "Come on, fella, we gotta hustle!" She removed the tray from the high chair and scooped the baby out.

"Why don't you just leave him here with me now?" Aunt Inga asked. "That would give you some extra time."

"Sure you don't mind? I don't want to take advantage—"

Inga wrinkled her nose. "Oh, child. Having the two of you around is what keeps us young. You get going now."

She nestled the sleepy baby against her shoulder. "And I have plenty of your milk in the freezer for him. You won't need to hurry back."

Lareana kissed Inga's wrinkled cheek and then her baby's smooth one. "Thanks again."

By the time she'd pulled her boots back on, sprinted to the sty, and balanced on the top board, she could contain her exuberance no longer. "A buyer!" she shouted at the crow in the top of a fir tree. "Hear that? We've got a buyer!" Samson barked, not sure whom she was talking to. Lareana leaped as far as she could, arms waving, ponytail bouncing. She hit the ground at a run, the sable dog at her side. *Wonder who it is?* The question crossed her mind when she stopped to open the aluminum gate. She shrugged it aside. *Who cares? Just so he has tons of money.*

※

"This is as bad as going into the show ring," Lareana muttered to herself as she parked her decrepit Datsun in front of the real estate office. She'd dressed the part of a successful businesswoman—tailored navy wool suit with a pearl-pink blouse. The pearl studs in her ears had been a gift from John one Christmas.

With a quick glance in the rearview mirror, she tucked a strand of golden hair back in the loose knot she had fashioned atop her head. More lipstick. A dusting of powder over her nose. "You're stalling," she admonished the direct blue gaze in the mirror.

With a deep breath, she slung her navy leather bag over one shoulder and stepped from the car. *Lord,* she prayed silently, *if I'm not doing the right thing, You slam all the doors. . .hard. . .so I know for sure what You want.* She eyed the pink polish she'd applied to her rounded nails. *But let me get my fingers out of the way first, okay?* Her quick grin toward the fleecy clouds was a soft amen.

A gray-haired man looked up with a smile when she walked in the door of the real estate agency. "I'll be right with you," he said as he finished his telephone conversation, giving Lareana a moment to study the seascapes on the walls. One—a sailboat, with red, white, and blue striped sails full and running before the wind—caught her eye. Someday she would do that, she promised herself. Sailing like that must feel like taking a horse over a jump—free and lighter than air.

Mr. Horton, his telephone business finished, put a stop to her daydreaming.

"Mr. Bennett should be along any moment now. Can I get you a cup of coffee or something?"

Lareana shook her head. "He's already seen the property then?"

"Yes. We went out this morning."

"And. . .?"

"And, ah, here he is, right on time."

Lareana turned, following the direction of the Realtor's gaze. Strains of "Some Enchanted Evening" whispered in her mind as her eyes widened in surprise.

The three-piece gray suit definitely did more for Trey than plaid shirts and worn jeans, but either way, he made an impact.

"Lareana Amundson, I'd like you to meet George William Bennett the Third, owner of the Surf and Turf restaurant chain."

Lareana extended her hand, but the greeting was stuck in her throat somewhere along with her carefully cultivated poise.

Her hand disappeared in his, its warmth familiar.

"I'm glad to meet you, Mr. . . ."

"Trey will do just fine. How would *you* like a moniker like George William Bennett the Third?"

She shook her head, a spark of mischief peeking from beneath dense lashes. "Trey?"

"As in three, the third. Trey to all my friends."

"So which is the real you? The hay hauler from last night or—" She paused to stare pointedly from his shiny wing-tipped oxfords up to the perfectly creased pants, marking the maroon and navy striped tie and the way the tailored jacket hugged his broad shoulders, then bringing her gaze level with his— "or is it the Wall Street executive?"

"Both. Neither. I don't really haul hay anymore. But Bud needed a helper, and I wanted to see how that end of the business was progressing."

"So you spent three hours unloading alfalfa, about six more in the truck, and you're back here this morning. Don't you ever sleep?"

"Some. These old bones didn't want to get up this morning, let me tell you." He massaged the muscles in his upper arm. "That's one job that'll keep you in shape."

"I take it you two know each other?" Mr. Horton observed dryly.

"Yes." Trey shifted his attention back to the Realtor. "Did you know this lady makes the best apple crisp around?"

"Can't say I've had the privilege." Horton opened the half gate and indicated two chairs by his oak desk.

"Won't you be seated?"

Trey placed his hand in the small of Lareana's back and ushered her before him.

Feeling as if she were one step off in a precision-marching band, she allowed him to steer her to the plush wing chair. The farmhand last night had been easy and relaxed, as comfortable to be around as an old shoe. This man, the owner of Surf and Turf, was known all over the Pacific Northwest as an up-and-coming tycoon, no doubt a wealthy one. One part of her resented the fact that he'd taken advantage of her. Might even be laughing at her now. But she looked up to find warm blue eyes silently appraising her, and she realized that no ulterior motives were hidden there.

Trey watched the thought patterns crossing her face like clouds on a summer's day. He could tell she was fighting feelings of discomfort, confusion. *Come on, Lareana,* he begged silently. *I'm the same guy you met last night. Don't let the titles fool you. And money doesn't mean a thing. Be open like last night.*

He hadn't been able to get her out of his mind. The long truck ride last night had given him plenty of time to think, to dwell on each word and nuance.

She was a special woman. He wanted to know her better.

Lareana turned to the Realtor as he seated himself and shuffled the papers on his desk.

"As I said, Mr. Bennett has already seen the property, Lareana." He turned to Trey. "Why don't you tell her what you have in mind?"

When he'd left home this morning, Trey had planned to make an offer considerably below the asking price, but not now. He was almost certain Lareana Amundson needed the money badly, or she wouldn't be selling. The parcel of land was a legacy from her grandmother, Horton had told him.

The sight of one pink-tipped finger massaging the knuckles of the other hand clenched in her lap decided him. "I'd rather show you," he said. "Do you have time to drive out there? We can talk over lunch."

He had a habit of turning questions into statements, Lareana thought, recalling his words of the night before. Now she barely had time to wave at the man behind the desk before Trey was leading her out the door and handing her into a sleek, silver Corvette parked at the curb. The maroon interior enfolded her as he settled her into the deep leather seat and hooked her seat belt.

"Whew!" Lareana whispered to herself as he slammed her door and rounded the front of the long, sculptured hood. "A steam roller is subtle compared to this man!"

"Comfortable?" Trey fastened his own seat belt and glanced at her before turning the key.

"Yes." She slid one hand down over the edge of the seat, luxuriating in the smooth grain of the leather. She sniffed the aroma of fine car interior mingled with just a hint of aftershave, a citrus-woodsy blend. She closed her eyes for a moment, enjoying the sumptuous atmosphere. A tiny chuckle, a fair song, escaped before she could stop it.

Trey watched her. He seemed to be doing a lot of that when she was around. She was all woman—one had only to look at her to know that—but her charm lay in that childlike wonder, her unabashed enjoyment of everything around her. His hand itched to tuck an errant strand of spun gold back into its fashionable knot. Twenty-four hours ago, he hadn't even known her. Surely love at first sight was only for the movies or in books. Surely. He closed his eyes, cautioning himself. He would have to take it slow and easy with this one.

"Why don't you show me the fastest way?" The turn of the ignition key brought the engine roaring to life. "I'm hungry."

Lareana gave instructions with only half a mind. When they were finally on the freeway and heading south, she leaned her head back against the headrest. Both the powerful car and its owner, who seemed suited for just such a machine, made her feel pampered and petite. It was an unusual feeling. All her life, partly because of her height and solid bone structure, she had been considered capable, competent, a leader. Her forthright manner only added to the illusion she had created, an illusion that had become a reality with the passage of time.

She felt anything but capable today, however. Selling land she had owned only a short time but that had been in the family for years was not on her normal agenda. But then, since John's death, she had been doing all kinds of things she had never expected to do. Good thing she had the faith to believe that God knew what He was doing, even when she didn't. A funny little muffled sound escaped, hovered in the rich air, and before dissipating, reached the ears of the man behind the wheel.

"Why the sigh?"

"I don't know." She shrugged, then added, "Too many changes, I guess."

He wanted to reach out and take her hands in his, to still the fingers that were still worrying the knuckles on the other hand. All his long-buried protective instincts surfaced as he saw her struggle to hide the tension.

"Change can be a positive thing."

"True. But sometimes I feel caught in the eye of a hurricane. Things are out of my control, things I didn't plan for, didn't anticipate. Didn't even want."

"Like—"

"Like John's death, of course, for one thing. Like selling this property for another—"

"You're getting a good price for it."

"Am I?" Talking with him in the warm cocoon of leather, she felt as if she'd known him all her life. She watched him from beneath lowered lashes, trying to concentrate on the business at hand. Instead, here she was, baring her soul.

"But you see, I've never owned anything before. No, that's not strictly true. I owned my cows. But this is land. There's something—" she stopped to marshall her thoughts— "something about owning a piece of land that's permanent. You may be able to change the top layer, but it will always return to its natural state, if given the chance. Land is *real*."

"That's why I still have my ranch at George. Guess you and I are farmers at heart. The land is part of us." He shifted his gaze from the ribbon of concrete to smile at her, an intimate smile that drew them closer. "Lovers of land."

She nodded.

"I'm going to buy your property." He turned his attention back to the road.

"Just like that?"

"Just like that."

"No dickering? I thought you were supposed to make an offer, and I'd make a counteroffer. I'm all prepared."

"I've already left a down payment with Horton. We can close the deal by the end of the week."

The enormity of what he was saying hit her like a shower of sparklers and lit her eyes with miniature candles. He was going to buy the land! She gave a decidedly unprofessional bounce in her seat. Visions of new dairy stock, mortgage notices marked PAID, and badly needed repairs vied for first place in her head.

"Lareana?"

"Hmm?" She wrestled her thoughts back from the farm and focused her attention on the man beside her. Impulsively she laid one hand on his arm. "Thank you, Trey. You have no idea what this means to me."

He felt the warmth of her hand through his jacket sleeve and turned to smile into her glistening blue eyes. But his gaze strayed to her mouth, which was slightly atremble with the intensity of her feelings. The urge to stop the car and take her in his arms was overpowering, and he had to clench the wheel with both hands. *Slow down,* cautioned his brain. *Don't forget to take it slow. She has no idea how you feel.*

"You're welcome," he said. "Want to know what I plan to do with it?"

"Sure." Lareana realized she hadn't inquired into his plans at all. All her thoughts had been on herself and her needs. She was instantly contrite. "I don't suppose you want to farm it?"

"No." He took the exit to Tenino, turning the car into the service road at the property line after they crossed the freeway. He stopped, switched off the ignition, and leaned muscular forearms on the wheel, staring out at the flat ground covered with pine and tall fir trees. A rusty barbed wire fence sagged in some spots, was nonexistent in others. One of the ancient cedar fence posts leaned drunkenly on the wire for support. He turned to look at her. "Have you ever been to Knott's Berry Farm?"

"Yes." Lareana's puzzlement showed on her face. "Years ago. Why?"

"Because this—" he made a sweeping gesture— "is Timber Country."

"Those trees aren't big enough to log yet."

"No, no! Timber Country will be a theme park. All my life I've dreamed about a park like Disneyland or Knott's Berry Farm here in the Northwest. We'd have a log ride through a timber mill and lumber town, a lumberjack museum, skid rides behind mule teams, a family restaurant. All the other rides could imitate logging procedures—" He shoved open his door. "Here, let me show you."

Lareana blinked as he slammed his door and rounded the car. A theme park? What a dream. Here? "But it rains all the time," she said as he opened her door. "At least, it rains a lot of the time. How can you build something like that here?"

Before she could question further, he had tucked her arm in his and was leading her through the knee-high grass to the straggling fence.

"The restaurant would be over there." He pointed to an area dominated by ancient stumps with young trees growing from them. "We'd need a huge parking lot. The log ride would start right between those two giant firs. I'm going to keep as many of the original trees as possible."

"Trey!" Lareana laughed as his enthusiasm caught her like a whirlwind and lifted her off the ground. She tried seeing the site through his eyes, but rain clouds kept obscuring her vision. "But what are you going to do about the rain?"

"Rent umbrellas. Build covered walkways. I don't know, but I do know I can make this work." He hugged her to him with one arm around her shoulders. "One of my favorite writers, Dr. Robert Schuller, says, 'Dream big. God honors big dreams,' so that's what I'm doing. Can't you just see it?"

Once, as a teenager, Lareana had been to Knott's Berry Farm. There hadn't been many sightseers, so she and a friend had ridden the log ride again and again. She could still feel the thrill of the last steep swoop and the swoosh as they hit the water's surface. "You'd build all kinds of logging scenes for the log ride?"

"It could be an historical ride from early days to modern methods. I don't know. I have to think about that. But there has to be a place where the loggers blow a logjam apart. I've been recruiting people from Disney and Six Flags. I've told them my dreams, and they're drawing tentative plans. We meet again next month."

"Next month? But you don't even have the land yet."

"I know."

"You're crazy."

"Yup. Certified. . .certifiable. . .which is it?"

"I don't know." Lareana felt bubbles of laughter welling up within her. "I don't care!" She paused, her gaze roving over the property. "Timber Country."

She chewed on her lip, thinking hard. "Have you ever ridden on a Percheron?"

The question took him by surprise. "No, why?"

"I've always wanted to ride elephants, but here you could sell bareback rides on Percheron horses—the bigger the better. And Smokey the Bear could walk around greeting the kids and, and—" Her gestures grew wider. "Are you going to have Paul Bunyan and Babe the Blue Ox and—?" Her words tumbled over each other.

"In the rain?" He turned, smiling down at her. Her face was flushed with the bloom of excitement.

"So sew monstrous ponchos!" She flung her arms wide to encompass them all.

Trey threw back his head, his deep laughter rolling over the rocks and Scotch Broom. He grabbed her with both arms, his hug lifting her feet from the ground.

Without another thought, he bent his head and planted a laughing kiss on the softness of her uptilted lips.

Chapter 3

In the exuberance of the moment, the kiss didn't register in Lareana's mind even when Trey set her back on the ground. They stood, arm in arm, and surveyed the land, both dreaming the dreams of what could be.

"Can't you just see it?" he asked. "I've been imagining it for so long, it's like the finished product in my mind. I can hear kids shouting and bands playing, chain saws roaring and even a rooster crowing."

"A rooster crowing?" Lareana turned to him with question marks in her eyes.

"Sure. There'll be a petting zoo, Ole's Barn. They had to have milk and eggs and stuff at the logging camps. Besides, a rooster is nature's alarm clock and—"

"And—?"

He grinned at her like a little boy with his hand in the cookie jar. "I just like chickens, banties especially. I'll have families of them running all over the park. You know, males of every species could take parenting lessons from banty roosters. They—"

"A chicken man!" Lareana shook her head, trying to keep from bursting into gales of laughter. "And banties at that! Somehow I never pictured—" She covered her mouth with one hand.

Trey assumed an air of injured dignity. "You can be assured, madam, that I will not buy you chicken for lunch." He offered his arm with a bow. "Shall we go?"

At the solemn look on his face, Lareana lost her composure. Peals of laughter broke forth, startling a blue jay watching them from the safety of a nearby alder. She tried to stop, but one look at Trey as he saluted the scolding jay caused her to hang onto his arm and bury her face in the gray wool of his suit.

Trey kept his own response under tight control, but his eyes delighted in her joy. When she raised her face, the urge to wipe her tears away with his fingers swept over him. Instead, he pulled out a snowy handkerchief.

"In the books, the hero dries the suffering maiden's eyes." He tipped up her chin with one hand and carefully blotted the moisture from her sparkling eyes. "I have a feeling this is a portent of things to come."

"Meaning—?" Lareana swallowed another giggle. She clamped her lips together, but her eyes refused to give in.

"Meaning our friendship. . .we're *both* crazy."

"Thanks a lot. Just because we're a cowgirl and a banty boy!" She placed her hand dramatically over her heart.

Trey drew himself up to his full six feet, three inches. "Banty boy? I resent that, ma'am. You're calling *me* little?"

"No, no. I meant banty. . .as in chicken."

"So. . .I'm a *chicken*."

Lareana shook her head, chuckles still escaping like feathers after a pillow fight. "I give up." She raised her hands in mock surrender.

Trey tucked her hand back in the crook of his elbow. "Let's go eat."

Once she had won the battle of the seat belt and the car was roaring its way back up the freeway, Lareana let her mind float back to the scene at the property. It felt good to laugh again, to share a joke with a man, an attractive man at that. She touched her fingertips to her lips. Such a simple gesture—a kiss. So long since her lips had been warmed by another's.

She shifted her gaze to the man beside her. Relaxed as he was, the power in his muscular body was only leashed, not tamed. His hands, bronzed from hours in the sun, held the wheel with an easy touch. His only jewelry was a square-cut black diamond on his right hand. Scattered hairs escaping immaculate shirt cuffs caught the sunlight and glinted fire.

She studied his face, a friendly face but with a square jawline that spoke of bulldog tenacity. His nose would be classic except for the slight bump, maybe a memento of childhood scuffles. The sight of sculpted lips reminded her of shared tenderness—lips turned up in laughter, lips touching hers—

With a breath that filled her lungs and further relaxed her shoulders, she leaned her head back against the plush seat and allowed her eyelashes to drift shut. Everything felt so good—the car, the man beside her, the sale of the property, the money to expand Three Trees. . . But what about the price? They'd never really discussed it. How did one gracefully bring up a subject like that? Her eyes flew open as her mind toyed with the options, and the musings sent shadows flitting across her forehead.

"Tell me about yourself." Trey broke into her concentration. "Start way back."

Lareana thought for a moment. *What could a man like Trey want to know about me?* "I've always lived on a farm, loved my freedom, my cows, a horse. Oh, and my family, of course."

"Where did you go to school?"

"Well, I grew up over by Puyallup—"

"I meant college."

"I started out to get a home ec degree at WSU, but when I realized how much I liked specialty cooking, I transferred to Willamette Institute's chefs' school in Portland."

388

"I've hired several people right out of that school. It's good. Did you go to work somewhere then?"

"Three Trees. John and I were married right after school. I practiced on him. But if I could be a chef in a really good restaurant and never leave my farm, I'd be perfectly happy. The two don't seem to fit, though."

"If the dinner last night was any indication—"

"That was nothing. I just threw some beans in the Crock-Pot and whipped up an apple crisp. I use a lot of apple recipes since we have so many fruit trees. Entered one in a contest one time."

"And you won first prize?"

"Nope. Honorable mention." She turned to face him. "I'll have to make it for you sometime."

"I'd like that. Did you come up with that recipe?"

She nodded. "I experiment sometimes, and I really like collecting old recipes. Some of them I adapt, others I keep in a file. Someday I'll put together a cookbook. They tell you a lot about the life and the people way back when."

"Have you ever cooked for crowds?" The seed of an idea sprouted in the back recesses of his mind.

"Just hot dishes and stuff for potlucks. That's always a good place to try something new. You get immediate feedback. If they don't like it, you take a full pan home. Why?"

"Oh, just a thought. How does lunch at the Falls sound?"

"Great." She tightened her lips, but the grin refused to be hidden. "Are you sure there's something besides chicken on the menu?"

A few minutes later they were seated at a window table overlooking the narrow Tumwater River. The water cascaded over stair-step falls, swirled between boulders, and paused in shallow pools before rushing to meet the southernmost tip of Puget Sound. In the country park off to the side, two children played on the swings while their mothers visited at one of the picnic tables.

A man, hands clasped around bent knees, sat on one of the flat rocks jutting over the spilling waterfall. Off to the left, the Olympia Brewery towered above the hillside.

Lareana's feelings of contentment grew until they flooded her inner being.

"Welcome back," Trey said softly when she finally turned to him.

"It's beautiful, isn't it?" A tiny smile played at the corners of her mouth. "Watching water in motion always has a soothing effect on me. I love the music of rivers and creeks, the rhythm of the ocean. There's a creek back of our woods where John and I used to go for picnics or just to sit and relax."

"I'd like to see it someday." Trey recognized in himself a growing need to bring her peace and contentment, to see that tiny smile flirt with the corners of her mouth, to share more moments like these with her.

She smiled dreamily. "It seems you've pulled the stop on all my secrets. Now it's your turn."

"First, what have you decided to eat? Our waiter is coming."

Quickly she scanned the menu in front of her. "I think the shrimp-stuffed sole with spinach salad. Iced tea to drink."

"What about chicken cordon bleu—" A passerby would never have recognized the dig from the serious look in his eyes. Only a tiny muscle twitching in his cheek betrayed his mirth.

Lareana wrinkled her nose at him but refused to rise to the bait.

As he gave the order to the waiter, her attention wandered back to the scene in the park below. A man had joined one of the women and her child. Then with the tot between them, stretching up to hang onto his parents' hands, the family ambled away toward the parking lot.

A swift stab of sorrow pierced Lareana's mood. She and John would never swing little Johnny between them, would never tumble him through the leaves or teach him to pump a swing high to the heavens. She chewed on her lower lip, fighting to keep the tears from sneaking around the lump in her throat.

You will not cry, she ordered herself sternly. She swallowed hard and blinked to banish the threatened overflow.

Trey watched her silently, immediately aware of her distress and the cause of it. All he'd had to do was follow her gaze to the little family walking across the parking lot.

If only I could say the magic words for her, he thought, *I'd make it all go away*.

"A wise man once said," he began softly, reaching one hand across the table to cover hers, "that a burden shared is halved and a joy shared is doubled. Earlier we doubled our joy. Now. . .let me walk through this with you, too. Tell me how you feel."

Lareana turned her hand, clutching his strong, warm fingers. "It still hurts," she whispered. "When I saw that family down there. . .I know better. . .but that could have been John and Johnny and me in a couple of years. Sometimes I get so jealous I want to scream. I want to shake people and tell them not to take what they have for granted." The tears turned her eyes to pools like those in the river below, shimmering in the sunlight on the surface, but hiding secrets in their depths. Her fingernails bit into the palm of his hand.

"I'm afraid taking things for granted is normal for most people."

"I know. And now I think it's one of our worst offenses." A tear lurked at the edge of her lashes, in spite of her control. "I have to remind myself that God knows what He's doing, because I sure don't."

"Do you blame God for John's death?"

She pondered for a moment. "No. . .it's not that. God didn't make that man drink himself senseless and then drive a car. Bad things happen in this world. But I always thought they happened to *other* people."

"To someone you don't know," he prompted.

"Yes, that's part of it. I guess I *did* blame God at first." She stared down at the salad plate that had appeared before her, then lifted her eyes to his. "Sometimes I even blamed John for leaving us. Isn't that silly?"

It was all Trey could do to remain in his seat. All of his instincts were to take her in his arms and try to absorb some of her pain, to shield her from the past. He'd never felt this way before.

"No, not silly. Just part of the grieving process." His thumb gently stroked the side of her hand. *I know how you feel, gallant lady,* he thought. *One loses, on either end of marriage.*

Lareana took a deep breath. Calm returned to her face, chasing away the tension, covering her sadness. She lifted her chin a fraction, a gesture Trey was discovering meant "I can handle it myself now."

"Thank you." She squeezed his fingers lightly, then released them. Picking up her napkin, she placed it in her lap and folded her hands over it. Obviously the time of sharing was over.

Trey watched her compose herself. He saw only golden threads swirled into the knot on top of her head as she bent to give silent thanks for the food. With her the gesture was completely natural, part of her being. Trey found himself thanking God more for the woman across the table from him than for the food.

They continued to eat in silence, but it was the silence of two people who have shared something important and are secure with each other and with themselves.

❧

Half an hour later, when they were back in the car, Lareana leaned against the seat. "Thank you for both the lunch and the shoulder."

"You're welcome, and while it may sound trite, please know the shoulder is available at any time." Trey crossed his arms on the steering wheel. "My father died years ago. While I hurt a lot, I remember my mother crying for what seemed like forever to my young mind. I had thought that men aren't supposed to cry, but one night she heard me sobbing into my pillow. She held me and I held her, and those tears—the ones we cried together—seemed to make things better from then on."

When he turned to look at her, Lareana felt her heart tug at the sight of moisture filling his eyes. She reached out her hand and laid it over his. This time it was his turn to accept a gesture of comfort.

Guiding the Corvette back toward the freeway, Trey said, "I've got an idea, and while I keep trying to push it to the back of my mind, it refuses to leave.

Want to hear it?"

"Of course." He had definitely pricked her interest.

"Would you bake up some of your apple recipes and maybe some of the old ones you've collected?"

"Sure. When?"

He consulted his pocket calendar. "How about a week from Saturday?"

"Why?"

"I'd like to sample them."

Lareana thought for a moment. "Then why don't you come early and stay for dinner, around six?"

"It's a date." He eased his car into a parking place by the real estate office. "Lareana, I paid the asking price for your place. Sign the papers as soon as Horton has them ready, and the check will be waiting."

"I can't begin to thank you—" She stared at him, wanting to say more, but unsure of how to express the churning emotions. She just knew she was glad she would see him again.

❧

Lareana flung open the door of her aunt and uncle's home. "The property sold. . .for full price! Can you imagine that?" She greeted her aunt with a mighty hug. "Now we can buy some cows and fix up a bunch of stuff around here."

"Slow down, child." Inga patted her niece's arm.

"How was Johnny? Did he behave himself?"

Inga looked at her as though she'd misplaced a marble or two. "Our Johnny?"

"Of course. He isn't always the angel you insist he is." Lareana grinned. "He's been know to pitch a fit once or twice." They both turned as tentative gurgles signaled the baby's awakening. *Cinderella's back to normal*, Lareana thought as she went to pick him up.

❧

The following Monday a tube-shaped package arrived in the mail. When Lareana opened it and unrolled the poster, she burst into laughter. A golden banty rooster, feathers cloaking his legs, clutched the top rail of a weather-beaten fence. His flapping wings lent strength to his morning pronouncement. Lettered across the top of the picture were the words: "This is the day." The familiar verse concluded at the bottom: "which the Lord has made."

"I couldn't resist," read the masculine scrawl on the back, with the signature, "George William Bennett the Third."

Lareana taped the poster to the door of one of the kitchen cabinets. Every time she looked at it, she could hear the crow of a rooster, accompanied by the sound of laughter.

On Thursday a station wagon with a large red plastic bow adorning its roof drew up into the yard. When Samson refused to stop barking, Lareana had to go outside to quiet him. The courier got out, went to the rear of the car, and let down the tailgate. She grasped a knot of strings and began the tug of war to extricate a bobbing bunch of helium-filled balloons. One at a time, they bumped and straightened, hearts and squares and circles, a rainbow of colors cavorting in the sun.

Samson barked in a frenzy of warning as the courier handed the strings to Lareana. Hanging onto the balloons, trying to shush the dog, and somehow thanking the delivery woman between her own howls of merriment gave Lareana no time to read the card. She didn't have to. But later she read the inscription attached to one of the balloons: "Saturday at 3. Trey."

Maneuvering the unorthodox bouquet into the door of the house posed another problem. Lareana finally tied them to the stair post—all but the one she fastened to Johnny's swing. The baby's eyes grew nearly as big as the balloon.

"As he said," she told the staring baby, "he's crazy." She shook her head at the riot of color, and at one balloon that had broken free and was bumping the ceiling. "And who cares?"

❧

By noon on Saturday she was ready. Sourdough biscuits were rising on the counter. Homemade blackberry jam, apple butter, and honey from the Three Trees' hives filled the three crystal jars on the lazy Susan. Beef stew simmered on the back burner of the stove, the vegetables, carrots, and potatoes from her garden waiting their turn. She had thought about fixing chicken and dumplings, but she couldn't bring herself to do it.

Blackberry cobbler would be ready for the oven when they sat down to eat, and her specialty, apple pizza, steamed on the rack, spicing the air with tart apple and pungent nutmeg.

As she sat curled in her chair with a cup of herb tea, Lareana rubbed Samson's back with one slippered foot, enjoying a rare moment of leisure.

When she had picked up Trey's check the day before, the sight of so much money had nearly unnerved her. What would it have looked like in cash? She smiled, imagining a stack of bills. The way things went around here, one of the cows would get out and start munching the stack away. The ridiculous picture brought a chuckle.

On the dot of three, Samson barked at the door. A car had driven into the yard. Lareana let the dog out.

"That's okay, Samson, " she called as the tall, broad-shouldered man stepped from his car. "He's a friend."

The dog's plumed tail wagged in welcome, escorting the visitor into the yard.

Lareana waited on the porch, enjoying the scenery—man and dog. A navy pullover sweater hugged Trey's broad shoulders, his light blue shirt collar visible under the crew neck. Jeans rippled over his legs as he strode up the walk, but the smile stretching the corners of his mouth and lighting his eyes arrested her full attention.

In like manner, Trey relished the picture she made, framed by the porch posts. Her dusky rose sweater and matching slacks set her cheeks aglow and hinted at the pleasing curves underneath. Trey forced himself to greet her casually. He couldn't sweep her up in the embrace he imagined, not this time.

"Thank you for my house decorations," she said as he came up the walk.

"You're welcome." He stopped abruptly. "What smells so good?" His nose wrinkled in appreciation. He sniffed again, one foot on the bottom step. "Woman, how can you look so relaxed when my nose tells me you've been cooking your romantic heart out?"

"You asked me to use some of my recipes. I aim to please!"

He took her arm. "Let's see what you've been up to."

Johnny stopped his jabbering when he saw the tall man enter the door. Lareana stooped down to pluck the baby from the swing seat. As she rose with him in her arms, she made the introductions. "Trey, I'd like you to meet Johnny."

The baby stared at the man, glanced back at his mother, then waved a chubby fist, his toothless grin announcing his approval. He kicked his feet and twined his other hand in his mother's hair, all the while jabbering and drooling, his two latest accomplishments.

"I think I passed," Trey said softly.

"With flying colors." Lareana winced and reached to free her hair from the baby's fingers. When his attention switched to her gold chain and heirloom cross instead, it was easy. "Sorry, young man," she said as she put him back into the swing. She picked up an assortment of toys from the floor and dropped them in the tray. Johnny beamed up at her, then attacked them with both hands.

As Trey watched, envy and desire and pleasure chased each other through the corridors of his mind. The picture surrounding him was all he'd dreamed of, his goal for a lifetime—a loving woman, a beautiful, healthy son, fragrances of cooking that spoke of caring, time to grow together. A prayer passed unbidden from his subconscious. *Somehow, God, make this mine. Please don't give me a glimpse of perfection and take it away.*

"Would you like to see what I've made?" The sound of her voice drew him back. "Or would you rather wait until dinner? I thought if you got here in time, we could go for a walk. I'd like to show you my farm."

Trey nodded. "I'd like that. What about Youngstuff here?"

"We'll just put him in his backpack. I'll even let you carry it."

Trey was amazed at the speed with which they were loaded and out of the house. It was obvious Lareana had done this many times. He paused on the step, adjusting the straps. Mount Rainier beckoned in the east. Down at the barn, some of the red and white Ayrshire cows had started to line up for milking. Samson took his place as escort, every once in a while sniffing the hand of the man allowed to carry the dog's precious charge.

Lareana pointed out the sights as they ambled down past the barns and into the old orchard. An ancient log cabin was slowly sinking into oblivion in the shade of a huge walnut tree.

"That's a shame," Trey commented, pointing to the rotting frame.

"It was too far gone when we moved here. I would love to restore it, but that takes big bucks. The fruit trees are responding, however." She nodded at the trees branching above them. "It's taken lots of pruning and spraying. At first I thought we'd killed them, John cut them back so far. This year we got a good crop, especially the Gravensteins. Nearly every morning I can look out my kitchen window and see deer grazing here and farther down in the pasture. Once we even saw a bear."

The pastoral scene suited her, Trey thought, as he watched Lareana. The breeze had tugged strands of hair loose from the leather slide she wore and teased her face with the tips. Her sky-blue windbreaker matched her eyes and brought out the translucence of the skin over her cheekbones. His fingers itched to tuck back an especially determined sweep of gold.

"Lareana, do you want to hear about my idea?"

"Of course, but you make it sound so solemn."

"That's because it's really important to me." He shifted the straps as Johnny bounced in his carrier. Trey correctly interpreted her questioning look. "No, he's not bothering me. I need someone to develop a menu and specialty dishes for my restaurant at Timber Country. I thought of you." He raised his hand. "Now, hear me out before you say anything. I think I've covered all the bases."

Lareana nodded, locking her hands behind her as they strolled back up the hay road.

"I want a distinctive flavor, as we've discussed. You already have a good glimpse of my dream, you collect the kind of recipes I want, and you're trained to cook for a commercial establishment. In addition, you said your dream—"

She nodded again. "I remember."

"You wouldn't have to leave the farm, especially in the early stages. You could do all the experimenting and researching from your kitchen. Then when we decorated, you could have a hand in that, too. What do you think?"

"You mean I can talk now?" Her grin erased the sting in her words.

"Only if you'll say yes."

They had reached the gate to the yard. Lareana swung it open but turned to gaze at the mountain before she entered. "One thing I want you to know. . .I never make a major decision—and you must admit this would be major—without praying about it first. My inner reaction is, 'Yes! Yes! Capital yes.' But I have to consider what's best for Johnny, too."

"I thought of that. That's why I pointed out that so much of it can be done right here. I believe it will give an even stronger sense of the early days since you would be operating out of your own kitchen." He paused when her grin widened. "How am I doing?"

Lareana didn't answer right away but turned and led the way into the house. "Would you like a piece of apple pizza to hold you over until dinner?" She lifted Johnny from the backpack and set him in the high chair.

"Apple pizza?"

She chuckled at the tone of his voice and offered a bribe. "I'll even warm it in the microwave for you. But come look before you make judgments you might regret later."

The pastry filled a pizza pan, but there all resemblance ended. Spirals of apple slices filled the thin piecrust. Crunchy topping finished it off, making Trey's mouth water.

"I think I love apple pizza!"

She sliced a wedge-shaped piece, slipped a paper plate under it, and set the microwave for thirty seconds. It was worth the short wait. After one bite, the only sounds Trey made closely emulated the gustatory satisfaction of a third-grader.

"I thought apple pizza might become a hallmark of your Timber Country. You know, with stands all around the park: 'Get your apple pizza here.' Like other parks have done with snow cones." She waited for his reaction.

Trey licked the pad of each finger with careful deliberation, then located a drip of topping in his palm. Finally his tongue cleaned each smidgen of flavor from his lips.

"You could always have another piece." Lareana nodded toward the pan, her voice breaking as she swallowed her delight. "I won't even charge you."

"Where did you come up with an idea like that?"

"I take it you like the product?"

"*Like* is an understatement. You, my dear young lady, have been hiding your talents under a bushel. . .of apples!" He settled back against the counter. "How much would you suggest we charge for each slice?"

"Well—" A hint of a frown creased her forehead as she pondered. "I'd thought maybe seventy-five cents, but I'm sure it could go for even more than that. I'd cut the pieces generously."

"Of course."

She glanced up to catch a ghost of a smile lurking in his eyes. "Are you serious about this or just leading me on?"

"I'm serious! I'm serious!" He held up his hand like a traffic cop halting oncoming cars. "It's just that I can't imagine your doing anything ungenerously."

"I think that's a compliment."

"I think you're right."

"Then. . .thank you."

"You're welcome."

He's so good for me, Lareana thought as she cut him another piece of the pizza. *I haven't laughed this much since. . .since I'm not sure when. He was right when he said we're both crazy. And I love it!*

The dinner hour came and went as Trey raved about all the different items Lareana had prepared. The sourdough biscuits were a keeper, Trey commented, the kind of item that could be unique. And the blackberry jam and cobbler. Well!

"I have no doubt," he said as they finished clearing the table, "that you could put together a prize-winning menu." He stopped her with a hand on her arm. "Lareana, please. Really think about my proposal. List all the questions you come up with and we'll discuss them. I know you caught part of my dream—"

The pull to answer yes right then was almost overwhelming. It would be a real challenge, one that she'd have to work into an already crowded schedule. She had enough to do on the farm. But. . .maybe. . .by hiring more help. . .and winter was slow anyway. . . . Working with Trey would be fun, too, and designing a restaurant was something she'd always dreamed of. In fact, his dream dovetailed with her own. But she had said she would pray about it, and she would. That was the bottom line. *Wouldn't it be nice if all this turned out to be God's will in action?* a small voice whispered from somewhere deep down inside.

"Thank you for your vote of confidence." She smiled up at him. "Let's go dream in the other room where it's more comfortable."

Johnny immediately nuzzled against her when she picked him up on her way into the living room. "Hungry, hmm?" She turned the tape deck on, picked up the baby's blanket draped over the back of her rocker, and settled herself down. As she leaned back, one foot automatically reached to twirl the stove handle, and strains from *South Pacific* filled the room.

"Have a chair." She pointed to the other rocker in front of the wood stove. She snuggled the baby down in her arms and covered him and her shoulder with the patchwork blanket.

Samson left his spot at Lareana's feet and padded over to lay his muzzle on Trey's knee. Trey obliged, stroking the sleek head. The dog sat at his side, requesting, never demanding, attention. A brass floor lamp with a Tiffany shade in rusts and yellows occupied the space between the chairs. An oak magazine rack flanked the more masculine chair, while a basket with yarns and crochet hooks sat beside her own.

I've come home, Trey thought. *I belong here. John, thank you for this gift. I promise to take good care of them. They won't want for anything, I assure you. We have so much love to share.*

Trey turned his attention back to the woman across from him. Lamplight and firelight vied for the privilege of bathing in her glow.

Feeling his gaze, Lareana looked up from her contemplation of the infant in her arms. It seemed so right. The man in the chair across from her, one hand stroking the dog. *He cares for us!* She felt a small shock. She had never thought about another man coming into her life. John was the only man she had ever wanted.

Wasn't this too soon? John hadn't really been gone that long. Or did feelings take time into account? *God, You must have brought Trey into my life for a reason. Guess I'll just have to wait and see.*

She felt a smile leave her heart, lift the corners of her mouth, and wing across the warm air, asking admittance to the heart of the man. Nothing was said. Everything was understood.

Chapter 4

The following morning Lareana had a hard time concentrating on her chores. Her mind kept dancing back to the evening before. She and Trey had put the baby to bed, then sat in front of the fire sharing all the important events of their lives. They had so many mutual interests—Rodgers and Hammerstein musicals, frosty nights, the smell of new-mown hay, riding a good horse through the early morning dew. And both of them loved the mountains.

She knew now how he could relate to her sorrow. His pain had been caused by losing a woman who decided she hated both him and his farms.

"We got engaged right out of high school," Trey had said. "We were starry-eyed and sure we had the world by the big toe. But I was determined to make that farm a paying operation before we married. The longer we waited, the more Jane decided she couldn't stand living 'out in the desert,' as she called it. And since I didn't feel I could live anywhere else—besides the fact that our livelihood would come from those hayfields she hated—she left."

Lareana watched as the memories flitted across his face. "Did you try to persuade her to come back?"

"She refused to talk with me. Why, I didn't even know where she was for a while." Trey clenched his fist on the arm of the rocker.

"That must have been hard."

"Mostly on my pride." Silence reigned, but for the hum of the blower on the stove.

Lareana tapped the floor with her toe as the rocker moved gently.

"The funny thing is," Trey continued, his eyes staring into space, "it was not long after that I entered the restaurant business. Now I have a condominium in Seattle. I don't spend all my time there, but I can't stay at the farm in George all the time, either. As far as I can tell, I have the best of both worlds."

"And it doesn't hurt anymore?" Lareana leaned her head against the back of the rocker, watching carefully for any signs of pain on his face.

"No. I've come to realize how different we were. I don't think—" He leaned forward, hands clasped on his knees. "Have you ever known someone who just couldn't seem to be happy? As if nothing was ever good enough or large enough or shiny enough?"

Lareana nodded.

Trey shrugged. "Now all I feel is sorry. . .for her, for people like her. I like making people happy, Lareana. That's one of the joys for me with Surf and Turf. People come to my restaurants and get away from the things that bother them. Just for a little while, they're happy. Timber Country will do the same thing."

Lareana watch the glow from the fire play games with the shadows across his face. *This is a man,* she thought, *who dreams big. He doesn't just stop with wishing. He goes after what he wants.* Yes, Trey would make his dreams become a reality.

"You've made *me* happy," she whispered across the space between them. And it occurred to her that she wanted to make him happy, too.

❧

Lareana finished feeding the calves and didn't remember a bit of it. A soft glow suffused her face, lending extra color to her cheekbones. She caught an amused smile from Uncle Haakan and wondered what she had done.

As she neared the house, Lareana's step slowed. With a shrug, she adjusted the backpack. Johnny had fallen asleep, and his dead weight caused the straps to bite into her shoulders. Turning at the gate, she glanced toward the mountain, but low clouds shrouded the peak.

"Father," she continued the prayer that had been on her mind all night and all morning, "what is it You want me to do? Is this job with Trey in Your will for us? It seems so to me. It came out of the blue, something I wanted but hadn't slaved and planned for. Sometimes I wish You would speak through a bush again—" she eyed the rhododendrons lining the fence—"or on the wind. . . Somehow, I have to know exactly what You want." She waited as if hoping for a sign. The breeze stirred the tall firs behind her and lifted the tendrils of hair, fanning her face, but there were no words she could understand.

A sigh seemed to start in her toes and work its way up. Johnny stirred, a tiny whimper reminding her she had other things to take care of. Samson nudged her hand with a cold, wet nose. The scent of wood smoke drifted down from the chimney on the tall white house, calling her back to what she had in the here and now. A second sigh, this time lighter and only from her diaphragm, turned into a whisper. "Patience has never been one of my virtues, has it? Thank You, Father, that Your plan is already in motion. Just clue me in when I need to know, all right?"

The breeze chuckled through the trees overhead.

Prayers for knowledge of the Father's will floated on both her conscious and subconscious mind for the next couple of days. During her devotional time, Lareana searched the scriptures for some indication of what direction she should go.

When she allowed her mind free reign, she could picture the restaurant, taste the delicious items on the menu, and hear the customers laughing and having a good time.

Trey's words came back to her: *I want to help people be happy, even if only for a little while.* It seemed as good a reason as any for a business.

Finally, one morning she called her mother. After the customary greetings and questions about the baby, a silence fell. Lareana cleared her throat. "Mom, how can I know what God wants me to do in a given situation?"

"What's wrong, dear?" Her mother's warm tones quieted the pounding of her daughter's heart. Lareana had heard that exact question many times in her life. But this time she hadn't told her folks about Trey's offer. She had told them about selling the property and about the buyer, but—

Lareana took a deep breath. "I've been offered a job designing a menu for a brand-new restaurant and helping set it all up. The owner—"

"Who?"

"Who what?"

"Who's the person who offered you this job?" Margaret Swenson's voice was quietly insistent.

"The same man who bought the freeway property. Remember, I told you he wants to build a theme park there—Timber Country. It will have a family restaurant." The words spilled out in her enthusiasm. She finally wound down, "And I can do most of the preliminary work right here, so I wouldn't have to leave Johnny or the farm."

She waited, knowing her mother was praying at this very moment. Lareana had learned from her mother long ago that there was no need to rush.

"Oh, babe." The childhood endearment came softly over the wire. "You have so much to do now. How can you think of taking on one more thing?"

"But, Mom, this is what I went to school for, a dream I've had for years. You know that."

"Yes. I know."

"But that's not the real question," Lareana persisted. "How can I tell this time what God wants me to do? Besides, with the extra money from the sale, we can hire some more help around here." She stuck the last in as an afterthought.

A chuckle warmed her ear. "Remember what Pastor Benson said that time? 'God can only guide you when you're moving.' Maybe this is one of those times when you'll have to step out and pray He will close the doors if you're going the wrong way."

"But I don't want to make a mistake."

"No. But then we learn by our mistakes, too."

"Hurts more that way."

"Yes."

"Are you saying I should try it then?"

"Have you made a list of all the arguments for and against?"

"Yes. There's a lot to be said on both sides." Lareana mentally reviewed the lists she had compiled the night before. "They seem to balance each other out."

"Then the question here is what's best?"

Lareana's smile lent love to her reply. "Mom, that was the question in the first place."

"Well, if it doesn't violate anything in Scripture, if you've prayed to be in God's will, I guess—"

"The answer is. . .step out."

"Right. But be prepared to change course if God closes a door."

"And get my fingers out of the way—quick!" Lareana could picture her mother's warm smile as the familiar chuckle again reached her ear. "Thanks, Mom. I love you."

"Bless you, babe. Keep us posted."

Lareana hung up the receiver. Now to get in touch with Trey. His instructions came back to her. "Call my secretary. She always knows where I am." He had stuck his business card on the corkboard by the phone. Lareana stared at the embossed gray card for a moment, indecision skittering through her mind like maple leaves before an autumn wind.

Johnny called her from the bedroom, his awakening voice changing from a gentle query to a specific demand.

Lareana welcomed the interruption. "Coming, son." She went into the bedroom and picked up the squirming baby. "Good grief, you're soaked!" She held him away from her shoulder until she could lay him on the changing table. The aroma of baby powder soon filled the air, along with his contented coos.

Lareana settled Johnny on his tummy in the middle of a large quilt on the floor before she reached for the phone again. This time nothing stopped her as she dialed the Seattle number.

"Surf and Turf Enterprises," a professional-sounding voice answered.

"May I speak to Mr. Bennett?" Lareana asked, her fingers clenching the receiver.

"Who may I say is calling?"

"This is Lareana Amundson."

The voice immediately warmed. "I'm sorry, Mrs. Amundson, but Trey isn't here right now. He'll be calling in any time. But he said to give any message from you first priority."

"Thank you. Tell him I'm at home." Lareana hung up the phone with a twinge of disappointment. Was this some kind of answer to her prayers? Was she not supposed to take this job after all? Maybe Trey had changed his mind and didn't really want her for the position. The doubts grew with every passing moment.

"Stop it," she commanded her runaway feelings. "You're making Mount Rainiers out of molehills."

❧

It was evening before Trey returned her call. Just the sound of his voice in her ear brought her worries back to sea level. "I'm glad you called."

Trey cradled the phone against his shoulder and spun his chair so he could look out over Puget Sound from his tenth-floor office.

Seattle had donned her evening finery, including the diamond necklaces circling the blackness of the Sound. A ferry on its hourly traverse between Bremerton and Seattle sparkled like a brilliant emerald-cut jewel against the velvety darkness. Trey rubbed a tired hand over his eyes as he listened to Lareana's soft voice in his ear. The tiredness vanished in an instant.

"You accept? You mean you'll really do it?" His voice rose with excitement. "Oh, Lareana, this is fantastic. What a team we'll make!"

He listened a moment, a grin creasing deep valleys in the tanned skin of his cheeks. "No, I don't presume to play God, but I really felt this was meant to be. Thank you." He glanced at his calendar. "How about if I take you out to dinner tomorrow night? We can talk over the arrangements, salary, that kind of thing."

"Why don't you come here instead?" Lareana pushed her bangs to the side as she cradled the phone on her shoulder. "I could fix a picnic lunch, and we could ride out to the back forty by the creek." She felt a momentary twinge. A swimming hole had been one of her and John's favorite spots. Did she really want to share it with a new man? She took a deep breath. "Bring your swimsuit if it's a hot day."

"What else can I bring? Salad? Dessert? How about some French bread and cheese?"

"Bread and cheese will be fine. See you about three?"

"Two, if I can make it by then. And, Lareana, thanks for the invite."

Lareana replaced the phone, her mind already on what she would serve the next day. She attributed the rising bubble of excitement and the grin she could feel dancing with the sparkle in her eyes to a chance to cook something special. It couldn't be the guest himself. Or could it?

❧

By the time Trey arrived the next afternoon, Lareana had dinner stowed in a backpack and two saddle bags. She had debated on whether to take Johnny along, then opted for a call to Aunt Inga. Yes, she would gladly baby-sit her favorite grand-nephew. Lareana hugged both of them as she ran back out the door, delight in her freedom, in the ride ahead, and in her new friend lending springs to her step.

"Any room for this?" Trey eyed her as she sat between the packs on the porch.

He handed her a wrapped package, then stepped back to take in the whole picture.

Sunbeams seemed trapped in her hair, and wild roses bloomed on her cheeks. Her smile of welcome flashed brighter than the sun. A blue plaid shirt, knotted at the waist, and rolled-up long sleeves showed off both the sky-blue tank top underneath and the golden tan of her arms.

"You look like pieces of the sun and sky came earthbound just for my enjoyment," Trey said softly.

Lareana looked up from finding a place for the extra package. "Why, thank you." She slipped the leather strap through the buckle. Her smile widened. "You don't look too bad yourself."

She saw that the *Gentleman's Quarterly* look had been exchanged for one straight out of *Western Horseman*. She rose and handed him the filled backpack, then whistled for Samson as she hoisted the saddlebag over her shoulder.

"I've already saddled the horses up in the corral." Lareana closed the gate behind them.

"How many horses do you have?" Trey asked as he settled the backpack in place.

"Three. My mare, Kit—she's a Morgan-saddle bred cross—and John's quarter horse gelding. He used Mike for rounding up the steers and cows."

"Mike?" Trey's eyebrows nearly disappeared into his hat brim.

Lareana laughed. "John believed in basic names. Nothing fancy."

"That's two."

"The third one is that little Welsh mare down in the pasture." She pointed to a small gray figure toward the woods. "We bought her when we found out I was pregnant. John thought we should breed her when the baby was born so the colt and kid could grow up together. Maybe I'll still do that."

Thoughts of John's dreams that had crashed in the fatal collision took over for a moment. She couldn't always find the enthusiasm to make them happen without him. Like getting the mare bred. Time whipped by like a whirling dervish. She was so busy trying to keep up that the extras, the special things they had planned together, often didn't get done.

Trey resisted the urge to interrupt her memories. He watched her face carefully, ready to intervene if she needed him. He, too, remembered stillborn dreams.

They reached the aluminum gate to the corral without breaking the silence. Both horses nickered when Lareana spoke to them. She handed Trey part of a carrot. "Give Mike this carrot, and he'll love you forever." She pointed to the bay with a white blaze who had his head turned expectantly. The deep sorrel mare beside him flung up her head and slammed an impatient foot into the dust.

"Easy, girl." Lareana rubbed the horse's satiny neck and palmed a carrot for her mare. "You need a good run, don't you?" The mare's answer was a sharp nudge in the chest.

"A bit high-strung is she?" Trey unclipped the lead shank and turned Mike toward the gate.

"Not really. Just has a mind of her own." Lareana finished, tying the saddle bags down. She checked the girth for tightness and swung aboard. "Dad says she's mean clear through, but I've always been able to handle her. I like the challenge, I guess. Besides, she has the easy gait of a saddlebred, pure heaven to ride." She leaned forward to hug both arms around the mare's neck. "You old sweetie, you." The mare nodded and pulled on the hackamore, ready to go.

On the ride to the creek, riots of scarlet vine maple screamed, "Look at me." Tall elms and firs shared their flickering sunlight and shadows with the errant breeze whispering secrets in their branches.

Trey drew in a deep breath of air, redolent of fir spice and falling leaves. He leaned the heels of his hands on the saddle horn and raised himself in the stirrups, both knees and elbows locked. "Ah-h-h-h." His whoosh of escaping breath spoke his delight as mere words never could.

A cock pheasant called from back in the underbrush. Lareana searched carefully, finally able to point him out, nearly invisible in the foliage surrounding the stump he perched on.

"This certainly is different from the hills around George," Trey said. "The only trees on a thousand acres are the ones I planted myself. But they'll have to grow some to beat this."

Lareana tried to see the overhung logging road through his eyes. "Guess this is another one of those things I take for granted. But I love it out here. Anytime. Any season. There just never seems to be enough hours in my day. Gotta check the fence lines soon."

The chuckling creek announced itself before they rode into view. A grassy glade banked one side while the other side hid under the drooping maples. Sunlight bounced shafts of diamonds off the ripples and peeked into the shadowed nooks and crannies, transforming the moss to emeralds.

"Just drop your reins. They're both trained to ground tie." Lareana swung out of the saddle and unknotted the latigo securing the saddlebags. "If you want to swim, the hole is on the other side of that enormous elm." She caught the questioning arc of his eyebrows. "I'm just wading today."

"Too cold, huh?"

"Well—"

He shrugged out of the backpack. "Even I'm aware that this is October, and you've already had a frost here. Let's just eat and wade. And especially the former."

Later, after they'd frozen their feet in the creek water and devoured the gourmet dinner carefully packed in plastic containers, Lareana retrieved two cans of pop from the creek and handed him one. A comfortable silence dropped around them as they leaned against a moss-covered root and watched the play of light and water.

"May I ask you a question?" Lareana turned to regard the man beside her.

"Um-m-m." Trey nodded without opening his eyes. "As long as I don't have to think too hard."

"How long did it take you to get over losing Jane?"

Trey pondered for a time. "I'm not sure. As the months passed, I found myself fretting about it less and less. I worked hard to keep any bitterness from developing, and I deliberately chose to forgive." He turned his head to look into her questioning eyes. "I found out that forgiveness means forgetting, letting go. And it meant forgiving myself, too. That was probably the hardest part of all."

"No 'if onlys'?"

"That's right. And no 'might have beens.'"

Trey wished he could tell her more about his newfound feelings, but he said nothing as he watched her lean her head back on the mossy root. *If only. . .* He smiled inwardly as he caught himself playing that game. *If you were ready to hear about the love I have growing for you. . .One day,* he promised himself. *One day.*

"You know something I've missed the most?" She faced him again.

"What?"

"Times like this. Having a man for a friend. John and I were friends first."

She thought a moment. Talking of John and the experiences they'd shared made her feel good this time. Maybe the healing really was beginning. "Thank you." She laid her hand on Trey's.

"For what?"

"Oh. . .for talking, sharing." Her voice softened. "For being a friend."

The setting sun was casting deep shadows as they rode back to the barns and Trey said good night.

❧

It was the next morning before Trey realized they still hadn't discussed anything about her job.

He made his phone call from the airport, since he had a flight to catch and wouldn't be back in town for a week. "May I take you out to dinner that Monday night?" At her answer, a frown replaced his grin. "Sure, we can make it an early night. Why didn't you tell me the trial was coming up?"

Lareana slumped in her chair by the phone. "I don't know. I guess I wasn't sure—" She chewed on her bottom lip. "Trey, this has nothing to do with you. It's my problem. . .well, not really. . .it's the law's problem. I don't have to go. I just want to. That man *must* be put behind bars before he can kill anyone else. His record stretches from here to next winter, and all because he drinks and drives." She stopped a moment to listen. "Yes, I'd like to have you go to the trial with me. As far as dinner goes, I'll see you about five that Monday. Thanks, Trey. . .for everything."

⤸

Lareana started getting herself and the baby ready early, but Johnny decided to help her out on the dressing table, kicking and laughing, making it nearly impossible to work his feet into the legs of his suit. Impatience was sneaking up on her, driving away the joy she usually found in the active baby.

"Johnny, sometimes—" She planted a kiss on his apple cheeks.

While she was struggling with the fastenings, Samson's deep bark announced company. She picked up the baby and dashed for the door, at the same time mentally counting the things she had left to do. At least the apple pizza had come out of the oven, its nutmeg aroma wafting outward as she opened the door. Trey could snack on that while she finished dressing.

"I seem to make a habit of this," Trey greeted her. "But what smells so heavenly?" He sniffed again. "It couldn't be. . .apple pizza, could it?"

"Whatever happened to 'Hello' or 'It's nice to see you' or even 'Hi, Lareana'?" Her grin matched the one dimpling the baby's cheeks.

"Should I go back and start again?" Trey laughed, a rich baritone that caused the baby to wave his fists in delight. "My nose always seems to precede my mouth. Anyway, it's all your fault. You did the baking."

Lareana leaned against the door frame, resting Johnny on her hip. Her gaze ran appreciatively over the man in front of her. He had said "casual," but his casual look had come right out of the latest men's fashion magazine: what every well-dressed businessman wears on a date. Camel wool slacks were topped by a navy cashmere sweater. Its softness invited her to stroke the nap. One finger hooked the collar of the camel windbreaker slung over his shoulder. Her mind assessed all this in the minuscule pause between one breath and another.

"Would you care to sample while we finish getting ready?" She stepped back, inviting him to enter. "Youngstuff here hasn't been too cooperative."

"You look fine to me." Trey reached out one finger for the baby to grab. "I could take him for you, if that would help."

Johnny didn't hesitate as he was transferred from one pair of arms to the other. His mother managed to wipe the drool from his chin with a dishcloth just in time for him to lean forward and chew on the finger he gripped in one hand.

"Maybe I'd better wash my hands first, if I'm going to be part of the main course." Trey raised his eyebrows, the question mark intended for Lareana. She laughed as she left the room.

"Just remember, you asked for it."

Johnny continued his chewing as Trey snaked a chair out with his foot and parked in it. He transferred the baby to a place on his lap and laughed at the antics of the young charmer. Johnny responded with a belly chuckle of his own but didn't release the finger of the man holding him.

"Ouch." Trey drew his finger back. "Lareana, he bites."

"Don't be silly," she responded from the bathroom. "He'll gum you to death but he can't bite. He doesn't have any teeth yet."

"Sure sharp for gums," Trey muttered as he pulled down Johnny's bottom lip. He paused, a grin deepening the creases in his face. "Want to bet?"

Lareana erupted from the doorway and pried open the baby's mouth. "He's got a tooth? Well, what about that? It broke through." Johnny twisted away, reaching again for Trey's finger. She dropped a kiss on his downy head. "Your first tooth. . .what a milestone. And you couldn't care less, could you?"

Her eyes met the lapis blue gaze of the man above her. "You don't need a Band-Aid or anything, do you?" she asked mischievously. "I mean. . .he did bite you." She chewed her bottom lip, trying to keep a straight face.

"Since I'm sure a tetanus shot is not in order, I'd settle for a piece of apple pizza, if it's not too much trouble." Trey tried to look soulful but failed miserably.

Lareana got to her feet, her teal wool skirt swishing softly as she stood. "You're sure that's all you need? No coffee or tea or something to go with it? Maybe you'd like a topping of ice cream or whipped cream?"

"Enough. I surrender. Just get yourself ready, woman. Johnny and I have been waiting forever—"

Lareana shook her head again as she placed the slice of dessert on the table in front of him.

Trey glanced from her to the dessert to the baby in his lap and back to the woman standing in front of him. Both his hands were occupied—one holding the baby, the other in the process of having a finger shortened.

Lareana just shrugged her shoulders at his predicament and walked off. "Mothers use three hands all the time," she commented as she left the room.

When she returned a few minutes later—hair swirled into a loose knot on the top of her head and silver loops in her ears—Trey had found a solution. The apple pizza had disappeared and now he was attempting to settle the gurgling Johnny in his car carrier. The baby even had a sweater and cap on.

Lareana watched for a moment as Trey bent over and nuzzled the baby's cheeks. One tiny fist tangled in his thick roan hair. Trey disengaged himself and kissed the tiny fist before rising to meet her eyes. "You two are something else," she said softly.

"Mexican all right?" he asked a few minutes later when they were all buckled in. Getting the baby's seat ensconced in the back had been no easy chore. The low lines of the Corvette precluded buckling ease, even for Trey.

"Fine." Lareana shifted her attention from the baby to the man beside her. "I haven't had a good chimichanga for a long time."

She ignored the countryside flashing by outside the car and let her thoughts roam instead. How much easier it was getting ready when there was someone else to help with the baby. Since she'd been a single parent from Johnny's birth, having another adult around was heavenly. She knew she could be spoiled quickly. Was God trying to give her some kind of hint? She really enjoyed being with this man, enjoyed not only his companionship but also his caring. But John hadn't been gone that long. She'd never planned on a relationship with anyone else. Back to square one—

Let's face it, she told herself. *Johnny will need a male role model in his life, someone who'll teach him how to be a man.*

She gave herself a mental shake. What was she thinking of? Trey wanted to hire her to help with his restaurant, not marry her. But still. . .no, he was a friend, nothing more.

Los Amigos tried to live up to its name. The tables were so close together the patrons became acquaintances whether they wanted to or not. Obviously, the tiny café was noted for its food and not for elegant atmosphere.

"We're in luck. We get a *booth*." Trey bent close to her ear to be heard above the mariachi recordings. They followed their hostess to a back corner where a large pink, bull-shaped piñata hung suspended over the table. When she set Johnny's car seat on the orange padded bench, he stared, entranced by the bright colors and the flickering candlelight.

"This is one of those places I've always wanted to come to and never took the opportunity." Lareana looked around, delight sparkling in her eyes. "I guess because I can't get used to going out alone. Thank you, Trey."

"Better wait to thank me till you've sampled the food. But the last time I was here, it was almost as good as what I had in Mexico City."

"When did you go to Mexico City?" Lareana asked over the top of her menu.

"A couple of years ago. I was toying with the idea of opening a Mexican restaurant, so I did some research." He glanced up at her. "Do you want something to drink? They make excellent margaritas."

"No, thanks." Her tone stiffened. "You know I don't drink, Trey."

"Do you mind if I have one?"

Lareana's forehead creased in a tiny frown. She started to say something, paused, took a deep breath, and started again. "I don't try to force my feelings on others. I. . .ah. . .I mean I know I can't change the world. But when John was killed, I swore I wouldn't drink again, that I wouldn't serve any alcoholic beverages in my house, and—" she stared at him across the table—"that I wouldn't ride with anyone who had been drinking."

"And you say you don't try to force your feelings on anyone else?"

Lareana straightened her spine and squared her shoulders. Her chin assumed its determined angle. "Is a margarita so important to you?"

Trey eyed her warily. "No. . .it's not. But I think you need to be realistic. People can enjoy a drink or even two and not suffer any ill effects. That doesn't make them drunk or drunkards."

"I know that." Though her voice grew softer, it still held a warning. "Can we drop the subject? Agree to disagree? I won't change my mind, and I have a feeling you aren't planning on changing yours, either."

Trey nodded, but when the barmaid came, he ordered soft drinks for both of them.

"Thank you." Lareana smiled across the table at him, but the serious look never left his eyes. The piñata cast a shadow on his face, making it hard for her to read it. *Maybe this is what he looks like when business decisions don't go his way,* she thought. *I'd sure hate to be on the other side if he really got angry.*

"Have you decided?" His voice remained clipped.

"The chimi." Her smile entreated his return to their earlier enjoyment. "I've wanted one for a long time. They don't taste the same when I make them. But then, I'm not very good with Mexican food." Lareana felt she was babbling.

Trey struggled with his feelings. He hated to make her unhappy but. . .she was being unrealistic. And unfair. He'd never had an accident. In fact, on the few occasions when he'd had too much to drink, he had been wise enough not to drive. He wasn't stupid. He studied the face of the woman across from him. Flickering candlelight highlighted her cheekbones, sending her expressive eyes into shadows. The gold in her hair deepened into honey where the shadows fell.

I know you're coming from a difficult situation, he thought, *but I sure plan to do something about where you're going. Somehow, Lareana love, you have to come to grips with the way the world is. People can drink and still function.*

He reached across the red and white-checkered tablecloth and took her hand in his. His thumb stroked the fine skin, forcing her to relax. He watched as her shoulders dropped, the relaxation traveling up her arm and down to the toes of her shoes. *I love you,* he wanted to say. *Lareana, I love you with all I am capable of loving and then with whatever extra abundance God gives me.*

He took a deep breath. The time wasn't right. Not yet.

Johnny decided he was due for some attention, and interrupted their study of each other. When they ignored his suggestions, he switched to the demand that always got action. Immediately, his mother turned to him, her gentle voice belying the turmoil of only moments ago.

Lareana picked Johnny up and reached for the diaper bag. "Bet you need dry britches, don't you?" Then, to Trey, she said, "We'll be back in a couple of minutes. Start without us if your dinner comes." She made her way to the restroom, grateful for the quiet when the door closed behind her.

On her return, a man from a nearby table stopped her. "Hi, Lareana." His flushed face testified to his diversion for the evening. "You finally come offa your farm?"

Lareana recognized one of the salesmen from the feed store. "Hi, yourself, Frank. It's nice seeing you. Enjoy your dinner." She continued toward her table with Johnny, who was staring at everything from the vantage point of her shoulder. She thought she heard something about "widow-woman" from Frank's table, but she wasn't sure.

"Who was that?" Trey asked as she settled Johnny back in his car seat.

"A man from the feed store. He usually loads the truck for me." Her dinner had arrived and she bent her head for grace, then continued. "He's always been polite, kind of quiet. I was surprised when he stopped me."

Trey glanced back at the table where Frank and several of his buddies were ordering another round of drinks. One of them slapped the waitress on her derriere as she left to fill their order. She glared at them, then giggled. Trey glanced at Lareana, but she was engrossed in her dinner and had missed all the byplay.

Their earlier ease in conversation seemed to have escaped to the Bald Hills and refused an invitation to return. Trey finally pushed back his plate, his dinner half-eaten.

"Don't you like it?" Lareana asked. "Mine's delicious."

"Guess I'm not too hungry, after all. Want me to take Johnny while you finish?"

Lareana wiped her mouth with the napkin. "That's okay. I'm stuffed."

"Dessert, folks?" Their waitress stopped at their table. "Our flan is really good tonight."

"None for me, thanks." Trey smiled up at her. Lareana shook her head also. "Just bring me the check, please."

Lareana picked up Johnny and began to button him into his sweater for the trek home. Her first inkling of trouble came when a slurry voice interrupted her.

"If I'da knowed you wanted to go out, I'da called ya."

"What?" Lareana whirled around, her senses reeling under the miasma of alcohol fumes.

"Just a minute, fella." Trey rose to his feet. "You have no reason to bother her."

"Buzz off, buster, I'm talking to the widow-woman here." Frank leaned both arms on the table, obviously needing the support.

"I said, 'on your way!'" Trey's voice deepened to a menacing growl. He grabbed the man's elbow with steely fingers and spun him away.

With surprising accuracy, considering his state of inebriation, Frank swung his other arm around and connected with the side of Trey's head. Only Trey's quick reflexes kept the punch from landing on his face.

"Stop it! Frank, you idiot!" Lareana felt waves of horror, generously spiced with pure anger, roll over her.

Two other men hustled the drunk out the door before anything else could happen. Trey glared after them, one hand rubbing the point of contact.

"Are you all right?" Lareana wasn't sure when she had gotten to her feet. She found herself standing in front of Trey, reaching with one hand to inspect the bruise.

"I'll be fine. That idiot was too drunk to do much damage." Trey waved aside the apologies of the manager and Frank's friends. "Are you ready?"

Lareana nodded, but before she could pick up the baby's seat, Trey had it in one arm and his other hand securely around her elbow, ready to guide her out to the car. Two uniformed officers met them at the door. By the time Trey convinced them he didn't want to file charges, Lareana's anger was beginning to boil again.

"Why not?" she demanded as they drove out on the street. "He needs to be taught a lesson."

"Granted." Trey's voice was still tight. "But I wanted you out of there...before someone really got hurt."

"But—"

"No buts. Do you want this kind of garbage spread all over the papers? That's what would happen if I pressed charges. I can't afford that kind of publicity, and you certainly don't need it."

Lareana stared at his clenched jaw and equally tight fists clamped around the steering wheel. "Trey?" Her question was tentative, seeking to soften the tension, as was the hand she laid on his arm.

"Oh, Lareana—" His voice broke. After a pause, he began again. "You could have been hurt...you and Johnny. I'd never have forgiven myself."

"It wasn't your fault."

"I took you there."

Lareana rubbed his arm and kneaded away the anger from his taut shoulder muscles.

"It was the alcohol," she said softly. "I wish—"

"Now what?" Trey thumped the steering wheel with the heel of his hand. Flashing blue lights were reflected in the rearview mirror.

Chapter 5

Trey checked the speedometer.

At the same moment, his foot came off the accelerator, but it was obviously too late. He couldn't argue. As soon as the Corvette rumbled to a halt on the narrow shoulder, he pulled his driver's license from his billfold.

Lareana watched, a tiny smile playing hide-and-seek around the corners of her mouth. When Trey glanced her way, she chased it quickly out of sight. Staring out her side window, she listened to the discussion between Trey and the officer.

It was a typical scenario. "Seventy miles an hour in a fifty-mile zone." The officer sounded stern. "What's your hurry?"

"I'm sorry, officer." The control was back in Trey's voice. "I guess I was thinking of something else."

Darn right, Lareana thought. *That fight back there would have broken anyone's concentration.*

The officer took the proffered license and returned to his car. Silence held court in the Corvette while they waited for the verdict. Lareana tried to think of something to say, but the frown on Trey's brow precluded any easy conversation. The rhythmic thrumming of his fingers on the steering wheel intensified the silence until Johnny squirmed in his carrier. Lareana turned to rock the seat with one hand, appreciating the diversion.

"Thank you," Trey said as he signed the ticket. The officer had been sympathetic, reducing the speed to 65 so the ticket was only for speeding, not reckless driving.

"Now you take it easy, Mr. Bennett," the officer admonished. "Your family needs you around for a long time." As he strode back to his patrol car, Trey glanced at Lareana. "Family, huh?" He turned the ignition. "Sounds good to me."

Lareana felt the smile return from its hiding place as she watched Trey's right eyebrow arc and the corner of his mouth twitch. The stern look he'd worn for the last hour dissipated like fog in the sunlight.

"I've always wanted a knight in shining armor," she said, "but I never dreamed mine would ride up in a silver Corvette."

"Or fight for your honor in a Mexican restaurant?"

She thought back to the pathetic drunk taking a swing at Trey. Her smile died. "I hope someone is driving Frank home." She turned in the seat. "They wouldn't let him drive, would they?"

"The police probably booked him for drunk and disorderly conduct. He's sobering up in the cooler by now." Trey reached for her hand. "Don't worry. He's not out on the road."

"It happens so easily," Lareana mused after a time. Her fingers had finally relaxed in Trey's palm. "One drink follows another. . . Nobody makes sense. . . Those men were laughing and having a good time. Before anyone knew it, things got out of hand. I—I don't even want to face him the next time I go for calf feed."

"It wasn't your fault."

"I know that, but—" Her voice faded as she leaned her head back against the seat. Six months ago the trooper's voice had had that same air of authority. She heard his words again. "I'm sorry, Mrs. Amundson. There has been—"

Tears welled in the corners of her eyes and slipped silently down her cheeks. She swallowed, trying to dislodge the lump that suddenly blocked her throat. *Dear Lord,* she screamed in the quiet of her mind, *how can there be such joy and laughter one minute and such pain the next? Sometimes I wonder why You allow things like alcohol in this world. All it does is cause pain and unhappiness.*

"Lareana, let me in." Trey massaged the back of her hand with his thumb. "Share your thoughts, your feelings with me so I can help you."

She turned her face, and the light from the dashboard caught the shimmer of tears. "Trey, I loved him so. John was not only my husband, he was my best friend. Sometimes I—" Trey waited for her to continue. He wanted to take her in his arms, to wipe away the tears and erase the pain. *A knight in shining armor,* he thought. *Maybe I can slay dragons but not the memories that cause her grief.* "Lareana, love."

He stopped his runaway thoughts as he realized what had slipped out. *Lareana, love.* Had she heard him? Would it make a difference? Love could make a difference, couldn't it?

He turned the powerful machine into the long, poplar-lined driveway of Three Trees Farm. Only Samson's halfhearted barking broke the silence when Trey turned off the ignition. He rested both wrists on the steering wheel, his square-tipped fingers hanging loose and relaxed. The beam from the mercury floodlight illuminated his features in sharp angles of black and white.

The light fragrance of her perfume teased his senses, and he closed his eyes for a moment, savoring the tiny whispers of her breathing, the warmth of her body so near and yet so far away. The officer's words came back: "Your family will need you for a long time to come." When would be the right time to acquaint Lareana with his feelings? She and Johnny were already his family, and he loved them.

Slowly he turned his head and looked into her eyes. Their warmth penetrated his thoughts. Anyone else would have questioned him, moved to gain his attention. Not this woman. She waited, giving him all the time he needed, giving him the kind of peace he'd been searching for, a feeling of coming home, of belonging.

He reached over the console and, concentrating all his love into the movement of his hand, picked up one of hers. He tipped his head forward and gently brushed his lips across the tips of her fingers. "I'll pick you up at eight-thirty, okay?"

She gave in to the temptation to stroke the wavy hair bent close over her hand. Her fingers threaded through its thickness, following the waves, brushing back the lock hanging over his forehead. It felt so right.

Trey closed his eyes, glorying in the thrills running down his back as her tentative touch grew confident. Angel wings grazed his forehead as she brushed back his hair.

"If you're sure you want to."

"What do you mean?"

"Well, I know how busy you are. . .I hate to take up your time—" Her voice trailed off as his head snapped up.

"Lareana, do you want me there?"

"Yes."

"Fine. I'll be there." He opened his door, turning to wrestle the baby carrier out before Lareana could reach for it. *One thing I'm going to do*, he promised himself as he bumped his head on the door frame, *is bring the van when we take this young man along. Fitting Johnny and his paraphernalia in this car is the pits.*

Trey set the sleeping baby in the carrier on the kitchen table. Then he turned and tried to communicate all the love he felt into one hug. "Good night."

"Good night, Sir Corvette." Lareana hugged him back and stepped out of his arms. "See you in the morning."

Trey started out the door, but a thought caused him to turn back. "Lareana, at Timber Country you'll never have to worry about a scene like the one we just experienced. We won't allow patrons to get drunk, I promise you that."

Lareana shook her head. "Why should it be a problem there?" She stopped as the harsh realization dawned. "Do you mean you're going to serve liquor at the park?"

"Only beer and wine, no hard stuff. And it would be in restricted areas. I thought maybe applejack would be something different." Trey clamped his lips shut on any more explanations. The warm woman he had held moments ago had turned to glacial ice.

"I thought you understood. I cannot work for a place that encourages drinking." Winter had frosted her eyes. "Good night, Trey." She closed the door with a click.

Tears of disappointment ran rivers down her cheeks as she tucked Johnny into his crib. They dripped onto her nightshirt as she crawled into her own cold, lonely bed. After blowing her nose for the umpteenth time, she plumped her pillow and shook her head. "Well, so much for that dream." She frowned at the moonbeams highlighting the oak flooring. This time the sigh came from her toes. *Wonder if I'll see him again, either? We're sure farther apart than I ever dreamed. Can't he understand—* Her musings were cut short by the ringing telephone.

A curt voice broke off her greeting. "Lareana, this has nothing to do with *us*, with *our* relationship. I won't let it. Now, in the past, we've agreed to disagree. Can't we do that now? Put all discussion of liquor at Timber Country on hold until I can do some more research?" He stopped, aware that she had not responded. "Lareana?"

"Yes." She felt a chuckle starting.

"Well?"

"I said yes. What more do you want?" She clamped her lips to keep the joy from spilling out.

Trey sighed, letting all the fear and antagonism drain away. She was being agreeable. They could work together. "You scared the living daylights out of me."

"Me, too. Trey, please understand how strongly I feel. . .I—I can't work with booze."

"No more of this tonight. I'll see you in the morning. Good night, Lareana. . .love."

The dial tone buzzed in her ear.

❦

A crowd had already gathered on the courthouse steps the next morning when Trey and Lareana arrived. Clouds scudded across the slate sky, harassed by the same wind that encouraged people to wrap their coats more tightly around themselves and seek the protection of doorways. Tired maple leaves plastered themselves on low-growing shrubs, hoping to end their dance of despair.

Lareana hunched deeper into the collar of her mauve down coat, grateful for its protection. The gray day matched her spirits. She had awakened that morning without her usual bounce, and as if that wasn't enough, Johnny had fussed when she left him with Aunt Inga. She told herself he'd be all right but. . . The sight of her mother and father waiting in the hallway broke her train of thought.

"Oh, Mom." Lareana hugged the gray-haired, slightly rounded woman. But for the age difference, the two could have passed for sisters.

"It'll be all right," Margaret comforted her daughter.

"I'm Carl Swenson." The deep voice matched the size of the man who patted his wife's and daughter's shoulders before extending his hand to Trey.

"I'm sorry." Lareana turned, embarrassment warming her cheeks already flaming from the wind. "Trey, meet my mom and dad, Margaret and Carl. Everyone calls Dad Swen." Swen and Trey sized each other up as she finished the introductions. "George William Bennett the Third, Trey to his friends." The smiles on the men's faces informed the two women of mutual approval.

Trey gestured toward the courtroom down the hall. "We'd better go in. They must be close to starting."

The jury had been selected the day before, so the trial was about to begin. But all the Perry Mason courtroom scenes hadn't prepared Lareana for the actuality. Only the color of the familiar flags broke the somberness of the wood-paneled room. The court reporter casually cleaned her glasses in front of the imposing bench against the far wall. All of the actors were in place and rose on command as the judge entered and was seated.

Silence fell like an oppressive cloud as the roomful of people found their seats and stared straight ahead at the drama about to unfold.

Seated between her mother and Trey, Lareana felt secure.

Finally she had the courage to look at the man seated next to his lawyer at a table in front of the black-robed judge. Daniel Greaves was not a monster. Clothed in a dark blue suit with a white shirt and burgundy tie, he appeared the small town businessman he was. No red bulbous nose, no hangover-slouch. Only the twisting of his thin fingers revealed his tension. Today the jury would have a hard time believing him to be the drunk his record proclaimed him to be.

"The state of Washington versus Daniel Greaves. The charge: vehicular manslaughter while under the influence of alcohol."

The judge looked at the man seated before him. "How do you plead?"

At the man's "Not guilty, your honor," Lareana felt a tiny flame flare to life in the region of her heart. She forced herself to sit still, even while the fidgets twitched at her arms and legs. As the trial progressed, the aura of unreality grew, and the tiny flame burned hotter and brighter.

This was the man who had killed her husband. And there he sat as if he hadn't a care in the world. When the judge agreed, "Objection sustained," Greaves smiled at his lawyer. When objections were overruled, the man only shrugged or didn't respond at all.

During the lunch recess, Lareana paid scant attention to either the food or the conversation. Trey watched her covertly as he became acquainted with her parents. What he saw made him uneasy, but it wasn't until the women left for the rest room that he got a chance to ask some questions.

"She took John's death extremely well," Swen responded to the first. "We figured it was God and her faith getting her through. But sometimes I thought she handled his death—the grieving and taking over the farm, the baby—almost too well. My wife says it was because farm women have learned to be strong, to recognize the seasons of life."

Trey nodded in sympathy. " 'A time to be born, and a time to die,' " he quoted.

Swen took another sip of coffee as if giving himself time to think. "It wasn't that she didn't cry and grieve. . .she did, but—"

Trey leaned forward, nodding again to encourage the other man's reminiscence.

"Sometimes grieving includes anger. Hers never did. She claimed she forgave the man—"

"But you don't think she did?"

"Time'll tell, Trey. Time'll tell."

Trey watched as the mother and daughter joined them by the cash register. Lareana answered when spoken to, but her usual sparkle was as frozen as the ice in her eyes. Her chin held its imperial angle, secured in place by an invisible steel brace.

Back in the courtroom a small group of people had gathered in the hall, blocking the door. A powerfully built young man imprisoned in a wheelchair laid a hand on Lareana's arm.

"Mrs. Amundson?" His voice was polite but assertive.

"Yes?" Lareana paused. "What can I do for you?" Trey moved closer to her side, ready to intervene if needed.

"My name is Brian Campbell. This—" he gestured at his wheelchair and useless legs—"is the result of my encounter with Daniel Greaves. I was his first victim. . .I think."

Trey sensed rather than saw Lareana's reaction. He wanted to put his arm around her, offer her any encouragement he could, but her icy reserve screamed, "Don't touch!"

"I'm so sorry," Lareana said softly.

"I just wanted you to know that we want him off the highways as badly as you do."

Lareana raised her eyes to meet those of a young woman standing just to the right of the wheelchair.

"I'm Cathy Hanson. I spent three weeks in the hospital after that drunk ran a red light. I'm still fighting with his insurance company. Daniel Greaves spent six weeks in the detoxification center. He's back on the road."

"Why. . .why are you telling me this?" Lareana stared from one to the other.

"We're going to get him." Brian clenched his fist on the arm of the chair. "If Greaves is convicted on this charge, we'll be at the sentencing. Hopefully he'll be sent up for a long time. In the meantime, there'll be a civil suit."

"It'll cost him." Fire and threats flashed from Cathy's eyes. "It'll cost him plenty!"

Lareana nodded. Trey felt her trembling through the down coat. He gripped her elbow a bit more tightly and motioned her toward the door. They re-entered the courtroom, finding their places just before the judge was seated.

Lareana kept her eyes focused on Greaves as the drama continued.

A state patrolman took the stand and introduced the evidence of a Breathalyzer test. The level of alcohol in the defendant's blood had been well above acceptable limits. Yes, he'd been drunk.

Greaves leaned back in his chair. Sometimes he scribbled notes on a legal pad. Never once did he appear regretful for his actions. It was as if someone else was on trial.

As the afternoon progressed, the tiny flame flickered and grew, licking up the sides of the cauldron steaming inside Lareana. Invisible even to those who loved her, it nonetheless began to bubble and spit.

"Forgive. . .that your Father may also forgive you." The Bible verse blew cool reason in through the windows of her mind, but instead of dousing the fire, it fanned it more.

Forgive, Lareana thought. *What a joke!* The man had been forgiven over and over and look what had happened! More people had been hurt, maimed. *God, where were You when this was going on? What good did John's death do?* She forced her hands to remain folded in her lap. Cautiously she ran her tongue over her aching teeth. They had been ground together too long.

The angry cauldron finally boiled over when she reached the outside door after court had adjourned for the day. The trial would reconvene at ten in the morning. Prosecution was nearly finished.

"He killed John and injured those other people, and he doesn't even care." She rammed her fists deep into her coat pockets, her navy pumps pounding out her venom as she descended the stairs.

A television crew was rolling their cameras as one of the reporters held a mike to Lareana's face. "How do you feel about the trial so far, Mrs. Amundson?"

Lareana never paused. "Hanging is too good for the man."

Above her head, Trey's and her father's eyes met. An imperceptible nod caused them both to take her arms and hustle her away.

"Later," Trey answered a persistent newspaper reporter. Robot-like, Lareana followed instructions as Trey placed her in his car. She hooked her seat belt before folding her hands in her lap again.

"We'll follow you," Swen said as Trey walked around the rear of his car. "Margaret will stay with her tonight."

"Good." Trey nodded his approval. "I don't think she should be alone."

Lareana's responses on the ride to the farm were monosyllabic. No matter what Trey said, Lareana refused or was unable to reply. Her mouth looked pinched and her eyes vacant, as if she'd retreated to the far corners of her mind. One finger rubbed the cuticle of another. Back and forth. Rhythmically. The gesture accompanied the beat of the windshield wipers after the rain started to fall.

"I've never seen her like this," Margaret said after Trey settled Lareana in her chair before the wood stove and returned to the kitchen. Margaret dialed the phone. "Maybe when Inga brings Johnny over, it will help."

Lareana hugged the baby fiercely, as if he, too, might be snatched from her. When he started to fuss, she handed him back to her mother and went upstairs to change clothes to feed him.

Seated in her chair with the baby nursing contentedly, Lareana leaned her head back and closed her eyes. She could hear Trey and her parents in the kitchen, no doubt discussing her, the case. She didn't care. The steaming cauldron within had settled to a simmer. . .except for the moments she allowed herself to remember Daniel Greaves. Then the flames licked higher.

"I'll pick you up in the morning." Trey laid his hand on her shoulder.

Lareana nodded.

Trey paused as if searching for something else to catch her attention. With her eyes closed and the slumbering baby in the crook of her arm, she looked completely defenseless. At least the frozen look was gone. *Thank You, God, for small favors,* Trey prayed. *I don't know how to help her, so that leaves that ball in Your court.*

"Why don't you spend the night?" Margaret asked as Trey was about to go out the door. "It would save you some driving."

Swen nodded his agreement. "Then you could take both the girls to the courthouse in the morning. I have to go home now for chores. I could just join you in the courtroom tomorrow."

"There are plenty of beds." On any other woman, the look Margaret gave Trey would have been pleading, but on her it was the look of a gracious hostess.

"Thank you. I will." He opened the door. "I'll just get some things out of my car."

Dinner was a silent affair. Lareana pushed her food around her plate, then excused herself.

Trey helped Margaret clear the table, all the while engaging her in conversation. He found her sense of humor delightful, her common sense far above the norm. He could tell where her daughter's strength originated.

Lareana was back in her chair, the firelight painting golden highlights across her cheekbones and dancing sparkles in her hair. The tilt of her head shadowed her eyes. She might have been asleep but for the listless hand stroking the dog by her side.

Her mind kept returning to the wheelchair-bound man and the woman, Cathy Hanson. Their injuries were permanent, just like hers. No matter what happened to Daniel Greaves, life would never return to what it was before. Brian would never walk again. John was dead. And Johnny would never see his father.

But Daniel Greaves—he walked and talked and laughed and even drove a car. And drank. And smashed people's lives. And lived to drink again. And drive again.

Red fury misted the backs of her eyelids. The cauldron spat and foamed, threatening to overflow.

"It won't help, you know." Lareana heard her mother's voice as from a great distance. "I mean it, Lareana. You can't carry the burdens of those others. You can't even carry your own."

"I know. 'Let go and let God.'" Lareana's tone reflected the weight of the ages. She opened her eyes. "But, Mother, I've been doing that, and what has it gotten me?"

Margaret refused to answer the question.

I'd like to answer for you, Trey thought. *It's gotten you a gallant spirit that takes life's knocks on the chin and comes up laughing, a son you adore, a man who loves you and wants to take care of you, and a God who will never let you go. Even though this plan B that we're in is not the one you started out with, it will be good. Believe me, Lareana, love.*

"You'll know again one of these days," her mother said. "You'll know."

❧

Lareana woke with the rending and smashing of cars screaming in her ears. She thought the whimpering was from someone in the accident, but it was her own agony that filled the quiet room. Samson thrust his cold nose into the icy hand she dropped over the side of the bed. When she didn't respond, he pushed harder.

"It's okay," she murmured as she rolled over, wiping the moisture from her forehead on the pillowcase. "Good boy, Samson." She rubbed his ears and muzzle. With the fastest tongue in the West, he swiped the salt from her cheeks. After she stroked him one more time, he lay back down on the rug.

Call on the name of Jesus, she commanded herself. *Put Jesus in your mind, and there's no room for nightmares.* Closing her eyes again, she visualized the Man from Galilee sitting on a rock beside a flowing stream. Over and over she whispered His name, "Jesus, Jesus, Jesus." Finally she sank back into oblivion, a smile now curving her lips.

Lareana awoke in the morning with the smile intact. The song had come back into her heart until the events of the day before resurfaced in her mind. She lay in bed, willing the image of Daniel Greaves to disappear. It didn't.

Keep Jesus in your mind, a tiny voice whispered in her ear. It had worked during the night. Why not during the day?

Lareana threw back the covers as Johnny's questioning voice called for a morning meal.

"One thing about babies," she muttered as she shrugged into her royal blue robe. "They demand to be fed no matter what's going on." She patted the region of her own growling stomach. "Yes, I hear you. I'll feed you, too."

Trey breathed a sigh of relief when she entered the kitchen with a smile on her face and a beaming Johnny cradled on one hip. She'd taken time to run a brush through her hair and clip back one side with a barrette. With blooming color back in her face, she was the antithesis of the ghost inhabiting her body the evening before.

Oh, Lareana, he thought, *if only you can hang on to your smile for the rest of the day.*

She did.

Until she saw Daniel Greaves in the courtroom.

At the sight of the blue-clad man leaning nonchalantly back in his chair, visiting with his lawyer, the color drained from her face. When Greaves laughed at some remark, the cauldron inside her bubbled to a full boil once more.

Trey sensed the change immediately. So did her mother.

As the spectators settled themselves after the judge had been seated, Lareana glanced around the room. Both Brian Campbell and Cathy Hanson were there, along with a full contingent of reporters.

As the witnesses testified to the character of Daniel Greaves, his morality, his business credentials, Lareana remained frozen in place. She hardly appeared to breathe, but her darting eyes missed nothing.

When the counselor from the Alcohol Rehabilitation Center stated under oath that Mr. Greaves had responded well to treatment, her jaw locked in place.

They left for the luncheon recess, and a blatant headline from the newspaper stand across the hall grabbed their attention: " 'HANGING'S TOO GOOD FOR THE MAN!' SAYS GRIEVING WIDOW." A photo of Lareana leaving the building was centered on the page.

They waited for the explosion.

But Lareana clung stoically to her control.

Late in the afternoon, Daniel Greaves took the stand. His air of innocence endured until the prosecuting attorney began his barrage of questions. "I don't remember. . .I only had a couple of beers" became his litany. At no time did he even begin to acknowledge any responsibility.

Trey, watching carefully for any sign of response from Lareana, perceived the dilation of her eyes. One eyebrow lifted. *Hang on, love*, he thought. *Hang on.*

After the lawyer's closing remarks, the judge gave the jury their instructions, and the somber group filed from the room. The wait began.

Greaves rose, stretched, and shook hands with his attorney.

Lareana stood.

Greaves turned. He glanced around the room, casually, as if he hadn't a care in the world.

Lareana stared, waiting.

His eyes locked with hers for half a second, the blink of an eyelash. The contact severed. He moved on.

A wheelchair halfway blocked the door. Greaves brushed by without acknowledging the occupant.

The trial was over. Or was it?

Chapter 6

A door slammed in her mind.

As the corridor to reason closed, Lareana allowed Trey to lead her from the courtroom. With a slight nod, she acknowledged Brian Campbell and Cathy Hanson. Reporters hovered around them, breaking away to follow her and her family.

The late-afternoon sunshine was temporarily blinding as Trey and Lareana paused a moment on the top step of the courthouse. Flashbulbs added to the glare as they descended. Some of the crowd waved signs proclaiming: "TOUGHER LAWS FOR DRUNKS," "DOUSE THE SOUSES," and "DRINKING AND DRIVING DON'T MIX."

Lareana ignored the reporters, brushing through the crowd as though it didn't exist. Her eyes were riveted on a male figure slouched against a late-model luxury car. Greaves finished lighting his cigarette and clicked the lighter shut.

The staccato beat of Lareana's high heels on the concrete sidewalk captured his attention. And everyone else's. She halted a couple of feet in front of him. Head high, honeyed hair tossed by the wind, her glacier eyes bored into his.

"I have a baby who will never see the father who loved him." Her voice carried clearly on the crisp air. "John is dead! You killed him! You and. . .your—" she strangled on the words—"couple of beers!"

The cauldron boiled over. The glacier melted in streams of tears as she turned into the circle of Trey's waiting arms. Trey waved the reporters away as he gently steered her toward the parking lot.

"Ah, Lareana," he murmured. "Cry it out, love. Cry it out."

"I hate him!" She hiccuped between words. "I hate him and all he stands for. He's not even in jail." She turned stark eyes on Trey. "What's to keep him from doing it again. . .drinking and d–driving that monstrous car of his?"

Trey shook his head. Nothing. He knew she didn't want to hear that answer. Nothing would happen unless a policeman picked him up again. Then Greaves would get another of his innumerable tickets. And maybe spend the night in the slammer, until his lawyer bailed him out again. No. It didn't seem fair to Trey, either. He wiped a tear from her cheek with a compassionate forefinger.

"How long do you think the jury will be out?" Swen asked as they reached the cars. "Should we wait or go on home?"

Trey settled Lareana, wrapped securely in her mother's arms, into the back seat of his van. "You wait here and I'll go check."

Lareana felt like an empty reservoir, drained by the tempest of tears. Her eyes stung and her nose continued to drip. She blew into a handkerchief and burrowed closer to her mother's shoulder.

Trey rejoined the others. "It's so late today that we won't hear a verdict until tomorrow morning at the earliest. I asked someone to call us when the time comes."

"You'll call me as soon as you know anything, then?" Swen rubbed a work-worn hand through his thinning gray hair.

Trey nodded. "You won't come with us for dinner?"

"No. My cows need milking, trial or no trial." He reached inside the car to pat Lareana's shoulder and clasp his wife's hand. "You two take care now. I'll see you tomorrow."

❧

Johnny took advantage of all the attention that evening. He found that tasty finger he'd enjoyed before, pulled at his grandmother's earrings, and tangled his fists in his mother's hair. Samson got slobbered on when he pushed an inquisitive nose near the baby's dimpled chin.

Lareana felt as if she was viewing the scene through binoculars, backwards. *Here is one life,* she thought, *and the trial today was another.* Traveling those miles in between was like going through a time warp.

After dinner, nursing Johnny in her chair before the crackling fire, she could hear Trey and her mother moving about the kitchen. Their soft conversation, with its indiscernible words, lent a soothing background music.

"I love her, you know," Trey was saying. "I have since the day I met her."

Margaret nodded. "We could tell."

"I haven't told her yet. I won't until she's ready."

"Six months isn't very long, you know. . .for grieving, that is." She hung up the dishtowel and sank into a chair by the table.

"I agree. But I've waited years for a woman like her." The depth of his feelings reached out and assured Margaret's mothering heart.

"You've been divorced?"

"Yes."

"I hate to sound narrow, but the Bible and our church don't condone divorce."

"I don't, either. It wasn't my choice."

"Yes, Lareana told me." She stared down at the embroidered daisies on the light blue tablecloth. Before the silence became burdensome, she patted his hand, rose, and went into the other room. She turned back in the doorway. "Your bed is still here, if you'd like."

Well, that wasn't so bad, Trey thought. *But I'll bet she doesn't change her mind easily.*

⁓

The call came early in the morning. The verdict would be announced at eleven. Lareana packed Johnny into his car carrier and strapped him into the back seat of Trey's silver and black van. Johnny's grandmother buckled herself in beside him.

"Sure is easier than that Corvette," Lareana whispered in the baby's ear before returning to her place in the front. The roomy interior offered sheer comfort.

Though the familiar flames flickered to life as they entered the chambers, Lareana doused them with buckets of cold reason. Screaming and hollering did no good. There had to be a better way. Trey kept a close eye on her as they found their places.

She held Johnny tightly as the foreman of the jury rose. He took a piece of paper to the judge and returned to his seat. In the quiet, she could have heard even a feather float to the floor.

The judge looked up. "Would the defendant please rise?"

Daniel Greaves pushed himself to his feet. Gone were the nonchalant air, the doodling, and the whispered comments. One hand plucked at the knot in his tie. He forced himself to stand straight.

"The jury finds you. . .guilty as charged." The gavel slammed against the bench.

Lareana felt relief take the weight from her shoulders, giving her the freedom to smile up at Trey standing tall beside her. She squeezed Johnny close. The courtroom buzzed. Everyone seemed to breathe more easily. Except for the ramrod-stiff man in front of the bench.

The judge rapped for order and glanced down at his calendar. "Sentencing will take place in two weeks."

That means it's still not over, Lareana thought. *He'll still be free for another two weeks.* "What does it take to get someone like him locked away?" she asked no one in particular. "What's wrong with our laws?"

"I can answer for you." Cathy Hanson had come up behind her. "People have to care enough to make tougher laws. We've been too lenient far too long."

Brian Campbell wheeled his chair up as she and Cathy entered the aisle. It made a good picture for the evening news—a woman with a baby in her arms and a man in a wheelchair.

Trey ran interference for them as they made their way to the car. He was never rude, but he clearly made his point. They had provided enough copy for the media.

"Thanks for being here with me." Lareana hugged both her father and her mother. "You've been super." She gave her dad an extra hug and whispered in his ear, "Thanks for letting us have Mom the last couple of nights. I know it was lonely for you at home."

"You'll be all right now?" Swen grasped her shoulders.

"Yes." The confident ring was back in her voice. She waved Johnny's tiny fist in the air as the grandparents drove away.

⁂

"Do you have to rush away?" Lareana asked when she and Trey returned to Three Trees Farm. "I thought maybe we could go for a walk or something."

Trey assumed his familiar pose, wrist draped across the steering wheel. He transferred his attention from the glorious sun making a last-ditch stand against the rains of winter to the woman beside him. Blue shadows under her eyes and a weary sag to her eyelids testified to the strain she'd been under. She looked as if she needed a long nap instead of a walk.

"If you'd like," was all he said. He rose from his seat and, bending nearly in half, walked to the rear seat of the van to unstrap the sleeping baby.

Lareana opened her door. Someone, somewhere, was burning leaves. The tang on the air drifted in. There was no mistaking the fragrance. A plaintive moo-o-o caught her ear. One of the cows had probably been left behind the herd as they grazed in the far pasture. Samson whined, front paws on the bottom step of the van. The snowy ruff around his neck needed a scratching.

Mount Rainier guarded the end of the hay field and the man halfway down the fence line. Uncle Haakan was hard at work on the endless task of repairing the miles of fencing on the farm. In novels, this scene would be called pastoral, Lareana thought.

A weary smile kissed the corners of her mouth. *Thank You, God for these surroundings to come home to.* She inhaled a deep breath, expelling the last vestiges of the courtroom and breathing in the peace of home.

Trey watched the transformation in silence. With the baby carrier in his arms, he had no hands to help her down. But now she didn't need that support. He was glad and sad at the same time. Like everyone everywhere, he needed to be needed.

A companionable silence surrounded them as they reached the apple orchard a short time later. Johnny had gone back to sleep in the backpack strapped to Trey's shoulders. Lareana chose two perfect, blush-kissed King apples and tossed one to Trey. One crisp bite, and she had to wipe the juice from her chin. He shared her grin as he wiped the remaining drip from the side of her smile. The urge to kiss it away prolonged the silence.

Lareana felt breathless, as if all the world was waiting in the wings for the next move. She stared into the depths of the azure eyes above her. Trey bent his head; she raised hers. That fraction of space remained until the sweetness of their breaths mingled, drawing lips and hearts into mutual surrender. Her lashes fluttered closed as his warm mouth covered hers, tentatively at first, then securely when his hands rose to grasp her shoulders.

Trey raised his head just enough to give them breathing time. "You taste like apple and honey and all things sweet," he whispered.

"The apple is understandable." The sparkle had returned to her eyes. She stood on tiptoe to return the offering and gave him three feather-soft kisses, one on each corner of his chiseled lips and one in the middle, prolonging the moment. "But when finding honey, beware the bee sting." She gently nipped his bottom lip.

Trey's chuckle was buried in the strands of tousled gold as he wrapped both arms around her and hugged her close. She fit just right against his heart and under his chin. Would that she could stay there forever.

They followed the cow path down the fence line to where Uncle Haakan stretched barbed wire, pounding staples to secure it to a newly replaced cedar post.

Lareana detailed the happening of the trial while Haakan pounded away. His nods served as vocabulary until he noticed baby Johnny stretching and yawning.

"Good day to you, too, youngstuff," he said, a calloused forefinger caressing the baby's cheek. Johnny grinned, his new tooth gleaming in the sunlight. Arms and legs flailing, he reached for the old man's finger, ready to chew away. Haakan chuckled and turned back to his fencing.

"Nice to see you again, Trey." He paused between one staple and another. "Those apples good this year?" He winked at Lareana and resumed his labors.

Lareana thumped him lovingly on the arm as her peals of laughter answered his dig.

That sly old fox, Trey thought. *Doesn't miss a thing, does he? Wonder if that meant approval? Sounded like it to me.* Trey caught Lareana's sidelong glance, smothered in mirth, as they continued down the cow path to the woods.

A deep drainage ditch traversed the field in front of the line of Juneberry bushes and wild rose canes. Bright red rose hips made the bushes a banquet table for the birds Trey and Lareana heard calling to each other. They followed the rim of the ditch back to a culvert in the road. Crossing over, Trey glanced up at the sky in time to see a hawk wheeling above the tall firs in the background. His screech floated down to them, one more note in a perfect symphony.

They traversed the rutted road among the alder saplings and scrub brush and stopped at the edge of another large hay field, this one bounded by second-growth timber of fir and alder. "This is one of my favorite places to ride."

"Besides the creek?"

She nodded as she scuffed one booted toe in the grass. Then, hands in her back jeans pockets, she raised her face to the sun. "We'll go again if my new slave driver of a boss gives me any time."

Trey smiled as he snuggled her in his arms. "The other day I was a knight in a shiny Corvette, today I'm a slave driver. Make up thy mind, woman."

Lareana slipped her arm around his waist as they turned and started back up the road. "We can go by and see the horses if you like. They're pastured on the other side of the milking parlor." She tried to adjust her stride to his longer one. "Next time we'll go riding up on the logging roads into the Bald Hills."

Later that evening, after Trey had left and Johnny was fast asleep, Lareana finally allowed the morning's drama a place in her thoughts. *There must be something I can do,* she thought as she climbed the stairs to bed, *some way to publicize the need for tough laws to protect people against drunk drivers. Funny, you never pay attention to things like this until you're caught right in the middle.*

And in the middle was where she found herself the next morning when she answered the phone.

"Appear on TV?" Her strangled gasp adequately communicated her shock. "You've got to be kidding!"

The voice on the other end assured her such was not the case. "And it would be a help if you brought your baby. It should be a simple interview. Because of the Daniel Greaves trial, we're doing a weeklong series on the effects of drunk driving. I know you're concerned about this problem.

"But. . .but—" Lareana thought back to the night before. *I didn't pray for this, did I?* She took a deep breath, feeling like a diver about to leap. . .into a teacup.

"Of. . .of course. What do you want me to do?" she asked finally. After the conversation, it took a supreme act of will to remove her permanently clamped fingers from the phone.

Trey thought it was great. "You've got a story to tell. Go for it."

Easy for him to say, Lareana thought. *He's not doing the interview.*

In three days Lareana found herself and Johnny standing just off the set, waiting for their turn in front of the camera. Trey had an important business meeting scheduled, but he had promised to tape the television show on his VCR. Then he and Lareana could watch it together. Her parents and aunt and uncle were parked in front of their sets at home.

Black hair and snapping dark eyes proclaimed the Hispanic heritage of the woman approaching her charges. With spritely grace, Juanita Evans crossed the cable-strewn floor, all the while chatting sociably to put Lareana at ease.

It didn't help much, even though she was already getting to be an old hand at this TV stuff. Juanita and her crew had been out at the farm the day before, taping scenes of Lareana and Johnny at home on the farm. The news team was trying to include a real human-interest angle without being morbid. The grin on Johnny's face as he waved and slobbered definitely wasn't morbid.

When they taped those first scenes, Lareana had been on her home turf. The camera had worked around her and her daily schedule. An interview on set was a completely different story, or so the butterflies and all their cousins cavorting in her midsection informed her.

"Can I get you anything?" Juanita asked. She seated Lareana and Johnny on a sofa. When the floor director clipped a microphone to the lapel of Lareana's indigo blazer, Johnny's chubby fingers zeroed in like a hawk diving for prey.

Lareana disengaged his fist and dug into his diaper bag for one of his favorite toys. She waved the bright red ring enticingly in front of him, but there was no thrill like a new thrill for the inquisitive baby. Back to the mike. Lareana's finger became the pacifier as Johnny guided it to his mouth and proceeded to chew. He paid no attention to the cameras, but smiles creased the faces of the circumspect crew. He took the finger out of his mouth, studied it carefully, jabbered and drooled, and stuck it back in again. Lareana was concentrating so hard on keeping her son occupied she had no idea what a picture they made.

A still frame of John and one of their wedding flashed on the screen, after the segments from the farm. Lareana's honesty in answering the questions revealed not only her own feelings, but the universal feelings of drunk-driving victims everywhere.

"I'm having a hard time looking at alcohol dependency as a disease right now," she said. "And it's almost impossible not to hate the man who caused John's death. It might have been different if this had been Greaves' first offense—" she paused, glanced at Juanita, and continued—"but then again, maybe not."

"What do you see as necessary changes?"

"Tighter laws. If people were afraid of heavy fines and automatic jail sentences, maybe they would slow down their drinking, or at least not drive when they've been drinking alcohol. It seems drinkers can't tell they've had too many until it's too late."

"And now the phone lines are open for your calls." Juanita turned toward the camera and smiled. "Hello, you're on News at Noon."

A male voice came over the wire. "My wife was killed by a drunk driver—" When he went on, the huskiness in his voice had deepened. "Now I'm raising three children by myself. I agree with you. Sometimes it's hard not to hate. I can't get dependable help. What do you say to toddlers when Mommy doesn't come home? It's tearing me up—" His voice broke.

"Thank you for calling." Juanita's tone was like the kiss of caring.

Lareana felt tears burning behind her eyelids. She blinked rapidly, using Johnny's blond head as a shield. The remaining calls were similar. All were stories of tragedy, shattered lives, and broken people.

"Our guest tomorrow will be Brian Campbell, another victim whose life was changed by drunk-driving." Juanita closed with, "Thank you for watching News at Noon."

After the floor director completed the countdown, Juanita turned to Lareana. "You were wonderful. How do you feel?"

"The time zipped by. I have so many more things I'd like to say."

"Well, thank you again. And—" Juanita's voice softened—"I know what it's like to be on the other side of the fence. My father was an alcoholic. I lived in mortal fear that he would injure someone else or himself. Thank God, he always made it home in one piece, car and all."

"What finally happened?"

"He went to Alcoholics Anonymous. Hasn't had a drink in ten years."

Lareana squeezed the woman's hand. "Your story has a happy ending. Maybe you need to share that kind of result in your special report."

When Lareana and Johnny got out to the car, she started to strap him in his seat, but his nuzzling mouth told her what he wanted. Food. Making herself comfortable, she flipped the blanket over her shoulder. "At least your fast-food chain is portable. Wonder what we could call it. Mom's? Milk on Demand?" She smoothed the downy cheek snuggled against her breast. "Oh, Johnny boy, I love you."

When his long lashes fluttered closed and stayed there, she put him back in his seat and headed for home.

❧

When Trey arrived that evening, he grabbed her and spun her around. "You were wonderful! Here—" He plugged in his VCR and slipped in the cassette. Instantly, Lareana and Johnny, slobber and all, appeared on the television screen in full color.

When the program was over, Lareana leaned back in her chair and turned to look at Trey. He was sitting with elbows on his knees, hands folded steeple-like under his chin.

"I heard of a new organization today." He tapped his two index fingers together.

"Oh?"

"It's called CORD—Citizens Organized for Responsible Drinking. Some of the restaurant owners were talking about it." He rubbed his hands together slowly. "You might consider getting involved in it."

"Are you going to?"

"I'm thinking about it. It might be a place to start lobbying. The legislature is where laws are changed."

"I think I'd better start at the library." Lareana switched off the TV set. "I don't really know much about all this—the laws, the proposed changes, or even what works in other places."

The phone rang. Lareana's eyebrows arched toward her hairline.

"Not the first, huh?" Trey locked his fingers behind his head, spreading wide the lapels of his gray silk suit jacket. As usual, he looked as if he had written and produced an ad for menswear, then starred in it.

"Nope. Guess this makes me a celebrity." Her grin deepened the dimples in her cheeks. "But the real one is sound asleep in there."

She answered the phone and came back. "You should have heard his grandma. Grandpa, too. They couldn't stop talking long enough for me to get a word in edgewise. Ah, well, I'll enjoy it while it lasts."

"You wouldn't by any chance have a cup of coffee or something out here, would you?"

"If by 'something' you're referring to goodies, you're in trouble. But I have coffee or herb tea, if you prefer."

He rotated his head, seeking to release the tension in his shoulders. "Tea sounds fine."

"If you'll sit in here where I can reach you, I'll rub your neck for you while I'm making the tea."

"That's a deal no one would pass up." He rose to his feet. Removing his jacket, he folded it carefully over the back of a chair.

Lareana had the teakettle on the stove and the mugs down before Trey entered the kitchen. When he sat in the straight-backed chair, she began her ministrations. Her hands, accustomed to hard work, were strong, and she knew how to pinch, press, and pummel each muscle and tendon into submission.

Trey let his head drop forward, the relaxation permeating deep into his neck and shoulders. When the teakettle shrieked, he jerked, aware that he'd almost fallen asleep.

He smiled at her over the steaming mug. "You're a woman of many talents." He inhaled deeply. "What is this?"

"My own special blend. They say that if you like the aroma, you'll love the flavor. I like honey with mine." She set a hand-thrown honey jar in front of him. A tiny clay bear straddled the lid.

"I suppose you made the honey, too?" He twirled the wooden dipstick around and held it over his cup. The golden syrup flowed into a thread-thin stream.

"Uncle Haakan did. Or rather his bees did. That's one of his hobbies. Sure helps our orchards out, too."

He sipped from the rim of his delft blue mug. "This is good. . .really good. You people are remarkable. Are there any of the old crafts you don't do?"

Lareana appeared to ponder his question. "I'll tell you a secret. . .that is, if you promise not to divulge it to the world."

"Trust me. I have my Agent 0010 badge from my Toastie Flakes box. That makes me irreproachable." He leaned forward, one hand cupped behind his ear.

Lareana lowered her voice to a conspiratorial whisper. "I don't make soap."

"I'm crushed." He clutched one hand to the general region of his heart, and waved the other hand, barker-like, "I had planned on a Super Soap Service at Timber Country. All homemade. Gentle enough to soothe the complexions of the fairest of the fair damsels. By the way, were there damsels in the lumber camps?"

"I think all the damsels stayed in Europe. Along with the knights in shining armor. Or so they say."

He sat his mug down with a thump. "Have I told you about the meeting next week? The one with the think tank executives from Six Flags and Magic Mountain?"

Lareana shook her head.

"I want you to be in on it, at least while we're discussing plans for the restaurant." He rose and went back into the living room to retrieve his jacket. Removing the calendar from an inner pocket, he checked the dates. "We should be covering that part of the planning by Wednesday. Could you come for the day?"

"I—I suppose so." She mentally counted off the days. "Will you be free for the sentencing?"

"No, but I'll be there anyway." He checked his calendar again. "If you want to bring Johnny and stay overnight at my condominium the day of the Timber Country meeting, it might make it easier for you. My housekeeper, Ada, would love to watch him for the day while we're in the meetings."

Trey watched for her response. *Almost blew that*, he thought. *Please don't misunderstand, Lareana.*

Lareana stared over the rim of her mug at the man sitting across from her. He made it all sound so simple. Just come up there. No problem. She'd have to wean that son of hers pretty soon.

She shook her head. "I'll come for the day. But that's all. Saturday Aunt Inga and I are having a recipe test day with the antique recipes I've collected so far."

"Sounds great. Wish I could come taste." He shrugged into his jacket. "I've got to get going. I'll call you tomorrow."

Lareana rose and stepped into his arms like a homing pigeon come to roost. The warm pressure of his lips on hers elicited a soft sigh, a whisper of surrender, the breath of love.

But Lareana didn't know it yet.

Chapter 7

W ho can that be?"

Samson's barking had reached a piercing pitch by the time Lareana opened the door. A clown wearing a red costume with white polka dots on one side and the reverse on the other tipped his fireman's hat, honked a horn tied to his belt, and handed her an armful of stuffed bear. The bear's T-shirt barely covered a rounded tummy.

"Pooh Bear?" She looked back at the clown. He nodded—vigorously. He touched his head with one finger as if he'd just remembered and drew a card from a huge pocket sewn on one pants leg. With a flourish, he presented the card to her.

Samson growled in the background.

Already laughing at the clown's antics, Lareana maneuvered around the bear to open the card. "A honey jar always needs a Pooh Bear. Trey."

Lareana wasn't sure if the tears in her eyes were from laughter or— She extended her hand. The clown c-a-r-e-f-u-l-l-y wiped his hand on his suit, both down the leg and across the chest, then gave her hand a single shake. He tooted his horn and leaped off the stairs, clicking his heels on the way.

❧

Hugging the toddler-sized Pooh Bear to her chest, Lareana stood in the doorway until the rainbow-hued van drove out of sight.

The man's crazy, she thought. *And how I love it!* Something stirred just on the edges of her subconscious. She paused, waiting for it to come nearer. It was something good, she could tell. But what? When nothing further materialized, she went about her day, mentally ticking off her tasks. She'd start with a phone call to a certain businessman in Seattle.

Trey was out of the office. "Would you please give him this message?" Lareana asked. " 'Pooh's stuck in the honey again. Now what?' "

A brief silence preceded the secretary's strangled "Of course."

❧

The next morning found Lareana up to her elbows in cornmeal, flour, and more apples. She carefully read the brief instructions for scrapple, a breakfast staple in the old logging camps. "Mix sausage with cornmeal mush and let set overnight. Slice and fry." Should she fry the sausage first? What did one put the dough—the mess—in to set? How much cornmeal? As in the past, she waited for Aunt Inga. All her years of cooking school, and she had never learned to make scrapple. She grinned inwardly.

Maybe she'd have better luck with apple pan dowdy. She reread the recipe. And then again, maybe not.

When Inga arrived, the two women attacked the matter at hand. Step one: Decipher the recipes.

By the time several hours had passed, the results of their labors lined the counters. The scrapple filled a bread pan in the refrigerator, ready to slice and fry then serve with syrup. Lareana had decided her apple crisp recipe was far superior to apple pan dowdy.

"I agree," Aunt Inga said as she relaxed at the table with a cup of Lareana's herb tea. "We ought to try cornmeal griddlecakes one of these times. As I remember, they were really good. Filling, too."

"I've tried buckwheat pancakes before." Lareana sipped her tea while she wrote in her comments on the recipes. She kept a record of all her experiments— both the successes and the failures—in a blue notebook. "But I think sourdough pancakes will be our hottest seller. I talked with one of the menu planners for a chain of pancake houses. We agreed that the restaurant should offer several kinds. One of those diaries I found said the logging cooks varied the kinds of flapjacks but didn't have more than one kind on any one day."

"It's the toppings that will sell. Your blackberry syrup beats anything I've tasted." Inga glanced toward the kettle bubbling gently on the stove. "And that hot apple compote. . .my, my."

Lareana flashed a grin at the compliment as she continued to write. "It's not as if I came up with that one myself. Seems to me you had a hand in it. You and your 'pinch of this' and 'touch of that.' Hard to measure those amounts."

"Lareana?"

The golden-haired young woman raised her head at the question in her aunt's voice. "What?"

"You've been seeing a mighty lot of that young man lately, haven't you?"

Lareana nodded.

"You know we want nothing but your happiness." Inga reached over and patted her niece's hand.

She nodded again and waited.

"It's just that John hasn't been gone too long. We wouldn't want you to be hurt or. . .well. . .for people to talk."

Lareana could tell it was hard for her aunt to give unsolicited advice. "Don't worry." She turned her hand and squeezed Inga's gnarled fingers. "He's just a friend. A good friend."

Sunday morning arrived along with a rainstorm that didn't slow Trey down. He wheeled the van around the drive in plenty of time to take Lareana and Johnny to church. When she opened the door, he brushed her lips in a brief hello.

This could get to be a habit, she thought as she inhaled the scent of his after-shave. Before she could react, he had picked up the baby carrier and packed it out to the van, all the while exchanging absurdities with the bouncing baby.

"Would Haakan and Inga like to ride with us?" he asked as he strapped the carrier into place.

"They're almost ready." She slid the diaper bag in next to the seat. As Trey settled her in the front seat and shut the van door, she had the strongest urge to reach over and kiss him again. Definitely habit-forming.

On the ride to the little country church, Trey charmed Haakan and Inga with stories of hay ranching in George. When they entered the front door, the crowd began to buzz about their local television stars, and Johnny was passed around and cooed over.

Their interest in Trey came more in the form of sidelong glances from the women, handshakes from the men, and snickers from the teenage girls. He was a real eye-catcher in a navy suede blazer and gray wool slacks. Light caught the raindrops in his hair and sparkled sienna. Her eyes were drawn to the laughter beaming from his eyes and then to his mouth, curved in an engaging smile, ask-ing to be kissed. So much for objectivity.

In the sanctuary, the organist was playing a medley of Lareana's favorite hymns. A hush descended over the congregation as the pastor bowed his head before the altar and began the service. When Johnny fell promptly asleep, Lareana found her attention drifting to the man beside her. She'd jerk it back to the order of service, only to find it roaming again. She'd forgotten the simple pleasures of tall shoulders next to her own, a masculine hand helping to hold the hymnal, a deep baritone voice belting out the hymns. And again the scent of his aftershave drifted by her.

Pastor Jensguard emphasized the words of scripture: "Beloved, let us love one another, for love is of God—"

The words leaped out at Lareana. That's what had been at the rim of her consciousness. She didn't just love Trey as a brother or a fellow human being. She was in love with him. And this kind of love was also from God. Trey had come into her life so unexpectedly, but just when she needed him. And yesterday she'd told Inga he was "just" a friend. Hmm.

Suddenly Trey sensed a new air of wonder in her. He'd been intensely aware of her from the moment he arrived at the farm. The winter rose tone of her wool crepe dress brought out the bloom in her cheeks and complemented the clarity of her complexion. Tendrils of goldenrod hair called to his fingers. Her slightly gathered skirt whispered against him when she crossed her legs. The haunting fragrance of her perfume drifted unseen, but never unsensed, around her, summoning. . .no. . .demanding, his attention. Sitting next to her was joy, was agony, was where he always wanted to be.

They stood for the closing hymn.

Back in the van, Lareana was delighted when Haakan and Inga accepted Trey's invitation to dinner. Wasn't she? The desire to tell Trey of her new discovery warred with the knowledge that he'd never said he loved her. Or had he? Wasn't he showing it by all he did? Her mind flitted back to their conversations. What had he called her? "Lareana, love"? Did it mean what she thought, or was it just a nickname?

She refused to replay those "love me, love me not" games of her teen years. Her internal instructions were adamant. She would discuss her knowledge with Trey that day. A thrill of anticipation tuned every sense to concert pitch.

Dinner at the Oyster House in Olympia met that restaurant's usual good standards. It wasn't their fault that Lareana thought the service was slow.

And Haakan and Inga were just being their normally gracious selves when they invited her and Trey in for coffee and dessert. Weren't they?

Now I'll get Johnny down for a long nap so we can talk, she thought as they finally arrived at her own door. But Johnny had been napping already. Instead, he woke up. . .screaming. When she changed his diaper, the heat from his restless body nearly burned her fingers.

She tested his temperature. The look on her face warned Trey there was trouble.

"It's 104 degrees," she said softly.

"You're calling the doctor?" When she nodded, Trey picked up the crying baby. "I'll hold him."

"I'll meet you at my office in fifteen minutes," Dr. Pat's calm voice reassured Lareana's racing fears. "It's probably an ear infection if it came on that fast. You say he hasn't been sick until now?"

"Just drooling and a runny nose once in a while. I figured it was from teething."

"That'll do it. See you as soon as you can get there."

It was, as Dr. Pat had suspected, a simple ear infection. But someone forgot to tell Johnny about "simple." He cried and fussed in their arms. Even laying him down caused a knee-jerk reaction. He'd start to doze off, then cry again, until finally the drops began to take effect.

Trey hated to leave, but he had to be at his office early in the morning. He waited until the baby's cries had turned to whimpers. Lareana walked with him to the door, Johnny snuggled against her shoulder.

"I'll call you in the morning," Trey whispered, dropping a kiss on each of their foreheads. He started down the stairs, then turned. "Are you sure you'll be all right?"

Lareana nodded. "Dr. Pat said twenty-four hours. You heard her." *So much for telling him my feelings,* she thought. All her lovely dreams. . .well, babies came first.

He slipped a hand beneath the hair on her neck and brought her lips to his. Johnny moaned again, one tiny fist clutching the collar of her blouse.

Trey saluted with three fingers to his forehead and left.

❦

Dr. Pat was right. By the next morning Johnny was feeling much better. Lareana, however, felt as if she'd been up most of the night, which she had. So she decided to take a nap when the baby did.

Even though she was worn out, thoughts of Greaves intruded on her rest. The anger hadn't died, it was only banked. She shut her eyes again. She'd deal with that later. She just as resolutely pushed away any thoughts about forgiveness. The ringing of the telephone brought her back from a lovely dream. There had been sunshine, birds singing, and she and Trey, alone on the grass beneath a tree. When she heard his voice on the phone, it was as if the dream continued.

"Good morning, love. How's the patient?"

"He's better."

"Did I wake you?"

"Um-m-mmm." Lareana stretched both arms above her head, the phone clamped on one shoulder. She twisted, reveling in the almost sinful treat of waking halfway through the morning. "But that's all right."

"Has he been there yet?"

Lareana was instantly awake, the dream banished.

"Who?"

"If you have to ask, he hasn't."

"Trey, what are you talking about?" A low laugh came through the wire. "Trey!"

"Enjoy your day, lady fair. I'm off to slay dragons." The dial tone filled her ear.

Lareana shook her head. Crazy man.

Shortly after noon, Lareana found out who "he" was. Samson heralded the arrival of Dan's Deliveries, a van painted bright red with a sign in iridescent letters: "We deliver anything. . .anywhere." The "anything" a cheery young man pulled from the back doors would please any little boy's heart. A toddler's rocking horse, more like a rocking cart, complete with seat belt, came first. The red and white painted pony sported a card that read, "To my second favorite TV star. Rock on."

The toddler-sized red cowboy hat was trimmed with white as were the chaps and vest. The hat on the cuddly teddy bear matched the child's outfit. "You gotta dress for the part," read that card.

Fits of hilarity attacked both Lareana and the deliveryman as they carried the booty to the house.

"That must be some proud daddy," he said. "I've never seen such a layout." Lareana never bothered to correct him.

❧

"Trey is out of the office," his secretary intoned.

"Tell him 'Hi, ho, Old Paint, and away.' " Lareana had a hard time keeping a straight face.

"R–Right," the woman stammered, her tone questioning.

❧

On Wednesday morning Lareana dressed in her most businesslike attire. She needed all the confidence she could dig up before the meeting. Whenever she thought about it, her resident troupe of butterflies turned handsprings.

She started out with her navy suit, but remembering Trey had seen that, she switched to gray. The soft, untailored jacket topped a silk turquoise blouse and a loosely pleated skirt. She loved the casually elegant feeling the outfit gave her. Silver chains and hoop earrings, suede pumps, and matching purse tied everything together. She swept her hair back into a French twist with her bangs brushed to one side and stared at herself in the full-length mirror.

"Not bad." She added a little extra teal eyeshadow. "Not bad at all." She had already taken Johnny over to Inga's. With Lareana gone so much, the older couple had hired the extra help the farm needed. Uncle Haakan could never have kept it all up by himself.

But it would be this way more and more. As she drove out the leaf-encrusted drive, she thought, *I'm becoming a businesswoman now.*

She held on to that thought two hours later as she parked in a garage in downtown Seattle. The ride to the tenth floor gave her no time to adjust to city speed before she entered the Surf and Turf executive offices.

"Mrs. Amundson? I'm Sandy." An energetic young woman rose from behind the reception desk. At Lareana's nod, she continued, "Mr. Bennett said to bring you to the board room as soon as you arrived." She started to lead the way down the hall. "Can I get you anything before we go?"

"No, thank you." Lareana controlled the tremor in her voice.

Following the receptionist down the hall gave Lareana time to glance at the textured oil paintings of the Northwest lining the walls. Pictures of Surf and Turf restaurants surrounded a sign boasting "Timber Country" in carved wooden letters on the end wall.

"Here we are." Sandy opened a solid oak door and motioned Lareana to precede her.

The board room looked as if it had just been lifted out of a business magazine. High-backed, leather-padded chairs surrounded a long oak table. To Lareana, it looked oblong enough to seat a football team and their families for Thanksgiving dinner. At the far end, picture windows overlooked Puget Sound, gray today like the clouds overhead.

Lareana took a deep breath and raised her chin a bit higher than normal. Her smile securely in place, she crossed to the head of the table.

The meeting was already in session, but Trey rose immediately at Sandy's touch on his arm. His eyes lit up at the sight of Lareana.

"We'll take a break now." He motioned to the group and took Lareana by the arm. "How's Youngstuff doing? Any trouble on the way up? How's the farm? It's so good to see you." He stopped talking to stare at her, longing to take her in his arms.

"Fine, no, great, and I agree."

Trey looked at her, dumbfounded.

"I was just answering your questions. You didn't give me a moment."

Trey threw back his head, his laughter drawing the attention of the people around the coffee cart. "Come on, fair lady, let's go meet the experts."

Soon her mind was a muddle of names and faces. The one person who stood out was Mrs. Quinelli, Trey's secretary. Lareana smiled at the expression on the dignified woman's face and extended her hand. "I'm glad to meet you—especially after the messages you've been passing on through me."

"Excuse me for a moment," Trey said. He flagged down one of the board members, leaving the two women to get acquainted.

"My dear, you've certainly touched his life in a special way." Mrs. Quinelli nodded toward the man who stood half a head above the others. She squeezed Lareana's hand once more. "Can I get you something? Coffee, rolls? We have about anything you could want over there."

"Thanks. I'll see." The two of them made their way through the group. Trey was calling the meeting back to order, so Lareana took a glass of orange juice and sat beside him as he gestured for her to do. Mrs. Quinelli was on her other side, carefully recording the proceedings.

"Feel free to join the discussions any time," Trey spoke into Lareana's ear as he took his place beside her again. His hand had brushed her shoulder as he pushed her chair in.

Lareana smiled her thanks.

The hours until noon melted away faster than snowflakes on an upturned cheek. Lareana listened carefully while she studied the charts and diagrams posted around the room. Possible layouts covered one portable easel, and schematics of existing theme parks were tacked on another. An artist had been commissioned to paint a watercolor of the entrance to the park. Two bark-covered logs held up a third, with "Timber Country" carved in bas-relief. It looked tall enough for Paul Bunyan to walk under.

At the word *restaurant*, Lareana's full attention snapped back to the discussion. As they referred to "the restaurant" time after time, Lareana cleared her throat. "I'd like to suggest a name."

Trey nodded at her. "Go ahead."

"Why not just the 'Cookhouse' or 'Cookshack'? That's what they called the dining areas back then."

Trey pondered for a moment. "Why not 'Swen's Cookhouse'? We have 'Ole's Barn' for the animals."

Lareana beamed her appreciation at his use of her father's name. "And the outside should be rustic, with vertical rough-sawn boards and a shake roof. A wooden porch with a slanted roof could extend along the front. No matter how large your building is, it would look authentic."

She laid a picture from an antique book on logging camps on the table before them. Her description was indeed accurate.

Trey nodded to the architects, halfway down the table. "You got that?"

At that point, others chimed in with ideas, both for the cookshack and other eating establishments on the grounds. Swen's Cookhouse, however, would be the only one with a sit-down dining room.

"Will the saloon be in the same building, or in a separate one?" asked one of the architects.

"You might want to have both," someone else added. "A lounge at the cookshack and then a separate building with a false front and swinging doors for the saloon."

"You're right on target," Trey responded. Lareana felt as if she'd been run over by a two-ton bull. With each word, she felt hooves pounding her into the ground.

No, Trey, you can't do this! She wanted to shake him. Waiting for the confrontation, she retreated to the depths of her chair.

Sensing her stillness, Trey dismissed everyone for lunch, inviting them to gather in the room down the hall. The meal would be served immediately. As they all filed from the room, still discussing the plans, Trey turned to Lareana.

"Okay, what's the problem?" His direct attack brought her eyes up to meet his.

"What do you mean, *saloon*?" She tried to keep her voice steady. "I thought we agreed that this was to be a family park."

"It is. What we agreed to was to disagree until I could do some more research."

"I thought that since we hadn't discussed it anymore, you'd changed your mind."

Trey crossed his arms over his chest and slouched on the arm of the chair next to her.

She was adamant. "Is it really so necessary to offer liquor?"

"Lareana, you know from your chef's training that most of the money made in a restaurant is from the bar. Good food and good service are imperative, but it's the bar that makes the profit."

"It doesn't have to."

"No, it doesn't. But you know my restaurants have a good reputation. My bartenders are trained in all the latest techniques for discouraging drunk driving. This wouldn't be any different."

Lareana chewed on her bottom lip, one finger rubbing the back of another. She didn't want to be involved in a place that served drinks. She just couldn't. What if a drunk left the park and murdered someone else? Someone with a family? Wouldn't that make her an accomplice?

But she did want to help build this park, create a fun place for people to enjoy themselves. She sighed. She was beginning to sound like Trey.

Trey watched the emotions play tag across her face. *Come on, Lareana. We can work something out.* He wanted to reach over and take her in his arms. Instead, he waited. "Can we again agree to disagree for the time being?" he asked. "And go eat? They'll all be finished before we get started."

Lareana stared at him, her eyes dark with indecision. With a barely perceptible nod, she rose to her feet.

The rest of the day wasn't much of an improvement over the first part. Lareana contributed her ideas, and everyone was quick to agree that lumberjack breakfast served all day would be a unique feature. They liked the thought, too, of wooden covered wagons with one side raised for serving soft drinks, cider, and apple pizza. Trey promised them all free samples at their next meeting.

But her participation didn't help to ease her own apprehension. She just couldn't get the thought of the saloon out of her mind.

When Trey dismissed the group for the day, Lareana rose and went to stand in front of the windows. The low-hanging clouds were spilling their despair in drifting sheets of rain over Seattle and the Sound. Lareana felt like joining them.

After finishing his discussion with a member of the think tank, Trey came to stand behind her. He circled her waist with his arms and drew her back against the length of his body.

With a sigh, she leaned against the solid wall of his chest and closed her eyes. His warm breath stirred the feathery wisps of her bangs as he touched his lips to her temple, once and then again. She covered his clasped hands with her own and offered up another sigh, this one from her feelings of discouragement, frustration, resentment. She wasn't sure which.

"Do you want to talk about it?" His question came softly against her skin.

Did she? She wasn't sure. Maybe discussing it would help them reach a compromise, but then again, was a compromise possible? All she knew was that she didn't want to make any decisions right now. She shook her head. "Just hold me."

Trey knew he'd have no trouble with that request. They watched the lights dress up the curve of the waterfront. Headlights flashed, bumper to bumper, on Alaskan Way below them, but they were high above the clamor of the rush-hour traffic. The only sound in the paneled room was their steady breathing—unless one considered the thudding of their hearts worthy of mention.

Trey thought back over their conversation about liquor in restaurants. As a decision tightened his jaw, he turned her around to face him. "Lareana, I have to show you something. It won't take a great deal of time, and it's right on your way home."

"What is it?"

"I'll show you." He took her arm, handed her her purse as they passed the chair, and marched her out the door.

"Trey!" Lareana pulled back. "I've got to get home. Johnny will be needing me."

"As I said, this won't take long."

Once in the elevator, Trey leaned back against the wall, allowing the weariness of a week of day and night meetings to seep through him. The plans were going well, but he'd found his energy divided, part of him wanting to be with Lareana. He slipped an arm around her waist and drew her to him. "Have I told you today how lovely you look?"

"No, but thanks, and I agree." She grinned. "That is. . .you do, too." Glad for the change of topic, she tapped him lightly on the navy and crimson silk tie he still had knotted loosely around his neck. She reached up and softly brushed his lips with hers.

Trey gathered her closer. This was surely what he needed after a long day—this woman not only in his dreams but in his arms.

"Where are we going?" Lareana asked against his lips as the elevator door opened.

"It's not far. You can follow me in your car."

"Trey—" the insistence in her tone was wasted on her escort. He merely continued to his own car.

A few minutes later, they pulled into the parking lot of the downtown Surf and Turf. Their difficulty in finding a parking place only proved the popularity of the establishment.

Trey led her into the lounge.

As her eyes adjusted to the dimness, Lareana looked around with interest. A carved antique bar with a cut-glass mirror behind it dominated one end of the room. Comfortable padded chairs circled small round tables. While most of them were full, the sound of conversation was only a low rumble. Waitresses, dressed in long burgundy skirts and tailored white blouses, added another touch of elegance.

Trey stopped at the bar and waited for the busy man behind the bar to have a free moment. "Lareana Amundson, I'd like you to meet Ted Crofton. He's been with me since this place opened." Lareana extended her hand, and it was engulfed by the large paw of the beaming, bald-headed man.

"I'm pleased to meet you." Ted's deep and powerful voice matched his body. "Can I get you something?"

Lareana glanced at Trey. "A diet cola would be fine. . .if you have it?"

"Ted, I'd like you to show Lareana the things we do here to encourage safe driving. Is there someone who can take over for you for a few minutes?"

After Ted called over one of the waitresses to fill his job and poured the diet drink, he turned to Lareana. "You know, of course, that Trey is the president of a group of restaurant owners organized to promote safe driving?"

Lareana shook her head. *I wonder what else I don't know about this man,* she thought.

"And I suppose he's told you about the equipment we've installed, the Breathalyzer, the—"

"No." She glanced up at Trey.

"That's what I want *you* to do," Trey said. "I have a phone call to make. Be right back."

"Come right this way, Ms. Amundson." Ted smiled at her.

In the following minutes, Lareana received a complete lesson in the state-of-the art techniques the restaurant employed. She learned how the Breathalyzer worked, how quickly alcohol moved into one's system, and some of the tricks people used to try to fool themselves and the machines. A sign above the counter read: "The management reserves the right to call a taxi for anyone deemed too inebriated to drive." The bartenders also refused service to patrons at their discretion.

"Do you find that some still get by you?" Lareana was quick to ask.

"Sometimes," Ted nodded. "But we tell the waitresses to keep track of how many drinks a patron has had, then the Breathalyzer is used. And we're all pretty good judges of people by now. Besides, we've been known to call the cops when someone refuses to comply." He nodded wisely. "Word gets around."

"Hasn't hurt your business?"

"Surprisingly, not much. If someone deliberately goes over his limit, the cabbies will cooperate. Trey has his parking lots patrolled, so if a car is left here, it's safe. As I said, word gets around."

Lareana glanced toward the corner as a ripple of guitar chords announced the evening's entertainment. A young woman with cascading midnight hair perched on a tall stool and adjusted the microphones. Her voice was mellow and haunting as she broke into the opening bars of a well-known love song.

Lareana listened for a moment. For a change, the volume wasn't turned up to deafening proportions.

Her attention was caught by a man about to leave. At the same moment, Ted left her side and approached the patron. At the bartender's insistence, the man blew into the mouthpiece of the plastic meter. As the reading showed too much alcohol in his bloodstream, he handed over his car keys.

"The cab'll be here in about five minutes," Ted informed him.

"Time for another drink?" the man asked, his smile beatific.

Ted poured a cup of coffee and set it on the counter. "On the house."

"Thanks, Ted," Lareana said as Trey re-entered the room. "You've taught me a lot."

"Any time."

"Can you stay for dinner?" Trey asked as they left the lounge. "We can get something quick. They rush the service for me when I ask."

"I'm really not hungry, and I've *got* to get home. Thank you, anyway."

"Okay, but you're missing out. I hear the food here is something to write home about." His easy smile invited an answering one. "I'll walk you to your car."

"Oh!" She turned back after unlocking the car door. "Are you going to be able to make the sentencing on Friday? It's at eleven."

"I'll be there," he reassured her. "If something comes up that I can't get out of, I'll let you know." He leaned on the door as she slid in and buckled her seat belt. "Call me when you get home?"

She nodded. "After I get Johnny down."

"Give him this for me." Trey kissed the tips of his fingers and laid them gently on Lareana's mouth. "Good night, Lareana, love."

The drive home was a kaleidoscope of sensations that left Lareana feeling more confused and worn out than before. She had a job that filled a lifelong dream, but Trey was still asking her to accept the sale of liquor on the premises of the park.

But remember, the little voice from somewhere in her mind admonished, *you said you wouldn't force your views on anyone else. And he is doing all he can to keep drunk drivers off the roads. If more restaurateurs had his sensibility—*

Lareana rubbed her tired eyes. Spotting a fast-food place ahead, she turned off at the Fife exit and stopped for a cold diet drink. Back on the freeway, she at least felt more awake. But that didn't slow her internal dialogue.

And that's not all, another voice whispered. *You have fallen in love with someone who has been divorced. How are you going to work that out? I can just hear Aunt Sigrid now.*

Flashing red taillights from the screeching cars in front of her finally registered above the internal muddle. Lareana slammed on the brakes. Her car fishtailed and skidded, sliding to a stop with the front tires on the grassy median. She had no idea how she'd missed the car in front of her in the line of stopped vehicles.

"Thank You, God," she whispered as she waited for her heart to settle back into its customary position. She took a deep breath and pried her fingers from around the steering wheel.

After assuring the state patrolman she was all right, she pulled out to pass an accident. That had been too close a call.

When her doubts started nagging her again a few miles down the road, she deliberately turned on one of her tapes. She sang the rest of the way home. The problems weren't resolved, but she turned, safely, into the drive at last.

❧

Even after her long phone conversation with Trey that night, Lareana didn't sleep well. Of course, Johnny's demanding an extra feeding in the middle of the night didn't help. Thoughts of Greaves continued to nag at her, along with the possibility of a saloon at Timber Country.

"If I didn't know better," she muttered as she turned her pillow over and thumped it into shape, "I'd think I was worrying. But since I have never been a worrier. . .pictures of the creek in the evening come into my mind." Even that failed. Greaves was in the way.

Thursday didn't go much better. Lareana and Johnny trekked to the library for books, articles, any kind of information on drunk-driving laws. She came out with armloads of reading material.

When she got home, put Johnny down for a nap, and started reading, she couldn't concentrate. The material wasn't exactly inspiring, especially the statistics.

When she went to bed that night, she sadly decided that the best thing about the day was that it was over. Sadder still was the fact that this was a positive thought.

❧

"You want to go in with me?" she asked Inga on the phone the next morning. "The sentencing shouldn't take long." *At least, I hope not.*

"If you need me, I will," Inga replied. "But today is my quilting day—"

"And you'd rather not miss it. That's okay. I'm taking Johnny, so I'll talk to you later." She finished getting ready and bundled the baby and all his trappings into the car. Trey had said he'd meet them at the courthouse.

More protesters had gathered outside the white building when they arrived, all of them carrying signs and parading back and forth. The chill wind hadn't seemed to dampen their spirits, but Lareana drew a blanket over Johnny's face to protect him from the cold and hurried into the building. Her mother and father were waiting for her inside.

After hugging them both, Lareana asked, "Have you seen Trey yet?"

Margaret looked up from making grandma noises with Johnny. "No. Was he coming?"

Lareana nodded. She walked back to the doors and stared out the glass. The crowd had grown. She held the door open for Brian Campbell to wheel in his chair. Cathy Hanson followed him.

After greetings were exchanged, Brian unzipped his jacket and spread the opening wide. "How do you like my new T-shirt?" It was marigold with bold red letters across the chest spelling out CORD.

"Hard to miss, that's for sure." Lareana smiled.

"Have you thought of joining?" Cathy asked. "We can always use more members. It would give you a chance to do something about people like Greaves. That's why I became a member."

Lareana was saved from answering as her father called her to the courtroom. The proceedings were about to begin.

Chapter 8

The judge entered.

Since their seats were in the back row, Lareana didn't see Greaves until everyone sat down. At the sight of his familiar slouch, all the anger she'd been shoving out of sight boiled up again. Her stomach clenched against the roiling. Her throat went dry.

She stared straight ahead until she felt a person take the seat next to her. At the same moment her concentration broke, Trey lifted her hand in his and squeezed. The sight of his face smiling encouragingly at her and the warmth of his body penetrated the coat of ice beginning to form around her power of reason.

The two lawyers who had been conferring with the judge took their places. The final act was about to commence.

"Will the defendant please rise?" the court clerk intoned.

Daniel Greaves pushed himself to his feet. He pulled his shoulders erect and, with a visibly expelled breath, looked straight at the judge.

"Mr. Greaves, the bench finds that you have received an unprecedented number of driving-while-intoxicated citations. You have caused four accidents involving bodily injury to innocent people. Also, you have been the recipient of every form of counseling and rehabilitation the state offers, all to no avail."

The judge looked over the rim of his glasses at the defendant. "Now you have been convicted of manslaughter in the death of John Amundson. I have no choice but to sentence you to no fewer than five and no more than ten years in the state penitentiary, sentence to begin immediately. Court dismissed." He banged the gavel.

The iron that had been holding Greaves upright melted. The man slumped in his chair, one hand over his eyes. A petite woman, tears streaming down her face, pushed open the swinging wooden gate and gathered him into her arms. A uniformed guard waited at his elbow.

Lareana felt no mercy. She didn't feel much of anything. Brian and Cathy gave her the victory sign when they caught her attention, but she couldn't respond.

Trey gathered her to him with one arm around her shoulders. He tried to turn her toward the exit, but she braced against his concern. Her attention remained riveted on the scene in the front of the room.

Greaves's lawyer shuffled his papers into his briefcase and, after a short conversation, clasped the man's shoulder and left.

The guard said something to Greaves. The convicted man replied, hugged the woman one more time, and just before he turned to go, raised his eyes to meet Lareana's. The unspoken request for forgiveness from this man who had been too proud to plead met the inability of the woman to forget.

Daniel Greaves left the courtroom through a back door with two guards in attendance.

A soft voice at Lareana's side stopped her as she was about to leave the room. "Mrs. Amundson?"

Lareana turned. "Yes?"

"Daniel asked me to give you this," said the woman who had been hugging Greaves. She held out a plain white envelope. "And I want you to know how sorry I am. . .for the death of your husband." Her voice broke. "My Daniel. . . well, he's not a bad man, you know. It's just when he's been drinking—" Her pale eyes pleaded for understanding.

A cooling draught of compassion released some of the tension coiled in Lareana's body. She took a deep breath and patted the woman's hand that lay on Lareana's coat sleeve. "Thank you for speaking with me." Almost as an afterthought, she took the envelope from the unhappy woman and slipped it in her pocket.

Trey carried Johnny as they left the building. Most of the crowd had dispersed. Only a lone TV camera and crew remained.

"I don't know how I feel," Lareana responded to the questions. "I thought I would feel wonderful, glad that Greaves got what he deserved, but—" she looked directly into the camera's all-seeing eye—"it won't bring John back. And while I can rejoice that no one else will be injured because of that particular alcoholic driving the highways, what about all the others?"

"You'll be all right?" Margaret asked when they reached the cars.

"Yes, Mom. I'm fine. You go on home. I know you have all kinds of things to do." She hugged both her parents. "Thanks again for coming in."

"I'll call you Sunday with plans for Thanksgiving," Margaret spoke through her rolled-down window.

Swen stepped close to Lareana. "You're not going to get involved with that CORD group, are you? Carrying signs and that kind of thing."

Lareana gazed pensively into his face. "I don't know, Dad. I just don't know. You've always told me to stand up for what I believe. Maybe this is the time I have to do that." She hugged him once again.

"I don't think he liked eating his own words," Trey whispered in her ear as the older couple drove off.

Lareana smiled. "No. They'd like to wrap their little girl in a down comforter and protect her, if they could." She shrugged. "But life isn't that easy, is it?"

That was one of those questions without an answer.

"Can I take you out to lunch, or would you rather I followed you home? We have to talk."

I'm not sure I want to talk, Lareana thought. *We might say things neither one of us is happy about.* She finished strapping Johnny's carrier in place. "I don't feel like going out to lunch." She shut the car door. "Guess I'll see you at the farm then."

Some reception, that, Trey thought as he followed her little car through the traffic and out to the country roads. A drizzle had started, graying the ageless hills and obscuring the mountain.

When they arrived at Three Trees, Lareana set the baby's seat on the floor and automatically put the teakettle on. As she shrugged out of her coat, she heard a crackling in her pocket. Remembering, she pulled out the envelope. It looked like her mind felt right now—blank. She tossed it on the table.

When she returned from hanging up her coat, Trey held the letter, idly tapping it against one forefinger. "Don't you want to see what's in this?"

Lareana removed Johnny's bunting and lifted him to her shoulder. "I'm not sure." Holding the baby in one arm, she took mugs out of the cupboard with the other. "Coffee or tea?"

Trey watched for a moment as she tried to do three things with one hand. Then he went to her and removed Johnny from her arms. "At least let me do this for you." He sat down on one of the kitchen chairs and cuddled the baby on his lap, one arm tucked securely around Johnny's middle.

The baby gurgled and waved his fists, then aimed for the finger that had proved so tasty before. "Is he ever going to quit chewing?" Trey asked. "And slobbering?"

Lareana paused in her preparations and watched the man and the baby. They had taken to each other as if they'd known each other all the baby's short life, instead of for only a month. Had it really only been a month since she met him? It seemed like a lifetime, so much had happened. Only it wasn't just that—

"You will know," her mother had said years ago, "when you meet the right man, the man God intends for you to marry, to be happy with."

But, Mother, she thought, *John was that man. You felt it as much as I did. And what do I feel now?* Well, God said He would supply her needs. She should be grateful. *I will be, Father God. I promise I will.* She set their mugs on the table and slumped into the seat.

They sat in silence, sipping their tea. Trey played with the baby, and Lareana stared out the window. Even her chrysanthemums in the boxes lining the porch failed to color the gray afternoon. The clump of lilac had lost its leaves and reached bent fingers toward the lowering sky. Samson whined at the door.

"I'll go change," Lareana said when Johnny started to fuss. "He's getting hungry."

She returned in a plaid flannel shirt and jeans. "I forgot to ask if you'd like some lunch." She finished tying her hair back with a Chinese-red scarf. "I can make you a sandwich."

Trey handed Johnny to his mother. "Why don't you feed him and I'll feed us? Just tell me where the fixings are." He walked into the living room, calling over his shoulders, "I'll just build this fire up first."

Lareana settled into her chair and drew the baby's quilt over her shoulder, cocooning Johnny in the warmth of her arm.

Trey left the stove door open, as he knew she liked, and returned to the kitchen. It was pleasant to hear him working around out there, frequently asking where things were and what she liked on her sandwich. Cupboard doors banged, the teakettle whistled, and Johnny nursed contentedly. When Samson whined again, Trey let him in with a pat and a friendly word.

"Do you want to eat in here or in the kitchen?" he asked, leaning one shoulder against the doorjamb. He had removed his navy blazer that revealed a sweater vest the same blue as a lake under intermittent clouds. He'd rolled the sleeves of his white shirt up to the elbows and done away with the tie. Wool slacks matched the sweater, a grayed blue but with the promise of clear skies somewhere, sometime. "Hey, are you there?" Trey's smile brought her back to his question.

"Whatever." She returned his smile. "I can't make any major decisions today."

No, I bet not, Trey thought as he returned to his duties. *You look about done in.* Those shadows under her eyes appeared as if they'd been painted on with indelible ink.

On her way back from tucking Johnny into his crib, Lareana picked up the envelope from the table and brought it into the living room. Trey had arranged their lunch on the coffee table in front of the L-shaped, oatmeal-colored sectional. As she bit into the ham sandwich, she discovered just how hungry she was. Reaching for the envelope, she slit it open and began to read.

Dear Mrs. Amundson,

I know you will have a hard time believing this. I am aware of the animosity you feel toward me in the death of your husband, and I don't blame you. But I wanted to tell you how sorry I am. I know it doesn't do any good after the fact like this, but if sometime you can find it in your heart to forgive me. . .

Lareana found herself trying to read through a veil of tears. She wiped them away with one hand and continued:

I can't even promise never to drink again, but I have been going to AA

*and haven't had a drink since the night of the accident. I can guess how I
would feel in your place. God be with you.*

*Sincerely,
Daniel Greaves*

Lareana's shoulders shook with the force of the sobs that wracked her body.
She drew her knees up to her chest, curling into a ball of pain. The letter drifted
to the floor.

At the first sign of her distress, Trey reached for her to take her in the shelter
of his arms and comfort her, but her rigid form refused to yield. He watched her
agony in silence, one hand stroking the back of her neck.

When the letter left her fingers, he picked it up and began to read. *Oh, my
love.* His desire to bear her pain burned within his heart. *I had hoped this could be
over by now but. . .*

Her weeping didn't lessen.

When his soothing hand didn't help, Trey turned and picked her up, cradling her in his lap whether she wanted it or not.

"I can't forgive him."

He could finally make some sense of her words.

"I've tried and I. . .I just can't." A fresh storm unleashed more incoherent
ramblings.

Trey didn't try to decipher them. He just held her.

"Wh–what kind of person. . .what kind of Ch–Christian. . .am I that I can't
forgive someone. . .when he asks?" She drew in a shuddering breath. "Today. . .when
he looked at me, I—I knew what he wanted. J–Jesus says to l–love your enemies. *I
can't do that.*" Her hands clenched and pounded on his chest. *"I can't."*

Trey continued the murmurings she didn't seem to hear. It made him feel he
was doing something, anything. He wiped the tears from her face and smoothed
her hair back again and yet again.

He had no idea how much time had passed when the sobs turned into
sniggles and the sniffles turned into the sleep of utter exhaustion. *Oh, my love.
How can I help you?* His thoughts followed the rhythm of her breathing, periodi-
cally broken by a leftover sob.

Jesus, Trey prayed in the quiet of his mind as he held her, *only You can help
her with this thing. I know You can because You helped me.*

Twilight had deepened to dark when Lareana awoke. She was huddled on
the couch under a crocheted afghan. A friendly pool of lamplight drew her eyes
to the man sitting in the rocking chair across from her. Trey had Johnny cuddled
against his shoulder. Within one minute, thumb popped in his mouth and eyes

half closed, the baby was enjoying the steady motion of the chair. Trey's eyes, at half-mast, held the same contented air.

Lareana's own eyes felt as if someone had thrown dust in them. Her throat was raw, and when she moved her head, an anvil took over, its beat pounding out the ebb and flow of her pulse. Her gaze turned to the letter lying open on the oak table.

She clenched her eyes against the sight of it, trying to wish away its existence. Before the letter, she could convince herself that Daniel Greaves didn't care, that he was beneath the human emotions of love and concern. No longer.

Father in Heaven, she prayed in the quiet of her mind, *I've come up against another one of the places that I can't, don't even want to, handle by myself. You know me. I've tried to do it. . .no. . .I'll be honest. I haven't tried to forgive Daniel Greaves. I was too angry. Now all I can ask is Your forgiveness and for You to forgive him. Thank You, Father.* Her quiet "amen" definitely meant "so be it."

I'll just lie here and rest a moment, she thought. *Then I'll get up.*

Her moment stretched until the phone rang at nine-thirty. She heard Trey answer it. This time when she raised her head, the blacksmith had taken his anvil elsewhere. "Who was it?" she asked when Trey came back into the living room.

"Inga. She wondered how I made out feeding Johnny."

"Feeding Johnny?"

"Yes. You do that when a baby starts to cry." A warm smile deepened the creases around his mouth. "I called her and she told me where to find the bottled milk in the freezer. You really are efficient, you know." He sat down on the couch, pillowing her head in his lap. "I didn't know you could save breast milk like that."

"You learn all kinds of things on a dairy farm."

"As if that had anything to do with it." He stroked the hair back from her forehead.

"So where's Johnny now?" She wasn't sure if she wanted an answer or not. She hated the idea of moving.

"In bed."

"In bed?"

"Lareana, are you hard of hearing or something? You keep repeating everything I say." A ghost of a proud chuckle over his accomplishments floated through his words.

"You know what I mean." She thumped him on the knee. "How did I sleep through all that?"

His stroking continued as he tried to sound offended. "We were *very* quiet. I explained to that young man in there that his mother had just had a very hard time and needed some rest. He agreed. And we were. . .quiet, that is."

"Just like that?"

"Well. . .sort of."

Quiet reigned again for a time.

"Thank you." Lareana knew she should get up and get going, but a pleasant lethargy had invaded her limbs. The warmth of Trey's thigh under her cheek, the gentle pressure of his fingertips blazing a line from her temple up into her hair, combined to keep her in a capsule of comfort.

"Trey?"

"Um-m-m?"

She pulled herself up to lean against his shoulder, her hair brushing his cheek. "I have something important to tell you."

His fingers stopped their soothing pattern. "Well?" His arm drew her closer, if that were possible.

"I love you." There, it was out. A simple declarative statement. She raised her eyes to watch for expressions on his face.

"Are you sure?" It wasn't the response she'd expected.

"No. I go around telling that to strange men all the time."

Trey smothered his laugh in the sweet fragrance of her hair. "Oh, Lareana, my love. Just don't go finding any other men to say that to. This man's going to be all you can handle."

"Does that mean you love me?"

"Since the day I heard you messing up poetry for your cows. It was like a light went on in my life." He lowered his head so his lips were a hairsbreadth above hers. "And it's been getting brighter ever since." Their lips met and Lareana reached one arm around his neck. The kiss changed from one of confirmation to one of growing passion.

Trey raised his head. "I think I'd better be on my way." He dropped a light kiss on the end of her nose. He repeated it after he had his coat on and was going out the door. "Good night, Lareana, love."

Lareana hugged herself with both arms as she trailed up the stairway to bed. She had barely crawled under the covers before sleep, a deep, restful sleep with no nightmares, claimed her.

❧

That same air of peace and relaxation greeted her in the morning when Johnny's wake-up call informed her that mommies should feed babies—immediately. The peace stayed with her through her morning devotions. Now, when she prayed, her words seemed to go directly to the heart of God, not to ricochet off the ceiling. Daniel Greaves was not in the way anymore.

When she thought of Greaves, she no longer saw the arrogant defendant at the beginning of the trial. All she could see was a broken man crying in his wife's arms.

By the next morning, Lareana had succumbed to her inner prompting to write him a letter. That would bring the act of forgiveness full circle. It wasn't as hard as she had thought it would be. By the time she finished, she had written one to his wife, too.

I'm glad for you that Alcoholics Anonymous is helping. Rest assured that I forgive you and I know that if you ask, God will, too—

In the following days, Lareana was to deal with the forgetting part of forgiveness. Pictures of Daniel Greaves leapt into her mind at the oddest times. Every time that happened, she replaced the pictures with one of Jesus. But just when she thought Greaves was vanquished from her mind's eye, he would reappear.

"I'm working at it, Mom," she said one day when she called Margaret. "I know I'm getting better because the anger's gone. It seems to come easier every day. When I remember Greaves, it doesn't hurt anymore."

"I'm glad," Margaret said. "People aren't made to live with hate and bitterness. They die from it. . .or maybe drink. Then, too, maybe this is God's way of reminding you to pray for Mr. Greaves."

Lareana felt her resentment flare up. "Mother!"

"I know you'll do the right thing." The pattern of her speech changed. "Now, about Thanksgiving—"

Lareana was glad for the change in subject. They spent the next couple of minutes planning for the holiday. It was Lareana's turn to host this year, so dinner would be at Three Trees. Margaret would take care of inviting the relatives. Thanksgiving was one of the few times during the year when all the aunts, uncles, and cousins got together. They usually fed about thirty people.

"I'm glad you feel up to it," Margaret said. "I was afraid there for a while—"

"I think I can do it now. During the trial I was so busy I had no time to think."

"Will Trey be there?"

"I hope so, but we haven't discussed holiday traditions yet." The silence lasted more than a moment. "He loves me, Mom."

"I know."

"And I love him."

"Yes."

"And you and Daddy approve?"

Margaret's sigh came from the depths of her mother heart. "We really like him, you know that. And we appreciate all he's done for you—"

"But?"

"Well, it's very soon after John's death."

"We've talked about that, Mom. I think John would approve of Trey."

"And Trey's selling liquor, Lareana. You know how the church feels about that, how we feel about it. We can't condone it."

"I know." Lareana sighed. "Give Dad a hug for me."

She gently replaced the receiver.

❦

In the next few weeks, Trey was so busy with meetings about Timber Country, Lareana felt she never saw him. Talking on the phone every day wasn't enough. One day she called her aunt who was a florist in Seattle and made a request.

When Trey arrived back at his office after a lengthy meeting with financiers for the theme park, he found a crystal vase filled with pink and fuchsia bleeding hearts and lacy asparagus fern on his desk.

"My heart bleeds for you. Love, Lareana," the note read.

"Ditto." Trey said when she answered the phone. "Can you come up here? There's no way I can get away right now, except in the middle of the week."

"I know. And you need your sleep. If I came, how could you fit me into your schedule?"

"We'd at least have lunch together." He studied the calendar. "How about Tuesday?"

"Uncle Haakan and I are going to a farm dispersal sale that day. We're finally getting some new stock."

"Thursday?" The silence warned him he wouldn't like her answer.

"I have guests coming for lunch—Brian Campbell and Cathy Hanson. They're bringing some people they think I should meet."

"CORD?"

"Yep."

"You're joining then?"

"I still haven't decided. That's what this meeting is all about. I've been reading reams of stuff on alcoholism, drunk driving, and the various programs and laws."

Trey's sigh could have been one of exasperation or defeat, Lareana wasn't sure which. She wasn't sure she wanted to know, either. "You'll be here for Thanksgiving, won't you?" she asked as the silence stretched between them.

"Of course I will. I get back from San Francisco on Wednesday evening. Can I bring anything?"

Lareana mentally reviewed the menu and who was bringing what. "Not that I can think of. Just yourself. And, Trey," she whispered before she hung up, "come as early as you can."

❦

Lareana's meeting with the CORD group gave her plenty of fodder for thought. While Citizens Organized for Responsible Drinking seemed more fanatical than she wanted to be, she could see lots of good coming from their program. Mostly in public awareness.

They discussed the tough new laws in Oregon and the need for changes in Washington, too. All agreed that mandatory jail sentences would cut down on offenders. But as one of the legislators had said, "Where do you find the jail space?" There were certainly no easy answers.

One thing Lareana did agree to do. She would make herself available for television interviews. But she didn't promise to take Johnny every time, even though one person applied some pressure along that line.

❦

In church on Sunday, Lareana wished Trey could be with her instead of in California. Having him with her in church was so special. There was something about God's order of things when a family worshiped together. There. She'd referred to him as family again. How could anything that seemed so right be so wrong?

Pastor Jensguard probed a sensitive spot with his sermon topic. "Love your enemies. . .and pray for those who. . .persecute you," he read from the Bible in front of him.

"God has never called His people to the easy road," the pastor said. "Loving those who love you isn't hard, at least not usually." His smile encouraged the congregation to laugh at themselves a bit. "But praying for someone who has done you wrong. . .that's where God's grace comes in. He never expects us to grow by ourselves. But He does expect us to open ourselves to His channels of love and let that love pour through us."

Lareana would have liked to be able to shield her thoughts from God as well as she hid her feelings behind her "all is well" facade. *All right, so I'll pray for Daniel Greaves. I get the point. You don't have to hit me over the head with a two by four.* She smiled to herself.

❦

"How's the heart, fair lady?" Trey's phone call late one evening was welcome, even if it was a poor substitute for the real thing.

"Still bleeding." Lareana cradled the phone against her ear and snuggled down in the blankets. "How's the dragon-slayer?"

"Lonely. Frantically busy. Beat. California may be sunny, but I haven't had time out of these offices to find out."

Lareana's heart went out to him at the weary timbre of his voice. "Oh, Trey. I wish there were something I could do for you."

"You could hop a plane."

"I meant right now, silly."

Their conversation extended over an hour. Nothing changed in their circumstances, but one more block was laid in the foundation of their growing love.

"Come home soon," she whispered as she laid the phone back in the cradle.

Chapter 9

Lareana was out of bed before the birds on Thanksgiving morning.
Trey would be arriving today. . .but when? *I wonder what's early to him?* Her thoughts took off on flights of their own. She made her way downstairs to start the stuffing for the thirty-pound turkey she'd purchased.

Johnny heard her out in the kitchen and added his queries to her busy schedule.

"If you get such good response with a yell or two," Lareana muttered as she wiped her hands on the dishtowel, "what's going to happen when you can talk?"

When the baby caught sight of her, his happy grin joined flailing arms and jerking legs. His actions banished any twinge of annoyance. She hugged him close and then laid him on the changing table. By the time he was diapered and dressed again, Lareana could see the tinges of dawn cracking the cloud cover in the east. Grays turned to mauve, to violet and pink—joyful banners heralding a new day.

Johnny did not get a thrill out of the sunrise. He wanted to eat. . .now! And he told her so. Lareana sighed and turned from the opalescent dawn.

"One job finished," she breathed as she set up the playpen in the kitchen and settled him inside on his tummy with his favorite toys. She returned to the stuffing. Wrestling the huge bird into the sink so she could insert the stuffing reminded her of other Thanksgivings. John had always helped stuff the bird. The thought caused no pain, only a vague impression of sorrow, like looking into an ancient mirror. She shook her head at the realization. The healing she'd been praying for was progressing.

She glanced at the clock and mentally calculated the time needed to bake the bird. Right on schedule. Without taking a break even for a cup of tea, she checked on Johnny in the playpen, added a few more toys, and flew back upstairs to get dressed.

Trey's coming. Trey's coming. Her thoughts beat time with her heart. She chose an amethyst wool shirtwaist dress out of the closet and threw it on the bed. Hers might have been the shortest shower on record.

She'd just finished clipping the sides of her hair up with mother-of-pearl combs and inserting amethyst studs in her ears when Samson activated his early warning system. A quick glance out the window confirmed her hopes. A familiar silver Corvette was parked by the front gate.

Her softly billowing skirt brushed the backs of her calves as she descended the stairs. She could hear Trey in the kitchen carrying on a conversation with a jabbering baby. They sounded perfectly content without her.

It may have sounded that way, but the look in Trey's eyes when she entered the kitchen dispelled any qualms she might have had.

Woman, you're definitely worth the wait, Trey thought when he saw her walk through the door. *I was afraid you were a figment of my imagination. Huh! If Seattle was too distant for us even to have lunch, California might as well have been the moon.* He rose from his kneeling position in front of Johnny, his eyes never leaving hers. When he opened his arms, she stepped into them.

"Ah, Lareana, love." He twined his fingers in her hair and raised her chin with the heels of his hands planted caressingly along her jaw line. Kisses, lighter than the brush of hummingbird wings, closed each eyelid, cherished each dimple, and greeted her waiting lips.

"You smell like roses in springtime," he breathed when he drew back an infinitesimal distance. He brushed his lips back and forth across hers, igniting nerve endings wherever he touched. "And just in case you didn't suspect, I love you, I love you—"

"I love you." They shared the last declaration together, two minds, two hearts in unison.

They drew back, hands still locked around each other's waists as if afraid of letting go.

"I'm glad you define early like this." Lareana reached up to breathe a kiss into the cleft of his chin, something she'd dreamed of doing for quite some time. She rested her forehead against the thunder of his heart.

"Lareana."

"Um-m-m." She lifted her face to his, the smile she bestowed on him rivaling the dawn and causing his heart to constrict.

"I have something for you. But first I have to ask you something."

Lareana nodded.

"I wanted to do something spectacular. Maybe skywriting or fireworks. But I can't. I thought of sending it with a troop of clowns, but you mean too much to me."

His voice grew husky. "Maybe poetry would help, but I didn't want to wait long enough to compose a poem. Lareana, will you marry me?" His eyes searched hers for any sign of hesitancy.

Her simple "Of course" rang bells of joy through the corridors of his mind. "You're sure?"

"This is a repeat of another conversation I remember. I don't go around accepting marriage proposals every day of the week." She threaded her fingers through the waves of hair on the sides of his head. "So you're just stuck with me," she said between kisses.

Johnny banged his chain of keys against the edge of the playpen.

"Or rather with both of us."

"A package deal, huh? Something along the lines of love me, love my son?"

"And dog, cows, horses, and you have no idea how many relatives, many of whom will be here before we know it. Are you prepared to meet the troops?"

"I will be once you put this on." He drew a velvet box from deep in his pocket.

When he opened the lid, Lareana gasped with pleasure. The glinting diamond on an etched gold band was surrounded by chips of amethyst, cleverly designed to make both rings inseparable when locked together. He slipped the engagement ring of the pair on her ring finger, then raised her hand to his mouth and kissed the ring into place.

Lareana felt a tingling clear down to the tips of her toes. "Thank you," she whispered, wishing she could find words to tell him how she felt. "The ring's beautiful and. . .and so are you."

Marriage, she thought. *I'm. . .we're getting married. But when? Am I ready to remarry?* Her thoughts froze. *What will the family say?* She bit her lip. *Knowing them. . .they'll have plenty to say.*

She held out her hand, letting the stones catch the light. The ring certainly did look lovely. "You have excellent taste."

"I know." He kissed the corner of her mouth. "I know."

Lareana laughed, a carefree sound that called up all the desires within him to protect her, to cherish her, to bring the song of laughter to her lips and help her share it with her world.

Johnny, tired of being ignored and ready for a bit of a snooze, interrupted their idyllic moment.

"Have you had breakfast yet?" Lareana asked after putting Johnny down. "I have cinnamon rolls in the freezer. They warm up quickly in the microwave."

"Sounds good. You'll eat with me?" She nodded. "Then we'll set up the tables."

❧

The living and dining rooms had become a banquet hall by the time they set up the three tables borrowed from the grange hall. With orange candles and fall fruits and vegetables, Lareana created a centerpiece on each table. There wasn't a lot of room to move around, but everyone would have a place to sit.

"How many people are you expecting?" Trey eyed their labors dubiously. "It looks like you could accommodate an army."

"You'll think it *is* an army by the end of the day." Lareana clicked a tape into the stereo. Strains from *South Pacific* filled the air. "Not exactly a holiday piece, but it sure means a lot to me."

"What if we went there on our honeymoon?"

"Went where?" She laid out napkins.

"To the South Pacific. Spending February on warm, sunny beaches sounds like a bit of heaven to me."

Lareana stopped what she was doing. "Is that when you want to get married?"

"No. I'd like to marry you tomorrow or next week at the latest, but February's the earliest I could get away for any kind of a honeymoon. You know how much trouble we had getting together for lunch."

"We didn't make it."

"What'd I tell you?"

Lareana came around the table and, slipping her hands around his waist, leaned her cheek against his chest.

❧

Turkey perfume greeted all the arriving guests after they'd been heralded by Samson. The house was soon full of laughing relatives, from young children who made a beeline for the haymow in the barn to elderly Aunt Karren who held court in the corner. The noise level rose accordingly, but it was a cheerful hubbub, a gathering of relatives who loved each other and showed it—most of the time.

"I've got something special to tell you," Lareana said, hugging both her parents when they entered the house. But someone interrupted with a question right then, and she got sidetracked. Lareana regretted that later.

Each group of relatives that arrived put more food on the tables. "Looks like we're feeding all the troops at Fort Lewis," Uncle Haakan said. That statement was his annual contribution to the festivities. Most of the time, he was an observer.

Trey met them all with a smile on his face and a special comment for each one of them. Within an hour they all felt they'd known him for years.

Lareana watched from the doorway as he sat with her aunt Karren, listening to tales of her trip to Norway. *Sure made her day*, Lareana mused as she watched the sparkle in the dimming eyes of her great-aunt.

"Where'd you find that hunk?" one of her cousins whispered. "He's a knockout."

"Would you believe in the milking parlor?" Lareana bit her lip to keep from laughing aloud at the expression on her cousin's face.

As the hot food was being transferred to the tables, Lareana sent one of the kids down to the barn to round up the others. When they were all assembled, Uncle Haakan asked the blessing.

Lareana had a hard time keeping her mind on the words his rich voice offered up. She was too full of her own thanks. And all of her gratitude had to do with the man standing beside her. Trey was not only filling in the gap left by John, he was already creating a place for himself. At the universal "amen," everyone sat.

Lareana's ring went unnoticed until she joined everyone in passing platters and bowls heaped with food around the table. Her cousin, sitting directly across from her, neatly dropped the platter she was holding. "Lareana!" The astonishment in her voice effectively halted all conversation. "Is that an engagement ring on your hand?" All eyes stared at the flashing diamond on her finger.

Trey and Lareana exchanged a glance that said quite clearly, "Well, the fat's in the fire now." Together they stood. Lareana nodded at Trey.

"This morning I asked Lareana to marry me and she accepted." His voice carried to every ear in the room, even to half-deaf Aunt Karren.

"But she hardly knows him," the old woman's querulous voice responded. "And John's only been gone a few months."

The silence was brief but spoke volumes. Uncle Haakan rose to the occasion. "Congratulations, Lareana; Trey, welcome to the family." The buzz of conversation resumed, but the announcement was not mentioned again.

I was afraid of this, Lareana thought. *Guess I know this bunch pretty well after all. I should have warned Trey.* She peeped sideways at his handsome profile. *And it'll probably get worse before it gets better.*

If the groans and moans from around the tables meant anything, dinner was a huge success. When the men exited to the sofas and chairs, the women began clearing the table. Trey didn't join the men. He pitched in with willing hands, carting dishes and food back to the kitchen.

Once he overheard two women whispering, "How long has John been dead now? Only eight months, isn't it?" asked the first. "Yes, and this man's been divorced, too, you know," replied the second. "How can Margaret bear that?"

It's not Margaret's problem, Trey wanted to say. *It's mine and Lareana's and we don't consider it a problem. Why should you?* But he knew the answer. These older people had lived with such dictates for a long time.

Lareana heard the whispers, too. And caught the speculative glances cast her way. One aunt took her aside.

"Lareana," she said, her eyes stern above an equally serious mouth, "you know the saying, 'Marry in haste; repent at leisure.' I can't bear to think of you rushing into marriage with that man, no matter how charming he is." She shook her graying head. "Can't you at least wait awhile?"

Johnny whimpered. *Saved by the bawl,* Lareana punned as she excused herself to retrieve her crying son. *The old bat. Who does she think she is?* Another voice answered the first. *Your Aunt Sigrid, that's who.* It was like a debate going on in her head. Aunt Sigrid had always been one of her favorite people.

"But she doesn't mind telling me what she thinks." Lareana closed the debate as she changed Johnny's diaper in the quiet of his room. She settled herself in a rocker by his crib and let him enjoy his Thanksgiving dinner.

Her thoughts winged upward. *Lord, I know what I want to do here, and I believe You sent Trey to me. You talk about love and forgiveness. That's what You've made me learn. Forgiveness.* A smile smoothed the worry lines from her forehead. She nodded. *Thanks.*

When she re-entered the living room, she felt a definite coolness in the air. While dusk was falling, no one but Uncle Haakan had made any move to leave.

She drew her mother out into the kitchen. "I wanted you and Dad to be the first to hear about our engagement," she said. "That's what I was referring to when you got here. I know how you feel, but—"

"Lareana—" Margaret put her arms around her daughter—"you know we love you, no matter what. We're afraid you're taking on some tremendous problems, but our love for you comes first."

"Thanks." Lareana hugged her back. "I know that, but it always helps to hear it." She took her mother by the arm. "Now, please back me up while I stand up for what I believe, okay?"

Lareana assumed a relaxed pose in the middle of the area where the adults had congregated. For once, it wasn't women in the kitchen and men in the living room. "I have something I'd like to say to all of you." She glanced from person to person, catching her relatives' attention.

Trey watched from the sidelines, proud of her spirit, but unsure what she planned to do.

"You all stood 'round me when John was killed. Some of you stayed with me." She smiled at her aunt Karren. "Others came and helped with the chores, even the haying when Uncle Haakan and I needed you." Several of the men nodded. "You have called me when I was in the dumps and helped me with the canning when Johnny and I first came home. You're a wonderful family, and I feel proud to be part of you."

She glanced at Trey long enough to get an approving nod. "But I have learned something in the last few months that I'd like to share with you. With Trey's help, I had to learn to forgive the man who killed my husband. Aren't we all given chances to begin again? I believe this is our chance, mine and Trey's, and I don't think time or the past should stand in our way. Anytime is always the right time for love." She paused, her eyes going to the mantel where a picture of John was displayed. "And I know we have John's blessing." No one moved. No one said a word. Lareana found her mother's eyes swimming in tears, and her father dropped his head.

Trey swallowed hard to dislodge the lump her words brought to his throat. *With a woman like that in my corner, how can I lose? Thank You, Father, for this second chance.*

Lareana moved to his side. "There's fresh coffee in the kitchen if any of you would like some. And plenty of leftover pie."

It was as if her words released the spell that had held them all motionless. Some stood and stretched. Others started visiting with the people next to them. Aunt Inga came over to where Trey and Lareana were standing.

"Now don't you worry." Her chirpy voice radiated good will. "They'll come around. You just wait and see. And, Lareana, I agree with you wholeheartedly. Welcome to the family, Trey."

The evening sped by as some left and others refilled their coffee cups. Lareana's parents had to go home but shared hugs with both Lareana and Trey as they left. Johnny woke up again, delighted with all the opportunities to entertain.

"That's one of the friendliest babies I've ever seen," Inga remarked. "He almost never cries."

"If I didn't know how prejudiced you are, I'd think you were the proud grandma," Trey teased her gently.

"Couldn't love him more if I were." She tapped Trey's arm with a gnarled finger. "There's an extra bed at our house tonight if you'd like. Save you a long drive."

"Thank you. I accept." Trey felt warmth and approval in Inga's display of hospitality.

Even Aunt Sigrid hugged the pair of them before she left.

"Please listen to the love in your heart," Lareana whispered in her aunt's ear during the embrace, "and accept him."

"I'll try, child. But I just don't know." The elderly woman shook her head as she walked down the steps.

"What a day." Lareana collapsed on the sofa after the last guest had departed. She kicked off her shoes and leaned against the backrest, yawning and stretching.

Trey resisted the urge to join her until she lifted the drift of golden hair from her neck with both hands and let it fall. He gave in, the lure of gold too great.

"Enticing is against the rules if you want me to make it to Inga's house tonight," he murmured against the sweetness of her lips.

"My, how you talk, sir." Her eyebrow arched, reminiscent of bygone days when women hid behind fans. "But then, talk is cheap. Or so they say."

"Then let's stop talking if you rate it so poorly."

"And—?"

"Do this instead." His lips took the place of his words. The kiss was worth the wait.

※

If Trey and Lareana thought they'd been busy before Thanksgiving, they were in shock afterwards. They discovered again, much to their dismay, that the distance between Seattle and Yelm didn't lend itself to easy commuting, especially since they were both going ninety miles an hour in different directions.

Lareana awoke the first Saturday in December to two inches of snow creating a fairyland outside her windows. By the time she called Trey and invited him to go with them to cut the Christmas tree, it was twice as deep.

Just before he arrived, the sun came out, painting the world in diamond glitter on fluffy ermine. Lareana had Johnny all ready in his backpack. She handed Trey the saw and shrugged into the straps of the pack.

"I'll take the kid, you get the tree. Even trade." His smile rivaled the icicles on the trees for brightness.

"Which way?" Trey took her mittened hand in his. He held the handsaw up toward the sun, studying the pointed edges. "This doesn't look sharp enough to cut pussy willows."

"Well, since pussy willows won't be out for a time, you can practice on a pine tree and develop your muscles."

He studied the saw again. "Maybe it'll cut butter—softened, that is."

"Gripe, gripe, gripe." She shifted the backpack. Johnny kept bouncing and kicking every time Samson ran by, frolicking in the snow.

Choosing the tree was not an easy task. Lareana had to look at every one, at least once. As they meandered back and forth through the woods, Lareana and Trey kept up a steady discussion of Timber Country, farming, CORD, and their wedding date. The last topic occupied most of the conversation.

When Lareana finally decided on the perfect tree, Trey sawed it down and hoisted it to his shoulder. . .for a distance of at least a hundred feet. Then moved by common sense and a complaining back, he dragged it the rest of the way.

"Did you have to pick out the biggest one?" he puffed as he maneuvered the tree through the barbed wire fence. "Where are you going to put such a monster?"

"You'll see" was her pert reply—just before she pelted him with a snowball.

"You'll get yours, when you don't have that guardian on your back."

The tree did fit right in the stairwell as she'd planned. And it was a beauty, full and permeating the house with pine perfume.

"My 4-H club is coming tomorrow to decorate it." Lareana stared at the boxes of decorations she and Trey carted down from the attic. "That'll be the first of my entertaining for the season. I love it."

"What other parties are you planning?"

"CORD and the Homemakers Club." She thought for a moment. "And the Dairy Wives."

"Would you like to hostess a party for me?"

"Are you serious?"

"Of course. Ada will do all the preparations. You just bring your natural graciousness to make everyone feel at home. Since you do that without trying, it should be a fun evening."

"I'd love to." She snuggled under his arm. "When?"

When became the operative word. The days ran by like sprinters going for the gold.

Lareana had her first taste of distress when the women from her Homemakers Club brought a bottle of brandy to put in the eggnog. That had been the custom in the past and Lareana had forgotten to inform them any differently.

Then on the night of the CORD gathering, someone brought homemade butter and rum for hot buttered rum. When Lareana questioned it, they looked at her as though she'd lost her senses.

Cathy took her aside. "We don't say that people can't drink. You know that, Lareana. We try to help them learn to drink with moderation. . .responsibly."

Lareana swallowed back her retort and got out the Christmas mugs. She and John had bought them for parties just like this. . .for hot buttered rum, as a matter of fact.

But resentment over her inability to stay with her decision of no liquor in her house nagged at her. She could have kicked them all out. Or tossed the alcohol out the back window. But where did her rights end and theirs begin? Surely she should be able to make the choices in her own home.

It seemed everywhere she went, people were offering "holiday cheer." Had it always been this way? She thought back. *Yes, it had. I just didn't notice because I like eggnog and hot buttered rum, too.* There, the admission was out. Now what?

Trying to keep her life in balance and remember the real reason for Christmas seemed harder as the day approached.

She still hadn't decided on a gift for Trey. All her other gifts were either made or bought, already wrapped, and placed under the tree.

Johnny thought the Christmas tree enchanting. He sat for hours watching the flickering lights and brightly colored ornaments.

Next year, Lareana thought, *we'll probably have to put the tree in the playpen. Or hang it from the ceiling.*

Trey watched her frantic pace with concern. He wasn't too excited over her continued frustration with the serving of alcoholic beverages, either. Every time they talked about Timber Country, somehow the subject gravitated back to the saloon.

"I'm tired of talking about it!" he flared up one night. "Can't we leave it alone for a while? It's still a long time until the place opens."

"But the architects are designing it now. I just don't see how I can support a place that serves alcoholic drinks, much less help plan it." She rubbed a tired hand across her forehead, much like a weary child. The blue circles had reappeared under her eyes.

"Lareana—" His voice flicked like the tip of a bullwhip. "Let's drop it." He rammed his hands into the back pockets of his jeans and went to stand in front of the window. The twinkling lights draped around the porch roof cast shadows of blue and red across his face.

He turned to her, remorse written like a banner across his face. "I'm sorry. I'm just too tired to argue, and so are you. And besides, I love you too much ever to want to fight with you." He walked back to her and drew her into his arms. "It'll work out, love, somehow. I promise."

I don't know. Lareana tried to keep the doubt out of her mind. At that point, it didn't seem possible.

Chapter 10

It didn't get any better.

The day of Trey's party, Lareana wanted to call in sick. She'd spent the morning taping a town hall-style discussion for a television program to be aired between Christmas and New Year's. A heckler in the studio audience had managed to get in a few slurring remarks like "self-righteous prohibitionists" and "do-gooders" before he was hustled out. While the knowledge that starting the tape over was supposed to make her feel better, it didn't help a whole lot. The producer tried to reassure her after the taping. The program looked good and would be very effective, or so he said.

She still hadn't found that perfect present for Trey, and Christmas was only a week away.

She left for Seattle early and, on an uncharacteristic whim, stopped at an arts and crafts fair at the Tacoma Mall. The covered mall was packed, both in the many stores and the wide decorated aisles. Tinny Christmas carols tinkled faintly amid the hubbub of harried shoppers.

The perfect gift, displayed on a navy velvet cloth, appeared to be waiting just for her. The artist cast his work in bronze and had many pieces on display, but Lareana failed to notice his other wares. The *gift* stood out.

The bronze depicted an early logging scene. The burly lumberjack, a perfect replica down to his suspenders, knit stocking cap, and an ax handle across his shoulder, stood watching a giant fir tree in its death plunge.

Lareana could hear the cry of "Timber!" the shattering of branches. She could smell the pungent scent of fresh fir and sense the logger's satisfaction.

The artist waited patiently on the other side of the U-shaped table. "You like that one."

Lareana raised her eyes to encounter the far-seeing gaze of an outdoorsman. He might have doubled as the model for the piece. "Yes, it's just the thing." She pulled out her checkbook. "Are you, by chance, a logger?" she asked as she wrote. "You create such vivid images." She touched the screaming branches forever captured mid-fall.

"Have been." His answer, though short, was not abrupt, but demonstrated an economy of words.

Lareana studied several other pieces. "And a fisherman. . .and a farmer?"

The man smiled, the kind of smile that deepened the weathered creases around his mouth and crinkled the crow's-feet at his eagle-keen eyes, a smile that invited her response. "Whatever's at hand." Lareana nodded, her smile deepening in imitation of his. All the while her fingers were busy exploring, comforting the dying fir tree.

"I'll be getting in touch with you," she said, as she finished writing her check and slipping his business card in her billfold. "I know just the showcase for your work." *Maybe*, she thought after wishing him a Merry Christmas, *he'd like to cast his scenes right there at the park.*

While the bronze was no more than eight inches tall, it was heavy enough that Lareana was glad she'd found a parking place up close. All in all, the excursion had taken only twenty minutes. She would arrive for the party early.

Trey had given her good instructions, so she was able to drive right to the underground parking garage of his condominium. Lareana unhooked her garment bag from the back hanger and picked up her carryall. Though thoughts of a country mouse arriving in the big city played in the back of her mind, she conveyed an air of poise and assurance. She alone knew it was fake.

Trey hadn't told her that the tenth floor was the penthouse. He hadn't warned her of ankle-deep carpeting in the hall or carved double wooden doors at the entry. This country mouse wanted to turn tail and run.

Lareana pushed the buzzer.

Ada fit her name. When the housekeeper answered the door, she took one look at the lovely young woman standing in the hall and beamed a welcome that would have melted a heart of concrete.

"My stars!" She held the door wider. "If you aren't everything Mr. Trey has been raving about. Come in. Come in." She shut the door again and took Lareana's hand. "My dear, I'm so happy to meet you." Lareana felt she'd just been made part of the family.

"Mr. Trey said for you to make yourself ready. He'll be here a bit later." Ada led her charge down a hall to a bedroom decorated in royal blue. The bathroom matched, with dark blue fittings and thirsty blue towels.

"I'll hang up your things, and you take a bath or whatever you like. If you're hungry, I'll bring you a tray." Ada stopped chattering to repeat, "I'm so glad you're here."

Lareana was, too, as she slipped into the tub redolent with rose-scented, bubbling bath oil and settled her head against a foam neck rest. With her hair pinned on top of her head, she let herself relax for the first time in days.

She had finally managed to tear herself away from the luxury of the Jacuzzi tub and was standing in front of the bedroom mirror, nearly ready, when Trey knocked at her door. "Come in," she said as she clipped on a dangling crystal earring.

Lareana turned for his inspection, glittering in an ice blue satin, floor-length gown. It fell freely from slight gathers at her shoulders, grazing her hips and swishing as she floated across the floor and into his arms. The modest, draped neckline seemed to draw attention to sparkling dangles in her ears.

Trey finally brought his lips to hers, ending the ache of abstinence and calling into being the joy of reunion.

"I think we have to go, my lady," he whispered in her ear, his breath sending tremors of delight rampaging through her system.

I'd rather stay right here. Lareana leaned closer rather than breaking the contact. *Let them have their party without us.*

Trey dropped a last kiss on her forehead. He began humming, softly, only for her ear. . . "Some Enchanted Evening."

Lareana ordered her internal aerial exhibitionists back to the wings. *I feel more like "We're Off to See the Wizard. . ."*

To Lareana, the living room seemed about an acre in size. The decorations were magnificent, a striking advertisement for the florist who had created the scene. A flocked tree, resplendent in shimmery gold and cut glass ornaments, glistened against the back of a wall-long window. Fat white candles, surrounded by flocked greens and golden balls, graced the mantel of a white marble fireplace and marched down the laden dining table. The caterers, too, had done their job well.

The holiday decorations matched the sophisticated décor of the steel-gray room with black and white accents. *One would never know the real Trey by studying the place where he lived,* Lareana thought.

By the end of the evening, she felt that way about his guests, too. Polite and pointless conversations had never held any enjoyment for her. She smiled in all the right places and repeated all the right words, but deep inside she felt someone screaming to be let out.

Is this what my life's going to be like? Lareana thought, leaning her back against the coolness of the fireplace. Trey ran a multimillion-dollar business, and these people were his friends and associates. She grimaced inwardly at the shrieking laughter of a svelte woman in a deep-cut black dress. But the eternal smile Lareana had ordered never left her face.

How could I meet them again on a business day and not remember what fools they made of themselves tonight? Is it all because of the liquor? Or is that just a convenient excuse?

"Down the hall and to the right," she answered the question without a break in her inner monologue. *Lord, I don't want any part of this. . .this circus. But I love Trey and I want to marry him. And entertaining is important to his business.*

Lareana played the perfect hostess. The role became her, but it remained a role, at least for this audience. She even had Trey fooled until he took a moment to refill her glass of sparkling water and brush a kiss across her icy lips.

"Are you all right?" He handed back her glass.

She nodded, not trusting herself to speak.

"That's my lady fair." But he gave her a questioning glance before he turned to a guest requesting his attention.

It took all her grace and humor to put off the overtures of one slightly balding banker. She did it without even offending him. She heard him expounding her virtues as a conversationalist a bit later.

As the hour grew late and the drinks flowed more freely, the din assaulted Lareana's ears until she could no longer bear the tumult. She returned to the lovely room where she'd dressed and retrieved her coat from the walk-in closet. Shrugging her arms into the sleeves, she crossed to the sliding glass doors and let herself out onto the rooftop garden overlooking Shilshol Bay. She ambled over to the half-wall and leaned her elbows on the railing.

But even out there she couldn't get away from the party.

"So you couldn't stand it anymore, either." A slurry voice announced the man who spoke at her side.

"Oh! You startled me." She turned to find the architect who'd been the chief proponent of the saloon at Timber Country.

"You're beautiful." He stepped from the shadows enough to peer at her with bleary eyes. "That Trey is one lucky fellow."

Lareana murmured a "thank you" but couldn't think of anything else to say. She needn't have bothered.

Charlie—he'd introduced himself—did all the talking. "I don't usually drink like this, you know. It's all her fault."

Lareana was afraid to ask who, but she succumbed to politeness. . .and curiosity.

"My wife. She left me. Took our kids, the dog, and the best car. Says I'm married to my job." He shook his head. "Can you beat that? All these years I've been supporting her, working my tail off for her and the kids." Sniffs accompanied his tale. He rested his forehead on his clasped hands on the railing. "That house is so empty, I hate to go home."

Lareana felt tears welling up in her throat at the man's confession.

"And so I drink. It takes away the pain."

Until tomorrow, Lareana wanted to tell him, *until you wake up again.*

"D'you ever need to get drunk?" His question caught her by surprise.

"No," she responded simply, "I try to let God take care of my troubles. Works better that way."

A long pause broken only by the hoot of a departing freighter gave her time to wish for more brilliant words.

"Good night, Lareana." He touched a limp hand to his forehead. "I need another drink." He stumbled back toward the brightly lit room.

Lareana shivered in the brisk wind blowing off the sound. She pulled her coat tighter around her. *Lord,* she continued the prayer she'd started earlier, *isn't serving alcohol to someone like that aiding and abetting? Doesn't that make Trey just as guilty? What am I going to do?* She stared out at the pinpoint lights of the town of Winslow and its ferry terminal on the tip of Bainbridge Island. The dark waters in between seemed like the chasm dividing her lifestyle from Trey's.

She was about to go in when she overheard Charlie muttering his good-byes.

Trey answered with a question. "Where are your car keys, my friend?"

Charlie had grown obnoxious. His answer made Lareana's ears burn.

"I don't care," Trey responded. "No one leaves my parties drunk and drives home. I've already called a cab for you. The fare's on me. Just give me your car keys. One of my men will deliver your car tomorrow."

Charlie's expletives were becoming more creative.

"It won't do you any good. The doorman will only put you in a cab. My orders." They moved out of earshot.

"Thank you." Lareana whispered the words against Trey's lips as he kissed her good-bye in the garage later.

"For what?"

"Oh, for living up to what you say." She planted another offering in the region of his cleft chin and snuggled closer.

"I wish you'd stay." He tipped her face up with one finger. "I hate to see you driving at night."

"I know." She got in her car and closed the door. Rolling down the window, she asked with a smile, "Would you call a cab for me, too?"

❧

Lareana sang along with the stereo the afternoon of Christmas Eve. She played the carols over and over, never tiring of either the music or the message. She checked the time. . .again. Trey had said he'd come early. One of these days she'd learn to set times for things. To her, "early" was like Thanksgiving morning. What a nice early.

She stopped wiping the counter. *"What child is this, who laid to rest. . . ?"* How *I love that baby of mine,* she thought. *Mary must have felt the same way.*

Samson's barking jerked her back to the present. She checked the window. Sure enough, her biggest Christmas present had arrived. She met Trey at the door, her long red skirt a-swirl and her lips promising love for the ages.

"Merry Christmas!" He hugged her, his arms wrapped around her as if she might disappear in a puff of smoke.

"You smell of—" he buried his nose in her hair—"roses and spice and. . .you."

He stepped back. "This has been a mighty long week. Let's not have too many of these."

"Meaning you want to tie the knot—"

"Or jump over the broom—"

"Would a vacuum cleaner work?" She batted her eyes at him. "I'm a modern woman. . .no brooms."

He swept her up again. "Woman, today we set a date."

Lareana didn't argue.

"I have something for you," he said as she took his coat. "Do you want to open it now or later?"

"Silly man. You should never offer me a choice like that. My mother always made us wait until after Christmas Eve services." She drew him into the living room. The packages under the tree covered up the lower branches, a colorful pile that spoke of love and devotion.

"Good grief." Trey stared at her in dismay. "Are *all* your relatives coming tonight?"

"No, just us."

"Then who are all those presents for?" She laughed up at him. "Old family custom. Deliver all packages on Christmas Day. That way no time for hanky-panky."

Johnny's summons interrupted their tryst under the mistletoe. "Let's go get him and open our presents now," Trey whispered in her ear.

Lareana leaned back, pretend shock written on her face. She giggled. "I won't tell if you won't. But just the ones from each other."

Johnny had more fun with the paper than with the cuddly pink pig that was his gift from Trey. But when his mother took the paper away, he found the pig's ear equally satisfying—in his mouth, of course. Trey and Lareana left him to his chewing and proceeded with their own presents.

Trey didn't say a word when he opened the package containing the bronze. He couldn't. He leaned over and touched her lips with his, his gratitude implicit in the caress.

"The business card is in the box, too," she said between kisses. "The man's a natural for Timber Country."

Trey placed a large box on her lap. "Your turn."

Lareana picked it up and shook it. "Light and no noise. You're trying to make me think something is in here. Right?"

Trey nodded. "Just open it."

The first thing she found, after tearing the red foil wrapping aside and lifting the lid, was an envelope. The card inside read: No liquor will be served in Swen's Cookshack. Timber Country Saloon will specialize in sparkling cider, root beer, sarsaparilla, and other soft drinks—served in icy mugs, of course, as befits a saloon."

Trey held her in his arms until her tears dried. "That's supposed to make you happy." He stroked her shoulder with a loving hand.

"I. . .it d–does. I always cry when I'm happy." She wiped her cheeks with her fingertips. Eyes still shimmering, she stared for a moment deep into Trey's soul. "Why?" she asked softly, her hands covering his. "What made you change your mind?"

"I've been changing and unchanging my mind, so I've had long talks with many of the family amusement park owners from across the country. The general consensus is, no liquor in the parks. The ones that have it serve only beer and wine, and in very restricted situations. So I went against the recommendations of my designers and—"

"And I love you, Mr. Timber Country." Lareana threw both her arms around his neck and nestled her lips just beneath his ear. The box flew to the floor in her enthusiasm.

Before his mind was totally absorbed, Trey picked up the box and set it back in her lap. "There's more."

She dug farther in the box. Another envelope. This one contained two tickets to Tahiti for February 15.

"Do you think we can make it? The three of us?" Trey wiped her tears away this time, and his own eyes had a suspicious shine.

"Um-hmm." The stars in her eyes rivaled the ones in the heavens. "I can't think of a better way to celebrate Valentine's Day than with a wedding, especially when it's ours."

After Johnny interrupted their embrace this time, they took turns wiping each other's eyes. The baby ignored them, however, when Samson joined him on the floor in front of the sofa. All that long, golden dog hair was too good an opportunity to miss, and his baby fingers took advantage of the situation. Samson sighed, his fine head between his paws.

Trey kissed his wife-to-be once again, on the tip of her nose. "There's more."

Lareana shuffled tissue paper around until she found a tiny box way down in the corner. It was oblong and velvet, covered in deepest blue. The three sapphires inside winked in the glow of the tree lights, one on a fine gold chain and the other two mounted on gold studs for her ears.

"I've always thought these would match your eyes," he said as he latched the chain around her neck. "And now I know." He turned her face with the tip of his finger so the jewels twinkled again. "They do." He breathed kisses where each sapphire rested, then trailed matching caresses over her jaw line, covering her mouth with his, warming her with the strength of his caring.

Lareana felt herself soar with the clouds, searching the far reaches of the heavens but always remaining in the unbroken circle of Trey's love.

Later, shoulder to shoulder with Trey in the candlelit church sanctuary, Johnny sound asleep in her arms, Lareana listened to the old, old story with a special joy in her heart. Her life had certainly changed since last year at this time. The songs flowed around her. "It Came Upon a Midnight Clear". . .a different enchanted evening.

Epilogue

T-i-m-b-e-r-r-r!

Lareana flinched as the fir tree crashed to the ground. With a rattle, the huge chain barring the front gate dropped to the ground. Three plaid-shirted men with suspenders that hiked logging pants above cork boots stood ready. One with a washtub and thumping stick, one with a kazoo, and the last with a tin horn, they would lead the proper band. Proper, that is, with instruments, but with costumes as individual as the loggers themselves.

The band burst into a toe-tapping rendition of "Oh, Susanna," the parade began, and Timber Country, Trey's dream brought to reality, was officially open to the public.

Riding in the gilded wagon behind the huge gray Percherons and waving to the crowds lining the street was easy. Keeping Johnny from climbing up to the driver's seat and corralling Trish in her lap at the same time was *not* easy. In fact, it was downright impossible. Lareana was already feeling more than a bit warm. A trickle of perspiration joined other drops down her spine. How did those women of early years manage?

When Trey swung aboard, she breathed a sigh of relief. Tricia waved her arms and chortled her approval at the handsomely bedecked man across from her.

He doffed his beaver top hat at her and checked the time from a golden pocket watch complete with looped chain.

"Right on the minute." He grinned at his wife, equally resplendent in a washed silk dress of royal blue. She had a hard time keeping her black lace-trimmed matching parasol upright. Trish loved the handle. . .in her mouth.

Trey's jacket and Lareana's dress matched in hue if not in fabric. . .Johnny and Trish, miniatures of their parents, ignored the period costumes. The sights were more fun.

"Here, let me take her," Trey said, gathering the squirming infant into his arms. At seven months, Trish didn't want to be gathered. She wanted to get to wherever the action was. . .preferably under her own power.

Lareana breathed a sigh of relief. She straightened herself and her skirts and turned her attention to the park. A group from CORD waved their banners and cheered as the wagon passed. Lareana waved back, proud of her work in the organization and the changes they were promoting.

The aroma of freshly baked apple pizza was already drawing crowds to the chuck wagons like kids to an ice cream vendor. One of the men from the grange raised his slice of pizza in salute.

As the wagon passed the log ride, she could hear riders screaming their delight. She shivered as she remembered their trial run. The drop into the millpond would thrill the most adventurous.

Next to the blacksmith shop, the creator of Trey's bronze logging scene was patiently explaining the process of his art to spectators as he designed another piece. He waved to Lareana as the wagon passed by.

After winding their way through the entire park, the wagon delivered them to the front door of Swen's Cookshack. As they stepped onto the wooden porch steps, Lareana glanced up at her husband. Behind him a sign boasted the old-time delicacies to be enjoyed within. She remembered all the hours, the successes and failures of experimenting with recipes to fill that menu. Even Aunt Sigrid had finally pitched in.

Trey circled Lareana's waist with one arm, trying to hold Trish with the other. He managed it, even when she stuck one baby finger between his teeth. Her deep belly laugh was the kind that demanded everyone to join in. And everyone did. All the relatives gathered on the porch chuckled together; even Uncle Haakan couldn't resist.

Lareana glanced up at the sign, Swen's Cookshack, and then at her mother and father. The pride in their eyes caused tears to blur the scene for her.

Thank You, Father, for this day and all the people around us, she prayed silently. *And for the dream You gave Trey to bring happiness to so many people.*

She reached up and planted a kiss on the corner of Trey's mouth and another on the baby's fair cheek. She leaned over to drop a third on Johnny's forehead.

"Hoorah for Timber Country!" she echoed the cheers of the crowd as Johnny, holding monstrous scissors and guided by his grandfather Swen's hands, cut the ribbon across the door.

"That's some boy, that son of ours." To be heard above the cheering, Trey spoke directly into her ear.

Lareana turned her head just enough to brush a fleeting kiss across his lips. "Takes after his dad."

The joy in Trey's eyes promised years of laughter and new dreams to build.

LAURAINE SNELLING

Lauraine Snelling is an award-winning author who is best known for her Red River of the North series starring the Bjorklunds; *Dakota;* and her most recent series, Dakotah Treasures. In *The Healing Quilt* Lauraine shares more of her own life's story with her readers. A talented writer, teacher, and conference speaker, she lives with her husband in the Tehachapi Mountains of California.

A Letter to Our Readers

Dear Readers:

In order that we might better contribute to your reading enjoyment, we would appreciate your taking a few minutes to respond to the following questions. When completed, please return to the following: Fiction Editor, Barbour Publishing, Inc., P.O. Box 719, Uhrichsville, OH 44683.

1. Did you enjoy reading *Washington*?
   ❏ Very much—I would like to see more books like this.
   ❏ Moderately—I would have enjoyed it more if _____
   _____
   _____

2. What influenced your decision to purchase this book?
   (Check those that apply.)
   ❏ Cover   ❏ Back cover copy   ❏ Title   ❏ Price
   ❏ Friends   ❏ Publicity   ❏ Other

3. Which story was your favorite?
   ❏ *The Neighborly Thing*   ❏ *Race for the Roses*
   ❏ *Talking for Two*   ❏ *Song of Laughter*

4. Please check your age range:
   ❏ Under 18   ❏ 18–24   ❏ 25–34
   ❏ 35–45   ❏ 46–55   ❏ Over 55

5. How many hours per week do you read? _____

Name _____

Occupation _____

Address _____

City_____ State_____ Zip_____

E-mail_____